I know you're out there listening to me.

And you'd better *bee-leave* I'm in here listening to *you!*

Your name is Godley Creme, and you're a transplanted Brit in NYC, working for one of the Murdoch rags, pumpin' out that social distortion for all the fine young cannibals. At age thirty-three, you're already well acquainted with the Infinite Melon Collie, and you know tomorrow is just an excuse away. Your girlfriend's name is Darcy Citrouille, a half-French/half-Senegalese piece of dollparts lovecake, and she's a translator at the UN. Right now she's offline, busy setting up the annual Francophone gathering in Benin, so you're on your own this weekend afternoon.

Which explains why you're sitting on a bench in Washington Square (site of a colonial-era paupers' graveyard and hanging-tree; could it actually be th-th-this very one you're sittin' under?), watching the freaks and ponces and prams perambulate. You're bonin' up on your latest assignment by reading a faint nth-generation xerox of a paramilitary manifesto, *Operation American Viper*, and eating a tongue sandwich seasoned with red hot chili peppers (but the you always did like your pleasure spiked with pain, and of course the more it hurts the more we know you really *care*), when outa the bush behind your bench comes a voice: "Everything's zen? I don't think so!"

Out from concealment within that innocent shrubbery now pops a character whose general weirdness makes him stand out even in this mix of ten thousand maniacs. (He's an expat Serbian name of Pedrag Fishzoup.) At six-five, his bald pate is tattooed with the gridwork of a Pentium chip. Gotta mean face makes Henry Rollins look like Boy George, angry eyes throwing off sparks like mazzy stars. His bare chest sports two nipple-rings in the shape of the Worm Ouroboros. He's wearing baggy shorts and hi-tops. And before you can move or scream for the cops, he thrusts his menacing mush right down into yours and hoarsely inquires, "Do you know the way to San Jose? LA was too much for the boy!"

Before you can answer, he reaches behind his back, and you know he's going for a knife or a gun! But wait — life and death don't mean a thing until those angels sing! Cuz what he brings forth is — a liddle ol' buh-buh-book!

The title burns itself down your danger-boosted neurons: *Ciphers, A Post-Shannon, Rock 'n' Roll Mystery*. "Wanna wee peek inside?" says the madman sweetly. Before you can answer, he's opened the front cover.

Under that garish lid is not your old-fashioned Guttenberg Galaxy of fixed print, but sum kinda cyberbook screen! And pictured on it in full-color, full-motion glory is your girlfriend, Darcy Citrouille! Darcy's naked and bound, and sitting inside one o' them big ol' Kannibal Kooking Pots, up to her slim waist in simmering water! Around her, wild cartoonish savages cavort like Solid Gold, Soul Train, NPG bacchantes! She seems to see you now thru the screen, and calls, "Godley, help me! It's El Scorcho!"

You jump to your feet, yelling, "Darcy, don't shed your skin and dance around in your bones just yet! I'm coming!"

Instinctively, you snatch the book — your only link to your Missing Mayte — out of Pedrag's grip. Even as you do so, the screen-image changes, cycling thru a montage of madness: snakes, saints and silicon wafers; rainbows, rivers and records; quantum equations and Quicktime Quim. The confusing display enervates you, sapping your will. You drop back down to the bench.

Pedrag sits beside you, draping a solicitous bare arm over your shoulder. "Don't give up now, my man," he counsels. "We've only just begun!"

# Ciphers

A NOVEL

PAUL DI FILIPPO

# Ciphers

A NOVEL

## Paul Di Filippo

A Post-Shannon Rock'n'Roll Mystery

Composed partially by
Sampling, Splicing, Channeling
and Reverse Transcription

A joint publication of Cambrian Publications & Permeable Press.

Copyright © 1997 Paul Di Filippo.

Front cover, spine, and page 497 photographs by Rotislav Košťál (special thanks to Vàclav Kříž for his assistance in Brno, Czech Republic). Author photograph (back cover) by Mark Ostow. Chapter photographs by Andy Watson. Trina—San Jose's fabulous exotic/erotic contortionist/dancer—featured on page 407. Book design by Brian Clark & Andy Watson.

First Edition

ISBN 1-878914-02-2 (cloth)
ISBN 1-882633-30-X (paper)

Library of Congress Card Catalog Number 95-075546

Cambrian Publications
P. O. Box 112170
Campbell, CA 95011-2170

Permeable Press
47 Noe Street #4
San Francisco, CA 94114-1017

http://www.cambrianpubs.com/DiFilippo/Ciphers.html

*This is dedicated to the ones I love.*

*This goes out to the ones I love, a simple prop to occupy my time.*

# M E T A S T A T E M E N T S

## 00000000

"The very first characteristic of a folktale is economy of expression. The most outlandish adventures are recounted with an eye fixed on the bare essentials. There is always a battle against time, against the obstacles that prevent or delay the fulfillment of a desire or the repossession of something cherished but lost. Or time can stop altogether....

"If a straight line is the shortest distance between two fated and inevitable points, digressions will lengthen it; and if these digressions become so complex, so tangled and tortuous, so rapid as to hide their own tracks, who knows— perhaps death may not find us, perhaps time will lose its way, and perhaps we ourselves can remain concealed in our shifting hiding places."

—Italo Calvino

## 00000001

"Art consists in going the full length. If you start with drums, you have to end with dynamite or TNT."

—Henry Miller

Chapter 00000000

# Recursions

A m I live or am I Memorex?
Soup or spark?
Patient Zero, or just a patient zero?
Or maybe Nowhere Man.
I'm a loser, why don't you kill me?
My head hurts.
Quit jammin' me! Radio Kaos! I'm just an old radio head! Communication Breakdown! Call it superbad, static across the band! Put up the filters, run a Hartley transform, erect the noise gatings to cut the hiss! All hands on deck, no rebel cells allowed! Prepare to repel pirate phages! All together now, all together now, reverse time's arrow, pluck its feathers, Funky Chicken, smooth out the signal, don't be overwhelmed by sheer numbers, five and a half billion transmitters—

Holy Melchisidek, Sophia and Thomas the Contender. It seems over—for now. Thank you, Tathagata, for showing me the sparkle of your china, the shine of your Japan. I am now indeed in control. It appeared for a time that I was becoming autistic, one toke over the line, Sweet Jesus. Then I'd be an autistic caustic Gnostic, just a clue in an acrostic, or a Zen xenophobe, a liddle ol' gene-sequence just a-waitin' for the probe.

Shit. The crosstalk is getting worse. Inductive interference, phantom circuits, frayed insulation, myelin and ectoplasm worn thin. I really don't know how much longer I've got on this plane.... The Tao is roiled like a stormy sea, maximum disorder, minimum information, everything permissible, every configuration or message equally likely, everything unpredictable.

My work is well underway now, though. I have not forgotten the Vow. A hundred different schemes and plots, movements and conspiracies, programs and subroutines, some simple and brutal, others complex and delicate (and a few that are simple and delicate or complex and brutal ((and one that is all four, plus self-organizing to boot!))). They will—they must—all lurch or zigzag or flow smoothly toward completion on their own now. No longer will I be the one who must make it all right, talk it out till midnight, and yet keep it all in. My ticket's been punched, I've bought the farm. I'm outta here, I'm history! Papa's got a brand new bag....

One of the most annoying side-effects of the crosstalk is a tendency to lapse into the dominant vernacular. I was not brought up this way. I had a classical education. My mother secured the best tutors for me. (Don't call me daughter, not fair to!) I am indeed too old to indulge in this kind of secular slang, pop argot or juvenile jive. It is most unbecoming behavior in a gentlemanly relic of my stature and innately reserved disposition.

But the girl can't help herself! She's Little Miss Can't Be Wrong! She's got rockin' pneumonia and the boogie-woogie flu, the hip-hop hives and dem ol' Kozmic blues! I am a DJ, I am what I play.

## THE RELIC'S RAP

Yo! Old Man, on a crooked track,
Don't go sayin' our talk is wack!
You be dissin' us left 'n' right,
On 'n' off 'n' outta sight,
Sayin' the old days was better'n now,
You'll put us on the Way, you'll show us how,
Make us be just like you—
Well, Old Man, you can go screw!

Don't get me wrong. I like young people. All five and a half billion of them. It's just that there are so many of them, and only One of me. I get overwhelmed sometimes. Now I know how Joan of Arc felt, when the flames rose around her and her Walkman started to melt. If only there were another person I could really talk to....

Where is my twin?

A recursive rule in language is one which can be used repeatedly on the same finite number of elements to generate an infinite number of different sentences.

In mathematics, recursive functions are such that their very definition is in some sense part of itself. Either the procedure invokes itself (direct recursion) or it invokes another in which it is itself required (indirect recursion).

Lonely, I apply endless linguistic recursions to the one-member set which contains myself, and generate an infinite set of interlocutors. But they only satisfy temporarily, as they all end up sounding and tasting like myself.

Lonely, I reiterate myself times without number, directly and indirectly, and generate information-dense self-similar patterns, all of which bore me, since I apprehend their deep structures instantaneously. (Here we are now, entertain us!)

Bodhidharma warned me about this.

There was a time I thought he might be my twin.

I could feel him stirring in southern India, a Big Soul sending massive waves through the Bohmian implicate order. I had never sensed anything like his presence, not in all my years. I knew I had to meet him, although I could already predict with near-certainty much bitter disappointment. I came fully awake for the first time in ages, and, without much effort, took the throne of the Celestial Kingdom for myself, as was my right, so that I would have a suitably impressive platform from which to greet the holy sage.

He took years to reach Nanking. Travel was primitive in those days. But at last he stood before me.

By his first words, I knew he wished to duel, to test my realization.

"Is a single snowflake the storm?" asked the Bodhidharma. "And if not one, how many?"

"One is the loneliest number," I replied.

"Can I put a droplet of this new stuff on my tongue, and imagine frothing dragons?" countered the Bodhidharma.

"If we particularize," I answered, "then are we not like the conditioned ones? Let me ask you, who speaks these words? 'I am the first and the last. I am the honored one and the scorned one. I am the whore, and the holy one. I am the wife and the virgin. I am the mother and the daughter. I am she whose wedding is great, and I have not taken a husband. I am knowledge and ignorance. I am shameless; I am ashamed. I am strength, and I am fear. I am foolish, and I am wise.'"

I believed he would not recognize these words from the West. But his knowledge was immaculate.

"*Thunder, Perfect Mind.*"

"You know Valentinus, then."

"From Paul through Theudas did he receive the dharma."

I descended from my throne and hugged the Bodhidharma to my bosom. "Soul man!"

I almost knocked off his cap, and he laughed.

"Ain't never gonna do it without the fez on!" he replied.

We broke our embrace. "Let us retire to the courtyard. We have much to discuss."

Beneath a mulberry tree in which the royal silkworms noisily munched, we sat on carven stools of teak. Servants brought coffee imported from the Mayans, which we sipped from delicate cups of blackware. For a measureless time we were outwardly silent, exchanging information along the channel of the Tao. After we had tasted deeply of each other's samadhi, the Bodhidharma spoke.

"You have been an arahant too long, concerned only with your own salvation. It is time for you to switch allegiances. Bodhisattva now you must become."

I laughed. "You would have me take the Vow? I, who have seen more of mankind's blind foolishness than you ever will? Why should I commit myself to universal redemption?"

"You underwent gnosis, but stopped short of apolytrosis. The demiurge still holds you, if you are not indeed Saklad himself. Surely you must realize this, after all these years of no progress, of stagnation. Recall the Buddha's Parable of the Raft! Once you have reached the Yonder Shore, you are a fool if you continue to carry on your back the raft that brought you."

"What a fool believes he sees, no wise man has the power to reason away," I countered.

"Sophistry," exclaimed Bodhidharma, "and I ain't talkin' Sophia! No, you are trapped on this earth by your selfishness. There will never be individual release for you, as long as you are concerned only with yourself. You won't get no satisfaction, though you try, try, try. If you ever want to escape perpetuity, you must take the Vow."

The Bodhidharma's diagnosis of my situation shook my nerves and rattled my brain. I knew on a deep level his unutterable wisdom and the truth of his estimation of my character. Yet still I sought to deny it by ridicule.

"It is you who are the egotist. Who but a puffed-up self-important saint would imagine he could actually carry out the Vow? 'However innumerable sentient beings may be, I vow to save them all. However inexhaustible the evil passions are, I vow to destroy them all. However immeasurable the sacred teachings are, I vow to learn them all. No matter how difficult the path of Buddhahood may be, I vow to follow it to the end.' What arrogant altruistic nonsense!"

The Bodhidharma stood. Under his serene countenance, I could tell he was distressed. "You are a perversion, Zen without Zen. I wash my hands of you."

Man, I was really pissed off. For this confrontation I had come so far, waited so long? I gained my feet and opened the royal purse that hung from the belt of my embroidered robe (not yet the Maitreya's garment for me), and withdrew some paper money.

"Here," I said, stuffing the money in the Bodhidharma's hand. "Here is your fee. Go now, and buy yourself some more cheap philosophy."

The Bodhidharma stared at the cash in his hand, then smiled like Hotei. A tendril of grey smoke coiled up from the money, ascending heavenward like breath from a dragon's nostril. It carried an incredible stench. Then the bills flared into white flames that caused me to close my eyes.

When I reopened them, the Bodhidharma was gone. But I got one last message from him along the Tao.

*If a man's skin is unbroken, he may hold poison in his hand. And you can't buy me love. Whoever wants to see me through form or to seek me through sound is on the wrong track, and will never meet the Tathagata.*

I abdicated the throne then, passing the Empire to a distant relative who took my name. The Bodhidharma had to spend nine years in a cave, gaze fixed on a rock wall, recovering his composure, before taking up his missionary work. I returned to my sanctuary, my mind unchanged.

Forever thereafter and continuously all I could smell was the Hell Money burnt in the four corners of the kingdom, sent to console the ancestors in the afterworld.

*This is Hell, nor am I out of it.* I met the man who wrote that.

Little did I realize it then, but the seed of change had been planted within me, though it would not blossom until 1948. I should have known not to mess with the Missionary Man. For in that year, with a distinct impression of Bodhidharmic laughter at the back of my mind, I finally took the Vow.

What a long, strange trip it's been.

Or as the Georgia Peach once sang:

Oh, you hear church people say,
We are in this holy way.
There are strange things happening every day.

I remember the dead and dying outside the Shang capital, the screams of disemboweled horses, the bloody armor and crushed plumes and trampled little flowers. (Where have all the flowers gone?) I sat astride my own royally caparisoned steed, surveying all, ready to order the sack of the defeated city. I had recently had a certain revelation in my father's study, the full import of which had not penetrated yet. Seeking confirmation of my powers, I took a small book from beneath my lacquered breastplate and opened it at random.

At that instant in the sky appeared a vision which stopped all motion on the field of battle.

An enormous celestial dragon—its whiskers splitting into whiskers, which in turn sprouted more whiskers, down into fractal infinity—filled half the heavens, along with the ideograms signifying *in hoc signo vinces.*

The dragon extended its forepaw toward me. Miles and miles it stretched, until the tip of a claw hung in front of my face. Miraculously, somehow by the time it reached me the scaled paw was merely the size of a big man's hand.

Then the dragon scribed its beastly number into the flesh of my forehead. The number was One.

Suddenly the scene of carnage sickened me to the depths of my soul. I had a proleptic flash of my future meeting with the Bodhidharma, foredoomed to sterility, and I wailed the plaint of the Emperor of Ryo: "Alas, seeing, I saw him not; meeting, I met him not. Now I repent and bemoan it as much as I did then." Or would then.

Dropping my Book of Dreams, I wheeled my horse and fled back to my own version of a contemplative cave.

Oh, my little flowers sing this song, dada, dada.
The circle-jerk is infinitely long, oh, the dada day.
Gwine to run all night, gwine to run all day.
I bet my money on a Nag Hammadi, somebody bet on a lay.

The world drags me down, and when it's running down, you make the best of what's still around. Was I wrong to pass on the temporal power to my self-engendered son and to my brother, and secret myself away to plumb the extent of my new-found cosmic knowledge? Who would sanely say I should have remained the King of Pain?

For so long I abstained from power and control, till it was forced into my hands. Flatfoot Floogie with the floy-floy, that's me. Dirty deeds done dirt cheap! Wouldn't I have preferred to remain a smiling coolie, just like in that song?

Little Chinkie Chinaman came to town,
Walked around in his nightgown.
Little Chinkie Chinaman, what you say?
"Hong Kong, billabong, Judgment Day!"

Blood. Blood is a special substance. The Bodhidharma preached his *Bloodstream Sermon*. There's blood on the tracks, and tracks in the blood. But blood makes noise.

Suddenly I don't want it to end. No, I've changed my mind. Hit the rewind button! Cue up that song again! Go into an endless loop! Let's try a second, third, fourth take! Give me just a little more time, and I will surely change!

If only this night could last all day....

But wait— The disc is slotted into the dragon's mouth like a communion wafer, and I am summoned. I must leave you now. But there's a little time left.

Just enough for a short tale.

# Refrigerator Magnets

# K L U E S

00000000
"Ah, it must indeed be admitted, we're in bad, we're in terrible shape when it comes to time."

—André Breton

00000001
"History has a stutter."

—The Mekons

00000010
"Take the serious side of Disney, the Confucian side of Disney...."

—Ezra Pound

00000011
"I grew up in step with the recording industry."

—Peter Medawar

That this sophic, stochastic, Shannonesque era (which, like most historically identifiable periods, resembled a nervous tyro actor insofar as it had definitely Missed Its Cue, arriving when it did precisely in July, 1948, ignoring conventional calendars and expectations, which of course dictated that the *Zeitgeist* should change only concurrently with the decade)—that this era should today boast as one of its most salient visual images the widely propagated photo of a barely post-pubescent actress dry-humping a ten-foot long, steel-grey and olive-mottled python thick as a wrestler's biceps (and what a cruel study for any wrestler, whether to fuck or pinion this opulent opponent)—this fact did not bother Cyril Prothero (who was, after all, a product of this selfsame era) half so much as that it (the era) seemed—the more he learned, the more wickedly perverse information that came flooding into his possession—to be exquisitely poised, trembling, just awaiting A Little Push, on the verge of ending.

Along with The World As We Know It.

(Yet Cy still feels fine!)

The sun comes up; it's Tuesday morning. Springtime in Boston. Okay, so it ain't Paris. (And although Paris had the world's first telegraph system, a semaphore-style, pre-electromagnetic kludge, Boston could boast of having implemented the world's first extensive telephone system. So there, you Febrile Frogs!) Neither is it possible to imagine that this contradictory city—where stark reflective towers overshadow their shingled and slate-roofed Colonial ancestors like mutant sons and daughters, where leather jostles fur, and where the incredible rankness of unwashed flesh and the Charles River frequently mingles with the intoxicating odor of Fresh Folding Money of Large Denominations—is any longer the Athens of America (you *can* log on to Delphi from here, tho), even if that title was ever anything more than incredibly primitive nineteenth-century PR, or blatant disinformation.

But could This Olde Towne possibly still be—the Hub? Well, yes, at this juncture, with the weird and important folks Cy is about to tangle with being present, the prosaic Home of the Bean and the Cod just might qualify for that Kozmic Distinction.

In any case, Cy likes his city in this Madcap Month of May. Sitting on a grafitti-decorated bench in the Public Gardens, sipping coffee from a styrofoam cup (he's so wired up, he really don't need no coffee in his cup, fourth of the day), he admires all the various kinda little flowers that are blooming odoriferously, masses of pistils, petals and pollen, colored like a whore's paintbox. (Cy thinks as he gazes at the banks of blooms: *Pretty strange to cultivate something living for its sex organs,* but that's just how Cy's mind works, nothing to worry about, the lad is actually pretty normal, same as you 'n' me.)

Even as he tries to relax, Cy's caffeine-jazzed nervous system has him fidgeting where he sits. With his free arm draped over the seat-back, he runs his fingers idly over the slats that comprise the bench. His deft digits encounter a deep depression that intrigues him. Epidermal info, like a Chinese armpit-reader from the pages of *Weekly World News!* He swivels his butt so as to take a gander.

The depression goes all the way down to the bare wood, revealing in irregular strata about twenty layers of varicolored paint. Incised in obviously ancient characters at this deepest layer is the motto:

ELVIS IS GOD

*Hmmm*, thinks Cy, *that's an interesting change on an old riff. Always knew that Elvis was King, but never that he was King of Kings. . . .*

As Cy ponders this prehistoric grafitti, he notices nearby a slightly shallower pit in the paint. Carved here is the message:

CLAPTON IS GOD

*Hoe-kay,* Cy avers, *I shoulda seen that one coming. Wonder if the whole sequence is here. . . ?*

Shure enuff, an even shallower depression states:

ENO IS GOD

'Fifties, 'Sixties, 'Seventies—what corresponding blasphemy exists for the recently vanished 'Eighties? Cy's itching to find it, it must be here, he's examined now every square inch of the seat, finally he's up and around to the backside of the bench, still nothing, he's getting more and more shooby-doo-ANXIOUS for some reason, he literally tosses himself to the ground, looking up at the cobwebbed, gum-spotted underside of the bench— And there it is, hidden from all but the elect:

PRINCE TALKS TO GOD

Weh-hell, fair enuff. Cy gets to his feet, ignoring the stares of his fellow citizens. He'd like to linger all day, examining this park-bench palimpsest, but time won't let him. He crushes his cup, and ambles on.

The famous Swan Boats, with their exaggeratedly Serpentine necks, are busy ferrying noisy tourists to nowhere, beneath a cloudless sky. I told you about the swans, how they live in the park.... Lovely lady lawyers—wearing company blazers emblazoned with the initials of their firm, J, L, K, G, S, H, D, H, L, S, G, H, O, E, P & G—are lazing on their lunch-hours. Even the street-people Cy saw earlier, who hang out daily at Faneuil Hall—those who managed to survive a mean tussle on the icy pavements with that dreaded Winter-Snake, Fafnir—looked relatively pleasant, as they waited to pounce on discarded containers of salad, yogurt, tofu-burgers, or What Have You.

On the far side of the stone footbridge above the lagoon of the Swanboats, Cy's gaze is attracted by a gleaming coin on the ground. (Odd, how *alien* lost coins on the pavement look, unlike anything else. Is it their perfect, minted and milled symmetry, or the host of values we attach to them that causes such sensory dissonance? Or is it.... SOMETHING ELSE?) Why, it's a p-p-penny, a coppery talisman of Good Luck! Nice way to start the day.... Cy stoops to retrieve it.

The penny is much scratched and gouged by assorted heels 'n' wheels, revealing that it's copper thru 'n' thru. Funny.... Cy looks at the date: it's this year's model. Why isn't the middle of the coin zinc? Cy scopes out the mint-mark, below the date: AZ.

Arizona?

There ain't no Federal Mint in Arizona.

Is there?

Pocketing the coin, Cyril forgets the minor riddle. But his enjoyment of these beguiling pastoral vistas has been disturbed. He sought out the Common this noon in an effort to forget his troubles—Ruby having to abandon her chosen calling and take that lousy temp assignment just so they could make the rent, he himself being stuck in a nowhere job—among the multitudes of his fellow citizens. Instead, his muzzy ponderings and idle voyeurism have led to no Great Insights, and he has merely created, he now suddenly realizes, another problem for himself. Because Cy is now—

LATE FOR WORK!

Oh, shit!

(Being late for work, of course, is a prime existential problem, representing one version of that Most Basic Dilemma: the absolute incongruity of Time and Space. In this case, too much Space to traverse and too little Time to do it in. Time keeps on slippin', slippin', slippin' into the future.)

And don't forget, of course, that TIME IS MONEY!

Yessir, Cy's pullin' that old White Rabbit routine now fer shure, little bit of Disney-contaminated imagery here, fat snowy anthropomorphic hare in plaid waistcoat and cravat, yanking out that big ol' turnip watch on its gold chain, goggling at the crazy-handed face, which leers back (everything's alive in the Disney universe, of course). Rabbit starts to pipe up in some nutty Bill-Thompson-type voice, "I'm late, I'm late, for a very important date! Feed your head!" and pops down that ill-omened Hole, Alice following.

(And what do *you* think that famous hole represents, in the context of a Victorian girl-child poised on the knife-edge of puberty, and knowing of Carroll's pedophilia? Huh?)

Cy's watch manages a feeble red leer with its LED face, and Cy represses the requisite Startled Exclamation, not wishing to act out the Part Entire. Having no Rabbit Hole to dive down, he settles for the subway entrance, corner of Arlington and Newbury, next to the Ritz Carlton, hops on the Green Line and—

—quick as that gets out, sorta dazed by the swift passage from greenery to meaner scenery, in gritty Kenmore Square. The square is the confluence of Commonwealth, Beacon and Brookline, the noisy nexus midway between Fenway Park and the Charles. It's a river-redolent billboard-heaven. Ch-ch-check out that huge CITGO sign, fixture for years, red triangle on white background, visible from half the city, towering over an Army-Navy store, J. S. Masterson's Funeral Home, and the B. U. Bookstore. As per usual, Mister Butch, itinerant black street-musician, is a-twangin' his guitar on the corner, singing The Wonder Stuff's "Give, Give, Give Me More, More, More."

"I hope I make more money than this in the next world...."

Five-three-six Commonwealth is home to Planet Records (its sign showing the RCA Victor Dog with a Mohawk), where Cy, despite the dubious wisdom conferred by approximately ten years of Higher Education, is the lone weekday afternoon clerk.

At the door of the shop, Cy is greeted cheerily by Yates "Straight Arrow" Yarrow, who obviously has been keeping an Eager Eye peeled for Cy.

"I can't believe it!" declaims Yarrow histrionically, before Cy can even fully enter the store. "You knew I had a doctor's appointment today and you still show up late! This is too much!"

Cy contemplates Yarrow's blade-nosed, excited, red face. Yarrow resembles an anorexic Ichabod Crane with dandruff adhering to the strands of his sparse blond hair like sugar on straw. His breath could warp vinyl records (and has). He lives with his mother. He is not interested in any music composed during this century, and disdains managing anything other than the store's small classical stock, leaving the majority of the work for Cy. (Just t'other day f'rinstance, Yarrow was trying to get Cy to listen to a boring score by Mendelsohn called "The Fair Mellow Scene," or sumpin like that there.) On his good days, Yarrow is merely supercilious. Detmold loves him as a son. Today, Cy could kill him.

Cy ends up locking gazes with his morning counterpart, whose watery blue eyes are magnified about twice lifesize behind enormous lenses. The contest is decidedly unfair, since Cy has his Ray-bans on, thus rendering himself Impenetrably Cool, not to mention nearly Orientally Inscrutable. (The rest of Cyril's outfit consists of a T-shirt for the group X ((a crowned cartoon snake coiled around that enigmatic letter)), a black sportscoat and jeans.)

The binary decision now is, should Cy opt for belligerence or placation? Cy's synapses, close to overload already, thanks to Various Personal Dilemmas, flip and flop and come up belligerence.

"Get off my case, Straight. I'm here now, aren't I? If your appointment's so important, then don't waste time arguing with me. Go get your herpes treatment, for Christ's sake."

Cy slides past Yarrow and inside the store, which is a dark warren full of customers and music, its walls plastered with promotional posters. There is a vertical rack bearing rock fanzines like Boston's own *The Noise*; the Steely Dan zine, *Metal Leg*; the George Clinton zine *New Funk Times*; one called *Caffeine*; and some ecological journals such as *Buzzworm*, not to mention an outa-place Krishna handout ("BACK TO GODHEAD" indeed!).

Yarrow's back is quivering with suppressed anger. Cy gets himself safely ensconced behind the counter, official-like, master of all he surveys. Trying to appear busy, hoping Yarrow will disappear, Cy straightens out the piles of free stuff atop the counter. A bumpersticker that demands EXPAND THE CHANNEL! (The Channel, Cy well knows—or thinks he knows—being a local niteclub pressed for space); another that argues REVERSE THE FLOW!, in opposition to the Army Corps of Engineers plan to reroute the nearby Blackstone River; some giveaway buttons for local faves The Mudmen.

After fussing as long as feasible, Cy looks up. Yarrow is still frozen at the door. But not for long. The moment Cy's eyebeams touch his back, he explodes, whirling to confront Cy from across the room.

Yarrow is rippin' at the disclosure of his secret affliction, especially considering the embarrassing circumstances of its contraction. Yarrow is the only person in the world ever to have picked up a case of herpes from his pet hamster, which he was wont to hold and cuddle of an evening in his naked lap. (But hey, all life shares the SAME CODE, so why not?)

"I've had it with you, Prothero!" froths Yarrow. "You've gone far enough! I I I'm not covering for you anymore! Detmold's gonna know!" Detmold being the manager of Planet Records, and resident ogre.

Having delivered this threat as neatly as a Stage Villain flourishing the Mortgage, Yarrow exits, accompanied by slamming door.

Cy thinks, *Considering that I do not relish having my ass chewed out by master ass-chewer Detmold, nor do I wish to lose this job, perhaps diplomacy would have played better.*

Facing the rows of wide vinyl record and narrow CD bins and the customers interspersed thereamong—all of whom (customers, that is) have been silently and attentively enjoying this farce—Cy says, "Okay, folks, show's over, back to browsing and idle discussion, please. If anyone actually wishes to make a purchase, give me at least a week's notice, or my heart might not be able to take it."

The assorted skinheads, punks, grungesters, aging hepcats, slumming Harvard types, nerdy future music critics studying liner notes, giggling high-school girls in spandex, mods, greasers, street-hustlers, dope-fiends, and pasty-faced hippies lookin' like they just crawled out from under the Big Rock of the last two decades with the flowers of the Summer of Love still threaded in their hair, but now as dessicated as any matron's pressed prom corsage—in short, all those less productive members of society with plenty of free time on their hands and a seemingly inexhaustible need to have New Waveforms pumped into their brains via their aural members— these good folks graciously comply, anxious to retain members' privileges here in this Country Club For Indigent Music-Lovers.

Just then the Kiwi record currently playing on the shop's aging turntable (whose cartridge-maker has gone the way of sliderule factories, ensuring a slow descent into entropy for the faithful machine) dissolves into a scratchy sound signifying the needle's exhausted tracking into the *cul de sac* of the spiral groove's terminus, the end of every song.... Cy, feeling the definite need to hear Some Old Standard that will lift his spirits, riffles through the available records under the counter and come up with Just The Thing. Unsleeving the disc, he drops it on the turntable, cues up the tonearm, and lets 'er rip.

Wotta mistake!

Cy imagined he could get away with playing the Beatles' *Abbey Road*. Boy, he must be growing feeble-minded! How could he have forgotten the awful dissension those onetime Moptops can still cause? Just like all them decades ago when we was Fab, the fighting's still between those who revere them and those who disdain. Thing is, those who revere are now the old, and the opposite camp's the young.

Some rowdy punk with hair dyed an achromatic white with pinkish undertones cries out, "Shut those senile buggers up!" Another yells, "Argh, wotta buncha noise!"

One of the more excitable hippies, wearing overalls and a primo ZZ Top beard, tosses a punch, explaining, "Your bad karma excuses this violence!" The non-violent, positively Gandhian fist connects, the punk goes flying, the hippie is leapt upon by assorted defenders, who in turn are buried under the hurtling forms of others eager to join the fray, some to score an ideological point, others just for fun.

Heh-hey, suddenly it's big-time wrestling comes to the narrow aisles of Planet Records! Complete with grunts, thumping falls, and cheers from the bloodthirsty spectators. Either that, or it's Armageddon! And you tell me it's not the Eve of Destruction!

Nimble as Jumping Jack Flash himself, Cy disengages the tonearm, thereby defusing the immediate problem, leaps the swinging gate set in the counter, wades into the violent storm of bodies and, with help from a few of the more cool-headed patrons, restores some semblance of order.

After catching his breath, Cy regards the somewhat contrite, bruised and bleeding folks and says, simply, "Major uncoolness, folks. Really lame. Let's get with the program."

Point well taken by all, the now thoroughly humbled combatants kiss and make up, after a grudging fashion, before returning to their sundry pursuits.

And, thinks Cy, I never even got to hear my favorite line. (Which, of course, is: "Tuesday's on the phone to me.")

Back behind the counter, Cy makes a less controversial choice: Elvis the Younger, beloved by all those In The Know, intellectual and lyrical enough for the old, and raucous and disrespectful enough for the young.

Straightening up as the sound swells out (Elvis mockingly welcoming one and all to the working week), Cy's eye catches on the poster hanging above the audio system. Seen daily, it has become unseen. But something today causes it to register anew.

Blown-up from an Avedon spread that originally appeared in the October, 1981, issue of *Vogue*, the graphic image quickly became the first Big Poster Of The 'Eighties. It depicts the young (even younger at that time) actress, Nastassia Kinski, who is nude save for a white bracelet. Lying on her right side, facing the camera with a drugged look, hair pulled back, pink lips slightly parted, her skin an overall roseate perfection, left arm shielding her breasts, little-girl belly an innocent curve disturbed only by dimpled navel, chubby kid knees slightly bent, she is draped with an enormous snake which emerges from between her legs so as to hide her pubic area, droops in coils on her torso, has its head poised on her shoulder, and extends its tongue almost into her ear, as if whispering unspeakable secrets, knowledge of an arcane sort.

The tattered, dusty poster, marred with yellowing tape, doesn't have quite the impact it once had for Cy, when he first saw it there. Still, it is inarguably a striking image, seeming to hint at Deeper Significances. Oh, sure, it's an obvious restaging of the old Garden of Eden Shtick. But beyond that.... Cy remembers that the text accompanying the photo in the magazine featured this disturbing nugget: "The picture, as you see it, was Nastassia's idea...." Oh, really.... You don't say.... Who is the seducer here? Could this possibly be a tableau in which Mutual Complicity plays no little part? Is there ever any seduction where the line between seducer and seduced is completely clear? Doesn't Mister Snake, now that we look twice, appear a little sheepish and cowed (if such a menagerie of metaphors is permissible)? And why does Cy, every time he looks at this poster, wish that he could see little Nastassia's back? It's certainly not that's he's such a fanatical ass-man, it's just that he keeps having this weird intuition that there's Something Hidden that the camera has deliberately not shown. It's the same impulse, he suddenly realizes, that made him look under the park bench half an hour ago....

Ambiguity, thy name is Woman.... Or maybe just Avedon.

(Cyril, having mostly outgrown his juvenile urge to paw a copy of *Playboy* from time to time, might have seen in—and been intrigued by—the March, 1989, issue the image of LaToya Jackson in the exact same pose, an example of Redundancy in Black, bookending with Nastassia the decade of Snake with Woman....)

But thinking of Woman brings Ruby to mind, and Cy feels renewed sadness at the memory of how she's had to hustle her assorted clerical skills as a temporary Gal Friday, putting aside the one thing she really wants to do....

They met at school, Northeastern that was, its grotty urban middle-class campus sprawled out by the Fenway. Cy, being older than Ruby, had already had time to change his major three times in five years, pretty solidly establishing his eventual decade-long dalliance with *La Vie Académique*. By this time, though, he had stumbled into the field that was to claim him irredeemably as its own, like a shameless barren bawd adopting some gutter-waif to serve drinks in her plush bordello.... (We're talking about Crazy Clio, History Herself, and her rat's nest, jackdaw charms, but her effect on Cy's warped outlook is really matter for another time.)

The class was an intro to West African history, spring semester. Cy strolled in late for the first session, stopped uncoolly dead in his tracks, stricken with the looks of this chick seated up front. Gotta be one of these here Mixed Bloods, skin colored just the way Cy takes his coffee, hair a cascade of kinky waves down to her shoulders, and, wow, when she turns around to see what sort of fool is showing up ten minutes into class, Cy was floored by *blue eyes to die for*....

My Cinammon Girl!

Cy flopped into a seat whence he could scope out this lady's not inconsiderable other charms. *Wotta bod*, sighed Cy to himself. Hello, I love you, won't you tell me your name.... Who *is* this lady? I would love to take her home....

Prof callin' that sacred roll, everyone laying on the old geezer their most sincere I'm-an-A-student "Present, sir!" and Cy just waiting to learn this mind-boggling mulatto's name. When the name was actually uttered, each incredible syllable twitched the hook in Cy's cheek expertly, so that the barbs sunk in without possibility of removal.

"Ruby Tuesday?"

"Here."

RUBY FREAKIN' TUESDAY!

After class, Cy wasted no time in coming on strong.

"I take it the folks were heavy into Mick and the lads."

Smile that said: I've heard this line a thousand times before, but what the hell....

"Well, yes, actually they were...."

Wotta mellow voice! Cy could listen to her for the rest of the day. And did. . . .

DeeWanda Lovingood—who resembled a young Lena Horne with a forty-inch chest—lived up on 116th Street in that New York City. An Angel of Harlem doin' that old Harlem Shuffle from one worthless job to another. Now leading a boring existence as a waitress in a coffee shop. Few tips, plenty of drips. Celebratin' Sunday on a Saturday nite, drinking her dinner from a paper sack. Lookin' for A Way Out with all her heart. You dig it, I'm sure. Turns out the times were primed to provide release.

She never cared much for the Beatles, but when the Stones blew into town nearly thirty (thirty!) years ago (Mick had recently left the London School of Economics; it was June 2, 1964, and they were riding on their one semi-hit, a remake of the old Buddy Holly tune, "Not Fade Away"), she was, well, heavily radicalized. Left her job and became the most earnest camp-follower, groupie, plaster-caster and sometime toter of Marshall amps the Stones ever had. Never regretted for a single minute abandoning her old life, to become the stuff of legend. (DeeWanda, it turns out, being the actual inspiration for that down-and-dirty ditty, "Brown Sugar.")

In the Stones entourage at this time was one "Smackwater" Jack Tuesday, who, thanks to the ill-health of Ian Stewart, had lucked into the job of playing miscellaneous keyboards with the group on this tour, irradiating those 88s. He and DeeWanda struck it off nice right from the start, even though in the beginning they never actually Made It. Theirs was more of a bond forged from the music and the mystique. Which was probably why, when DeeWanda found herself pregnant (possible father being any of two dozen fellows from Mick on down in the pecker—ah, excuse that—pecking order), she chose to marry Jack.

Anyway, DeeWanda Tuesday's pregnancy caused her and Jack to leave the tour. Can't risk no innocent fetus getting them broken chromosomes from various sonic and chemical assaults. Happened they were passing through Boston just then, and they stayed.

When the baby, a girl, was born months later, in 1965, DeeWanda named her after her favorite aunt whom she never saw much anymore, one Ruby Rybofunken, who had married a German businessman named Rudy and moved to the little Black Forest town of Bad Attitude.

Two years later the Stones would go gold with their tribute to the little girl they had jointly fathered.

It was a good popular reassuring name, Ruby Tuesday, and sorta helped the Tuesday family fit into their surroundings too, the Roxbury ghetto tending to boil over from time to time during these heady days, when interracial couples were a decided, and not completely endorsed, rarity....

"So," said Cy, setting down his Ruby-colored coffee after a sip, "you might be Mick Jagger's illegitimate daughter...."

Ruby's face got serious all of sudden, and Cy's heart clenched. Jesus, out of everything she had just told him, he had to fasten on that one fact, which was probably a sore point, and thus hurt her. Wotta friggin' idiot!

Big ol' crocodile tear started to squeeze out the corner of one eye and her chin trembled. Cy was ready to cry himself when Ruby said:

"Is it—is it my lips that make you say that?"

Weh-hell, Cy did two and a half double-takes, as about a dozen racial stereotypes compressed and inverted, then burst out laughing, as did Ruby.

Wotta girl!

Thus, ten years ago now, began The Perfect Relationship. Oh, there were a few bumpy spots in the road, natch. While Ruby's folks heartily approved of the match, having been thru all this Mixed Breeding hassle themselves, Cy's Mom 'n' Dad, Rhiannon and Tyrone, had positively freaked. Only Anna Tina, Cy's fraternal twin sister, had stood by him. (Tho, come to think of it, Anna's hubby, Alan Condor, had been kinda cool too.) Needless to say, with such prejudice casting a heavy chill over the prospect of a big marriage, and what with neither Cy nor Ruby being much for social conventions, Ruby had never got her Golden Wedding.

But such familial grudges were nothing compared to the troubles associated with getting and spending, art and the world.

Ruby's major was film history, little microcosm of Cy's more wide-ranging

Cliometric interests. Her ultimate dream was to *make* films. (She had tried to get into the NYU fast-track, but failed.) In her senior year, with some second-hand video equipment they scraped the money together for, she had begun producing nifty and enigmatic little tapes with various co-conspirators. A few had played at student shows to enthusiastic acclaim.

A year after graduation, she was still taping, making better videos than before.

But no one was showing them anymore. Student outlets were closed to alumni, and few others existed for aspiring non-professionals.

Hence, many tears, arguments, years of starvation and postponed dreams, plans made and abandoned, and final gloomy submission to a temporary clerical job with Wu Labs, some kinda hi-tech firm out on Route 128.

(All of this foregoing summary excluding Cy's own troubles, which had caused no little tumult on their own....)

Wotta life! Oh, Ruby, when will I ever earn enough for us...?

A pimply-faced kid is standing patiently at the counter, awaiting Cy's attention. The suburban metalhead is wearing a Whitesnake tee-shirt. Exiting his reverie, Cy responds minimally.

"Yeah?"

"Mister." Cy hates being called "Mister"; he feels old enough lately without kids only five (well, awright, maybe ten, okay, okay, fifteen) years younger than him tossing it up in his face. "Mister, someone's switched the dividers around again."

"Oh, shit," opines Cy. Why must they do this when he's on duty? Here's this amazingly wonderful system—maybe you've heard of it, been around for a while, called the alphabet—which represents the perfect way to organize such things as records and CDs. But Someone hates this system (an anarchistic young punk, a blissed-out brain-damaged hippie?), and seems intent on subverting the carefully arranged Order of It All, as if the system has personally wronged him, and this so-far-uncaught Someone, at random intervals, introduces some pure Gaussian White Noise into the system, rearranging all the black or white plastic record-dividers, causing utter confusion, chaos and mental anguish.

(This record-store rearranger might actually, I propose, have been implementing some stochastic resonance: the paradoxical practice of adding a moderate amount of noise to a transmission in order to make the signal stand out clearer.)

"Okay, I can't come out and fix it now, I've got a new shipment of stuff I gotta unpack. You'll just have to deal with it. Jesus, you kids practically live in here, you think you'd know where everything is by now. What're you looking for?"

"Human Sexual Response."

All the bins bear tamper-proof numbers stenciled on their sides against just such an occasion as this. "Bin Nine," says Cy. The kid doesn't leave.

"Well?" prompts Cy.

"I need some quarters for the videogame too, Mister."

Over in one corner is an ancient hulking Centipede that belongs in Boston's

Museum of Computer Science. Cy rues the day it was ever installed, as the demand for change is never-ending.

"Okay, okay, gimme that dollar." Cy opens the register and scoops out four quarters. But hey, this silver's alive! The quarters somehow slip out of his nervous fingers and hit the floor, bouncing and rolling out of sight, tails chasing heads in some binary cascade, mimicking the flight of some elusive truth. The coins are as skittish as if they had a mind of their own.

"Let's try again," says Cy, and this time manages to hand over the change. Satisfied, the kid scoots off.

Bending down, Cy comes up with a heavy carton of PRODUCT that has just arrived this morning, as it does every Tuesday. Naturally, Yarrow didn't take the time to verify the contents against the packing list, but left that little chore for Cy. How Yarrow cons Detmold into thinking he does all the work around here is beyond Cy.... Oh well—*Excelsior!*

Which is what Cy finds when he rips open the box. Not, of course, the old-fashioned straw packing of his youth—that is long gone, along with nickel candy bars and ten-cent comics—but these here new-fangled white styrofoam pellets, shaped variously like snowy Cheetos, teensy-wheensy elf-maiden diaphragms, and empty marrow-bones, which Cy absolutely hates. They're so useless, sheer noise....

Cy dips his right hand into the packing material, trying to scoop it out and into the trash. But he must be full of static today, since the annoying little buggers stick to his hand, refusing to drop off. Cy shakes his hand, but the alien critters are now crawling up his jacket arm.... What's this, have they divined his hatred toward them and vowed to retaliate? Are they heading for his head, possibly to eat his brains out?! He frantically tries to brush them off with his left hand, and now they're on that arm too! Jesus Christ, this is creepy! They seem to be multiplying too, or perhaps more are leaping madly out of the box to join their brothers. What's he gonna do, some're on his pants now, heading for his heritage, alien DNA gobblers zeroing in on the prime source of naked DNA, his balls.

YOWWW! Was that a *bite?* This is too much!

Cy whips off his contaminated jacket, balls it up and stuffs it in the trash. Grabbing a longbox CD out of the carton, he uses it like a trowel to scrape the voracious styrofoam off his legs. When his precious body is at last clean of these artificial alien leeches, he pushes them off the shrink-wrapped new PRODUCT back into the box and slams the cardboard flaps down. The box goes once again under the counter. Let Yarrow deal with this extraterrestial invasion tomorrow. He'll be safe enough, having no balls to be attacked. Detmold is not paying Cy enough to risk his life like this.

Everyone, Cy realizes, has been watching this performance of his. Shux, maybe it *was* a little crazy to freak like that, but—fuck 'em. They weren't the ones being attacked. He presents his back to his audience and notices that he is still holding his makeshift trowel. Turns out to be the latest release from the Bushmasters. Great, maybe just give this a little spin when Elvis finishes advising us to "blame it on Cain."

Cy's thumb is covering the UPC code on the album's back. The black and white stripes show from beneath his digit. Nothing strange here, except.... *He can feel the bars, right through the shrink-wrapping!* Like some sorta digital Braille, the lines are being read by his thumb as actual ridges, tiny troughs and crests which, even if they exist in actuality, should be imperceptible by such a gross instrument as his blunt thumb.

What the hell is going on here?! This is a day for major weirdness....

Cy rubs his thumb slowly back and forth across the UPC code. This fills him with the queerest sensation.... Apparently, new circuits have been established in his body, turning him into some sorta supermarket checkout scanner. He is getting *information* through his fingertip, odd, disturbing data, definitely not the prosaic serial number of the album, no, it's much heavier than that, recomplicated, highly coded stuff that lingers just on the edge of his comprehension....

The room begins to fade from Cy's senses. Strokin' that ol' barcode faster 'n' faster, suckin' in the bits, runnin' all sorts of decoding, decrypting, deciphering routines on the data, Cy is plunged into

### THE POPPERIAN REALM OF PURE NUMBERS

Where do numbers come from? It seems the ultimate human egocentricity to insist that they are merely products of the human brain (although this is a camp to which roughly half of all mathematicians—number experts—belong to). No, it makes much more sense—in addition to absolving the human race from the nasty things numbers have been responsible for (identification tattoos inked into concentration camp victims; formulas underlying atomic destruction)—to maintain the position that numbers have some objective, Platonic, empirical existence, apart from human perception of them.

The light in the Realm of Pure Numbers is perfect, sourceless, pearly and eternal. Cy floats somewhere in the no-space, a disembodied point-of-view. Below him is.... something. His brain is having *mucho trabajado* interpreting what he is "seeing." It appears to be some sorta.... ocean. Yes, that's what it is, a heaving, frothing, whitecapped sea of numbers, the primordial *Urschleim* out of which all numbers known to mankind are abstracted or perceived.

And the sea is binary.

OF COURSE!

Binary, the simplest method of representing numbers that exists. Occam's Razor, right? Why should every possible number from every conceivable system—decimal, hexadecimal, what-have-you—exist up here in Number Heaven in its human-dictated form when it is ultimately representable by ones and zeroes? And that's just what Cy is contemplating, an infinite seething extent of ones and zeroes, out of which every possible human-recognizable number is formed.

And l-l-lookit those little rascals just enjoyin' themselves up here in Number Heaven. The ones zip through the ineffable medium like streamlined pikes, the zeroes wallow like Disney whales. And whenever a one pierces the center of a zero—why, a new one or zero is born! It's the Sea of Love! These are copulatin' digits, folks, breeding like mad—which of course makes no difference in the total population of numbers, which is already infinite.

Cy then notices that there is another kind of birth going on here. Strings of ones and zeroes are clumping together out of the primal soup—the exact same way theorists imagine self-replicating molecules first formed in earthly oceans—and segregating themselves from their companions. Look, there's such a string now: 1000000. Why, if Cy remembers his powers of two, that's 64! Someone down on earth needs a 64, and so this little guy's gonna be born! Sure enough, even as Cy watches, the little string wiggles like a snake and disappears.

Cy's vision, growing more acute, now penetrates to the bottom of the number sea, which, while infinite in extent, is not very deep. Down at the bottom, he witnesses the return of used-up numbers. Hordes of decimal figures pop up into Number Heaven and are briefly perceptible before losing their earthly forms as they dissolve back into zeroes and ones.

It makes such sense. In nature, all is conserved. Matter and energy perform their ceaseless dance of changes, but nothing is lost. Everything that goes down a black hole comes out a white one. The Tao receives back what it has temporarily loaned. It has to be the same with numbers. Once used up and discarded, they return to this realm, to regain their essential purity.

So they're all here, home at last. The serial numbers from the myriad junked products of a consumer age; numbers that flicker on cash-register displays and disappear; numbers preprinted on checks; discontinued telephone numbers; abandoned highway numbers (Get your kicks on Route 666); the random numbers that drive videogames; reams of laborious measurements now discarded: the numbers the architects of the Pyramids and Chartres calculated, data from experiments whose observers are now dust, all the numbers Einstein tried and abandoned before settling on 2 as an exponent; numbers employed by children jumping rope or chalking hopscotch patterns; lucky or unlucky draft-lottery numbers; item-numbers from old Sears catalogs; all the Big Primes used to encrypt secret information, lost once the information was decrypted. The single digit, mispunched into the autopilot, which caused Flight KAL 007 to stray and be destroyed by the Russians. After every imaginable use to which numbers can be put, every perverse or positive application, when their mundane existence is run, back they come, just like homing salmon.

What's more, Cy realizes, the numbers bring back news from earth with them. Dissolving into the whole, they release this information into the circulating medium, where it is quickly disseminated to every cavorting zero or one.

Lately, all the returning numbers can talk about is what these crazy humans are up to in terms of new uses for numbers. Ya see, these gross physical creatures just lately got the idea of using numbers to represent *every possible kind of information*. Thass rite, no longer do numbers merely stand for quantities or vectors or such-like abstract things. Nosirree, nowadays numbers can represent anything! It's Numbers' Liberation! Dig it, digits, digitizing is in! Music, words, money, anything can be digitized! Coded, sent down channels, decoded, stored, compressed, reproduced, optimized, manipulated, strung, unstrung.... Everything's gettin' to be numbers down there, gang! It's just one big Numbers Hoedown on ol' earth these days.

All this chatter is becoming infinitely seductive to Cy. Forget how he can understand it. All he wants to do is groove on this numerical gossip.

Somehow he wills his point-of-view to sink lower, lower.... He is nearing the surface of the sea. Flying-fish ones leap up to greet him, piping, "Welcome, human, welcome!" Now Cy's actually touching this puissant fluid, he can feel his sense of self melting, melting, dissolving into a complex string of ones and zeroes, miles long, goodbye, goodbye....

The phone is ringing insistently, loud as a chord from the latest thrash classic. Cy is back.

Noise, imperfect, necessary human noise, has saved him.

Still half-lost in Number Heaven, Cy shakily picks up the receiver, giving a garbled "Plannit Wreckers" acknowledgment. His head is still woozy from his recent unexplainable epiphany. He is definitely not prepared for the crackle and mush that pours out of the earpiece. The static that rushes in to fill his brain is incredible. Sounds like AT&T has tapped into the telemetry from Pioneer out at the edge of the solar system. Cosmic grunge, interstellar leftover background radiation from the Big Bang, alien beeps, whistles, burps, hisses, pops and crackles from the Heaviside layer almost totally obscure the familiar voice that says, "Hello, Cy?"

"Yeah, Ruby, that you? Oh, jeez, Ruby, I'm glad you called. Listen, the strangest things have been happenin' to me today. Let me tell you about it—"

The voice at the other end of the channel says something Cy can't decode. "Ruby, you gotta speak up, I can hardly hear you. We've got an awful connection."

Another customer other than the pimply-faced kid stands at the counter. This one's a person Cy has never seen before, a bluff, tall, red-haired older guy with knowing green eyes. The old fart's wearing charcoal-grey slacks and a blue blazer. His tie is patterned with some little animal. Very incongruously, he's also jangling some loose Gay Pride Rainbow Freedom Rings in his hand.

Not wishing to alienate anyone further than he has already today, and somewhat humbled by his recent Kozmic Vision, Cy says into the receiver, "Hold on a minute, Ruby, someone wants me. Yeah, what is it?"

"Where would I find Genesis, boyo?" Real cornball Irish accent on this joker, probably some relic of Boston's fabled Irish past (the Irish have had a lock on the Boston mayoral seat for over forty years; if ever, say, a Wop was to win the office, the Final Trump might sound). This doofus has probably been holed up in Dorchester all his life with a potato growin' in each ear and a sixpack of Guinness in hand.

"Bin Four." Back to the phone. "Ruby, are you still at work? What's going on?"

"[Bizzz] .... work. But Cy, I can't [shhhh] .... anymore. There's something really [brak-brak-brak] on here. It's creepy. I'm [CRACK] .... ing. I left a note [zeezeezee]...."

"Note? Screw notes, Ruby, what's goin' on? If you can't hack it anymore, leave. We'll manage somehow.... What the hell do you want?"

This last remark is directed at another importunate customer. Whoo-wee, real doll we got here, some striking chick, but still she's interrupting Ruby. Petite Oriental gal with glossy crow-black hair down to her pert ass, which is encased in snakeskin pants, also she's got them wicked red nails and lips, your typical dragon-lady outa *Terry and the Pirates*, a honey-and-venom cocktail in every kiss, you bet. From her wafts the scent of that chic new perfume, White Eternity. Femme Fatale, indeed: she'll build you up, just to put you down, and before you even start, you're beat! Possibly one of the many Hmong from the Golden Triangle who've settled in Boston lately....

"Hey Joe, you have anything by The Slits?"

"Bin goddamn Ten! Ruby, Ruby, are you there? Listen, Ruby, meet me at home and we'll compare notes. This all must mean something, you and me both weirdin' out today. I'm leaving right now."

"[Bleepbleepblat] .... don't know if they'll let me leave, Cy! They told me to report to [pop-pop-pop]."

"They, who's they? Where are you supposed to go? Ruby, listen— What now, for Christ's sake!"

Little Miss Slant-eyes musta brung her older male cousin with her. No, that's typical Western blindness, Cy, can't you see this guy's of a different ethnicity, Filipino maybe?

"So sorry to upset your phone call, sir. But please to direct me to Univers Zero, group of a French jazz-type nature on the Black Saint label."

"Bin freakin' Sixteen! Ruby, Ruby, exactly where are you calling from?"

"I'm [hahaha] .... here at Wu Labs. I've got a cordless phone in the john."

Phoning from the ladies' room? What kind of craziness is this? "Ruby, I— What the fuck do you want?!"

The new guy, fourth intruder, on the other side of the counter jumps a foot. He's a weaselly looking creep with slicked-back hair and a greasy grin. His ferret's face is all a-twitch with involuntary tics. Looks mean and wiry, narc-shifty under a veil of innocence as rotten as a gravecloth long buried. "Huh-huh-hey, Muh-muh-mister, I juh-juh-just need to fuh-fuh-find this here al-al-album...."

"Can't you see my life's falling apart? Who, for god's sake, who?"

"Young Neal and the Vipers."

"They're a local group, Bin One. Uh, sorry about the expletive, bro, no need to mention it to the management.... Ruby, Ruby, are you still there?"

"Goodbye, Cy. I hope this all works out okay.... [wheepwheepwheep]."
The line goes dead. Cy's brain is flip-flopping around like a gaffed electric eel.
He slams the phone back down in the cradle. What the hell is going on there at Wu
Labs? Four twenty-five an hour don't entitle no one to mess with your head. Cy is
determined to rush out there and perform some feat of derring-do when he remembers that Ruby said she left a note at home. Better check that out first, might explain
everything. Maybe he's over-reacting, the connection was bad, he was just coming
outa his funk, maybe nothing's wrong. Yeah, definitely check out the note first.

"All right," bellows Cy, "everyone out! Store's closed!"

Confusion greets this announcement, and, irritatingly, no one makes a move
toward the door. Cy sees a blood-red haze dance before his vision.

He's out from behind the counter, sweeping everyone toward the door. "Hey,
bro', lay off...." "Watch your hands, you old fart!" "But I want to buy this one, really,
I do...."

Just as Cy herds the last ne'er-do-well out, someone else slips in. Cy turns to
wither him with a scorching blast, then stops.

It's Augie Augenblick, Cy's best friend.

Obviously sensing Cy's manic condition, the beefy Augenblick holds up a clear-
plastic-cased compact disc between them, at arm's length, as if to explain his daring
to venture in. Standing there with the rainbowed silver disk in outstretched hand,
he looks like some stupefied Roman footsoldier who's just found his shield miraculously shrunken in the face of an enemy charge, or maybe Doctor Strange employing his Mystic Amulet.

"Augie, I'm sorry, you gotta leave, something's wrong with Ruby and I'm closing up."

"Fine, okay," temporizes Augenblick, employing the kind of voice one might use
to coax a weak-kneed jumper down from the ledge. "I just wanted to exchange this
disc I bought yesterday. It's a dud. I put it in the player and all I get is a buncha
noise...."

Cy snatches the disc out of Augenblick's hand and stuffs jewel-case and all into
his rear pants pocket, ripping one seam nearly all the way. The disc pokes precariously out, held by some threads. Cy immediately forgets it.

"Catch you later," offers Augenblick, hastening to depart the company of this
madman.

"Right, fine," says Cy, locking the door behind them, once outside.

The subway ride home seems endless. Cyril feels entombed in the belly of some
subterranean snake, doomed to crawl forever beneath the earth.

Eventually the torture ends. Cy dashes off the train, up stairs, down half a mile of
sidewalk, up more stairs, to the door of his apartment. His and Ruby's apartment!

Banging, hoping she's beaten him home. "Ruby, open up, it's me! Ruby are you
there?" Nothing. Keys out, fumbles, finally lets himself him.

Two states: Ruby, no Ruby.

No Ruby.

She—Ruby Tuesday—has not managed to escape whatever she feared. Somehow, Cy knows this with utmost certainty. You're lost, little girl....

Empty home echoes to his calls. The note. Where? Their usual message drop, the fridge!

Cy runs to the kitchen, confronts the refrigerator—and is given pause.

Wotta frigging mess!

The appliance is almost hidden under paper. Articles and pictures ripped from magazines, old handwritten reminders, receipts, bills, photos, lyric sheets from albums, crayoned color-by-number drawings from his nephew Arthur, Anna's son.... It's like a closet filled with junk.

The papers themselves are in turn obscured by dozens of little magnets. There are magnets that look like realistic fruits and vegetables, magnets that look like cookies and pieces of cake and pie. There are cat magnets, Buddha magnets, worm magnets, hamburger magnets, sheep magnets, record magnets, butterfly magnets, dog magnets, music-note magnets, and plain-magnet magnets.

This quotidian surface strikes Cy suddenly almost like.... noise. Visual noise! How could such insidious confusion ever have taken root right here under his nose, flourishing with his actual complicity...?

Cy begins frantically ripping stuff down, searching for The Note. Magnets hit the floor and roll off like mechanical mice, into hidden corners and out-of-the-way spots, where they'll lie for years to come....

He has it, at last. Why'd she bury it so deep?

*Cy—*
  *I've stumbled onto something really strange here at work.*
*I didn't tell you about it because I didn't want to worry you,*
*knowing you had your own troubles, but I wrote this note in case*
*anything should happen to me. If you're reading this, then I'm*
*afraid something has. Play the tape labeled P.O.P. to learn more.*
  *Goodbye.*
  *Ruby*

*P.S. If you try to come after me, please be careful.*
*P.P.S. I love you.*

Shit. *Your own troubles....* Wotta jerk he must have been lately, if Ruby felt she couldn't even bother him with something this big. Shit.

Cy falls into a chair like a bag of broken bones. Wotta black day! Just then the phone cricket-chirps. He slips on a magnet jumping for it, goes down WHAM! flat on his back. Up painfully, grabs the phone, hoping—

It's Detmold. "You're fired," intones the ogre.

"I guessed," agrees Cy.

# Mekong Melusine, That Kampuchean Kutie

# K L U E S

## 00000100
"Information is not knowledge, knowledge is not wisdom,
wisdom is not truth, truth is not beauty, beauty is not love,
love is not music. Music is the best."

—Frank Zappa

## 00000101
"It's not that I don't care for snakes
But oh what do you do
When a 24-four foot python says
'I love you?'"

—Shel Silverstein

## 00000110
"The Serpent Princess offered the Buddha a pearl and
passed straight through to nirvana."

—*Konjaku Monogatarishu*, a Japanese Folktale

## 00000111
"You must understand this. Before you were born, you
were zero. Now you are one. In the future, you will die and
again become zero. All things in the universe are like this.
They arise from emptiness and return to emptiness. So zero
equals one, one equals zero."

—Seung Sahn

F ifty-Four was a really happening year.
Not as wild as 'Forty-Eight, natch, but we can't get into that yet.
Anyhow, just consider these Significant Events from one crucial year of the decade which conventional wisdom (an oxymoron if ever there was one) would have you believe was brain-dead.

*Brown vs. Board of Education* had just been decided. Segregation was dead, man, altho the corpse would kick galvanically for 'bout twenty years. We're gonna mix them races up, you bet, and hybrid vigor will be the rule of the day. New information thru recombination is the hidden imperative behind the politics, and even Southern Man—even the Grand Dragon of the KKK—can't stop it now....

The first Bilderberg Conference, named after its original meeting place, the Bilderberg Hotel in Öosterbeek, Holland, was taking place that year. Organized by Dr. Hieronim Retinger, the conference would meet annually from '54 on. Its attendees comprised the movers 'n' shakers of the world, political, financial and mediagenic (Marshall McLuhan would be there in 1969.) The proceedings were strictly private; no minutes were ever published. Bill Clinton would attend for the first time shortly before being elected. Surprise! This is the same guy, natch, who said, "We were all born for the information age. This is a jazzy nation, thank goodness, for my sake, that created be bop and hip-hop and all those other things. We are wired for real time."

The Grim Reaper's Top Draft Choices for that year: Alan Turing commits suicide, and von Neumann learns of his ultimately fatal cancer.

On other fronts, the folks at Texas Instruments had this here brainstorm. Gonna take that nifty little gizmo, the transistor (invented, not coincidentally, in 1948, by Shockley, Bardeen and Brattain at Bell Labs, same year that Claude Shannon published "A Mathematical Theory of Communication"; but I promised not to digress), and deploy it in its very first mass-market appearance. Cue the fanfare here, please, while two lovely Vegas-lookin' gals—legs up to their ears, breasts barely covered by rhinestone straps—whisk the wraps off an object balanced on a short Doric column, revealing.... THE FIRST TRANSISTOR RADIO, the TR-1, cool molded-plastic case with sweet lines concealing primitive hand-wired boards, first cheap and portable disseminator of nooze, vues, and tunes, which device would immediately begin selling like lemonade in Death Valley. Eager white teens, already chafing under the Big Sleep of Eisenhower, started scarfing up millions of the neat-o gadgets, holding them continuously to their collective Ear, or perhaps using those hokey but state-of-the-art, bowling-pin-shaped earplugs for an even more intimate connection. Kookie, lend me your comb! I just couldn't resist her, with her pocket transistor!

They all seemed to be waiting for a crack in the façade of gooey pop music (them Andrews Sisters, man, like Dullsville), having sensed the subterranean tremors intuitively. Something new was a-borning, all right, but the lineaments of the strange creature were shrouded as yet....

And fer shure, no one quite visualized the savior as a hillbilly truck driver *cum* usher with a sneer and a pompadour who was about to cut his first record on, of all days, July Fourth, Independence Day, of that very same year.

Meanwhile those crazy Negroes with their African music were laying their claim to the new device as well. R&B stations were pumping out soulful wailing that filtered from thousands of urban speakers, and Bird Parker had one more year to live and was playing like he knew it.... (Hank Williams had died the previous year, not even getting to enjoy the success of his last hit, "I'll Never Get Out Of This World Alive.")

And The Third World—or as it was still known then, the Colonial Possessions— why, they were gonna be absolutely flooded with transistor radios, with dramatic results, in less time than it took your local Ambassador to cable home THE NATIVES ARE RESTLESS....

(In Jamaica, for instance, Radio Jamaica Rediffusion would begin blasting New Orleans jazz, among other forms, into the ears of calypso-crazed Rastas, with explosive theological-musicological results.)

But wait.... those clever buggers at Texas Instruments, even as they unwittingly trigger one revolution, are already worried about the next one. Ya see, them damn transistors, teeny as they are, are TOO BIG. Can't get enough of them together in the same device to do anything really wild, cuz the waste heat fries the device up. Wotta we gonna do, it's in our genes to minaturize and recomplicate, have we hit some Natural Limit, has our glorious March of Progress come smack up against a brick wall? *No!* shout all the engineers in a resounding chorus. *No, we shall not let it be!* And one Jack Kilby starts dreaming of.... Integrated Circuits. Thousands of transistors on a single slice of silicon.... But a lot of hard work—dead-ends pursued, seeming victories crumbling to ashes—lay ahead, before such a dream could be realized....

Meanwhile, Eckert and Mauchly would be grateful for even *one* transistor in their ol' Univac. Univac's been around since 'Fifty-one, but it hasn't improved that much. Still got all them vacuum tubes. Every new task required physical rewiring! (Programming, what's that? Oh yeah, Von Neumann's wild idea....) Know how the Univac transmitted ones and zeroes, on and off? Delay lines, macroscopic tubes of mercury which propagated liquid pulses.... Holy Alchemy! Can you dig it, digits, actually surfing on mercury waves? Maybe the new Whirlwind computer being installed this year at MIT will herald a new generation. Probably does about ten operations per second, ha-ha!

The biological community was still reeling from last year's double revelation. The smaller explosion was caused by the proof offered by John Carew Eccles of Oxford that brain activity was mediated by chemicals (acetylcholine being Eccles' chosen subject; he'd pick up the Nobel in '63). Hmmm, lotta food for thought here.

Could we mess with the chemical balances, and thereby influence thinking? Lithium, you are to the future as flint spears are to H-bombs....

The second, more stunning discovery was made by those youthful, disrespectful clowns, Watson and Crick: the double helix structure of DNA. (And what of the rumors that Rosalind Franklin ((no relation to Aretha)), disgusted with their show-manship, had gone to work for a minor concern known as Wu Labs, prior to her untimely death?) But even the Dynamic DNA Duo weren't hep yet to the possibility that a good portion of the structure of DNA consisted of redundancy and noise, nor were they yet thinking in terms of metastatements and reading frames, jumping genes and mini-families, nor, Unktehi forbid, REVERSAL OF FLOW.

And neither, yet, can we.

How-some-ever, yes, ahem: seemingly meaningless interjections have a grammar and utility of their own, in language and genes.

No, the big headaches—and prospects—of bioengineering were yet to arise, and your average biologist, after a nod toward W & C, was more preoccupied with developments on the vaccine front. Seemed a really effective polio vaccine was at last to hand. (Tho Salk and Sabin were still dukin' it out over live virus versus killed.) The Third International Poliomyelitis Conference was meeting in Rome, where the bloodthirsty, hubristic humans were bent on declaring war against that li'l ol' killer virus....

Peanut M&M's were introduced in '54, but at first only in brown. Post-segregation, it was deemed Good PR to make them ALL COLORS.

'Round the world from America, the French had just gotten the John-the-Baptist treatment: they had been handed their heads on a platter at Dien Bien Phu, and been forced to sit down in Geneva for some of that disgusting peacemakin'. (Vice-president Nixon claimed we coulda rescued our allies with a few well-placed "tactical nuclear weapons," but somehow the idea didn't go over too well. Oh, we'll all go together when we go, every Hottentot and every Eskimo....) The United States was already making reassuring noises about picking up the reins in Indochina.

Right next door in Cambodia—sleepy land of jungle-crowned Angkor Wat and steaming rice paddies, lithe women like willows and smiling men riding elephants—the French had also just been ousted, albeit by less violent means: a general revolt of the populace aided and abetted by the ruling royalty. Compelled to pull out its administrators and grant the country its independence, the wily and crafty Gauls still managed to maintain a forceful diplomatic presence and general behind-the-scenes influence in the tiny, tranquil, backwater capitol of Phnom Penh, a place where, if you studied the heuristics and logistics of the mystics who lived there, you would learn that their minds never worked in a line....

And where the very minor Foreign Service officer, Phillipe deClosets, age twenty-four, sat bored outa his skull, not a little frustrated and angry too, and just basically Ripped At Everything.

Behind his scratched embassy desk, deClosets had his feet propped up on an open drawer. His wheeled wooden chair with the swivel base was tilted back precariously. Mounted on the ceiling, a big-bladed fan lazily stirred the humid air. It was mid-September, almost the end of the rainy season, and deClosets, still in his first year at this abominable Cambodge posting (this was no HOLIDAY IN CAMBODIA, fer shure), had already learned to hate the very sound of dripping water. Even a leaky tap was enough to set his nerves on edge. It was like Chinese Water Torture! What an execrable and unwanted change from his last assignment.... If only things hadn't gone so bad in Dahomey.... The dry savannas of French West Africa had never seemed so beckoning as now, nor the dusky thighs of the King of Dahomey's favorite wife....

DeClosets held a small pocket-mirror in one hand, angled to reflect his face. Although he should have been attending to the official papers with which his desk was laden—communiqués, reports, order forms, lists of equipment, all the noise that spewed out of diplomatic channels—deClosets was busy practicing his sneer.

There was this basic Bad Attitude newly in the air that Western Civilization breathed, ya see, big changes in the works. Stewart and Fonda, they were old models, man, zero information content because utterly predictable. A new esthetic was being formulated. Brando, Dean, Belmondo were all current exemplars, Bogart the breadboard model. (Every generation's got its own disease.) Guy couldn't be *too* tough or *too* cool, had to get the basic blank-eyed, tough-as-nails look down pat, complete with curled-lip sneer for moments when squares did something particularly dumb or chicken-shit. This cultural wavefront had struck deClosets recently with the force of revelation—even at this far outpost of Western Civ—and it immediately became imperative for him to cultivate this look.

Thus the faces deClosets now tried out in the glass. Whoa-ho, nice curl on the stubble-dark upper lip that time, eyes could be a trifle more beady tho, couldn't hurt to clench his strong jaw muscles more aggressively either, since more'n one lovely lady had fallen for his strong profile already....

The door to deClosets' tiny office opened without warning. Trying to lower his insouciant feet with some alacrity, he caught his heavy boots (which he was forced to wear against the omnipresent mud, contrary to all stylistic considerations, when he really dreamed of winklepickers) on the lip of the drawer. Thanks to the inevitable laws of physics, his thwarted actions were translated into movement of his chair, which disturbed his delicate balance. The chair tipped up on its rear two wheels, and deClosets went over backwards with a CRASH!

DeClosets quickly scrambled unhurt to his feet. Major blow to the image here, gotta recover best as one can.

Facing him across the width of his desk was Etienne Groshorloge, his immediate superior. Groshorloge was a distant cousin of deGaulle's. He had been through the *Ecole Nationale d'Administration*, and therefore ranked as Cadre A. (DeClosets, having entered the Foreign Service via an exam for civil servants, was relegated to Cadre A Prime, and he and his peers were continually looked down upon by the alumni of the *Ecole*, a source of much teeth-grinding tension among the juniors.) Exhibiting a familial resemblance to his famous cousin, Groshorloge reminded deClosets of *une foie gras stupide avec la dyspepsie.*

"I take it you are not exceedingly busy," said Groshorloge.

DeClosets twitched his upper lip in a subtle manner that would fail, by the merest hair, to get his ass reamed yet still manage to soothe his disgust. He hated this well-respected man.

"I am always active, both for myself and the greater glory of France," contradicted deClosets.

"Yes, well, half of that predicate I will accept. In any case, I have a new assignment for you. You are to wander inconspicuously throughout the city and secure information about the activities of the Americans. Since independence they have become increasingly bold, and their interests in Indochina no longer coincide entirely with ours."

"I see," said deClosets. Lord, this piggish Groshorloge was fanatically suspicious of the Americans. In that regard, however, he was no different from many of his countrymen. Anti-Americanism was on the rise in France, and deClosets failed to see why. Hadn't the Americans liberated their very homeland? (Then fourteen years old, deClosets had been hooked on Yank style and goods from his first comprehension of their wisecracking speech and his first taste of a Hershey's bar. This infatuation had waxed over the past decade, culminating in his Brando imitations.) Also, hadn't American money helped to rebuild France from the rubble? Ah, ingratitude! What was that line from Shakespeare, heard during deClosets' sole London visit, at a performance of *Lear* that Cockney girl had dragged him to....? Oh, right, "How sharper than a serpent's tooth...."

DeClosets tried to scope out the full extent of his assignment. "Am I permitted to issue bribes, suborn, cajole, or intimidate officials, or perhaps seduce secretaries? If the former, I will need some American dollars. If the latter, I am already fully equipped."

Groshorloge nixed such schemes with a wave of his hand, popping one wild instant daydream deClosets had been enjoying where he played some sorta Bogart-type role, *à la* Casablanca. "Don't be nonsensical. I merely want you to keep your ears open, perhaps have a drink with one of the laxer Americans, ask some of the natives what they know. Under no circumstances will you do anything to get us in trouble. Do you understand? You are to function strictly as a receiver."

"Of course.... Am I dismissed now?"

"Yes. Oh, one more thing. If you can think of any scheme that would cause tension between the Americans and the Khmer, you will let me know. If I find merit in the suggestion, we might implement it."

"Yessir," said deClosets.

*Fuck you*, thought deClosets.

Groshorloge left, deClosets donned a trenchcoat against the miserable drizzle, packed a notebook and pencil in his pants pocket, checked out his appearance in the small mirror, practiced a final sneer, and stepped out of the Embassy into the streets of Phnom Penh.

Gotcha typical Former Colonial Possessions street scene here, of the lighter variety. The Cambodian capitol, circa 1954, was a pretty bucolic place, lacking the reeking poverty, spiritual degradation and general funky political malaise of Saigon to the southeast. (The main hardass malcontents, the Khmer Serei, or Free Khmer, are right now holed up in them Cardamom Mountains, only a few hundred strong and dwindling, thanks to the general Good Times now underway, which made them seem like raving anarchists. And since deClosets's personal motto is *Laissez les bon temps roulez,* he ain't too sympathetic to the guerrillas' plight.) Everyone, thought deClosets as he walked through the persistent mist, seems more or less happy with their new independence and the benevolent, albeit loony, rule of King Norodom Sihanouk, who indulged such penchants as making rambling three-hour speeches over the radio and playing saxophone in local jazz clubs. (And although no Bird, the King did possess a moderate sense of bop.)

Thin-shanked men pedaled *cyclos* through puddles, ringing tinny-sounding handle-mounted bells. Old women wearing traditional red-and-white-checked cotton *krama* head-cloths sold mangoes from trays.

Snakes in bamboo cages, their mouths sewn shut, were the fixin's of a yummy supper. (Melchisidek, forgive them, for they know not what they do....)

Here 'n' there an occasional European, Australian or Chinese national could be encountered, and these foreign interlopers, contrary to their usual uptight ways, seemed to have been mellowed by residence in this pleasant country.

DeClosets, of course, for all his determinedly nurtured hipness, failed to see himself as an outsider in no wise different from these other white-skinned folks, reason being that the French had been in *Cambodge* for ninety years, and, well, just belonged here. His world was just naturally divided into the colonizers and the colonized.

Nor did deClosets at this point in time believe that this country had the ability to change him in exactly the same manner as it had changed and was yet to change so many others. And the stubborn young Frog would have denied it if you pressed him.

DeClosets moved along the busy streets bordered with pastel-colored Riviera-style low-slung balconied buildings, which were interspersed with your basic Weird Tropical Vegetation, to wit: silk-cotton trees, palms, rambutans, bamboos and, by the water, mangroves. His mind was busy trying to figure out how best to carry out the orders of Groshorloge.

Trouble was, deClosets had no contacts as yet in this city, no reliable sources of information. In the few months he had been here, ever since the screwup in Dahomey and subsequent transfer, deClosets had done little except piss and moan and practice his drop-dead stare. Not the best method of grounding oneself in the subtleties of the native mentality, politics and culture. Now he was at a loss regarding whom to pump for the information Groshorloge demanded.

Faced with a dilemma of such magnitude, deClosets did the only thing he could. He decided to go get wasted. That much he could accomplish, having made a point immediately upon arrival in Phnom Penh of learning the location of all the dives, roadhouses, niteclubs, gin baths, cathouses, juke joints, shooting galleries, casinos and opium parlors, which, while not as numerous as those of Saigon, were not nonexistent.

It was toward an establishment of the last sort that deClosets now turned his steps.

Madame Chantal's opium parlor was the primo member of its class. Exquisitely decorated, boasting the finest dope and women, run with elegant discernment by the ageless Madame Chantal herself (rumor had it that she was the widow of the owner of a rubber plantation, who ((the husband)) had been beheaded by a tribe of cannibalistic Khmer high up on the Mekong some fifty years ago; she however had been spared when the tribesmen found her wearing, behind her left ear, the long-life charm of a banyan leaf), the parlor was frequented mostly by journalists, diplomats, and members of the Cambodian ruling class, not barring the royalty themselves. (Further rumors asserted that, for special clients willing to pay a special price, Madame Chantal would arrange a liaison in a third-floor room with a masked woman who was in reality Monique Sihanouk, wife to the King himself.)

So deClosets stepped inside, doffed and checked his coat, combed his damp black hair in a gold-framed mirror, and joined his fellow lowlifes and hopheads for a lost, somnolent hour or three of cheerful puffing, chasing the dragon, hoping that when he emerged from the cloudcover his problems would have been miraculously solved.

'Course nothing so simple as that happened. But what did was even more Significant.

Round about three o'clock, guy blew in and didn't even stop to take off his coat before bursting into the smoking room. DeClosets looked up stuporously and blearily focused on Harry Covair.

Covair was an American diplomat of deClosets' grade, and of the same basic age and attitude. He seemed an agreeable type, and deClosets would have enjoyed seeing more of him, but Covair was kept pretty busy in the American Embassy down on the banks of the Bassac, and seldom got out to such officially frowned-upon places as Chantal's.

Right now the brown-haired, skinny American was dripping water in a puddle while he clutched a flat package wrapped in plastic. "Hey, you dope-fiends, wake up and give a listen to this platter! It's all the rage back home. Just got it from a friend Stateside."

From the uncharitably described patrons arose a sleepy murmur of assent as from a flock of rockdoves. What was playing on the hi-fi now was some half-heard abomination like "How Much Is That Doggie In The Window?", Madame Chantal's taste in music tending toward the sentimental, this being the one unpleasant feature of her hospitality.

Covair clumsily dragged the needle across the still spinning disc, producing a horrid screech that generated instant alertness along dope-flooded neurons, causing everyone to sit bolt upright. Then he dropped the new forty-five down and cued up the arm. "Hold on to your hats, fellas, you ain't ready for what you're gonna hear! This is Number One in Memphis right now!"

And shure enuff, they weren't ready—at least not deClosets.

Out of the speaker came this southern US hillbilly voice similar to accents he had heard from various GI's, sorta like the oral equivalent of white lightning, and it just electrified deClosets. He couldn't even concentrate on the lyrics, so mesmerized was he by this new and powerful combination of rhythms and delivery, by the sophic impact of this novel method of musical encoding. (Eventually, he would learn that the song was "That's All Right Mama" ((B side: "Blue Moon Of Kentucky")), sung, natch, by one Elvis Presley.) But right now, during this initial encounter, deClosets was too shaken and stunned to wonder about such minutiae. He was groovin' on the song as a gestalt, and it seemed to enter his veins like the dope he had been recently ingesting.

When the song was finally over, deClosets got to his feet and approached Covair. The other patrons, while seeming mildly appreciative, had obviously not been hit as hard by this musical revelation, and had already sunk back into snakelike torpor. Most people just ain't got the receptors for the gnosis/satori ligand.

Covair was lifting the disc as if it were his firstborn and carefully repackaging it protectively against the insidious moisture.

"May I hold it?" asked deClosets.

Sensing his sincerity, Covair allowed the young Frenchman to cradle the licorice pizza with its simple black and yellow label that bore the legend SUN and a triumphantly crowing rooster. And what a new sun it was! DeClosets closed his eyes and basked in the afterglow.

Finally handing the sacred object back, deClosets said, "This is the music of a new age."

"You ain't just gassin' there, cuz," shot back the Yank. "I been waitin' for something like this to happen for years now. A white man singin' black—I just knew somebody else hadda be listenin' to the same stuff I was."

DeClosets was puzzled. "You mean there are precedents for the voice and style of this man?"

"Precedents!" howled Covair. "Where you been, Jim? You think this hillbilly came outa nowhere?"

"Well, whom would you name?" asked the earnest European. He took out his handy notebook and poised his pencil above a blank page.

Covair grinned. "Oh, just one or two folks. Such as Hank Ballard, Bobby 'Blue' Bland, Dorsey Burnette, Johnny Cash, Ray Charles, The Clovers, Arthur 'Big Boy'

Crudup, Fats Domino, Bill Haley, Etta James, Robert Johnson, Albert and B.B. King, The Moonglows, The Orioles, Johnny Otis, The Penguins, The Platters, Little Esther Phillips, Lloyd Price, The Ravens, The Robins, The Spaniels, Big Mama Thornton, Joe Turner, Dinah Washington, Muddy Waters and Howlin' Wolf. 'Course, those are just the big names, there's a few dozen others less well known. Say, you done scribblin' yet?"

DeClosets' pencil had been burnin' up the page, but he had managed to get down all the strange names. "Yes. I must now apply myself to acquiring the recordings of these musicians."

"Well, you ain't gonna find 'em anywhere in this neck of the woods, 'cept back at my pad."

"May I take that as an invitation?" trepidatiously quavered deClosets, not daring to hope.

"Can Marilyn Monroe fuck?" cryptically quipped Covair, in what deClosets took to be affirmation.

By that evening, DeClosets felt a new friendship was cemented forever.

In the following weeks, Covair and deClosets spent almost all their free time together. Each man told his superiors that he was spying on his counterpart, and Groshorloge and his American alter ego, one Dixon Ticonderoga—referred to by Covair as "a pencil-necked geek"—both rubbed their hands gleefully together, anticipating great results and advantages.

Of course, the two bosom buddies were doing nothing of the sort. Mainly they wandered around the delightful riverine city staggering drunk, after consuming innumerable bottles of San Miguel beer, or lounged at Madame Chantal's, listening to the newest releases forwarded by Covair's Stateside pals. Once, under the guise of field reconnaissance, they borrowed a car from the French pool and rode up Route 26 to the Tonle Sap, the Great Lake (which REVERSED ITS FLOW during every September monsoon), for a couple of days' fishing. (A spill of palm-oil had rendered it a Greasy Lake indeed: no good for swimming, but the fish came out pan-ready!)

Eventually, however, the bosses of both Kool Kats, growing understandably impatient, demanded to see some positive results from this fraternization. DeClosets and Covair were initially strapped for a plan to cover their tails. After an inspiring session at Madame Chantal's, during which repeated listenings of "Good Rockin' Tonight" served as mental tonic, they came up with a plan.

Giggling like a couple of drunken schoolgirls, the two went shopping, then split for their respective embassies. That night they met under a new moon by the gurgling Bassac, and carried out their scheme.

In the morning, the city awoke to joint consternation on the part of both the French and the Americans. On every building owned by the Americans, and in various public locales, the slogan FARK YOU! was painted in large red letters. (FARK, of course, standing for *Forces Armées Royales Khmer*, the national army, with whom the Americans were busily trying to ingratiate themselves.)

Not unscathed, the French buildings—and any plaza wall not bearing a FARK YOU!—were decorated with BONJOUR TRISTESSE. "Bonjour" was Cambodian slang for graft, bribes, and kickbacks, and the French had been trying to stamp it out for ages.

Weh-hell.... Covair and deClosets were both alternately congratulated and chastised. A nice bit of psychological warfare, but still....couldn't you have discovered that the other side had something similar in mind?

Suppressing their delight, each just bashfully lowered his eyes and curled a lip in that by-now patented Presley sneer.

October rolled around and the rains ceased. DeClosets was feeling on top of the world. Say-hey, bro', doncha know that's just when you gotta be on your guard, cuz the Kozmic Doorman is likely to chose that very moment to pull the red carpet right out from under ya!

War broke out in Algeria.

Consternation, panic on the Quai d'Orsay, refugees flooding the motherland, everyone runnin' around like headless geese, tremors and repercussions from Papeete to Cochin China....

Groshorloge called DeClosets into his office one lovely October morn. All unsuspecting, the Presley-besotted youth entered.

"Sit down, please, Phillipe. I have important news for you. Because of your African experience, you are being reassigned to Algeria. No, no, make no protestations of your humble unworthiness, you have exhibited such initiative that I am sure you will live up to our expectations and become quite an asset to the Algerian corps. That's all, Phillipe, you may go now."

Stupefied, deClosets left the complacent Groshorloge without ever getting the chance to utter any protests against this probable death-sentence. (French diplomats were being croaked by the Algerian rebels faster'n they could breed 'em back home. The *corps* was rapidly becoming *corpses*. The vets who survived, of course, were called *pieds noirs*, or black feet, a title which hardly seemed sufficient recompense for the dangers.)

DeClosets headed straight for Chantal's.

There he found Covair.

The problem was quickly explained. DeClosets grew more and more angry and despondent as he spoke.

"Do you think I could defect to your side, Harry?" finished deClosets.

"My side? What the hell are you talkin' about, cuz, we're all on the same side, ain't we? NATO and all that? You show up in front of Ticonderoga lookin' for sanctuary and he'll hand you back to Groshorloge so fast your head'll spin. No, buddy, I'm afraid there's no refuge there. It's one tough row to hoe, and I can't see no way out...."

DeClosets was silent for a minute. Then: "I am going under the fence in that case, Harry."

Little bit of noise here in the translation made Covair wrinkle his eyes and say, "Huh? Oh, 'over the wall,' you mean. Well, can't say I blame you. Sure as hell hate to be on the scene of one o' them guerrilla wars myself. Heard they can get real nasty. Thank Christ that'll ever happen here! Where you gonna go, buddy?"

"I don't know, Harry. Truly, I don't."

"Well, good luck, Phil. Let me know if I can getcha any supplies by five-finger discount...."

DeClosets and Covair shook hands. DeClosets sought for some sentiment to convey the depths of his feelings for the American.

"Harry, if I ever have a boy-child, I will name him after you, and you will be his godfather."

"And I'll take him every weekend to the Apollo Theater, you betcha."

They parted for the last time.

DeClosets wandered for a short time throughout the city, up Norodom Boulevard, through the Post Office Square, past the Royal Hotel, pondering his options. Definitely not an appealing lot. Sure, he could resign from the diplomatic corps—he wasn't in the army after all. But—and a big but it was—such notices of resignation moved through normal channels extremely slowly even during peacetime, and now, all channels being clogged with the noise of war, he'd probably be dead in Algeria before he was officially released from his post. No, not an appealing risk.

Let's see: he could simply refuse the transfer, in which case Groshorloge would probably find some pretext to jail him for insubordination or even treason, he'd be shipped back home and, amid wartime hysteria, find himself kneeling beneath the guillotine. (DeClosets was being a little hysterical himself here, but for some reason—perhaps connected with persistent memories of the rumors of how Madame Chantal's husband had lost his own noggin—he couldn't dislodge the notion of beheading from his head.)

No, his only safe course seemed to be flight. But where to? Saigon seemed the likeliest bet. Hide his ass away amongst the various slimy underground elements there until this whole mess turned around and he could emerge. When to scoot? If he could grab a car under cover of night, he might have eight hours or so until he was missed. That should give him a long head start....

Ending up back at his embassy, deClosets made like nothing was wrong.

"*M'sieur* Groshorloge, perhaps you could share with me the bounty of your superior knowledge concerning the Algerian situation...."

"I would be delighted, Philippe. By all means, sit down...."

*Gladly on your face, you overstuffed Napolean*, mentally riposted deClosets.

Night came. DeClosets, ditty bag full of stolen victuals, drugs, snakebite-antivenom kit, and black-marketable goodies in hand, snuck into the auto pool, where shadowed Citröens dreamed oily wetdreams of lubejobs given by mechanics dressed in chrome suits and equipped with big hot greaseguns. He hesitated, keys in hand. This city, to which he had come so reluctantly, herein to unexpectedly experience the major musical epiphany of his life, had grown on him like a bromeliad on the limb of an unwary tree. He was surprisingly reluctant to leave.

Turning his back on the vehicles, deClosets resolved to spend a few last hours saying goodbye to Phnom Penh. Couldn't hurt any, could it?

No one was at Chantal's except a languidly limbed, honey-colored, thirteen-year-old girl clad in translucent silk undies who lay on the thick Moroccan rug, druggily blissed-out, with a long bolster off the couch clamped between her thighs and gripped against her small chest. Her head rested against one of the couch's four feet, which were carved in the shape of an animal claw grasping a ball. DeClosets, that jackdaw of trivia, knew that the motif was an ancient Oriental conception, representing a dragon's foot clutching the Pearl Of Wisdom....

DeClosets experienced a sudden urge to replace the cushion with his own horny body, but instead merely prodded the girl awake and asked where everyone was.

"The King—he plays tonight and all have gone to hear...."

Weh-hell, deClosets was up for some music and he set out to find the sax-tootling King.

At a smoky club called *Le Serpent*, deClosets discovered half of the city's *haute monde* clustered noisily at tables whose tops were obscured by lipstick-smeared glasses, empty bottles and full ashtrays, while the King and his pickup jazz band jammed onstage under blue and red lights. They were slammin' out "Java Jive," a slinky chanteuse caressing the lyrics.

"I love coffee, I love tea, I love the java jivin' it loves me...."

Looking around for Covair, deClosets failed to spot him, chose therefore to sit with some agreeable strangers, ordered up a Hanoi Highball ("One sip, and you turn Red."), and settled back to relax prior to his hegira.

One thing led to another, as they so often do, and before deClosets knew it, the time was three AM. Forcing his reluctant feet to support him, deClosets bade a fond farewell to his new friends and prepared to split. Gonna be no one at the carpool now, fer shure, start 'er up and hit the road, Jack, don't look back or turn to salt like Lot's wife....

DeClosets scooped up his change from the wet tabletop. Heh-hey, what was this queer coin, big silver cartwheel emblazoned with a dragon on one side and phoenix on the other, stamped 1923.... Why, it was the famous suppressed Chinese Imperial Dollar, minted but never circulated because it invoked too many Imperial sentiments in tumultuous Republican China.... Well, wherever this coin had been in the intervening thirty-one years, however it had escaped destruction and ended in his possession, deClosets chose to regard it as a lucky omen. If he were brave as a dragon, he too would be reborn like the phoenix....

Somehow, without any conscious effort on his part, deClosets found himself driving through the tropical night southeast on Route 1, heading toward that old Saigon. Trouble was, he could barely keep his eyes open, and after a few dozen kilometers or so, he had to pull over and go to sleep.

Morning arrived in birdsong and the distant lowing of water-buffaloes amid the paddies. DeClosets awoke, rubbed his gritty eyes, and continued his maladroit escape.

Doncha know, deClosets's shameless swilling and toe-tapping last night had definitely worked against him. Groshorloge—pissing mad more at the theft of an official car than at deClosets's abdication—had had time to radio ahead and set up a roadblock at the junction of Routes 1 and 15, outside Neak Luong, after Route 1 crossed the Mekong. DeClosets came upon the French soldiers doing eighty KPH. They had their rifles pointed in his direction. He slammed on the brakes and the car went into a skid, barrelling through the soldiers, who threw themselves aside.

As soon as the car had stopped, deClosets floored the pedal again and roared off. Only thing was, he now roared north on Route 15, back into Cambodia.

Definitely more than a minor screwup.

Faced with no choices, deClosets kept barrelling north. At the next roadblock, where 15 joined 7—all these numbers, man, some kinda conspiracy, or what?—the troops (who by now were convinced that innocent deClosets was some kinda Commie spy on the run) started shooting when they saw his car. DeClosets, windshield glass in his hair, rolled out of the moving auto while still a hundred yards away from the troops and hightailed it into the surrounding paddies.

The novel sensation of having bullets whiz by one's ear instantly served to transform certain information in deClosets's possession—namely, that his country was at war in one part of the globe, and that they were former colonial masters in this land, trying to maintain influence now by chicanery, bluster and intimidation—into stone certain knowledge (knowledge, of course, being merely information with strings attached, incorporated into a formal scheme and exhibiting interconnections with other facts).

Using the helpless and scared peasants, who had halted their labor and now stood in shock, as visual noise between himself and the marksmen (there is no shame when running for your life), deClosets splashed across the broad paddy with his hide intact and into the welcoming outliers of jungle.

Run, run, run thru the jungle, boy! He ran crazily for hours, nearly hanging himself on snaky lianas several times, until he seemed to have finally lost his pursuers. Then he dropped to the moist earth.

Gradually, the noises of the jungle returned: chattering, chirping, chittering, and cachinnations, some kinda crazy animal party-line.

When deClosets regained his breath and his legs felt less rubbery, he set off aimlessly again.

In the following days, deClosets encountered no people, but did meet the following animals: a tiger, a panther, two leopards, a bear, a herd of wild oxen, grouse, egrets, and ducks. Thanks to incredible patience, he managed to catch one of these latter, wring its neck, and eat its half-cooked, still pin-feathered flesh. Worst company, tho, was them slithery, slippery, sneaky snakes. Cobras, king cobras, banded

kraits and Russell's vipers. Also, another, seemingly venomless type whose discon-
certing habit was TO DROP OUT OF TREES ON YOUR HEAD! Whoa-ho, like to give a
feller your basic cardiac arrest....

After a drink from a stream induced wicked diarrhea, deClosets started to feel
pretty shitty. Seemed like he had this here fever, too. But he just kept stumbling on,
not knowing what else to do. Talk about your basic Bungle In The Jungle. He who
made kittens made snakes in the grass....

Rubbing his "lucky" coin absentmindedly, he hoped alternately for either a pool
of quicksand or rescue by a beautiful American female archaeologist.

So on about the fourth afternoon, sunlight slanting greenly through the leafy
canopy above, deClosets underwent the further alienating experience of being cast
as the lead in one of your archetypical Myths of Western Civilization, namely

DISCOVERY OF THE RUINS OF A LOST EMPIRE,
COMPLETE WITH SURVIVING PRIESTESS!

Parting a screen of waxy foliage, deClosets halted in shock. Before him reared
several enormous spired stone structures scattered across a clearing. The buildings, composed of huge blocks cunningly fitted together, were partially covered
with vines and full-sized trees with their roots gripping cornices and lintels. The
clearing was uncannily silent, with no one in sight.

After a moment of initial disorientation, during which he could not be sure he
hadn't somehow mysteriously been transported around the world to the jungles of
Central America, with their Mayan temples, deClosets stepped out, leaves thwacking
together behind him, and began to wander among the buildings in astonished pe-
rusal.

Okay, what we've got here, deClosets dizzily decided after an extensive survey, is
your standard Ancient Khmer Ruins, circa 1100 AD, just like the vast Angkor Wat
complex north of the Tonle Sap. Except, unlike those temples, the intricate, inter-
laced, thick Indian-style carvings on these buildings were almost entirely of....snakes.
Thass rite, snakes of every conceivable size, shape and disposition, engaged in various unsavory pursuits, such as swallowing whole cows and men, or, can it be, just
pull aside these tenaciously tentacled creepers here, wow, it is, a huge snake seemingly copulating with one of them traditional celestial maidens, what're they called,
oh yeah, an *apsaras* ....

Well, this was all very interesting and historical, like, but it didn't put any butter
on deClosets' bread, of which he had none anyway. Let's see, the fact that this site
was relatively growth-free must mean that it was known to the natives at least, who
probably kept it clean out of ancestral pride or some such motive. If he could find
a path out, it would probably lead to some hamlet, in which he could solicit shelter
and food for an indefinite time....

Circling the clearing, deClosets sought such a trail. At the northern edge, he came upon a curious construction. Some kinda big walled pit inna ground, looks like. Gonna just stand on the edge here, careful-like cuz of this light head, and look in....

At first deClosets had trouble believing his eyes. Some sorta febrile hallucination, gotta be.... At last, tho, he was forced to admit the reality of what he was seeing. The frieze he had just seen had come unfrozen.

Gorgeous native gal lay naked on her back on the dirt floor of the pit, brown nipples enticing the sky, feet planted firmly, legs apart, and, and, THIS TITANIC PYTHON HAD ITS HEAD BETWEEN HER THIGHS, LICKING AT HER BUSH! As deClosets's jaw hit his chest—unhinging rather like a snake's—the python left off licking and slithered its length up the woman, and now the gal—who's got legs and knows how to use 'em!—had the snake clamped tight and was humping furiously away, and suddenly deClosets couldn't tell if there was only one snake in the pit, or two!

It's the Union Of The Snakes! Ride that snake to the ancient lake! He's long, seven miles long, he's old and his skin is cold....

Hold on just one minute! Ain't no crazy snake-rape gonna happen while an exemplar of Gallic chivalry was nearby. Without even stopping to think, deClosets grabbed a nearby stick, jumped into the ten-foot-deep pit and began just a-whackin' away at the oscillating scaled back, and Ol' Mister Snake—who appeared to like his humanality-type sex only under less insulting conditions—quickly disengaged from the maiden. As deClosets braced himself to meet an ophidian assault, the snake surprised him by slithering away and vanishing into a small arched hole in the side of the pit.

DeClosets looked down at the rescuee. The gal, eyes shut, was writhing with unsatisfied, tho mute, lust in the dust. Thick cords of viscous snake sperm dribbled from her quim and asshole. She seemed not a whit either pleased or displeased by deClosets's actions, so consumed was she by her trans-species desires.

Well.... DeClosets, stimulated to the most rigid erection he had ever known, did the only thing he could. Which was to jump her bones right there, despite tremendous aches, hunger, fever and queasy bowels, and indulge in sloppy seconds.

Thus was deClosets welcomed to Nokor Wat.

When deClosets regained his post-orgasmic senses and disentangled himself from his new acquaintance, pulling up his ragged, shitty pants in the process, he was faced with the interesting and far from academic problem of exiting the well. DeClosets sure wasn't about to follow *M'sieur* Snake down his hideyhole—even assuming it broached aboveground—and he really felt too weak to even leap for the rim of the pit, much less pull himself up.

Left with only a single option, deClosets managed, by signs, to convey to the woman—who now stood beside him, with sweat runneling her dusty skin, and who apparently understood neither French nor his limited Khmer—that he would boost her out, whereupon she should contrive his escape.

Over by the wall, deClosets made a cradle of his hands, the gal stepped in, deClosets hoisted her with what little strength remained to him, she gained a purchase, levered her strong arms—and quick as a wink disappeared from deClosets's limited horizon.

"Hey," said deClosets weakly and ineffectually, contemplating the air. Maybe this hadn't been such a good idea after all.... The sun beat down on his unprotected head. He turned to look at the snake's burrow. Nothing. So far. What did it matter, tho? How long would he last in this hole without water, without food? No, as Johnny Mathis always sang, "Chances are my chances are none too good...." Most likely, Mister Python would be literally jumping deClosets's own bones soon enough....

A vine thwacked the brick side of the pit. DeClosets looked up, found ol' *Mamselle* Snakehips standing with feet braced ready to pull him up. Shoulda known once these native gals get a taste of French lovemaking they'd never desert their man....

With much travail deClosets half hauled himself, was half pulled, out of the serpentine well. And then there he stood, faced with the dark Asian eyes of this mysterious jungle princess, two far more enticing and seductive wells which he did not, or could not, at that moment or any other future moment choose to escape. He had fallen in love with a slant-eyed lady.

Now, had deClosets read his H. Rider Haggard, he'd'a known not to mess with Ayesha. But as it was, his soul was bagged.

Gal took him into one of the ruined buildings, deClosets allatime tryin' out these truly absurd, insulting pidgin phrases in an effort to get her to speak or at least register signs of comprehension. Stuff like: "Me you fickyfick, now we *bon amis*, chop-chop." Gal showed no emotions, unless completely self-assured complacency counted as such, just led deClosets into a chamber that was obviously her home, grass mattress, coupla clay jugs, wooden bowl, not even a candle to disperse the shadows that hung from the shrouded ceiling, through a rift in which lanced a beam of sunlight filtered by vegetation.

Making deClosets lie down, and satisfying herself that he wouldn't get up—truth was, he really couldn't—the woman left the room. DeClosets pondered his fate while she was gone, and decided that it topped even his dreams of a glamorous American archaeologist, who probably woulda been harder to get in the sack anyway....

Gal returned with an armload of fruit and a piece of bark, whose pulpy inner layer she made deClosets chew. After consuming as much of the fruit as he could, along with some water, deClosets felt an insidious sleepiness overtake him, and succumbed.

What had to be days later, he awoke alone, refreshed, rejuvenated, renewed. Wow, that stuff beat out even Coca-cola, gotta be a small fortune to be made in the pharmaceutical trade there, if only he could find out what tree the bark had come from....

As if mentally sensing his alertness, his naked nurse entered and proceeded to administer the second stage of his treatment, which consisted of pinning him to the grassy mat and screwing him royally with the same unconstrained fervor of their first encounter, accompanied by odd modulations of his various ganglia deClosets hadn't known he'd possessed.

DeClosets cooperated wholeheartedly, and on the whole felt he acquitted himself rather better this time, being in full possession of faculties.

When they—or rather when she—was finished, as if a compact had just been sealed, or some sort of obscure bonds irrevocably formed, deClosets came into possession of the knowledge that he would be staying with this woman for quite some time.

Somehow he felt disinclined to disagree.

Where else did he have to go anyhow?

During that first fully conscious day of his stay in Nokor Wat, deClosets continued to try to get the woman to talk. No go. All she'd do is quirk her lips in an enigmatic smile that had deClosets's own artificial smirk beat all hollow. She seemed to regard his verbal gymnastics as some particularly laughable birdsong. Least she must answer to some name.... DeClosets ran through some local *noms des filles*. Boupha, Kunthea, Tevy, Chantrea....Nope. Well, deClosets had to call her something, if only for his own sanity's sake, and not being Tarzan, he didn't want to settle for your plain generic label, such as "Girl," so remembering what the celestial maidens were called in ancient Khmer myth, and taking into account this woman's resemblance to same and also her knowing grin, he chose to call her Sara Smile.

As deClosets's time with Sara lengthened, he decided he might have chosen her first name more wisely than he knew.

For one thing, Sara was obviously worshipped by the neighboring natives, who came calling from time to time with gifts of fish, rice and wine. These visits initially made deClosets nervous, for he suspected that he might be resented as a trespasser, but when it began to appear that in the villagers' eyes he shared Sara's aura, he grew relaxed and came to look forward to the company the smiling, albeit timid villagers represented.

In between such calls, deClosets simply lived. Freed from all the carking cares of civilization, he went the whole Gauguin route. Laid around all day noshing on breadfruit, durian or jackfruit, tossed the empty skins at monkeys and laughed at their recriminations. The clouds alone provided hours of study. Rainfall meant it was bathtime. Building up a slow buzz on native wine could take the whole day. Because the sky is blue, it turns me on....

And of course there was continual fickyfick with Sara. Between her tawny thighs deClosets found all the answers and anodyne he needed. Gal could really do it, no questions there. Falling asleep in her arms at night, after a strenuous bout, deClosets felt completely happy.

'Course, at those times when he awoke in darkness to find his companion gone, he did feel a little queer and uneasy, knowing but not admitting that Sara was probably down in the pit with his rival, Old Lucifer. But.... Man can't have everything, and the concept of fidelity was stretchable, if one really needed it to be.

Thing deClosets missed most was music, but even that was provided for when he contrived to teach the villagers a few pop tunes. Bangin' 'n' strummin' away on their simple instruments, they soon became quite adept at producing a funky kinda Indochinese Rock 'n' Roll, and these songfests completed deClosets's happiness.

'Bout four months into his stay, deClosets noticed Sara putting on a little weight.

"Gotta watch that breadfruit, babe," he warned nervously. "A-and maybe you need a different kind of exercise."

Sara only showed the smallest temblor of a smile, maybe a .1 on the Richter scale for amusement.

Soon it was unmistakable: Sara was pregnant. DeClosets freaked out at first. It wasn't so much that she was knocked up— The real issue was:

### WHO WAS THE FATHER?

Sara's unshakeable calm soon restored deClosets's sanguinity. It seemed to be a normal pregnancy. Sara had never looked more ethereally beautiful or healthy. She was so radiant, in fact, that at times she seemed too good to exist in this vale of tears, this cruel, crazy, beautiful world. Every morning when you wake up, hope it's a big blue sky—but some day, I'll have to say goodbye....

And hey, what could he do about the parentage anyway, at this late date? Kid was gonna be born and that was that. If it looked like him, fine. If it had scales—well, we'll deal with that when the time comes.

Came the day, as it always will.

Sara on the mat, her face glowing in some sorta apotheosis, legs apart, straining without sound, vagina he had plumbed so often now dilated out of recognition, deClosets poised to help, uttering soothing noises, and HERE IT COMES, snake or human, it's human! Little girlbaby, squalling and bloody, in deClosets's hands....

He was just trying to deal with the umbilical when there came a soft implosive POP and the cord lost its tautness.

DeClosets looked up.

Sara Smile had vanished.

Well.... He set the baby down and started running around, yelling, calling her name, generally going insane. Finally gave up, emotionally exhausted. Went back inside. Kid was still there, sleeping with preternatural grace. Unable and unwilling to ignore this small piece of Sara, last proof of her mortal existence, deClosets tended to the baby, tying off the cord, cleaning it up as best he could. Hey, kid's gotta eat! But what?

For the first time in several months, DeClosets left the ruins. In the village, his appearance caused a ruckus. The villagers seemed surprised by, but resigned to, Sara's disappearance. Eventually, a lactating woman was tapped to come live with deClosets until the baby should be weaned. Thankfully, he still seemed to be charmed, due probably to the kid's being Sara's daughter.

So thirteen years passed while Daddy deClosets tried to raise his little girl like a good father should.

It wasn't easy. At first he was reluctant to depart the ruins for good, as he knew he should have, expecting that Sara would return any day. After a couple of years, when his hopes had faded, it just seemed like too much trouble. Little Melusine— for so he had romantically christened "his" daughter—seemed happy there, and deClosets couldn't bring himself to uproot her. And besides, there was still his accumulated bad karma with the French Diplomatic Corps to contend with.

Day by day, his daughter revealed more and more of her mother's heritage. Her long black hair that hung to her tailbone, her ginger skin, her limber limbs, all recalled, sometimes quite painfully, Sara's form and ways. Luckily, Melusine exhibited none of her mother's muteness. Quite to the contrary, she became precociously fluent in both French and Khmer, and delighted deClosets with her loquaciousness. In addition, deClosets thought to detect some of his own genes expressed in her prominent jaw.

The one thing deClosets found disturbing about his daughter was an odd sort of amorality, an uncanny inability to fathom certain restrictions and admonitions he urged on her. On second thought, considering her maternal background, maybe it wasn't so odd after all.

So here it was, nineteen-sixty-eight already, how time flies when you're bringing up kids! All was quiet at Nokor Wat, as usual. Outside, however, things had changed. The old Cambodge that deClosets knew was mostly gone, or going. You got your VietCong in their sanctuaries all along the border, and pumping supplies in through the port of Sihanoukville. Americans got kicked out in 'Sixty-four, and French are barely an influence any longer. Yessir, big ch-ch-ch-ch-ch-changes. (Time may change me, but I can't change time..)

One day DeClosets noticed a big change underway right beneath his nose. He had been getting kinda withdrawn and abstracted lately, hardly even screwed willing women from the village anymore, even though he was only, what, thirty-seven? Geez, the life of a hermit.... Anyway, coming out of a daydream one afternoon, deClosets saw Melusine dabbing blood from her thighs with a palm leaf.

He was up on his feet and by her side in a second. "Are you hurt, *mon cher?*"

"*Non*, Papa, this happens each month now...."

Oh-ho, man, wake up! Little Melusine, whose perpetual nakedness deClosets had grown to hardly notice, ain't so little anymore, got them curvy hips and budding breasts, just like any Saigon Sweetie.... DeClosets felt incestuous stirrings. Maybe if he could convince himself that she wasn't really his daughter, but belonged to Ol' Mister Snake (who, by the way, hadn't been seen since Sara's departure).... No, forget it, man, this is your kid.

As best he could, DeClosets tried to get across The Facts of Life. Insofar as he understood such a weighty topic.

After explaining the, um, ballistics of balling, the chemistry of copulation, the physics of phucking, Daddy deClosets tried to convey some of the emotional tenor of Courtship and The Act.

"Well, honey, it's like the way you feel when you dance to the music of the villagers."

Melusine cocked her head quizzically, so deClosets tried to elaborate. He essayed a few tentative shuffles with an imaginary partner in the dust of the clearing. "You see, you check him out once before you make your move."

"*Oui....*"

"Then you put your bodies in the groove."

"I see....I think."

"Hit the floor and put the rhythm in your pocket."

"Like this?" said liddle Mel, wagglin' her hips.

"Right, right. Then worm on in, and on the beat you can lock it."

"Then....you arch your back, don't even cut no slack."

"You've got it! By George, I think she's got it!"

DeClosets and his daughter had come together now, and were boppin' around the temple, caught up in a trance, singing in unison:

> *"Freeze and tease and ya spank it like ya please*
> *Curve dat backbone as you swivel side to side*
> *And in between strokes you can add your slide*
> *Take it to the stage from the spank to the worm*
> *Add some extra jollies for the Funkadelic Sperm!"*

The two collapsed in a sweaty heap. Mel's downy pussy rode DeClosets knee, and her small breasts pressed into his belly. Feeling an erection sprouting, the dutiful Daddy disentangled himself and retreated to his quarters for a heartfelt wank.

This discussion and exhibition, deClosets soon had reason to believe, maybe hadn't been such a good idea for either of them. But what choice had he had?

A few days later, deClosets found Melusine lying, eyes closed expectantly, at the bottom of the snakepit.

"What—what's going on?"

"I am just taking the sun, Papa."

"Well, get up out of there, it's dangerous," deClosets adumbrated.

"How so, Papa?"

Not wishing to say, deClosets merely pulled at his beard and ordered her out again. Could be he shoulda told her.

Very next day he found her there again.

Trouble is, the Big Bopper was there too, the *ne plus ultra* of pythons, slithering slowly out of its hole.

Feeling immense *déjà vu*, deClosets grabbed a branch and jumped in.

Recumbent Melusine, hearing the THUMP as her father landed, opened her eyes, saw the snake, and jumped to her feet. DeClosets advanced fearlessly on the snake and proceeded to whack it as before, succumbing to The Redundancy Of Things.

Snake, however, was not so cooperative this time. We're talking about one horny snake now, thirteen years of abstinence bottled up inside his length, the object of his affections within sight. So he just flipped a couple of coils around deClosets and squeezed the life out of him.

Our hero deClosets, crushed by tumblin' time, cuz time will crawl!

All this time Melusine stood as if frozen. Sad to say, she helped her father not at all—not that her efforts would have availed much against the huge serpent.

When the snake was done with deClosets, he advanced on Melusine and had his way with her, as snakes will. (And if Mister Snake *was* Mel's Dad, then it was incest as well as humanality he committed!)

Thus was deClosets ushered out of Nokor Wat, and this life.

Thus was Melusine ushered into womanhood.

For the next two years, Melusine lived alone at Nokor Wat. The villagers continued to supply her food. Sex she got from the snake. The things Melusine learned from that snake! Some kinda hot information! The secret of Four-Way Hips, the Eleven Intractable Pressures, the Sinewave Oscillations, the Celestial Comeon.... Knowledge that would stand her in good stead in the days to come, for Melusine's world was about to be radically altered.

Nineteen-seventy. Sihanouk had just been ousted, whereupon he allied himself with the rebels he had long been fighting, who now called themselves FUNK, the National United Front of Kampuchea. The Secret War being waged by U.S. forces had been underway for a year, starting with the "Great Dragon" surveillance over-flights, followed by the actual bombing runs and incursions of disguised American soldiers under the codename of Operation Daniel Boone.

Melusine was sitting quietly one day in her clearing when this figure burst in. Clad in VC black pajamas, carrying Charlie's trademark AK-47, the man was anomalously Caucasian. He spun around, as if scoping for enemies, then, reassured, moved toward Melusine.

In bad French he said, "Whose side you on, honey?"

Totally confused, Melusine tried to explain her life.

The man seemed not to care. He was obviously taken with her nudity. When Melusine had faltered to a halt, he said, "Honey, I gotta get to the border, and you're gonna be my guide. And when we get back to Saigon, you can be my girl. Alla whores there got the Black Rot, and you're the neatest thing I've seen in a hound dog's age."

Melusine tried to explain that she had no desire to leave, but the man ignored her, grabbed her arm, and hustled her off.

Snake was nowhere at hand to perform a rescue. Phlegmatically, Melusine said goodbye to her old life.

For the next seven days the pair worked their way toward the border. The man seemed not to care about Melusine's inutility as a guide, since her performance each night was extremely adequate. The only trait of Melusine's that he objected to was her pleasant, wordless singing, which he ordered her to stop, claiming he hated music. Other than that, he seemed to become quite besotted with her, and eventually told her his life story, in broken French.

He called himself Sergeant Nick Fury, after some figure out of American myth. Once his name had been Harry Covair. He had been a naïve young diplomat—a veritable Teen Angel compared to his current fiendish condition—in Phnom Penh until the Americans were banished, whereupon he was recruited by the CIA for his knowledge of Asian ways and turned on to The Real State Of Affairs, which he was given to understand consisted of continual war between Us and Them, Us being the CIA and Them being everyone else. Now he headed Operation Daniel Boone, whose men were landed by helicopter inside "neutral" Cambodia, along with a team of natives, with the mission of reconnoitering and capturing VC. They weren't supposed to penetrate further than thirty klicks inside the country, but Fury's squad had been ambushed and he himself, the sole survivor, hounded further into the country.

Melusine tried to comprehend all this strange information, but succeeded none too well. In any case, she knew what was required of her when Nick Fury dropped his pants, and obliged, tho it *was* a little kinky to do it with a man.

So Nick Fury and his trusty sidekick were nearly at the border—one dreaming of the bars of Saigon, the other reminiscing wistfully about Dad, Snake, and the quiet days at Nokor Wat—when they ran into a little bad luck. As Fate would have it, they ended up

## SUR LA BOITE

Back in South Vietnam, ya see, at the Bien Hoa airbase, the Americans had received their daily orders from SAC. Feeding the secret ciphered information into their Olivetti 101 computers, they deduced the Cambodian coordinates for that day's illicit bombing. As the B-52's, which had flown all night from Guam, arrived overhead, these illegal coordinates were radioed up to the bombers, while fake ones within North Vietnam were recorded on datasheets, for public consumption. (This practice was known as dual-channel reporting.) Armed with the deadly numbers, the bombers continued on their way toward the target "box," which this time happened to contain, in addition to the other hapless victims, Nick Fury and Melusine.

First warning the man and the girl had was an awful basso droning like a swarm of maddened bees in the deceitfully cheerful blue sky. Fury said, "Oh, Mother of Christ!" and threw himself under a bush. Melusine, not knowing why, did likewise.

Then the planes were upon them, filling the air like pterosaurs. From their bellies, like a string of ones interspersed with the dead air of zeroes, fell the bombs, numbers made manifest in high explosives. The first ones hit with digital cruelty, ripping into the fertile earth. The roar was tremendous, and the earth seemed to suck in Her Gut in peristaltic pain. Melusine shut her eyes and began to wail. Let's all sing a chorus of the Amerasian blues....

During an anomalous second of silence, she looked up to see Nick Fury on his feet, some distance away in the open, shaking his fist at the sky. Apparently the irony of being bombed by his comrades, after suffering so much hardship on their behalf, had driven him round the bend, beyond all towns, all systems. Like some mad king, he now berated the uncaring air, until flying splinters from a tree punctured his chest and stretched him out on the churned ground, his only bier. Teen Angel, you're at peace now....

After a seeming eternity, the bombing stopped.

Melusine rose, unhurt.

For lack of anything better to do, half in clinical shock, she stumbled south.

Well.... the sight of a naked girl traipsing out of that hell on earth was enough to take even the seasoned ARVN troops aback—but only for a moment. Quickly seizing on the main chance, some of the more enterprising soldiers co-opted Melusine for their own use. When they were rotated back to Saigon, they took her with them and sold her to a bordello owned by Madame Nhu, the Dragon Lady. Melusine, exhibiting her mother's stolidity and other talents, didn't complain, but endured, and even flourished. Thanks to her unique training, she soon became legendary, commanding the highest fees. In time, she found that Saigon couldn't hold her, and she ended up in the Philippines, at Subic Bay, where she entertained the many Yank and Aussie boys who flowed in and out on R&R (Rimjob Resurrection). Along the way she found time to pick up a little martial arts for self-protection, including mastery of the infamous Dragon's Touch.

Word of Melusine's exquisite talents filtered up the ranks, through grapevine channels, and she eventually pulled a stint at CINCPAC in Honolulu, keeping the brass that ran the war free of annoying tensions. There she learned in the beds of majors and generals (who were never happy unless they had a war) certain information that allowed her to make her fortune and insure her independence. By wisely investing in the operations run by a certain yakuza of mixed Israeli-Japanese blood (one Lao Cohen by name), Melusine was enabled to gross over a million dollars in the business of illicitly trans-shipping integrated circuits to the Red Chinese. With her money, invested partially in Dragon Airlines of Hong Kong, she moved back to the Philippines and established herself as Madame of Manila's classiest bordello, with branches in the Patpong and Soi Cowboy districts of Bangkok, lovely city bisected by the Chao Phraya River, where other girls did the mattress-work and Melusine merely supervised.

It was 'Seventy-five by then. The American involvement in Vietnam was winding down. The Cambodians, driven mad as a nation by incessant and internecine warfare, were about to attempt to destroy the past and launch their Year Zero by filling the innocently beautiful Mekong with a Mayan-style display of corpses and severed heads, which would make this kinda radically funky soup.

Mekong Melusine, a hardened twenty-year old, was sitting behind her mahogony desk in the office of her bordello, fan-blades agitating the steamy air, bored outa her mind like her father twenty years before, contemplating how she was going to pass what amounted to her retirement. A buzzer sounded, and Melusine called, "Come in."

Turned out to be this slicker 'n a rat's tail Filipino, name of Epifanio Pagano. Melusine had him sit, served him a drink, chit-chatted a bit before getting down to business.

"I understand you represent a certain Wu Labs, Mister Pagano...."

"Very correct, so to say, Miss Melusine. My employer, Doctor Wu, enjoys to make you an offer. He wishes to buy your business from you, lock, stock, and cock-ring."

"What's the price?" Mel asked.

Pagano quoted a figure equal to ten years' gross on all her houses. Mel was floored, but tried not to show it.

"Why so high?"

"The Doctor seeks to establish his cordiality, so as to enlist the special services of you personally, along with a few of your more talented flowers."

Pagano handed over a computer printout, which Mel swiftly scanned.

"Vivian Vervain, Grace and Gloria Numinoso— These are high-priced ladies, Mister Pagano."

The Wu Labs rep made an elegant bow from his seat. "As are you yourself, Miss Melusine. But the Doctor's plans require such. Let me explain in some detail...."

The proposition, once described, turned out to be the most intriguing that she had ever heard. And when you consider the business Melusine was in, you realize *we're really saying something*, and that the magnitude of intrigue involved had to be gauged in mega-Hoovers (the standard unit for measuring paranoia, secrecy, deceit and transvestism).

Later, tho, when she was lying on the gynecologist's examining table, feet stirruped, legs apart, she had a moment's doubt about letting them insert the IRS up her pussy, which, tho much plumbed by approximately 2000 cocks, had never held anything quite like this.

But it was over before she could hesitate, and then when they had her flip over on her belly, her naked rump in the air, and employed the tattooing needle on her groceries, it was much, much too late to back out.

# MAX PARALLAX, P.I.

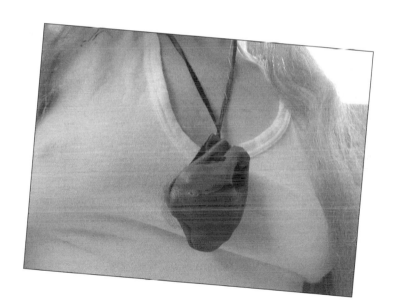

# K L U E S

### 00001000
"Religion has the same relation to man's heavenly
condition that mathematics has to his earthly one.... Belief in
God and belief in numbers.... One wants so much to find the
biggest number."

—Vladimir Nabokov

### 00001001
"Paranoia is an illness of power."

—Elias Canetti

### 00001010
"I wish we were in the dark, you can talk to me in the
dark, in the light you tell me things like....zero doesn't
exist....or bad money drives out good."

—William Gaddis

### 00001011
"It's in me, and it's gotta come out."

—John Lee Hooker

On the trash-rescued coffee-table beside the Salvation Army couch that sits on the Building 19 smoke-sale rug in Cyril's living room lie some objects, dropped there precipitously upon his hasty Ruby-frantic entrance. A handful of change that he found himself carrying after fumbling out his key; and Augie's rejected CD that miraculously accompanied Cy home in the tatters of his rear pocket.

His back is to these objects now, so Cy does not see what is happening among them.

From the Arizona-minted penny, composed of Holy Copper born of the Sun, mined by hand from ancestral Indian lands and formed into shape by workers at a modern-day collective whose roots lie in the old Indian leagues, and known as the Dyadiac Intertribal Gathering of Indian Talismanic Archons and Loas, blessed by an assortment of sages and brujos right down to those holy Zuni fools known as mudmen, rises a thread of smoky ectoplasm the color of semen. The wisp of spirit-cum probes the air for a few seconds until it senses the presence of the compact disc. Then it dives like a striking mamba down through the jewel-case and into the receptive randy hole at the center of the disc. At the exact moment of this Mystical Union and Sacred Conjugation the amorphous stuff takes on a shape, anchored in the two objects.

L-l-look! It's that foxy old Zuni Serpent of the Sea, Kolowissi—unless of course it's Quetzalcoatl or any other of a dozen Amerindian snake deities. Ain't much more than a penny's worth of difference 'tween 'em all, so we'll just call him K.

K smiles, his whiskered mouth opening to reveal venom-packed fangs which lower into striking position like the flaps of a landing F-17. Superabundant astral poison drips from their tips. The snake's body wavers and flows across the room, moving closer and closer to where Cy stands all unwitting.

When the Sneaky Snaky is within striking distance, it rears back and thrusts forward, firmly planting its ghostly incisors right in our hero's ass and shooting its toxic wad!

Cy absentmindedly scratches his rear. Funny how you get these anony-mous itches....

K retracts, his substance sucked back into penny and disc. For now.

All of a sudden, Cy feels faint. It's the stress of the situation. Pressure, under pressure, feeling like you want to scream, *Get me out*.... Jesus, he's awkward as an Irish nun at a French lesbian orgy. He is having one *hell* of a time trying to carry out Ruby's instructions and thereby resolve this whole Crazy Mixup (although what the exact nature of the mixup might be, or if there even is one, Cyril cannot yet say).

Just gonna fumble this here tape labeled *P.O.P.* into the camcorder's slot and sit down for a little matinee that's gonna explain everything, thinks Cyril nervously as he tries to figure out exactly how the undersized eight-millimeter cassette fits into the device. The mating is tricky, and Cyril feels like some kinda third-party pervert assisting at this intimate juncture of male and female machine-parts.

(Sometimes, watching Ruby deftly perform such tasks as this, Cyril found himself subject to the most inexplicable and unbearable hard-ons, as if he had just witnessed a particularly raunchy movie. Usually such erections led to satisfyingly outrageous sex with his lady-love. But Cyril could never quite bring himself to explain afterwards what had gotten his hormones coursing. Sorta embarassin', doncha know, to confess to finding any *inanimate object* erotic ((garments excluded, natch)). ((And while we're on the subject, how about the erotic properties of the various members of the plant and animal kingdoms, hey? On second thought, the topic's too big. Let's table it till we get this movie over with.)) But today, of course, with Ruby being unaccountably and forlornly Among The Missing, there is no possibility of such an outcome to any gadget-stimulated arousal. So why don't we stop thinking along these lines, *right now!*)

There, Cyril's got the stupid and obtrusive cassette aligned properly and socketed home. (The horny camcorder is whispering subliminally, *Oh, honey, it's in so deep, it fills me up,* but Cyril refuses to listen.) Now, gotta snake this cable behind the set and jack it into the television (entirely different operation from jacking off—*or is it?*).... Whew, he's sweating from the whole operation, but the equipment is finally all hooked up for viewing, and his faintness seems to be fading a little.

Looking up from his work, Cyril is suddenly struck by how desolate the apartment seems. The yellow lace curtains Ruby picked, which now are filled with late-afternoon sunlight like wet nets full of wriggling golden fishes, the worn old couch, the half-visible kitchen table with her breakfast dishes still on it (gal never could pick up after herself, and Cy usta get angry once in awhile about it, but now, now he wishes only that she were in the bedroom going through all her drawers and tossing clothes left and right, like most mornings)—everything in the four rooms seems to whisper Ruby's name. Where is she? What can possibly be going on? Cyril wants to dash out of the house and over to Wu Labs to demand some answers. But who would he speak to, what would he say? You've kidnapped my girl, or at least spooked her somehow into hiding out? What if Ruby's on her way home, and they missed each other coming and going? No, best to follow Ruby's note before taking any other action.

Cyril spins the television's dial to channel three, then stabs the power button. The screen flares into an orgasm of visual white noise, while static crackles from the speaker. He taps the camcorder's PLAY key, and the screen settles down as the tape begins spinning.

Flopping into a spring-shot chair, waiting for explanatory images to appear on the tube, Cyril has what seems like a mini-eternity to consider his plight. His mate apparently missing, his job lost, his brain suddenly subject to bizarre and uncontrollable hallucinations, his best friend Augie doubtlessly thinking him insane— hey, what more could any guy want? It's a wonder he isn't chewing up the carpet in

Frothing Mouthfuls. (Thing Cy don't understand is just *how easy he's still got it*....)
But such Nebuchadnezzar-like maniacal grazing just isn't an option for Modern
Man. Too primitive and spooky.... So instead he's sitting calmly before the electronic hearth, as if it were any old Saturday night, just a-waitin' for the latest injection of mass-produced entertainment-type information. It's wonderful, absolutely
wonderful. All his animalistic flight-or-fight instincts have been utterly eradicated by
Civilization, Mass-Communications, and Over-Stimulation. He should be out bash-
ing someone over the head with a club to get Ruby back. Instead, he's paralyzed
until a stream of electrons strikes a phosphor-coated glass plate and triggers a
cascade of photons which his eyes will pick up and transmit to his brain.

Suddenly Cyril feels himself falling into what he is already coming to call a "fugue
state." (Nice little synthesis of musical and psychological terminology here.) This
one's relatively mild, tho, not such a pain, really, kinda nice to have this non-phar-
maceutical outlet from reality, long as it doesn't get too scary, like, or interfere with
essential activities like eating and screwing. Hold on now, the room's disappearing,
here we go-o-o-o-o-o....

PLATO'S CAVE, PART II

Cyril's inside a cave with no exit. It's a moist cave with glistening, red-grey, veined,
pulsing walls. Occasional drips of some kind of chemical broth fall from the ceiling
onto his head. Some trickles down his face and into his mouth. Whew, whatever that
stuff is, it tastes awful! But boy, does it pack a kick! The juice causes Cyril's brain to
flood with random images that register powerfully before disappearing: a tree, a
snake, a snatch of music. When these inner flashcards are gone, Cyril concentrates
on his new surroundings. The light is dim, almost non-existent, but somehow Cyril
can make things out well enough. After puzzling over the texture and configuration
of the biological elements that make up the cave, Cyril realizes where he is. He's
inside—his own brain! (What organ did *you* think he occupied? Aren't you ashamed
of yourself?) Cyril has been reduced to a miniscule homunculus or manikin im-
mured deep within his own brain, huddling blindly and powerlessly in a chamber
carved out of neurons, synapses and dendrites, waiting for regurgitated, massaged,
twice-handled information to filter in in the form of neurotransmitters, which signals might, just might, help him decide how to act.

Instead of Plato's Shadows of Knight, all we can really know is a Funky Joseph
Campbell's Soup.

A burst of noise shatters Cyril's prison, plunging him back to his apartment and
his uncomfortable seat before the television.

While Cyril was Away On Business, a picture must've snapped onto the screen,
and sound now emerges from the set.

At first Cyril can make no sense of either.

The display is mostly black, with an out-of-focus image filling a circle centered on the screen. The soundtrack is a garbled collection of voices, typewriter clatter, ringing phones, and Muzak. Cyril watches for ten minutes. Nothing changes. Then one voice rises above the background buzz, although even this speaker is distant and muffled. The voice says something like, "Tuesday, lass, we need another body here, pronto." The image suddenly jerks into motion, the point-of-view shifting crazily, blurry objects that might be desks, file-cabinets, word-processing workstations, swirl kaleidoscopically around. The movie, Cyril realizes, was obviously made by Ruby at work. But how? Then Cyril has it.

Poor as they are, Ruby and Cyril both determined recently to indulge themselves in the areas that each valued most highly.

Using most of their pitiful savings, Ruby got herself a brand-new Canon H800 eight-millimeter camcorder with built-in fuzzy logic, contributing her old equipment as a trade-in. The sleek 'n' sexy gadget's tiny cartridges hold two hours' worth of film, its built-in electret mike and CCD imaging system make it state of the art, and it weighs only a few pounds. Ruby was so happy with her new toy and so convinced that she would be able to make better tapes than ever before, that Cyril hardly winced when he heard about the fifteen-hundred dollar price-tag.

His own new CD player, which he had deemed extravagant at a tenth of that cost, now seemed like an absolute bargain.

The camcorder, Cyril realizes, is small enough to have fit in that big leather shoulder-bag Ruby owns. A dime-sized hole punched in the side would have allowed the lens to pick up what Cyril was seeing. What Ruby hadn't been able to fully compensate for, though, was that the camera's infrared autofocusing mechanism would be screwed up beyond redemption by even the onboard chip, and that the resulting shots would be almost indecipherable.

Now the POV is floating herky-jerky-like down an aisle of fuzzy shapes that might be desks as seen from about waist-height. (Cyril can imagine how uncomfortable Ruby must've felt toting around her cam-laden bag on its strap. What freaky things could have been going on down there at Wu Labs, that she felt she had to tape them to get anyone to believe her?)

There is a big blurry figure leading Ruby down this gauntlet. Seems to be a guy with red hair. Wish he'd turn around so I could see his face. Probably couldn't make out his features anyway, though, focus is so awful.

The ghostly figure of the man comes to a door and keys a security code to get in. Can't see the sequence of numbers, natch, just in case gotta bust in there to rescue Ruby, like Secret Agent Man. Gonna walk like a man, talk like a man. . . . The door closes softly behind Ruby and the guy, silencing the Muzak and other aural garbage. Now the only sound is Ruby's heels clicking on the tiled floor.

Guy says, "I realize this little chore is above and beyond your standard duties, Miss Tuesday, but the company appreciates your cooperation."

Some helluva thick accent on this joker, but it's muffled by Ruby's bag. Irish, Welsh, Scottish? Kinda reminds Cyril of someone's he's heard speak just recently, but he can't place it.... Oh well, what's one more mystery when added to all the others?

Ruby replies, "I don't mind doing a little extra work, Mister O'Phidian, but I hope it's nothing like that last task you gave me, with the petri dishes. It was awfully messy. I ruined a perfectly good pair of shoes."

Hearing Ruby's voice drives a cold spike of grief through Cy's heart. Is she gone, will he ever see her again? He wishes she would turn the camera on herself, just so he could have one (last?) glimpse of her. He has to force himself to master his feelings and pay attention to the sense of her words.

"Yes, well, lass, the biotechnology division did get a little sloppy on that one. But I promise you that today's session won't be like that. We need you simply as an observer."

"I guess that's okay then, Mister O'Phidian. Uh, do you think I might get a raise out of this? I have been here six months and all...."

"We'll see, darlin'. The company rewards those who show some initiative and help us with our plans."

*"Darlin'!"* thinks Cyril. Wotta conceited sexist pig! If he knew Ruby was putting up with such shit.... If she comes home, she's never going back!

The floating POV has arrived at another door. Same ritual of keying in a code. Betcha ass must be something that rates Kozmic Secrecy, all right, to be hidden behind all this security. Cyril conjures up a buncha deadly, illicit possibilities: cache of nuclear weapons, laser death-rays mounted on mobile tripods (Cyril is Gene Barry holding them off with Sheer Bravery and Cunning), intelligent computer bent on taking over the world.... For the first—but not the final—time, Cyril thinks, hey, this could be heavier than just Ruby's fate alone....

The door is opening. Cyril holds his breath. All possibilities are still latent in this never-to-be-duplicated moment of videotaped *Now*, but soon they will evaporate (for Ruby, have already evaporated) in the hot quantum flash of Heisenbergian observation, condensed by the observer's sensory apprehension into a constrained single timetrack beyond whose narrow borders lurk all the myriad shadow universes where things went differently and were seen to do so. (All messages are embedded in a context of possibility; the wider the context, the greater the uncertainty. The greater the uncertainty, the more information is conveyed by the eventual selection of a single message out of the many.)

And it's, it's, it's—

A doctor's office?

Hey, man, wotta rip! Getcha self all worked up for Sinister Nastiness, and wotta ya slapped with? A Rubber Chicken in the shape of the same old sterile examining room everybody's been familiarized with since childhood.

Some other blobby figures are standing around in the room, revealed as Ruby pans her shoulder-bag. Then the camera focuses on the occupant of the tissue-sheeted examining table. Holy Guccione, it's a Nekkid Lady! Cy's sure of it, despite the fuzziness of the scene, having spent plenty of time trying to catch flashes of T&A on the over-the-air channels that are scrambled with the industry-standard Cipher II system.

"What is this?" Ruby says coldly through the speaker. Atta girl, Rube, you tell 'em! "What's going on?"

"Now, now, Miss Tuesday, please don't get the wrong idea," says the unctuous O'Phidian. "This woman is an employee of Wu Labs. She's here today for, ah, a regular examination. However, the company nurse is out sick herself—ironic, isn't it?—and the law requires that there be a, how shall we say it, a female chaperone during the exam. I'd like to call on you to play that role."

"I just—I don't know. I wasn't hired for such things...."

"Remember what I said about the company helping those who help us, Miss Tuesday. Besides, you're here now, and this poor lass is getting mighty chilly."

"I don't—oh, let's just get it over with, then."

"Wonderful, I knew you'd come 'round. Doctor Black Elk, you may proceed...."

Gal on the table hasn't said word one through all of this, as if she's bored or reluctantly playing along. You think in such a situation she'd either say she was grateful for Ruby's presence,or deny she needed her.... Odd, the whole setup is just plain odd.

The doctor blob is now between the gal's stirruped legs. Hey, no one said this was gonna be a gynecological exam.... Cy the Voyeur feels mighty odd, watching all this on tape, and can well imagine how Ruby must have felt actually being there. Heh-hey, this exam is getting weird, doctor's pink finger blobs (no gloves—is this AMA-approved?) probing excessively deep between tufted carnadine softness.... The whole thing is like watching a pornographic movie shot through a lens covered with a whole jar of Vaseline, all it needs is some kinda hokey disco soundtrack. Blurry as it is, Cy is getting sorta Worked Up.

Whew, Doc seems to have found what he was looking for, cuz he's out from between the patient's legs, holding between two fingers some kinda Concealed Weapon he must've retrieved, and None Too Soon either, from Cy's perspective, since it was almost time to Start Taking Emergency Measures. (What a jerk, Cy berates himself, getting turned on when all your thoughts should be for Ruby!)

"The iris appears in good condition," says Doc Elk. "Although of course, she will not be needing it anymore."

Iris? What the—?

"Fine," says O'Phidian. "If you'll just drop it off at Data Retrieval, Doctor, I'd appreciate it. Agnes, thank you, that'll be all for now. You'll be receiving new orders from Mel in the near future."

"More of the same, Paddy?" queries Agnes, legs still a-gape.

"No, darlin', something new."

Agnes gets up from the table. "Mary be with you," she says.

"And may the Woman Who Knows The All guide your own footsteps, lass," replies O'Phidian.

Mother Mary? wonders Cy. Are these nuts sum kinda Khristian Kooks?

As the woman named Agnes passes in front of the camera, Cyril sees a patch of black on the "patient's" backside, just above the cleft of her buttocks. A tattoo? Wow, we're dealing with some kinky people here....

Pretty soon the room is empty except for O'Phidian and Ruby. The latter is the first to speak.

"What was that all about?" she demands coldly.

"Why, I told you—"

"That's bullshit. That woman didn't want any 'chaperone.' She's been through this a hundred times before. You know what I think, I think you're testing me. You wanted to see how I'd react to the idea of having that, that gizmo put up me! You're trying to recruit me for some crazy scheme!"

"Miss Tuesday, what a ridiculous idea."

"I don't think so. I think I've hit the nail on the head."

"I suggest you return to your desk, Miss Tuesday, and consider what you've seen before jumping to any conclusions. And just remember that if you refuse this assignment, the next one offered might not be so palatable."

After that, there is no more talk between Ruby and O'Phidian. They retrace their route, and Cyril watches ninety more minutes of film that show nothing but the innocuous office-type activities around Ruby's desk.

Cyril replays the pivotal scene five or six more times, getting nothing more out of it than he did the first time. This don't explain bo-diddley-squat! Where's Ruby? Has she consented to whatever O'Phidian had in mind, and been sent away? Or has she been silenced cuz of what she knows? Either alternative abruptly seems plausible to Cyril's confused mind.

The sun is setting now over the Charles, throwing long Fu-Manchu-like skeletal fingers of gloom into the apartment. Cy stands up wearily, feeling a strange kind of will-less enervation, as if his brain has been overloaded with too much obscure data and his muscles drained of energy. Ruby should've been home by now, if she were returning at all. What can he do? What if she's left him of her own free will? What if this tape was her way of telling him goodbye? But he still loves her, damn it! He might as well admit it, he's just a slave to love, addicted to love.... What can he do? He has to continue to believe that what they had between them still exists.

Cy has only one idea left. He goes to the phone, dials a number. Hello, Operator, can you help me place this call? Pennsylvania 6-5000. Beechwood 4-5789. 853-5937. 867-5309. 634-5789 (Soulsville, U.S.A.)....

"Good afternoon, Wu Labs."

"Hello, may I speak to Miss Tuesday, please? She's a temp."

Pause. "I'm sorry, we have no employee by that name, temp or otherwise...."

The phone slips from Cy's hand and swings crazily from its cord like a hanged man, final as a Tarot reading. Cy sits back down. Pretty soon the irritated whooping and recorded voice issuing from the receiver ceases. Pretty soon the whole apartment is dark. Here comes the night! Cy still sits motionlessly, cloaked in blackness, in a room where no light can find him....

Comes a banging on the door, followed by some hollering.

"Cyril! Cyril, are you in there? Can't you hear me knocking? Let me in!"

Cyril just keeps on a-sittin. Poor boy ain't even in no fugue now, just a-wallowin' in the meanest kinda mindless blue funk you ever seen, makes a galaxy-sized black hole look like the LaBrea Tar Pits. Even Billie Holiday's never been this low. He's way down now. The clocks will all run backwards and Thursday night and Friday will be on Tuesday night instead....

"Cy, goddamn it, I know you're in there, open up! It's me, Polly! Ain't no stranger!"

Polly, yeah, I knew a Polly once, Augie's girl and one of the Four Musketeers of Northeastern U....

Cyril blinks once, twice. Has he blinked at all in several hours? Thought only snakes could stare like that.... Whatever happened, his eyes feel like sandpaper. Exerting every erg of energy, gets to his feet and shuffles to the door, hesitates a second, then opens it.

It's Polly all right, revealed in the yellow low-wattage hallway light. Nice to know someone still tells the truth.... Hey, what's this, Polly's crying! Strands of her long ash-blond hair are pasted to her finely sculpted cheeks and her driftglass-green eyes are red-rimmed. Seeing Cyril, she throws herself sobbing into his arms.

Holding this crying woman ain't doing nothin' to alleviate Cy's melancholy, and before he knows it, he's wailin' to beat the band too. Wotta soggy state of affairs! Hey, hold on a mo': Boys don't cry! But he's driven to tears, lonely teardrops. They're cryin' a river, a river of tears.... Take me to that river and wash me down....

After a few minutes pretty Polly gulps down her last tears and manages to say, "Oh, Cyril, Augie's missing! He never showed up for supper and didn't phone, and you know him, he's just not like that, and I've called the police, but he wasn't in an accident, and I tried to get you on the phone, but it was always busy, and I, I, I don't know what to do!"

Weh-hell, Cyril feels like an actor might who hears someone else uttering his best lines on opening night. Exactly what the fuck is going on here?

"Ruby's missing too," explains Cy.

"Oh, no, they've run off together!"

Despite his troubles, Cy cracks a little smile at this. Polly has always been a bit jealous of Ruby's exotic non-WASP looks (Polly being your standard Caucasian Girl Next Door herself), and could never quite believe that Augie had eyes for no one but her. She's made this kind of half-jokey, half-serious accusation before. But tonight, there seems to be more weight behind it than usual, as if Polly knows something she's not saying, and Cyril makes a mental note to probe her more on this.

But for now—and possibly for his own peace of mind—Cy hastens to reassure her. "I seriously doubt it, Polly. I think Ruby was in trouble long before today, and it has nothing to do with Augie. And anyway, when I saw Augie today—"

"You saw Augie today! When?"

"He came by the store to return something, around one. I only talked to him for a few seconds, but I could tell there was nothing wrong. He was just his old self. No, if he's missing, then it's not anything he planned, with or without Ruby."

"Then what's going on, Cy? Do the two disappearances have anything to do with each other? How are we going to find out? What should we do?"

"Answering those questions," utters Cy with utmost solemnity, "must become our Number One Priority."

Polly is silent for a moment, and Cy is convinced she's floored by his Zen-Master-perfect reply, its Koan-like Kompleteness, delivered in his best Voice of Wisdom. Then she speaks.

"You big idiot," ventures Polly, "that's so obvious it's no fucking help at all."

*₂ℓℓℓ*

That Polly! Swell female-type, good friend, lotsa laughs 'n' all that—but boy, not exactly the one person Cy would've picked to sleep with last night, of all nerve-weary, soul-wracked nights.

And let's just get it straight that "sleep with" is to be construed literally here. Perhaps if the verb's other, coded meanings had come into play, the night wouldn't have been so bad. But they hadn't. Not that Cy was up to such sacktime shennanigans. Nope, all he wanted was to sink into oblivion and forget about his troubles for eight hours or so. But he hadn't counted on Polly saying let's spend the night together.

Before Cyril knew quite what was going on, Polly had sacked out on the couch. Having exhausted speech and thought, she deemed it the only thing left to do. Well, Cyril felt the same. So he retreated to the empty bedroom and stretched out. That was when it all began.

First off, the bed was too big. No Ruby in it. (You're so far away from me, I'm tired of makin' out on the telephone. You been in the sun, and I been in the rain....) Cyril hugged a bolster, flailed his arms and legs around until the cold sheets were totally tangled, shed a few tears into his pillow, felt sorry for himself, wondered what Ruby was doing, and was finally drifting off to sleep—when Polly started snoring.

We're not talking any kind of demure, lady-like cat-purring sounds here, either. It was Major Sawmill-Processing-A-Redwood Time. Cyril came awake as if doused with cold water. At first he couldn't believe his ears. How did Augie stand it? On second thought, how come Polly didn't wake herself up? The noise was tremendous. But Cyril didn't have the heart to go bug her about it. He lay and suffered in silence. Hey, at least the sound meant he wasn't totally alone.

Cyril passed an essentially sleepless night before dropping off into a light drowse. Cold dawn light filtering in finally put an end to the farce. Woke up, it was a Chelsea morning.... But how can it be a New Morning without you, Ruby? It ain't no beautiful morning, each bird singing his own song, as long as you're gone.... He got out of bed around six, with the sounds of the awakening city beginning to compete with Polly.

In the kitchen he set some coffee perking in an old-fashioned pot on the gas-range. The heavenly odor made him feel somewhat human. Ah, that Java Jive! Oh, slip me a slug from that wonderful mug!

Cy's mind begins to wander down to Juan-Valdez, coffee-achiever, Taster's-Choice-Kute-Kupple country.

Jesus, what would Civilization do without coffee? Its European discovery and dissemination had come just when the Industrial Revolution was cranking up, producing that lifestyle we all know and love today. The two went hand-in-hand. Couldn't have one without the other. Life would be unbearable, no one would go to work, no one would stay up late, nothing would get done. We'd all be living like Savages, in a land gone to flowers, nothing but wild, bad, lightning seeds! Cy's mouth starts to water, his nerves itch for the coffee to be done. He starts a-dreamin' about coffee....

Coffee, intrinsic component of Modern Man's blood! Wake up and smell the caffeine in your bank account! Coffee, Lubricant of Society! Coffee, the cheapest, legalest buzz around! The whole family can share it! Sittin' around the breakfast table: "Good morning, dear, here's your coffee." "Thanks, honey. What flavor do we have today?" "Guatemalan Coaxihuital, dear." "Great! Say, where's Junior's mug?" "Coming right up, dear. I've only got two hands, you know. At least until I've had my second cup of coffee." "Hey, Mom, don't forget some java for Sis!" "I won't, Junior. Here it is. Drink up now, little girl, you've got to be on your toes for kindergarten." "Okay, Mom—but where's Fido's coffee?" "Oh, darn it, that dog's a terror, he's been through three cups already. Yesterday I had to peel him off the mail-lady. Here you go, Fido." "Woof!" All right! Swallow that hot black gold down, folks, get yourself around a pot or two. Or else—hey, why not! Fill up one o' them California-type hot tubs with a few hundred gallons of the stuff, not too hot, just a comfortable-feeling bath. Put three or four five-pound bags of sugar and a ladle by the side, along with a couple o' watering cans full of cream. Find yourself a few friends who all take their coffee the same way (can't have no one what likes it black arguing with those who want *cafe au lait*), then....JUMP RIGHT IN! Ah, bliss! Pure Pig Heaven! Wallowin' in the Primal Pool of Coffee, sticky with sugar and rich cream, colored just like Ruby's skin, slurpin' it down, letting it run out of your ears and between your toes, the broth gradually getting flavored with various humans secretions, until it was this kinda funky soup....

"Is that coffee I smell?"

"You betcha, Miss. Take off your clothes and jump right in!"

"Cyril—what the hell are you talking about?"

"Sorry, Polly, just day-dreaming. Pull up a chair, the brew should be done. I take it you slept well....".

Polly eyes Cyril narrowly as he pours their mugs full. Her white cotton blouse and black slax—which she has slept in—are totally wrinkled and bagged out and her hair is a hayrick. (For the first time in their long relationship, Cyril notices that Polly sports, well, you'd call them, he guesses, sideburns, pale though well-defined delicate feminine featherings of hair extending down alongside her seashell ears. It's sorta sexy, this here-comes-Billy-in-a-skirt androgyny....)

Polly seems particularly feisty this draggy mateless morn. "And just what is that supposed to mean, buster?"

Seating himself, Cyril holds up a placatory hand. "Nothing, nothing, just a pleasantry. Here, drink this. Maybe it'll take the rough edges off."

Polly sips, the coffee does its trick, and she instantly mellows out. "I'm sorry I snapped at you Cyril, it's just that I was afraid you were going to make fun of my, my—you know."

"Hey, no problem. Sometimes I clip my fingernails into the kitchen sink and forget to rinse 'em away. Now, are there any other personal quirks we should discuss before we get down to the important stuff?"

"You mean, like what happened to Augie and Ruby?"

"That's it. Polly, listen, we've been friends for years. I know you weren't mad at me just now. You're worried about Augie. Well, I'm worried about Ruby, so let's lay those two preoccupations on the table right from the start, and not let them interfere with how we get along. Something tells me that we're going to be spending a lot of time together, before we solve this mess. And we can't let ourselves get sidetracked with irrelevant personal stuff."

Polly regards Cy for a moment with an indecipherable expression, and he wonders if he's hurt her feelings (he flashes on all the stupid things he's inadvertantly said in his life, like that gaffe during his first conversation with Ruby), and just when he's convinced that Polly hates him, she gets up, throws herself into his lap, and locks her arms around him in your basic Can't-Get-Enough-Of-This-Guy Hug.

"Oh, Cy, I knew I did the right thing to come to you for help! And if I had known about Ruby being missing, I would've been here even sooner! I don't know what I was thinking. I was just—oh, I can't even put it into words, worried, maybe, that somehow our relationship was going to change, because our mates were missing. Does that make any sense?"

"Yeah, I can dig what you're saying. Now, how about letting me breathe...."

Actually, Cy can breathe okay, it's just that there's this Glandular Problem making itself known in his jeans, and what with Polly counting so much on their Eternal Platonic Friendship, he'd prefer her not to notice. (God, it seems that since all this weirdness started, he's been incredibly horny! Perhaps it's some sort of Darwinian biological imperative to scatter his seed before his imminent demise....)

Polly says, "Oh, sure, sorry," and gets outa Cy's dangerous lap. Back in her own chair she asks, "What did you mean about this mystery taking a lot of time to solve, Cy?"

Relieved, Cy responds, "Well, it's like this. There's a lot more going on than you know about, and I bet Augie's somehow become involved. Look, we've gotta start from the same base of information. Let me explain. Then there's a tape you've gotta see."

So Cyril launches into a recitation of all he knows. His eyes held by Polly's, he lets a small portion of his mind reminisce....

Way back when, shortly after Cy and Ruby had become an Item, they started going to a lot of campus activities together. It was football season, and they managed to catch every home game. Naturally, they knew the name of Augie Augenblick, star quarterback and prodigal mathematician.

Augenblick was renowned for the complexity of his plays. Beneath his stolid and somewhat dumb-looking exterior lurked the mind of a tactical genius. His inspiration had been to realize that the mathematics of the Mandelbrot Set could be applied to football. Under Augie's guidance, the fractal scrimmage completely unnerved all opponents. It was said that he had developed his own coding system to diagram his inspirations, the old, conventional way being too simplex. Took three blackboards and a personal computer just to explain to the team how to move. Even the coaches didn't quite understand what he was doing, but his strategies won games, so they left him to call the shots.

Linked inextricably with Augenblick's name was that of Polly Peptide, sports reporter for the school paper. Polly wrote a column for the *Northeastern Norbert* (named after Norbert Weiner, who had once made a large donation to the school) called "Peptide's Peptalk," in which she capsulized the collegiate sports scene. Polly had been hooked on sports from an early age by her father, who had season tickets for the Bruins, Celtics, and Red Sox, and had even been known to squeeze in an occasional game of the Pawtucket Red Sox, the Boston farm team. Lacking a son who could accompany him, he had tapped Liddle Polly to be his sporting companion.

Polly and Augie became romantically hooked after a locker-room interview which continued till the place gradually emptied of players and coaches—Augie raptly rapping about strange attractors and such, Polly hanging fascinated on every word— and which degenerated—or maybe es*calated* is a better description—into a torrid joint shower and coupling that continued, after a stumble-stuttered, kissy-touchy walk back across campus to Augie's dorm, until the next morning.

When Ruby was commissioned by Coach Bubba "Brass" Balzac to capture some of the team's infinite regresses on tape for the Coach's personal archives, and the cocoa cinematographer got to know Augie personally, it was only natural that the four kids should get friendly and start hanging out together. (And Ruby did such a good job of taping, she had Brass in her pocket.)

Objectively viewed, they made an odd quartet: Cynical Cyril, the perpetual student, half his head in the past, half in some nebulous future; Awesome Augie, master gamesman; Recordin' Ruby, video-camera seldom out of hand; and Petite Polly,

Co-ed Lois Lane. But there was some chemistry among the four that defied conventional expectations, and they soon became fast friends.

(Antibodies, curiously enough, are composed of four proteins. The instructions for these proteins reside in four separate locations in the nucleus, labeled "Variable," "Diversity," "Joining," and "Constant." An easy mnemonic for our purposes might be "Victim," "Dakini," "Jock," and "Clerk.")

In retrospect, Polly had been the one who had held them all together. She had forged the bond of emotion and enthusiasm that united the quartet. She was a deep gal, that Polly. Cyril still remembered, for instance, how surprised he had been to learn of Polly's actual major. It wasn't journalism. No, something much more abstruse. Imagine Cy's expression when he heard that Polly's field was—

"Semiotics? And a minor in communications engineering? You've got to be kidding."

"No, why should I be kidding? Do you think they're stupid fields?"

"No, no, of course not. It's just that that stuff's too much for my poor head. Signs, signifiers, the signified.... And personally, I never wanna know more about radios than where my favorite station is."

"Listen, semiotics is quite simple. You see—"

"No, ma'am, don't even try...."

Cyril made a point of never underestimating Polly again after that....

And so now that he's done explaining as much as he can, he hurries to show Polly Ruby's tape, hoping she'll be able to shed some light on what it all means.

When Polly's done watching, she says, "I'm more confused than ever. But I am inclined to agree with you about the serious and complicated nature of at least Ruby's troubles. About Augie, I'm still not so sure."

There it is again, that undercurrent of Hidden Meaning in Polly's tone. Cy resolves to get it out in the open.

"Whadda ya mean, Pol? Is there something you know about Augie's vanishing that you're not sharing with me?"

Polly looks bashfully at the floor. "Well, yes. You see, Augie and I haven't been getting on too good lately. There's been a lot of tension and arguments. So I'm still not sure his disappearance isn't just a personal matter between the two of us."

Cy feels awful. "Gee, Pol, that makes me sad. I always thought that you and Augie were the perfect couple. Uh, can I ask what it's all about? Is it, like, um, sexual in nature?"

Polly's blush makes Cy wish he hadn't raised such a touchy topic, especially since his hair-trigger tumescence is manifesting itself again at Polly's demure embarrassment.

"No, nothing like that. It's about work."

"Jeez, wouldn't you know it. Work sucks so bad! Is it your job or Augie's?"

"Neither. It's a potential job for Augie that's causing the trouble. You know how he's been working for the Lottery, right?"

"Yeah, under that crazy Jap."

"Cyril, please. Hokyo Zammai is not crazy, he's just eccentric. In his own way, he's a genius."

"Face it, Pol, the guy's elevator doesn't go to the top floor. Anyone who could think up that last game—"

"You mean the one where the player's number was determined by a combination of body moles and EEG readout?"

"That's the one. You shoulda seen the lines at the local dairy store. Buncha half-naked people all wired up with 'trodes—"

"Well, all of this is beside the point. Augie recently received a letter from the En Ess Ay, offering him a position there."

Cy vaguely recognizes the acronym as that of a government agency. "Is that Social Security?"

"No, that's Ess Ess Ay. En Ess Ay is the National Security Agency, a real bunch of bastards, thousands of times worse than the Eff Bee Eye or Cee Eye Ay. They employ more mathematicians than any other organization in the world, mostly as cryptologists. I don't want Augie to get involved with them, but Zammai's quirks are getting a little much, and Augie tends to see the En Ess Ay job as a challenge. We fight about it all the time lately. He's stormed out more than once on me. But"— Polly starts to sniffle—"he's always come back before."

Cy's up and by Polly's side, strokin' her hair as she snivvles. It's time to cry again.... She reaches up to hold his head and barely—by accident?—brushes his denimed erection. Cy disengages before things go Too Far.

"Now listen, Pol, don't go blamin' yourself. I've got a solid hunch that Augie's disappearance is connected with Ruby's. I say we attack the problem from that angle, and see what we come up with. Whadda ya think?"

Polly erases with a finger the tracks of her tears, and smiles up at him. "Okay, I'll go along with that. It's better than the alternative."

"Good, good, that's more like the sensible Polly I know. Now, where does that leave us?"

The gal's all business now, emotion momentarily shelved in favor of clear-headed strategy. "As I see it, we've only got two choices. We can try a frontal assault on Wu Labs—"

"But they've already stonewalled me on the phone—and despite the way everything looks, they might not even be involved."

"Right. Which leaves the possibility of enlisting some outside help."

"The police?"

"Useless. I already talked with them last night, a guy named Officer Pupp, and they can't do anything until the person's been missing for a week. Even then, all they do is put 'em in a file. No, I had in mind someone like a private detective."

"C'mon, Polly, this isn't some television show!"

"No, I'm serious. Listen, we won't stop looking ourselves. But it wouldn't hurt to have someone else looking too. I even know one—he worked for my father once. Industrial espionage with a twist. Not only were secrets leaking out, but his employees were being deliberately infected with some kind of Industrial Disease."

Paul Peptide, Senior, owns a biotechnology firm, GreenGenes, based in Cambridge (the firm's motto is a question: "Is the grey cell green, or the green cell grey?"), and is quite well-to-do. All them box-seats ain't handed out with Government Cheese, ya know! Recently, he's inked an agreement to take over his erstwhile competitor, Seragen, in Hopkinton, thereby acquiring the rights to their new anti-AIDS discovery, IL-2 Fusion Toxin.

"Well, I still don't know. How are we gonna pay this guy? I told you I lost my job, and I don't even know how I'm gonna make the rent."

"Oh, Cy, don't worry about that, I'll hit Daddy up for it. And your rent too. After all, what are friends for?"

Cy goes all kinda mushy inside. This gal can really pull off an Emotional Rescue. If he weren't so in love with Ruby....

"Okay, you've convinced me. What's this guy's name?"

"Parallax. Max Parallax."

"Oh, God, what a hokey— All right, all right, enough said, it's your money. Or anyway, your Dad's. Let's move it. The sooner we get to the bottom of this, the quicker we'll find Ruby and Augie."

"I have to have a shower first, Cy. I'm just filthy."

"Right through there. I'll be waiting."

Listening to the sound of running water (splish, splash, I was takin' a bath) and trying not to picture what's going on inside his shower stall (where's that lucky bar of soap slippin' and slidin' right now?), Cy wanders about the living room. Hey, here's the compact disc Augie returned and which Cy mindlessly carried home. Ruined a good pair of pants over that photonic platter.... Cy picks it up. Is this the last token of poor Augie, Cy's final contact with him? What was Augie interested in, musically speaking, before his disappearance, huh? Was it the new Sinéad O'Connor that Cy tried to turn him onto (hoping the new disc would eschew Irish Harridan Hype in favor of recapturing the virtues of her sterling debut on *The Lion and the Cobra*)? Cy examines the label. It's some old blues, fittingly enough, John Lee Hooker, "Crawling Kingsnake," etc....

Boy, these CDs are really something amazing, digital miracles, although lately there have been Rumors of eventual disintegration and decay, scams to sell gold-plated models, superstitious attempts to improve sound quality by marking the discs with felt-tip pens.... (When you believe in things that you don't understand, that's superstition.) Sometimes Cy wonders if these Digital Donuts really are an improvement, or if it's a case of bad sound driving out the good.

Gee, everybody's jumpin' on the Hooker bandwagon lately, since he did good with *The Healer* a few years gone by. *Who's responsible for this re-issue?* wonders Cy with professional curiosity. Don't recognize the label, Dying Dragon records (big lizard pierced with a lance, expiring melodramatically in a pool of blood). One mo', bro', tiny print says—

A wholly owned subsidiary of Wu Labs.

Whoa-ho, slow down a minute, this is TOO MUCH. Cy feels kinda faint. This is a new connection all right, another piece of the puzzle.

Cy feeds the disc into his player and starts it spinning beneath the laser eye. The queerest symphony of hoots, blats, beeps, wails, lost chords and sour notes spills out of his speakers. Ain't John Lee, fer shure. Couldn't even be Philip Glass. That's right, Augie claimed the disc was defective. IS IT THO? What if IT'S JUST MISLABELED? What kinda information is coded on the shiny platter with its trapped spectrum? Definitely not music. What else could it be?

Polly emerges wrapped in a towel, dripping. "What's that godawful noise?"

Cyril fills her in.

Polly's face grows solemn. "That's it, then—the missing link. This disc is important somehow, Cy. It's obviously been released by mistake, and now Wu Labs wants it back. They came after Augie looking for it—but he didn't have it anymore, and so they kidnapped him."

Cy shuts the player off and removes the disk, handling it as if it were radioactive. "What do you suggest we do with it?"

"We've got to hold onto it. That disc might be our bargaining chip, to get Augie and Ruby back."

"Wait a minute," Cy pleads desperately. "Aren't we getting just a little paranoid here? Discs full of secret information, plots, kidnapped people...."

Polly's just staring at him, and Cy trails off. "I guess not," he finally admits.

"I'll be ready in a sec. And remember—we have keep that disc with us at all times!"

"Yessir!"

"Can the witticisms and let me dry my hair."

So the doubtful duo, suitably coiffed, disc in Polly's purse, soon depart the apartment and are out on the streets of the North End.

If that disc don't shine, it's gonna break that heart of mine!

There are a lotta subtle and not-so-subtle hassles associated with a lady of Ruby's complexion living in this (red)neck of the woods, but all in all, things aren't unbearable here, and the rent's still relatively cheap for this expensive city. Also the atmosphere is Ethnic, Quaint and Historical, and this appeals to Cyril's sense of the past. Hey, lookee-here, we even got Old North Church—you know, one if by land, two if by sea, primitive cryptogram of a former Third-World Independence movement.

With Polly leading the way, the pair soon find themselves at the end of a subway and out on the greenly glorious Common. It hasn't even been twenty-four hours since Cy was here last, but the scene already wears an unwonted look, as if he is viewing it through X-Ray Spex or cardboard 3-D glasses with the red and blue plastic lenses. The place is hoppin', as usual, with music blastin' and bums roastin' in the sun, portraits bein' painted by street-artists and sacramental sacks of drugs bein' ceremoniously surrendered, upon the exchange of greasy, germy bills. Following von Neumann's law known as The Irreducibility Of Real Things (to wit, any real object, such as a tree, is not capable of being ultimately and fully described by any formulation one bit less intricate than itself), the whole scene is essentially irreproducible. (Down here, you see, the poets don't write nothing at all.)

Cy and Polly cut across the park, neither talking, both preoccupied with thoughts of the dear departed ones. (Cy wishes he could stop thinking of Ruby and Augie this way, but their absence is such a palpable sensation that he is compelled to view it in such terms.)

Standing at the juncture of several paths is a crimson-robed guy carrying a sign on a stick. More oddly, the freak's got a pet *peacock* on a leash! (His name—the guy's, not the bird's—tho Cy can't possibly yet know it, is Paavo Pavonine, and he's a Finnish expatriate of dubious merits.) He looks like some kinda cartoon, and Cy is initially not inclined to take him seriously. But when he gets a gander at the guy's message, he is given pause. This pause sneakily transmutes to a shiver.

A KALPA IS TEN BILLION YEARS

SCIENCE CLAIMS THE UNIVERSE IS TEN BILLION YEARS OLD

ARE YOU READY FOR THE CHANGE?

Cy grabs Polly's elbow and speeds her up past the prophet before the bearded crazy can buttonhole them. No point in hearing more bad news, even if it is nonsensical. This ain't no Tale Of The Ancient Mariner, and they ain't no wedding guests.

Well, seems like everything's coming in binary pairs for Cyril lately, cuz no sooner is he past this obstacle than his eye falls on some disturbing grafitti spray-painted in runny letters on the side of some old geezer's statue:

AIDS WAS SOMEONE'S MISTAKE

Okay, I give up, thinks Cy, addressing the God of Synchronicity. If you want me to know what *that* is supposed to mean, you'll have to tell me, cuz I can't figure it out. Does it mean that catching AIDS involves making a mistake, or does it mean— Nah, it couldn't be....

To divert his mind from such morbid speculations, Cy asks Polly, "So, where's this Parallax guy have his office? Some grungy industrial building, no doubt, in keeping with the image of his profession."

"Not exactly. He's located in the Ritz."

"In the Ritz?"

"Well, it's where he lives, he's one of the permanent tenants. He doesn't have an office *per se*—he works out of his residence."

"This I have to see. I hope your father has deep pockets, Polly."

Pretty soon they're at the Ritz. After a brief altercation about the way Cy's dressed, they're allowed to contaminate the place with their presence. They ride the elevator to the tenth floor. They walk down a long carpeted corridor to Room 1010. Outside the door, Polly doesn't even knock, but just turns the gold handle and pushes it open.

"You're such good friends?" cracks Cy.

"It doesn't do any good to knock, since Mister Parallax is deaf."

Say what? Cy is so stunned, you can probably knock him over with a feather, provided the rubber chicken were still attached. This is great! A deaf detective. Hell of a disability for someone in the business of professional eavesdropping. How's such a guy gonna help them? Hire the handicapped is okay as a motto, but lives are at stake here! Well, things could be worse.

And soon are.

Inside the single room, centered on the expensive, Arabian-patterned rug, is a big cushioned chair. In the big chair is a big white guy—over 300 pounds big. Whoa, this guy makes the Shakyamuni Buddha look anorexic! He's got the same kind of phlegmatic serenity as the Enlightened One. He's wearing an expensive white suit and dark glasses (altho the room is not overly bright).

He does not rise to greet them. For a minute, Cy wonders why. Then Polly approaches the seated detective and takes his hand in hers. When she starts inscribing characters on the guy's palm with her fingertip, Cy worst suspicions are confirmed.

This guy is blind too! A big Blind Melon!

An immobile, blind, deaf detective! Too freakin' much!

"Polly," Cy gently suggests, "this is fucking insane! What can this poor helpless schmuck do for us—"

"Quiet! Can't you see I'm trying to explain our problem to Mister Parallax? This takes a lot of concentration."

Thus reproached, Cy wanders idly about the room while Polly draws hieroglyphs in Parallax's palm. The place has as few personal possessions as a monk's cell. Hey, check out the clothes, all Brooks Brothers. Guy must either have inherited money, or actually somehow come through for his clients to justify his pay. Don't see how, tho.... Hey, one thing definitely missing is extra shoes. Guess the Fat Man don't wear out much sole-leather in the course of his work. Can we even call him a Gumshoe?

Cy's back in front of Parallax, and Polly's just finishing transmitting her coded message down the channel of Parallax's nerves. She steps back and waits for something, Cy can't figure what. He uses this interval to quiz her.

"So, what's the story with this dude, Polly? Is he for real? How'd he get this way? Has he been blind and deaf since birth, real Helen Keller, like? Talk about a Def Jam...."

"No, this happened to Mister Parallax in the Korean War. He was captured by the North Koreans and tortured. That was when he lost his sight and hearing. But apparently, while still a POW, he was taught certain secret Oriental skills by a friendly guard, who took pity on him."

"Gah-rate," Cy droll-ly counterpoints, "so now we got the Shadow on the case." But underneath his skepticism, he's not so sure of himself. This enormous seden-tary guy projects a certain aura of competence, for all his defects. Hey, who knows, them Koreans are weird folks. Definitely the only country in the world with *I Ching* hexagrams on its national flag.... Maybe this guy does have some secret sources of information.

Cyril sits disrespectfully on the arm of Parallax's chair. All of a sudden Cy gives a little strangled squeak and jumps half outa his skin, for Parallax has reached up and unerringly grabbed Cy's earlobe, tugging his head down as if he, Cyril, were Penrod or sumpin'.

"You," says Parallax, in a resonant voice, "are a doubter. Nonetheless, for your friend's sake, I will try to help." Parallax releases his ham-handed pinch and Cy, straining against it all this time, teeters backward. Major weirdness here, awright, but who knows—maybe that's just what they need in the fix they're in. Fight fire with fire, doncha know....

With this curt evaluation of Cy's character, and the accompanying promise, their first session with Parallax is succinctly over.

On their way out they encounter a bellhop wheeling in a trolley piled high with dome-covered plates, lookin' like a little Moon colony spread out on the white linen Mare Serenitatis: Parallax's lunch. Must be enough there for three people. There's even some triple-zero caviar. Hey, poor guy's gotta enjoy something, Cy supposes.

Back on the street, Cy says, "And this clown's actually come through for your father?"

"He found out which employee was passing on secrets to a competitor when no one else could, and who was spreading the bug among the workers."

Cy just shakes his head. "Okay, it's only money, I guess. Speaking of which—"

"That's just where we're heading next."

Cy and Polly hop the Red Line (Cy's so busted Polly's even gotta buy his token) and in no time at all are standing outside the Cambridge house belonging to Polly's parents.

"Daddy's home today, so we'll be able to see him with no trouble. Sometimes he's sorta hard to reach at work."

"Uh, Polly, maybe you'd better talk to him alone. I don't wanta look like I'm pullin' some con on him or something. Say, does he even know Augie's missing?"

Polly looks dejected. "My parents don't approve of me 'n' Augie living together. They think he's wasting his talents working for Zammai. So I haven't even told them. They'd only say something nasty, like he ran out on me. Which for all I know, de-spite that Wu Labs disc, might still be true."

Cyril feels immediate empathy. He still can't forgive *his* Dad for calling Ruby a "quadroon" or "octaroon," or whatever the fuck wacky old-fogey term he had used. He still remembers with immense gratitude Twin Sister Anna letting Dad have it with both barrels over that crack. Gotta see Mrs. Condor one o' these days soon. Maybe she'll have some insight into this mess, and help him 'n' Polly feel not so lonesome they could cry....

"Hey, sorry to hear it, Polly. I didn't know your folks were as bad as mine...."

"I don't like to talk about it. Talking doesn't solve anything."

"Agreed. Should I wait out here?"

"No, that's foolish, you can come inside."

So here's Cy a-kickin' at the carpet again, doin' the Left-Out-Of-Things Shuffle outside the door to Mister Peptide's study (glimpse of the man himself sittin' behind his desk smokin' a pipe out of which wreathe snakes of smoke; looks like a Master Salesman). What's an exec like him do all day, anyway? Count up his CD's? (That's Certificates of Deposit, natch, not Compact Discs.)

Shattering Cy's bored musings, all of a sudden there comes this haunting wail from the depths of the house. Hey, Body, turn that heartbeat over again! What *is* this? Is his life turning into a bad novel, or what?

The ululations stop. Cy waits, but they don't resume.

Polly emerges shortly thereafter from the study, waving a check. "We won't have to worry about money for a while, at least. Here's plenty for Mister Parallax's retainer, and any possible expenses of ours."

"Fine, wonderful," says Cy half-heartedly. He wonders how to broach the topic of the screams to Polly. This is not a subject he's ever seen covered in etiquette manuals. Does one say, *Excuse my impertinence, but do you have a torture cell in the basement where you grill the bioengineering competition? Or is it perhaps some Hideous Botched Experiment, Rage In The Cage?* Kinda sticky....

Polly says, "I want to see my brother before we leave. Do you mind?"

Brother? This is something else he never knew about Polly. All kinds of new information comin' down the channel today, fer shure.

"No, no, 'course not." Play it cool, man.

Polly brings him to an upstairs bedroom.

In the room, huddled in a corner on the floor, is a kid about seventeen. He's wearing one of them padded fiberglass biking helmets, and he's got boxing gloves on his hands. He doesn't look up when Cy and Polly enter. Cy notices a snaky river of drool running down the kid's chin, and his eyes, tho open, register nothing. Don't take no Max Parallax to peg this fellow as the source of the weird keening.

"This is Paulie Junior," explains Polly. She's down on her haunches, hugging the boy, who totally ignores her. "He's been autistic since age four."

Christ, what a cruel world! Where was God when this kid's brain was being wired? Cy knows a bit about autism, having just read an article on it. Tagged in 1943 by one Leo Kanner. Lately, thought to stem from the brain producing too much of one neurotransmitter, serotonin. Result is withdrawal, compulsive physical behavior such as hand-flapping or head-beating, accompanied by severe tantrums and language retardation. Strikes in childhood, makes kids totally unmanageable and unsocializable. One theory has it that their brains are unable to properly process the flood of sensory data everyone else takes in stride, and that their bizarre behavior is their attempt to cope. November spawned a monster....

"Isn't there a new drug—"

"Fenfluramine. But it hasn't helped much in Paulie's case. No, he'll be like this for the rest of his life. And because we can't stand to institutionalize him, my Mom doesn't work, but spends all her time caring for him."

Cy's left shifting from foot to foot in embarrassed sympathy while Polly croons wordlessly to her brother, trying to communicate some primal emotional vibes to him. Cy focuses on the kid's blank face, attempting to penetrate beyond the stony facade, figure out just what it's like to be trapped helplessly inside your own skull during a continuous sensory barrage, it's slippery going, can't find a handhold, wait a minute, what's this crack, just gonna slip thro-o-o o o

Cum on feel the noize! Noisenoisenoisenoise, scratchy white blanket wrapping whole skin from head to foot, my hair hurts, can feel each one tugging at my scalp, gonna pull 'em all out, couldn't hurt any worse, but my hands are trapped in mush, stiff mush, beat it away, get away, waves of stink and heat, a thousand, thousand smells, putrid, rank, garbage filling my mouth, puke it up, wet piss filling my lap, someone squawking, pressure on my chest, can feel all my internal organs like watermelons, can't breathe, too many, too much, flood of light and color and movement, where's the still center, it never stops, even in sleep the bitstream overflows its banks, caught in random feedback loops that I can't get out of, noisenoisenoisenoise—

"We can go now, Cy."

Shakin' his head—his *own* head!—Cy recovers. "Uh, okay, right, I'm with you."

Somehow hours have passed by unnoticed. Seems like it was just noon at Parallax's, but now dusk is falling. How long was Cy inside Paulie's head....? Good thing he could get out *at-tall!*

Walking down the shadowy streets back to subway stop, Cy and Polly are silent. Words seem useless or unnecessary just now. Talk solves nothing....

Looking up idly at the telephone poles, Cy notices a cord threaded among the coaxial (coaxihuitl?) cables. He usta wonder what that rope was, until a Jewish friend named Morty Anguipede explained. Seems that certain really Orthodox sects forbid travel beyond the limits of one's house on Sabbath. Great, but don't that sorta contradict the idea of attending temple? Oh, yeah, right.... How we gonna get around that one, Rabbi? Hmmm, lessee, how's 'bout we string up this cord called an *eruv*, said cord functioning as a metaphysical extension of the house's boundaries. Now everyone can walk with impunity within the perimeter thus defined, without offending The Big Guy.... Strange to contemplate that cable, carrying its religious information, strung up there with the phone wires....

Around them now, one by one, the streetlights are coming on. Cy's brain chooses this moment to burp up a memory he hasn't inspected in ages. So strong is it, that he feels compelled to share it with Polly.

"When I was a kid," says Cy without preliminaries, as they stroll, "I used to fantasize about how the streetlights were controlled. I pictured this big control panel, Streetlight Central, y'know, with millions of dials and readouts and one master switch—the kind of big knife switch you see in old horror movies. There was one guy—an old guy, with a long white hair 'n' beard, real grandfather image, I guess—who was in charge of Streetlight Central, altho he had lots of assistants, too. Sorta like Santa Claus and his elves, maybe. Anyway, this old guy would monitor the intensity of the sunlight all day. And if it was cloudy, or mainly, of course, when it got to be dusk, the level of light would cross some lower threshold and he would walk to the panel, real proud and dignified like, amid the admiring gazes of his assistants, and—throw the switch! All over the city, all the streetlights would come on instantly, as the signal raced down the wires, disspelling the darkness."

Cy pauses. This is really choking him up, for inexplicable sentimental reasons, and he's not sure if he can go on, or if Polly even wants to hear this.

Seeming to sense his uncertainty, Polly grabs his hand. Well, he's started, so he's gotta finish.

"It got to the point where I actually believed in this guy. Believed so much that I would peddle my bike around the city, looking for Streetlight Central. Then one day, someone—I forget who, maybe another smartass kid—told me how the streetlights really worked. Each one had a photo-electric cell, and triggered itself. Well, Jesus, I was totally broken up. The picture of all those autonomous idiot lights, unconnected, isolated, turning themselves on, no mind behind it, no master plan or motivator—I cried that night, I'll tell you, and the streetlight shining into my bedroom was no comfort at all. I always kept the curtains closed at night after that. Damnedest part of the whole thing was, I couldn't quite convince myself that the Master Streetlight Man had never existed. I felt like I had killed him by failing to believe in him."

Cy's convinced he's made an utter ass of himself, till Polly says:

"And if he existed, Cy—"

"Yeah?"

"If he existed, would he help us, or wouldn't he even care?"

Weh-hell, the normally wise-mouthed Cy has no comeback for this depressing question, and so he and Polly continue to walk slowly back along the residential sidewalks of Cambridge to the T-stop. They do not release their handclasp, and Cy hopes Polly is getting as much innocent comfort from it as he is.

Polly speaks. Seems Cy's sharing of his childhood fears 'n' fantasies has triggered a similiar flood and need for release in Polly.

Her story, tho, consisting as it does of actual Weird Doings, pushes Cy's dreamy episode right offstage.

"Even Augie doesn't know what I'm about to tell you, Cy. No one does except my parents—and maybe one other person, if he's still alive. So I'd appreciate it if you don't spread this around. I don't want people thinking I'm some kind of New Age loony like Shirley MacLaine."

"No, no, of course not, I won't tell a soul, cross my heart and pleased to meet me," promises Cy, a little nervous at the prospect of being burdened with some Horrible Secret that he'll have to carry around for the rest of his life.

"Not even Ruby?"

"Not even Ruby," he further affirms, feeling despite himself a kind of delicious erotic treachery. Polly's hand is suddenly almost too hot for comfort.

"Good. And even between the two of us, I'd prefer not to mention it again. What I'm about to tell you is just too weird, and has too many painful associations for me. You see—I remember being in my mother's womb, and a little bit of a past life."

"Holy fuckin' snakeshit!"

"Oh, that's nothing. It's worse than that. You see, Cy—" Polly chokes up a bit. "I—I killed someone too."

Cy, doubly a traitor now, instinctively tries to drop Polly's hand, but she's got his clenched so tight he can't. So he squeezes back in what he hopes is a reassuring way.

"My first real memory is one of floating blind and breathless in a warm fluid. Sound came to me distantly, unintelligible. My belly was anchored to something. I had no real freedom. I could only kick and stir my feeble arms. So I let my mind roam, roam where it wanted to. And where it wanted to go was to a past life. I couldn't remember much of it. The transition to this new form was already blurring it. The only thing that was really clear was my death. It hadn't been a natural one. No, I, a woman then too, had been murdered, strangled by a jealous lover. The terror of it was still fresh enough to make my undeveloped heart pound. I remember feeling grateful for an instant that I had escaped the clutches of this man.

"Then, with an awful shock, I realized I hadn't.

"He was there in the womb with me, my fraternal twin. The karma of our past lives had bound us together in this reincarnation."

Cy is shocked. "You're a twin too, like me 'n' Anna? How come I never knew? Where is this other brother?"

Polly stops walking and stares Cyril straight in the eyes. They are between streetlights, in a pool of leafy shadows, and Polly's own eye sockets look blackly hollow.

This bosky binocular occultation makes her look Real Spooky.

"He's dead. He's the one I killed.

"You see, I was the older child, by a few seconds. My egg had gotten fertilized first. I was fractionally more developed than he was. Just enough to let me—to let me—"

Polly starts blubbering again, just like last night, and Cyril has to hold her close for a minute before she can speak.

"We were reversed in the womb somehow, oriented head to feet. And I—I put a kink in his umbilical. Wrapped a little leg around it and cut off his blood supply."

Polly takes Cyril's hand and places it on her upper left thigh, apparently the murderous leg itself. Funny, it don't feel like a Deadly Weapon, more like a sweet firm inviting hunk of love-flesh. Cy lets his hand linger just long enough to show he's got no repulsion or aversion for the Murderous Limb, then withdraws it before he creams in his pants.

"He died," continues Polly, "and decayed and was mostly scavenged out right there in the womb with me. Momma had to eat for two, not three, in the last few months of her pregnancy.

"You know how different things were back when we were born. No ultrasound or anything. So primitive, it seems now. No one ever knew my mother was carrying two embryos. When I was born, nobody thought twice about some extra afterbirth.

"The shock of being born wiped out a lot of these memories for a while. My first few years were pretty normal. But around age three, just when the human brain is passing a critical von Neumann complexity level in its development, it all flooded back to me.

"Along with messages. Messages from my dead twin."

Cyril starts them walking again. This story and the shadows have made his surroundings CREEP CITY, and he wants to hasten back to the comfort of home.

"I'd hear him as plainly as if he were by my side whispering in my ear, but no one else could. He told me he was coming to get me. He hadn't been reincarnated yet, he was still in limbo, a bardo state, but pretty soon he'd get a body and whenever he was able to, he come kill me again.

"Well. You can imagine the effect this had on a three-year-old. I couldn't eat, I couldn't sleep, I'd scream at the slightest surprise. I started to sicken. My dead twin was killing me even without the benefit of a physical body.

"I had told all this to my parents, of course. Naturally, they didn't believe me. They took me to every specialist imaginable. Finally, they had to admit it was 'psychological.'

"It was then that my father did something I'll always be grateful to him for. Despite being an absolute materialist, very scientific, he decided he had better fight this battle on a different level. After all, nothing else was working.

"He and I flew to New Orleans. There, we visited the Hoodoo Guru.

"He was a member of the Wild Tchoupitoulas tribe, a group of Amerindians who had been interbreeding with runaway slaves ever since the sixteen-hundreds. An old man even then, he'd be a hundred if he were still alive. He had matted grey hair and a grey beard. He lived in a shack on the bayou—had been born on the bayou and never moved. We had to reach it by swamp boat.

"The shack was decorated with goatskulls on the outside. Inside, it was jammed with old fashioned apothecary bottles on shelves. They were filled with all sorts of weird things. Rattlesnake tails, colored liquids, teeth and animal abortions.

"After examining me, nodding wisely all the time and muttering to himself as if he saw this type of trouble every day, the Guru began to mix up a potion. When it was done, he began the ceremony. It was surprisingly short. All he did was sprinkle the liquid on me—boy, did it stink!—lay his juju hand on my head, and chant a couplet:

"'Zing, zing, zang and cha dooky do! Old Tchoupitoulas kick de ass ub dis anjonu.'

"An 'anjonu,' I later learned, is a vengeful spirit of the recently dead, similar to the Chinese Hopping Ghost.

"Then, from someplace I couldn't see, he took this—"

Polly reaches down the front of her shirt and pulls out a small leather bag on a drawstring that runs around her neck.

"It's my fetish. It's juju against the anjonu. I've never taken it off since that day in the shack. And I've never been bothered by my twin since."

Cy is like totally WACKED OUT! He don't know whether to shit or go blind. Dazed and confused.... The things you never know about people. Maybe he can get used to this. She's still the same old Polly, sure she is. Just your average twin-murderin', fetish-wearin', Voodoo Witchy Woman.

Cy tries to show he's unflappable. "Wha-what's in it?"

"I don't know," says Polly. "I never dared look. But—"

"Yeah?"

"Sometimes it moves."

# DaHomey, Sweet DaHomey

# K L U E S

00001100
"A strange notion, that divine immanency, instead of doing men good, enfeebles them or disorders their senses."

—Apuleius

00001101
HOBBES: "Do you think there's a God?"
CALVIN: "Well, *somebody's* out to get me."

00001110
"Each cell in your body has the evolutionary status of a former colony."

—Stephen Jay Gould

00001111
"Funk can be anything. Funk is an idea; it's whatever it needs to be in order to survive. We don't have to take nothing as our bag. *Everything* is our bag."

—George Clinton

Once you go around the Benin, thought Claude Lollolo ruefully, you can't go Dahomey again.

(But hey—why be surprised when confronted with the reality of that truism? I always knew that Wolfe cat had some sorta Secret Tap into the Kozmic Wavelength, what with all his allusions to THAT WHICH COULD NOT BE SPOKEN.)

Seated behind his desk, Lollolo shook his noble head sadly and gave vent to a mournful chuckle. His youthful and handsome mulatto features, carved as of tawny wood torn from the secret heart of some rare tropical tree, were traced with lines of emotional pain, betrayal and a wee touch of consequent cynicism. Could be the kid was overplaying his role a little, but lissen up—we're talking major bummer of a letdown here, occuring to a figure of positively royal lineage, all of which circumstances tended to impart to Lollolo an aura of tragic Byronic Gloom 'n' Doom that was a trifle more justifiable than it might be if you or me exhibited same.

*What a pathetic way*, Lollolo continued to ruminate, *for a grown man to spend his time!* Particularly a sharp young dude with more'n his share of snap and hustle, who already bore the impressive, albeit empty title of Information Minister for the newly socialist republic of Benin.

Hey, all you young dudes, put down your 'ludes, and swallow a little history! Benin had gone Red three years ago, in '74. It had still been called Dahomey then, that ancient and honorable name. After a year of the experiment, when President Kerekou (as recently as 1972, before the coup, merely French Paratrooper Kerekou) had noticed his new economy was spiralling downward, converting a formerly prosperous land to a Marxist-Leninist miasma of poverty, he had changed the country's name, much as certain tribal peoples around the globe would don a disguise, even the clothes of another sex, to cheat some malignant fate.

Prior to the ascension of Fearless Leader K, Benin had been an independent, capitalist and monarchical liddle slice of the Third World, and doing quite well, thank you, under the name Dahomey. Before that, it had been the positively well-off French colony Dahomey, whose citizens were among the best-educated in Africa. And even more formerly, roughly the same territory had been the ancient and mighty sovereign empire of Danh-ho-me....

End of lesson, dude, cuz I don't know much about history, don't know much about geography.... No, I try to forget the past, can't change it anyway, go back and tell the Bodhidharma I'm sorry. It's all past....past....past....

Echo-chamber effect here, with Narrator's voice gradually fading away, becoming more and more ghostly, until it is hardly anything but the whisper of a dead man's thought, ghost in the machine, cross-talk on the wires, finally stabilizing to the sepulchral but nervously frantic tones of an amphetamine zombie.

The past. Where is it? What is it? Is it true, what Faulkner said and believed and seemed to live by? "It's all *now*, you see. Yesterday won't be over until tomorrow, and tomorrow began ten thousand years ago." If all time is somehow *now*, then the past is not nonexistent, but only separate from us down some imperceptible dimension, and its inhabitants—those we commonly call "the dead"—are *still around somewhere.*

How to reach that nebulous territory of the dead, though, or be reached by it? Every culture has had its intermediaries between living and dead, shamans and witch-doctors. (And I am yours: Ding dang walla walla bing bang!) Is there a shaman in the house?

The dead *are* trying to reach us, tho. I know it. Daily I apprehend it anew. Their land is dotted with myriad ghost-manned sending stations that keep a-pumpin' out half-decipherable messages which, traveling down the long, long channel of Time, reach us full of static and erasures; or, what is worse, Time might be a binary symmetric channel, one in which all transmission errors do not necessarily produce erasures—gaps which are at least recognizable as such—but instead produce *false bits*, pernicious disinformation, and how the fuck can we deal with that curveball from the past, what's the Kozmic Checksum....?

Stop, hold on, get in control.... Paranoia, the destroyer! They'll roll you for a nickel and stick you for the extra dime.

Pop up the narrative from the task-stack.

Lollolo did not relish resting on his duff in his dilapidated office (which still bore many ancient traces—bullet-shattered plaster, boot-prints in brown dried blood, broken panes of glass patched with cardboard—of the Coup of '72), making up bad puns (a weakness of his) about the plight of his country. But there was little else he could do, given the constraints of his current situation.

If it weren't for his second career—the ace up his sleeve, the derringer in his boot, the knife strapped to his thigh—as an agent for the slightly sinister and mysterious, but decidedly good-paying and cutting-edge-keen Wu Labs, Lollolo would feel even lousier about his prospects, and those of his beloved country—*Fuck Benin! Dahomey forever!*—than he already did.

It was December, 1977, and it seemed to Lollolo that this era of his maturity, although outwardly moribund, was one hell of a fermentatory period. And that was even discounting the radical changes in his own land. ('Course, maybe everyone just turned twenty-three—Lollolo's age—thought their own particular era the most heady of times.) Still, the observation appeared to Lollolo to have some objective truth to it....

What else could one make, f'rinstance, of the goings-on in that imperialistic and monstrous You Ess of Ay (which nation was currently number one knock-'em-down straw man in Dahomey, although Lollolo couldn't quite hew to the party-line here, either)? Just a few years ago, in '73, Boyer and Cohen had performed the first successful recombinant DNA experiment there. Now, word was, them crazy gene-freaks was tryin' to insert human genetic material into....yeast and bacteria! Holy Legba, talk about your Kozmic Level perversion! Bestiality paled in comparison. Might be a world-wide oil shortage goin' on, but no way they were runnin' out of their stockpile of good old hubris back in the land of the free (which last year had celebrated the bicentennial of its own Independence, by the way).

Meanwhile, at MIT, the math and bio boys were going wild. Ronald Rivest, Adi Shamir and Leonard Adelman, using huge prime numbers, were perfecting trapdoor ciphers, work which the NSA would soon seek to classify. Next door to them, Philip Sharp had discovered the editing of messenger RNA, an event many experts would in later years come to call "the true beginnings of molecular biology," and for which he would in 1993 win the Nobel.

And l-l-look at that old lion, Great Britain, which Lollolo retained more than a passing interest in, seeing as how in the days of her empire, the insatiable bawd had had more than a trivial role to play in turning Dahomey into Slave Dispatching Central. (More on this pertinent topic anon.)

Seemed the mangy ancient beast had a few new fleas itchin' at her skin these days. Buncha lads callin' themselves The Sex Pistols, and also dey ragged bred'ren, yahso! Currently, the Pistols' novel brand of noise, as embodied in "Anarchy in the U.K.," was toppin' the charts. Lollolo had gotten an early live tape of the group through his Wu Lab contacts (Wu seemed to have some hand in the group's financial backing, as filtered through Malcolm McLaren), and played it frequently, whenever he needed a dose of reassurance that the First World had its discontents too. No future, no future, no future for you!

And at Cambridge (England, not Massachusetts, now), Sir Frederick Sanger and his co-workers at the British Medical Research Council labs had just deciphered the entire genetic text of an organism for the first time in history. True, the organism under discussion was only a liddle ol' virus known as OX174—only made nine proteins, for Sakpata's sake—but still, its whole repository of possibilities, its very essence, was now an open book.

Turned out the book was full of puns.

Sanger's most important discovery was that of "reading frames." Every nucleotide in the virus's DNA could be interpreted in two ways, depending on where the mechanism of interpretation started reading. It was as if every novel had another novel hidden inside it; or as if a reader, having finished with a novel, might need to go back and read it again, starting with a different chapter, to extract its full meaning.

As Sanger himself said, "Something rather subtle seems to be at work," inside the nucleus.

Oh, yeah, and let's not forget certain subterranean stirrings which were reminiscent of the twitchings of Nidhoggr (literally "dread biter"), the snake coiled around the roots of Yggdrasil. (This Lollolo lad was something of a scholar of snakes in myth, history and legend, for good and compelling reasons.) These uneasy rumblings and abortive movements were manifesting themselves among the many unaligned countries allied with Dahomey. There was a general, albeit unformed call for something that was to be known as a "new world information order," reversing the dominance of North over South, said area of agitation being under Lollolo's purview in Dahomey. Lollolo and his Third World counterparts elsewhere were currently pushing for the item to be put on the UNESCO agenda.

Yessir, definitely big changes brewin'—and that was taking into account only the topside stuff. If Lollolo factored in the outrageous ultra-umbrageous data he had been able to glean from his service to Wu Labs (and such data were frustratingly scarce and fragmentary)—

Who-whee, there was gonnna be some crazy shit goin' down in the next decade or so!

Understandably, all this made Lollolo feel a little uneasy. Being involved in world-shaking trends and plots tended to have that effect on him.

Playing those my-eye-eye-ind games forever. But it's all in the game....

Time to check in with the *Afa*, thought Lollolo, for a little guidance.

Reaching for the handle of a drawer, Lollolo tugged at the pull, only to have the reluctant wooden desk fight back. Shit! This drawer was swollen shut from weeks of autumnal rain just now ending! Sometimes Lollolo hated the rainy season—tho the torrid and enervating harmattan winds now beginning were no picnic either. Just the price one paid for living in exotic, darkest Africa, he guessed.

But couldn't the country afford to supply one of its upper-echelon ministers with a metal desk? Lollolo silently implored the framed photo of Fearless Leader K that hung on the wall. An errant shaft of hot Porto Novo sunlight thrust through the window and graced the official portrait with an incongruous corona. Made the crazy bastard look more like a madman than ever. In any case, so what Lollolo's Ministry boasted no other employees than himself? 'Least he could have A Modern Office Environment, couple o' framed abstract prints to hide the bullet-holes, nice zebra-skin couch to bang his nonexistent secretary on, all that'd be pretty cool....

With mighty exertions worthy of one of his royal ancestors preparing to decapitate a sacrificial victim, Lollolo got the drawer open at last, revealing....a little hide bag closed with a drawstring.

Removing the bag and leaving the cantankerous drawer extended like an insulting tongue, Lollolo undid the closure and spilled the contents of the sack on his nearly bare desktop.

Sixteen polished palmnuts, incised with various runic lines, the *Afa-du*.

Scooping up the nuts in his right hand, Lollolo felt himself falling into the familiar *Afa* state. He conceived himself with absolute certainty to be intimately linked to the entire matrix of the universe, a mere extrusion of the underlying substratum of seamless information that manifested itself as the illusory unconnected world perceived by the senses, what the Hindus called *maya*, the Zen monks *samsara*. The nuts in his hand and his hand itself were both connected inextricably to every other atom in the infinite universe. Energy flowed into his muscles from distant suns. His identity was subsumed by those of birds and beasts, snakes and women. He partook of totality. Thus the predictive throws he was about to make were in no way arbitrary or random, but instead ineluctable and revelatory consequences of the nature, position and intention of every molecule in the infinite cosmos, all of which were tugging at his hand and (the) nuts.

The universe was a huge cellular automaton, fashioned out of an infinite number of smaller CA's, changing its state with each tick of the Kozmic Klock, and Lollolo would now divine its current status. Or so preached Saint Fredkin, currently at the California Institute of Technology, MIT's twin.

Kinda made a guy feel part of something big, but humble at the same time. And, f-f-folks—don't knock it if you ain't never tried it!

With a practiced cast, Lollolo tossed an arbitrary number of nuts from right hand to left. One remained behind. Setting it aside, Lollolo picked up a pencil and drew a pair of vertical strokes on a piece of paper. Next he repeated the cast, from left to right hand. A single nut stayed back again. Beside the double stroke, Lollolo penciled in two more, some distance away. Third cast: two nuts lagged, and a single line was drawn beneath the first brace. (Neat kind of parity logic involved here, all right.) After eight throws, Lollolo had a figure that looked like this:

$$|| \quad ||$$
$$| \quad |$$
$$| \quad |$$
$$|| \quad ||$$

*Ode-Megi.*

Not bad, an overall positive pattern, full of promise tinged with risk.

*A stranger will come seeking gifts. Although the slave is a trifling man, his master is one to be reckoned with. Do not refuse the emissary, though he ask for the king's favorite leopard-wife. There is no blame. Consult the Dahngbwe-no for further details.*

The Snake Mother....

Lollolo pensively stroked the small but deep tribal scars on one cheek with a fingertip. (These scars, restricted to those of royal lineage, were a straight line superimposed on a circle, sorta like a one piercing a zero.) Anything involving the Snake Mother was heavy stuff.... Could it be connected with those rumors that had been filtering down the WL grapevine lately....?

Rebagging the vatic nuts, Lollolo turned to other tasks. May as well check the schedule for the week's broadcasts by the capital's—indeed the country's—only radio station—

There was an unexpected knock at the door. Who could it be? Lolollo's post was so unimportant—Fearless Leader K handled all the really major pronunciamentos—and so out of the mainstream of Dahomean politics, that he seldom received a visitor.

"Enter, please," said the dubious *Afa-du* dude.

100 ∞ Di Filippo

Door swung open and in came a khaki-clad white guy wearing a pith helmet and wraparound shades. Man, was this fellow beat! First off, his face and exposed arms and legs were covered with mosquito bites and leech scars. There was a swollen abcess on one jaw and two fingers were in a splint. He wore a large waterproof satchel slung across his back. A Swiss Army knife hung from his belt. The guy was pushing a bicycle in worse shape than him. Its frame was bent, both tires had patches on every inch and more'n a few missing spokes, and the seat was worn down to bare metal.

Guy said, "*M'sieur* Lollolo?"

"*Oui*," said the cosmopolitan Porto Novan.

"Package for you from Wu Labs, via the Pasteur Institute."

The messenger unslung his satchel and fished out a metal box 'bout as big as an unabridged dictionary.

Lollolo accepted it, nonplused. "I don't—how come—who are you?"

The messenger straightened with a show of pride. "Robert Norbert Aubisson, at your service. Otherwise known as King of the Messengers, or *Roi* Aubisson. We share an employer."

"But what has happened to you? Was there fighting, *peut-être,* on the way in from the airport?"

"I did not come from the airport."

"Certainly you have not—"

"Yes, all the way from Paris. By ferry from Spain to Morroco."

"But why?"

"Conventional modes of transport were deemed insufficiently secure for the package I carried," explained Row-bear Nor-bear.

Lolollo just shook his head. Unbelievable.... Yet he had come to expect the bizarre from Wu Labs, and this situation, though beyond his understanding, must be accepted.

Producing a receipt book, Aubisson said, "If you will just sign here, *M'sieur*, I'll be off. No reply is expected."

Bemused, Lollolo signed. "Have a safe trip, Robert. Frankly, I cannot imagine what it will be like."

"Only the lonely know how I feel, *M'sieur* ."

After Aubisson had left, Lollolo opened the unlocked box.

Inside, packed in styrofoam chips, was a petri dish filled with nutrient agar, several strange discs, and some kind of mechanism seemingly complementary to the discs.

Lollolo studied the contents for a while. The discs were small shiny rainbowed platters (Holy Aido!) labeled with the names of, Lollolo supposed, musicians: THE SEX PISTOLS (well, natch), THE JAM, THE RAMONES, THE CLASH, THE TALKING HEADS.... Okay, suppose they were some strange kind of record, and this was the player. What was he supposed to do with them? It hardly seemed likely that *Roi*

Aubisson would have been dispatched across two continents solely to provide for his personal enjoyment....

Lolollo suddenly recalled the strange envelope he had received six months ago, with the commemorative Australian postmark of the Aboriginal snake-god Bobbi-bobbi, celebrating the hundredth anniversary of the first extermination of a whole Abo tribe. It had contained nothing but a circular piece of filter paper.

A piece exactly the size of this petri dish.

Rummaging through his desk, Lollolo retrieved the envelope. He uncapped the petri dish and, tentatively, laid the filter paper atop the agar medium.

Pale purple words immediately appeared on the paper disc.

*EYES ONLY!*
*You are holding*
*a colony of OX174*
*modified to produce a non-natural cytokine—Protein*
*Ten—which reacts with the stain in your*
*filter paper. The viruses have been fixed in a matrix,*
*and each one has been programmed to produce*
*the appropriate on/off pixel.*
*STERILIZE AFTER READING!*
*Dear Claude: Please*
*play these discs at regular*
*intervals over the*
*government station.*
*Signed: P.O.P.*

Nana Buluku, these people at Wu Labs were all maniacs! Deliveries by bike through the jungle, messages spelled out by viruses, Aboriginal filter paper, all timed to arrive just when he was contemplating the station's schedule.... Sometimes he swore they did all this just to keep him off balance, maintain a certain smokescreen level of complexity.

Well, the request seemed harmless enough. He would send the discs and player to the station and let the engineers figure out how to work the new technology.

Leaving the office momentarily, Lollolo returned with a bottle of bleach taken from the janitor's closet. He poured some into the petri dish. Adios, OX174!

Now, when could he program the new music? Maybe he'd just cross out the entry in this three-hour, three-AM slot on "Increasing Grain Production by Dedication to Socialist Methodology." No one in the government would probably notice, and if they did, Lollolo could claim it was some snafu by one of the engineers. Little lively music probably *would* do the poor country more good than lectures, no matter what other plans it would also further....

Lollolo signed the sheet to authorize the change. Then, spinning his chair to the left, he fed the same paper into an ancient manual typewriter, prior to pecking out his name below his signature. Lollolo hated this machine, and frequently issued requests for, if not one of them new-fangled word-processors from Wang, at least an electric typewriter, fer Kpo's bloody sake! Why, lookee-here, half the keys on this spavined contraption were busted. In order to type his own name, Lollolo had to use the one and zero keys: 1011010. One wise-ass over in cryptography had started to call Lollolo "Mister Binary." What a joke! Often his memos went out with half the letters of each word missing.

```
Att nt n: m mb rs f th g v rnm nt ar n t t sp ak t w st rn
r p rt rs w th ut auth r zat n fr m th s ff ce.   1011010
```

Now what kind of respect was such a message going to command, Lollolo demanded, even if it could be understood (thanks to language's built-in redundancy)? It was enough to make a guy mighty despairing....

After dispatching the altered radio schedule, discs and drive via a half-naked urchin named Andriambahomanana who had attached himself somehow to Lollolo, sleeping outside his office door and running errands for him in return for the occasional coin, Lollolo worked a bit longer. But despite his best efforts, in the end he just couldn't concentrate and decided to take the rest of the day off. That ethereal bulletin from the *Afa-du* and the transcontinental package had shaken him more than he realized. And the latter was probably not a fulfillment of the former, since the *Afa* had spoken of someone *asking* for gifts, not *giving* them. That meant there was more to come....

One advantange to being simultaneously the lone underling and supervisor, thought Lollolo as he descended three flights of stairs (damn elevator was down again), was that he could ask himself for a break, grant it, and notify the rest of the staff to cover for him without ever speaking aloud.

Out on the noisy streets of Porto Novo Lollolo dodged black boys on mopeds and white Russian advisers in Army trucks to cross to the banks of the Porto Novo Lagoon, the estuary on the city's southern periphery. He began to follow the curve of the Lagoon north, toward the main market-place, having no particular destination in mind, but only wanting to think.

Lollolo did not pass unnoticed through the small city. (Cotonou, to the west, was three times as large, and even that metropolis held only 350,000 souls.) The barbers and customers at "COIFFURE DINGO STYLE Specialists des cheveux modernes" whispered as he passed, as did the junk-recyclers hammering tin cans into funnels. Among his fellow *Beninois*, too many people (too many people going underground, on an endless trip) recognized him and knew his romantic story for anonymity to obtain.

And it went like this....

Back in 1864 came a visitor to Dahomey, emissary of Queen Victoria. Guy name of Richard Burton: crazy-as-a-bedbug Arab impersonator, searcher for the headwaters of the Nile, rogue, adventurer, and major cocksman. Burton's mission was to deliver Victoria's message to one Gelele son of Gezo, then King of Dahomey. This official burden did not stop him from co-habiting with any number of assorted swarthy, cone-breasted maidens he encountered along his way. In fact, although he never mentioned it in his official memoirs of his trip (where he *did*, however, toss out this hint: "If I say too little, it is for fear of expressing too much."), Burton's major purpose in accepting this boring mission was to compile raw data for his monumental but never-to-be-published *magnum opus*: *The Amatory and Copulatory Habits of the Races of Mankind, containing much heretofore unrevealed matter of a libidinous nature.* (The manuscript for this valuable work was burned by Burton's tightass widow, much as twelve of the sixty-four Nag Hamadi codexes were burned by their discoverer, Muhammad 'Ali, leaving only the fifty-two we know today.)

So anyhow, Burton screwed his way into the interior from the coast village of Whydah (contemporary Ouidah), dodging leeches (infested! the planet's infested!) and malaria mosquitos all the way. (The British had a liddle ditty: "The Gulf of Benin, the Gulf of Benin / Where few come out, though many go in.") Arriving at the King's village of Abomey (contemporary Abomey), Burton, besides being forced to witness a gruesome sacrifice or two and exhibit his dancing and singing prowess in ritual celebrations, had the shock of his sexual life.

Dahomey, you see, was home to the Amazons. The actual living, fighting model for Greek myths. Half of Gelele's army was composed of women, many of whom were physically more impressive than the male warriors. Burton, naturally enough, couldn't resist the sexual challenge presented by these belligerent gals, and resolved to seek out the most formidable of them for an extended mattress throwdown.

Came the night he had chosen for his conquest.

Burton sneaked out of his native hut and ventured into what he was confident was the Amazons' compound.

Or so he thought.

Being a newcomer wandering about unfamiliar territory in pitch-blackness, he had inadvertently ended up at the royal quarters housing the King's thousand or so wives. Over the log palisade and once inside, Burton discerned his mistake, but whe-hell, too late to back out now, doncha know, just gotta pull off that old infidel-in-Mecca routine without a hitch, fer shure.

A sound behind Burton.

He whirled.

It was the King's chief wife (Burton had been introduced earlier), coming back from using the primitive WC. She held the guttering torch she had been using to light her way. A former Amazon, she towered an inch or two above Burton. Half her head was shaven, the other half covered with a beaten silver plate held in place by leather thongs. She was spectacularly and blackly naked save for a horse's tail, held on by a cord running around her waist and between her legs, projecting insouciantly off her rump.

For an eternal moment she and Burton locked eyes, and he waited for her to bring down the house with a scream.

She turned without uttering a word.

Burton followed the twitching tail.

What ensued utterly demoralized Burton for the rest of his life. Every maneuver he tried to pull on this gal to establish his masculine sexual superiority was out-flanked. She knew every last trick he did, and more, matching him orgasm for orgasm. (Burton had learned how to achieve multiple male orgasms from Mai Won Song, the wife of the Ambassador to England from the ancient Kingdom of Choson. While we're in parentheses, we might parenthetically remark that in Victorian times, climaxing was referred to as "spending.") Not even the Bedouin Camel Trot, which had never failed him before, could prevail.

In the end, he was forced to admit defeat. He slunk back to his hut around dawn, luckily undiscovered by the King or soldiers. (This crestfallen and soured attitude can be discerned in the second volume of Burton's book about Dahomey, as op-posed to the first.)

Not long thereafter, Burton departed, aboard Captain Wilmot's ship, *H.M.S. Rattle-snake*.

Nine months later, imagine Gelele's surprise while attending the birth of his new coffee-colored son. Sure don't look hundred-percent Yoruban, do he?

The guilty wife escaped death by the hair of her shaven head. The son was ban-ished from the line of succession, but managed to achieve fame as a *Min-gan*, or Captain, in the frequent wars of Danh-ho-me.

So. 'Bout ninety years went by. Burton's genes, much diluted, were now repre-sented chiefly by, of all redundant coincidences, the current King's favorite wife, a gal named Kwatzanna. (Quite a bit of near-incestuous royal interbreeding in ol' Dahomey.) The country was currently part of French West Africa, here in the Nine-teen-Fifties. Lotsa diplomats visited Abomey to get the King's cooperation and ap-proval.

One of 'em was named Phillipe deClosets.

During his first royal reception, deClosets was smitten by the bedroom eyes of this Burtonian descendant. (Kwatzanna was standing behind the King, holding the royal umbrella over him and wiping his brow.) DeClosets was confident, from cer-tain wordless signals, and from the cocksureness of youth, that any overtures from him would meet with acceptance.

At the first opportunity, deClosets hit on this winsome lady. Kwatzanna practi-cally knocked him off his feet. Seemed like them long-buried Anglo genes was just a-yearnin' to form some kinda NATO alliance with deClosets' Franco nucleotides. It was as if Kismet, Fate and the Norns had all stirred the pot.

How-some-ever....deClosets was not to be as lucky as Burton. Him and the regal paramour got caught *in flagrante delicto*, which is Latin for "with her feet up in the air." Ensued deClosets' banishment to Cambodge, and all that followed. Papa was a rolling stone, wherever he hung his hat was his home.... Nine months later....you got it. One Claude Lollolo came squalling into this world, a child automatically disinherited from the throne, which today was held by his cousin, King Agoli-Agbo.

(And did Lollolo realize, in this year 1977, that he had a Mythic Female Kounterpart, a little half-sister halfway 'round the globe, who was busy taking sailors round the world? Nope, not an inkling of a thinkling!)

When the revolution was heating up in '72, Lollolo was approached by the conspirators. His royal support would be greatly appreciated.... (Left unsaid was what would happen if he refused.)

Hey, why not? Nineteen-year-old Lollolo was sorta drifting at the time, having just returned from his first tedious semester at Oxford (them fractional English genes having exerted their call), and was looking for a change.

You say you want a revolution? Weh-hell you know, we all wanna change the world....

If he had known exactly what a minor functionary he would still be, five years later, he might've responded differently. Still, his life wasn't unbearable. Especially since he had made his connections to Wu Labs....

Lollolo had arrived at the market: acres of spontaneous booths and bamboo mats spread with merchandise: liter bottles of gasoline, shoes, grilled bananas. People and stray pigs thronged the narrow paths between vendors, pausing to inspect and sample. Stepping over a pile of bleached animal skulls used in various Vodun rituals, Lollolo nicked a hot doughnut from a brass tray (the vendor smiled his pleasure; such a condescension from one of even disgraced royal blood would be good for business) and penetrated deeper into the bazaar.

Amid the various spicy smells and wind-borne dust, Lollolo came upon a common enough tableau which, today, affected him strangely.

A scribe with cheap pen and tablet of colored paper in hand was composing a letter for an illiterate tribesman—dressed in bright hues and wearing a straw cap—who was dictating hesitantly. Struck by the poignant manner of the customer, Lollolo stopped. The whole transaction reminded him of something he couldn't quite put his finger on. Scribe, transcribe, transcription....

Genes. The reproduction of genetic information. The customer was the DNA template, the scribe was RNA, and words the resultant proteins. Both processes mirrored each other almost exactly. Carry it even further: the recipient of the letter would function like reverse transcriptase, translating the information back into a form that would be assimilated into the brain. Language as virus, who said that....?

Too much!

Lollolo seemed unusually aquiver today to normally imperceptible signals. Imagine witnessing some kinda cellular mechanics on a gross macroscopic level, all humanity and its vaunted cultures reduced to nothing more (nor less) than the transcription and reproduction of numinous information.... Gotta be the after-effects of tapping into the *Afa*. He felt as if he were suddenly able to discern a myriad of heretofore hidden patterns and interconnections. Every mote seemed pregnant with significance, every human gesture an encyclopedia of meaning.

Lollolo focused his attention even more intensely on the scribe and his customer. Hey, what was going on now? Oh, the letter was finished and sealed, and finally the scribe was getting paid. Money....what a crazy thing money was. Wasn't money, come to think of it, a kind of....INFORMATION? Sure as Gbwe-ji slithered, it conveyed meaning from sender to receiver: *I value your labor or products to this extent.*

Wait a minute, we're getting in awfully deep here, possibly well over our confused heads. Let's start from square one. The illiterate tribesman dictates information to the scribe, who copies it down in another form and then hands it back to the customer, who in turn passes over more information in the form of money to the scribe, but now the scribe has in his head the information dictated and in his wallet the information in the form of coins, but that seems grossly unfair, he's got more information than the customer, who's only got the same information in two different forms....unless the information contained in the letter is useless to the scribe, which would imply a hierarchy of information, all information is not created equal, some information is knowledge, and above knowledge, some information is....wisdom?

Whoa-ho.... This is too intense. Can't deal with these concepts with only a doughnut in my stomach, gotta wrap myself around a drink or two of palm-wine, and maybe a plate of *igname pile*, mashed yam yummies.

With an effort, Lollolo wrenched his eyes away from the scribe and rechanneled his thoughts. His gaze fell then upon the vendor on the far side of the busy scribe. What in the name of Bo—?

There was one hell of a weird black man operating this booth. Dressed in appliqued native robes, the guy had utterly Caucasian features capped by a fake Afro wig (kinky Afro, gonna have to kill some brother today!). The wig was of such bad quality that it looked more purple than black—a purple toupée—and from beneath it poked flaming red hair. True, his face and hands and sandaled feet were black, but an artificial black, like shoe polish or somethin'. Was this dude crazy, or what? Good way to incite a riot, appearing in blackface in newly People's-Revolutionary-Party-governed Benin.

As a duly appointed representative of the government, Lollolo took it upon himself to go straighten out this madman. White man in Hammersmith Palais don't play here....

Lollolo walked over to the booth. What was the guy selling? Eight-track tapes, how hokey, man, that was yesterday's technology. Africa always got sold the dirty end of the stick all right, impractical baby formulas, unsafe drugs (live polio vaccine had been field-tested on this continent, and rumors abounded that it had since MUTATED), quadrophonic stereos, carcinogenic pesticides, high-tar cigarettes, and now eight-track tapes. *We're always the West's dumping ground for old products*, thought Lollolo. *Wotta one-way street! When are we gonna originate something new that we can give to the rest of the world?*

"You, sir—" Lollolo started to say in his Anglo-accented English (his French was Parisian, his Fon Abomeyan), when the vendor interrupted.

"Claude, lad, how wonderful to see you again," boomed the idiotic-looking fellow. "I understand you got my package today."

Lollolo was taken aback. Suddenly the bright sunlight seemed hollow, the salty, Lagoon-scented air unbreathable.

It was the Irishman, Paddy O'Phidian, his main contact with Wu Labs. Previously they had met only in England, or elsewhere in Europe. And whenever Lollolo had information to send from Dahomey to Wu Labs, he had transmitted it out of country through certain discreet channels. Never before had he encountered this high-level representative of his secret employer here in his native land.

He realized now that he had made the tacit and reassuring—but dangerous—assumption that he was the highest representative of Wu Labs in his country, that Dahomey was his assigned branch of their worldwide operations. How could he have been so foolish? Obviously, an organization like Wu Labs would never let a part-time native operative like himself run things unsupervised....

Had all his actions and reports been counter-checked against duplicate information from other sources? Thank Dahngbwe he hadn't fudged much....

"I—Paddy, what—" Lollolo tried to master his emotions. He had nothing to fear from this visit, did he? "What are you doing here?" Lollolo at last managed to say.

"Simply trying to unload some surplus merchandise for my employer," said O'Phidian, indicating with a wave the various bulky cartridges spread out on the bamboo shelf.

Lollolo regarded the tapes. Pretty wide selection of the most bombastic rock groups of the decade: Yes, Genesis, Eagles, Supertramp, 10cc, Boston, Electric Light Orchestra, all those whose style had been instantly rendered ridiculous by the pared-down noise flooding from the London clubs.

(Rock 'n' roll, you see, represents the evolutionary triumph of a superior form of musical encoding over older pop organisms. The ease with which rock was able, in a mere ten or twenty years, to drive dinosaur forms off the airwaves is a testament to rock's highly efficient syntax, its seductive compatibility with the brain's hard-wiring, and its greater bit-per-second transmission rates. And punk was a mutant throwback to the progenitor sound, necessary in the scheme of things to kick stagnating 'Seventies music out of its predicatable rut and up a quantum level.

(Certainly, speaking on a personal level now, rock has expunged nearly all prior musics out of *my* old head; I simply cannot recall much of the pre-classical, classical, folk, swing and jazz pieces I once knew, just snatches from Before Presley. A bit of Mozart, an old darky tune, some Glenn Miller— That's all I retain from the hundreds of thousands of symphonies, chants, plainsongs, ballads, Tin Pan Alley

Broadway Musical hits, Aboriginal laments, ragas, Chinese court songs, *Ave Marias*, and roundelays. Strong memes expel the weak.)

Trying to sound hip, forgetting the package he had so recently received, Lollolo said, "Yes, I'm sure cassettes will soon antiquate this medium."

"Lord, boy, who's talking about cassettes? We're already looking at optical encoding of digitized sound. Didn't you recognize what I sent you today?"

Lollolo flushed with shame. And he had heard rumors about this too—

"And"—O'Phidian winked obscenely—"optical encoding of other digitized information."

You gotta excuse Lollolo for not being on the tip. No real shame there, cuz only a few dozen people in the world at this time would have been able to distinguish O'Phidian's loose-lipped bullshit from the Shinola on his Hibernian face. Why, shucks, t'weren't even any of them personal computers, home VCRs, or Walkmen in that primitive decade.

But Lollolo recovered quick, sharp lad that he was, shook his head in agreement, waiting for O'Phidian to volunteer more information, which he obligingly did.

"'Course, I was also waiting for you to walk by."

"G-a-a-a-h!"

This statement was almost too much for Lollolo's hyped-up consciousness, and he nearly turned and fled. Talk about steretypes, he felt like Steppin' Fetchit fer shure.

Sensing Lollolo's trepidation, O'Phidian reached out a big hand and plopped it on the African's shoulder before he could move, and Lollolo was frozen in place.

"Let me just gather up my stock, Claude, and we'll find someplace quiet where we can have a little private talk."

O'Phidian bundled up his assortment of outdated music in a colorful native cloth. The ramshackle booth he abandoned to any takers.

The two men began to walk through the marketplace, O'Phidian drawing many hostile stares which only Lollolo's presence served to defuse.

The Irishman seemed oblivious to the repercussions of his pathetic disguise. Could he really be such a simpleton, or did his buffoonery conceal deeper purposes?

As if he had somehow managed to overhear Lollolo's earlier thoughts, O'Phidian now said, "Fascinating, the byways of commerce, don't you think? All this exchange of money and services that one finds in all modern cultures. Good thing your people have abandoned cowries, though. Rather cumbersome, carrying all those strings of shells around, I would think. Although of course, it's still reflected in your language. The nomenclature for numbers is what I'm referring to."

Lollolo knew very well what O'Phidian was referring to, but he couldn't fathom exactly what he meant by it. In Fon, all numbers above one hundred literally translated as "x cowries." There was no way to denominate a quantity above one hundred without implying money. It was a strange linguistic quirk, all right. Was money all that was worth counting? Is that what O'Phidian was trying to say? How the hell was he supposed to know? Best just to ignore the remark.

The odd-matched pair had left the bazaar behind now, and O'Phidian steered Lollolo toward an open-air cafe. They sat at a table, beneath an umbrella spiked into the earth, and ordered drinks.

"*Pitto*," said Lollolo.

"Argh," said O'Phidian with exaggerated disgust. "How can anyone drink beer made from rice? Waiter, I'll have a Guinness."

"A Guinness? You can't get—" began Lollolo.

"Yes, sir," said the waiter, and left.

Lollolo stared at O'Phidian, who held a shit-eating grin for thirty seconds before saying, "Private stock. I come here often."

His worst fears confirmed, Lollolo waited to experience utmost despair. Instead, to his surprise, he felt curiously liberated, elated almost. This game of spying he had been playing, ever since he was recruited at Oxford, had, he realized, started to pall, to seem small potatoes, not worth the candle. Now, with his efforts authenticated by O'Phidian's presence as absolute reality, with major resources apparently invested in his country by the enigmatic Wu Labs, his second career seemed to offer all the promise that his first did not.

Emboldened by the realization that he and his country mattered somehow, Lollolo said, "Can't you at least take that obscene makeup off, O'Phidian? It's liable to get both of us beaten up. I expect you to fall to your knees and start crooning 'Mammy' at any moment."

O'Phidian countered, "I'm afraid the disguise must stay. It serves its purpose."

"And what could that possibly be?"

O'Phidian grew suddenly serious, leaning toward Lollolo. His normally outrageous Mick accent even disappeared.

"It's noise, Claude, sheer noise. All racial stereotypes are noise masking the truth of the individual personality, you see. Now normally, my Irish façade is enough to disarm people. In your country, however, that mask doesn't evoke the same response, and I've got to push things even further. I'm working the edge of the envelope today, lad. Think of it as disinformation, Claude."

Straightening, O'Phidian resumed his usual voice. "Here's our beer, boyo, let's drink up."

The waiter deposited Lollolo's amber-filled glass and O'Phidian's nearly black brew with its tan head. Lollolo was momentarily struck by the visual incongruity of himself, the black man, drinking a pale beer, and the white man a dark one. Then O'Phidan was proposing a toast.

"To the success of our venture."

Lollolo clinked glasses in agreement, although he couldn't have defined exactly what their venture was. Then, although he never intended to, he offered O'Phidian

the traditional Dahomean salutation:
"*Oku.*"
Immortality.
"*Oku de'u,*" responded O'Phidian.
You too, pal.

After the first sip, Lollolo ventured courageously to ask, "I assume you've been sent by Doctor Wu...."

"Ah, that's quite possible. The Doctor is a deep one. No one actually sees him much. Orders come down the channels, and we hop to it—'we' being you, me and every other employee of Wu Labs. Who's to say who's at the other end of the line? Could be Doctor Wu, could be myself, or—could be no one's there. Could be there once was a Doctor Wu, but he's long gone. Perhaps the orders generate themselves spontaneously, meaningful strings arising by chance from a random-numbers generator. Stranger things have happened. Who can be certain of anything in this world? Have you ever seen Pinter's *The Dumbwaiter?*"

"What?" These were hardly the reassuring words Lollolo had been hoping to hear, nor did he expect to be quizzed on his theater-going experience. Kinda queer not to know your ultimate employer, or whether he even existed or not.

"Well," shot back the confused Lollolo, "you must at least have come here with something definite for me to do."

"Ah, now that's a point we can agree on."

"Well?"

"Well what, Claude-me-lad?"

"What do you want from me?"

O'Phidian told him.

Lollolo sprang to his feet.

"You're crazy! I can't do that! It's sacrilege, I'd be put to death!"

"But if the Danghbwe-no agreed?"

Weh-hell, *that* question stopped Lollolo dead. He had never thought of that possibility.

"How—how will I find out if she agrees or not?" asked Lollolo, already knowing and dreading the answer.

"You'll just have to ask her, won't you?"

"*Y-e-e-gee!*" exclaimed Lollolo.

My fucking father indeed!

Thereupon did the nasty, self-satisfied, O'Phidian—having thoroughly screwed up Lollolo's entire conception of his (Lollolo's) place in The Scheme Of Things, and having also placed upon the stalwart, albeit inexperienced young Minister of Information's shoulders a tremendous burden—noisily quaff his Dublin Poison, wipe the froth from his lips (at the same time inadvertently removing a broad smear of facial dye, transforming his blackamoor disguise into the customary "blackface" with outlined mouth), arrange with Lollolo where they should next meet, after the

successful (hah!) completion of his mission, and finally, standing, depart with his shouldered burden of outmoded rock 'n' roll, leaving Lollolo metaphorically cryin' in his beer, with them Memphis Blues again.
Oh, Mama, can this really be the end...?
We're really back on the chain gang now!
After the ingestion of a dozen more ricey beers had sufficiently altered his skull-soup, Lollolo decided boozily that there was no point in postponing his doom. He got up shakily and meandered hazily through the harmattan-heavy, white-stuccoed city, arriving at last at the government garages. He signed out for a Citröen 2CV and fell into the driver's seat. Say-hey, where's that tricky ol' ignition hiding, c'mon out, you slippery bugger, ah, there it is, who'd ever think to look for it on the steering column....?
Lollolo brought the engine to life and backed out, laying rubber (tuff trick in reverse, but this kid had a lot on the ball) and narrowly avoiding a sentry's foot.
Before he was technically clear of the city-limits, he had killed two chickens and turned a goat into burgers. And he still had 150 klicks to cover before reaching Abomey. (Whole country was only as big as Tennessee, but the distance seemed almost insurmountable under current mental conditions.)
Gonna require extreme mental and sensory concentration and a display of all Lollolo's kinesthetic and proprioceptive skills to make this trip alive, especially since this heap didn't even have a radio with which to pass the hours. Only one thing to do.
Lollolo reached a hand inside his shirt and withdrew, hanging from a leather cord around his neck....his fetish.
Said object was the ugliest effigy imaginable. Horrible-lookin' little grinnin' priapic demon with outstretched tongue, carved outa wood from the *hun-ti* (or bombax) tree, and then liberally slathered with animal-blood until it achieved the permanent nightmare patina of an abattoir floor. This gruesome sucker had been shaped by the royal Buko-no during an *Afa*-trance upon the birth of little Claude, and shortly thereafter fastened around the infant's neck, never to be removed during his life-time. Lollolo's ELDRITCH EIDOLON was both the repository of his vital *anima* and also his guardian or tutelary spirit. In times of trouble, the fetish could be called upon for solace, protection, guidance, and general good vibes.
Figuring that now, if ever, was such a time, Lollolo acted to invoke the fetish's protection.
He popped it in his mouth.
The fetish bulged out Lollolo's left cheek like three walnuts, and the cord dribbled out between his lips like limp brown spaghetti. Looked kinda stupid—to Western eyes—but it sure made him feel good, to be a-suckin' on little Big Prick, who had been in his mouth on and off again ever since his first memory. His nerves became supple and easy, unknotting and unkinking, surging with cosmic *qi* energy; his senses cleared and his mind was emptied of anxiety; his whole self became nothing

but the automatic pilot for the highway-eating roadster.

Hey, folks, what say we leave Lollolo now as he journeys north, past boabab trees (under one of which stood a strange small white boy) and termite nests, himself a temporarily mindless zombie, and capitalize on his seemingly senseless and regressive Third World oral-fixation as a springboard for religious discussion?

Dahomey's animistic faith was, of course, at the root of Lollolo's actions. It was an ancient faith, and one familiar to most Westerners under a debased name: *voodoo*. Tho here in Dahomey, its birthplace, if you're smart you won't get caught calling it anything but *Vodun*.

*Vodun* was a rather unique theology in that it had at its center a vacuum, or big gaping zero, known as Mawu-Lisa (originally borrowed from the nearby Aja tribe). Mawu-Lisa was an androgynous she-male, deaf and blind to all supplications (so *sor*-ry, sir, that *num*-ber is no longer in *ser*-vice), who had created the universe and promptly lost interest in it and disappeared, rather like a hack writer with her latest airport-rack bodice-ripper, or a painter of motel-room art. (If you want to cloak this concept in a dead language, the Latin term is *deus absconditus*, the absconded god. Cf: Faulkner's negligent "Old Moster" ((sic)) and Nabokov's uncommunicative "Person Unknown.")

Unable to rely on this schmuck for anything (he-she was probably too busy fucking him-herself), the Dahomeans had populated the earth with more accessible spirits. There was Kpo, the leopard deity; Bo, the patron of warriors; Xoxo, the maker of twins; Takpwonun, the hippo god; Legba, the fertility god (who, whether sculpted as male or female, liked to have his/her genitals anointed with palm-oil); Gbwe-ji, the boa; Aizan, the god of commerce and markets; Aido, the rainbow, or Heavenly Snake (Stone Cold!); Sakpata, the god of smallpox.

And, first among equals, Danh, or Danhgbwe, python-god. Occasionally known as Steely Danh. Formerly kept by the hundreds in special huts, in squirming brownish-yellow and white-mottled masses. (Burton called this snake "the happiest animal in Dahomey.") Why, those crazy natives grooved on this scaly critter so much, they even named their country after him. Danh-ho-me. In the belly of Danh. Above the earth, Danh has 3,500 coils, or *xasa-xasa*, and below the same. Together, they support Mawu-Lisa's creation....

It's 1561, three years before the birth of Shakespeare. Sir John Hawkins—many-times-removed ancestor of Screamin' Jay—sails into Dahomey and is greeted by the King.

"Hey, Kingie, whatcha gonna do with those POWs ya got corraled there?"

"Sacrifice them to Danh. Kill them by beating them over the head with one of their own severed legs."

"Whoa-ho! Yer kiddin', right? You sound like them wacky Mayans. Sure you're on the right continent, Kingie?"

Kingie raises ceremonial broadsword menacingly.

"Hey, no offense, man, I can see yer serious. Well, seems a shame to waste so much potential brute Negro labor like that. Wouldn't Danh be just as happy with three or four victims, if his Kingie was liberally supplied, like, with plenty of cowries and trade-goods? I thought he would, that wily ol' serpent knows a good deal when he sees one."

So Hawkins stuffs his hold full of bodies and returns to England, where Queen Liz, appreciating the favorable impact of this new commodity on the balance of trade, issues the first royal patent for slaving, opening the floodgates for the eventual forcible relocation of millions of warm bodies.

Sail away, sail away!

Thus began the Triangle Trade (not the Golden Triangle; we'll get to that later): slaves, molasses, and rum, the booty Cy's Boston was built on. (It is pertinent to note here that John Dee, Liz's court Wiz, possessed a magic mirror brought back from The New World: a slab of Aztec (possibly Mayan) polished obsidian, which he would consult for advice. It is not recorded whether he ever saw the face of Quetzalcoatl in it....)

In due time, some of these discombobulated Yorubans and Fon end up on the isle of Hispaniola, where they promptly set up such of the old gods as haven't spoiled during shipment. The idiot honkies had obliged them by inadvertently bringing along plenty of shamans in their holds.

Legba and company offer some small consolation to the slaves, forming a comforting subtext to the grafted-on Christianity of their masters, and the hidden set of correspondences, or double meanings, reminds them of their native land every time the crazy white priest speaks. (Cf: *Macumba* in Brazil and New York, and *Santeria* in Puerto Rico and Miami.)

Danh—or as he is known in the new world, Damballah (not to be confused with Shamblalah), has come along too, along with his rainbow consort, now known as Wedo. Together, they'll do their best to comfort and eventually free their adherents. Let my people go-go!

Damballah's Catholic cognate?

Saint Patrick, he who paradoxically drove the snakes from Ireland.

The whole episode is a tribute to the persistence and longevity of information. Tho of course that ol' signal-garbler, Time, has added some noise to the message. As we've seen, in Haiti *vodun* mutated to *voodoo*. In addition the old magician's title, *buko-no* has become *bokor*, whereas *yevogan*, or priest, has altered to *houngan*. But the essence remains.

And along with their religion the reluctant slaves also managed to retain an African relic even more insidious and, ultimately, more vital and relevant, a kind of deadly information-virus which, spreading from hidden tropical nooks wet as love, will, in the twentieth century, come to conquer Western Civilization with a delayed poetic revenge, and which, even as you read these words, is probably filling some nook of your brain.

Negro, or mixed-breeding, music.

Jungle rhythms.

Drum-talk.

Tribal chants.

Rhythm 'n' blues.

Proto rock 'n' roll.

Ur-funk.

(The very word "funk," of course, in its musical sense, is Africa-derived. From the Ki-Kongo language came "lu-fuki," meaning "body odor." Out of a subsequent mingling with the Creole "fumet," odor of food and wine (slave connection), came our modern "funk," which if you gotta ask what it means, you ain't never gonna know.)

These Dahomeans, man, are wild dancers and musicians, ya see, just like their other Yoruban kinfolk. By Prajnaparamita, you wouldn't believe—

But why don't we just take a look?

Lollolo arrived in Abomey toward dusk. The Makhi Mountains brooded in the distance like insensate godlings. The drive had sobered him up, and he had spat out his fetish a few miles back, letting it hang slobbery against the outside of his khaki shirt.

Now he was cursing himself for a fool. Whatever did he have in mind, rushing up here like this? He could have postponed the whole ordeal for at least a week, during which time anything could have happened to save him, such as a megaton meteor impacting with the earth and destroying all life. Each hour of existence was sweet and not to be forsaken. Why was he rushing toward his certain doom? Was it still possible to turn back—?

No way. There was a huge welcoming committee around the King's palace, composed of all the assorted court functionaries and hangers-on, as well as hundreds of commoners come for the festivities. How had they known—?

Of course. There stood the King's ancient Master of *Afa,* divinatory nuts in a bag hanging from his belt. Sand-bagged by prophecy, oh yeah.... Got dem ol' Sophic Blues again!

When the crowd spotted Lollolo they commenced with these wild ululations interspersed with shouts of *"Tamule!"* ("Brave man!" Yeah, easy enough for *them* to say....)

Parking the Jeep, Lollolo got out, resigned to his fate and determined to show some royal panache. He performed this impromptu little gonzo dance to indicate how honored and happy he was. Crowd went wild. Then, escorted by various dignitaries, he proceeded through the gate known as *Ako-chyo-'gbo-nun* ("All the world must pass through here") and was inside the royal compound, several palisaded acres of trampled earth dotted with huts of varying dimensions—the larger ones quite impressive, with porches attached and many wings—and with dozens of altars, each bearing a different paste-slathered efficacious effigy.

The largest building was the royal residence. Over it towered a massive acacia tree, which looked like nothing so much as a nerve terminating in a myriad twisty dendrites, as if the Earth Herself had extruded a bare synapse to grok what was going on.

Seated on his throne, which was set outside the palace door, was King Agoli-agbo, Lollolo's cousin.

Kingie was fat as an *agouti*, or native bush-pig, quite dissimilar to his slim cousin. (Standing side by side, they looked like the number 10, ha-ha!) The King was bare to the waist, exhibiting womanly tits, and wearing a silver nose-plate (to protect from spirit inhalation) and armlet.

(One reason the Dahomean King got to be so big was that he was really two persons in one. Agoli-agbo was king of the urban population. His alter-ego was the Bush King. The Bush King even had a separate capital a few miles away, along with a discrete court and customs. This binary life was kinda hard on the waistline, what with having to attend twice as many feasts and all.)

Bad, bad Agoli-agbo looked mean as a junkyard dog. Even the presence of the royal jester, or *Ai-hun-da-to*, seated at his feet failed to alleviate his somber mien. This was his natural condition, so Lollolo wasn't overly scared yet. Plenty of time to quiver and shake after he made his outrageous proposal. It would be many hours before he would get to speak to the titular ruler of Dahomey, and he prepped himself mentally for the wait.

Conducted to a carven stool placed behind a long table, Lollolo allowed himself to be seated with the other members of the court, facing the King some yards away, the air filling with darkness like a shroud. Servants then swarmed out, bearing huge platters laden with food: yams, plantains, pawpaws, pineapples, roasted goat and chicken, *wo* pudding, there was enough to choke an *agouti* here, can't say Cuz doesn't know how to throw a party.

Everyone next fell to chowing down. Two of the King's wives stood before him, shielding his face from view with a cloth, while a third wife fed him. His many daughters stood nearby also.

When darkness began to hinder the activities, servants kindled a huge bonfire in the center of the courtyard. (Bodyguards bearing archaic rifles emerged and ceremoniously shot it full of holes.)

Upon completion of the meal, the part of the ceremony most awaited began.

Music. Dancin'. African Bandstand.

The royal band took center stage. There were about a dozen musicians, equipped with horns, bells, drums, rattles fashioned of gourds strung with snake's vertebrae, and....electric guitars! Wild, when had those been added...? Oh, yeah, Fela, Hugh Masekela and King Sunny Ade had all stopped by last year.

A generator roared to life. The rattlers started shakin', the guitarists twangin', the trumpeters blowing like Dizzy, the drummers percussin', and the rifftide engulfed Lollolo and the others in sonic syrup that made their blood vibrate and their feet twitch. Talk about your Phil Spector Wall of Sound, folks! Before you could say

"Got a nice beat and you can dance to it," all the folks, including Lollolo and the King, were up and stompin' and swayin', boneless as jellyfish.

It was minutes into the song before the sweaty, bootie-shakin' Lollolo recognized the tune as a funkified version of "Black Magic Woman." Far out! Talk about your feedback loops! Hey, screw worries, let's Dance This Mess Around!

And now it is the Land of 1000 Dances! The Funky Chicken, the Cool Jerk, the Watusi, the Twist, the Freddie, the Frug, the Mashed Potato.... Hours passed in a rhythmic haze. The tireless band never let up, segueing right from one tune into another. "Gimme Shelter," "Black Snake Blues," "Grazing in the Grass," "Good Lovin'...."

Lollolo danced his pants off. (Literally. Somehow he just lost 'em, shirt too, ending up clad only in flower-printed boxer shorts over his sheened cocoa skin. Lotsa other folks were half naked too.)

At last, however, the music ceased. Lollolo collapsed to the trampled ground, semi-conscious. The bonfire, having dwindled unattended, cast a wan light over the recumbent forms of the exhausted dancers. Lollolo gazed glassy-eyed into the hovering blackness beyond the fire's perimeter, which seemed now to define the entire universe.

After several minutes he recovered enough to realize that his audience with the King was at hand.

Crawling across the clearing to the throne, where the imperturbable, albeit sweaty Agoli-agbo once more was seated, Lollolo made the ritual obeisance by heaping sand over his head. Then he stood—royal blood had some prerogatives—and began his address. Ho-boy, gonna have to fling some powerful lion shit now!

"Honorable cousin—" began Lollolo.

The Yevogan, standing on the King's left, turned to the Buko-no and said, "Exalted Master—"

The Buko-no faced the King from the right and said, "Celestial Wisdom—"

What the—? Oh, yeah, Lollolo had forgotten how no one except the Buko-no was supposed to speak directly to the King. Gotta go through channels. What a joke. Oh, well....

"I," continued Lollolo, "come here today in all humility—"

"I approach the supremely powerful throne with a sense of awe—"

"I crawl to your feet with the craven mein of a jackal caught stealing from the leopard—"

"—knowing that yours is the power of absolute rule—"

"—knowing that my life is in your hands—"

"—fully cognizant of the fact that I stand in relation to your highness as a fly to a willful boy, and that if you so wish, you will decapitate me with one mighty stroke as I kneel gratefully before you, kissing your feet—"

"Hey!" Lollolo was pissed. "I didn't say that!"

"I was embroidering your pitiful speech," claimed the Buko-no.

"No you weren't, man, you were screwing it up, adding noise, making me look like an asshole."

Say-hey, where's this effrontery coming from? Lollolo didn't know, but it sure felt good. All his life he had labored under his mother's disgrace, her dalliance with Papa deClosets, kowtowing to his cousin. If he were going to die tonight, to make the transition to *Ku-to-men*, or Deadland, then....well, fuck it, he'd at least go out as a man!

"Just back off," said Lollolo. "I'm talking to the King myself from now on."

Shocked murmurs from the audience. Screw them too, the bleeding monarchist sycophants! What did they know about the new protocol of socialist Benin?

The only one who seemed to be on Lollolo's side was the wacky Ai-hun-da-to, who, come to think of it, was the sole individual besides the Buko-no who was permitted, in his role of sacred buffoon, to address the King directly. The hunchbacked jester was winking broadly at Lollolo and miming the actions of a man who had just gotten kicked in the balls. Encouraged by his goofy ally, Lollolo plunged on.

"Your Highness, I've come because someone I trust,"—oh, really, trust O'Phidian?—"a man of wisdom, although a white, has told me that the Danhgbwe-no wishes to speak to me and confer something on me. I now formally petition you that I may enter her hut."

Utter silence.

Holy Legba, my ass is grass now, thought Lollolo. No one *ever* entered the hut of the Danghbwe-no, save the young girl she nominated in her old age to be her successor. Even the priestess's food was left outside. Neither did she ever exit, issuing her predictions, advice and Delphic oracles from within the shadowy interior.

The painful silence stretched like taffy. The air seemed suddenly chill, peeling the moisture from Lollolo's skin. He knew he was gonna die. Not only that, but he felt like an idiot, wearing only his underwear. Nearly stripped of clothing, he felt shorn of all European camouflage, once more utterly native and hence subject to all sorts of irrational fears and compulsions which only a fool would ignore.

Agoli-agbo raised a hand, palm up.

The Buko-no reached within his robes and withdrew a machete-like blade, the royal instrument of decapitation. It was flecked with dried brown flakes.

He placed its grip in the King's hand.

Lollolo bowed his head, resigned.

"Stop."

The voice came from beyond the fringes of firelight.

Everyone knew it was the Danhgbwe-no.

Outside her hut.

For the first time in tribal memory.

The world was ending.

"Send the boy to me," she demanded.

Weh-hell, you never seen anyone hop to it like these folks. The Yevogan and

Buko-no clamped Lollolo's arms to his side and hustled him through the shivering crowd. At the edge of the firelight they thrust him out into blackness.

Lollolo landed on his knees and hands. He found himself staring at two bare muscular feet. The ankles above the feet were encircled by cuffs. In the dim illumination, Lollolo thought to make out the cast forms of tiny snakes with tails in mouths.

Then the small snakes spit out their tails and slithered off the priestess's ankles. Gbwe-ji!

Lollolo jumped to his own feet as if goosed. The Danhgbwe-no had turned, and was walking calmly back to her hut. She appeared naked, save for a horse-tail, which beckoned Lollolo to follow.

He did.

Old Burton genes, don't fail me now!

Lollolo covered the distance entranced. At the entrance of the hut he brushed past the frondlike foliage that served as the only door the Danhgbwe-no needed to preserve her privacy, and was fully inside.

The windowless structure was lit by a small scented candle shaped like Legba. The wick came out his prick, which stood straight up, taller than his head. (Burton said the god "crouched before his own Attributes.")

On the rafters dozens of pythons were coiled, as if on branches. Betcha this gal don't have no problem with mice or lizards, no-sirree! A couple flicked their tongues idly in greeting.

Lollolo was too shocked to be scared.

The Danhgbwe-no turned to face him.

She was agelessly beautiful. Her ebony nudity was compelling as terror. She seemed made of something rarer than flesh. Affixed to her forehead in some inexplicable manner were two small helical horns, taken from the diminuitive Dahomean antelope.

The Danghbwe-no seemed to have passed beyond speech now, into an existential territory where only actions signified. Cuz next she folded down gracefully onto her plaited sleeping mat, went to her back and spread her legs, revealing her wiry bush. Reaching down with both hands, she parted her fur and the glossy convoluted lips hidden within. Her upper arms pushed her heavy breasts together.

Weh-hell.... Talk about getting straight to the heart of things.... Seemed like a fairly unambiguous invitation to Lollolo. Tho what it had to do with his mission he couldn't say. Hey, wait a minute, despite lack of known social intercourse, this bold lady seemed somewhat conversant with making the beast with two backs. Hmmm....

Who gave a care for such mysteries now? Ever since gazing upon the priestess's glories, Lollolo's music-heated blood had been surging south to produce an erection of positively Legba-like proportions. (I hesitate to mention this next fact—sounding as it does like sheer stereotypical Racist Myth—but Lollolo was rather Well Endowed, possessing a penis that extended a full twenty-five—erect centimeters, that is.)

When Love walks in the room, everybody stand up!

So. Lollolo's erection actually unsnapped his shorts, and they dropped to the floor, as did he. Crawling between the Danhgbwe-no's legs, Lollolo was stopped at waist-level by her hands on his head. Still speechless, she pushed his face back down into her wet snatch.

Nowise averse, Lollolo began to lick.

Who-whee, this gal had the most wonderful musky juices Lollolo had ever tasted! It was almost as if some exotic element existed in her system and no other woman's. The funky taste was addictive, and Lollolo, her sweet cunt his embouchure, played her like an instrument for what seemed hours, while overhead the watching snakes lashed their tongues in imitation.

Lollolo had a fleeting vision of himself as a giant catfish on the floor of the mighty Niger River, Dahomey's northern border, just a-suckin' down that funky soup of sediment and wholesome nutriments.

Eventually Lollolo couldn't settle for foreplay alone anymore. Levering himself up and over the straining woman, he drove his prick deep up her. Jam up, jelly tight!

With Lollolo in her, this brown sugar gal became pure tantric energy, bucking and gyrating like a syncopated snake. Where had she learned these moves? Lollolo felt his spine turning into *wo*-pudding. It was all he could do to hold back his orgasm, but he could sense the Danhgbwe-no wasn't ready to climax yet, and he bravely plowed on.

Finally Lollolo knew their joint moment was at hand. He picked up the speed and power of his strokes.

The Danghbwe-no opened her mouth in silent exultation—

—and popped out of existence.

Lollolo crashed face-first onto the mat, bent and scraped his enormous boner, howled, rolled over on his back, grabbed his wet cock and sprayed gouts of jism uselessly but with some small pleasure ceilingward, toward the watching snakes.

When he was done cumming, he paused, naturally enough, for thought.

Trouble was, he had no idea of what anything meant, nor where the Danhgbwe-no had gone, nor whether he had fulfilled his mission.

There came a stirring outside the door. The voice of the old Buko-no tentatively said, "Dearest Favored One of Danh, did you get what you sought?"

Propping himself upon one elbow, Lollolo replied, "I guess."

It was only when he was dressed and driving home, still somewhat dazed, that Lollolo realized the most obviously significant repercussion of his actions:

His country, for the first time in recorded history, had no Danhgbwe-no. No successor had been nominated, unless it were himself. The sacred hut was empty, even the snakes having fled back to the jungle. The world really *was* ending!

Back in Porto Novo, Lollolo impatiently rode out the time until he was scheduled to meet with O'Phidian. He still didn't know whether to report failure or success. He had met with the Snake Mother, as O'Phidian had ordered, but he had been expected to bring some sorta information back from her, and he hadn't. Or had he? Lollolo harbored this sneaking suspicion....

Came the day. O'Phidian showed up at Lollolo's apartment after work. He wore his normal skin tone and Western clothing, as if preparing to return home. Lollolo certainly hoped so. The Irishman had brought nothing but trouble.

"So, lad, tell me everything that happened...."

Lollolo recited the bizarre events.

O'Phidian remained quiet throughout, contenting himself with nodding his head. When Lollolo had finished, O'Phidian stood. "You've done it, all right, me bucko, and a fine job of it too. The Snake Mother received her deserved apolytrosis, thanks to you. Now there's only one little chore left."

The Irishman reached into a pocket and removed a small capsule which he swiftly swallowed dry. Smiling, he explained, "Just a small dose of ibogaine, lad, to facilitate all necessary celestial connections."

Lollolo blanched, knowing that the powerful hallucinogenic West African drug was nothing he himself would ever take so cavalierly.

Following this statement, O'Phidian dropped his pants and shorts, standing palely naked from the waist down.

Legba, even his pubic hair was an alien red! Lollolo reared back in horror. "What—?"

"You've got to pass it on, boy, what you took from the Snake Mother, and I'm the carrier. Now, if you'd be so good as to bugger me, your share'll be done. No, don't worry about harming me with that enormous John Thomas of yours—which I've read about in your files—I've been trained from youth by the Holy Fathers of the Order of Saint Draco to take just such pleasant abuse."

"This is insane! I won't!"

O'Phidian managed to outstare Lollolo, despite the disadvantage of being half unclothed.

"You wouldn't be reneging on your agreement with Wu Labs now, would you?"

Lollolo considered the implications of that question for about fifteen seconds. Then he reluctantly unbuckled his belt.

O'Phidian kneeled on the handwoven native carpet—with its traditional motif of snakes swallowing monkeys—and presented his ass.

Suddenly, Lollolo, who, up to that very moment had been utterly disgusted by the whole prospect, experienced a surge of unwholesome mean lust, triggered by nothing so much as the color of O'Phidian's skin. He realized just what an archetypical scene he was enacting here. The white man, conquerer, enslaver and colonizer, kneeling before the animal whims of his former slave, who, newly independent, had years of subjugation to avenge....

Little did Lollolo know then that a mere thirteen years later, Africa would finally be free of its last colony, thanks in part to his actions here today.

Lollolo's prick swelled as he advanced on O'Phidian.

The Irishman began a weird keening: "Zoxathazo a oo ee ooo eee oooo ee oooooooooooo oooooo uuuuuu oooooooooooo ooo Zozazoth!" The ululation sent a quiver along Lollolo's nerves, but he didn't hesitate. Lowering himself behind the compliant Irishman, he wet his cock with saliva and placed its dusky head against the man's rosy anus. Ebony and ivory! The juxtaposition of their two oppositely colored skins sent Lollolo whirling away into a fugue as he inched it in....

Black. Everything that black stood for, all that it meant, its heavy load of symbolic freight. Complete negation, yet infinite depth. Mystery, secrets, riddles, enigmas, ciphers. The blackness of space, where white galaxies lay like pools of sperm. The blackness of underground rivers, miles below the living earth. There is water underground.... The blackness at the bottom of the sea. The blackness of a twisted heart or soul or mind. The blackness of night.

There was the Black Budget, the U.S. Defense Department's secret allocations for unnameable projects. The Black Box from KAL Flight 007. The Black Diet consisting of water alone, which tortured prisoners the world over knew. The Black Bag Jobs of the CIA. The Black Rose, a collective of Boston anarchists. *Film noir* and the dreaded *bête noire*. The presence of British Black Watch troops in Guyana during the Jonestown mass suicide. The blackouts of World War II, when rockets arced, following Gravity's Rainbow, otherwise known as the Heavenly Snake. The Black Rod of the British Parliament. (Lollolo's Black Rod stroked in and out of O'Phidian's Rosicrucian ass.) The Black Hundred, early Russian revolutionaries. The defunct East German television show, *Schwarze Kanal*, or Black Channel. Satanism, the Black Religion. The Black Rain that fell after Hiroshima. The Black Death. Black Heroin from the Golden Triangle. The Black Madonna of Poland.

The Beatles singing "Baby's in Black" and "Blackbird." The Stones singing "Paint It Black." The Hollies singing "Long Cool Woman in a Black Dress." Los Bravos singing "Black is Black." Steely Dan singing "Black Friday" and "Black Cow." Public Enemy rapping "Black Steel in the Hour of Chaos." Led Zeppelin singing "Black Dog." The Grateful Dead singing "Black Muddy River." Cream singing "Big Black Car." Wynton Marsalis blowing "Black Codes." AC/DC singing "Back In Black." Pearl Jam singing "Black."

The new American Express Black Card, more prestigious than the platinum one, with a credit line of half a mil. The British soldiers known as the Black and Tans, who subjugated Ireland, and the Black Taxis of Belfast. Commodore Perry's Black Ships, which opened up Japan to the West. (And did those conquistadors never imagine that the flow would not always be One-Way? Hadn't they conceived of Feedback then?) The Black Market that flourishes as the Binary Brother to every aboveground economy, where all transactions are cash or barter, and there ain't no returns....

The black of the tomb and the black of the womb (which latter is probably more accurately described as a smoldering crimson-purple, but we're talking common misinformation here.)

And, thought Lollolo as he bit his lip and felt himself preparing to flood the Blackness of O'Phidian's rectum with his white sperm, there is the black of ink on paper....

And ink, as the *1001 Nites* tells us, "is the strongest drug."

# Is Your Ass Dragon?

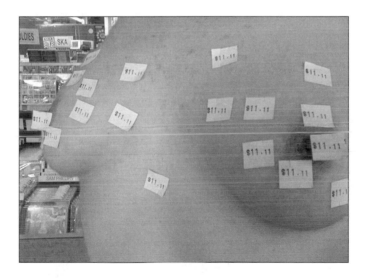

# K  L  U  E  S

### 00010000
"But if I say I'm incredibly successful and that I'm really
richer than beyond my wildest dreams, there'll be people that
want to buy into my successful aura and perhaps then it'll be
like a snake swallowing its tail or something, or some sort of
nameless void rolling on a double helix and I'll be able to
actually make some money and buy some new shoes."

—Stan Ridgway

### 00010001
"A tragic sigh. Information. What's wrong with dope and
women? Is it any wonder the world's gone insane, with
information come to be the only real medium of exchange?'"

—Thomas Pynchon

### 00010010
"Lord of the Americas, the Money God, the god of gods,
the clay of clay, nullity on high, zero with ninety-seven
thousand decimals fore and aft."

—Henry Miller

### 00010011
"To get my picture taken, I'd wear a black suit with yellow
polka dots and green stripes over that, with a purple scarf
around my neck, white ruffles on my sleeves, pants with
white pleats on each side above white shoes, a snake around
my neck and a bone in my nose."

—Screamin' Jay Hawkins

There is the problem of money.
Always.
Call it, as Cy does, Auric Angst.

Cyril hates sponging off of Polly. He doesn't know exactly how big the check from her father is, but he knows it's not inexhaustible. And even if it were, he'd still feel lousy about riding on her generosity.

Cy has This Thing about money, ya see, as do 'most all of us.

Money, goddamn it, defines his self-conception to far too great an extent. It limits what he can eat, where he can live or travel, what CDs he can buy, and what clothes he can wear. When he's got a pocket full of cash, he feels great. When he's flat, he's down. Money is the internationally standardized and capacity-packed wavelength at which transmissions are made in most socio-cultural situations. Without money, one is a dead transmitter, a station off the air, a message source where entropy has triumphed totally, overwhelming all meaningful information. At the same time, of course, money is the message itself, as well as the frequency, both the information transmitted and the channel down which it is sent.

Kinda hard, doncha know, to overestimate the value of that old valuta, the capacity of cash, the bang of bucks, the weight of wealth, the guilt of gelt, the span of spondulix.

Take that liddle matter of rent, f'rinstance.

Today is Thursday, the twenty-seventh of May, the day after the Dynamic Duo's visit to Parallax, the Pinball Wizard P.I., and the Midnight Confessions of Cy's Streetlight Delusion and Polly's Twin Murder. (Most reluctantly, Cy was convinced to actually handle Polly's fetish. Thank God, it had been in a quiescent mood and hadn't stirred, remaining a shapeless leather-covered lump in his palm. After Polly deemed Cy had familiarized himself sufficently with this vital, albeit hidden side of herself, she had lifted the bag by its thong and slipped it back beneath her shirt, there to nestle between those attractive, apparently unfettered boobs Cy had never seen but could not help involuntarily visualizing. ((The slope of her tits as she emerged from her shower clad in a towel, the feel of her thigh copped under the streetlight—)) If only he were in that bag, and could live on Sugar Mountain.... Actually, contact with the fetish *did* serve to diminish his fear a bit, tho he still tended, less than twenty-four hours after the startling revelation, to view Polly somewhat askance.)

Any-hoo, a few days from now, the rent'll be due. Cy was counting on his Planet Records check, along with Ruby's Wu Labs pay, to satisfy the quite reasonable expectations of his landlady, Mrs. Scozzafava. (Ruby, Ruby, where could a girl like you be? Tuesday Heartbreak, fer shure! Don't walk away, Renee! Cy's praying every minute that a girl in trouble is a temporary thing....) Ruby's pay is of course beyond reach, and Cy has little stomach this morning for trying to track down Detmold and get his own check, tho he supposes he'll have to attempt it sooner or later.

Oh, sure, Polly has already volunteered to cover the rent. But that don't make Cy feel any better. Worse, in fact.

It was only fair, Fairfaced Polly said last night, after they returned sleepily to Cyril's digs. She couldn't go back to her own abandoned apartment, which she claimed was too spooky-lonely, what with the ghost of Augie always peering over her shoulder (not literally, both she and Cy hastened to assure each other), and so she was gonna make her move into Cy's pad semi-permanent, for the duration of this Mess of the Missing Lovers. (All the old Italian ladies in the neighborhood, thought Cy, were gonna be ecstatic that the nice young Prothero boy had finally ditched the black girl and gotten himself a regular white one. My Mom says cuz she's black, don't bring her round... but we're bigger than the pain! Louie, Louie, Louie, Lou-ay, makes no difference if you're black or white, long as you know what I mean....)

But Cy still cannot reconcile himself completely to the notion of relying on Polly to pay all his bills. It's a form of monetary impotence he finds unsettling.

All of the foregoing is meant to explain why, this fine morning, Cy and Polly are having this kinda circular conversation so familiar to members of The Deadbeats' Club everywhere.

"Let me get this straight," queries Pol, sippin' her cuppa brew in the sunny North End kitchen. "You can accept money from your sister without guilt or worry, but not from me?"

"Well, no, not exactly. I mean, I'll worry about paying her back all right. It's just that I've been borrowing money from her all my life, and I owe her so much now, that it won't worry me quite as much or in the same way that owing you money would."

Polly eyes Cy sneakily over the rim of her cup before lowering it to clatter in its saucer. "So it's not the fact that it's a woman helping you out financially that's the issue."

Cy's indignant. 'Specially since Pol's dart is not too far off the bullseye. "Of course not! What kinda jerk do you think I am? I got no hangups about that. Leastwise, no conscious ones. Jeez, Ruby's always earned more'n me, and I never thought twice about it. No, if push came to shove, I'd be happy to use your money. But if there's a chance I can contribute, then I'd like to."

"Well, I still don't see any practical or ethical differences between my money and your sister's, but if it eases your conscience...."

"It does, it does!"

"Well, when can we go see her?"

"How about right now? We don't have anything else on the docket, till Parallax comes up with something. And Anna works at home, so I know we can catch her there."

"Let's go, then."

Mister Penurious Prothero and Miss Prosperous Peptide are shortly boppin' down the hill to the subway stop. On the way, they pass Sigmund Vincent's Pawn

Shop, a local institution, three gilt balls above a window full of people's bad luck. "Maybe," says Cy, "I'll even have the money some day to redeem my guitar." Polly expresses the appropriate commiseration. "Gee, Cy, I'm sorry. I didn't know things had gotten that desperate."

"Yes, sad to relate, but I'm in hock to Siggy Vincent."

Just then a local girl Cy knows emerges from the store. Her name is Janey Mercurio, and she's carrying a gun.

"Yo, Janey," says Cy, "what's happenin'?"

Mercurio's normally sweet face is grim, her eyes red-rimmed. "I caught Jeremy cheating on me."

"Well now, jeez, that's not *so* awful....," Cy temporizes, eyeing the gun warily.

"With another guy," adds Mercurio. "Now I'm going to kill them both."

Before Cyril can protest or reason with her, Mercurio stalks off.

Janey's got a gun, and she's getting serious! This could be Sweet Jane's Revenge. Don't mess with these local girls....

Sobered into silence, Cy 'n' Pol continue on.

Under the Central Artery, Grafitti Bridge carrying Route 93 that separates the North End from downtown, pass Pol and Cy. Before you can say "ungena za ulimwengu," they're on a train heading for Newton, a cozy bedroom community west of the city.

Cyril's fallen silent, thinking about his vanished past and uncertain future. Polly seems likewise absorbed. The train's running aboveground now, nice change from being buried. Trees, birdies, traffic, billboard advertising MELCHISIDEK LITURGICAL SUPPLIES: INVERTED CROSSES, LIVE MALE GOATS, VIRGINS....

Train keeps a-rollin' till Newton's here. A handful of folks get off, Polly 'n' Cy among them.

"We can walk to Anna's, it's not far."

Wide sidewalks, big bushy maples and oaks, tykes on trykes, it's another Pleasant Valley Sunday, such a change from the grubby city that Cy feels dizzy. Will he and Ruby ever live like this? It seems impossible they'll ever be able to afford anything half so nice. Anna's been lucky. Money changes everything....

The Condor home is a big white three-story Victorian at 128 Blue Jay Way. Turrets, gingerbread, the whole Bux-Deluxe-Restoration-Special. Cy ascends the steps and rings the bell. He's a little nervous, now that he's here to supplicate (ain't too proud to beg, are you, Cy?), and he grabs Polly's hand for reassurance.

"It's just that I want to hold your hand, Pol."

(Are your sure that's all you wanna hold, Cy?)

The door is opened.

It's Cy's fraternal twin, Anna.

The familiar disorientation sweeps over Cy upon seeing Sis. She looks as much like Cy as two non-identical siblings can. Mirror in the bathroom, can I take you out tonight...? God, she's even gotten her hair cut same as his! For the first time in years, he has a recurrence of that ol' childhood telepathic flash where he's inhabiting Anna's body, feeling T&A&C from the inside for a change, observed and observer switching roles in Heisenbergian trade-off. Whoa-ho, hold on tight, this is weirder than going inside Paulie Peptide's skull, it's a head-to-toes out-of-body experience....

Hey, I've got my period! Cy realizes. And my breasts are *sore*....

"Cyril!" exclaims Anna, then tosses her arms around her brother.

The contact restores Cy's sense of self. He's back in his own body again. Which is kinda not so good. Cuz all this mammarial/gluteal/menstrual awareness has given him a painful boner (or did Anna get into his skin while he was in hers and *turn it on?*), which now presses uninvited into his very own sister's leg. (She's up a step from Cy.)

God, what a monster he is! It's not bad enough that even while his Ruby is missing he's harboring lustful thoughts about his best friend's girl—no, now he has to develop the hots for his own sister! What kind of depraved beast *is* he?

Anna releases Cy, who does an adjust-the-drape-of-the-pants-crotch shuffle. "Come in, come in," she insists. Polly and Cy comply, entering a spacious living room filled with comfortable if pricey old furniture set on a rug big as the Far-Eastern country of its origin.

"What brings you out here, Cy? You haven't visited in months."

Too embarrassed to state his real need immediately, knowing also that it would be unwise to divulge Ruby 'n' Augie's disappearance, Cy says, "Oh, I just thought it'd been too long since I stopped by. What's up?"

An elbow digs into Cy's ribs. "Hey—Oh, yeah, right. Anna, this is my friend, Polly. She went to school with me 'n' Ruby."

The two gals clasp hands, draw together and make an air-kiss above each other's shoulder. Cy gets a strange sensation, watching them. He was in the womb once with Anna, just like Polly was in the womb with her brother. Could Anna have chosen to croak him, as Polly did her sib? Does he owe his existence to his sister's embryonic generosity?

Life. And women. Too mysterious for words.

Polly and Anna disengage.

"Well, you're in luck. Alan and Arthur are both home today. Alan had a late premiere last night—he's still sleeping, in fact—and Arthur's got a cold, so I kept him out of school."

Noticing a powered-up monitor on a desk across the room, its screen full of text, Cy says, "Oh, man, you're working already. Sorry, Anna—"

"No problem. Give me just a few minutes to edit this file, and I'll be ready to visit. Why don't you go see Arthur while I finish?"

Anna retreats to the corner of the room set up as an office, file cabinets, modem, fax, etc. She dons a pair of headphones—love of music runs in *this* family, boy—and gets to tappin' keys in time to some silent beat.

"What's your sister do?" asks Polly.

"She's an editor at Shambhala Books."

"Are they local? I don't recognize the name."

"Yup, they're right here in Boston. She worked for years in London, for Serpent's Tail Books, but was always looking for a job back home. And she found a sweet one. Anna don't even hafta commute, 'cept now and then for meetings. She does all her work over the wires. Pretty soon, when they get teleconferencing installed, she won't even need to go out for that. It's like total Information Highway."

Polly wanders over to a wall of bookshelves. "Are these some of the titles she's worked on?"

"Yeah, she's in charge of the Shambhala Dragon Editions. They're all like primary texts."

Polly runs her fingers over a range of Taoist/Hindu/Buddhist/Zen/Gnostic/Egyptian/Coptic/Mayan/Rastafarian volumes. "Sort of New Age?"

"Well, not really, unless you consider ancient religions new. Like I said, they're all translations of old stuff."

Polly takes down a book and starts leafing through. "Gee, this is fascinating.... Do you mind if I—?"

"No, go right ahead. I'm gonna say hello to my nephew."

Cyril goes upstairs to Arthur's bedroom and knocks.

"What's the password?" a somewhat congested, pre-pubescent voice calls out.

"Um, 'Darkman?'"

"Moldy oldy, Unca Cyril."

"'Bozo the Clown?'"

"No bozos on this bus."

"'Mariah Carey?'"

"Word up! C'mon in!"

Cy opens the door and enters.

Arthur Condor is a pudgy ten-year-old with curly blond hair, wearing plastic-framed eyeglasses. He is sitting up in bed, legs under the covers, surrounded by the accoutrements of a day out of school. Cy sees a pile of comix, something called *Big Numbers* uppermost, a Nintendo control, a Walkman, a stack of videotapes, a Chinese Checkers board, and a TV remote. The television and stereo are playing simultaneously. Arthur wears a T-shirt bearing an image of the chemical structure of the caffeine molecule, somewhat distorted into perhaps a new molecule by the rolls of his stomach.

"How ya doin', Art?"

"Okay, Unca Cyril, 'cept for this lousy cold."

"What's the movie?"

"*A Better Tomorrow.* Chop-socky flick from that Hong Kong guy, John Woo."

Cy quivers a bit at the coincidence. Like a masochist peeling back a scab, he says, "Um, great. What about the music?"

"Danzig. 'Snakes of Christ.'"

Whew! No Freaky Synchronicity there, as far as Cy can tell....

Now it's Arthur's turn to query. "Hey, Unca Cy, whatcha listenin' to lately?"

"Oh, a little of this 'n' a little of that."

"You heard Metallica's newest?"

"No, I can't say—"

"Megadeth?"

"Well, I—"

"Guns 'N Roses?"

"No, you see—"

"Nitzer Ebb, Skinny Puppy, Nine Inch Nails, Sonic Youth, Porno for Pyros, King's X, Tackhead, Rage Against The Machine, the Genitorturers, G.G. Allin, Soundgarden, Fishbone?"

"There's so darn much—"

"*Billy Joel?*" sneers Art Condor.

"Hey, now, don't be a smart-ass."

"Sorry, Unca Cyril, but someone's gotta keep you on the edge."

"Yeah, well, I was on the freakin' edge before you were born."

"Use it or lose it, Unca Cy. Hey, can you help me with my homework?"

Arthur has skipped two grades, and is now in an advanced seventh-grade program at a private school, the Babbage Academy. Cy sits on the edge of his nephew's bed and considers this fact carefully before replying, "Uh, sure, I guess."

"Awesome." Arthur rummages through the debris on the bed and comes up with a folder. He opens it and shuffles some papers. "Okay, we'll start with history, your specialty. What Russian ruler had a thing for horses?"

"Catherine the— Hey, are you sure the teacher asked you that?"

"It's a special unit on Russian depravity. Did you know that Rasputin was a member of the *khlysty*, a sect of religious nuts who handled snakes?"

"No, I didn't...."

"Okay, enough history, we'll switch to comparative religions. Now, for the prize behind Door Number Two, Mister Prothero: What do you know about the Maitreya Buddha?"

Cy cups his chin and cudgels his brain. "Isn't he the avatar known as the 'Future Buddha, the one yet to come?' Sort of a savior figure, still living in Tushita Heaven?"

"Sounds like primo bullshit. The teacher'll lap it up. Let me write that all down." Arthur scribbles away. "Okay, now dig this. The ancient Chinese believed in a class of holy men called *hsien*, people who had become immortal through mystical revelations or through magic elixirs. The highest class were the *t'ien hsien*, or celestial immortals, who frequently made the transition to heaven by vanishing even while people watched. But you also have the *ti hsien*, or terrestrial immortals, who continue to inhabit the earth, offering advice and wisdom to mortals. Now, the question is, If such beings really existed, where would you find one today?"

"In, um, a monastery in Tibet?"

Arthur makes an annoying noise, like a game-show buzzer. "Wrong! My teacher, Ada Black, says they'd be right under your nose, doing something completely modern. Well, you didn't do too good on religion, Unca Cy. I hope you never need it for anything. Let's finish my English homework now. We're reading *King Lear*. Okay, what are the dominant metaphors in the play?"

"Uh, well—"

"Snakes and dragons, ghosts and flowers. What is the role of Lear's Fool?"

"To transmit wisdom?"

"Good. Why doesn't Cordelia receive her share of the kingdom?"

"Because she can't speak...?"

"Right, the message doesn't get through. What does 'the face between her forks' refer to?"

"I don't know."

"Goneril's pussy."

"Art, please, keep it down! Your Mom'll kill me if she thinks I'm teaching you to talk like this."

"You can't teach me anything I don't already know, Unca Cy. All right, finally, what do these closing lines of the play mean? 'The weight of this sad time we must obey, / Speak what we feel, not what we ought to say: / The oldest hath borne most; we that are young / Shall never see so much, nor live so long.'"

"I don't know."

"Me neither. I think the guy just couldn't figure out how to end his story. It's a common failing among authors who bite off more than they can chew."

Cy stands up. "Well, Art, I'm glad I could help you. I gotta go talk to your Mom now. Hope your cold's better soon."

"Not me, I love being home." Art activates his Nintendo. "See you next time you need a loan, Unca Cy."

Cy stops with his hand on the doorknob. Is it worth denying what's so obvious, just to salve his pride? Nope.

"Art, if you ever live to maturity, you will learn to exercise more empathy for other people's problems."

"Hope I die before I get old."

Downstairs, Polly's still engrossed in her book. Anna's standing by the computer while it transmits her work. His sister, Anna, works in an electronic cottage, she never stops, she's a go-getter....

Seeing Cy, Anna says, "I'll put on some fresh coffee for us. The smell should wake Alan up."

Polly looks up from her book. "Anna, could I borrow this?"

"Sure, which one is it?"

Polly flips the front cover Anna-ward.

Cy catches a look too.

THE SERPENT REPENTS
An Ana(tetra)gram(maton)
by
Sally Salonika

"Oh, that. You know, sales have been very disappointing on *The Serpent*, and we had such high expectations. Our modern titles never sell as well as the classics, but we had hoped to catch the semiotics crowd on this one."

"I could tell. It's my field."

"Well, you're quite welcome to borrow it."

Out in the kitchen, coffee drippin' from the expensive combination Braun espresso/cappucino/goat-cheese processor, Anna breaks out some fresh croissants, her regular morning delivery, and pretty soon they're all noshin' 'n' joshin', rehashin' old times. After a while, the kitchen door swings open and Alan Condor, bathrobed and slippered, trips in.

Anna's husband is a good twenty years older than she and Cy. He's bald on top with a ruff of wiry hair that led his son to nickname him Bozo. Alan Condor is quite well-off. He owns a chain of cinemas, those giant mall megaplex kind as well as an art-house or two. Last night he had been at one of the latter, officiating at the opening of a Peter Greenaway Festival, starting with that director's *A Zed and Two Noughts*.

"Mornin', dear. 'Lo, Cy. Coffee, please. Who's your friend?"

Cyril introduces Polly, who smiles prettily. Cy asks, "How's everything, Alan?"

"Not bad. The opening went well. Though I had a hell of a time fending off well-wishers with drinks."

Alan has a history of alcohol abuse. Nothing too grim, but enough to make him recently join AA. Twelve Steps lead up (but thirteen steps lead down).

"You deserve a lot of congratulations, Alan. I think you've got it licked."

"One day at a time, Cy."

The conversation resumes. Polly and Alan soon discover that they can talk sports, and they're off rappin' about point-spreads on the Sox. Cy takes this opportunity to hit Sis up.

"Anna, you think you could see your way clear to lending me a few hundred—"

Alan, unfortunately, has overheard, and now jumps in.

"Cyril, I suspected money was the reason for your visit. I've been wanting to talk to you about this for a while, and now's as good a time as any."

Cy braces himself for the usual lecture. He'll endure anything to get the cash. But he's in for a shock.

"Cy, Anna and I feel you're wasting your life. You're very bright, you've got a degree from a good school, and you still insist on living the lifestyle of a student. You're wasting your time in that record store, working for minimum wage. You could have a good job teaching. Or I could easily get you into a management-training program with one of the corporations that sponsor my festivals. You're not getting any younger, you know. You simply can't continue to throw your life away like this."

"You know I burnt myself out on history. There's no way I could teach it."

"There's a lot of other fiscally responsible jobs you could hold. And I'm afraid that until you show us some sign of maturity, we're not going to lend you any more money."

Cy stands up. "Anna, is this your decision too?"

Anna's snifflin', but shakes her head yes.

"Okay, it's your call. But I don't have to hang around with people who don't understand me. I mean, it's my life and I'll do what I want! C'mon, Pol, let's get out of here."

Cyril half-drags Polly out of her chair and toward the front door.

"Nice to have met you both—"

Anna catches up with her brother on the front steps.

"Cy, please don't be angry with us. We love you, you know, and we're just trying to help."

She gives Cy a kiss on his cheek and at the same time stuffs something in his pants pocket. Whoa-ho, don't get bit by the trouser snake, Sis!

Cy stalks off, all wounded feelings. It's not till they're back at the T station that he thinks to check the contents of his pocket. It's three crumpled fifties, loose change around the Condor house, probably Arthur's weekly allowance. Well, it's not much, but at least he can supplement Polly's money. On the train, Cy apologizes. "Sorry to drag you on this useless trip, Pol."

"No, not at all. I got to meet your sister and her family. And, I latched onto this great book."

By the time they're back in the city, Cy has reached a decision. He's still fixated on getting some funds for their Kwest, and he's only got one place left to turn.

"Pol, I'm heading out to the record store to collect my last paycheck."

"Good luck. If you don't mind, I think I'll get back to the apartment and read. Maybe Max will call."

"Catch you later, then."

So. Tired of trains, Cy is once more hoofin' it cross-town to Planet Records, just like that fateful Tuesday walk. Besides being good exercise that might help vent his sour feelings about his relatives, it saves some subway-fare too.

The day is hot and the distance from downtown to Kenmore Square is a good hike, down monoxide-heavy streets jammed with broken heros on a last-chance power-drive. Cy passes the time thinking about that CD of Augie's—

Why would it be full of noise? Could it be that he's decoding it wrong? It might only emit noise when played through the wrong machine. If he played it somehow on a laser video-disc setup, what, if anything, would he see? Yeah, gotta try that as soon as he can lay his hands on such a machine, might be the clue that would solve everything....

Time comes he's arrived at Kenmore Square. How strange the familiar turf looks, after only a two days away. It's as if everything it once meant to him—a relatively enjoyable, mindless job, where he could forget the self-inflicted anguish he had experienced in his last few months at school, and recover from his semi-nervous breakdown, amid music that he loved, while he and Ruby plotted their future—all this significance has been locked away, the scene encrypted in a code to which he lacks the key....

Say-hey, they've even changed that big billboard, that perennial fave, which used to advertise CITGO. Now it demands:

EXPAND THE CHANNEL!

And below that, the puzzling formula:

$$C = W \log \left( 1 + \frac{P}{NW} \right)$$

Those crazy rockers, whodda thought they'd go so far as to rent a billboard to advertise their expansion plans? Altho what the math stuff is all about, God only knows. Maybe they're trying to attract the MIT crowd....

Immediately forgetting the message, Cyril pushes through the door of the shop and looks around. All is as before, the crowd of idlers, the decibel level of the music blasting out of the shop's speakers (sound-track to *Purple Rain*), and Cyril wishes he could still fit in. But somehow he knows there's just no going home again.

No one's behind the counter at this moment. Has Detmold hired Cy's replacement yet, or is Yarrow holding down the fort for thirteen hours a day? It'd be just like Detmold to coerce Yarrow into working the extra shift for straight pay, just so he (Detmold) could save on another employee's fringe benefits (which were almost nonexistent to begin with).

Waiting for someone to show up from the back of the shop (hey, even Yarrow should be permitted to take a leak now and then), Cy leafs through a stack of rock fanzines near the register: *The Noise, Bucketfull of Brains, Forced Exposure*, et cetera, hey, what's this one, never seen it before, appears to be called *Laocoon*, looks kinda interesting....

Since no one's watching him, Cy just folds and stuffs the xeroxed zine in his pocket without, you know, paying for it, placating his conscience by reminding himself that Detmold owes him for all the indignities he's put him through in the past.

Just then Yarrow steps through the curtained rear storeroom entrance. Luckily for Cy, the myopic "Straight Arrow" is polishing his greasy glasses on the hanging tail of his plaid shirt, and so does not spot the theft. He'd be sure to tell Detmold about it, and Cy'd probably end up doing ten years in Walpole for aggravated mopery or some such.

Donning his glasses, Yarrow sights Cy.

"Wha-what do you want?"

"My pay. Did Detmold leave it for me?"

"De-de-detmold says you can't have it, cuz you quit without notice."

"Quit! I didn't quit, Detmold fired me!"

"I don't know anything about that, I only kn-know what Detmold told me to tell you...."

THIS IS TOO FREAKIN' MUCH! On top of his brother-in-law's tight-ass Tuff Love, this insult pushes Cy over the edge. He experiences Complete Mad-Dog Anger, tinged with Total Insanity. The absolute nerve of Detmold! But, Cy realizes, it's only what he himself deserves, he rolled over like a puppy when Detmold fired him, and now he's reaping the results of his wimp-out. It may be too late to recover his pay, but he can still get some satisfaction outa this joint, cuz now

HE'S GONNA WALK IT LIKE HE TALKS IT!

Cy's hand falls on the first available object within reach. It's a price-gun, lying on the counter. Made of yellow plastic, the device has a handle and a trigger which, when squeezed, shoots out a sticky little white price-label.

Gun in hand, Cy advances on the quivering Yarrow.

"Let's Go Crazy" begins to play, Prince's guitar sounding like a chainsaw eating nails.

"Wha-what are you doing? No, stay away, you'll regret this, put that gun down, no, don't—-"

"Yaaaargh!" screams Cyril the Barbarian, and launches himself through the air. He lands on Yarrow and brings him to the floor, sending the slovenly sycophant's glasses flying. Then he begins to paste Yarrow's pimply face with stickers. The gun is set to $11.11 (man, these cassettes are getting expensive lately—or maybe it's set for cheap CDs), and as Yarrow's blotched complexion becomes covered with these hash-marks, he starts to look like a human barcode.

Yarrow's screams begin to irritate Cy, so he glues his mouth shut to match his eyes. Gonna mummify this sucker, yeah! Osiris-ify him! However, his victim's calls for help have already attracted some of the customers to his aid. (Unbelievably, others continue their browsing, deeming the scuffle none of their concern.) The bystanders try to pull Cyril off the hapless Yarrow, whose face is now almost hidden by black 'n' white stickers. At the first touch of their hands, Cy erupts up from the floor.

He's wild! He's unstoppable! He's a human hurricane of price-stickin' mania! Boy's got about a hundred hands, like Kali, each holding a price-gun. The wall of sound that Prince is laying down complements his frenzy. Take that 'n' that 'n' that, you worthless suckers! Gonna put the new Mark Of The Beast on your foreheads!

Say-hey, think I'll lay a pair of $11.11s right across this chick's chest, price-pasties masking her fear-rigid nipples, yeah!

Shouts and screams and frantic advice fill the store. "Kall the Kops!" "Grab his arms!" "Turn up the music, I can't hear it with all the noise!" People are being trampled as they try to escape. The whole scene is just like when Harpo grabs the customs-stamp in *Monkey Business* and lays about, branding passengers and customs-agents with OFFICIAL APPROVAL. Man, this feels good! Might not get my money back, but hey, your cash ain't nothin' but trash!

Oh-oh, sirens are a-soundin' down the block. I been runnin', poe-leece on my back! Sunday, Monday, Tuesday, Wednesday, Thursday, Friday, Saturday, poe-leece on my back! Lousy cowards, all of them put together can't even deal with one brave desperado and his trusty price-gun. Well, fuck all these sheep, he'll take on the cops too!

BULLHORN-AMPLIFIED VOICE: "Okay, Prothero, we've got the place surrounded. Throw down that price-gun and come out with your hands up!"

SNARL OF A CORNERED DENIZEN OF THE MEAN STREETS: "Screw you, coppers, you'll never take me alive! I'm a bookkeeper's son, I don't wanna hurt no one—but I've got a case of dynamite, and I could hold out here all night! If you want me, come 'n' get me!"

STUTTER OF A TOMMY-GUN: *Buddha-buddha-buddha-buddha-buddha-buddha!*

Well, wonderful as this sounds in his imagination, Cyril is overtaken by sensible trepidation. What good will he be to Ruby in prison? He really should split, better part of valor and all that. But first he leans over the silent Yarrow and hisses harshly into his unpasted ear, "If you tell them who did this, I'll come back somehow, I swear, and use your withered balls for a necklace!"

That'll just have to do it, thinks Cy, as he hightails it out of the empty shop.

Tramps like us—baby, we were born to run!

Directly outside the store Cy barrels down the subway stairs and hops the Green Line heading home. It's early in the day and already his nerves are strung tighter than Eddie Van Halen's guitar-strings. This being unemployed ain't all it's cracked up to be. Where's all them hours of sitting lazily at home in front of the tube, swilling vodka bought with food stamps? Could be that part'll come later. But, Cy realizes, he's been in on the edge of slippin' into a funk. He's almost forgotten that his true role right now is that of Tuff 'n' Seasoned—but Noble—Private Eye, on the trail of his missing two friends. Maybe his loyal albeit deaf 'n' blind assistant, Parallax, has turned up a lead. Best to get home and see what Polly has heard from the Big Guy.

Meanwhile, Cy's gonna pass the ride by reading that fanzine he stole. As the car rocks and screeches around underground curves, garbled words issuing from the train's PA like clots of unmasticated peanut-butter, he digs the sheaf of papers from his pocket, smooths the crumpled mass and begins to scan it.

Hmmmm, mag calls itself *Laocoon*, got crappy production qualities, smeary xerox of characters produced by a faint typewriter ribbon, crude graphics consisting mainly of an oft-repeated emblem composed of buncha blobby human figures struggling with a sea serpent looks kinda like Ollie, of Kukla, Fran &, enough to make Polydorus, the original sculptor of this same legendary scene, spin in his grave. Okay, credits? Entire contents seem to have been written and drawn by one Hyman Numinoso, address unknown. Articles got such titles as "The Trilateral Commission and Ozzy Osborne: Who's the Puppet, Who's the Master?"; "I Ended Up in the Cutout Bin of Life"; and "Boston's Vault: Club for Execs, or Colloquium of Secret Masters?"

After reading the text, Cy looks up—he's one stop from home—exceedingly puzzled. Altho pop music forms an integral subtext to all these articles, their basic thrust is toward viewing the world as a vast conspiracy. This Numinoso guy is plainly buggy as a roach-trap, seeing the hand of nefarious, Fu-Manchu-type operators behind every innocent nuclear Chernobyl meltdown or Exxon *Valdez* spill or minor Bhopal-grade catastrophe or Siege of Sarajevo NATO-inaction. According to Numinoso, one can detect and/or predict the schemes of these various cabals through interpreting pop lyrics.

The words of the prophets are written on the subway walls and tenement halls (and zine pages)....

Such a view, in Cy's estimation at least, is totally untenable, if only for the single reason that anyone holding it is bound to end up either committing suicide or becoming a monk or hermit. Even during his worst Clio-engendered depression, Cy never subscribed to this kind of industrial-strength paranoia. No, this stuff is too far out on the fringe....

And exactly what *does* constitute the fringe nowadays, in these overly eclectic and standardless times? Cults, the underground, the far extremes of left and right—they used to be so easy to identify. (Why, Cy, that old fart, even remembers when one could confidently call *Rolling Stone* an underground mag!) When there was an inflexible mainstream to stand in opposition to, underground information used to be easy to spot. Reproduced in small quantities, under-funded, espousing philosophies guaranteed to piss off the middle-class— These were once the hallmarks of cultish media and thoughts. But today the real underground seems dead. "Cult" is now defined as a movie costing a couple of million at least and playing in scores of Alan-Condor-owned theaters around the country. So much for limits on small and cheap. And as for shocking the bourgeois— Well, the goddamn bourgeois just won't play the game anymore. They consume everything mindlessly, without discrimination or shock, positively wallowing in information overload.

Novels: secretaries and housewives swallow like so many bonbons graphic sex scenes that once would have merited Supreme Court decisions, and college students doze through the printed subversive rantings of ancient leftists.

Movies: VCRs turn everything into television, allowing Mom 'n' Pop to spend their weekends watching either porno flicks once confined to Times Square strokehouses or French anti-movies that once played only Cambridge Art Pits.

Painting: Eric Fischl's scenes of implicit bestiality and David Salle's split-beaver shots hang in the MFA.

Music: ah, here's the saddest case of all the arts, shure enuff. Rock 'n' roll, the great unwashed devil, is now The Nation's Music, used to hawk cars and food and clothes. How dreadfully sad....

And even if a piece of insanity like *Laocoon* does represent some real subterranean impulses, it's still co-optable. Give the guy a grant and a word-processor, and, before long, he'll be right up there with *The New York Review of Books*....

The train pulls into Haymarket and, leaving the underground, Cy abandons his underground train of thought.

Short walk home. Cy eagerly anticipates finding Polly waiting for him. Recalling how he felt that afternoon when he raced home to find Ruby missing, he doesn't know what he'd do if he had to step into the empty apartment each day, and he can well understand why Polly abandoned her crib.

Gee, that Polly's swell. Look how understanding she was with his dumb brother-in-law. Cy had temporarily forgotten in the last year or so just how nice she was. The two couples had, as people will, drifted apart a bit after graduation, their visits declining to once a week or so. Why, come to think of it, Cy doesn't even know if Polly's still got her old job. She hasn't been going out to it for the past two days. Have to ask her. Maybe she'll be taking a nap, naked, and he'll wake her up, and she'll peel back the sheets and say....

Cool it, man! You're gonna enter with an irresponsible and unwelcome hard-on, and spoil everything. There, that's better.

"I'm back!"

No response. Jesus, don't tell me—No, hold on, kid, get a grip on yourself, there's no conspiracy, no one's stealing all your friends one at a time. Aha, see, here's a note, right next to *The Serpent Repents*. But wait, what's this, Polly's laid the paper in a pool of water leaking from a vase of flowers, and half the letters have bled indecipherably:

*De  r Cy,*

   *M  x cal ed w  s me inf rm t  n he di  n't wa  t to re  e  t ov r the ph  ne.*
*Me  t   e t ere.*
*Po ly*

After much conning of the half-obliterated message, Cy gets the gist and rushes out to Parallax's tenth-floor headquarters.

Up in Room 1010, much to his relief, Cyril finds His Female Sidekick busy scribing into Parallax's pudgy palm. To be fit for the Ritz, Polly has changed into a white T-shirt tucked into a black leather miniskirt, black nylons and—

Yes, she's wearing a pair of pink HI-HEEL SNEAKERS!

This footgear is all the rage this season. Invented by a self-trained Puerto-Rican designer who calls herself Muchacha Linda—"Beautiful Girl," or, for short, "Mucha' Linda"—these shoes resemble Converse High Tops, but feature heels of varying heights. Even guys are wearing the shorter models, and the low spark of high-heeled boys is everywhere these days.

Polly's shirt advertises THE FLYING KARAMAZOV BROTHERS, whose logo is a winged heart flanked by cobras.

She finishes her transcription and unbends, pulling her tawny hair back from her face, as Cy asks, "What's happening?"

"Max has unearthed someone for us to talk to. A former employee of Wu Labs who apparently left on bad terms. Max feels there's a chance that this man—he's holed up in a cheap hotel—might be able to tell us what Ruby and Augie possibly stumbled on, and what, if anything, Wu Labs has done with them."

"Jesus, lotta 'mights' and 'possiblys' and 'chances' in there. Can't we get anything more certain than this 'apparently' shit? What are we payin' this guy for?"

Max Parallax now speaks. Altho Cy believes he is most certainly deaf and blind, he seems to have sensed Cy's disbelief somehow, perhaps the same way he learns things without ever stirring from the hotel.

"There is no certainty in the transmission of information, young doubter. Every fact you seek to obtain has been contaminated by noise in its journey from sender to receiver, and its reception at all is chancy. Every message resolves itself out of the continuum of all possible messages, but shadow messages still remain. Yet this is as it must be. Were there no noise, there would be no information. Any message that is *a priori* certain can contain no information at all. Noise is the necessary yin to information's yang. You may minimize it, but you will never—*must* never—do away with all noise or uncertainty. This is a lesson we all must learn. And it is this lesson that I fear those at Wu Labs are daring to ignore or contravene."

Cy stares at Parallax for a second, seeing himself reflected in the Fat Man's dark glasses. Shux, Cy's really watching the detective now. Polly's filing her nails while they're dragging the lake.... Is this to be a Moment Of Sheer Epiphany, folks, in the Eternal Nowness of which Cy realizes his kinship with Parallax in particular and all other animate and inanimate objects in general? Will Our Hero attain satori, enter samadhi?

"What," Cy finally interpolates, "the fuck is this birdbrain talkin' about?"

Guess not. Looks like Our Hero takes a fall.

"Oh, Cy," sighs Polly, "I'll explain later. Let's go now. I've got the address, and the quicker we get some answers, the sooner we'll get Ruby and Augie back."

"Right. Catch you later, Mister Parallax, sir, 'n' thanks for the mumbo-jumbo."

"Oh, Cy!"

Outside Cyril says, "So, where are we heading?"

"It's a hotel in the Combat Zone," replys Polly.

Cy gags on his own saliva. "What? Us two? You 'n' me? Why? I mean, what for?"

"Because that's where this person can be found, silly."

"Oh."

Weh-hell.... Pretty soon the intrepid pair are down on Washington Street, among the daytime lowlifes who throng them topless-bottomless-middleless bars where strippers contort themselves into the Worm Ouroboros, and who patronize the loopbooth joints and two-dollar-admission, 24-hours-a-day thee-ay-ters and cocktail lounges where the LADIES' ENTRANCE is outlined in hot-pink paint.

They're down at the end of Lonely Street now, standing hesitantly outside the incredibly decrepit and raunchy HOTEL ALHAMBRA. (They discern the name of the illustrious establishment by reading the glass shapes of the neon sign, which is lit even at this hour. However, were one to interpret only those letters or portions of letters that are actively glowing, the sign would read: HOT— L-AMI-A.) Next door is a porno video store advertising the collected works of Vivian Vervain, including *Djean Djinni's Blow-Djob*.

"Well," offers Cy after a moment, "we're not getting anywhere just standing around out here."

"No, we're not," says Polly determinedly. "Let's go in."

The small dim lobby is all one would ever expect from the exterior: torn, filthy, faded carpet; sag-bottomed upholstered chairs with soda-stains on their arms; fly-specked plastic plants; sand ashtrays overflowing with butts; a cigarette machine. There're three or four smelly bums asleep in the chairs. Place looks so sleazy that Marlowe would ask Spade to back him up before he went in, while Archer and McGee covered them.

Cy spots the registration desk, lit by a bare forty-watt bulb and manned by a spiffy black man. This older guy has slicked-back wavy hair. He wears a black suit with yellow polka dots and green stripes over that, with a purple scarf around his neck, white ruffles on his sleeves, and pants with white pleats on each side above white shoes. A-and, is that a snake around his neck—? Nope, the shadows played tricks with Cy's eyes. It's just one of them old-fashioned Bone-Phone gadgets, conducts radio sound through bone-vibration. Oh, yeah, the guy has a pierced nostril and wears a stud shaped like a golden tibia.

This dandified dude is perusing a hardkover kollection of Krazy Kat Komics, and kwietly laughing to himself.

"Let me handle this," Cy says. "What's the name of this guy we're looking for?"

"Lantz. Ferdie Lantz."

"Okay. Stick close."

Cy saunters over to the desk.

"Sign in, stranger," the clerk growls.

"Not what I'm here for."

"Beat it, Jackson."

"No, no, listen, I'm looking for someone—"

"Look thru any window."

"Hey, now—"

Polly lays a restraining hand on Cy's arm. "Mister, my friend's a little upset because he's lost his girl—"

The clerk snickers in an oily fashion. "Barbara Ann?"

"No, actually—" begins Cy, but the clerk cuts him off with a rapid-fire litany.

"Peggy Sue? Linda Lou? Denise? Black Betty? Angie? Peg? Josie? Rosalita? Layla? Lola? Rita? Little Latin Lupe Lu? Roxanne? Suzie-Q? Proud Mary? Sweet Loretta Martin? Polythene Pam? Suzi Creamcheese? Bertha? Sugar Magnolia? Shanghai Lil? Cross-Eyed Mary? Candy? Madame George? Lucille? Avengin' Annie? One-eyed Fiona? Hey, why not love the one you're with?"

Polly persists in a sensible tone. "Please don't make fun, Mister, this is serious. We believe that one of your lodgers can help us find her. Won't you please tell us what room Ferdie Lantz lives in?"

"A white room, with black curtains."

"C'mon!" yells Cy, unable to restrain himself any longer.

The clerk finally seems somewhat chastened by Polly's obvious concern and sincerity, or perhaps by Cy's anger.

"Twenty-five," he says. "Or six-two-four."

"Well, which is it?" demands Cyril.

"Number nine," says the clerk. "Number nine, number nine...."

"He's nuts," says Cy. "Look, I'm just gonna check the register." Cy grabs the book out from under the clerk's nose, expecting resistance. But the strange fellow appears to have lost interest in them, nodding off with chin on chest. Krazy Kat lies klosed in his lap. In the cheap hotel, time stands still.

Cy flips back a few pages, then starts reading forward.

"Here he is, number sixty four. Let's find out if he's in."

A clanky old elevator with an accordian-cage door brings them to the sixth floor. Walking down the corridor they are subject to a gauntlet of sexual moans 'n' groans issuing from behind each door. Some heavy S 'n' F goin' on here, and that don't stand for no sci-fi!

A snatch of speech filters out: "Hey, baby, I dig U better dead...."

Cy feels his ears heat up, and he can't look Polly in the eyes. In the poor illumination, he believes she's blushing. House of the Rising Sun.... Boy, hope ol' Ferdie ain't similarly engaged, could be kinda ticklish....

At room 64, they halt and knock. No answer. Cy looks at Polly, tries the handle. It turns and the door swings in. Tentatively they step inside.

The ragged and cracked shades are down, outlined in white sunlight that allows Polly and Cy to make out a man lying on the bed.

The man is fully clothed. In fact, he's over-clothed. He must be wearing about a dozen layers of garments, including gloves. Stepping closer, the investigators notice that the man's ears are stuffed with cotton. A-and, what this, over his eyes he's got them teeny swimmer's goggles, only the lenses have been painted black!

Polly breaks the silence first. "I've seen these symptoms before. This man's suffering from AIDS."

"Gaahh!" shouts Cy and jumps back instinctively. Shoulda known he'd encounter such hideous viruses if he came down here. Squeeze the sleaze and you find disease....

Then Cy upbraids himself, feeling somewhat ashamed. Like everyone else, he knows AIDS ain't contact-contagious, but the word is so scary he responded automatically. Say-hey, come to think of it, he's never heard of such bizarre behavior associated with the disease before. Maybe he misheard Polly...?

"Is—is this a stage most victims go through?"

"Yes, it is."

"Gee, I didn't know. Is he hoping all those clothes will help him ward off, uh, opportunistic infections that might compromise his immune system?"

"Of course not. What are you talking about?"

"You know, AIDS."

"AIDS doesn't have anything to do with the immune system."

"It doesn't?"

"Not the disease I'm thinking of. What are you referring to?"

Cy tells her.

Polly smacks her forehead. "What a dummy! You know how specialists wear blinders sometimes...? Well, all I could think of was semiotic AIDS, not biological AIDS. I should have known we weren't talking about the same thing." Polly's skin darkens a tinge. "And of course, Augie and I being so monogamous for years, I haven't had any practical reason to think of that awful disease...."

"Well, what's this semiotic AIDS acronym stand for?"

"Ambient Information Distress Syndrome. Otherwise known as channel-overload. It's a strictly twentieth-century psychosis associated with the information explosion, getting more and more common every day. The victim basically feels overwhelmed by all the information pouring in on him. He begins to tune out, falling into fugue states from time to time. He tries to escape all stimuli, hence the goggles and cotton. In the most developed cases, the victim approaches catatonia."

This news don't exactly please Cy, especially the reference to fugues. Could it be that he himself...? Aw, screw it, they're here to learn what happened to Augie and Ruby.

"Let's see if we can stimulate this guy into talking a little," says Cyril. The two move to the bedside and prop the man up with some pillows. They strip off his goggles and unplug his ears. Their actions don't even register. Cy gets some water in a dirty, fingerprint-smeared glass and forces a few drops through Lantz's lips, pouring the rest over his head.

Spluttering, the guy opens his eyes, taking in his visitors with a stolid kind of fear.

"Okay," says Lantz, "I'm ready. Take me back."

"We're not taking you anywhere," Cy hastens to assure the man. "We're not from Wu, we're friends. We think Wu Labs is involved in the disappearance of some people we know, and we want your help."

The man buries his face in his hands. "Why can't everyone just leave me alone? I don't want to know anything else, I just want to forget. Go away, please, go away."

"We can't leave until you tell us what you know," Polly says.

Lantz raises his head. His eyes are rimmed with black paint from the goggles, and he looks like some kinda Rocky Raccoon.

"What can I tell you? I was only a programmer. I just wrote the macros, I didn't know what they were going to do with them, I swear it."

"Macros? For what?"

Lantz is starting to get overly excited, one might almost say hyperfrantic. Sweat pops out on his face. Them layers of clothes must be sweltering!

"It was just a few subroutines, I didn't even work on the mainline logic, you know I didn't. Neural nets have always been my passion, and they were doing things no one's ever tried before. And the paycheck— They pay so well, you know. But I didn't do it for ideological reasons, I wasn't one of the committed ones, like O'Phidian."

"Yes, we know that name. Ruby's boss. What can you tell us about him?"

"He's carrying the bug. He's the only white man." Lantz slurs the next sentence; to Cy it sounds like: "He got clawed."

"What kind of fellow is this O'Phidian?" asks Polly. "Can we reason with him to get our friends back? We think we have something he might want. Would he bargain for it?"

"All depends on the state he's in. He's not himself lately. I think the bug's eating away at him, myself. He's holding it until the engineers can make it perfect. They had one failure already, you know. What am I saying, of course you know about that, who doesn't, and so they're awfully leery, the bioboys, they don't want another screwup."

"What kind of bug? A programming bug?"

Lantz looks sullenly at the wall. "Don't jerk me around! You know."

"Honest," Cy maintains, "we don't."

Lantz says nothing.

"Let me try something," suggests Polly. "Ferdie—what can you tell us about the Eye Are Ess?"

The phrase from Ruby's secret tape triggers Lantz's logorrhea again. "It's in hundreds of dragons, all over the world. Melusine's the head of the corps, she reports directly to O'Phidian. They tattoo them, you know, right above the butt, with a dragon. That's the Wu Labs trademark, natch, Dragon-brand disks, Dragon-Write software, oh, yes, but Wu's the chief dragon...."

"Doctor Wu? What's he look like, what's his past?"

The sound of Doctor Wu's name off a strange pair of lips appears to have an effect on Lantz's nerves similiar to mainlining 100 CCs of caffeine. In the dusky room Cyril believes he can see Lantz's pupils dilate and his skin mottle. Ho-boy, guy's gonna have a textbook myocardial infarction or sumpin, maybe this here programmer's programmed to self-destruct, huh, like a trashy Jon Land thriller, paperback writer, yeah.

But Lantz effortfully reasserts some degree of control over his body, although his mouth seems exempt.

"His past and his plans— Ha! You don't want much, do you? What makes you think I'd know such things, a guy low down on the corporate scale, sitting in front of the tube, coding all day? But here's the joke—I do know a few things. Things I've overheard, information I've picked up here and there, social engineering in the cafeteria, hacked from files I couldn't resist looking at, from drunken talk with my co-workers in other departments. That's why I had to get out, I knew too much, I couldn't work there anymore, I couldn't even sleep." Lantz leans forward conspiratorially, his black-ringed eyes burning. "Did you know that at the end there my Mac—the old faithful Mac I had worked on for so many years—started *whispering* to me. That's right, whispering *obscene things*, things I can't repeat—"

"Hey," chimes in Cy, "the Vee Cee Are did that to me the other day—"

"Quiet, Cy, let Ferdie go on."

"It's all right, I don't mind. What were we talking about, I can't keep track of things anymore. Did you tell me your names? No, don't bother, it's just more information, information I can't handle."

Lantz drifts off, staring mindlessly at the water-spotted wallpaper.

"It's the AIDS," whispers Polly to Cyril.

Cyril is completely creeped out by Lantz's bizarre behavior. "We're not going to get anything out of this basket case, Polly. Let's split."

As if to refute Cy, Lantz begins talking again, more calmly.

"Doctor Wu. He's at the center of it all. But the center is empty. No one sees him. Who knows if he even exists anymore? Perhaps he's fled, bored with the whole enterprise he's put in motion. Maybe he'll show up when the run is over. The universe is a computer, you know. *But no one's figured out what the computation is for.* Yet we still keep flipping the switches, pushing the bits around. Orders still come down, but who issues them? Maybe O'Phidian's running the whole show. He seems to occupy the highest level. All the directories are open to his password, there's no cipher to which he doesn't have the key. But Wu—how can we know anything about him except what we make up ourselves? He seems to have fallen below the event horizon, into a black hole. No information comes out anymore, it only gets sucked in. The company bears his name, the orders carry his signature, but we never see the man himself. And all those years—! He's been around forever, you know. No one remembers a time without Wu, he's older than history, they say. As for his plans— Everything is part of his plans. He wants to conquer space and time. He has an infinite number of schemes. Oh, sure, some are more important than others. I stumbled on one. The Eye Are Ess—that's fairly high up there. But the bug is tops. If they ever perfect the bug, you can kiss your ass goodbye, sugar! And so can everyone else."

As Lantz winds down, Cy looks to Polly and says, "Shit, Polly, this sounds really bad. I'm more worried than ever about Ruby and Augie now. I say we bust in on this Wu asshole and demand that he he tell us what he's done with them."

Polly shakes her head. Cyril has never seen her pretty features so distressed. "We're too powerless, Cy. We can only follow the course of no-action, *wu-wei*. Forceful moves will have to be our last resort. No, we need more facts, something to either bargain with or bring to the authorities. Ferdie—do you have anything concrete, something extra we could bring to the trade for our friends?"

Lantz flops back on the sex-stained covers. "No, go away now, I can't help you, I don't have anything you could use, just leave me alone, I only want to forget." Lantz redons his goggles, shreds a kleenex and stuffs it in his ears. "Come back in a week, yeah a week should do it, I'll have something for you then."

"We can't wait a week," says Cy angrily, but Lantz is gone, lost in the thundering surf of his AIDS-clogged mental channels. Shux, it seems they can't get no satisfaction *at-tall* today!

"C'mon, Cy, we'd better leave."

"Gee, Ferdie," Cy sarcasms, "thanks for the information. I know it's only a Combat Zone, but still...."

Out on the street they head toward the subway, both silent. It appears they've hit one hell of a dead-end, fer shure. Unless Parallax can turn up something new, Polly and Cy are stymied, no closer to recovering their mates than they were on Tuesday.

Then Cy remembers the thought he had earlier, about playing Augie's CD on a different mechanism. Excitedly, he explains his theory to Polly.

"So, we always suspected that CD was important somehow to Wu—that's why they took Augie—but now we might have a way of learning what's on it."

Polly's spirits seem bouyed up by the possibility, tho Cy notices she's shedding a few tears at the mention of absent Augie. But brave Polly bucks herself up and says, "My father's got a videodisc player, we can use his."

With a lighter stride they reach the subway and head back to the North End to retrieve the disc, before riding the Red Line to Cambridge.

On the clattering train they refrain from talking, and Cy has a chance to ponder what he's learned from Polly about this alternate AIDS. Can it be that he's developing this new kind of neurosis himself? Sure as hell sounds like it, what with falling into fugues 'n' hallucinating 'n' all. Cy's always liked to be hip and *au courant*, but he'd gladly pass up the latest in diseases if he could. He feels sorta queasy thinking about ending up like Lantz, and he resolves to unburden himself to Polly.

Back in the apartment, Polly gets the CD from where she's hidden it in the bedroom, while Cy idles in the front room, wondering how to broach his fears. When Polly reappears, he still hasn't hit upon any subtle strategy, so, much to his own surprise, he just spills all his worries in a gush.

Polly's ash-blonde eyebrows vee down in concentration as she listens. She absentmindedly rubs a sideburn in a gesture of thoughtfulness. When Cy's finished, she hesitates a moment, then says gently, "I'm afraid you do have an incipient case of AIDS, Cy—"

Cue the melodramatic ham here, folks. We all know everyone secretly practices their reaction for when they're hit with the news that they've got The Big C or some other particularly twentieth-century ghastliness, and Cy is no exception. Now's his moment, and he's not gonna waste all those prior mental rehearsals.

"That's it then, I'm dead meat, I've had it. I'm sorry, Polly, but you'll have to carry on alone. If you ever find Ruby and Augie, tell them that I did my best, I went down fighting, and I—I always loved them. You'll all come visit me, Polly, won't you, when I'm lyin' catatonic in the bughouse? Just play a little of my favorite music in my ear, and maybe I'll smile...."

"Oh, Cy, take it easy, it's not as bad as all that."

"It's not?"

"No, it's not. Sit down a minute, and I'll explain."

Taking a seat at the kitchen table, Cy awaits Polly's reassurance.

"First," asks Polly, "what do you know about information theory?"

"Zip."

"Well, it's a complex subject underlying much—or all, if you believe some theorists—of modern science, and perhaps the whole cosmos. You heard Lantz claim that the physical universe is literally a computer. That's the theory of Ed Fredkin, whom I got a chance to hear when he was at MIT. But in your case, this needn't concern us now. Basically, if I can simplify somewhat, the main premise of information theory concerns the transmission of messages. Each message starts with a sender, is encoded for transmission down some channel, where it is subject to degradation by noise-sources, and then is decoded and interpreted by a receiver. I think you'll immediately recognize this process as happening in a hundred different forms every day."

"Okay, I'm with you so far."

"Good. Now, Ambient Information Distress Syndrome arises when a person's mental channels become burdened beyond their inherent capacity. It's not caused by a virus—like that other kind of AIDS you reminded me of—it's strictly a structural limitation of our brains."

"Whew, that's a relief, that I don't got some bug in my system."

"No, you don't, if you mean a virus. But in a way, you do have a 'bug,' a flaw in your wetware. You're feeling the effects of information overload, our century's probable undoing. Your brain isn't built to handle the mass of facts and perceptions that you're subject to each day. You see, while it takes no energy to acquire information, paradoxically it does take energy to destroy it. That's the fact that allowed Leo Szilard to undermine the possibility of Maxwell's Demon."

At this exact moment, the fetish under Polly's Karamazov T-shirt makes a little jump. Cy shoots out of his chair and skids backwards halfway across the room. "Cy, I warned you it did that from time to time. We can't let ourselves be distracted. Now, get back here. Good. Look, this simple formula explains everything." Polly scribbles something on a napkin:

$$C = W\log\left(1 + \frac{P}{NW}\right)$$

"Oh, yeah," Cy says, poised to move fast again, "clear as Dylan lyrics." The formula does tug at something within him, tho, as if he's seen it in another context.

"No, really, let me explain. $C$ is the capacity of any channel, $W$ is the bandwidth—about fifty bits per second in humans—$P$ is the power input and $N$ is the noise. So if we want to unclog your channels, we have to either widen the bandwidth, increase the power behind the message, or lessen the noise. The first two are impractical, given the physiological limits of the brain, so we'll have to concentrate on the third. We need to simplify your life, cut down on the noise and restore some certainty to things. And by trying to recover Ruby and Augie and discover Wu's plans, we're doing just that. So—hang in there, Cy. It might be tough going at times, but thing's are bound to get better."

"If I don't go down first."

Polly reaches across the table to squeeze Cy's hand. "Well, we won't count on that—although it sounds interesting."

Embarrassed, Cy squeezes back, then releases Polly's hot little hand, tho it feels so good he just wants to keep on squeezin'. Stop, in the name of Platonic Love!

Seeking to edge away from dangerous ground, Cy picks up the CD. There's the dying dragon logo he noticed the other day. He examines it more closely.

The Wu labs dragon, natch, is not your standard Western model, but rather the whiskery, serpentine celestial Chinese variety, a much more potent critter. Your Chinese dragon, or *lung*, ain't no Disney-fied bumbling mortal creature, but a divine being representing supreme wisdom. The product of some kind of ancient gene-engineering, it bears the horns of a stag, the head of a camel, the eyes of a demon, the neck of a snake, the scales of a fish, the claws of an eagle, the pads of a tiger, the ears of a bull, and the whiskers of a cat. It was a hoary ol' dragon what emerged from the Yellow River to reveal the secret of yin and yang to one of the first Chinese emperors, who thereafter named the imperial throne the Dragon Throne. Lao-tzu, the *hsien*, was called a dragon for his wisdom. To this day, when it rains, Chinese peasants claim that a dragon is coupling with the earth. ("Yo! Take cover, comrades, hell of an ejaculation comin' down!")

Cy stands. "Let's find out what's on this disc. And then we'll kick Wu's ass."

Polly's parents aren't home. Paulie Junior is at the Jormungandr Behaviorial

Institute where he spends much time without any apparent improvement.

With great anticipation, Cy and Polly pop their disc into Mister Peptide's top-of-the-line deck, which can play any size platter. At last they're ready.

Cy flips on the TV and the player and steps back, ready for instant enlightenment.

Completely unintelligible flickering rainbow patterns blaze into life on the wide screen and stereophonic static roars from the speakers.

Despite much fiddlin' 'n' diddlin' with the controls, this is all that can be coaxed from the disc.

Cy whacks the top of the television with the flat of his hand. "Shit! I was so sure we had it! But it's just more noise. What the *Christ* kind of information is *on* that disk, if it's not audio or video?"

Pretty Polly looks kinda down-in-the-mouth herself, as if she'd like to cry but is holding back for all she's worth.

"We've got to think harder about this, Cy. And don't forget that Parallax is still working for us."

"Let's face it," opines Cy, "we're fucked up the butt." As if to illustrate, Cy rubs an old itch on his own ass.

Cy wanders glumly outside. He feels like Absolute Crap. Might as well give up now, and save any future heartbreaks. Write off the rest of his life as an empty book. There's a Heartbreak Beat in my neighborhood, and it's Nineteenth Nervous Breakdown time, yeah....

The Peptide house has a yard in back, surrounded by a waist-high wooden fence. Cy ambles into the grassy plot. Beyond the fence, in the adjoining yard of a neighbor, children are playing. Aimlessly, Cy leans on the fence to watch.

There are about ten children under twelve, playing raucously. Their otter-like pre-pubescent androgynous bodies are covered by one- and two-piece bathing suits. (How dumb, those bras with nothing beneath. What a culture!) They have two garden-hoses hooked up, one to a long plastic mat or runner, down which they skid on their bellies, the other to—*a Wham-O Water Wiggle!*

Cy hasn't seen a Water Wiggle since his own childhood. He didn't even know they still made them. The device is a goggle-eyed green monster-head that caps the hose. Jets on its side allow the hose to dart through the air like a living thing. The children shriek and giggle as they alternately run from and advance on the crazily writhing hose.

Cy feels ultimate nostalgia for the scene. How many sunny suburban hours of his own youth were spent in just such mindless delight? Such days seemed infinitely long, with no problems, nothing that could disturb his ecstatic peace of mind, no dark clouds of separation and loss hovering constantly overhead. When I was a boy, everything was right.... I used to be a little boy, but now the killer in me is the killer in you.... If only he weren't too old for such things....

BUT WHO SAYS HE IS?

"Look out, kids! Cowabunga!"

Cy's over the fence in a flash, he's launched himself low into the air, hands outstretched in a diver's pose, KER-SPLASH, he's sliding fully clothed and belly-down on the slippery vinyl runner, ruining the hundred-dollar snakeskin Adidas that were a present from Anna, just a big happy adult otter come to join the young'uns.

Weh-hell, give these kids credit for being cool. In these days of baby-molesters and child-kidnappers, you'd think they'd freak at the intrusion of an apparently insane adult into their midst. But either they sense Cyril's completely sincere abandon, or they're disarmed by the fact that he's arrived from the Peptide house, a familiar locale.

In any case, they do not run away screaming, but instead pile in an enormous heap on top of soaking Cyril. Cy wrestles with the kids, rolling around on the fragrant wet grass. Already he's completely forgotten about all his troubles....

Then something gives him a whack on the head.

It's Mister Water-Wiggle! Oh-ho, sneak up on me from behind, huh? Cy's upon his feet, clutching WW by the throat, take that, you vile serpent! He's being liberally sprayed, the kids are goin' wild, high-pitched screams, yelling advice and WWF tips, the hose seems possessed of supernal strength, it twists madly, aiming a jet of water right in his eye, causing Cy to yowl and loosen his grip.

Wiggle escapes and does a crazy dance of victory, weaving through the droplet-filled air, where each drop holds a tiny rainbow.

Cy's a-rubbin' the soreness out of his eye, and so he don't see that WW is mighty pissed-off. (Cowpoke's Lesson Number One: If you grab a buzzworm by the throat and start a-chokin' it, pardner, don't a-let go until you're done!) Summoning up all his hydraulic strength, Mister Wiggle flies through the air and passes right between Cy's legs, under his crotch! Who-whee, felt like a rocket skimming his balls! Where's that Ol' Wiggle now...?

"Christ, look out, Mister, it's comin' back!"

And indeed Wiggle is loopin' back, this time passing over Cy's shoulder and twice around his waist, so that now the hapless victim's got a coupla coils of hose around his middle and between his legs. Hey's, this is getting serious! Lemme lay a hand on that flyin' snake!

"Cy, what in God's name is going on?"

"Polly, help, I'm being hogtied!"

In a sec, Polly's by Cy's side, herself getting throroughly drenched by Wiggle's venom as she trys to untangle Cy from the rubbery coils. Before either can cry "Uncle!", however, the evil Wiggle, faster than the eye can follow, greases Polly's hip like a big truck, scoots between her nyloned thighs, thrice around her waist, then once around the joint package she and Cy comprise, pinioning their arms to their sides. Shit, gotta be about a hundred yards of hose here! Cy and Polly are now inextricably yoked together face to face, helpless as two bound kittens. Next thing they know, they lose their footing and crash to the wet turf.

Now Wiggle hovers motionlessly in the air, sensing his moment of triumph. Polly and Cy stare up at the leering painted face, hypnotized, waiting for the end. Wiggle arches back his neck prior to striking, darts forward—

—and falls detumescent to the ground, dribbling a few futile spurts of water like the Devil's Eighth Diurnal Ejaculation.

A boy comes to stand over Cy and Polly. "Gee, that was awesome, Mister, but I figured I'd better shut it off."

"Yeah, well, thanks, I would have had the thing under control in another minute." Kid ain't fooled, and Cy grins weakly.

Suddenly, he's intimately aware of Polly's body. Her miniskirt's up around her waist, her wet thighs are clutching one of his legs, and her stiff nipples are poking through the first A and the O in the Karamazov T-shirt and pressing into his chest.

Cy feels a hard-on growing, knows Pol must feel it too.

He looks straight 'n' long into Polly's jade eyes.

She stares back unwaveringly. Her lips part, and she slides her plump velvet mound along his leg, insofar as Wiggle will allow.

Cy practically faints. "Uh, kid," suggests Cy with quavering voice, "how's about loosening the hose?"

"No need to hurry too fast," adds Polly.

# The Snakes Of Ireland

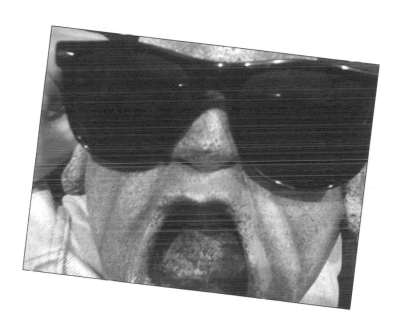

# K L U E S

## 00010100

"The light of heaven cannot be seen. It is contained in the two eyes.... The great One is the term given to that which has nothing above it. The secret of the magic of life consists in using action in order to attain non-action.... If a man attains this One he becomes alive; if he loses it he dies.... Therefore the adepts have taught people to hold fast to the primal, and to guard the One. If one guards this true energy, one can prolong the span of life, and can then apply the method of creating an immortal body...."

—*Secret of the Golden Flower*

## 00010101

"His mother, a real snake, had been a lousy mother."

—Kathy Acker

## 00010110

"The Tloque Nahoaque, the Universal Creator, created in a garden a man and a woman who were the progenitors of the human race. The woman was called Cihuacohuatl, the woman snake, the female snake. She bears twins."

—*Legends of Mexico City*

## 00010111

"Things went from bad to weird."

—Lou Reed

∫ tately and plump Father Declan Aloysius "Bogart" Gogarty was not. Quite to the contrary, he was a rather cadaverous sorta chap, kinda thin-shanked and knobby-wristed, with sallow skin that had seen too much artificial light, and in-puckered cheeks. Although he shaved these selfsame concave cheeks every day, by noon they would show a distinct stippled shadow. Dressed in the long bicolored robe of the Order of Saint Draco (half black and half white on the vertical were these traditional vestments of heavy monkscloth, with a dot of the contrasting color on each side of the chest), Father Gogarty looked nonetheless like a gangster. Hence his nickname, derived from his overall likeness to that rising young Hollywood star.

Despite his stern, even intimidating appearance, this spry and wiry youth—a mere 128 years old—was possessed of a keen and mischievious intellect befitting the head of an Order known for its deft hermetic probing into the mysteries of the Pleroma.

And on the whole, it was a Good Thing that Father Gogarty didn't look nor act like no effete Francis or Sebastian, them sniveling Christian martyr types. In Gogarty's purlieu, those pantywaists never woulda lasted long enough to preach Word One of the Demiurge's twisted gospels. Cuz it sure was hard to be a saint in *this* city.

Ya see, the central—nay, only—monastery of the Order of Saint Draco lay smack dab in the middle of the Liberties, Dublin's most notorious slum, home to every vice known to man (and a few known only to woman); habitat of such legendary bawds as Liverpool Kate, Piano Mary, Mrs. Mack, and Teasey Ward (all of whom, natch, charged a high BAWD RATE); a place where every conceivable object or service could be bought and sold, money changing hands like signals passing through repeaters, noise gatings and multiplexers, being boosted and merged, broadcast on encrypted carriers of untraceable origin; where despite all the tawdry activities the commonest thimblerigger could surprise the visitor with the sheerest poetry out of his Guinness-befoamed mouth ("Here only the English language is undefiled," said one writer of the Liberties).

Granted this environment, it was probably just as well that Father Gogarty looked Tuff Enuff.

Especially since the Order of Saint Draco maintained many of these illicit rackets themselves, funnelling the profits into their coffers and thence through various obscure conduits around the world. Money was never a problem at this monastery; the radio to heaven was wired to their purse.

So. It was December 31, 1937, (four years after the invention of Muzak), the final cold day in a cold, cold year. Ya had your basic Worldwide Depression still hangin' in there, of course. (Just a little trouble with creation, transmission and decoding of fiscal information, doncha know. Schizophrenia in the Money Mind. Brother, can ya spare a dime? But not to worry, the whole international network of monetary channels would be unclogged soon, once the Zionist/Illuminati/Vatican Bankers finish duking it out among themselves. That's all that money wants. Soldiers keep on warrin', world keep on turnin', cuz it won't be long, you hylics and mudmen, keep on dreamin' your lives away in ignorance, don't cultivate your own primal mindfulness or polish the Mirror of the Mind, forget you were born with Buddha nature, obey all orders, prove Milgram right, lemmings over the cliff, Gadarene Circean swine.... Assholes! You'll always get fooled again! How many times do I have to tell you: don't follow leaders, watch the parking meters, Johnny's in the basement, mixing up the medicine. You make a man want to forsake you, fuck her bodhisattva vows, all we seem to share is misery, yet still I want to build up a solid bond in your heart!)

Hit the reset button....

There was some fairly alarming action going down in Krautland at the same time. *Could be a serious rumble brewin' there,* thought Gogarty, calculating its potential impact on the Order. He had a stochastic flash of massive troop movements, burning greasy ovens, suicidal divebombers.... It might require the full force of The Andrews Sisters before the Allies could triumph. Don't sit under the apple tree with anyone else but me—said the Serpent.

Another thing to keep a reptilian eye on was the Japanese invasion of China. This year had seen Chiang Kai-shek make reluctant alliance with his Communist foes in the face of the invading Japs, who knew not what hoary possible dragon they were disturbing in its lair....

And finally, from America, a not entirely positive development this year, perhaps that singular country's most radical contribution to world culture so far. For 1937 was the year Bausch and Lomb introduced the first high-quality, mass-produced sunglasses for the general public: Raybans, to be precise. "Comfort against glare...." Hah! We all know what they're *really* for. Generations of hipsters, Mafia hitmen, South American generals, Arab sheiks, Kool Kats, Greek shipping tycoons, widows of slain American Presidents (I wanna be Jackie Onassis, and wear a pair of Big Sunglasses), Cambodian Prime Ministers, rock stars, FBI, CIA and DEA agents, high-flyin' Enola Gay aviators, junkies with pupils dilated, club-hoppin' I-wear-my-sunglasses-at-night trendies, Texas highway-patrolmen, Deep South sheriffs—all those yet unborn millions who, in a phrase, HAVE SOMETHING TO HIDE OR WANT TO GAIN THE UPPER HAND, and wish to suppress the information output from their eyes with a plastic filter—were receiving, in this momentous year of the waning 'Thirties, their biggest boon. *Kinda dangerous,* thought Gogarty, *to let the hylic ones replicate with technology even partially the famed Gnostic Whammy without the requisite mental preparation.*

Amid these less-than-pleasant or otherwise dubious developments, Gogarty was happy to note that his beloved Ireland was experiencing something of a rejuvenation. Seven hundred years of outside domination were finally coming to an end. (Ireland even had her own Prime Minister now, the aptly named *Taoiseach*.) True, things had been rough since '21 (note: the same year the Nine Powers were attempting to slip the thin end of the wedge into China's Open Door), but real independence seemed closer than ever. The new Constitution—which mentioned Britain not at all—had just been enacted two days ago, along with the inauguration of Hyde as Ireland's first President, and the establishment of Gaelic as the official language. (Pretty wild, changing a country's National Code with one stroke of the pen....) And Ireland being traditionally so poor, the Depression hadn't made as much of an impression here as elsewhere.

Yessir, things were definitely looking up for The Children Of Hibernia.

And for the Holy Order of Saint Draco.

Ever since Father Carpocrates O'Brien had returned from America—where he had picked the brain of a certain ingenious 21-year-old MIT undergraduate named Claude Shannon (ah, wasn't it truly wonderful how the Sons of the Old Sod everywhere hung together!)—a ferment of ideational excitement had filled the Order's cloisters.

After fifteen hundred years of laborious theological debate and speculation; after fifteen hundred years of studying the heavens and the depths of their souls for traces of the Demiurge's intentions, for the faintest message from Sophia where she dwelt in holy spermatic licentiousness in the Ogdoad, the Eighth Level of Heaven; after fifteen hundred years of painstaking minute spiritual progress, mocked day by day, as Jacques Lacarriere says, "by the maleficent substance of Time"— After this whole tragic secret history, the followers of Saint Draco finally had a scientific basis for their peculiar beliefs....

Father Gogarty stepped from the tenebrous doorway of the Order's headquarters (pocketing a small volume by Flaubert as he did so). The small and undistinguished building, denoted only by a corroded bronze plaque inset next to the door, crouched in the shadow of nearby Saint Patrick's Cathedral. It always amused Gogarty that the two structures, one tiny, one huge, bore the same physical as metaphysical relationship to each other: the small one functioning as an unknown and hidden codicil to the larger....

Into the miry, byre-y streets of the Liberties good Father Gogarty set his carefully polished brown shoes. (The area derived its name from the fact that, until 1860, when Father Gogarty had been a stripling of fifty-one, it had been the Cathedral's private fiefdom, not subject to secular rule.) The slit of sky glimpsed through the channel formed by the close-set dingy brick flats was a wintry leaden color, and some sort of insulting precipitation seemed imminent.

Gogarty wished he could hurry with his mission, and so be back in the musty comforts of the cloisters before he became drenched or chilled.

But trouble was, he didn't know exactly where he was going, or who he was looking for.

The deal was this: a member of the Order—Father Basilides Lehane, from Clonmacnoise—had just died, at the ripe old age of 256. (But wait—old Gnostics never die, they just Fade Away!) It now devolved upon Gogarty, as head of the Order, to choose a replacement. Since time immemorial, the Order had consisted of sixty-four monks, no more and no less. The number was sacred, deriving from an incident in the Order's history. As little time as possible should be allowed to pass before picking Lehane's successor.

That process, however, was essentially aleatory. Just as the new Dalai Lama was chosen by monks wandering throughout Tibet until they encountered an individual who exhibited the unmistakable holy signs, so was Gogarty bound by his beliefs to search the streets of Dublin—and if necessary, all the cowpaths of Eire—for Lehane's replacement, who would reveal himself by potent emblems.

*Saint Draco grant the search be not overlong!* implored Gogarty. *But if I have to swim a river, I will. And if I have to climb a mountain, I'll do that too.*

Shivering beneath his heavy zebra cassock—which was belted with a golden cord terminating in a snake's head—Gogarty set out, heading downhill toward the River Liffey.

And what a wild and woolly scene the Holy Father was thrusting himself into!

The slimy cobbled chilly streets were packed higgledy-piggledy with tweedy desperados and wicked women, ragtag urchins and crippled beggars, touts, thimbleriggers and drunken idlers. Horse-drawn carts carrying coal clopped and clattered by, nearly eviscerating unconscious gutter-hugging sots. From the pub known as *The Brazen Head* floated the obscure strains of caterwauled song, perhaps "The Foggy Dew." (Not for nothing was the harp Ireland's national symbol. Music was in her snaky, riverine veins.)

Up and down the crooked streets of the city did Father Gogarty wander, not neglecting to travel the avenue known as the Serpentine, his senses alert for the telltale ineffable portents that would reveal he had found his mark.

Wearying, he sat for a while by a gap in a wall. He noticed a rusty tin can and an old hurley ball. The innocuous objects somehow made his soul sad. He heard cards being dealt, and the rosary called, and a fiddle playing *Sean Dun nGall*. The music brought water to his eyes. Ah, there'll be whiskey on Sunday and tears on our cheeks, but it's stupid to bawl and it's useless to blame about a rusty tin can and an old hurley ball....

Bracing himself with a prayer to Saint Valentinus, Gogarty resumed his search.

Ay, and didn't the hours stretch and drag on, fruitless, deadening scores of infinite minutes without sight nor sound of Father Lehane's successor. *Curse you, Sabaoth, for ever consigning us to this time-bound mudball!* inveighed Gogarty.

At last he could walk no further on his long, parlous, parched journey around Dublin. The many hours of tromping had left him footsore and fatigued. Gogarty sought refuge in a pub: *The Feathered Serpent*, of propitious name.

Inside the strepent, seedy establishment, beneath dim yellow bulbs wreathed in smoke, Gogarty ordered a pint. At the bar, two aging bravos were boasting to each other.

"And wasn't it meself who was Pearse's right-hand man during the Easter Uprising?"

"Ah, go on with ye! How could that be when it was me own self that the great man turned to for everything!"

Gogarty suppressed a smile. Over the years, the 1500 rebels had swelled to tens of thousands. If these poor fools only knew the real meaning of the famous rebellion, which, besides occuring on a day symbolic of rejuvenation, had also taken place on *Shakespeare's birthday...!*

The good Father carried his drink to a table and took the weight off his feet beneath a placard that proclaimed:

ONLY GUINNESS SERVED HERE
GUINNESS IS GOOD FOR YOU!

The table was already occupied by three toothless, wrinkled oldsters smelling of peat smoke. They doffed their caps and nodded respectfully to Gogarty, lifting their own pints in token of shared enjoyment of the Heavenly Brew. Gogarty nodded politely back. As he sat, he was inspired by his fortuitous completion of the Sacred Quartet to converse with these hylics. Perhaps he could awaken the Sophic Spark within them with an appropriate parable.

"Would ye be after hearing a joke, gentlemen?"

"Ay." "For sartin." "As I live and breathe, Father, 'twould refresh me heart."

So Father Gogarty embarked on:

THE TALE OF THE DOPI HOPI, THE GUFI SUFI
AND THE OUTASITE OPHITE

"Well, there were three travellers once upon the pilgrimage to Jerusalem. One was an Indian—"

"Like the famous Buddha, then, Father?"

"Nay, an American Indian. He was of the Hopi tribe, and none too swift. Thus he was called the Dopi Hopi. The second member of the little band was a Persian—"

"Like the cat, Father?"

"Ay, like the cat. Or the rug, for that matter. Pray, let me get on with this joke, or I'll forget the punchline. Now, the Persian was a member of the Sufis, and, divine fool that he was, was called the Gufi Sufi. The last member of the group was an Irishman—"

"Ah, 'twas only to be expected!" "Wouldn't you know it!" "Only a crazy Mick would consort with such hay-thens!"

"Yes, well, we must have tolerance for other faiths, children, even though we are certain the Mother Church is the only true religion. Now, the Irishman belonged to the holy order known as the Ophites—"

"Are they Jesuits, followers of the dreaded Loyola?"

"No, they're not Jesuits! Now, listen! This Ophite had the miraculous power of making himself invisible at will—one of the six holy powers ascribed to bodhisattvas, and hence was called the Outasite Ophite."

"And did the Irishman, Father, then possess the other five miracles of the Tathagata also, namely clairvoyance, clairaudience, teleportation, ability to converse with the dead, and the power of flight?"

"Yes, yes, yes, by your mother's drawers he did! Where was I? Oh, right. So the three seekers found themselves lost in the desert on their way to Jerusalem, all a-thirst.

"'I'll get some water for us,' said the Dopi Hopi. And he began to chant and whoop and perform a rain dance. Well, the Indian danced and hollered himself to exhaustion, but nary a drop of rain did fall.

"Next the Persian said, 'By the Prophet's beard, I'll dig us a well.' He began to spin like a whirling dervish, faster and faster, the sand jetting up like a fountain around him, till he had drilled down out of sight. After several minutes the sand stopped spouting. Then the Gufi Sufi's embarrassed face appeared out of the hole. ''Tis dry all the way to China,' said he.

"The Irishman had been watching all the activity of his cronies with a smile. Now he said, 'Leave it to me, lads, and you'll find I've come across the desert to greet you with a smile, though my camel is so weary it hardly seems worth the while.' With this mysterious admonition, he made himself invisible and went off a ways, where he positioned himself by a track in the sand he recognized as a snake trail. Then he waited till a snake chanced to wiggle by, whereupon, knowing the serpent's legendary affiliation with water, he followed it unseen straight to an oasis. He went back to his mates and brought them to the oasis, where they all satisifed their thirst, sated themselves with dates, and then, when it was midnight at the oasis, proceeded to bugger each other silly."

The elderly gaffers looked at one another quizzically. One removed his cap and scratched his head. The other pulled on his chin. The third crossed himself. Finally, one spoke.

"Er, Father, the joke fails to assume its true aspect in me mind. Nay-ther virtuous nor humorous does it appear. For one thing, I cannot give credence to three holy men of whatever nature indulging in such sodomy on the way to the Holy Land."

"And if the Ophite could truly teleport like the Shakyamuni, then why didn't he just zip straight to Jerusalem?"

"Or fly up high and spot the bloody lake?"

Gogarty tried to explain. "You're being too literal. Don't ye see, lads? By a torn-down-à-la-Rimbaud dislocation of the six senses and a deliberate overindulgence in the treacherous pleasures of the flesh, conjoined with a flouting of Ialdabaoth's insane prohibitions and an opening of the soul's channels to messages from beyond the Hebdomad, one can achieve pure and instant realization and sanctification, and be lifted instantly higher and higher, until we're all like Buddha, Jesus and the Wizard of Oz?"

There was a moment of silence. Then one old man said, "Ah, now I see. The whole tale is more in the nature of a koan."

Another chimed in. "Glory, 'tis plain to me now also. The good Father's story is much like the old chestnut, *Why did Bodhidharma come from the West?*"

"Or *Does a dog have Buddha nature?*"

"To which, of course, the master's reply was the universal negative, *Mu!*"

"That reminds me of a good one, boyo. Does a cow have Buddha nature?"

"Moo!"

The old magi fell to laughing and chattering among themselves. Gogarty rose up in disgust. It was useless to talk to these hylics. Carrying his drink, he switched tables. He dropped into his chair with a despondent thought: *I believe in the Kingdom come, where all the colors bleed into One—but I still haven't found what I'm looking for!*

At this table Gogarty discovered himself seated next to a shabby old crone who was holding, partially wrapped in her shawl, a naked male babe—who sported an astonishing crop of downy red hair—against her withered bosom. The ancient virago crooned wordlessly to the shivering days-old infant, who was attempting to nuzzle the dry paps he instinctively sensed lay beneath her black shawl.

"Ah, poor liddle Paddy!" croaked the granny. "Ye'll find nothing there for ye. 'Tis a bloody shame ye've been desarted by yer maither, that hussy! Lord knows what will become of ye now!"

Out of apparent desperation, the woman dipped her finger in her foamy pint and offered the factitious tit to the fussy infant.

The baby immediately fastened on the finger and sucked it dry.

Encouraged, the woman raised her glass and tipped it gently to the baby's lips. The lusty lad immediately began gulping down the frothy brew with evident relish. His eyes closed in bliss, and his little uncircumcised penis swelled into a pitiful erection, validating whole textbooks on infantile sexuality.

The three old men had witnessed this precocious imbibing. "Holy Mary Magdalene!" "Saints presarve us!" "'Tis a miracle!" They rose *en masse*, filed to the table and proceeded to shower the babe and crone with gifts: a pocketwatch, a handful of coins, a crucifix which, tangled in its own chain, was hung upside down around the baby's neck.

The bar was filled with pious ejaculations. Outside in the street, a donkey began to bray, a cock to crow, and a crow to caw. Patrons crossed themselves in wonder.

Gogarty underwent a brief flash of satori. This had to be it....

"Hullo, good mother," Gogarty insinuated himself. "'Tis an astonishing prodigy of a child you dandle there."

Over the slurping noise the infant made, the woman replied, "I fear the lad is fated for hard times, Father, leastways if we judge by his first two days on earth. His mother has fled—the Pixies curse her!—leaving him with me, a poor old in-law she's hardly shared the time of day with before. And me with barely enough money to keep my own poor body and soul together."

"And who might the mother be?" asked Gogarty.

"And what would she be but one of them damned tinkers?"

The Tinker Tribes were Ireland's gypsies, tramps and thieves (that's what the people in the town they called us), distant relatives of the Romany clans, itinerant, wagon-dwelling ne'er-do-wells who made their precarious living though guile and craft, shuttling around the country like impulses squirted down Ireland's hoary synapses, camping on the banks of the Shannon, summering on the isle of Cephalonia. The Tribes were eight, or 2 cubed, in number: the Claffeys, the Sherlocks, the Driscolls, the Caseys, the Carthys, the Coffeys, the McQueens, and the O'Phidians.

"Young Oona O'Phidian's the strumpet in question," continued the crone, "and her without a husband of any sort at all. This babby is probably the son of Old Nick Himself, if I know me Oona! Well, whenever she passes through Dublin, she visits the old widow of her uncle, which you'll understand is meself. This time, she had the little bundle with her, naked as the day it was born. And when I wakes up this morning, she's hit the road again, leaving poor Aunty holding the babe, whom the mother called Patrick."

Gogarty pondered this information. A red-haired baby named after Ireland's patron saint and born on the very day the country had formalized its independence, and one, moreover, who guzzled Guinness like a trooper and promptly developed a willing albeit useless erection from the ambrosia....

What other signs would any believing man demand?

"Is there any chance Oona will be back for her son?" asked Gogarty.

"Nay, none at all. She swore to me that she was bone-tired of all the attentions men paid her, that her sweet little Lady Jane had brought her nothing but trouble and grief. And I can well believe her. There's been murthers done over that gell! Anyway, she claimed she was entering a nunnery in France, though I'll credit that when I learn the Pope's beatified her."

Gogarty needed to hear no more. "Mother, would you like to know that your great-nephew is well provided for, his destiny allied to the Holy Order I represent? 'Tis a fine devout existence I'm offering to sponsor this lad for...."

"But he's just an infant," hesitated the aunt.

"We would," offered Gogarty, "of course be willing to provide you with a yearly stipend of, say, thirteen pounds, as the infant's guardian."

"Make it sixteen," the crone shot back, "and ye've got a deal."

"Done," declaimed Gogarty.

Gogarty treated the whole crowd to another round to formalize the bargain. Little Patrick included.

Leaving the pub with babe in arms, Gogarty had a painful memory of his own bastard youth. His mother, Ruah Gogarty, had been a servant in the household of the

Babbage family of London. Their seventeen-year-old son, Charles, had knocked her up. When in 1809 her pregnancy became evident—that Unholy Swelling which mimicked the rotundity of the Pleroma—she had been quickly shipped back to Ireland. Gogarty's childhood, prior to his own initiation into the order, had been a rough-and-tumble one. He vowed now that this infant would know no such troubles.

The Holy Order of Saint Draco was restored to its Numerical Perfection of Sixty-Four Members. With what they had learned from Claude Shannon, they were going to kick some ass in the next few years.

Let the world beware—

The boys were back in town!

*lll.*

Once upon a time and a very good time it was there was a snakey-ake coming down along the road and this snakey-ake that was coming down along the road met a nicens little boy named baby Paddy....

Father Gogarty told him that story: the Father looked at him as through a glass darkly: he had a hairy face.

He was baby Paddy. The snakey-ake had come down the road where Saint Draco lived: Saint Draco had founded their Order.

*That old black magic has me in its spell,*
*That old black magic that you weave so well.*
*Those icy fingers up and down my spine,*
*The same old witchcraft when your eyes meet mine.*

He sang that song. That was his song.

When you first sip the beer it is mostly foam then it gets liquid. The Father gave him the black beer. It had a wonderful smell.

The story of Saint Draco was the very first thing little Paddy ever learned.

And a most strange and complex story it was.

To begin at the most obvious place (which of course was not, and never could be, THE REAL BEGINNING): An entry for Saint Draco could be found in the standard Catholic hagiography, right after Saint Dositheus and before Saint Drausin. Quite brief, it usually read something along the lines of:

*Saint Draco, born ca. 380 A.D. in Asia Minor. Canonized by Pope Celestine I for his missionary work in the Orient and Ireland, this enigmatic figure narrowly missed being branded as a heretic, fortunately dying before the creed he espoused was branded heresy at the Council of Ephesus, held by Saint Cyril in 431.*

So much for the official history.

(Paddy later learned that in ancient Ireland, when the roast was divided among the members of the court, the royal historian was accorded "a crooked bone." No explanation of the significance of this symbolic act survived, but it evoked for Paddy the whole twisted labyrinth of Clio's maze.)

The hidden threads of what Saint Draco represented extended back at least 500 years earlier, to before the birth of Christ, that purveyor of perverse parables and enigmatic info.

Cut to the Essenes. Crazy buncha Jews living the communal life circa 200 BC. Believed in some wild things, chief of which was attaining eternal life through sheer electric contact with the godhead, which they defined as Pure Wisdom. Enter the usual variety of persecutors and torturers. Exeunt the Essenes, early in the second century AD. (Although a rumor persisted for centuries that Jesus was secretly an Essene, which would mean that their teachings never did die....)

Torch was passed before then to the Therapeutae, an even tinier sect—neither overtly Christian nor Jewish—living on the shores of Lake Mareotis in Egypt, circa 100 AD. No one quite knows what they preached or practiced, although it is assumed that they held intact the doctrine of the Essenes in some form until Christianity was ready for it.

It was roughly at this point that the cultural wavefront or set of infectious memes we can now call Gnosticism began to be identified with individual personalities.

First of these was the infamous Simon Magus, he of Biblical invective and the monetary crime of simony. Simon wandered throughout the Middle East at the same time as Christ's disciples (later, he would visit Rome), preaching a counter-program, what he claimed were Christ's true teachings. With him always was a prostitute named Helen, whom he identified as Ennoia, or Sophia, both names meaning literally "Divine Wisdom." This boy wowed the crowd with magic, exhibiting all six of the bodhisattva's powers, at the same time spieling some wild stuff, including ideas on the mind's innate grammar which seem to have preceded Chomsky by a good millenia or two. Simon believed everyone could be God; he liked to say that the Rivers that flowed through Eden were still in all of us, four arteries, two of air, two of blood. "Thou and I are but One," he said in *The Great Revelation of a Voice and a Name.*

After Simon's "death" (multiple versions, no corpse), his two disciples, Saturninus and Menander meandered throughout the area, cultivating the seeds he had planted. They musta done a good job, cuz in the next two centuries Gnosticism exploded, coming to rival the fledgling Christian church everywhere. (It was only when Rome went papal purple, and the might of its armies was at the command of the Christians, that the Gnostics were finally "exterminated.")

The catalogue of druidic talmudic Arabic Gnostics and their sects just exfoliates beyond comprehension at this point.

I can mention a fella named Marcion (born 85 AD in Sinope ((little town just north of Synecdoche))). This guy was nuts, inspired, or both. He was so outrageous that his own father, the Bishop of Sinope, was forced to excommunicate him! Marcion was the inventor of the terms "Old and New Testament," and at one time almost succeeded in converting the church establishment to his views.

Then there were Carpocrates, Basilides, Ptolemy (yup, the famous philosopher; see his *Letter to Flora*), Valentinus, Epiphanes.... Groups calling themselves Peratae (Those Who Pass Through), Sethians (named after Cain's other brother), Phibionites (Humble Ones), Nicolaites, Stratiotici (Soldiers), Levitici, Borborians (Muddy Ones), Zacchaeans, Euchites (Lazy Ones) all flourished.

A particular Gnostic hotbed was Alexandria, city at the mouth of the holy Nile....

If we can synthesize a coherent creed out of the many Gnostic views (there was no such thing as heresy among Gnostics), it would go roughly like this:

This mortal world is a hellish botch, a murky parody of the hyperworld. It lies at the bottom-most basement of creation. It was brought into being by an inferior spirit, the Demiurge, son of Sophia, variously known as Saklad, Ialdabaoth, or Sabaoth. A host of other spirits—Archons and Aeons—populate this universe, in levels above ours.

(Sophia retains a certain measure of control over these Archons, control obtained through having fucked all of them, accumulating their sperm as a kind of karmic voodoo hostage. The Barbelognostics wrote: "She showed herself to them in impressive form, seduced them and collected their sperm with the aim of absorbing back into herself the Power that had become scattered in several different beings.")

The celestial architecture is mirrored in many natural phenomena, most notably the human eye. The clear white is the perfect hyperworld; the colored iris is the realm of the Archons; and the pupil is the Black Hole of this Earth.

Man too is a hideous abortion. He was originally pictured perfect in Sophia's mind. Her son, perceiving Mom's thought, fashioned his own version of man: "a naked weak thing who lay on the ground in the black waters, wriggling like a worm," according to Saturninus. Taking pity on this snakey subhuman, Sophia touched it and gave it strength to stand. Her spark remained in the race. We are spirits, spirits in the material world. And Time is the most hated sign of our imprisonment....

The Demiurge is the God described in the Old Testament. He is not the same one depicted in the New, Jesus's Heavenly Father. Nope, Jesus (and his Apocryphal twin brother, Thomas) are Sophia's boys, better offsprings than the Demiurge.

Saklad was a mean, malignant son of a bitch, loony as a burning bush, who could never be the Father of Jesus and Thomas. Simply put, the Creator was—and remains—evil (assuming, of course, that he even exists anymore).

The Old Testament became, then, to the Gnostics, a Book of Lies, all its villains heroes and vice versa.

What were man's duties in this scheme? Simply put, to cultivate the Sophic spark within him and disdain worldly creation. Central to the Gnostic doctrine, as their name implied, was the worship of knowledge. Information. Wisdom. Through contact with Sophia, the oh-so-carnal personification of Divine Wisdom, one could earn eternal life. Simple as that. Get juiced on enough wisdom, tap into the Holy Channel, and you're immortal. Okay, bro'! All right! Hand me the wire, beam me the signal, jack me into the Heavenly Network! I'm ready!

Implementation of this attitude took two opposite forms, however. (Hey, no one ever said the Gnostics were big on logic!)

First, you could become an absolute ascetic, eating as little as possible, eschewing fornication, terminating pregnancies (no one deserved to be born into a second-rate creation), refusing to be a part of society, eliminating all noise from the Heavenly Telemetry. (But pulling a Johnny Ace—what would seem to be a sensible exit from hell—wasn't encouraged, cuz suicide obviated your chance to improve your soul.) There were plenty of Gnostic communities like this.

The other course to gnosis lay through what Blake (a Gnostic if there ever was one, by the way) called "the path of excess." To "use up" or "shed" the corruptions of this world, to transcend them and achieve Grace and Glory, you had to experience the pleasures of the six senses without limit.

Eat to excess.

Dance like a dervish.

Pray till you fainted.

Fuck your brains out.

(Roll me in designer sheets, too much knowledge is not enuff!)

You can imagine the hysterical shit-your-toga reaction this latter path inspired among the nascent Catholic Church. Even more irritating was the fact that a Gnostic would recant whatever you asked him to, swear to worship any god the authorities put him in front of, and then, once released, calmly go back to his old ways. No martyrdom for these Kool Kats! We're too busy pumping hot loads of jism up any gal who'll stand in for Sophia!

As I mentioned, these insults to the Holy Roman Church were pretty much wiped out as the centuries advanced. The Gnostics actually helped in their own extermination, since they disdained organization, and had no infrastructure to match the Catholics. Oh, sure, over the next thousand years you had degenerate recrudescences of the pure Gnostic faith: Manicheans (Saint Augustine himself was an early follower, before recanting), Paulicians, Cathari, Bogomils, Nestorians, Albigensians, and Harold Bloom. But they're now all forgotten (?) and abandoned (?), unacknowledged castoffs of history....

But wouldn't you just know that the one exception to this general extinction was the survival of the farthest out Gnostics of all?

These were the Ophites (Followers of the Serpent). Remember, the Old Testament's villains were the real heroes, primal victims of historical revisionism and of the first recorded disinformation campaign. And who's the biggest fall guy in the Old Testament? Natch, Satan as snake.

The Ophites worshipped Mister Snake as the Promethean bringer of a knowledge forbidden to man by the Krazy Old Koot upstairs. You can imagine how this sat with the Pope. Toss in a little Oriental Kabbalistic mysticism and the aforementioned tendency toward orgies, and you've got your basic High-Explosive Theological Brouhaha.

(Check it out yourself by reading *The Tripartite Tractate*, *The Testimony of Truth*, *The Hypostasis of the Archons*, *Epistle of the Blessed Eugnostus*, or any other of the surviving Gnostic texts.)

Saint Draco was an Ophite Gnostic. Operating within the Roman establishment as a secret agent, he kept his true allegiances hidden as long as he could, fooling everyone so successfully that he even got canonized. Eventually they sussed him out tho, and when it looked like he was gonna take a tumble at Ephesus, he staged his own death and fell back to the safehouse he had set up years ago in Ireland, where he truly died dozens of lustrums later.

What better place to hide? We're talking ends of the earth at the time. Couldn't get much farther away from civilization than Ireland. Surrounded by his sixty-three loyal comrades, Saint Draco and the Ophites secretly kept the flame of Gaelic Gnosticism burning bright, worshiping the Snake in its phallic avatar.

(The sacred number sixty-four derived from the record amount of orgasms Draco had achieved in one eight-day period, cloistered with the wives of all the Roman Senators, who were too busy debating some trade bill or sumpin to keep their mystery-cult-maddened spouses satisfied. William Butler Yeats knew of the Ophites of Dublin on a surface level, thanks to his Golden Dawn connections. When he heard of this ancient incident, he quipped: "SPQR should stand for 'Stiff Prick up Quims Religiously.'")

Hey, boys and girls, hylics and pneumatics, we're back to the twentieth century all of a sudden. Hope you're not dizzy!

When Paddy O'Phidian was four years old, he began his Ophite training.

At first, he had only to assist the older monks in small ways as they tended the ATP. The Archon Tracking Platform was a small observatory set on the roof of the Order. With both optical instruments and primitive radiotelescopes, the Ophites kept track of Aeonic doings.

"Note the Great Serpent constellation, Patrick, how it winds through Ursus, its head pointing at the pole star, suckling at the navel of the heavens. Slow down now with the crank—that's fine. Ah, we're looking right up Sophia's skirts now, boy."

"Your lap hard, Papa G'arty."

"Never mind that now, Paddy."

Those frosty winter nights and sultry summer evenings scanning the skies were O'Phidian's earliest, sweetest memories, a time of innocence never to be replicated and soon to be shattered....

When O'Phidian was eight, Father Gogarty began a tradition. Each year on March 16, the sad anniversary of the slaughter of two hundred Cathari on a pyre in 1244 after the fall of their fortress of Montsegur, Father Gogarty would take him to the Phoenix Park racetrack for a day to practice his precognition.

"Who do you like in the fifth, Paddy?"

"I'll bet on Nag Hamdaddy."

"Are you sure, boy?"

"Yes."

"Well, I'm taking Bottle of Smoke."

The announcer's voice crackled from speakers. "Welcome, folks! The day's clear, the sky's bright, and they're off! It's Hamdaddy leading by a length— Wait, Bottle of Smoke is coming up on the left. Like a streak of light, like a drunken fuck on a Saturday night— It's Bottle of Smoke, at twenty-fucking-five to one!"

Gogarty clapped a hand on O'Phidian's shoulder. "You failed to look far enough into the future, lad. Never let sentiment over a name cloud your vision, Paddy. Come on, now, there'll be other races."

Young O'Phidian took the advice well to heart. Sentiment would never play a big part in his life.

Reading Gnostic texts with the Fathers, O'Phidian revealed himself to be an inquisitive, sharp-minded young neophyte.

"Why can't everyone in the whole wide world be a Gnostic, Father Borbelo? It would solve so many problems...."

"The mass of men are hylics, Paddy, mudmen with no interest in polishing the Mirror of the Mind. Hylics are actually a subspecies—one in the vast majority of course—genetically indisposed to satori, not true humans at all. There's no saving them, short of rewiring their brains. Remember: 'Mindfulness is the path to immortality. Negligence is the path to death. The vigilant never die, whereas the negligent are the living dead.'"

At age ten: "Father Simon, if Woman is the image of Sophia, why are there none in the Order? The original Gnostic communities were open to both sexes. Women would help us to focus our minds, wouldn't they?"

Father Simon squirmed a little. "Well, Paddy, 'tis true that the Female Principle is what we worship, but our Order—for reasons you shall one day learn—has decided that heavenly contact is best maintained through, ahem, unisexual bonding. Women tend to disturb the focus, rather than concentrate it."

"I see. I suppose...."

One day soon after, O'Phidian was found masturbating to the accompaniment of a picture of Lauren Bacall, torn from an issue of *Photoplay*. Brought before Father "Bogart" Gogarty, O'Phidian prepared himself for chastisement.

Instead Gogarty merely studied the spunk-stained picture and said bemusedly, "'Put your lips together and blow....' Paddy, my son, I think it's time we took you on a little trip."

The next thing O'Phidian knew, he was standing on the shores of France. Soon he was in a train, heading to the ancient forest of Columbiers in Poitou.

"We're going to visit an institution affiliated with ours, Paddy. It's the Nunnery of Saint Melusine. Melusine was the wife of Raymond of Poitou. The peasants called her Queen of the Fay, and said she was half-serpent, that half below the waist, though she was as mortal as you or I. She was really a Gnostic, and after her death a sisterhood was founded in her name. I've arranged for us to arrive on a Saturday, Melusine's Holy Day, so that we can witness an *agape*, or love-feast."

O'Phidian remained silent. His mind failed to create any images appropriate to the Father's words.

From the train they hired a horse-drawn wagon to bring them to the huge old nunnery building, a mossy chateau set on a large estate. A bomb-crater from the recently ended fracas Gogarty had foreseen ten years ago marred the lawn.

"There is a tragic history connected with this land, Paddy, which you would do well to learn.

"Melusine had two sons, Geoffroi of the Tusk, and Freimond. Geoffroi inherited all his mother's serpent-knowledge, but without the accompanying wisdom. That went to Freimond. During a quarrel, Geoffroi killed Freimond, much as Cain killed Abel. Since that time, the line has continually degenerated, although we have been keeping our eye on it for recurrence of a genetic predisposition to Gnosticism.

"Eventually, the family name became Aubisson.

"In the 'Thirties, there was one direct descendent of Geoffroi left. Her name was Regine Aubisson, and we had high hopes for her. But factors beyond our control intervened to spoil our plans.

"First, in 1929, she fell in love and married outside the proper gene pool. A Paris record store clerk named M. T. deClosets. Her father, acting under our instructions, promptly disowned her, hoping the shock would bring her to her senses. Such was not the case. She moved to Paris and out of our control.

"In 1930, Regine had a son, Phillipe. We are currently tracking his career, but his potential appears small.

"During the beginning of the recent war, Regine's husband was killed.

"Regine then fell in love with a German officer named Lambton Wurms. Wurms was part of the team—which included that famous Finnish quisling Paavo Pavonine—that was working on the mechanical ballistic calculating machines invented by Konrad Zuse, and known as S1 and S2, which were positioned in France to feed coordinates to the V-2 launching sites in Holland.

"At the same time, Regine was recruited by the partisans. She was able to supply them with important information on German troop movements.

"Soon, Wurms and Regine conceived a son, Phillipe deClosets' half-brother. They named him Robert Norbert.

"Just when the Nazis were in retreat, Wurms learned of Regine's 'treachery.' He promptly strangled her, finishing the evil deed just as a squad of Americans burst in and killed him. I do not doubt that the souls of these two lovers are still working off their bad karma in the realm of the hungry spirits, before being allowed rebirth.

"When Regine's widowed father passed away, the Sisterhood of Melusine acquired the family chateau. And as for Robert Norbert, we managed to gain legal custody over him. He is being raised in a Gnostic orphanage."

O'Phidian contemplated the lurid story for a time. "And the lesson, Father?"

"A Gnostic who denies his heritage will always come to a bad end, lad."

At the door of the convent, the boy and man were greeted by a tall black woman dressed in a rainbow-striped habit.

"Erzulie be with you," she said.

"And Damballah with you," replied Gogarty. "Here I have the youngest Draconian, Sister Michelle, now old enough to take part in an *agape*."

"You are just in time. It has already begun."

Sister Michelle guided them through empty halls, up to a large set of doors.

"Go in now, Paddy. Michelle, *ma belle*— I mean, the Holy Sister and I have, er, private business to conduct. I'll pick you up in a while."

And with this promise, the doors were opened and Paddy was somewhat roughly pushed forward, as if into a cell.

Before he knew what was happening, he had been stripped of his robe and lay naked on his back.

Looming over him were six or seven nude women, plainly possessed by Bacchantic passions. O'Phidian had never seen so much as a bare teat before. Now he was confronted with a dozen, and half that many "faces between the forks."

O'Phidian tried to lever himself up. He had a fleeting glimpse of the rest of the room. It was carpeted in writhing woman-flesh.

Then the Sisters of Melusine were atop him.

He was drowning in flesh, being smothered in flesh, soft, alien female flesh! He tried to scream, but a cunt capped his mouth while a mouth swallowed his tiny cock, teeth scraping along its length. (I want a pearl necklace....) Other bodies pressed up against every inch of him, pinning him down, rubbing against his knees, his elbows, his feet.

He had an orgasm, but he was too frightened to enjoy it. (The ones after the first were no more pleasant.)

When the original women were done with him, O'Phidian was passed around the room, like a cork bobbing on the sea. (A cushy cooze mosh-pit!)

He ended up in a relatively calm corner. Wet from head to foot with sweat and cunt juices, he simply lay sobbing, trying to catch his breath.

At last O'Phidian looked up.

Two women were sitting closely, facing each other. Each one had her feet flat on the floor, widely apart, and was bracing herself with an arm extended backwards.

O'Phidian couldn't believe his eyes. The women were linked by a snake! No, it was a rubber penis, double-headed, running from cunt to cunt. With their free hands the women worked it slickly back and forth, moaning, until they climaxed.

One of the women noticed him then. She had bright red hair, and seemed momentarily sane.

"What's the matter, little one?" she said in Gaelic. "Too much, isn't it? Come here, Oona will watch over you."

O'Phidian gratefully climbed into the woman's arms.

Which was where Gogarty finally found him, asleep.

"Oh, oh," said Gogarty concernedly.

"Yes," said the woman. "And no."

O'Phidian couldn't talk again for a week. When he had regained the power of speech, his first word was, "Why?"

Gogarty stroked the boy's hair. "Not out of meanness, lad, but simply to give you a taste of Sophia's insatiable appetites. When you touch a woman, any woman, you touch Sophia directly, and had best beware. With our sensitivities, we could not stand the sensual feedback that would develop between an advanced female and male Gnostic. That is why we here in the Order have chosen to make contact with the Godhead through the intermediary of the male snake, the one you keep in your pants. In a year or two, after further studies, you'll be fully initiated. Then you'll understand."

O'Phidian tried to believe. But his faith in Father Gogarty had been subtly undermined.

Which, he would come to see later, had been part of Gogarty's plan.

The promised gnosis happened sooner, not later.

It was the year 1948. Eleven-year-old Paddy O'Phidian sat in Father Gogarty's office, reading, from the Order's library, a copy of the 1935 pulp magazine, *The Mysterious Wu Fang*, which he had hidden in his assigned volume, *The Trimorphic Protennoia*. The office was windowless, buried deep within the moldering pile of the Order's decrepit Georgian-era flat. (The Order had last moved in the 1740s, as a safety precaution after Brother Lehane, one of the Hellfire Club's founders, had been publicly linked to that scandalous nest of debauchery.)

The stuffy room, with its smoke-stained panelling, held a massive desk, a visitor's chair, a hat stand, a faded velvet couch, all set on a threadbare rug whose barely discernible motif seemed to be the Hibernian Harp with snakes substituted for its strings. On the wall hung an 1897 painting by Franz von Stuck entitled "Sensuality." It depicted a fleshy naked woman half-reclining against a draped surface. A gigantic snake ran between her thighs, around her back, and over her shoulder, to peer straight out at the viewer with bared fangs. The woman's smile was precisely eight orders of magnitude more mysterious than Mona Lisa's, as rated by the Art Tyrant's Police, the same people who fix auction prices.

Cassocked Father Gogarty sat behind his desk, fingers steepled, contemplating young O'Phidian.

As the years had passed, Gogarty's resemblance to Bogart had only deepened (or could it possibly be the other way around?), mimicking the star's maturation down to the last wrinkle. The appearance of every new movie featuring the laconic actor seemed uncannily to heighten the similarities, as if Gogarty and Bogart were hooked into a feedback loop mediated somehow by the projection of film and the act of viewing.

Since the head of the Order had thrust him into the *agape*, O'Phidian had tended to regard him warily. *It sure is creepy*, he thought now, looking covertly up from his book, *to have Sam Spade as your surrogate parent, mentor, teacher and spiritual guide.*

Gogarty collapsed his spired fingers into an interlocked knot, leaned forward across the desk, and fixed O'Phidian with a lancet-like gaze, compelling him to lower his book.

This was the famed Gnostic Whammy. The light of the hyperworld channeled through the adept's microcosmic eyes. It was cultivated by learning to outstare snakes.

Trained by years of such ocular probing, O'Phidian neither winced nor flinched under the Celtic Ray, accepting the full impact of the Father's visual information-exchange. (One of the first lessons learned by members of the Order was how to establish, if not the sought-for dominance, then at least equality of eye-contact, at best superimposing one's chosen information content on an opponent, at worst defusing his.)

Having passed this daily test once more, O'Phidian waited patiently for Gogarty to speak. Ever since age four and those nights on the ATP, O'Phidian had come each day to these chambers to digest and be quizzed on a mixture of theology, history, and a science so new it didn't have a name yet.

Today he had no reason to expect anything different.

But Gogarty threw him a curve.

"Are you prepared," demanded Gogarty, "to enter the Order as a full-fledged brother?"

"If," weakly riposted the bewildered O'Phidian, "you think I am."

"Very well. Move to the couch."

O'Phidian did as he was directed.

Gogarty rose from behind the desk and moved to stand beside the youth where he sat. He lifted his robe.

Beneath it he was naked.

O'Phidian regarded the Father's genitals with suspicion. Although he had of course seen the anatomies of Gogarty and the other brothers in the communal shower-room, he had never witnessed an adult prick in this engorged condition. He realized now that the sight had been deliberately withheld from him.

"You are beholding knowledge," said Gogarty, "the knowledge which the mad god of the Old Testament sought to deny mankind, the knowledge which it is every human's birthright to exchange with as many and whatever kinds of partners he so chooses, the knowledge which the Holy Snake delivered unto us, and also the channel through which we may daily pierce Sophia's endlessly regenerative hymen and make brief contact with the numinous. If the Male One is not as beautifully empty and capacious as the Female Zero, it is yet potent enough. Did not Atum's sperm form the Milky Way? Take it in your mouth."

"What?"

"Put your lips together and blow."

O'Phidian tried. It was not as unpleasant as he had anticipated.

"That's enough. Lie on your stomach."

O'Phidian complied.

"Prepare to be informed," Gogarty advised, lifting the boy's robe and positioning himself over the youth.

Face pressed into the musty-smelling, dusty velvet, repressing a sneeze, O'Phidian had a dawning suspicion about what Gogarty intended....

"Yowwww!"

The boy's brain short-circuited in a sophic blaze. He returned from the hyperworld with a permanently altered state of consciousness, aware of two things: Gogarty's motions, and his words.

Never faltering in his strokes, the Father was intoning verses from *Paragenesis*.

"When morning dawned, the angels urged Lot, saying, 'Arise, old and impotent fool, you are the sole lickspittle citizen here who still obeys Saklad's capricious injunctions regarding the exchange of seed. The others seek to reach Sophia and become as gods, partaking of knowledge and eternal life. Therefore we grant thee further useless years of thy dull grey existence, as mockery of thy stomachless pusillanimity. For the rest, their time on earth is nigh over. Go now, for we mean to rain fire and brimstone down upon the Cities of the Plain, for the asses of these Gnostic catamites are as grass.'

"Thus did the Demiurge persecute and extinguish the noble and righteous Sodomites...."

At this point, Gogarty launched into a soaring Irish-tenor rendition of the eerie *Hymn of the Naasenes*, a millennia-old Ophite chant.

"Aaa ooo zezophazazzzaieozaza eee iii zaieozoakoe ooo uuu thoezaozaez eee zzeezaozakozakeude tuxuaalethukh."

O'Phidian verged on fainting, and could only wonder dazedly how much longer this torment would last.

On the final chorus Gogarty gargled the last syllables in a wordless shout as he climaxed up the boy and fell atop him heavily.

O'Phidian could feel the Father's Irish Heartbeat. He tried to extricate himself, but was unable to. Gogarty appeared comatose.

Just as O'Phidian felt he would suffocate, the Holy Father, seeming to realize his imposition, stirred just enough to allow the boy to breathe more easily. Then, his mouth close to the boy's left ear, the man began to whisper.

"I would have liked to wait for this moment until you were a bit older, lad, but I simply couldn't. The outer world has forced our hand, as usual. It's Shannon, don't you know. He's published. The Order no longer has a monopoly on his theories. We begged him not to, to give us just a little longer to work on establishing more efficient channels to the godhead, using his encoding theories. We know it can be done, we have evidence from the past, saints who have just *vanished*.... Laymen too. That addle-pated Fort, for instance, even had a glimpse of it: 'It is our notion that if they could almost *realize* they would instantly be translated into real existence.' And our native son, Bishop Berkeley, with his *esse est percipi*.... Close, very close. But Shannon wouldn't listen. He claimed the world needed his ideas. It's this last war, the madness and destruction of it all, it completely changed him, made him into a bloody idealist. He should know better. Hylic mankind isn't ready for such knowledge, nor ever will be. We must preserve it for the elect. Oh, certainly not just the Sixty-four. No, others too—but not everyone! It's insane. The world is going to become a Bedlam in the next few decades, with this information about information loose. We in the Order must be strong, to pre-empt our competitors for access to the numinous. We need to be operating at full strength. That's why I had to induct you now, lad. You do understand, don't you?"

O'Phidian, voice muffled by the rotten cloth of the couch, replied, "Partly, sir. I know I must trust you."

Gogarty withdrew his semi-flaccid member and pushed up off O'Phidian. The boy got to his feet and adjusted his robe. For the first time in years, he couldn't meet Gogarty's eyes. The Father seemed to understand exactly what was going on in O'Phidian's skull.

"Sit down, boy. The ceremony of indoctrination will not be quite finished until you understand something else."

Gingerly, O'Phidian lowered his rump to the chairseat. Whoa-ho, think I'll just levitate a few inches above, braced on my elbows.... And now, folks, came:

## A SERMON ON DECONDITIONING AND CONTROL

"What you have just experienced," Gogarty explained, "was a one-way experience of dominance and submission. I'll not call it rape, since there was no force involved and I received your consent, but it was certainly not a situation where mutually pleasant sensations were enjoyed by equals. And why was that? Do you have any idea?"

O'Phidian pondered. "Uh, well, sir, it was because, um, you knew what was going to happen and what it would be like, and I didn't. Just like during the *agape*, with those crazy women." O'Phidian shuddered at the memory of the icky females.

Gogarty smiled. "Exactly, my boy. You do not disappoint me, and I see I was right in my estimation of your intelligence."

O'Phidian felt proud, despite a lingering indignation and suspicion. "Thank you, sir."

"My pleasure, lad. Listen closely now. Superior knowledge, a greater quantity of information, allowed me to gain the upper hand over you. Although what we did today should not be diminished—it was indeed, on one level, an enactment of the Gnostic Sodomitic Sacrament—on another, more important level, it was a lesson in the way the world works. Put plainly, the one with less information always gets screwed. Whether it be an individual, a group, a generation, a community, or a nation, whoever knows less gets the boot in the rump. Just look at the history of our own poor land, or of any other colony, if you need an object lesson on a larger scale. The affairs of mankind always tend to fall naturally into such a pattern of control and subservience, and liberty is never gained until the imbalance of information is altered. That's one thing I want you to retain from today's encounter."

"And the other?"

"This precept: if you can dislocate your rational mind—through meditation, or, by receiving a shock from a master such as myself—you will sometimes find yourself making a breakthrough to a higher level of cognition. Learn to prosper from misfortune, love the blows from the Master's staff—or your blow of his staff."

Again, young O'Phidian experienced satori. Of course, it was all so plain, just as Father Gogarty described it.... Even his experience with the Sisters of Melusine made sense now.

He had the ticket back from Suffragette City!

He found he could hold Gogarty's gaze again, and did. "I won't worry anymore, sir, for I have seen the light in your eyes. In your eyes I feel the heat, I am complete."

And it was true.

After his inaugural deflowering and first enlightenment, O'Phidian assumed the full duties and perquisites of a member of the Order, including officiating at the elaborate Gnostic mass, where a snake was loosed to crawl on the loaves, thereby transubstantiating them, and Primal Soup was imbibed; and—special duty of the youngest member—wandering the city with senses alert for any information that might be of use to the Order. (Even at his tender age, O'Phidian was not naïve enough to imagine that he was the only such source of information the Order relied on or could tap, and he was certain that this assignment was, in part, just one more step in his training.)

This latter task in particular, whatever its rationale, pleased the youthful O'Phidian no end, and seemed more like play than work. His previous forays into the city had been drastically limited, and always conducted under the strict observation of one of the Fathers. He had seen practically nothing of the city of his birth, and now, his head filled from his leisure-time reading with grand tales of his country's—and especially Dublin's—past, he essayed the city's streets (the wide, statue-lined thoroughfare of O'Connell, the narrow lanes of the Liberties), intensely absorbing everything he saw, ready perhaps to encounter the Dragon who bit Leopold Bloom on the ass.

One of O'Phidian's favorite spots was down by the Custom House. The place drew him for several reasons. First, in its role as government offices, it represented a nexus of information flow that intrigued him. The building seemed at times almost visibly to pulsate with the constant passage and shuttling of documents and orders, reports and letters which the fanciful lad envisaged passing thru an infinite series of hands. Standing in front of the alabaster-columned façade, he would grow dizzy trying to imagine what went on inside, of having access to all that information....

(Without realizing it, without being able to halt the progress of the disease if he had realized it, O'Phidian, poor kid, was already hooked on information. At this stage a junkie, he was not far from becoming a pusher, and one of the biggest at that. ((Can you really blame him, after the upbringing he'd had?)))

The architecture of the Custom House intrigued O'Phidian also. It was a baroque yet classical edifice, proud and impressive. Its column-tops were elaborately carved; many represented fanciful Celtic river gods, with fish sprouting from their beards and mussels from their hair. And what better deities to adorn a building that perched so precariously on the banks of the Guinness-dark River Liffey that its whole image was mirrored in those depths?

O'Phidian adored the Liffey. The way its sinuous length threaded the city, constantly in motion, yet unmoving.... It spoke to him wordlessly of travel and footloose wandering, of the sea and other continents washed by that sea, stirring his Tinker's blood, the river bounded by banks calling to the blood-river bounded by flesh.... You don't pull no punches, but you don't push the river.

For hours would young O'Phidian sit gazing into its flow, contemplating such stories as floated to his mind, such as the first English invasion of his land, in 1169, led by the turncoat Dermot MacMurrough, who, in a frenzy of decapitation, had three hundred Irish heads laid out on the Wexford battlefield before him....

It was now June 16, 1954. (Little subterranean holiday called Bloomsday. Across The Big Pond, Art Blakey was inventing hard-bop with The Jazz Messengers.) Seventeen-year-old O'Phidian was leaning on a rail beside the Liffey, lost in thought (specifically, how the aging Yeats came to be fixated on quack rejuvenation schemes, and whether he had been an honorary member of the Order or not). The world had gradually faded away from O'Phidian's daydreaming mind. He barely felt the iron rail beneath his forearms. His unvarying day-to-day routine, the stability and familiarity of the Order's long-term scheming, the unchanging, history-soaked city, all these things conduced toward frequent such intervals in the young acolyte....

An explosion sounded not far away, jerking O'Phidian out of his fugue. Another quickly followed, more distant, then a third on the second's sonic heels. Sirens began to wail, citizens to scurry, and the city to bestir itself.

Alarmed, O'Phidian left the Liffey and headed back toward the Liberties.

The density of pedestrians and traffic increased steadily the closer he got to the Order's building, a human disaster-tropic gradient mimicking the physical topography of the city and conveying information O'Phidian could not bear to acknowledge....

The strait brick channel leading to the Order's door was clogged with people, some fleeing, others pushing forward to gawp.

O'Phidian underwent an overwhelming and uncontrollable epiphany, mixed with terror, experiencing the scene as if the terminii of the alley were synapses, the chute itself the inter-synaptic gap, and the people merely units of neurotransmitters carrying inhibit messages.... His vision clouded, as if with an Aryan Mist.

The crackle of flames could be heard, and smoke scented. O'Phidian still tried to believe the worst hadn't happened.

He turned a corner.

The Order's centuried building was rubble swathed in flames. Fireman vainly battled the inferno. Anyone inside at the time of the explosion—and O'Phidian had no reason to believe most or all of the sedentary Order hadn't been within—could never have survived.

A toothless old man by O'Phidian's elbow said, "Ah, those murtherin' IRA bandits, what won't they stop at, attacking holy men who never harmed a soul."

A second codger claimed, "Nay, it must have been that team of Protestant terrorists, the Orange Krush."

A third one proposed, "I fear 'twas the Algerians."

"Algerians?"

"Ay, have ye not heard? They are rebelling against the French."

"And what would they be doing in Dublin, then?"

"Doesn't everyone end up here sooner or later?"

O'Phidian ignored the old men, knowing it had been none of these factions. The Order's enemies were not political. They were those who wished to keep the world in ignorance, who profited from the blindness of the hylics. The Establishment, the Organization, Black Hats working for The Clampdown. This was the work of someone who knew the true nature of the Order, and had reason to want to see them fail.

Six years into Shannon Time, and the action among Those In The Know was heating up.

Helpless, helpless.... How can you run when you know....? Paranoia strikes deep, into your life it will creep.

Tears filled O'Phidian's eyes. He felt sick, as if someone somewhere were sticking pins in a voodoo doll modeled on him. That's how it begins, you feel those Needles and Pin-zuh, a-hey now, a-hey now....

(Later, much later, half glimpsing a familiar stubbled Sam Spade face attached to a memory-provoking black-and-white tuxedo, across a crowded room in a distant foreign city, at an embassy party, O'Phidian would wonder if this apparent destruction of the whole Order hadn't been staged by the Order itself, so that it might go further underground. Could an organization built on knowledge—and usually advance knowledge at that—which had survived millennia, really be so easily caught?

But then why hadn't they cut him in on it? An oversight? Deliberate? His loyalty and devotion was unquestionable. Was it commands from SOMEONE ABOVE? Was it cuz he was the youngest monk? Did Gogarty and other unnamed ones know even then— or were they able to *predict*—that his destiny lay elsewhere, down stranger paths? O'Phidian never pursued that face from his past, choosing ignorance over information for once, preferring to let that halcyon period remain unsullied by knowledge of what really had been.... Levels above, and levels below, that was the Gnostic universe.)

Weh-hell.... Here was a likely lad, clad in a now-meaningless robe that allowed every chance breeze to fondle his balls, facing the ruins of the only home he had ever known, with no money, no prospects, no friends, no salable skills, and no place to rest his head that night....

Sometimes I feel like a motherless child!

What could anyone do in such a situation?

The only thing Irishmen in distress had ever done:

Split. Burst the shackles of this crazy factional land. Like a river that don't know where it's flowing, I took a wrong turn and I just kept going. The silence-exile-and-cunning trip. Listen to them Tinker genes talkin' at you, man: make like a Kleenex and blow. This is, or soon will be, the era of Kerouac. Get on the road, you dharma bum! Take off!

But where to?

Where else?

London Calling! Ferry 'cross the Mersey, boyo!

So.... Knowing something of his past, O'Phidian took a chance and visited *The Feathered Serpent.*

Could it be? Yes, this incredibly ancient withered-apple-faced virago sitting in a corner with her pint must be his great-aunt. Mother Ireland, the sight of O'Phidian's unmistakable robe stirring her neurons into memory, fell weeping at O'Phidian's feet, mutterin' some kinda nonsense 'bout the Prodigal Son.

Before you could say "To Hell or Connaught!", O'Phidian was dressed in borrowed civilian clothes and sipping of the Elixer Of Life. Shortly after that, he found himself aboard the ferry to Liverpool with a small sum of the strange medium known as cash, looking back at a retreating green shore.

The whole world had long thought Ireland Snakeless.

Now, for the first time in centuries, they were right.

A momentous moment. O'Phidian felt he should shed a tear. But he surprisingly found himself dry-eyed, having emptied himself of sorrow earlier, and instead surprised within himself—as one might surprise a dozing snake baking itself on a rock—an incipient happiness and a sense of adventure. Natch and why not, the kid was still a kid, despite his weird upbringing.

He stayed no longer in Liverpool than it took to make train connections for London.

When he stepped out into Waterloo Station, tired and grimy, he still had no idea of his ultimate plans. Therefore he sought out a drink. Exiting into the Waterloo Sunset, he looked wide-eyed around at the sights of the metropolis. He bumped into a young boy and girl who weren't looking where they were going either.

"Are you okay, Julie?"

"Sure, Terry. As long as I gaze on you and the Waterloo Sunset, I'm in paradise."

The city was still high from the coronation of Liz Squared a year ago. Definite atmosphere of a new age dawning. Young monarch, no war, economy on the upsurge.... Proto-swinging London, perhaps. Soon to be filled with Mods 'n' Rockers.

("Are you a Mod, or a Rocker?"

"I'm a Mocker!")

In a pub randomly chosen, *The Sighbell Arms*, the overwhelmed O'Phidian ordered his usual and took it to a table next to a couple of fairly young guys having a spirited dialogue.

The men paused in their speech when O'Phidian sat down. They seemed gloriously flushed with triumph. Now one proposed a semi-facetious toast.

"To our success, Mister Watson."

"To our success, Mister Crick."

The men clinked glasses and drank.

O'Phidian sampled his own brew, and promptly forgot them, sunk in his own thoughts. After a few minutes, tho, something one of the men said caught his attention.

"—the Irish potato blight, for instance. The trouble there, of course, was monoculture, relying on one cultivar across the whole country. Once the bloody virus got in, blam! the whole crop was gone. No chance of a resistant strain of potatoes withstanding the disease, since there was only one strain cultivated. It was sheer lack of information, not enough genes in the pool, too inbred. Same damn thing with the upper classes here. If conditions ever change, they're ripe for extinction. Survival always favors the halfbreed. Mix those genes up, for Christ's sake!"

"Still, someday with what we've learned and the start we've made, perhaps we could even engineer...."

"Rubbish! That will always be beyond our powers...."

"Ah, well, such wild speculation is fine, but I suppose we should be getting back to the banks of the Cam and down to work."

"Do you think we should take that funding from DIGITAL?"

"We'll have to think more about it. Depends what strings are attached. We don't want to be anyone's puppets."

The men departed. O'Phidian stayed. He had been acutely stricken by the synchronicity of his chancing to overhear the particularly relevant conversation of these two men, whoever they were. Altho he didn't understand half of what had been said, the very topic, and the earnestness with which it had been discussed, seemed to be a sign that he must pursue the grail that he had first glimpsed in the Order.

Total Knowledge. Supreme Wisdom. Grace and Glory.

Five weeks later, O'Phidian had a job—and perhaps a career.

Turned out O'Phidian had a relative—of sorts—in high places.

And government places at that.

Brian "Blackie" Coffey was a member of the Coffey Tinker clan who had abandoned the traditional gypsy life and gone the Establishment route. (There were always a few black sheep in any family.) After securing an impeccable education at all the right schools, he had entered the civil service and now, twenty years later, headed a small and little-publicized branch of the government, known as the King's Messengers.

Whoops, 'scuse the slip, Liz. Queen's Messengers since last year.

Founded over two centuries ago, the Messengers were a unit attached to the Diplomatic Corps. They had one function and one function only: to physically convey written directives from home and back, in cases where the messages could not be trusted to other channels. Perpetually peripatetic, they roamed the globe, shuttling from one outpost of the dismantled Empire to another, bearing the secretest secrets, the holiest information, like privileged impulses traveling First-Class down the world's nerves, slipping like Mercury under tripwires, thus qualifying as the Quicksilver Messenger Service.

Armed with nothing but bravado and guile, they relied on an innocuous appearance and a certain steely blandness to accomplish their forays into quite often hostile situations. They could be recognized by one fraternal emblem: a tie emblazoned with greyhounds, symbol of their swift unerringness.

"So," said the Irish-accentless Coffey to O'Phidian, once the youth had taken a seat in the man's office, "you're Oona's son."

"Yes, sir," replied O'Phidian, fixing Coffey with his hyperworld gaze. "Although I've never met my mother. She abandoned me at birth...."

Coffey signalled with upraised hand to delve into such touchy matters no further. "It's all for the best, lad. Doesn't do for someone in our line to have too many ties back home anyway. Not married, are you?"

O'Phidian repressed any sign of the distaste he felt at such a notion. "No, sir."

"Very well, then, I'm willing to take a chance on you. You seem like a plucky lad. It just so happens that we have an opening in the ranks. Lost a man in Cambodia just a week ago. Beastly. Eaten by a snake, I believe, or some such rubbish."

"I see. I'm very grateful for a chance to prove myself, sir."

"It's the least I can do for the son of a Tinker, lad. And anyway, I'm sure you'll do right by the service. There are a few more of our kind among the Messengers. We seem to have a bent for this type of work.... Well, I suppose it's settled then, aside from a few formalities. Give me your hand, boy."

After shaking hands, Coffey opened a drawer and removed an object wrapped in tissue: the fraternal tie, an elegant product of Bond Street, the greyhound motif picked out in delicate stitches.

"Never disgrace this, O'Phidian. It stands for something larger than us all."

"I won't, sir. Thank you."

Outside the building, O'Phidian was accosted by an insidiously smiling Oriental of some stripe. (O'Phidian's as-yet undiscriminating eyes failed to identify the man as a Filipino, namely Epifanio Pagano, twenty years younger than when we last saw him, in the office of Mekong Melusine, where he was pitching his recruitment woo for Wu, the same mission, as you mighta guessed, which he was engaged on now. This boy keeps turnin' up like a bad penny!)

"You are to come with me, if you please, good sir."

"Bugger off," Freudian-slipped O'Phidian.

Pagano whistled a snatch of the unmistakable *Hymn of the Naasenes*.

"Where to?" politely inquired O'Phidian.

Cut to an old abandoned commercial bank building, down a little alley pompously called King George Street, on the banks of the Thames. (The river-smell engendered a head-spinning nostalgia in O'Phidian which he felt unable to cope with, on top of everything else at this moment.) Pagano led O'Phidian inside, into a dimly lit office that looked as if it hadn't been used in decades. Dust lay everywhere, and cobwebs adorned the rafters. There was a sweet smell present, as of ginger.

Someone sat in deep shadow in an old wooden swivel-chair behind a desk, back to O'Phidian. A man, it seemed.

Pagano said, "I've brought him, Doctor," then left, shutting the door.

"Please sit down," came a quiet yet compelling voice from within the dusk. "I have no time to waste, for time is money."

The voice sounded older than time. O'Phidian did what the voice said.

"Are you from the Order?"

"The order is no more."

Was there a spoken capital beginning that second word, or not?

"I represent myself alone. As yet, the cipher of the dragon is One."

Couldn't mistake the capital there. Did that mean the other word hadn't been? So much uncertainty....

"Uh, I see. Well, you asked me to come here to tell me something, I assume...."

"Yes. You are to work for me."

"Doctor Whoever-You-Are, I can't—"

"Your hexagram is Meng, Youthful Inexperience. 'I do not go and seek the youthful and inexperienced, but he comes and seeks me. When he shows sincerity, I instruct him.' There is no mistake. You are to work for me. Give me your tie."

"What?"

"The Messenger's tie. Give it to me."

Utterly cowed by the absolute assurance of this man, O'Phidian obeyed.

As he placed the tie into the wrinkled, long-nailed left hand extended out to the side and slightly back for it, he caught a glimpse of black plastic frames obscuring the man's profile. Was this guy wearing *sunglasses...?*

The tie disappeared from O'Phidian's view. A second later, it was seemingly offered again.

O'Phidian took it.

It looked identical to the one he had been given by Coffey, except....

Yeah! The tail of each greyhound now terminated in a snake's head!

"Go now," commanded the Doctor.

He went.

That was the only time he ever saw Doctor Wu.

(If he had even seen him that once. What *had* he seen, save for a form that could have been a mannequin, a waxy clockwork hand, a pair of dark glasses...? Eyes without a face, you got no human grace....)

But he went to work for the Doctor, all right, keeping his Messenger's job too. Quite the double agent was our boy O'Phidian, rushing around the world on both the Doctor's business and the Queen's. Put the message in a box, put the box into a car, drive the car around the world until your message is heard. But make sure, huh, that you're not on the Road To Nowhere.

Off he went to Egypt that same year (the year the Muslim Brotherhood, founded 1928, was outlawed), during the attempted overthrow of Nasser, where he delivered instructions which led to the negotiation of the Anglo-Egyptian Treaty that finally ended Britain's presence in that country. (And recruited into Wu's employ an exotic dancer—then only 13-years old, yet already possessing a Heavy Rep—known as Zona Pellucida.)

To Greece in 'Sixty-Seven, during the Papadopoulos coup, where he delivered vital information to the British Embassy there. (And enlisted a disheartened royalist named Agnes Agape. O'Phidian's sexual predilections helped him deal with these Sophic avatars from a certain position of lofty disinterest. Tho as we shall see, in Greece O'Phidian greased a different channel than usual....)

On that same Grecian jaunt, he detoured to the island of Cephalonia, where he made the acquaintance of Sally Salonika, expatriate British-Turkish Boho writer, one-time lover of Robert Graves.

And of course to Dahomey in 'Seventy-Seven—for what, we well know.

All this time O'Phidian moved higher and higher up the ranks of Wu Labs' employees, ostensibly never doing any more than following the Doctor's distant instructions, yet managing to pick up the slack reins of power and control left dangling by the unaccountably absent Wu, always bearing in mind his ultimate goal, established so long ago.

Came a time when no one in the organization was more powerful than O'Phidian.

Except Wu.

If he even existed anymore.

And, damn it, what *were* his ultimate goals?

# STOCHASTIC ORGASMS

# K L U E S

## 00011000
"I went so far as to claim that the world would end not with a good book, but with a beautiful advertisement for heaven or for hell."
—André Breton

## 00011001
"A woman is sitting on a dais above an immense carven desk; she has a snake around her neck. The entire room is lined with books and strange fish swimming in colored globes. There are maps and charts on the wall, maps of Paris before the plague. I lean out the window and the Eiffel Tower is fizzing champagne; it is built entirely of numbers."
—Henry Miller

## 00011010
"God sometimes plays dice with whole numbers."
—Gregory Chaitin

## 00011011
"People are trapped in history, and history is trapped in people."
—James Baldwin

"Oh! Strip me, Cyril—now!" hints Polly obliquely.

Weh-hell.... Cy has seen this coming, of course. The way Polly placed his hand on her thigh when she was telling him about her childhood, certain Veiled Glances she'd cast at him on the train back from the Condors.... Just one Look, that's all it took. It all added up to a growing interest in him as a Male, a non-Platonic affection which could only manifest itself sooner or later in a physical way.

Namely, doing the Wild Thing. Rocking the Cradle of Love. Dancing in the Dark. Moving with the Loco-Motion. Getting on that Groovy Train. Banging a Gong. Big Time Sensuality. Shaking, rattling and rolling. Stealing some Afternoon Delight.

Everyone wants to do the Horizontal Bop!

But altho this notion had been feverishly, recursively building on itself in Cy's mind, he'd hesitated to act on it. The appeal on Wednesday morning that Polly had made to his Brotherly Protection had stuck in his mind, an apparently insurmountable barrier to any Hot Love Action. In the past two days, his cock had hardened regularly for Polly (for anyone, actually, he sometimes guiltily thought), with the precision of a metronome, yet he had restrained himself from so much as goosing her pert little rump.

But now, here in Cy's living room, her words hanging like frozen fire in the air between them, a guy'd have to be as blind and deaf as Max Parallax not to realize that Polly has suddenly gotten as hot for him as he for her.

And even a blind and deaf man, wrapped up in that intimate tangle on the slippery earth-scented lawn, would've suspected something when he felt Polly's tongue in his ear, inserted slyly during their exertions, as the giggling kids sought to extricate the two adults from the now-flaccid rubbery coils of the insidious Mister Wiggle.

Cy remembers thinking: *I get delirious, whenever you're near....* Shux, this gal was like a brick to the head!

After being freed, Polly and Cy, too beat to scramble over the fence, went via the street back to the Peptide household, fully intending, they both knew, to Make It.

Frankly, Cy was surprised they'd had the self-control to get back to the house. The way Polly kept bumping her hip up against his led him to believe they'd end up Doing It In The Road, Dancing In The Street.

But make it back they did, if barely. They opened the front door of the Peptide domicile, stepped inside, locked limbs immediately in a clinch, Cy got ready to tumble Polly backwards onto the couch, Polly was grabbing his ass—

And Mrs Peptide called from the kitchen, "Hello, Polly, dear. Could you help me with the groceries?"

Shit! They disengaged just as Mrs Peptide walked into the front room.

Mrs Peptide, *née* Pressina Persephone, was the daughter of Greek immigrants, Kataibates and Ria Persephone, who hailed from Lowell, Massachusetts. (Polly's fair skin and blonde hair musta come from Dad's side—or the milkman's.) Now a trim and attractive forty-eight (she'd never even had to wear a girdle, thus making her Girdle Number equal to Zero), she had grown up next door to the Kerouac family, and in fact had had a childhood crush on Jack, who was of course much too old for her. She had met Paul Peptide in 1960, when he established his fledgling business in the old mill town and she had gone to work there. In that far-off year, natch, there had been no such thing as genetic experimentation, and the firm which was to grow into GreenGenes was known then as Mixed Coatings, Ltd., and specialized in making pills for the pharmaceutical trade.

"Gee, Mom, I can't, I'm *all wet*," Polly double-*entendred*, nearly causing Cy to faint.

"Goodness, what have you youngsters been up to?"

"W-w-we were playing with the kids next door," Cy, managed to gasp, "and we nearly got strangled by a rogue hose."

"I see. Well, you should change up, before you catch cold."

"Good thinking, Mom."

Upstairs, Polly snaked her tongue around Cy's uvula.

"Oh, Cy, I've got so much to give you. But not here. Let's get home."

"G-g-good thinking," stutter-echoed Cyril.

They went through separate doors—Polly into her old bedroom, still lovingly maintained by her folks as in her high-school days; Cy into Paulie Junior's untenanted room, a dishearteningly characterless cubicle.

Cy could still feel the heat of Pol's bod right thru the intervening wall. He had this mild semiotic-AIDS flash, as he peeled off his soaked clothes: a patch of wall starts to glow, first red, then yellow, then blue-white, finally dissolving into an irregular hole, through which steps nude Polly, surrounded by thermal-distorted air, emanating radiation of solar intensities from her jutting nipples and bush.

Needless to say, no such thing happened. (Whadda ya think this story is, anyhow—a FANTASY?!)

Naked, Cy decided to check himself out in the bureau-top mirror. Not bad for an old man a lot closer to thirty-two than to sixteen. Tight butt, good pecs.... He hoped Polly would like what he was looking at now....

Hold on a minute— What *was* he looking at?

The mirror above Paulie's dresser had gone smoky black, swirling with a moiré pattern of curdled clouds. Cy watched in fascination as the clouds stabilized into a scene as clear as HDTV.

Inside the foreground of the mirror was a man. His skin was bronzed, and he had eagle-like Meso-American features. He wore a necklace of tiny silver skulls on his bare chest, and a plumed head-dress. Behind him was a Hades-like scene, all excoriated figures writhing in torment. One poor soul was being devoured by an enormous worm.

The man spoke.

"Hey, kid, how ya doin'?"

"Gah-gah-great."

The immense flesh-colored worm behind the man had finished eating the damned soul, and was now crawling toward Cy's unaware interlocutor.

"Glad to hear it. Listen, the name's Tezcatlipoca. Call me Tez. I understand you're on the trail of my old bunkmate, Quetzalcoatl."

Now the worm was rearing up directly behind Tez, its enormous slimy toothy maw open wide as a volcano.

Cy's incredulous expression alerted Tez. He spun around, raising a barbed lash, and began to flail away at the worm.

"Down, Jormungandr, down! Back, back!"

The worm commenced yelping like a cartoon animal with its tail on fire. "Yip-yip-yip-yip-yip!" It humped swiftly away to bathe its flayed nose in a greenish pool.

"Fuckin' thing hates my guts. It's on Q's side. But you ain't, are ya, buddy?"

"I'm not?"

"No, you ain't. I heard it thru the grapevine. You don't like Doctor Wu anymore'n I do."

"Oh, Doctor Wu! Right, I don't! He's got my girlfriend and my girlfriend's boyfriend. I mean, Polly's boyfriend."

"Yeah, yeah, I don't really give a fuck about why you wanna nail Wu's tail, I just want to pay him back for how he screwed me over. If I've got anything to do with it, his days are numbered."

"What did Wu do to you?"

"I was the sun, and he knocked me outa the sky and turned me into a freakin' tiger. And after I let him fuck me up the ass, like we was Village People at the YMCA or sumpin...."

"Uh, right. Well, listen, where are you, how can we meet to plan our strategy?"

"I'm in *mictlan*, the Land of the Dead. My buddy, Mictlantecuhtli, is letting me crash while he's busy in the Gaza Strip. The whole Middle East needs a lot of attention. It's like, Beirut, Iraq, Iran. I speak very, very fluent Spanish: *cheveray, cheveray*.... Where was I? Oh, yeah, why don't you meet me here?"

"In the Land of the Dead...?"

"Yeah, it's not a bad place to visit, but I'd hate to live here. I'm an outdoorsy type myself, if ya know what I mean. Give me the open skies. But some folks groove on it. I remember when I brought Doc Dee here, I had a hard time getting him to go home."

"I don't know.... Can't you just give me some information right now that might help?"

"Sure, I guess so. Come close, tho, I gotta whisper."

Cy advanced to the mirror.

"Closer, closer, yeah, that's good. Gotcha!"

Two steely hands exploded from the mirror and locked around Cy's biceps.

"Welcome to Wonderland, Alice!"

"AIIEEEE!" screamed Cy, feeling himself being pulled into the smoky mirror.

The door to Paulie's room burst open.

"Cy, what—" said Polly.

"Holy Jaguar, it's Coatlicue! I'm outa here!"

Released, Cy, who had been straining against the pull, rocketed backward into Polly.

As soon as his body made contact with hers, everything disappeared.

Cy was left floating all alone, at the center of an infinite pearly fog. Was this the smoke contained in the mirror? He thought he had escaped.... No, it felt different, more like the tangible light of Numbers Heaven. There was no malevolence....

The mist was incredibly dense and tactile, altho the sensations it imparted were hard to describe. Cold, warm, wet, dry? None of the above? The mist felt very intelligent. It seemed curious about Cyril's presence. It adapted itself to his contours, pressing on him, deriving information from his form like a blind person running her fingers over a statue.

*Her* fingers? What made him say "her?"

The fog had apparently completed its surface examination. Now it began to insinuate itself into the Six Openings of Buddhist theology. It flowed up his nostrils and into his ears. Cy opened his mouth to yell, and the fog filled his mouth too. Heh-hey, what was going on, damned mist was poking at his privates! Oh, no, the proctological fog was up his asshole now! Butch dyke fog with a strap-on!

Cy suddenly realized something: the fog was horny and lonely. It couldn't keep its tendrils off him. Filling its whole sad universe, the numinous sentient fog welcomed its infrequent visitors, and only wanted to get to know them better. I didn't mean to turn you on, fog!

A feminine whisper filtered into Cy's brain.

Hi, honey, I'm Sophia, who're you?

Without waiting for an answer, the fog commenced stimulating Cy to an erection, while simultaneously stroking in and out of his ass.

*Hold on just a minute!* Cy tried to say, but it was no use. He had always thought the advice to rape victims about just lying back and enjoying it was incredibly stupid. But when your assailant was the whole universe, you didn't have much choice.

Just when matters were approaching a CRISIS, Polly's voice brought Cy back to reality.

"Cy, are you okay?"

Cyril opened his eyes.

Polly stood above him, gazing in wonder at his throbbing boner.

Cy jumped to his feet. So long, Sophie, whoever you might be.... For now.

"What's going on, Cyril? You blacked out when we touched. When I let go, you woke right up...."

"I— That Aztec— Sophia—"

"Cy, calm down. You're actually shaking."

Moving to the bed, Cy sat. When he could form a complete sentence, he said, "Polly, what did you see when you came in?"

"You were pressed up against the mirror, screaming."

"No one was pulling me in?"

"No, not that I could make out. It was just your own reflection."

"That's it?"

"Well, now that I think about it, I couldn't see your arms. I thought they were hidden by your body."

"No, they weren't. I was almost in the Land of the friggin' Dead!"

Cy recounted then his conversation with Tez.

"And the weird thing was, he got scared when he saw you. Called you Coatlicue...."

"Who's that, Cy?"

"I'm not exactly sure. One of the Aztec goddesses, I know that much from a class in Latin American history. But I can't be sure which one."

"How flattering. Well, if your vision was real, it's good to know that somebody else has a grudge against Doctor Wu."

"Yeah, I guess. But can we be sure that *his* enemies are *our* friends?"

Cy suddenly realized he was naked. He jumped up and began to wiggle into a pair of Paulie Junior's jeans and a shirt.

"What happened, though, after I came in, Cy?"

"It's like you said. As soon as I touched you, I went someplace else."

Cy gave Pol a highly edited version of his encounter with the lubricious mist. No sense letting Polly know he had cheated on her before he even had her.

Polly's sweet face was full of concern. She pondered a moment, then said, "It's the AIDS, Cy. You're experiencing peaks of information overload. Your brain is mixing up and regurgitating everything you know. You need to relax and forget your troubles for a while."

"Jeez, that's easy to say, Polly, but I'm a knot of tension. Our mates are missing, our ace in the hole is a blind private eye, we've just seen a pitiful victim of the terminal stages of my disease, and we've nearly been killed by a malevolent Wham-O toy. I'd like to know how I'm supposed to relax."

"Just cum with me," punned Polly.

Taking his hand again—Cy flinched, but nothing untoward occurred—Polly guided him out of the house and back to the subway.

All the way home, seated beside him, she kept her whole length pressed up against Cy. If it's just another train ride, why you lookin' that way? I thought you were a Sweet Thang when I saw you on the A Train.... The pressure was vastly reassuring, but at the same time eminently disturbing. What the hell was going on here? Sure, he and Polly had always had an unspoken subterranean attraction for each other, but they had kept a lid on it, knowing it could never be acted on. "Keep your hands to yourself," had been their unspoken motto. Why was their desire growing now? The more he thought about it, the stranger it seemed. It was almost as if they were being impelled by vast forces external to themselves, molecules caught in a catalytic enzymatic broth, binary components forced to express their complementarity....

And was this the wisest course? Guilt washed over Cy. She was his best friend's girl! (But she used to be mine. Wait a minute, what made him think that? 'Course not, she never was. Leastways not in this life....) The very Klicking of the Kars seemed to remind him of his potential betrayal of Augie. What were he 'n' Polly letting themselves in for? Would they regret it later?

The subject of love, Cy realized, was infinitely deep. Love could make you happy, and all you needed was love. But love was also a battlefield, love was a stranger, and love was a hurtin' thing. (Or, if you would, love was strange, love was a many-splendored thing.) Only love could break your heart. But you had to put a little love in your heart first. Love was like an itching in Cy's heart, like oxygen to his lungs. He had a whole lotta love, his love was bigger than a Cadillac, big enough for Polly and Ruby both.

Ruby.... How could he have forgotten Ruby? What a cheating heart he had! There on the rumbling train, he felt torn between two lovers. Ruby: he still loved her madly. Polly: could it be he was falling in love with her too? Who knew?! It was so complex! Sneaky feelings for slippery people! All he could be sure of was that he felt like makin' love to Polly. He'd fuck Ruby too, natch, but love was here and now she was gone.

By the time the train pulled into their stop, Cy had come to no conclusions about the morality of what was about to happen. He resolved to turn his mind off and let his body take over, in an attempt to defuse his AIDS. If—when!—he saw Ruby again, he was sure she'd be a woman who'd understand, she'd be a woman who loved her man.

And the plain facts were, Cyril was so randy from the constant contact of Pol's bod against his, he woulda jumped a snake.

It's the season of loving....

But—

Who *do* you love?

Why, the only flame in town!

They frenched feverishly for a while outside the door of the apartment. Then Cy backed Polly in—

—and stopped dead in his tracks.

The space looked as if a cyclone had been through it. Cushions were ripped open, posters torn from the walls, drawers upended, footprints in spilled flour.... Place looked almost as bad as when Ruby had misplaced her final senior project.

Finally seeing the mess, Polly said, "The disc, Cy. They were after the disc. Thank God we took it along!"

"We'll have to keep it on us at all times," said Cy, returning to nuzzling Polly's neck. He was actually less concerned over the invasion of his privacy than he would have anticipated being, had anyone told him a day or two ago that his apartment would soon be trashed. His hormones were still pumping, he was riding the Testosterone Rocket to the Mound Of Venus. "You'll have to put it under your ass while we fuck."

"Oh! Strip me, Cyril—now!" hints Polly obliquely.

Cy is nothing loath. He picks Polly up and carries her to the bedroom.

The room is lined with bookshelves filled with Cy's collection of history texts. A map or two occupies an odd niche here and there. Space is at a premium in the Prothero-Tuesday household, and the one spare room is devoted to Ruby's avocation (mixing and splicing decks, etc.), so Cy's obsession dominates their sleeping quarters.

Only when Cy sets Pol down does he notice what she's changed into, back at the Peptide domicile: a short sleeveless vintage summer dress, decorated with a motif of double Roosevelt dimes.

It's the famous PAIR O' DIMES SHIFT!

Cy grabs the hem of the shift and pulls it up over Polly's head.

She's wearing only a black lace bra and black panties, where a darker dampness spreads from her cleft. Her fetish hangs between her breasts. My black satin, black satin doll....

Polly's eyes have become smoky mirrors. *I've got a girlfriend that's better than that*, thinks Cy involuntarily. *She's got the smoke in her eyes. Tell her no, no, no....*

Fuck you, Konscience, I'm not backing down. I've got a dirty mind whenever she's around, and now we're gonna do it all night!

Cy runs his hands down Pol's back and hooks his thumbs in her panties. Dropping into a crouch, he drags the panties over the twin sinuosities of her ass, letting the soppy garment fall to the floor.

Polly steps out of them. Her hands on his head compel him to kneel.

You got me on my knees, girl—you just gotta let me lay you down!

Polly's long legs.... How many times has he watched these limbs, capped by a ridiculously short skirt, never imagining he'd be in this position...? Or, let's be honest, imagining but never daring to hope....

Polly's hands press his face into her crotch.

We're at the Headwaters now, fer shure, Burton's Nile.... Sweet cunt, juicy twat, itty bitty pretty one. Peptide Poontang. Ever-flowing headwaters of Good Head, river of life, fount of erotic info.... I visited the Doctor, I drank from the fountain....

Cyril nibbles at her fragrant mons and outer lips.

Weh-hell, this is apparently too much for moanin' Polly, cuz she drags Cy up by hands under his armpits and is outa her bra—but not her fetish, no, never that!—faster, of course, than Cy can undress himself—but not by much.

Both are naked.

The familiar apartment seems suddenly transformed into a liddle ol' Garden of

Eden by their nakedness, no snake around (or at least he remains politely off-stage).

Cy suddenly gets this—well, *mental transmission*, apparently from Polly. It's just like the way Sophia's voice earlier sounded in his very synapses, but this time unmistakably the voice of the woman whose bare waist he now grips.

Clothes are noise on the message of the body....

That's all very interesting in a theoretical fashion, like, but not now, okay, brain?

Cy is captivated by Polly's whiteness. It's been so long since he's seen anyone but his dark Ruby naked. (Ruby, you forlorn Goodbye Girl!) Polly's wavy pubic hair, a Golden Triangle, the pinkness of her nipples, her expanses of opalescent flesh.... This is....Kinda Kinky. It's like suddenly inhabiting a photographic negative, and Cy glances briefly out the window, expecting to see a black hole in the sky where the sun should be.

Somehow they are in the big brass bed.

Cy kneels on something small and hard and reaches down to remove it. The object is a refrigerator magnet, the one shaped like a musical note. How'd that get here...?

Polly pushes Cy down flat on his back atop rumpled sheets. Then she's kneeling beside him. Don't seem like he's in control here, exactly, not knowing what's going on from one second to the next. But to reiterate the obvious: who cares?

Suddenly Polly's swung a leg over Cy's head, and she's facing his feet.

Her cunt, that rare dewy incarnadined flower, is poised an inch or three above his lips.

Cy is hypnotized by one perfect drop of translucent moisture clinging in mysterious supension to a single pubic hair.

Why, this must be the fabled Puh-pearl Of Wuh-wisdom!

Cy tongues it off and swallows.

Heaven is a place on earth!

Then he's sucking her delicately convoluted cleft.

*You were just a liddle virgin, going to be wed, but you got into my bed, I gave you head till you were red, and you married* me *instead!*

Cy licks for dear life. His tongue feels as long and thick as the Stones' logo.

Polly's fine hair washes his thighs, then her mouth descends on his prick, her fetish dangling onto his groin.

Love me tender, Pol! He feels like he's tripping on those legendary Sex Packets.

F-f-folks, this is what's known as The Worm Ouroboros, the Snake That Bites Its Own Tail, Alchemical Sign of Immortality, The Ultimate Feedback Circuit, A Closed Loop Of Information. Neural signals travelling from transmitter to receiver to transmitter to receiver.... Good channels, unambiguously primal code, no noise. It goes round 'n' round 'n' round, and it comes out here!

And cum he does.

Cy's orgasm precedes Polly's by seconds. He tries to concentrate on bringing her off, but knows he's losing it. This blast is going to be a doozy!

But when it hits, he is totally unprepared for the intensity of it. His cock feels ethereal, as if it is made of numbers and spurting champagne. I was a free man in Paris....

Then, in the middle of the transcendental joy-explosion, everything simply stops. What the—?

Cy looks down at himself.

He's standing up, fully clothed. Polly's gone. He's in a strange room. There's a desk with a guy seated at it. Behind the desk are two huge banks of vacuum tubes and flashing lights, switchboards and mercury delay lines, partially encased in crackle-finish cases.

The guy wears a bloody Nazi uniform full of bullet holes. There's a wound in his forehead. He seems perturbed.

"You are *schtupping mein frau, Herr* Prothero."

"I— What— Who—"

"The one you know as Polly. When she was mine, she was sorta kinda my best friend. Now she's gone Uptown, West End Girl with an East End Boy, and she didn't even have the decency to change the sheets! I never was the kind to make a fuss, even with you there sleeping in between the two of us! But I love her more now than when she was mine! You've given me a broken heart again. But this is bigger than you, *Herr* Prothero. Regine and I are fated to be lovers forever. I am merely waiting to be reborn. I cannot let you have her. Unfortunately, her fetish protects her and even you, so long as you are together. But as soon as I get you alone—well, let's query Spirit One and Spirit Two for the verdict."

The guy jabs some buttons on the antique computers, and they each spit out a punched card. He holds them up for Cy to see.

The punchmarks on one spell out GUILTY, on the other INNOCENT.

"Ah-ha, a split decision. Luckily, I can cast the tie-breaking vote. Guilty!"

The Nazi stands and draws a Luger, taking aim at Cyril.

"Hey, I thought you said you couldn't harm me—"

"It never hurts to try."

The trigger is squeezed—

Cy hurls himself under the gun at the Nazi's waist—

He's lying on a carpeted floor, staring at someone's tapestry-slipper-clad feet. There is a smell of ginger in the air.

Cyril stands.

The new room is poorly lit by a single green-shaded lamp hanging from a long cord over a baize-covered card table flanked by two metal folding chairs. Seated in one of the chairs, pushed back out of the lamp's small circle of radiance, is a man. Seems to be an old Chinese guy wearing sunglasses.

"If you are done playing with spirits in the night, please sit," says the man.

"Where am I?" counters Cy.

"Neutral ground," says the man.

Or was that "neural ground?" Guy's got an accented whispery voice like snake scales rustling over sand, makes it kinda hard to understand him.

Having no recourse, Cy sits.

From the old gent comes the noise of ruffling cards. "I so enjoy games of chance, Mister Prothero, but do not have many occasions to play. Perhaps you will indulge me now. I had in mind a hand of binary poker. You are familiar with it?"

"No, not really...."

"This deck holds sixty-four cards, thirty-two aces and thirty-two jokers. I will deal eight cards to each of us. Five of a kind beats four, six beats five, and so on. In cases where we hold the same number of like cards, aces beat jokers. In the rare event that we receive identical hands, we will play again. You may discard and draw once. Is so much clear?"

"Yes, but—"

"Now, as Mister Persi Diaconis has proven, it takes seven shuffles to truly randomize a deck. Just to convince you of my honesty, I will shuffle eight times."

The old guy whips thru eight Vegas shuffles.

"Here are your cards."

Doctor Wu—who else could it be?—deals sixteen cards faster'n a snake's tongue flickers.

Helpless, Cy picks up his hand.

Seven jokers, and a lone ace.

Can't make his hand any worse by discarding, and might make it better....

"I'll take one," says Cy, throwing the ace face-down.

The Chinese dealer flips a pasteboard to Cy. He picks it up.

Joker. Full house.

"I will stand pat," says the Chinaman.

Cy displays his hand triumphantly. "Eight jokers."

His opponent lays down eight aces.

"Shit," ventures Cy.

The old man gets up creakily. From behind his back he pulls a big hacksaw and advances on Cy, who sits paralyzed, unable to raise his eyes to the Doctor's face.

"I will now collect," says the Chinaman, laying the saw against Cyril's neck and beginning to cut.

Surprisingly, there is no pain. The sawing motion feels good, in fact, almost like an orgasm....

Polly's grinding her pussy insistently against his momentarily inattentive lips, while she continues to swallow every drop of his still-spurting jism.

More'n a little freaked, Cy manages to recover enough to bring her to climax with a tender tonguing.

Polly takes her mouth off Cy's prick, arches her back, grabs her boobs, and makes a lotta noise while nearly smothering him.

But oh, darlin', wotta way to go!

When she's done, she rolls off, panting.

Cyril waits an appropriately considerate time before saying, "Polly?"

"Yes?"

"Something wild happened just then."

"I'll say!"

"No, I'm not talking about the sex—although that was wild enough. This was something else."

Cy explains.

Poor Pol goes white. "My brother—the one I killed in the womb—he's still out there! I thought after all these years that maybe I was free of him...."

"Your twin brother is a horny old Nazi?"

"I told you, he was my jealous lover in my former life. I can't account for the old me's tastes!"

"Whoa, don't get excited, I don't hold it against you. He doesn't really worry me anyway. We're safe from him, thanks to the Hoodoo Guru's fetish. No, what bothers me is Wu. What was that poker game all about?"

Seemingly intrigued now, more like her old optimistic self, Polly scrambles around to lie same way as Cy. "You're right, Cy, the game with Doctor Wu is more important than my brother. My first guess would be that it wasn't a regular AIDS-type fugue, it was more like a stochastic projection of our struggle with Wu."

"Stow-what?"

"Stochastic, relating to probability. You experienced a glimpse, however subjectively symbolized, of the actual future—or one of our likely quantum futures, anyway."

"Is that possible?"

"Yeah, sure. You see, probability lies at the roots of information theory. It's a way of encoding 'missing information,' everything we don't know about a situation. And there sure is plenty we don't know about the fix we're in! Probability measures both knowledge and ignorance. Your brain seems to be assessing our knowledge and ignorance and assigning odds to our success. The binary nature of the game would seem to symbolize a fifty-fifty chance."

"That good?"

"Don't knock it, I wouldn't have placed it that high. This whole process is known as estimation, by the way. In estimation, you're usually dealing with a continuously varying function of time and space—which describes our situation exactly. And prediction is just an important special case of estimation, where the message of interest is the value of a random signal at some future time."

"Wow."

Pol looks puzzled. "Why the projection should assume the form it did, though—Why Wu wanted to saw off your head, that is, I can't say."

Cyril squeezes Polly's ass. "Maybe he was jealous of the head I was getting."

Pol blushes. "Or your head in my bush."

Suddenly the erotic tension is too much, and, unwilling just yet to initiate a second spin-the-bottle-five-minutes-in-the-closet-with-you, Cy tries to defuse it.

"I'm starving! How about you?"

"Yeah, I could go for, um, a pizza?"

"Great, I'll call."

One nice thing about living in the North End: pizza is never very far away. Cy dials his old fave, Pizzeria Regina.

"Montagnier's Pizza, home of the Faster Pasteur Pasta."

"Hey, what happened to Pizzeria Regina?"

"Out of business in a merger. May I help you?"

"Uh, yeah, sure, a large pepperoni with Green Onions."

"Be there in thirty."

Cy hangs up the phone.

The doorbell rings.

Hastily grabbing a floral-print cushion cover from the debris and wrapping it around his waist, Cy goes to the door.

An older guy with big shades stands there, holding a steaming pizza box.

"Mister Prothero?"

Cy is floored. "How—?"

"We're always running scared for our customers."

"All right, one second while I get some cash."

Leaving the pizza-man at the open front door, Cy goes for his jeans and his sister's money.

Polly appears naked in the bedroom door, sees the delivery man, and ducks back.

"Oh, pretty woman!" exclaims the guy.

"Hey, that's enough of that!" says Cy. He returns in a minute with the cash.

"Can you break a fifty?"

"Sure."

The guy hands Cy the pizza and takes the bill. He unslings a backpack, and fishes a plump moneybag out of it. The sack looks like something Daddy Warbucks or Uncle Scrooge would carry, right down to the big snaky dollar sign stencilled on it.

"Eighty rolls of new pennies. Thank you for trying Montagnier's."

Cy's juggling the pizza and the incredibly heavy moneybag. "Wait one darn minute—"

Too late, the messenger's slammed the door and scooted with Cy's cash.

"Fuckin' nut...."

Cy drops the bag and carries the pizza back to Polly.

"That was quick."

"No kidding. What'll you drink?"

"I could go for some coffee, if it's not too late for you...."

"Sure."

Soon they're having pizza and black coffee in bed. (It's espresso love!) Cy's wearing the cushion cover over his lap—don't wanna drop no hot mozzarella on the Fambly Jools—and Polly looks good in his old Doors T-shirt.

They're quiet while they eat. The meal is not serving to lessen the undercurrent of randiness, as Cy half hoped it would. Instead, to the contrary, all this biting and chewing and licking of lips and blowing on hot coffee is somehow magnifying the sensuality of the situation.

Finally, after they've gorged themselves, they start inevitably to fondle and play with each other.

"Oh, Cy," whispers Polly, "I want you—"

"I want you too."

"Yes, I mean that, but I want you—"

"Yeah?"

"I want you  "

"Go on."

"I want you to tie me up...."

"What?!"

Cy releases Polly, who stares shamefacedly at her hands in her lap. "There," she says, "I've spoiled everything. Go ahead, say what you're thinking. I'm a pervert, a deviant, disturbed. Pretty soon they'll be coming to take me away, ha-ha. . . ."

"No, that's not what I was thinking at all, Pol. It's just that you—you surprised me."

"I don't look like the kind of woman who likes getting tied up?"

"I don't know. What do those kind look like?"

"Well, I'm not. At least, I don't consider myself primarily such a person. I mean, I can get satisfaction without it, as you might just recall. It's only something Aug-Aug-Augie and I used to—used to do now—now—now and then!"

Pol starts weeping like a kid who's just had her kitten run over. She makes love like a woman, but she breaks just like a little girl....

"Polly, Pol, listen, stop your sobbing!"

She gradually does. "You, you don't think I'm awful?"

"No, of course not." *Mighty weird, yes, but not awful.*

"Well, you see, it was all an accident. One day, Augie and I were skipping rope for exercise. I got tangled in his jumprope, he got tangled in mine, one thing led to another, and—well, you know how these things happen."

"I do? I mean, sure I do!"

"So. Would you do it for me?"

"Uh, yeah, of course. What should I use?"

"Anything soft."

Cy rummages through the ransacked contents of his closet until he comes across a bag full of Ruby's silk scarves. Her perfume still lingers faintly in them. Traitor....

"Will these do?"

"Oh, yes...."

Lay, lady, lay, across my big brass bed. Pretty soon, Polly's spreadeagled on the mattress. Cy gently knots four scarves around her ankles and wrists and fastens them to the posts.

Despite the lascivious situation, Polly's looks reminds him somehow of Tenniel's classic depiction of Alice in Wonderland. (Oh, yeah, that's what that crazy Aztec in the mirror called *me*!) Weh-hell, now she's his Alice in Chains, his little Mudhoney, his sweet Hole, his Nirvana, fer shure!

"Is that, um, okay?" queries Cy.

Polly's writhes sensuously, straining against the bonds. Her eyes are getting that smoky look again.

"I can't get loose!"

"Pol, I'm sorry!"

"No, it's wonderful! Oh, Cyril, I'm tied to the promontory!"

Promontory...?

"Heap the covers up at the foot of the bed like a monster—quickly, please!"

Cy does as directed, excitement swelling in him, despite The Bizarreness Of It All.

"Help, help, save me! Someone help me! It's getting closer!"

Cy roars. Is he supposed to be the monster or the savior? Does it really make any difference?

He jumps on the bed, straddling Polly, his stiff prick bobbing against her bush.

"Oh, Saint George, Perseus, Mister Dragon! Love me two times, I'm going away!"

Polly spreads her legs as much as the scarves will allow, and Cy shoves his aching cock up her.

He's slippin' and slidin' between those Sugar Walls. And tho he would've sworn he could last forever after already cumming once, he shoots his wad within a minute, as Polly expires with a scream.

Frightened by her violent reaction, Cy quickly jumps up and unties this modern Andromeda.

"Polly, Polly, are you all right?"

Polly throws her arms around him and murmurs, "Now I know everything will all turn out okay, Cy."

Then she's asleep, snoring, fer shure, but not, Cy is grateful, so loudly as she is wont to.

Cy goes to take a piss.

When he returns, Polly is wearing a scarf around her neck.

It's a snakeskin-print.

There is no way Cy can sleep. He's all coffeed-up.

"Polly," he says, though he knows she is sleeping, "I'm aching and empty and I don't know why."

Oh yes he does. It's Ruby.

My little run-run-runaway! Since you're gone, the nights are getting strange, and everything is present tense! What do two fucks with Polly mean for their relationship? What about his friendship with Augie? Does Polly feel guilty too? Damn it, why did Augie and Ruby have to disappear?! It's all their fault!

Gazing down at Polly, tho, he thinks: Ain't love the sweetest thing? But: WHY DOES LOVE GOT TO BE SO SAD?

Cy covers Polly up with the remnants of the blanket monster. It's raining out now, he realizes, the storm sprung up out of nowhere in the formerly cloudless sky.... As far as I can see the sky is coal-grey. The water falls, it rains like a slow divorce, it runs in spontaneous guttered rivers, down drains and underground. Until the mighty rivers dry up, I'll be your man.... There is water underground, under the rocks and stones.... You may ask yourself, "How did I get here?" You may find yourself saying, "This is not my beautiful wife...."

Cy kisses Polly's brow tenderly and leaves to prowl the apartment.

Without so much as a pair of skivvies to garble his body's message (which is: residual nervous tension under a layer of sexually induced somatic ease), Cyril flops down in a chair before the television. Watch a little tube, catch a few rays from the Cathode Sun? Nah, might wake up Polly. And besides, who needs the extra information....

Cy feels the television then—even powered-down—to be a devilish double agent, representative of a hostile force. Ostensibly his servant, the little Mitsubishi (treacherous Japs who built the Zero!) is the prime operative in something known as "the information explosion," the cause of his disease. (I'm the tool of the government and of industry too. I am destined to rule and regulate you. I may be vile and pernicious, but you can't look away. I'm the slime oozing out of your TV set!) Along with a gushing flood of books, magazines, newspapers, videotapes, computers, satellites, radios, journals, databases, cassettes, discs, handbills, billboards, flyers, mail, zines, e-mail, grafitti, and official reports, his television supplies Cyril with more information per second than he can possibly digest. Every minute more information is generated than he could do justice to in a year of constant assimilation. It's the Red Queen's Race, fer shure.

But of course that's not the worst of it. The first thing you think of never is. No, the worst of it is that *this information doesn't go away anymore!* As Polly told him not long ago, while it's effortless to acquire information, it's bugger-all hard to erase it! Whereas in earlier periods information at least had a short half-life, disappearing in masses of crumbling, wormy paper, nowadays a revolution in storage has insured that *it lasts forever* (or at least for many, many human lifetimes, which is all that matters). All the information you couldn't handle when it was first produced now waits patiently on non-biodegradable tapes and imperishable optical discs. The weight of generations rests on our shoulders in the form of cassettes and microfilms and bubble memories. *Couldn't get to last Sunday's* Times, *so you threw*

*it out in the trash? Here it is on your computer screen, ha-ha-ha-ha-ha!*
What is this, tho, except the old problem of HISTORY, greatly magnified? History
has always been a curse. (Joyce: "History is a nightmare from which I am striving to
awaken.") There has always been so much more History than there is Present.
Every second of Now, once past, becomes History, a droplet of mineral-filled water
adding to the length and diameter of that stalagmite-dildo, History. (As Gertrude
Stein might've meant, "Today is as tomorrow was as yesterday will be as today is.")
History, Cy's old nemesis, has always—or at least for the last half-millennium or
so—been too vast for comprehension. The bane of all thinkers. How to make sense
of that space-and-time-Gödeling noisy tapestry, or even be sure that one has traced
all the relevant threads...?

And nowadays the present—thanks to the immense and unstoppable output of
an unprecedented number of living beings, equipped with a miraculous technology
developed almost in a somnambulistic, outer-directed fashion—has become as
ungraspable as the past.... The human brain simply isn't built to handle the flood.
Its channel-capacity is too small....

Cyril tries to get a hold of himself. This is the kind of thinking that led to his
dropping out of school from nervous exhaustion, without ever getting his degree.
(Ten years of his life wasted, flitting from one branch of history to another, never
being able to internalize or sort out the whole interconnected mess, obsessed, like
history-besotted Thomas Wolfe, with *number and amount.* Everything counts in
large amounts....)

After a minute or so of deep-breathing exercises, Cy feels in control again. Whew,
that was a narrow escape. Almost got sucked into the abyss. Can't let it get to me,
gotta take one thing at a time....

Outside the rain is hammering more loudly now, sounds like "Riders on the
Storm," by the Doors. Like an actor out on loan, a dog without a bone.... Kinda
melancholy, especially thinking of Ruby out somewhere in the downpour, and him
sittin' here like a fool in the rain....

Something in Cy's recent train of thought leads him to recall a phrase Polly has
just tossed out: "a continuously varying function of time and space." Why does that
sound familiar? Oh, yeah, because Ferdie Lantz said something similar. What was
the context? Hadn't they asked about Wu's plans? "He wants to conquer space and
time." What the hell could that mean? Take the binary pair separately. To conquer
time would entail....what? To be able to grasp all of the past....and the future? Or
even....to live forever? And what about space? It couldn't be anything so mundane as
literal absolute freedom of movement through space. The partial and tantalizing
glimpses he has so far gotten of all Wu's schemes seem to relate to knowledge and
information. To master space meant....to hold it all in the mind, perhaps, to have
instant and complete access to all present knowledge. Of course, that had to be it!
Omniscience, the only game in town, the information age's grail. The god-trip.

Say-hey, our boy's on a roll now, he's convinced of it. Granted that his speculations hold some probability, the next step is probably to return to Lantz, their only lead, and confront him with these accusations, hoping he'll spill something new.

Cyril gets up and begins pacing. Sleep—that blessed time when the brain accepts no new information, and passes what it has through the filter of dreams—is further away now than ever. How to pass the time till it comes? Music, maybe? He hunts for his Walkman, but can't find it in the mess. It's probably somewhere in the bedroom, and he doesn't want to wake Polly up by rummaging around for it.

Jesus, this is awful: even when your mind is super-saturated with information, it clamors for more. As long as you're conscious, the processing never stops, constant input demanded to feed the machine, more useless bits to add to the database, more branches on the decision-trees....

Cy's eye falls on a book on a table. It's a paperback with a garish cover. A fantasy entitled *The Riddle of the Dragon*.

Funny, it's nothing he ever bought. Maybe Ruby...?

Anyhow, the paperback is illustrated with a painting of a big-chested, raven-haired gal dressed like an S&M dominatrix in leather and metal. She confronts a crusty ol' dragon with an air of wanton invitation. The creature, its head lowered, seems interested in the heroine's crotch, its cavernous nostrils only scale-inches away.

What the fuck is it about dragons anyway that makes them so popular? Cy's heard the theory, natch, that young girls like 'em—same as they like horses—because they're eager for something hard and muscular between their legs. But, appealing as such a notion is to everyone's fantasy of The Concupiscent Teenybopper, there's got to be more to dragons than that. Wisdom? Power? Wealth? The metaphors are all overused, and Cy wishes somebody'd do something different with dragons, or shit-can them all together. Maybe this book'll be the one....

Cy picks it up and opens to the title page:

THE RIDDLE OF THE DRAGON
by
Zona Pellucida
A Post-Tolkien, Sword & Sorcery Mystery
Composed partially by
Scanning,
Stealing,
Copying,
and
Reverse Engineering
"This is adjudicated by the one-eyed love."

Looks promising, if pretentious. Let's read.

Good news: all the confusion he has endured recently hasn't caused Cy's literary standards to degenerate: it's plain from the git-go that this book, like most of its ilk, is a piece of shit. It reads like an amateurish, confusing, cliche-infested farrago.

However, much to Mister Prothero's surprise, the novel soon has him in its grip. In some mysterioso manner, it turns out to be an eerily *relevant* piece of shit.

The story goes like this:

The protagonist is the bimbo depicted on the cover. Yclept Melusine (a good old medieval name), she's the head of a buncha ruthless Amazons who are the secret power behind the throne of the nominal rulers of this particular Never-never-land. Basically, these Evil Bitches control the flow of information throughout the kingdom, keeping a tight rein on such Hot Fax as what troops are garrisoned where; what peasants are growing what crops and in what quantity (this knowledge having tremendous value in the marketplace, sorta like Wall Street insider tips); and what the various alchemists are up to in their fanatical pursuit of Divine Knowledge and the concomittant ability to get rich and laid often. Oh, yeah, the Amazons also function as tax collectors, a primitive IRS, which gives them mucho status and power. In addition, they have this arcane ability to enslave anyone they have sex with. Natch. What else?

The Amazons' living totemic beast is the ancient Lord Dragon, an incredibly wise and cunning being. He hides deep within a network of caverns, and no one ever sees him (friggin' deceptive cover art!) or even knows if he exists, save for the High Priest, a nameless Ophite Gnostic (say what?) who seems strangely immune to all the fleshy charms of the floozies he cohabits with.

Such plot as there is in this sprawling travesty concerns the elaborate and not-altogether-clear machinations of the Amazons to further tighten their control of the kingdom—mainly by screwing various ministers and generals and royalty, who become their LOVE-SLAVES, and by extorting money from merchants and peasants to add to their already overflowing treasury. Oh, yeah, there's also this nattering subplot about the alchemists trying to achieve transcendence and immortality.

Weh-hell.... For some reason, Cy is utterly transfixed by this hodgepodge, and before he knows it two or three hours have passed in rapt reading. He's gotta find out how it ends....

How it ends is—it doesn't. Not really end, that is, in the conventional sense of resolution. What happens, all within a few pages, is that the High Priest experiences an odd demise, Lord Dragon makes a brief appearance, utters some profundities before vanishing for good, and the alchemists accidentally (?) loose a new Black Plague on the world. Just to add insult to injury, the last chapter—number 64—is titled "Before Completion."

Say *what?* This book's pretty nervy for a piece of Pop-Lit. Where's this Pellucida get off, writing so obscurely, when all the audience wants is A Good Read?

Disgusted, Cy tosses the book against the wall, where it breaks its back and lies crippled on the floor. He looks at the red digits of the clock across the room: 1:11.

It was pretty stupid to expect illumination from such a source. But Cy has a nagging feeling that if only the book had been written more clearly, he might've—just might've—derived more of its message. What was the point of all that obscurity, redundancy and extraneous diversion? Was every novel doomed to exhibit such symptoms—sheerly cuz of the built-in limitations of the very form—eventually being overwhelmed by the noise inherent in the very act of transmission? Couldn't someone devise a better, more efficient code...?

And all that pseudo-medieval crap. New information demands new forms. Can't writers and readers see that such trappings are just useless noise, outmoded encodings? Why don't more writers stretch themselves, and try

## MESSIN' WITH THE CODE

Messin' with the code is every honest writer's responsibility as a message-sender determined to get the most information out of his chosen channel. But it is the task most often shrugged-off. Every advance in literature, every new mode and technique, derives ultimately from some Noble, Albeit Possibly Crack-Brained Experiment with the given structures.

Messin' with the code includes, but does not totally consist of, the following:

Utilizing puns, rebuses, riddles, ciphers, enigmas, puzzles, distractions, red-herrings, sleight-of-hand, anagrams, acrostics, skewed orthography (phunny spellink), KRaZy KApITAlIZAtioN, unorthodox punc(tu....a)tlon?!, veiled hints, parody, cryptic allusions, said-bookisms (he ejaculated), authorial interjections (see what I mean?), repetitious catch-phrases, the mixture of different modes such as poetry and prose, and the conflation of reality and fantasy.

It is interesting to observe that Messin' With The Code is primarily, tho not exclusively, a twentieth-century preoccupation. And those forms of art that arose with the century seem most at-ease with such experimentation. Two such vehicles are animated cartoons and printed comix.

Doesn't it sometimes seem as if cartoons more closely mimic reality than any other art? Who hasn't felt like poor ol' Wile E. at times? Cy sure has! And as for comix—weh-hell....

One of the primary Messers With The Code was one George Herriman, Kreole Mulatto, Kreator of Krazy Kat. His inspired play with words and visuals resulted in works of art not often matched for sheer gonzo revelations. But I don't have to tell you that, do I?

What is not so well-known about Herriman, however, is that during his indigent youth, he held the job of sideshow barker for a carny. The act he had to introduce was a pinhead eating snakes, and he would spiel thusly:

*Bosco, the wonderful! Bosco, the Silurian Senegambian Snake Eater! He eats them alive! He bites their heads off! He grovels in a den of loathsome reptiles! An exhibition for the educated! And a show for the sensitive and refined!*

(Question is: was this pro-snake or anti-snake propaganda?)

And you know what? If you're really daring, you can even fool with the Metastatements that govern Messing! But now we're starting to get into dangerously self-referential, recursive territory. Who knows, we might even end up by Messin' with the Messer!

So. That's Messin' With The Code. 'N' if you're an aspiring author, you'd better pay attention, cuz if you don't, all your work will be in vain, and you'll end up, Cyril realizes, smack dab in the middle of

## THE LAND OF DEAD GENRES

It is always the twilight preceding a dark and stormy night in the Land Of Dead Genres, a heavy dusk that lies leadenly on the country's castles and Gothic mansions, its primeval New England forests and Victorian city streets, its World War I skies and Wild West prairies, its Regency parlors and pirate galleons. Through these locales move the ghostly figures of abandoned characters, making no contact, alone in their uselessness, conveying nothing but dead information, everything they can do certain and hence valueless, their probability 1.00. Here, black is the color and none is the number. Natty Bumppo passes James Bond without a nod. The Spirit and Inspector Dolan sit in the station while rain drips from the windowsill. Ivanhoe finds no energy to tilt at G-8 and his Battle Aces. Tom Swift offers no rides in his gyrocopter to the battalions of nurses and governesses hanging dispiritedly about. The plight of chained princesses does not intrigue Sherlock Holmes. Ragged Dick has no energy to stop the runaway carriage containing the banker's daughter. Pilgrim Christian makes no Progress. (Welcome to the blank-screened theater, Pilgrim!) Tom Mix can't mix it up with them rustlers no more. (Who is that gaucholito, high in the Custerdome?) Marlowe smokes too much and is always drunk. Superman, Batman and the Shadow feel the dry rot in their joints. Ace reporters and cub copyboys uncover no scoops; all the underworld gangsters are too enervated to hatch any schemes. The conical hats of Cheech and Chong wizards droop impotently. Dragons try to ignite, but only burp and taste bile. Entropy is all that flourishes here....

# The Heads And Tails Trip

# K L U E S

00011100
"Doctor Sax was bellowing in fury, 'And now you will
know that the Great Snake of the World lies coiled beneath
this Castle and beneath Snake Hill, site of my birth, a
hundred miles long in enormous convolution reaching down
into the very bowels and grave of the earth, and for all the
ages of man has been inching, inching, inch an hour, up, up, to
the sun, from the unspeakable central dark depths to which he
had originally been hurled—now returning and now only five
or four minutes from breaking the crust of the earth once
more and emerging in the breaking boil of evil, full flaming
fury of the dragon....'"
—Jack Kerouac

00011101
"Nature is the ultimate underground chemist."
—Anonymous

00011110
"America is a combination of voodoo and bad politics."
—Mojo Nixon

00011111
"Whether exaggerated suspicions are paranoiac or true to
reality, a faint private echo of the turmoil of history, can
therefore only be decided retrospectively."
—Theodor Adorno

H oe-kay, kids, time to split the screen! Open up a new window in our Screwy
Gooey!

We're gonna make the big jump to two tracks now. I'll sound just like one
of those famous harmonizing duos: Simon and Garfunkel, Zager and Evans, Gaye
and Terrell, Brewer and Shipley, Peter and Gordon, Chad and Jeremy, Jan and Dean,
the Everly Brothers, Aztec Two Step, Seals and Crofts, Loggins and Messina, Hall and
Oates, Milli and Vanilli, Tuck and Patti, Mickey and Sylvia, the Indigo Girls, Pink
Lady, the Righteous Brothers, Sam and Dave, Ashford and Simpson, Peaches and
Herb, Sonny and Cher, Ike and Tina, Donny and Marie. Only I'll do it all myself, like
Sinatra in the studio, everyone else phoning their half of the duet in, just me and my
shadow, my non-existent twin, strolling down the Avenue of Time.

So set your mixers on stun, slip into some boss gear, don a pair of fab shades,
and journey with me now back to the year when monaural finally died, the year the
whole world almost went Gnostic, the year chemical satori opened a hell of a lotta
Third Eyes.

Trust me: Mister Pusherman.

No bummers.

You'll have a groovy trip.

## Track 0

On April 16, 1943—Shakespeare's birthday—Doctor Albert Hoffman, chemist
at the Swiss firm of Sandoz, accidentally absorbed thru his skin some lysergic acid
diethylamide, a substance he had synthesized five years earlier, and took humanity's
first LSD trip, thereby beating NASA and its Apollo moon landing by a quarter of a
century for the honors of farthest distance yet traveled by man.

(And does Cyril knows that in 1993 the world's had FIFTY YEARS OF SUNSHINE?)

## Track 1

Emmett "Eminent" Demesne had the ineluctable misfortune to be born spin-
dly and puny into a family and community as weird and unforgiving as a flock
of harpies.

The odd circumstances of his birth determined all he was to become.

Genes and History—

Set and Setting—

Nature and Nurture—

They'll get ya every time!

Going up the country, where the blue verbena grows.... Misty Mountain Hop!

Picture a forgotten village high in the Smoky Mountains of western North
Carolina, close to the Tennessee line, not far from Asheville (Thomas Wolfe's
home town, natch) and Black Mountain, perhaps near the hamlet of Scaly. Name

of the place don't matter. Just a collection of shotgun shacks scattered up and down the hollers. A place Old Moster forgot after he created the world. General store selling feed and grain, lazy houn' dogs snoring on splintery porches (ain't none of 'em never caught a rabbit yet), feeble-minded wuthless citizens shambling aimlessly among their pitiful crops, everyone living Close To The Bone, hardly ever bestirring themselves out of their sloth, except when it came time to attend church—

—each night.

EACH NIGHT?

Yup.

That structure that looked like a barn that'd been repeatedly hit by lightning, and which ain't seen a lick of paint since it was built, just a funky old shack set way back in the middle of a field, with its tin roof rusted—that place packed 'em in like the Asheville Odeon *every single night?*

You betcha asp it does, boy.

One mild mid-April night in 1943, the infant Emmett Demesne entered our world, this vale of tears, popping out of the everywhere and into the here.

Delilah Demesne—D.D.—lay on a corn-shuck mattress on the sand-scrubbed pine-board floor, straining and groaning with the effort of this birth, her first. An inquisitive breeze fluttered the ragged cotton curtains on the screenless windows. A yellowed calender from the seed company of DEMETER AND ZUSE, displaying April of the year 1928, hung on the wall. Outside, a whippoorwill called mournfully, answered by an owl.

Deedee Demesne's pain-contorted features were an intriguing multiracial mix, as were those of the whole inbred village, reflecting a secret history of which even the villagers themselves were only half-aware....

In the year 1561 (just as Sir John Hawkins was landing in Dahomey), a small party set out from the Yucatan, heading north. This intrepid band of travelers consisted of an entire Mayan clan, led by the legendary Tupac Shakur. The clan, a marginal one that existed on the fringes of Mayan society, traced its ancestry back to intermarriage between Chinese New World colonists (abandoned by the Celestial Empire during the upheavals of the Five Dynasties period) and members of the priesthood of Kukulcan.

Fleeing the Spaniards, they journeyed north, following the coastline of the Gulf. After many travails and much loss of life, they reached the mouth of the Mississippi. There, they fashioned boats and took to the water, paddling upstream. Round about what would one day become Memphis, home to Elvis and the ancient Greeks, after almost two years of wandering, they were attacked by Indians who worshiped Tawiscara, the evil twin of Ioskeha, both of whom were grandsons of the Moon. The ambush forced the immigrants to flee east, into the wilderness. Entering the Smokies, familiar Chichen Itza vistas, they felt safe at last.

Welcomed by the Cawtawba tribe, the Sino-Mayans settled down and proceeded to mingle their genes with those of the Indians. Roughly twenty-five years later, a Cawtawban-Mayan fishing-and-wampum-collecting party to the coast stumbled upon the English colony at Roanoke. Having a tuff time of it, the English settlers were convinced to ally themselves with the natives, and relocated lock, stock and hogshead to the interior, first making sure to leave behind a red herring pointing to Croatan.

There, in the Smokies, liddle Virginia Dare, first white girl born in the Americas, married handsome Chac Apaec, first male born to the conjoined North and South Cathay-Indians, thereby founding the line that culminated this moment in laboring Deedee Demesne....

Kneeling beside Deedee with phlegmatic concern was her overalled husband, Orvall (AKA "O.D."). The lambent light cast by a flickering kerosene lamp covered them as with a golden blanket.

"Keep bearing down, Deedee, it's a comin'."

"YEEEOOOOOW-OOOOOO!"

"Whoa, good enough, Deedee, you squirted him out slicker'n a watermelon seed—which he ain't much bigger'n. Lord, I seen ticks that weigh more'n this pitiful runt."

"Suh-sorry, Odie, I tried my best."

"Thass awright, Deedee, no matter his size, he's still another soul for the Church...."

"I—I'd sorta like to name him after my father, Odie—if'n it's okay with you."

"Emmett? Don't see why not. It's all the same in the Trickster's eyes."

Thus was young Demesne, all unknowing, immediately consecrated to both the past—symbolized by Deedee's Dad—and the future—symbolized by the church's eternal concerns with the afterlife.

### Track 0

In the year 1947, Doctor Werner Stoll of Sandoz published the first paper on the effects of LSD in the *Swiss Archives of Neurology*. (Note: the Swiss broadcast LSD and received money in the form of drug-profit deposits back; a clearer case of serpentine tail-in-mouth would be hard to find.)

### Track 1

A harmless garter-snake was placed in three-year-old Demense's crib. He began to wail and kick. Odie slapped him mercilessly across the face until he stopped. Demense retreated to a far corner of the crib, cringing from the serpent.

Deedee was crying also.

"Am I gonna have to whup you too, woman?"

"Oh, no, you done right, Odie. I'm a-cryin' at the thought of our son disgracin' us when it comes time to bring'm to services."

Track 0

Doctor Robert Hyde of the Boston Psychopathic Institute, an affiliate of Harvard University, took the first trip in the Western hemisphere, in 1949. In the next year, he and his colleagues would administer exactly one hundred doses of acid to volunteers, making Boston the ground zero of the American psychedelic revolution.

Track 1

The responsibility of representing both the past and the future seemed to weigh heavily almost from the start on young Demesne. After that early chastisement, he cried seldom, managing somehow to project an air of wordless, persecuted solemnity. Folks deemed it uncanny. Granpa Emmett, coming to view his namesake, pronounced his verdict: "Acts jest like a little judge. Eminent, sorta."

The nickname stuck. No one ever called the boy Emmett, but just "Em," which in their minds stood mostly for "Eminent." As a toddler, it was always, "Walk to Momma, Em." The skinny naked youngster, little pee-pee and little toes, staying up late to be with his parents after the nightly ceremonies, would comply with a comic air of utmost majesty, as if trying to live up to some vast responsibility. When he was a little older, it was, "Slop them hogs good now, Em." Carrying a pail nearly bigger than himself as if it were a pillow bearing jewels, the boy would proceed to fill the hogs' trough like a butler dispensing caviar.

When he was six, Demesne fell sick. Made particularly susceptible by overwork, he caught one of the most dreaded Scourges of this primitive decade in the middle of the twentieth century.

The disease was polio.

We're talkin' one hell of a mean virus here, folks, in case you've forgotten. Still runs rampant in Africa, where the hapless victims crawl thru the dust and are called "serpent children" for their legless method of peregrination. Gets right in the Central Nervous System, heading straight for the spinal cord, where it inflames and destroys, resulting in paralysis. (Awful what a little piece of naked DNA, hardly more than few tens of thousands of nucleotides long, just some basic Raw Information, can do, ain't it...?)

As it turned out, Demesne got off lucky. Just a little withering of his right leg, leaving him with a pronounced limp to add to his scrawniness. The whole incident served mainly to increase the boy's insular dignity. After recovering from his feverish months in bed, he exhibited an accentuated attitude of wary stiffness, going about his duties with a gimpy haughtiness, frequently casting a rearward look over his lowered right shoulder, as if hoping to surprise the malevolent Destiny that dogged him.

This air of seeming superiority didn't sit too well with Demesne's peers, who ridiculed him mercilessly. He was beaten, tricked, and humiliated. No one would pick him for their side during a game of *pok-a-tok*. But he was a rock, he was an

island, and a rock feels no pain.
Till he met that one girl who could love him like a rock.

## Track 0

General "Wild Bill" Donovan, head of the Office of Strategic Services, wartime predecessor to the CIA, initiated in 1942 a search for drugs which would serve as incapacitants and/or truth serums. Mescaline, marijuana, goofballs, and dozens of others were tried. Tips were taken from studies conducted by Nazi doctors at Dachau, and Third Reich surveys done on captured partisans by *Ubergrupführer* L. Wurms. By August of 1951, these inquiries and field experiments were being conducted under the name Operation ARTICHOKE. LSD was a mere curiosity to ARTICHOKE, not fully understood. The CIA cast its nets further afield; for a time, an extract from something called the "Caribbean Information Bush" was hot. Yahso! Good ol'-fashioned heroin smuggled by CIA-backed organizations from the Golden Triangle was frequently used. Then, on April 16, 1953, CIA Director Allen Dulles authorized Operation MK-ULTRA, whose main thrust would be toward refining the use of LSD for intelligence purposes.

(Quite a few of these acid shennanigans were helpfully co-sponsored by McGill University in Canada, where in 1949 neurologist Donald Hebb wrote his seminal *The Organization of Behavior.*)

## Track 1

When he could get away from chores and elude any of his peers bent on tormenting him, Demesne liked to wander along the bosky banks of Cripple Creek, the rock-studded, trout-leaping, waterdoodle-spotted stream that meandered along the outskirts of the village. By the purling waters, cripple limping along namesake stream, he could forget for a time all his troubles. Or most of 'em anyway. There was one big 'un that continually nagged at him.

Demesene passed a yellow-bellied blacksnake sunning itself on a rock; it calmly waited for the stranger to go.

Demesne shivered, and moved on. *King of the mountain, mountain in the shadow of life. You can say you're Peter, you can say you're Paul, but don't hang me up on your bedroom wall....*

Next year he would turn eleven, the age when children were formally inducted into the church. There was no way he could avoid it. But he would rather die than go to church. Weh-hell, screw it! A year was a long time. Maybe something would happen before then. He wasn't going to let fear spoil his day.

So the poor young country boy, Mother Nature's son, went barefootin' along, heading for his favorite spot, a small secluded clearing on a bluff above the creek.

When he pushed through the shrubbery surrounding the site, Demesne stopped dead in his tracks. There was a naked gal in his secret spot, sunnin' herself just like the snake he had passed.

It was Vivian Vervain.

The Vervains lived next door to the Demesnes: Hamilcar, Hanna and Vivian. Demesne knew the daughter as a headstrong, quick-witted girl, impetuous and lively. She had never paid him no mind, and he had barely said two words to her all his life, awed by her clear superiority.

And now here he was, gazing on her as she sprawled buck-naked!

Vervain, some three years older than Demesne, looked a ripe eighteen. She was built like the mythical brick shithouse, Daisy-May curves from head to toe. A direct descendent of Dare and Apaec, Vervain possessed the startling combination of wavy honey-blonde hair, cinnamon skin and slightly Oriental eyes. (All the best cowgirls have Chinese eyes.)

Spotting Demesne, Vervain sat up. She made no move to cover her considerable charms.

"Howdy, Em. Whatcha doin' out this-a-ways?"

Demesne was absolutely tongue-tied. "Juh-juh-just wuh-wuh-walkin'...."

"Well, come 'n' sit a spell with me."

Demesne did as he was bidden.

Vervain began to chatter about life in the village, inconsequential gossip. Her nudity, originally so startling, seemed more and more natural. Gradually, Demesne began to relax. No one had ever treated him like this, as if he were a real person. He began to participate in the conversation. Eventually, he found himself spilling his guts.

"Aw, shucks," reassured Vervain, "you shouldn't worry so, Em. Papa Kukulcan ain't got nothin' but your spiritual welfare in mind."

"Mebbe so. But what about the ee-niche-ee-ay-shun ceremony? I heard it's plumb painful."

Vervain giggled. "I don't know what they do for boys, but the girls' ceremony warn't so bad. It hurt at first, but felt right pleasant after. Here, let me show you."

She yanked at the twine belt securing Demesne's ragged shorts and slipped its knot. Then, before he could react, though he was still seated, she pulled his pants off like a magician whisking a tablecloth out from under ten full place settings.

"Hey—" said Demesne weakly.

Vervain was kneeling in front of him. "First a gal's got to kiss the snake," she said, lowering her head into his lap. Her abundant sun-dappled hair concealed what she was doing.

But whoo-whee, Demesne sure could tell by touch!

His liddle boner manifested itself in her mouth. Vervain was cupping his balls with one hand. The other was busy between her own legs. Just when he thought the pleasure had reached an unendurable level, Vervain lifted her mouth off and clambered atop him.

"Then the snake goes in here—"

Vervain was bucking like a locoweed-maddened she-goat atop him. Demesne couldn't believe how good it felt. Something that had been knotted in his abdomen all his life began to uncoil and spread. Kundalini energy flowed like floodwaters. *She's givin' me excitations, she's givin' me good vibrations!*

At last Demesne came, spraying the holy nectar *amrita* up Vervain's exquisite slit.

She rose and fell twice after his ejaculation, shuddered, yelled and stopped. *Up on Cripple Creek she sends me, up on Cripple Creek she mends me!*

*Down on the riverbed, I asked my lover for her hand—and got her bush instead!* (While a red-tailed hawk circled overhead.)

For the next year Vervain and Demesne talked and fucked every chance they got. She was his best and only friend.

Until everything fell apart.

## Track 0

CIA LSD experiments continued under the auspices of the Technical Services Staff. The TSS believed in immunizing all its agents against possible outside infection by Russian LSD, and so began a series of impromptu acid tests, spiking the drinks of their own unsuspecting spooks. Gearing up for extensive further experimentation, the Agency convinced the Eli Lilly company to begin manufacturing LSD. By the middle of 1954, Lilly had succeeded in decrypting the secret Sandoz formula, and production began.

## Track 1

Two men held Demesne down by the shoulders. His head was spinning from the potent kickapoo juice he had been forced to drink. *Red, red wine goes to my head, makes me forget I still need you, Vivian....*

He was naked below the waist.

A figure appeared in his field of vision. He had a flashback to the day he had lost his virginity. But this was not the pleasant apparition Vervain had been.

It was his own Granpa. His face and bare breast were painted in whorls and paisleys, sunbursts and snakes. He wore a tall head-dress of chicken feathers and a necklace of beaten copper plates. He carried a genuine ceremonial Shonen Knife.

"Holy Kukulcan, Giver of Breath and God of Winds, masked under so many diff'rent names, Damballah 'n' Quetzalcoatl, Leviathan 'n' Ananta, you who sprinkle the earth with your fructifyin' blood, accept now this pitiful soul unto your graces, make him your own horse, as he offers up a sacrifice of his mis'rable flesh, and bares forever the head of his own personal snake."

Granpa pinched Demesne's foreskin and begin to cut.

## Track 0

Doctor Sidney Gottlieb, Chief of the TSS, having learned all he could from intra-Agency trials, decided to expand LSD testing to unsuspecting American citizens.

## Track 1

Demesne's wound refused to heal. It pained him night and day. Vervain came by to see him. In his delirium, he told his parents to send her away. On the fourth day, however, she barged in regardless.

"Lemme look at thet sad ol' snake, you stubborn cuss." Vervain pulled the blanket off him and removed the bandages. "Jest as I thought. Them idjits musta not even boiled the knife like I tole 'em to. You wait right here, boy."

No problem....

Shortly, Vervain returned.

"I fixed you up a simple, outa the blue verbena. It's good for snake-bites and bit snakes. Just put it on twice a day, and you'll be fine."

"Thanks, Vi," whispered Demesne.

She kissed his hot brow.

"Don't you worry, Em. We'll be humpin' again right soon."

But this paradisiacal promise was not to be fulfilled.

Although Vervain's poultice stemmed the infection and allowed the natural healing process to commence, Demesne suffered tremendous scarification. Pissing hurt. Sex, attempted once, revealed itself to be out of the question, ecstasy transmuted into agony.

Vervain wept. Demesne too, for the first time since he was three.

"Em, what the elders done to you has decided me. I been chafin' here anyway in this hick burg. This place ain't big enough for what I feel inside me. I'm after wisdom, and all the Church's got is in-for-may-shun. I'm ready for takin' it to the streets."

"But, Vi—we're just two kids."

"It don't matter none. We can do anything we want, if'n we believe in it. Wotta we got here? Nothin'! Children, behave, that's what they say when we're together. An' watch how you play! They don't unnerstan! So we got to run as fast as we can, holdin' on to one another's hand! And freedom's just another word for nothin' left to lose."

"I jest don't know— What about the Church?"

"The Church has done taught me everything it can. I need some room to move."

"But—"

"My mind's made up, Em. I'm fixin' to leave, with or without you. I feel free, and freedom tastes of reality."

"Lemme think on it a little."

"Don't take too long," warned Vi.

But he did.

## Track 0

Doctor Gottlieb (a whole buncha doctors in this mess, ain't there?) enlisted the help of George Hunter White, an old spy. In 1955, White opened up a CIA-funded brothel in San Francisco. Thus began Operation MIDNIGHT CLIMAX: johns were dosed with acid, while White watched their reactions, sexual and otherwise, from behind a one-way mirror.

Deciding to film these trials, White recruited a blacklisted Hollywood director, Eric Engst. Engst soon became smitten with one prostitute, a young country girl. After a year's duty in the cathouse, the girl and Engst, having consumed approximately a hundred hits of acid apiece, split together.

## Track 1

Vivian Vervain had been gone a year now. The memory of her hardly hurt at-tall. Or so Demesne tried telling himself. It wasn't even the sex he missed so much: after all, his chawed-up pecker prevented that. No, it was the companionship. I'm not waitin' on a lady, I'm just waitin' on a friend.... What can make me feel this way? My girl....

His life had reverted to its lonely circumscribed routines. It was a familiar prospect, and he could have lived with it indefinitely. Except for one thing.

Church.

A hot August evening, crickets, beetles, katydids and other buggles making a racket in the woods. A quarter-moon rose above the pinetops like a Cheshire-cat grin.

It was time for the nightly gathering of the congregation of the First Therapeutic Antebaptist Prelapsarian Feathered Serpent Joyful-Noise-Unto-The-Lord Church. (Missionary work in the early twentieth century by Reverends Penniman, Burke and Greene had added the final layer to the village's syncretic beliefs.)

From all corners of the settlement drifted adults with their older children in tow, moving softly through the summer dusk, down streets of clay and dust.

Undersized twelve-year old Demesne limped along behind Odie and Deedee, whom the years had not softened. Man, he hated this scene. If only he didn't have to attend. Impossible, though, to live here and not belong to the First Therapuetic Etcetera Church. He regretted now the timidity that had kept him from following Vervain. Could he possibly catch up with her? How? He had no idea where she had gone. And the world beyond these mountains was completely unknown to Demesne. He wasn't sure if it even existed, or if beyond the farthest slope he'd wind up falling down the mountain and over the edge of the world....

Up the three rickety steps, across the warped boards of the porch that resounded to the tramp of leather soles, and into the cavernous, flame-lit interior.

There was no altar in this church, no crucifix, stations of the cross, pews or statues. Place was barer'n a widow's cupboard. Only furnishings were a few wooden folding chairs, and an old Victrola with flared horn. But the postulants of the FTAPFSJNUTL Church needed no such trappings, anymore'n they needed a minister or preacher. This was a charismatic church, ya see, given over to direct contact with The Holy Spirit, or Paraclete.

What was religion, after all, but a channel to the Divine, a pipeline for Heavenly

Information? What good did it do a man to put all those filters between himself and the Numinous? No sirree, you wouldn't find such decadent hindrances here. Just a buncha incarnate souls opening up the gates of perception and inviting the Big White Scaly Dove to fly in, a buncha horses for the *loas*.

Demesne took a seat to rest his sore leg. He watched his elders prepare the Sacrament. They poured it from big jugs into screw-top Ball jars. Despite all he had been told, it still looked like fruit-flavored corn likker to him.

Someone cranked the Victrola and put on the Church's one record: "The Viper's Drag," by Fats Waller.

Into the building now came Granpa Emmett, carrying the final prerequisites for the ceremony: two big gunny sacks that bulged ominously. As Demesne watched, fixated with his usual horror, the contents of the sacks wriggled furiously.

The bags were dropped in a corner, writhing.

Jars passed from hand to hand, among even the youngest children. When one reached Demesne, he only pretended to drink.

Pretty soon, the Spirit responded to the first petitioners.

An old woman fell to the floor, flopping about like a fish and speaking in tongues. (Who's got the Holy Key to this Cipher, f-f-folks? What Sacred Prime will reveal God's Plaintext?) After her, others quickly succumbed.

Some soon reached a stage where they regained control of their limbs but, with eyes showing only whites, still seemed zombified, still hooked into some Supernal Circuit, listening to Distant Orders. Ride your horse, Papa Kukulkan!

(*This is only the White Man's Vodun, Claude,* said Mel, thirty-five years later, as they watched a private screening of a similar ritual. *Nothing your average Afro-Kampuchean don't already know....*)

Demesne's father now exhibited the spooky signs of this paranormal state. He approached his son, who still sat miserable and shivering.

"The spirit ain't descended on you yet," said Odie sepulchrally.

"Nossir."

"You ain't hardly trying, though. In fact, you're puttin' up barriers to The Spirit In The Sky, ain't you? You'll never be one of the community, iffen you keep on like this."

Demesne attempted uselessly to explain. "I hate— I can't lose control."

"You gotta, boy. You gotta lose your mind to find it."

"I can't!"

Odie turned away from his son then in disgust, toward where people were rummaging in the sacks. He moved to share what they were disbursing.

Well, what else?

Snakes. Snakes of every sort. King, ribbon, pilot, hog-nosed, worm, rat, coachwhip, milk, bull, and water. Not to mention copperheads and moccasins. There were even baby snakes, or snakelets. (And, astonishingly, one hoop snake, that species which, tail in mouth, rolls down hills to achieve a certain velocity, whereupon, releasing their bite, they fly thru the air like an arrow toward their prey. Hoop snakes that miss their target can be found embedded in trees.) These, you see, were the necessary adjuncts to the services, the element that most floated Demesne's gorge up into his throat.

Following the words of Jesus (Mark 16:18—the same gospel where John is beheaded and the two fish are miraculously multiplied) which assured that the elect could handle serpents, the Therapeutics culminated each mass with aggravated assault upon a buncha helpless reptiles rounded up that day.

This was one freaky scene. Men and women both were kissing snakes and actually mouthing their flat scaly heads in some kinda mock-fellatio. Snakes were slippin' down shirt-sleeves and up dresses, getting Lord-knows-where. People were faintin' in holy ecstasy, as they was vouchsafed signs of their salvation and entry to the hyperworld. So far, no one had been bitten. But Demesne knew the possibility of a venomous attack was there. Past masses had infrequently culminated in a fatal attack or two.

While he was watching with horrified resignation as his own mother inserted a serpent down her flour-sack panties, his father snuck up on him and draped one around his neck.

"Yah!"

Demesne shot to his feet, dislodging the snake, and ran from the church.

Crouching outside in some bushes, he knew he'd have hell to pay tomorrow. A tear fell.... Don't let the Sun catch you cryin', boy!

What a canin' he would be in for, come dawn.

But, folks—

Sometimes, TOMORROW NEVER KNOWS.

The night filled suddenly with the sound of whirring blades. Spotlights lanced down from above. Young Demesne looked up, but was blinded. Thus he failed to see the insignia of the United States Treasury Department stenciled on the bellies of the descending helicopters.

It was the legendary squad of special Treasury agents, members of the division known as the Bureau of Narcotics and Dangerous Drugs, led by Colonel (Retired) Homer "Homo" Faber, and his notorious catamite and AIDS-de-camp, Private Duncan Idaho. Charged with capturing all malefactors who tried to deprive the government of any portion of its legal revenues, affiliated with Hoover's FBI, the CIA, the NSA, the SEC, AFT (Hello, Koresh and fellow Davidians!) and the IRS, Colonel (Retired) Faber and his men had been staking out the Therapeutics for several months now, waiting for just the right moment to make their move. Concerned primarily with the heretical evasion of distillery taxes, the Treasury agents were also—as a favor to the FCC— intent on busting the Therapeutics for Illicit Interception Of Heavenly Signals.

The choppers landed in the field surrounding the church and disgorged dozens of submachine-gun-armed and sunglass-wearing agents.

Before the God-besotted Muswell Hillbillies knew what the Christ had hit them, every last one—save for liddle Demesne—were all manacled, shackled, hog-tied, trussed, trammelled, chained, handcuffed, gagged, and found themselves being heaved like sacks of grain into waiting paddy-wagons, which had arrived with synchronized precision, having travelled over rutted mountain roads for the past twelve hours. The infants and toddlers left at home were shortly corralled and added to the catch.

Once the Black Marias were loaded, they roared off, carrying the entire population of the village to a mass trial and long jail sentences. (After being convicted on all charges up to and including High Treason, the entire village was incarcerated in the Addiction Research Center at Lexington, Kentucky, run by Doctor Harris Isbell, where, after much fruitless probing for a hypothetical "Holy Gland," they were all finally lobotomized.)

The nameless village, quick as that, was expunged from the face of the earth. We put the past on Fuji and erase it totally.... No more would its streets resound to the tramp of loamy shit-kickers, nor its church witness the orgy of snakely adoration....

Meanwhile the agents clambered back into their Hueys, which flew off after scattering several tons of salt. Colonel (Retired) Faber was left standing alone, his personal chopper idling under the tender care of Private Idaho, surveying his handiwork. He braced his legs wide apart, lit a post-arrest cigar, ran one hand over his buzzcut, folded his arms across his chest, and puffed contentedly.

Demesne watched all this in shock. Naturally, he was devastated. His entire universe had been shattered in the space of a few seconds. Much as he had disliked his parents and the other villagers, they were his kin. All he could think to do now was to remain in hiding until this last flatlander flew off.

When Faber said, "All right, boy, you can come out now," Demesne nearly fainted. His legs seemed subject to Faber's commands, for they carried him out to the waiting G-man.

"Why weren't you in there with the rest of them, boy?"

"I—I don't believe in that crazy stuff, sir."

"Don't underestimate them, bunky. They weren't fools. No, they were dangerous enough, messin' with the Divine like that. Potentially more deadly than H-bombs. Anyone who tries to let Sophia loose in this world deserves to get zapped like the Rosenbergs."

Demesne nodded, although he didn't know what an H-bomb was, nor who the Rosenbergs were.

Faber released a cloud of nasty smoke. "So, what are your plans now, son?"

"I—I don't rightly know, sir...."

"Think you're man enough to join us in our fight against tax evaders and information-leggers?"

It was as if a clear white light—the Sun of the Hyperworld that all his kin save him had always had access to—suddenly filled every interstice of his being. This was the invite he had been waiting for all his life, a chance to revenge himself on those who had tormented him, if not the exact souls, then others just like them.

"I'd like nothing more, sir."

"Climb aboard, then—Junior G-man," growled Faber the Conquistador gruffly. As Demesne boarded the copter, Private Idaho goosed him.

Thus ended the Night They Drove Old Dixie Down.

One thing was sure.

Demesne wouldn't be workin' on Maggie's Farm no more!

## Track 0

Captain Al Hubbard, former OSS man, former Treasury Agent during the glory years of Capone, now loose cannon and rogue agent, obtained LSD from his CIA contacts and, after his own lysergic conversion, immediately became an acid proselytizer. Soon known as "Captain Trips," he traveled around the globe, spreading what he referred to as "wampum" from his diplomatic pouch. In 1955, he turned on Aldous Huxley.

## Track 1

Weh-hell.... Before you could say "Up, up, and away!" Demesne found himself in the capital of the nation he hardly, till then, knew he was a part of. From Deedee to DeeCee was a short physical journey but an immense mental one. Demesne's head was left spinning.

(Later, at a time when his paranoia—or, as some would call it, COMMON SENSE— was measured in mega-Hoovers, he would wonder if this whole setup, from wiping out his entire community, to the handy father-substitution Faber offered, to the disorientingly speedy trip, hadn't been very carefully planned—or at least brilliantly improvised—in order to gain his absolute allegiance to a set of principles and goals which he might have been otherwise inclined to initially question. ((But how can I be sure, with such rascals?)) Whether deliberate or fortuitous, the scheme worked—for a time at least—inculcating in young Demesne an unswerving dedication to all that the Treasury Department stood for.)

Before dawn of the day after the raid, Demesne was brought inside the classi cally columned building at 15th Street and Pennsylvania Avenue. There, he was conducted to a dormitory in the basement.

He would spend the next six years of his life here, along with the rest of his classmates.

## Track 0

Henry and Clare Booth Luce both turned on frequently during this period. In May, 1957, *Life* ran an article on the wonders of "Magic Mushrooms."

## Track 1

Anticipating the need for young undercover agents which the growing wave of Immoral Beatnik Laxness and Mixed Breeding Music was causing, The Treasury

Bureau had begun several Operations. One of these was to recruit orphans directly into the Bureau at a tender age, molding them into perfect agents. After years of training in various weapons, disinformation, espionage, and disguise techniques, the co-opted orphans were to be sent into Rock 'n' Roll High Schools identified as trouble-spots, there to function as Junior Narcs. (Cue the Clash here, in a few anachronistic chords of "Julie's Been Workin' for the Drug Squad.")

Such was the plan—inspired brainchild of Colonel (Retired) Faber and labelled Operation FAGIN.

Such was what did occur.

Young Demesne underwent a grueling course of training that left him a finely honed tool of the Treasury Department, akin to a dope-sniffin' German Shepherd. He was subtly led to associate dope-fiends with the despised cult of the snake-handlers he had been reared in. (After all, both groups first got stoned and then indulged in all kinda bizarre Metaphysical and Karnal Hijinx....) He was transformed into a single-minded drug-huntin' machine, whose congenital seriousness was accentuated to an unnatural pitch.

## Track 0

1959: Allen Ginsberg took his first LSD trip, seeking to recreate his mystical Blakean vision of 1948.

1960: Ginsberg, Peter Orlovsky and Timothy Leary tripped on psilocybin in Newton, Massachusetts, not far from where the Condor household would one day be.

That same year the Narcotics Manufacturing Act was passed, amping the heavy law-enforcement-type responsibilities already assigned to the Treasury Department, namely its branch known as the Bureau of Narcotics and Dangerous Drugs. (Someone somewhere who had a reason not to want to EXPAND THE CHANNEL or REVERSE THE FLOW, and was perhaps extrapolating from ominous Hipster Jive, perhaps interpreting the subterranean messages coded into the burgeoning rock 'n' roll, perhaps experiencing a straight Stochastic Shot, was gearing up for the threatening popularity of the Industrial-Strength drugs that were coming down the pipeline, most of which had been developed under CIA supervision.)

Also in 1960, Ginsberg ingested the Aztec sacrament, *yagé*, and hallucinated himself covered with snakes, "Myself a snake vomiting out the Universe."

## Track 1

Faber and seventeen-year-old Demesne were sparring without gloves in the Treasury gym.

"Wiped—oof!—that rube—gotcha!—accent out yet?"

"Yes—ouch!—sir!—hrrnng!"

"Fine. Put your dukes down."

Demesne complied. Faber socked him in the breadbasket and the boy folded around the Colonel's (Ret.) fist.

"Well, in that case, as soon as you learn not to trust anyone, you'll be ready for your first assignment."

## Track 0

The pace of events began to accelerate.

1962: Timothy Leary—wild Irishman—dismissed from Harvard for turning his students on. His colleague, Richard Alpert, soon similarly ejected. LSD named by act of Congress an experimental drug without beneficial effects, and access to it limited.

1964: Millionaire William Hitchcock loaned his Millbrook estate to Leary and friends.

1965: LSD outlawed by Congress. Ken Kesey and the Merry Pranksters on their cross-country goof and, later, the San Francisco Acid Tests. Augustus Owsley Stanley produced the first of his approximately four million hits of acid.

After many, many trips, Leary released his major scientific finding: "God does exist; and the language of God is the DNA code."

## Track 1

Private Idaho said, "All right, Cadet Demesne, up off your knees."

Demesne dragged a hand across his sticky face. He was angry, sure, but he never lost his head, even when he was *giving* head. Memories of Vervain going down on him taunted him. His scarred cock throbbed and hurt, but there was no solace for it in this world.

## Track 0

1967: The Millbrook commune forced to disband, in the wake of a raid by G. Gordon Liddy.

## Track 1

It was the January of Love.

Demesne had been an agent for six years. He was twenty-four. His small stature allowed him to impersonate students as young as fourteen, although his somber manner somewhat detracted from the impersonation. Usually, though, the unsuspecting students just classed him as geek. He had assisted in approximately one hundred busts so far in his brief career.

Now he stood in the office of his mentor, Faber.

The office was decorated with a portrait-gallery of Faber's heroes: George Hunter White, J. Edgar Hoover, Tertullian, Cortez the Killer, Pisarro and Saint Augustine.

The crew-cut Colonel (Ret.) sized up his protegé approvingly for a few seconds before speaking, chomping on his cigar.

"Did you ever wonder, Demesne," queried Faber without warning, "why the Narcotics Bureau falls under the command of the Treasury Department? After all, the Department's nominal task is to oversee the printing and distribution of currency, and the collection of taxes. Sure, it makes sense for the IRS to be a branch of the Treasury—but the Bureau of Narcotics? Why is that, do you think?"

(The IRS, by the way, divides the US into eight—or two cubed—administrative regions. Why not seven or nine?)

After a day of arduous training, Demesne's crippled leg was paining him, but he tried to ignore it. He wished Faber would ask him to sit. None of this, of course, showed on his face.

"I have no idea, sir," Demesne replied honestly. "I've never given it much thought."

Faber puffed his stogie in a contemplative fashion before uttering his Delphic response: "Em."

At first Demesne thought Faber was calling him by his nickname. But that couldn't be. It must mean something else. Best to play dumb.

"I beg your pardon, sir...?"

"Clean your ears out, boy! You haven't forgotten your economics courses already, have you? I'm talking about M, the money supply."

Demesne remembered then. "Of course, sir. Em One, Em Two, Em Three...."

"That's more like it. But you've forgotten one."

"I have?"

Faber smiled knowingly around the cigar. "Em One: the value of all coins, currency and checking accounts. Em Two: Em One plus savings. Em Three: Em Two plus negotiable certificates. Em Four...."

"Begging your pardon, sir. There is no Em Four."

"That's where you're dead wrong, boy. There is a measure known as Em Four."

Demesne racked his brains. "Obviously, it must be Em Three plus something else.... Not—not drugs?"

Faber nodded smugly. "That's it, boy. Drugs. The one vital commodity most like money: easy to handle, comes in various denominations, universally accepted. Just as money flows in the veins of businesses, so do drugs flow in the veins of our citizens. They're the backbone of civilization as we know it. ('Scuse the mixed metaphor, Demesne.) Despite the official line we hand to the public, our society couldn't function without drugs. Just take nicotine, caffeine, alcohol and aspirins, for instance. Drugs are a necessity. Where would our goddamn security apparatus be without drugs?!

"But just like money, they have to be regulated. You can't just print up all the dollars you want, or they become worthless. Same goes for narcotics. It's our job to see that the value of Em Four stays within acceptable bounds, as dictated by those functionaries above us, mostly the folks at the Federal Reserve.

"And an enormous and thankless task it is, son, as you doubtless do not need to be told. Laying our hides on the line, just to implement Gresham's Law as it applies to dope: interdicting the bad before it can drive out the good. And of course we don't even get to indulge ourselves with the dope, as do those we protect, since we have to keep our minds and senses clear for the task at hand. At least, we can't indulge as much as we might like, hey, boy?"

Here Faber winked broadly.

Demesne did not know quite how to respond. Once more his apparently solid world was being inverted, all he had come to take as given being subtly twisted. And his leg— He felt like fainting—

"And the information load," Faber continued, "is just enormous. The only way we can get a handle on Em Four and stay on top of it is to record and analyze all drug production and subsequent buy-sell transactions. Thank Christ for this new generation of computers! That line of Wu Ten-ten's we just contracted for is going to make our life a lot easier. We'll be able to calculate Em Four right down to umpteen decimal places now...."

Demesne lost the last few words. His physical and mental endurance both ran out, and he crumpled in a semi-conscious heap to the carpet. Face pressed into the shag, he heard Faber rise and move to stand above him. There was the sound of a belt unclasping. He felt his own pants jerked off. Vivian....

Faber mounted him then and began to bugger him, still lecturing.

"You're a good agent, Demesne, but you need to learn more control. Self-control, and control from above. Always seek the upper hand, unless the upper hand is already holding a gun. In that case, submit. Until the hand's back is turned, when you can stab it. Uhnh!"

Faber came and dismounted quickly, with military precision.

Demesne lay where he was, wondering only what was next.

Faber obliged his protegé's curiosity. "New assignment for you, son, soon as you gather your wits. You're to take on a deep cover and penetrate the Haight."

Still reeling, Demesne interpreted the place-name as "Hate."

Poor little guy didn't know it was almost the Summer of Love.

"But first," said Faber, "I want to show you something. Get your sea-legs under you, bunky."

Demesne struggled to his feet and followed Faber.

Down, down, down, they went, deep into the sub-sub-sub-basement. The air was dry and hot, overlaid with an odd yet heady stench of burning.

Stopping at a certain point in the interminable corridor, Faber pulled open a massive asbestos-padded door.

Demesne saw a giant roaring furnace fed by multiple chutes, its many gratings forming a leering idol's face. Naked servitors shoveled at an endless stream of ash and clinkers, loading them into wheeled iron carts which they trundled away.

The furnace seemed to bellow when it spotted the visitors, as if eager for a human sacrifice.

Faber slammed the door. For once, the unflappable G-man seemed scared. He bent down and picked up a dollar bill that had escaped the furnace's maw, as if to divert Demesne's attention till he could recover.

"That's where old worn-out money gets burned up, son, along with excess drugs," said Faber, waving the buck. He's Mistra Know-It-All, a man with a plan and a counterfeit dollar in his hand. "We pipe the smoke four miles away into the ghetto and vent it through eight sets of scrubbers. Even filtered, it helps pacifies the darkies. One toke of the pure stuff is enough to keep you high for a year."

"Why—why are you showing me this?"

"It's also where we put traitors to the Bureau, son. Just thought you should know."

### Track 0

At this point, the CIA finally deemed acid useless for its purposes. (Or so they claimed. Whether they continued to finance and abet the spread of acid throughout the 'Sixties is still a matter for dispute.) The Agency's attention was focused now on some of the other 32,000 drugs it had catalogued. Quinuclidinyl benzilate, or BZ, capable of producing a six-week bummer, became a fave, and was eventually stockpiled for domestic riot control. (BZ was manufactured by Hoffmann-La Roche of Nutley, New Jersey, a firm not far from Bell Labs in Murray Hill.) But it was a liddle too late to put the acid genie back in the bottle.

### Track 1

Grab a flower, stick it in your hair, and let's go! Down to The New American Lotus-land, where the Kozmic Konsciousness is dawning! Quicker'n the American Breed can bend you and shape you, or Morrison the Lizard King can open The Doors of your mind and light your fire, or Garcia and The Dead can spike your Kool Aid, you 'n' me 'n' Demesne will jump across the continent, annihilating Time and Space, juh-jus' like the Atom, when he Gets Small and dials himself down the phone lines, a teeny conscious quantum wavicle riding them electrons....

Whoops, we seem to be picking up leakage from another channel as we zip down them Kontinental Koaxials. Is this cross-talk....music? Yup.

"You never give me your money/You only give me your funny paper/I never give you my number/I only give you my situation...."

Maui-zowie, we pop out of the mouthpiece and Get Big! Wow-wow-wow! Here he was! Outasite! Dig this scene, fellow Diggers! (Careful, Emmett, some of those DIGGERS might really be DIGITIZERS!)

There were Tribal Members hanging out, panhandling, tripping, making music, making love, grooving, goofing, putting the tourists on and putting them down, laffin' the plastic hippies outa town. (A favorite mind-blowing technique of the residents of the Haight was to hold a mirror up in their windows when bugged by nosy tourists.) There were Seasoned Hippies who had been that way since Mario and Berkeley (the school, not the Bishop, natch), and young kids fresh off the bus from Winnemucca and Sioux Falls. And all of them were dressed....outrageously. Styles from the past ten decades were jumbled together capriciously, reflecting

## THE THEORY OF PERPETUALLY EXPANDING ECLECTICISM

The Present sits atop a Mountain which grows daily, hourly, by the second. This Mountain is the Past.

The French economist George Anderla, using information theory, has devised the following chart of World Knowledge. One AD forms the baseline, the quantity of knowledge being represented as $x$.

| DATE | KNOWLEDGE |
|------|-----------|
| 1 AD | $x$ |
| 1500 AD | $2x$ |
| 1750 AD | $4x$ |
| 1900 AD | $8x$ |
| 1950 AD | $16x$ |
| 1960 AD | $32x$ |
| 1967 AD | $64x$ |
| 1973 AD | $128x$ |

The spooky thing about this chart, natch, is *the rate of doubling is itself accelerating.*

Once it used to be possible to ignore the Mountain, and pretend one occupied a featureless Plain Of Time, as empty and thin as Flatland. (Even in this long-gone, primitive era, tho, complete ignorance could never be maintained, and there surfaced from time to time rumors of Golden Ages and Other Days, when there was not so much to know). But such blissful ignorance is possible no longer, thanx to THE PERSISTENCE OF MEMORY—institutional and extra-cranial memory, that is. With the advent of better and more durable records, the spread of printing, the relative stability and longevity of societies and cultures and institutions that would preserve these records, the existence of the Mountain became more and more obvious and undeniable. The Past *never went away anymore.* One was forced to acknowledge it, to come to terms with the stupefying legacy of the dead. The task was awesome. It drove some people krackers. The smothering weight of past thoughts, speculations and accomplishments made it sometimes seem as if everything had already been done or said or thought. It became hard to create anything that seemed utterly new. There was too much information just a-blastin' down the channel of Time. (Scribes in ancient Babylon are on record as complaining of this.) One artist went so far as to propose that "Instead of museums and public libraries, I should like to see in the main square of every city a colossal statue of Oblivion. Let us abolish the past, and all that comes with it! And let us make art as if no human being had ever made it before." (Jean "Jimmy" Dubuffet, Margaritaville's own fave painter. Good luck with that one, Jimmy!) Most people didn't take such an extreme stand, of course. Instead, whether they knew it consciously or not, they used the Past like a giant grab-bag. They mined the Mountain, emerging from the time-quarry with campy nuggets from other eras to incorporate into their current art or lifestyles. Sometimes this strategy of accomodation with the Past made it look as if the Past was out to psychically colonize the Present, sending out mind-control signals as in some 'Fifties horror-flick. (Whoops, sorry about the simile involving a past decade, folks, just slipped in, like....) And the problem only got worse in the twentieth century. New methods of artificial memory—videotapes, magnetic tapes, discs, film, DIGITAL CODING—only added to the burden of History. The average person in the last few decades of our century could hardly be called contemporary insofar as he was an amalgam of the Past.... The styles and objects in the uppermost layers of the Mountain were almost all composites and hybrids of things that could be found in lower layers. (And there was no way to stop this Perpetually Expanding Eclecticism except *to destroy the race's memory*....)

All this by way of explaining why Demesne, functioning under Deep Cover, was wearing knee-high fringed leather mocassins like those of Natty Bumppo, jeans, an Edwardian frock-coat, a Louis XIV lace-fronted shirt, and a Revolutionary War tricorn.

Brown shoes don't make it here!

Demesne's hair, incidentally, was now shoulder-length, representing six inches of new forced growth in one week's time. This was the result of the application of a secret drug known as Peltanol. Basically similiar to Rogaine, which Upjohn Pharmaceuticals would begin to market two decades later, Peltanol had been developed in the labs of the FBI, out of the necessity for its agents to go undercover convincingly.

So.... Suitably attired, Demesne began the investigation. Get on the tail of them heads! Gonna crack the drug trade in this Hippie Shangri-la wide open, run it all the way back to the Golden Triangle, mebbe, in that there Indochina. He was still a little confused by Faber's revelation of the existence of M4, and its impact on his (Demesne's) very reason for being, but—screw it! He was just a lower-echelon operative with an assignment, no questions asked....

Idling down Haight around Divisadero, Demesne picked himself up a copy of the *Oracle*, the So-Cal hippie paper of record.

40¢

Galactic Edition

Published monthly by the Oracle Cosmic Joy Fellowship

"If Granny won't take acid, give her the *Oracle!*"

Groovy Day Glo illos, yeah! BUT— What's this?

FIRST HUMAN BE-IN TODAY!

Shure enuff, here were posters for it too, seen now that he was sensitized to the info: American Indian holding an electric guitar, seated on a horse, list of bands and speakers, including....Buddha? Really be something if the World Honored One Hisself showed up!

Continuing his trek down the Dirty Boulevard (where the TV whores were calling the cops out for a suck), Demesne headed toward Golden Gate Park, site of the festival.

By the time he reached the Panhandle, immense crowds had formed. There had to be over twenty thousand people here! Demesne picked his way thru the masses, heading for Hippie Hill. Once there, he commenced the tricky, elaborate, crafty process of insinuating himself into the community of dopers.

Kids, we're professionals: don't try this at home!

Demesne simply found a circle of tokin' jokers, flopped himself down on the trampled grass, latched onto the joint when it came around, and began to smoke same. "Doing a number," they called it. I got fat bags of skunk, I got White Owl blunt, and I'm about to go get lifted. . . .

Now, the prevailing Hippie Myth was that anyone who got stoned would, if a narc, reveal himself and/or convert to Hippiedom. But what they didn't know was that all narcs had previously been put through a rigorous course of drugs, re-educated if necessary, and ultimately TRAINED NOT TO ENJOY BEING HIGH OR TO LEARN FROM IT.

Thus Demesne could talk the talk and walk the walk without for one moment losing his dedication.

In-*std*-ee-us!

Having passed this test, Demesne was quickly taken for what he presented himself to be: an aimless Aquarian, footloose and free....

Slow down, you move too fast! Got to make the morning last. Wouldn't it be nice if we could wake up together, groovin' on a Sunday afternoon? Speakers spoke, bands played, everyone got mellow. The Be-In was a big success. No pigs intruded. Demesne did a hit of Owsley with minor trepidation—this was definitely Schedule One stuff—but managed to survive the inner lightshow with his artificial personality intact.

Came nightfall. Demesne turned to this groovy barefoot, tie-dyed and bell-bottomed chick lying beside him on a blanket in the park—at least he thought she was groovy-lookin'; kinda hard to tell, what with the dusk and dope and all. She was really young, tho: Sweet Little Two to the Fourth, just on the edge of seventeen.

"Uh, what's your name, babe?"

"Lady Sunshine."

"Like, where can I crash tonight, Lady?"

"Well, I live with Insurrectionist Resurrectionists. It's kind of a heavy trip. They don't groove on strangers, so you can't stay there. But you could try the Pixies, right next door."

Pixies? Man, these people were weird! "You mean, like, elves, fairies, hobbits, those kind of folks?"

"Hey, you're into Tolkien! Far out! Did you ever read Pellucida? No? Well, I'm not talking about fairies, I'm talking about a commune. The Pixies are sorta like the Diggers, they take in people, feed them, share their dope."

Paydirt! The first level of the Organization!

"Sounds cool. Whereabouts are they?"

"C'mon, I'll show you...."

Somehow Demesne found himself at the door of the Pixie commune. Lady Sunshine, revealed under a porchlight, turned out to be a real twentieth-century fox! Foxy Lady! The girl bade him an ethereal farewell, then went to the big seedy Victorian manse across the street.

Too bad she had to split; too bad his wang-dang-doodle was inoperative; too bad life sucked. She coulda been the Sunshine of his love.... Oh well, he had his mission to keep him warm.... Partin' is such sweet sorrow.... Them bell-bottom blues again....

The Pixie building was a giant ark of a house. It was decorated in pyschedelic patterns with what appeared to be any leftover paint available. A sign over the open door said:

THE PIXIES
IF THE SWITCH ISN'T ON, IT'S OFF

Hmmm, seemed to be some kinda variation on Kesey's "on or off the bus" schtick.... I can dig it. Okay, Demesne, take a deep breath and....FURTHUR! He walked inside.

### Track 0

John Starr Cooke, a polio victim sitting in a wheelchair in Mexico, directed his Psychedelic Rangers as they spread drugs around the globe.

The Diggers staged a march called "The Death of Money."

Owsley began to synthesize STP. "On/Off/Onoff/Onoff/Onoff/Onoff/Onoff/Ommmmmm," he said on the back of a Blue Cheer album.

### Track 1

In the Pixies's pad, Demesne encountered many people wandering about, some sacked out, others engaged in talk. Stereo was blaring out Hendrix's "Voodoo Chile": "Gonna chop down the Mountain with the edge of my hand...."

"Fredkin, turn it down!" yelled someone. "There, that's better. Now, like I was sayin': Ringo, he's the jester figure, you dig...."

Okay, nothing too strange here, I can handle it.

Demesne approached a likely looking character. "Hey, who do I see about crashing here?"

"Just do what moves you, man."

"Isn't anyone in charge, like?"

"Well, yeah, I suppose that'd be Jack."

"Can I talk to him?"

"He's not here right now, he's out trying to score...."

Better and better!

"Okay, that's cool, I'll catch him later. What's he look like?"

"Big guy with a beard."

Oh, great, that narrows it down to every other guy in the place. All this hair, man, it was like *facial noise*.

Demesne ended up falling asleep before he could track down El Supremo, Jack. He shared a bare mattress with five other people. During the night, responding to some wordless shared subconscious emanations, the sleepers formed themselves into an innocent kind of daisy chain, a closed circle of bodies. (And the chemist, Kekule, striving to unlock the secrets of the benzene molecule, dreamed of a snake with its tail in its mouth, and Eureka, it was so! Kekule had a better trip than Swedenborg, who dreamed of snakes crawling all over his head.)

He woke up in the morning thinking he was hugging his pillow. Turned out to be a gal's thigh. His own was similarly clutched by a hairy guy. Yuk! Memories of Faber's chain-of-command assertive assault surged up disagreeably in Demesne, and he extricated himself.

Demesne ambled out to the kitchen. On the wall was a Wes Wilson poster for a Fillmore show: pastoral landscape with a naked woman clutching a huge snake. Demesne averted his eyes.

There was a big hairy guy sitting at the table eating some peanut butter out of the jar with a spoon. He wore a striped caftan and exhibited a rather disconsolate air. Could this be—

"Jack?"

"Hrmrm."

"Howzat?"

"Um, 'scuse me."

Guy ran a thick dirty finger around inside his mouth.

"This peanut butter's sticky, y'know. Gotta get some milk for the fridge, but I keep forgettin'. There's so much to keep track of, and I don't get much help from all the goof-offs here. Wish Pavonine was still here.... Not that I'm complainin', that's their trip. Anyway, I just said, 'Hi, man.'"

"You *are* Jack?"

"Jack Flash. But you can call me Jumpin'. Want some peanut butter?"

Demesne was suspicious of the food, but recalled Junior Narc's Rule Number One: Never do anything to alienate the suspect. And besides, he had wicked munchies still from yesterday....

"Uh, sure...."

"'Fraid there's only this one spoon...."

"That's cool."

Well, here ensued the most far-out conversation Demesne had ever taken part in, in all his drug-consuming youth. No stoned four-way monologue had ever been so trippy. What with that ol' peanut-butter-heavy bent stainless-steel flatware spoon (serving-size, by the way) passing back and forth like a Skippy-Jif-Peter-Pan joint, and back molars bogging down in sweet aromatic goober-sauce, there occured the most mumbled, jumbled dialogue ever known to man. This had to be what the day after Babel was like. But, much to Demesne's surprise, after a while he found that—whether because he was on the same wavelength as Jumpin', or simply by using his drug-sharpened deciphering routines—he was able to make sense out of a conversation that went, in part, something like this:

"Islpthrrlssnite."

"Grtgrtmrm. Hwdjlikit?"

"Nizzplzz."

"Thnkz. Jsttrynfillaneed."

"Hrryagtsmmgddope."

"Ntthzzmnt."

You get the picture. Anyway, what Demesne learned was this:

Jumpin' Jack Flash had been as lackadaisical and unambitious as his followers only a year or so ago. At that time, in fact, there had been no such group as the Pixies. The motive for the formation of the commune had been Jumpin's epiphanical encounter with the new drug pixeldrine.

Unlike marijuana or peyote, say, and more closely resembling LSD, pixeldrine, far from being a naturally occurring substance, was the carefully engineered product of modern chemistry. Jumpin' had been turned onto it by his one and only source: a nameless Irishman who passed through town on an irregular schedule. The Irishman was extremely vague and contradictory. At times, he claimed to represent the Queen of England; at others, a large international firm called Wu Labs. Jumpin' somehow couldn't see Good Queen Bess the Second as being involved with the manufacture of pixeldrine—although was it mere coincidence that "LSD" stood for Pounds, Shillings and Pence?—so he assumed Wu Labs was behind it.

Demesne almost fainted at the magnitude of this information. Wu Labs, the respected giant manufacturer of computers and chemicals, software and fertilizer, multi-tentacled conglomerate, the very company that supplied computer hardware to the Treasury Bureau, involved in illicit narcotic production—! If he could prove this to be true, his fame and fortune would be made!

The spoon scraped the bottom of the jar noisily, and Demesne dislodged with his tongue the last of the peanut butter from the roof of his mouth. He still wasn't quite clear on the exact nature of pixeldrine. What about it had led Jumpin' to form the commune...?

"So tell me," Demesne inquired slyly, "what kind of high does this stuff give?"

Jumpin' got a dreamy look on his fuzzy face. "Well, first off, it changes the way you see the world. Everything looks like a computer-generated display. You know, composed of millions of little squares—pixels. Everything has little step edges on it. But that's only the most superficial aspect to the drug. What really matters is that it allows you to understand the true structure of the universe."

"That's a big claim."

Jumpin' shrugged. "It's just the truth."

Demesne bit. "Well, what is the true structure of the universe?"

Jumpin' leaned over the table, and so did Demesne. Their mutual peanut-butter breaths mingled. Jumpin' whispered, "Binary."

"Binary?"

"The universe, on an incredibly deep level we normally can't reach, is composed solely of binary information."

Demesne straightened. "Isn't that just the old yin and yang theory?"

(Remember: one had to speak in this fashion in the 'Sixties.)

"That's part of it. But I'm talking physics, something that's subject to experimentation and control. That's what pixeldrine shows. And it's the gospel I'm trying to spread. But there's even more to it than that. You see, everything in the universe is a component of a vast computer."

"Hold on now, man—"

"No, it's true, we're all just bits in the channel. And the computer is workin' all the time, workin' on a Problem."

"Which is?"

Jumpin' lowered his voice. "That's what no one knows. That's what I aim to find out. I estimate another few dozen trips will give me the answer."

Demesne decided to back off. He knew the sound of religious fanaticism all too well. "That's a wild theory, man. I'd like to learn more. When do you think this guy will come by with more hits of pixeldrine?"

Jumpin' shrugged. "Can't say. I thought we had an appointment to meet last night. But he never showed."

"Well, that's cool, time is on our side. How's about if in the meantime I hang around and try to lend a hand?"

"Sounds great. First thing is, let's get some milk."

"Right on!"

### Track 0

Owsley was busted. The Brotherhood of Eternal Love became the prime source of acid in the form of "orange sunshine" tablets.

### Track 1

Thus did Demesne take up permanent residence with the Pixies. At first, it was interesting, something different, even at times a lotta laffs. Thanks to his focused energies, he was able to assume a position of second-in-command to Jumpin', who appreciated the help.

Demesne heard many tales of the former second-in-command, one Paavo Pavonine, who, by all accounts, had been quite a character. In his late thirties, the man claimed to have been a former Nazi collaborator, partly responsible for the V-2s that had rained down on England. Now a pacifist, natch, he was embarked on a spiritual quest, and had lately left to take up residence with the Yazidi of Iraq, a Krazy Kult that worshiped Satan and his earthly rep, The Peacock Angel. They also propitiated both the Sun and the six-foot-tall statue of a snake, which they blackened with shoe-polish each day as part of their devotions.

"Weird, man," said Demesne with a irrepressible shudder to Jumpin'.

"But that ain't the weirdest part, man. The priests—they're all eunuchs!"

"Gah-ross!"

Any-hoo, the leader of the Pixies was again freed from daily running of the commune and could concentrate on trying to establish contact with his mysterious source.

But the ineffable Irishman was not to be found.

One day, Jumpin' took Demesne with him to visit the neighbors. Demesne was intrigued by the chance to see Lady Sunshine again. However, Jumpin's motivation was different.

"Maybe the Eye Ares know something about my contact," the desperate doper hoped.

At the door of the I.R. commune, Jumpin' knocked. A curtain twitched aside. This motion was followed by a shouted command from inside.

"Get back! You oughta know not to stand by the window, someone'll see you out there!"

The door opened as far as three chains would allow, and the snout of a shotgun poked out.

"Who the fuck is it!"

"Davey, man, easy! It's just me, Jumpin'."

"Okay, okay, hold on."

After much rattling, the door was cracked enough for Demesne and Jumpin' to enter.

Jumpin whispered a warning to Demesne: "Watch out for this guy. He's a wild street-fightin' man."

The obviously tripping white dude holding the shotgun wore a fur vest over bare skin, purple bell-bottoms and green suede boots. A headband restrained a Jewish Afro. A peace symbol hung from a leather thong around his neck.

Jumpin' made introductions. "Emmett, meet Davey Burnout, the Psycho-killer. He's living for the Revolution."

"It's just around the corner, man. The Establishment wants to wipe us out, now that acid's opened up a line to the hyperworld. The Romans did it to the Mystery Cults, man. But they won't do it to us. I heard of a van that's loaded with weapons, packed up and ready to go. Heard of some gravesites out by the highway, a place that nobody knows. It's coming any day now."

"Well, sure, man, but meanwhile, we gotta live. You heard anything about my Irish dealer lately, man?"

"Fuck that! This ain't no party, this ain't no disco, this ain't no fooling around. No time for dancing or lovey-dovey—I ain't got time for that now!"

"Gee, Davey, I'm just asking for a little help—"

"Listen, you heard about Detroit—there's a panic in Detroit—heard about Houston, heard about Pittsburgh Pee Ay?"

"No, I—"

Davey Burnout gestured upstairs with his gun. "I just transmited the message to the receiver, hope for an answer some day. I got three passports, a couple of visas, you don't even know my real name."

"I wasn't askin', man—"

"We've got computers, we're tapping phone lines. I know that that ain't allowed. We dress like students, we dress like housewives, or in a suit and a tie. I changed my hairstyle so many times now, I don't know what I look like!"

"Pretty bad, if you ask me."

Burnout seemed to collapse inward on himself. "My chest is aching, burns like a furnace. But the burning keeps me alive."

"Hey, *compadre*, don't lose your head."

"I can't even write my own name!"

At that moment, a dapper-looking black man wearing a knitted multicolored jumpsuit entered. Jumpin' hailed him.

"Hey, Watts, how's it hanging!"

They gave a soul shake. "Em, meet Harlem 'Motown' Watts, Davey's lieutenant."

"Hi."

"Reach out, I'll be there."

"Harlem, you heard tell of my connection?"

"He keeps you hangin' on."

"Right, right, I can't find him."

"He's really got a hold on you."

"Well, I guess. I could kick it if I wanted."

"Sometimes the hunter gets captured by the game."

"Hey, not me! This is strictly for science."

"I second that emotion. You're uptight, but everything's all right."

"Well, you know anything about him?"

"Ain't no mountain high enough to keep him away."

"Glad to hear it. I'll keep waitin' then."

"It's all in the way you do the things you do."

"Right on."

Bidding the pair of Insurrectionists *adieu*, Demesne and Jumpin' left.

"Freaky," said Demesne.

"Far out."

"Sick."
"Kicky."
"Ballsy."
"Flaky."
"Hung up."
"Put me thru some changes."
"Blew my mind."

## Track 0

Media overkill trashed the Summer of Love. The Haight filled up with fakes. A mock funeral was held, "The Death of the Hippie." Bad trips began to outnumber good, as set and setting deteriorated. Disaffection and madness filled the air; everyone saw the bad moon rising.

The clampdown was coming, fer shure.

## Track 1

Days and months went by without word from the bearer of pixeldrine. Without the stimulus and bond of the novel drug, the commune began to fall apart, and Demesne was soon having trouble maintaining any semblance of control over the transient residents. As those who had once sampled pixeldrine forgot the experience and drifted away, the house filled up with newcomers who held no particular allegiance to the gospel of World As Digital Information.

Jumpin'—who, having taken more doses of pixeldrine than anyone else, managed to maintain his belief—found his sermons (which began to sound more and more like gibberish) falling on deaf ears.

"Like, if man is five, see, then the devil is six. And if the devil is six, then god is seven!"

"Aw, you're fulla dogshit, man!"

Trying every last desperate scheme possible to hold the place together, Jumpin' rented some silent stag films one night, bought some acid, and tried to stage a "Free Love Freakout."

Demesne was put in charge of running the Super-8 projector. He tried to concentrate on the mechanics of reels and sockets and not watch the films or the flagrant fucking of the freaks, so as not to create a painful erection which he could do nothing about. But he invariably found his eyes drifting to the bedsheet that served as a screen.

The fourth film of the evening flared on.

SALAMMBO
FREELY ADAPTED FROM
THE NOVEL BY FLAUBERT
DIRECTED BY
ERIC ENGST

The city of Carthage is being beseiged by the Barbarians. The Carthaginians are going wild with panic. They offer sacrifices to the badly painted façade of Moloch, money, drugs and children. Lotsa X-rated debauchery during the ceremony. (Demesne swore he recognized Lady Sunshine in the crowd.) Cut to the the Barbarians. Ditto in their camp, represented by a single Army-surplus tent, as they anticipate pillage and rape. Back to the city. Obvious General-type paces the cardboard battlements in consternation. Finally slaps his forehead in inspiration. Dashes back to what is obviously his private residence. Goes into a bedroom. Beautiful gal is there. Blonde hair, lotsa Cleopatra-style makeup. (She looked kinda familiar to Demesne.) Father yaks his plan to her, she drops her eyes demurely, but finally agrees. Father leaves. Gal starts to undress. (Those tits— It was Vivian Vervain!) She goes to a window, tosses it open, and spreads her arms in supplication. A giant python drops down from above, falls onto Vervain's shoulders, tightens its black coils around her waist—

The film snapped, and the screen went white.

No one noticed but Demesne.

The next day he gained entrance to the I.R. commune and found Lady Sunshine. Wearing a Jersey "worm" dress from the New York designers Sibley and Coffee, she was so high Demesne feared her brains might run out her ears. After much questioning, he managed to ascertain that she had indeed participated in the filming of *Salammbo*.

"Vivian, where's Vivian?"

"Oh, man, she's split with Engst. She was in 'Frisco till a week ago, but she's gone now...."

"Where?"

"Asia, man."

Asia. Unbelievable. Life truly sucked....

Despite such stratagems, like a cloud below an inattentive angel, the commune drifted out entirely from beneath its founder. Demesne knew the worst had happened when he returned from shopping one day and found the ON/OFF sign gone from over the front door.

Jumpin' sat on a stained mattress holding his head and making mournful noises. Demesne felt just as bad. What of all his months invested on this case? What would Faber say? Could he possibly salvage anything?

Jumpin' looked up when he heard Demesne enter. The madness of withdrawal and abandonment and loss of faith had entered his eyes.

"There's only one thing to do," he announced. "We have to go to the source."

"Where's that?" asked Demesne hopefully.

"Wu Labs headquarters, in Massachusetts. We'll follow the Bee Gees! Are you with me?"

"That's all the way across the country!"

"So?"

So indeed. At this point, what'd he have to lose? The case was dead, unless he took drastic action.

"You bet."

"Then let's go."

The two piled into Jumpin's VW van—the Databus, the Magic Bus—and took off, just like that.

That was the 'Sixties for you, man. You'll never see a decade like that again, you poor unknowing hylic fuckers.

Sustained by uppers and music, the pixillated pair made it nearly to their goal.

Actually, as far as Peebles, Ohio, which ain't exactly next door to New England. Still, considering the lousy condition of the bus, they did pretty good.

"We're gonna throw a fuckin' rod, man!"

"Try to take it to the bridge, anyway."

Hoe-kay.... Here were these two frantic Young Americans—dirty, weary, hopeless, hungry, sleepless—abandoning their busted bus (pulled in just behind that bridge) and setting off on foot to complete a useless journey, and what do you think their first Emergency Measure was?

That's right.

Jumpin' reached in his pocket and took out a little case. "My last two hits of pixeldrine. Let's do 'em."

"All right," said Demesne.

They took the pills.

Shure enuff, a mile or so down the road the described effect took over.

Demesne looked around in amazement. It was all true.... Everything was binary info.... He could almost decipher The Problem....

Trudging through the digital landscape—where trees and boulders, cows and birds, clouds and houses, all exhibited step-like jaggy edges—the pair came out of woods onto a vast plain. The plain was dotted with manmade grassy mounds, the ancient labors of long-dead Indians. The biggest one was 1300 feet long. It represented a, a—

Demesne couldn't believe his digitized vision. The huge earthwork depicted a snake swallowing an egg.

The two had wandered into Serpent Mound State Park.

As Demesne gazed fixedly at the mound, he saw it start to split. Turves fell like scales from the mound. An enormous serpentine head poked through. It turned toward Demesne and opened its jaws, extended its tongue to taste the air.

"I am the One," it hissed, and Demesne felt Zero At The Bone.

Weh-hell.... Demesne just freaked. In one instantaneous and utterly devastating flashback, his whole serpent-tormented childhood washed over him. He flew right down that long and winding mental road. Stunned and amazed by his childhood memories. My city was gone! Way to go, Ohio!

Atop the pixeldrine experience, this manifestation was just too much.

Letting loose a piercing scream, Demesne dashed blindly across the plain, heedless of Jumpin's calls. He ran and ran and ran, at an angle to the mounds, with nothing in mind except to escape the awful image of the world-devouring snake. He might have run forever, had he not collided face-first with a chain-link fence.

Demesne bounced off as if the fence were a vertical trampoline and hit the ground unconscious, his face imprinted with a diamond lattice. Park rangers rushed from their building. Seeing the uniformed figures, Jumpin's paranoia went off the scale and he fled, leaving his friend to cope on his lonesome.

(Mister Flash never did make it to Wu Labs, his quest aborted by circumstance, but managed to settle down in Ohio, where, in the mid-'Seventies, he founded a firm specializing in hi-rez monitors known as PixieTek and made a pile of loot, thereby turning on its head the old adage, "Dope will see you thru times of no money better than money will see you thru times of no dope.")

Demesne—or some portion of that personality—awoke in a hospital. The man was totally burnt. He had broken on thru to the other side, but he hadn't made it back. After his condition became apparent to the doctors in charge, he was soon transferred to a state mental institution, or as such places used to be called, "a snake-pit."

One thing Demesne would've been proud of: his Deep Cover was never broken. Without identification, he remained a nameless charity case, and to his handlers at the Treasury Department, it was as if he had vanished off the globe.

### Track 0

August 1969: Woodstock.

December 1969: Altamont and Manson.

1970: Leary sentenced to twenty years. First Weathermen bombings.

Helter Skelter!

### Track 1

For the next three years, Demesne remained completely over the edge and beyond the pale. His main treatment consisted, natch, of more drugs. Not recreational, but taken from that class known as neuroleptics, including reserpine, derived from snakeroot. All these anti-psychosis drugs succeeded in doing was to give Demesne a permanent case of tardive dyskinesia. (Tardive dyskinesia is an interestingly bizarre condition wherein the brain's acetylcholine receptors—you remember how Eccles discovered them in '53—are screwed up, and the sufferer is subject to unending tics, twitches, stutters, and other involuntary movements occasioned by the noise in his brain's channels.)

Demesne probably would've stayed crazy for the rest of his life, had not Fate intervened in the form of a fellow patient newly assigned to his ward.

The guy was an Army flyboy of mixed Amerindian-Irish descent, named Hiawatha Du Danaan. Cashiered on a Section Eight, his insanity lay in the fact that he had tried to tell the truth about the secret bombings of Cambodia then underway in which he had participated. No one would believe that the US government, already fighting one immoral war, would embark on another totally undeclared one.

Being completely sane, this ex-soldier had nothing better to do with his time than listen to Demesne's ravings and make sympathetic comments. (These comments consisted of such jolly flyboy banter as, "Shux, fella, turnin' in your friends ain't nothin! Why, once, when I was high on orange sunshine, I bombed the shit out of a certain Box in gook-land that jes' so happened to contain a good buddy of mine, Nick Fury. I got a telepathic goodbye from him as he bought the farm. She-it, me and my Co-pilot Roland—you know Roland, he later lost his head in the tail-gunner position—we accidentally blew Fury's covert ass right to hell!")

This amateur therapy, as if establishing a beneficial feedback circuit that smoothed out the kinks in Demesne's neurosystem and convinced him that he was not the only heir to Original Sin, eventually restored the G-man to a certain functional level.

In 1975, after eight years in the loony-bin, Demesne, judged functionally capable, was freed, a twitchingly paranoid, shrunken remnant of his old self, with nothing to sustain him except a hardcore belief in the evil of drugs and the binary indifference of the universe.

He returned to the Treasury Department, only to find that the Drug Enforcement Administration had since been created to handle the duties once assigned to the Treasury. (And what symbolic significance did this administrative split have? Was M4 still being calculated and monitored? Demesne didn't really care. He just wanted to FIGHT DRUGS.)

In amazement, after verifying his story, the DEA took the former agent back.

Demesne went looking for Faber.

His old boss was dead. Officially tripping on an experimental compound known as TVC-15, he had tossed himself into the sub-sub-sub-basement furnace and become so much greasy smoke over the ghetto.

When Zero Tolerance became the official policy, Demesne laughed harshly to himself.

He could tolerate the Zero, all right.

It was the One that scared him.

Now a single-minded Monkey on the back of international dope-smugglers anywhere, he had no life outside the DEA.

And when, nearly two decades after his near-fatal encounter with pixeldrine, on the basis of disturbing rumors that spoke of a deadly new drug available in Boston, Demesne was assigned to that city, he just twitched both eyes and a cheek muscle, then took off, never suspecting that his old nemesis, Wu Labs, might be involved.

But then, neither did anyone else.

Chapter 00001001

# The Float

# K L U E S

## 00100000

"To transmit information means to induce order. This sounds reasonable enough. Next, since entropy grows with the probability of a state of affairs, information does the opposite: it increases with its improbability. The less likely an event is to happen, the more information does its occurence represent. This again seems reasonable. Now, what sort of sequence of events will be least predictable and therefore carry a maximum of information? Obviously a totally disordered one, since when we are confronted with chaos we can never predict what will happen next. The conclusion is that total disorder provides a maximum of information; and since information is measured by order, a maximum of order is conveyed by a maximum of disorder. Obviously, this is a Babylonian muddle. Somebody or something has confounded our language."

—Rudolf Arnheim

## 00100001

"Anyone who doesn't believe in miracles isn't a realist."

—David Ben-Gurion

## 00100010

"Everything spoke: their water jars, their tortilla griddles, their plates, their cooking pots, their dogs, their grinding stones, each and every thing crushed their faces."

—*Popul Vuh*

## 00100011

"Number helps more than anything else to bring order to the chaos of appearances. It is the predestined instrument for creating order, or for apprehending an already existing, but still unknown, regular arrangement or 'orderedness.' It may well be the most primitive element of order in the human mind."

—Carl Jung

Cy's gone in and out of the midnight hour while reading his trashy fantasy. Now Ol' Commander Clock says 1:11, urging our boy to GET SOME SLEEP, but he just can't. The body is willing but the head is freaky. I had too much to dream last night, just like Scrooge. Do all these recent hallucinations stem from just a Dickensian "blot of mustard, a bit of undigested beef?" That's what you get for eating a big Vanilla Fudge Sundae topped with Electric Prunes and a Chocolate Watchband just before bedtime....

The revelation Cy thinks he's just had about Wu's possible goals is whirling around in his brain. "To conquer space and time...." Omniscience and immortality. Breadth and persistence, depth and span, a brush dipped in knowledge and an infinite canvas.... Cyril can't wait till morning, so they can go badger Ferdie Lantz, poor AIDS-wracked bit-flipper, some more.

Meanwhile, tho, Cy's head is a pain in the ass (especially since that's where it seems he's been prone to keep it lately). The head, after all, is Prime Receiver and Processor of information, obvious nexus of the senses and the brain. Cy has often thought that decapitation (that most savage, final denial of information-processing) would be kinda nice, provided it didn't kill you. (*Too bad*, thinks Cyril, *I left Wu's gambling den before the Doc could finish sawing my head off, so I coulda taken it for a test drive, so to speak.*) Life would be like it was for those Martians imagined by Burroughs (Edgar Rice, not Bill), the ones who were born naturally with necks terminating in stumps, and relied on a separate species (which looked, natch, just like huge heads with little atrophied limbs) to sit on their stumps and guide them around, when they (the bodies) weren't just rooting blindly and mindlessly. Come to think of it, isn't there a similar image in one of Baum's Oz books? Sci-fi heads in bottles, brain transplants, cyborgs....

Weird archetype, fer shure....

Cy's mind is wandering like Moses. All he wants is to bag some zees, now that he and Polly are done Burning Down The House. (Watch out, Cy, you might get what you're after.... And wouldn't it be a Crowded House if Ruby and Augie suddenly turned up?) You're my Venus, you're my fire, what's your desire? I'll stop the world and melt with you! It's getting better, so much better all the time, since you've been mine. What a climax the Indoor Fireworks were to three days of blue-balls, which he assumes Polly was experiencing too. (What does one call unrequited horniness in women, by the way? Vexed vulva? Hot lips? Clit snit? It all comes loose, tho, when the levee breaks!) He's fairly certain Polly enjoyed that sixty-nine as much as he did, even with his episode of astral travel tossed in. Yummy, yummy, yummy, I've got love in my tummy, cuz she's a rainbow!... She sure seemed to get off on being tied up. Better brush up on his Boy Scout knots, if they were gonna make a habit of this....

Heh-hey, come to think of it, was it mere coincidence that Pol had gone all soft on him only when they were bound up in the coils of Mister Wiggle? Goddamn, he owed that stupid garden hose a lot!

But good as it was, Cy cannot escape the question of what the sex means for their relationship. How will they face each other in the morning, or face Ruby and Augie if (*when*, damn it!) they find them? Maybe they can pretend it never happened, or claim they fell into each other's arms out of sadness, seeking solace, in a one-time moment of weakness.

But that's not the truth. Cyril felt almost compelled by forces larger than himself to make it with Polly. And he's afraid he won't be able to resist doing it again. Oh God, what does sex mean to me, what does sex mean to society...? If I didn't love you, I'd hate you—

If, if, if! Contingencies are driving him nuts! He needs certainty, a clearness of vision. But instead, he can't resolve a single true message out of the spectrum of all messages. He's caught, trapped in

## THE NEST OF IFS

The Nest of IFs is a big Roc-sized assemblage woven of twigs and debris high up on a cliffside, littered with the bones of Sinbad and others. It's filled with Baby IFs, little naked wormy creatures with big eyes 'n' maws 'n' vestigal wings, all struggling and crying for food. Cy's in the middle of them now, they're wrapping themselves around him in their frantic hunger, and suddenly he can see that the Liddle IFs are printed with conditions and consequences, arranged like a crooked ladder around him in this sequence:

> IF they can find Ruby and Augie
>> IF they can get some information from Lantz
>>> IF he can get some sleep
>>>> IF his brain stops spinning its wheels
>>>>> IF he can get out of this fugue
>>>>> Then he can distract himself
>>>> Then he can relax
>>> Then he can wake up refreshed
>> Then they can bargain with Wu
> Then everything will be like it was.

The Baby IFs unwrap themselves from around Cy, for they've heard the approach of their Momma. Far off in the sky, a small form can be seen. It grows larger, larger, till it's big as the hellbound train, a giant flying snarling Momma IF, labelled on the one side Cy can see:

IF YOU LIVE!

Puff, the Magic Dragon! Realio, trulio, it's not Custard, Cy. This is Mission Control, Major Tom, end your EVA right now!

The rain has stopped and the sounds of heavy weather traffic have died down. His old living room—despite looking like nothin' but a house party's been goin' on—has never seemed so welcome.

Cy's up out of his chair and stalking back 'n' forth naked, his brain tearing itself apart like an unharnessed engine over this dilemma. He'd love to go out while Pol sleeps in, and walk off this energy, but he can't, cuz of what that Nazi said: only the closeness of Polly's fetish protects him. She's his Soul Asylum!

Not looking, he slams the bare toes of his left foot into the sack of pennies he dropped near the door. He hops around one-leggedly, holding the Injured Members, falling finally onto the cushionless couch.

Jesus, that hurt like a bitch!

It's too much, too much of everything. Let them all talk! Boy with a problem! I was born under punches! Keep it in, cut it up, kick it out! Psychotic reaction! Shock that monkey!

Cy collapses weeping. Boo-hoo-hoo, poor Cy's gotta cry like a baby.

Hey, fuck you! It's my party, I'll cry if I wanna!

Talking to himself. Bad sign, very bad. He's got to get control of his brain.... Wild mood swings bad, two legs good.... Are we not men? We are Devo!

A book. Maybe concentrating on another book would help him. (I read a book I never read, drank a beer and went to bed—but where did you *go?!?*) Whatever gets you thru the night....

*Riddle of the Dragon* lies broken-backed and accusatory on the floor where he flung it. What else? Here's a stack. There's Polly's borrowed copy of *The Serpent Repents*. Nope, too deep. How's about *Who's Had Who*, a history of sex—"lay lines"—among the rich and famous? ("If you've screwed anyone, you've screwed everyone in history") Too lightweight. Who wrote this book of love? Shawcross's *Sideshow*? More friggin' history! No, a book won't do. Cy sweeps the whole stack to the floor.

The noise don't even wake Polly, as he was half-hoping it would. Wake up, Little Suzie! he'd like to shout, and help me make it thru the night. But she keeps on dreaming, her snores having gotten louder, acquiring a magnificently mellow melisma.

Abruptly, Cy decides to flip on the television, keeping the volume low. He'll have to take a chance that the insidious instrument of Jap domination won't betray him. With any luck, traditional late-night fare will soothe him and put him to sleep....

Cy and Ruby never could afford cable—no 57 channels and nothing on for them—so he'll have to rely on what's broadcast for free. (And you get what you pay for!) Cy picks up *TV Guide.* Lessee, one AM:

[2] THE VIPER AND HER BROOD—Drama
Fine adaptation of the play by Thomas Middleton (author of *The Black Book, A Mad World My Masters,* etc., etc.), starring Cher, Sting, Dweezil and Moon Zappa, Michelle Phillips, Art Garfunkel, Apollonia, Glenn Frey and Phil Collins.

[4] HEART OF THE DRAGON—Documentary
Part Four of the series on China examines the founding of the Chou Dynasty at the decisive battle outside the Shang capitol in 1111 BC. Narrated by Doctor An Wang. Funded by San Francisco's PBS affiliate, KSOI.

[5] MOVIE—Drama [BW]
"The Snake Pit." (1948) Olivia de Havilland gives a striking performance as a mental patient who is helped out of her psychosis by a talkative roommate. With John Ramistella.

[6] MOVIE—Horror
"Lair of the White Worm." (1988) Director Ken Russell trowels on the sex and violence in this adaptation of the little-known Bram Stoker novel. Parental Discretion Advised.

[7] MOVIE—Adventure
"Snake People." (1968) Boris Karloff in a plot involving snake-worshippers, voodoo and LSD. With C. Shannon and R. Hartley.

[10] LATE NIGHT WITH DAVID LETTERMAN
Dave's guests tonight: Millbrook de Lysid, Tedham Porterhouse, Charles Westover and George Ivan. Musical guest: Shannon's Dress.

[12] MOVIE—Suspense
"Cat People." (1982) Contemporary remake with Nastassia Kinski. Theme song by David Bowie.

[25] MOVIE—Pornography
"Blacksnake." (1973) Another in Russ Meyer's big-tit cycle. Utterly without redeeming social value. With Marie Laurie and Mary Isobel O'Brien. Parental Proscription Mandatory.

[27] MOVIE—Action
"Enter the Dragon." (1973) Good, clean fun as Bruce Lee violently disarranges the features of all opponents.

[36] MONTY PYTHON—Anarchy
Pet shop skit; Queen on acid; Sir Richard Burton and actor Richard Burton lost in Dahomey.

[38] MOVIE—Comedy
"When Irish Eyes Are Smiling." (1954) Humphrey Bogart as a Priest Of The Old Sod riding herd over a monastery full of wacky monks! With Reginald Dwight and Richard Starkey.

[44] MOVIE—Mystery [BW]
"Sky Dragon." (1949) Charlie Chan and Number One Son solve "The Case of the Missing 78s," involving a crate of John Lee Hooker records lost in the Communist takeover of China. With James Osterburg and Louis Firbank.

[56] OUR PLACE IN THE SHADOWS—Soap Opera
This old chestnut is now celebrating its thirty-second anniversary. This episode:
Cheryl and Paul swap mates Robbie and Audrey.
[58] MOVIE—Federal [BW]
"G-Men Versus the Black Dragon." (1943) Heroic Treasury agents fight slant-eyed
spies. With Vincent Furnier and Ernest Evans.
[64] MOVIE—Educational
"Popul Vuh." (1993) Ancient religious text of the Mayas dramatized for modern
viewers.

Remote in hand, Cy begins to click between shows.

Nothing holds his attention. Ten minutes here, five there; a snippet of this, a
sound-bite of that. He just can't focus. Everything seems too alien, like a broadcast
from another planet.

As per usual, the commercials are the best thing.

1    CLOSE UP of actor who looks like YELTSIN, seated behind desk.

YELTSIN
(Shuffles papers stamped with hammer and sickle.)
Hello, Western Comrades! It is my big pleasure to invite you all to world's newest
amusement park.
(beat)
*Commieland!*

CUT TO:

2    EXT OF BLOCKS OF CRUMBLING APARTMENTS; GULAG VILLAGES SET ON FAKE
SNOW; STORES WITH LONG LINES OUTSIDE. COMMIELAND NEON SIGN CRACK-
LING AND SPITTING SPARKS, WITH ONLY HALF THE LETTERS LIT.

CUT BACK TO:

3    YELTSIN STANDING with roll of RED TAPE in one hand and reel of RECORDING
TAPE in other.

YELTSIN
Now that Russia is part of International Money Mind just like other countries, if
you want to relive marvelous exciting glory days of Five Year Plans, you must come
to *Commieland!* Watch tractor races, cram whole family into one-room apartment,
get simulated frostbite gathering wood. KGB men will spy while you have sex in first-
class Soviet Hotel with authentic lack of amenities. Book now! Hard currency only,

natchski! Discounts for members of the *khlysty*, White Brotherhood and *Bogorodechnyi*. Accommodations limited to several millions of captive peoples.
(Removes shoe and bangs on desk.)
We will bury you in fun!

One segment of the *Python* show does manage to snag Cy's interest for a time. It's the famous pet shop bit. Except it's not exactly as Cy recalls it. Seems like John Cleese is trying to return—a snake?

1   INT of PET SHOP.

JOHN CLEESE

This snake, sir, is dead.

MICHAEL PALIN

It's not dead. It's merely digesting a large meal.

JOHN CLEESE

(Wacks counter with board-like snake.)
Digesting a large meal? What did it eat, a bloody poker? I tell you, it's plainly deceased. This snake, sir, has gone to herpetological heaven. It's an offed ophidian. It's a senescent serpent, a torpid Tiamat, a quiescent Quetzalcoatl, a decaying Damballah. This snake, sir, is deader than the one baby Hercules strangled. It's a comatose cobra, a boa that should be buried, an antiquated anaconda, a rigid rattler. To put it quite bluntly, it's a pyss-poor python.

MICHAEL PALIN

(Unshakeable.)
It's not dead.

And he says it with such calm assurance in the face of Cleese's angry insistence that Cy shivers, and switches stations.

Finally, on snow-distorted UHF channel 64, Cyril, having exhausted all other shows, intersects the promised film version of the *Popul Vuh*. He comes in just as a title is disappearing from the screen:

PART EIGHT

Cy casts his mind back to his Meso American history class, conducted under the tutelage of Professor Balam Knight (a classy guy who drove a Jaguar). As Cy recalls, the *Popol Vuh* has only five parts. Now, this sacred text *does* mix earlier mythological tales with actual historical incidents (much like the Bible, come to think of it). Could it be, Cy thinks, that *some scribe or group of scribes has been continually updating the book in secret, ever since the Spaniards came?* Who knows? One thing fer shure, them Mayans are just weird enuff to perpetuate such a tradition secretly over the centuries.

Consider:

The Mayans worshipped Time, erecting monuments to commemorate the sheer passage of days. (The glyph for a day was the image of that day's god carrying a load on his back. Boy, you're gonna carry that weight a long time!)

The basic Mayan "week" lasted thirteen days.

There were twenty possible day names—all natural objects, such as "water," "dog," and "death"—which, combined with the thirteen day numbers, formed a Sacred Year of 260 days (not coincidentally, a period more or less equivalent to a human pregnancy). In addition, the Mayans observed a traditional Solar Year of 365 days (eighteen months of twenty days each, plus five intercalary days.) The 360 days without the extra five were called a *tun*. A *katun* was 7200; a *baktun*, 144,000; an *alautun*, 23,040,000,000!

Events were supposed to repeat in some fashion, from one cycle to another.

The Mayans, natch, are also famous for practicing human sacrifice, tho this appears to be something of a Bum Rap, at least when they are compared to their northern pals, the Aztecs. Combined with their worship of temporality, this practice has led to their being called, by some, "time vampires," as if they sought thru blood to conquer time.

Mebbe, mebbe not.

"All we can be sure of," said Prof Knight, "is that the Mayans were the most number-obsessed culture in history, as testified to, in part, by their independent invention of the Zero."

The title disappears now from Cy's sight, and he's into the film.

1    BOSTON 1954. INT shot of boardroom of UNITED FRUIT COMPANY. Bunch of WHITE GUYS IN SUITS sitting around long table.

SAM ZEMURRAY

Gentlemen, as President of UFCO, I'm happy to report that the CIA-sponsored invasion of Guatemala—Operation SUCCESS—will be getting underway immediately. The Commie government of President Arbenz, who dared to appropriate one percent of our untilled acreage for shiftless Indians to squat on, will soon be out, replaced by the puppet regime of Castillo Armas, whose dick is in our pocket. Boy, I'm still mad at Arbenz for interferring in 1948 with our highway construction plans down there! You know what that's all about....

(beat)

I am named One Death, the chief.

EDWARD BERNAYS

And as one of three PR men for this whole shebang, I'm proud of my lying, dissimulation, chicanery, flackery, hyperbole, scare tactics and bribery. It's a triumph of disinformation. We've got the whole Fourth Estate duped. The country is in a tizzy!

(beat)

I am named Seven Death.


JOHN CLEMENTS

You did a good job winning over the liberals, Ed, but it was only through my efforts that we got the hard-core conservatives in our camp.

(beat)

I am named House Corner.


SPRUILLE BRADEN

My job was the hardest! I had to pose as a disinterested ex-diplomat and make pro-UFCO speeches, even though I was on the UFCO payroll.

(beat)

I am named Blood Gatherer.


THOMAS CORCORAN

Hey, you three, don't forget how I lobbied all the senators and representatives down in DC, and disseminated official-looking but duplicitous "white papers" on the practically non-existent Commie presence in Guatemala.

(beat)

I am named Pus Master.


ALLEN DULLES

You did a good job, Corkie, but you never would have gotten anywhere if I hadn't backed you with my CIA. We got lots of practice overthrowing Mossadegh in Iran last year—tho those Yazidi waged a helluva fight for a buncha eunuchs—and we're just itching to put what we learned into play. Overthrowing governments is like eating salted peanuts: you can't stop at just one! Thank goodness the National Security Council granted us covert powers in 1948! With any luck, we can reverse the tide of postwar anti-colonialism and keep all the old maps just like they used to be. Hey, I wonder if the French could use our help in Indochina?!

(beat)

I am named Jaundice Master.


JOHN FOSTER DULLES

Hold on, little brother, that's for me, Secretary of State, to decide. Oh, I'll let Ike

in on it, but he's so busy shoving that huge cock of his up his secretary, Anne Whitman, wife of an UFCO officer, Edmund Whitman, or down some golf-course gopher hole, that it'll be basically up to me.
(beat)
I am named Bone Scepter.

### JOHN MOORS CABOT

As your assistant, Boss, I'll influence all my rich Boston friends in your favor.
(beat)
I am named Skull Scepter.

### HENRY CABOT LODGE

Good job, cousin. For my part, as ambassador to the UN and holder of a large block of UFCO stock, I'll ride herd on that bunch of wogs and gooks. They'll never get their new world information order. At least not for forty years, by which time we'll all be comfortably dead.
(beat)
I am named Trash Master.

### JOHN McCORMACK

I know that I didn't do much except read UFCO press releases into the *Congressional Record* in my Massachusetts Senator job, but maybe I could get something out of this too...?
(beat)
I am named Stab Master.

### ALLEN DULLES

We'll let you test some of the yagé we bring back, John!

### COLONEL ALBERT HANEY

Listen up, you simpering Senator Codfish! I'm in charge of this whole invasion, and you'll get what we give you. I just got back from running the CIA station in South Korea, and I know just how to deal with your type.
(beat)
I am named Wing.

### JOHN McCORMACK

I— You— This is outrageous! I'm a Boston Brahmin! I won't let some cheap soldier talk to me that way!

### COLONEL ALBERT HANEY

Oh, you won't, huh? Well, we'll just see about that. Rip!

ENTER RIP ROBERTSON.

COLONEL ALBERT HANEY

Rip here is my assistant. His favorite job in Korea was accompanying ROK guerrillas above the 38th Parallel and bringing back Chink ears. Rip, the banana!

RIP ROBERTSON

(Takes out an enormous BANANA plastered with UFCO STICKERS, and a TUBE of K-Y JELLY.)

Okay, Senator, we can do it with or without the lubricant, all depends on whether you give me any trouble or not.

(beat)

I am named Packstrap.

JOHN McCORMACK

No, no, get back— Ouch! Oof! Eeek! Yipes!

SAM ZEMURRAY

There's nothing I love better than money, but watching this asshole being humiliated is kind of fun, too.

(beat)

We are the Lords of Xibalba, the Land of Death.

CUT TO:

2    INT of OFFICE. Tropical vegetation visible out of WINDOW. MAN seated behind desk; two MEN standing.

JOHN PEURIFOY

(Seated)

We've got the go-ahead, boys. As US Ambassador to Guatemala, I've sworn to President Arbenz that we have nothing to do with any rebels.

BIRCH O'NEIL

And as CIA station chief, I've made sure to establish secure back channels, so that there's no evidence of contact with the plotters back home.

E. HOWARD HUNT

I've been helping with all the dirty tricks. For instance, the walls of Guatemala City are covered with the number 32, which everyone assumes is a reference to the thirty-second article of the Constitution, which prohibits political parties from having outside—namely Commie—affiliations. But we all know what two to the

fifth power really means.
(beat)
My assistants are super-tricky too. David Atlee Phillips has the country ringed with radio transmitters and jamming stations. Henry Heckscher, one of our old Nazis, is bribing Army officers to defect. And don't forget that Ambassador Willauer in Honduras is running the operations of Civil Air Transport, the former Flying Tigers and current CIA front, who a few years ago helped Chiang Kaishek in China. Unfortunately, the Commies won that one.

JOHN PEURIFOY

I feel confident of victory now, boys. By the time we're done, this country will be as fucked-over as Greece, where I just helped install a right-wing dictatorship.

E. HOWARD HUNT

This is good training for Nixon's 1972 re-election, which I stochastically intuit.

CUT TO:

3 EXT of RUINED TEMPLE, set in middle of jungle. These are the remains of the Mayan town of Rotten Cane. TEMPLE is covered with vines and trees. ZOOM in on empty WINDOW. POV goes INT. ROOM with walls and floor of stone blocks. ROOM is plainly inhabited: COUCH, WATER GOURDS, native RUGS, single SHELF with BOOKS. MAN is seated on COUCH in *zazen* posture. MAN is a *ladino*, part Indian, part European, with Indian predominant.

ENTER CROWD of INDIANS.

FIRST INDIAN

Do we dare disturb the daykeeper?

SECOND INDIAN

Are you batshit, man, of course we gotta! The future of the country is at stake!
(Shakes seated MAN out of his trance)

EIGHT SNAKE

(Instantly alert)
Why do you disrupt my communion with Sophia?

FIRST INDIAN

Holy Mother-Father, we had to! CIA-backed troops have crossed the border. They are going to overthrow our democratically elected government and replace it with lickspittle imperialistic lackeys.

EIGHT SNAKE

(Disdainful)

What does it matter who occupies Guatemala City? We have seen conquerors come and go over the centuries. Politics is all an illusion. You know that our true task is to worship time until the *alautun* changes. When the *kalpagni*, or burning fire of Armageddon, arrives, we will come into our kingdom.

(Lifts BOOK down from SHELF. BOOK is covered in jaguar-hide)

Let me read to you—

SECOND INDIAN

Holy Laughing Falcon, Boss, forget the scriptures for a minute, willya! It's easy for you not to worry, you don't got no family to feed! You can afford to go Blue Sky Mining, but the company ain't doing right by us. If we don't get some relief from those UFCO bastards, we're gonna starve. They don't even pay us in real money, ya know, just company scrip.

EIGHT SNAKE

You dare to dispute me, Eight Snake? Am I not a descendent of the Holy Grandparents, Xpiyacoc and Xmucane, of their twin children, One Hunahpu and Seven Hunahpu, and of their twins, One Monkey and One Artisan, Hunahpu and Xbalanque, and so on, down through the *katuns*? Do I not control the Hurricane and the Thunderbolt? Was not the dharma transmitted to me directly from Seung Sahn? I have been educated at Oxford and Paris, Boston and Alexandria! The mitochondria of Blood Woman live on in my cells!

SECOND INDIAN

That's cool, daykeeper, but it still don't help me when I'm caught in the crossfire. Whatcha gonna do for your people?

EIGHT SNAKE

I will perform a divination.

EIGHT SNAKE lights BRAZIER and smoke of burning COPAL and YARROW ascends. Takes BAG and spills CORN KERNELS on floor. Makes pass with RIGHT HAND over them, then scoops up handful. Pushes remainder aside, sets down reserved ones and begins to arrange them in groups of four. Remainder divided into a group of two and a single. EIGHT SNAKE studies groupings intently when done.

EIGHT SNAKE

Hmmm, I wish I could consult an *Afa-du* master on this one. Well, no time for that.

(Turns to audience of INDIANS)

The Lords of Xibalba are against us. They have sent their messengers, the Owls and Whipporwills, ahead of their agents. Down the Black Road, over the River of Churning Spikes, the River of Blood, and the River of Pus they have come, to cause tumult and disorder. The country will suffer for a *katun* or more before there will be any relief. There is nothing I can do.

SECOND INDIAN

Nothing! Call up K, why doncha!

EIGHT SNAKE

No, I must reserve Sovereign Plumed Serpent.

SECOND INDIAN

Well, we're dead meat. *El Pulpo*, the Octopus, which is what us superstitious Indians call UFCO, will win for sure.

EIGHT SNAKE

Not in the long run.

FIRST INDIAN

As John Maynard Keynes said: "In the long run, we'll all be dead."

QUICK CUT BACK TO:

4 INT of EIGHT SNAKE'S ROOM. EIGHT SNAKE is alone. INDIANS burst in.

FIRST INDIAN

Now the rebels have taken Esquipulas, home of the Church of the Black Christ!

EIGHT SNAKE

There is still nothing to be done.

SECOND INDIAN

I've had it! Bring in the heavy guns!

ENTER AL HUBBARD—CAPTAIN TRIPS—AND ERNESTO "CHE" GUEVARA.

ERNESTO "CHE" GUEVARA

I was a poor magazine and book seller in Guatemala City when this imperialistic UFCO war radicalized me. Now I intend to split for Cuba. But first, I will aid my comrades by transmitting my revolutionary virus to this revisionist dupe.

(Takes out Mao's *Little Red Book* and begins reading aloud)

AL HUBBARD
Hold him down, boys, I'm gonna give him 1300 mikes!

INDIANS pinion EIGHT SNAKE, while HUBBARD pinches his nose and pours liquid LSD down his throat. GUEVARA continues to read, voice gradually becoming distorted and alien.

CLOSE UP of EIGHT SNAKE'S FACE, which undergoes startling expressions.

CHECKERBOARD WIPE TO:

5   MONTAGE OF SFX: FLOWING COLORS, PULSING AMORPHOUS ORGANISMS, TENDRILS OF *QI* ENERGY. KUNDALINI SERPENT ERUPTS FROM EIGHT SNAKE'S ABDOMEN, COILS TO HEAVEN, PIERCES CLOUD AND UNLEASHES RAIN OF AUTONOMOUS PRICKS AND CUNTS. SWARM OF HUMMINGBIRDS WITH DRAGON FACES SURROUNDS EIGHT SNAKE'S HEAD. OTHER ASSORTED WEIRDNESSES. EVENTUALLY, LSD BEGINS TO WEAR OFF.

DISSOLVE TO:

6   CLOSE UP OF EIGHT SNAKE'S FACE.

EIGHT SNAKE
I have been blinded by the light, cut loose like a deuce, another runner in the night. I got down, but I never got tight, and I'm gonna make it tonight!

ALL INDIANS
Hooray!

EIGHT SNAKE proceeds to cast spells: *chakih mesa*, or "dry table," which causes emaciation in the victim, and *rax mesa*, or "fresh table," which makes the victim vomit blood.

CUT TO:

7   MONTAGE OF SOLDIERS DYING. PLAGUES ARE STOPPED WITH ADMINISTRA-TION OF ANTIBIOTICS.

BACK TO:

8 EIGHT SNAKE slumped in defeat.

EIGHT SNAKE

It's no use, men, I waited too long. The medicines of Xibalba are too strong. I dare not let Hurricane loose, or the country will be destroyed. And the day is named Death, not propitious for Sovereign Plumed Serpent. No, I fear the land is theirs now.

SECOND INDIAN

It's all right, Daykeeper, you did your best.

EIGHT SNAKE

(Recouping energies)

From now on, we'll just have to fight them underground, hit them where they're weakest. Men, back to your farms! It's time to plant the coca leaf.

CUT TO:

9    INT of EIGHT SNAKE'S ROOM. EIGHT SNAKE present, with naked honey-haired WOMAN. EIGHT SNAKE looks considerably older. ENTER TWO INDIANS holding THIRD INDIAN captive.

FIRST INDIAN

Holy Mother-Father, here's the leak. We caught him getting paid by the cops in town.

EIGHT SNAKE

I feel the need of some exercise. A ball game, perhaps.... Off with his head!

THIRD INDIAN faints, is dragged outside. SOUND of chopping blade hitting block. EIGHT SNAKE suits up in KILT, HIP YOKE, ARM GUARDS, PANACHE, HEADBAND.

EIGHT SNAKE

Will you join me, Vivian?

VIVIAN VERVAIN

No thanks, Snakey! I give head, but I don't play with one!

EIGHT SNAKE

You make an excellent pun, Vivian. As you know, the Mayan glyph system favors puns, since glyphs may be read either syllabically or iconographically. The *zacbal tzih*, or play on words, lies at the heart of our thinking.

VIVIAN VERVAIN

And don't forget that the concept of the DNA reading frame means there's millions of puns in our very cells.

EIGHT SNAKE
Excellently phrased. Well, I'm off to the game.

EXIT EIGHT SNAKE. VERVAIN passes time by reading *Popul Vuh* and frigging herself.

VIVIAN VERVAIN
(Closing BOOK and licking her FINGERS)
What a wild guy that Snakey is! To think he's gone from tribal shaman to head of Western Hemisphere drug traffic in a mere thirty years or so. He gives me the goldarned shivers. I'm a lucky girl to get this assignment....

ENTER EIGHT SNAKE. He is covered in splatters of blood.

EIGHT SNAKE
The ball is no longer suitable for play.... Ah, that felt good. Sometimes the responsibilities of running a worldwide drug cartel bring me down. I am grateful I found you, Vivian, for you help relieve the stress.

VIVIAN VERVAIN
Balling the Eight is what I'm best at.

EIGHT SNAKE
Another fine pun! Come to me, Little Prawn House.

CUT TO:

10  MONTAGE OF EIGHT SNAKE'S DUTIES. HE MEETS WITH NOTORIOUS ASSASSIN, MICHAEL DECKER, AGENT 0010, FORMER STOOGE OF THE UNITED STATES INFORMATION AGENCY; HE MEETS WITH THE FAMOUS SANDINISTA, COMMANDER ZERO; HE DISPOSES OF ANOTHER TRAITOR IN A PIT FULL OF SNAKES; HE SHAKES HEAD OVER BALANCE SHEETS. LOSSES SEEM TO OUTNUMBER PROFITS. MANY SHOTS OF BAILING OUT UNDERLINGS.

CUT TO:

11  LONGSHOT OF TEMPLE. IT IS SURROUNDED BY AN ARMY OF MEN CREEPING THROUGH THE JUNGLE, TRADING GUNFIRE WITH THE DEFENDERS IN THE RUINS.

CUT TO:

12  INT of EIGHT SNAKE'S ROOM. EIGHT SNAKE and VIVIAN VERVAIN present.

EIGHT SNAKE

This looks like the end of a *katun*, Vivian. My empire is collapsing around my ears. This new American War on Drugs is constricting M-4 too tightly. I can't figure out what they have in mind.... With Faber, I always knew where I stood, but his successor, Anguipede— No, the DEA cannot be trusted anymore. Aided by G-2, Guatemala's intelligence agency, they've knocked the props out from under me. We've got to relocate the operation, maybe lie low for a while.

VIVIAN VERVAIN

Sounds good to me, Snakey. But how are we going to get past these narcs?

EIGHT SNAKE

There is an extensive network of caves beneath Rotten Cane, and they lead far, far away, farther than you can imagine. But we are not descending into darkness this time, by the organelles of Blood Woman! We will rise up to the sun. But first, I need you to suck my little bird up and get the *qi* flowing.

VIVIAN VERVAIN

You want your bird in my bush?

EIGHT SNAKE

Not necessary. Just make it stiff.

VIVIAN VERVAIN begins to suck EIGHT SNAKE'S COCK, which protrudes from under his KILT. When it is stiff, she reluctantly disengages, dropping back onto to couch to frig herself. EIGHT SNAKE moves to an ALTAR on which lies the detached SPIKE of a stingray fish and a stone BOWL containing a single piece of PAPER. He holds his PENIS above the BOWL with one HAND, and, picking up the SPIKE with the other, pierces the HEAD of his PRICK, letting several DROPS OF BLOOD fall on the PAPER, which he then ceremoniously ignites. The SMOKE coils heavenwards.

EIGHT SNAKE

It should not take long now, Vivian. Gather what you need.

VIVIAN VERVAIN

(FINGERS in her TWAT)

I need you up me, Snakey!

EIGHT SNAKE

We have barely enough time....

EIGHT SNAKE and VIVIAN VERVAIN begin fucking. Just as they cum, a MAN ENTERS.

His face is alive with tics and twitches, he limps and carries a GUN.

                    EMMETT DEMESNE
    Vivian!
(Drops gun in shock)

EIGHT SNAKE disengages from VIVIAN VERVAIN, jumps up and socks EMMETT DEMESNE, who falls to floor.

                                            CUT TO:

13   LONGSHOT OUT WINDOW. A DOT IN THE DISTANCE SWELLS WITH EACH PASSING SECOND. FINALLY, IT CAN BE DISTINGUISHED AS KUKULCAN, SOVEREIGN PLUMED SERPENT, CREATOR OF THE UNIVERSE. KUKULCAN ARRIVES AT RUINS, THRUSTS HEAD THROUGH WALL IN AN EXPLOSION OF STONE.

                                            CUT TO:

14   INT of ROOM. KUKULCAN'S HEAD protruding, EMMETT DEMESNE paralyzed with fear on the floor. EIGHT SNAKE and VIVIAN VERVAIN clamber onboard their Civil Air Transport.

                    VIVIAN VERVAIN
    Oh, Snakey, this big guy feels so good between my legs!
(Rubs her bare wet PUSSY on K's broad BACK)

                    KUKULCAN
(With evident pleasure)
    Hissssssssssssss!

                    EIGHT SNAKE
    Farewell, Demesne. This round is yours, but do not count me out yet.

                                            FADE OUT.

Wow. Those were the best special effects Cy has ever seen.... And that Vivian gal was some sexy dish....
    "Cy, what are you doing? Haven't you slept at all?"
    Looking up, Cyril spies Polly. She stands in the bedroom doorway, wearing the bottoms belonging to a pair of fur pajamas Ruby gave him once as a joke. It's a wild

wild life.... There are rosy blotches on the flesh of her breasts and stomach, where the ridges of crumpled sheets pressed. She's pretty in pink, fer shure.

"Uh, yeah, I guess." Cy suddenly realizes he's got this enormous boner. Who ever woulda thought ancient sacred books could be so, um, stimulating? Guess it just takes the right director....

Cy stands and advances on Polly. Her eyes go wide.

"What, again? Now?"

Cy tries to growl like a jaguar: "Grrrrr." Comes out sounding more like Tony the Tiger.

He bumps crotches with her, and grabs her by the ass with both hands. She jumps up and wraps her legs around his waist. The fur pajamas make her feel like a big cat.

Cy walks the two of them backwards and drops Polly on the bed. The PJs come off, they fuck missionary style, and Cy collapses, brain and body sated at last.

"You sleep now," whispers Polly. "I'll stick to you like a stamp to a letter, my guy...."

Cy complies.

Four in the morning, woke up from outa my dreams. Nowhere to go but back to sleep, but I'm reconciled.

Peace like a river flows thru the city.

All too soon, tho, here comes the sun! The sun is shining brightly, like a red rubber ball. Wake up, wake up, get out of bed, and let the sun shine to your head! Sunshine, go away today, don't feel much like laughing. Ain't no sunshine when Ruby's gone....

Riding along on a carousel.... Will I ever catch up to you, Ruby? We're captives on a Carousel of Time. We can't return, we can only look behind from where we came....

Polly's not in bed. Cy can smell coffee, *soma* of the gods. He drags himself up, takes a leak, dons some boxers, and heads out to the kitchen.

There's a big day of detecting ahead, Cy knows. But he wants to untangle the relationship between them first. The guilt he felt last night is still a sour taste in his mouth, made even worse by his uncontrollable third attack of lust.

"Mornin', Pol," essays Cy.

Polly don't seem too embarrassed: she meets his eyes, smiles warmly. "Hi, Cy. Want some Hi-C?" She giggles. "I've been waiting years for a chance to say that."

Gee, Cy's not looking for a cynical girl, but this early morning exuberance could easily get on your nerves. He never knew how much he appreciated Ruby's matinal mopiness.

"Uh, thanks. Polly, before we do anything today, I want to get something straight between us."

"Already?"

"Polly, please. Don't you have any remorse for what we did last night?"

"Which time am I supposed to feel bad about?"

"Polly, I'm trying to resolve an ethical dilemma, and you're not helping."

"Are you a Catholic?"

"Polly—"

"Oh, I get it. This is marriage proposal. Should I get a Polly trousseau ready? Were goin' to the chapel and we're gonna get married?"

"Pol, c'mon!"

His substitute girlfriend goes all serious. "Cy, I know what you're getting at, and I'm trying to deflect it. I've been faithful to Augie for years now, as I bet you've been with Ruby. But Augie and Ruby aren't here now. They're out of the picture, they're a missing factor in the equation, and we need to concentrate on finding them. You were totally flipping out yesterday from your AIDS, and I did the only thing I knew of to calm you down. And it worked. Look, you feel pretty good this morning, don't you?"

Cy takes mental inventory. "Why, yeah, I guess I do. I got you, I feel good!"

"Fine. And if we keep on screwing like we did last night, maybe we can even wipe the AIDS out of your system entirely. Not that that's the only reason I just wanna make love to you. This isn't easy to put into words, so roll with me, Cy."

"I was gonna say—"

"No, listen to me. I'm attracted to you as a lover for yourself. You've always been one of my best friends, Cy. Now that friendship's become something deeper. I can't pretend to say what'll happen when we get Augie and Ruby back, anymore than you can. But one thing I know is that I won't torture myself with useless moral quizzes while there are more important things to worry about."

Cy is mollified. "Well, I just wanted you to know I don't take anything for granted."

"Oh, Cyril, I know that! Here, drink some coffee and smile."

"Okay.... Hey, Pol, I had a brainstorm while you were sleeping."

As he tells lubricious Polly now of his lucubrations, Cy gets more and more excited. His wild theory that Wu is seeking omniscience and immortality—based solely on that one phrase of Lantz's—seems more and more probable. Polly appears to think so too.

"Omniscience does tie in with information theory, Cy, and that esoteric discipline does seem to underlie all of Wu's actions. One could theoretically handle infinite information if one's mental channels were infinitely large, or if one could develop an ultimate encoding scheme. And Shannon's Second Theorem does allow the possibility of a perfectly efficient code. Of course, there'd be the problem of limiting biological noise.... And would omniscience extend into the future as well as the past and present? That's the stochastic angle. As for immortality—I don't quite have a fix on that yet. Perhaps it has to do with that secret project that Ruby filmed. Anyway, we can poke at Lantz's shell a little more effectively now. Let's go roust him out."

"Go for it!" exclaims our caffeine-juiced boy.

On the subway, Cyril remembers a question he had for Polly.

"Hey, Pol, you still got that same job?"

Upon graduation with her degree in semiotics, Polly had been about as employable as a buggy-whip maker. After hard searching, she had at last found a job dealing with signs: hanging billboards, with pastepot and brush.

"No, I gave it up just before Augie disappeared. It was too boring. My boss, Elias McDaniel, was real mad at me too. He had a big job coming up and needed me. Funny thing, the assignment was right in Kenmore Square, near your record store. Somebody bought the illuminated CITGO sign, and we were supposed to alter it." Polly gets a thoughtful look. "In fact, you know that equation about channel capacity I showed you?"

"Yeah...."

"That's what was supposed to go on the billboard. I didn't think much about it at the time, but now...."

"I knew I saw that formula someplace before! It's up there, bigger'n Godzilla, where the whole city can see it. With the hassle in the store, tho, I forgot all about it. Do you think Wu had anything to do with it?"

"Sure seems likely," avers Pol. "But what exactly is he trying to say?"

"Search me...."

"Right here?"

"Hey, Polly, don't, people are watching!"

Cy's forced to fend off Polly's tickling fingers like a skittish virgin, much to the amusement of their fellow riders.

That Polly—she's a hot number!

Soon they're in the lobby of the HOT—- L-AMI-A.

The same outrageous black clerk is behind the counter, reading a comic: *Hardboiled*. He's seated in a high-backed chair that looks like a coffin around him.

Looking up and spotting Cy, he sneers and says, "Welcome to the Hotel California, may we help you?"

"Listen, buddy, don't give me no lip."

"Lips like sugar? Sugar kisses? You need a *girl* for that. Bernadette? Evangeline? Sweet Caroline? Cracklin' Rosie? Windy? Allison? Carrie-Anne? Charlotte Ann? Miss Molly? Darling Nikki? Mustang Sally? Sweet Jane? Dear Prudence? My Sharona? Sexy Sadie? Jessica? Runaround Sue? Maybellene? Long Tall Sally? Short Fat Fannie? Jenny Jenny? Mojo Hanna? Miss Ann? Donna? Sherry? Sussudio? Sally Mae? Cecilia? Bony Moronie? Sweet Judy Blue Eyes? Gloria? Suzanne? Melody Cool? Aw, you're just Kathy's Klown."

"I'm gonna punch you out, man—"

"Cy, don't waste your time. Let's go see Lantz."

Upstairs all is as before, except a little quieter. Jesus, was it only yesterday that they were here? So much has happened. Time is tight, time seems unhinged. Should he be wearing a Dali watch on his wrist...?

Cy knocks on door 64. No answer. Has Lantz succumbed totally to AIDS, retreating into his autistic cocoon to escape the information tsunami? Cy pushes on the door.

It's unlocked and swings in.

They enter.

The room is empty.

"Shit!" says Cy. "He's cut out on us."

"He may have left behind a clue," pollyannas Polly. "Let's look."

Cyril picks an overstuffed chair piled with dirty clothes to investigate; Polly tackles the bureau.

Picking up each piece of clothing, Cy goes through the pockets.

Heh-hey! Here's a scrap of paper! And it says:

> Big Mama Thornton birthed God.
> Janis nursed Him.
> Carole King schooled Him.
> Madonna fucked Him.

Cy crumples it up and tosses it, not noticing the message's parallel to the park-bench palimpsest he encountered a few days ago.

Back to the pockets. Nothing, nothing, nothing, what's this? It's a coin....whoops, it's slippery!

The coin falls into the remaining clothes, and Cyril scrabbles for it. The coin retreats out of reach. Cy thrusts deeper for it. Oh shit, it's gone down between the cushions. Wedge your hand in, kid, down the black hole. Where the *fuck* is it?

Suddenly Cy experiences immense *déjà vu*. He's lived thru this before. When? Oh, yeah, when the boy asked for change in the store, and all the coins spilled and skittered off. Does life always repeat, "first as tragedy, then as farce?" Is Cy doomed to cycle thru events again and again? He supposes duplication underscores the point, insures correct reception, but is it necessary to live always in

## THE LAND OF REDUNDANCY

In the Land of Redundancy, everything repeats. Everything happens twice in the Redundant Land. People get up in the morning, then they get up again. They get up twice. They have breakfast once, then another. Two meals. They drive to work, turn around, go home, then drive there again. Two trips to work. Telephones always ring twice, a double ring, or else multiples of two. People verify facts, then check them again. Doublechecking. Two lunches. One, then another. Two coffee breaks. A first, and a second. When it's time to drive home, they do it once, go back to work, then home again. Twice as much commuting. Two suppers. Dinner times two. They watch a TV show, then its instant replay. They see it two times. Everyone cums twice with their mate. In the same position, of course. All dreams happen twice. Dream reruns. In the morning, it's another day. Another day. The national motto of Redundant Land is:

$$R \overset{\Delta}{=} 1 - \frac{H}{H_{\text{max}}}$$

The people explain themselves by saying, "You must have redundancy to gain complexity; complexity only comes with redundancy. Allow me to reiterate: redundancy kicks complexity kicks up, complexity is boosted by redundancy."

Or in other words, Go back, Jack, and do it again.

But them dummies don't even know the difference between context-free and context-sensitive redundancy!

Contact with the coin brings Cy back from his fugue. Hey, these trips are getting to be no sweat. Kinda interesting, actually. Imagine, such a crazy place....

"Polly, I found something!"

"Me too!"

Cy brings the coin to Polly and they examine it together. It's a big silver cartwheel emblazoned with a dragon on one side and a phoenix on the other, dated 1923. Well, so what? Don't mean a thing to either of 'em. Cy pockets the coin regretfully.

Polly's find, however, is potentially more interesting. It's a brochure for one of them crazy flotation centers.

ZAQUICAZ AQUA RETREAT
251 MENLOVE AVENUE
ESCAPE YOUR CARES
EXPERIENCE RELIEF
RATES:
"I'D GIVE YOU EVERYTHING I'VE GOT
FOR SOME PEACE OF MIND."

"You think they know Lantz there?" queries Cyril.

"Worth a shot."

They set off.

Underground, in the arteries of the city, Cyril, waiting on the platform, idly takes the mysterious coin from his jeans. How did a down-and-out bum like Lantz, living in a flop-house, come to have such an obviously rare coin? Was it a remnant of his former respectable life as a well-paid data-processor? Why would he hold on to this one possession, after losing all others? What was its significance? Would it help them recover Ruby and Augie?

Cy, despite subconsciously knowing better, begins fingering the bas-relief dragon on the coin. (Is the dragon heads and the phoenix tails, or vice-versa? Ain't like no US currency. Both animals got heads, both got tails. This here is a redundant coin that swings both ways!) Oh-oh, watch out, boy! The tactile stimulation from this history-rich object is inducing the by-now familiar fugue-state, and Cy's soon off spinning into

## THE LIFE OF IMPY, THE IMPERIAL DOLLAR

Minted in 1923, Impy—as he was called by his friends—was doomed to a life of frustration. Bearing the discredited symbols of the Dragon Throned Emperor—who had been forced to abidicate in 1912—Impy was deemed too subversive for circulation. Impy and all his brothers and sisters were impounded under orders by Sun Yatsen.

For years Impy sat forgotten in a dark bank vault in Nanking, the provisional capitol, itching to be out in the world, taking part in the flow of commerce, conveying value, performing as legal tender, passing from wanton, won-ton hand to hand, being used and abused by strangers, fondled and adored, cursed and bitten—Impy almost orgasmed just thinking about it.

But such a conventional life was not to be for Impy and his cousins.

It was early October, 1934. The Nationalists under Chiang Kaishek were fighting the Communists under Mao. Mao's troops were desperate for funds. A task force was dispatched to raid the bank where Impy moldered. They took severe losses, but mananged to make off with a large haul. Impy saw the light of day for the first time in a decade.

Setting out to join Mao in the south, the party was ambushed by a gang of Triad Society thugs.

The Triad Societies—or tongs—were remnants of Taoist mystery cults. Over the millennia, they had devolved from seekers of immortality and wisdom to mere criminal mobs. There were many different Triads: The Society of the White Lily, the Hung Society (*well hung*, I would venture), the Incense Burners, the Origin of Chaos, the Origin of the Dragon, the Society of Heaven and Earth, the Green Lotus Hall, the Heavenly Queen Hall, the Great Blending Hall, the Extensive Conversion Hall, the Shaolin (martial artists supreme, masters of the Dragon's Touch, the founder of the Shaolin monastery having been Bodhidharma).... They retained certain mystical trappings, such as the Thirty-Six Vows of Initiation. (No. 20: "If a brother gives away the secret ceremonies of the society, may he have his eyes bitten out by a snake.") The Boxer Rebellion, led by a mad Chink who claimed he was Jesus's twin, was an example of the kind of force Triads could wield.

The tong that attacked the party carrying Impy was based in Shanghai. Known as the Sick Poppies, they dominated the opium (or as it was called, "foreign mud") trade. Led by a mysterious figure known only by his Society Number, 415 (4 x 15 + 4 = 64 hexagrams in the *I Ching*), the Sick Poppies had learned of the bank robbery and now planned in their apolitical fashion to help themselves to the spoils.

A pitched gun-battle ensued. A remnant of the Communists escaped, taking some of the Imperial Dollars with them. (These coins would accompany Mao on his entire Long March, thru thirteen provinces, eight forests ((whoa-ho, China Groves!)), sixty-four cities, over sixteen mountain ranges and across thirty-two rivers, eventually ending up in the Communist redoubt in the Caves of Yenan, far in the north, near the Great Wall.)

Impy, however, was part of the loot left behind.

Number 415 picked him up. "This is my *mebil*, my *churinga*, sent to me by Sovereign Plumed Serpent, sacred token that speaks to me alone, source of my ice-blink luck. No one may look on him. The words are in my belly." Number 415 pocketed Impy.

Gah-rate.... In the dark again, no possibility of fiscal promiscuity. What was this, a seraglio for silver? The other, luckier Dollars now embarked on a kind of shadowy half-life (when compared to their aboveground government-sanctioned peers), passing from thief to whore to opium-dealer, and others on the fringe of the economy, the black market.

Impy, meanwhile, had to content himself with an occasional fondling from Number 415 during moments of tension.

April, 1949. The Communists—under Liu Bocheng, the One-Eyed Dragon—succeeded in taking Shanghai from the Nationalists in a massive battle. Number 415, attempting to flee the city, was killed when he wandered into a shootout near the Park Hotel.

Number 415's corpse was heaved onto a pile of bodies.

Impy fell out of his pocket, and into the open mouth of another corpse.

The corpse stirred.

He gulped convulsively and swallowed Impy.

Done coughing, the man dragged himself to his feet and staggered off.

A Chinese man of indeterminate age, the swallower of Impy was dressed in antique embroidered robes and wore the once-traditional, now despised, pigtail, or queue.

By various shifts and stratagems, the man escaped to Formosa.

On the boat, with great pain, the man passed Impy in a costive bowel movement.

On Formosa, Impy, none the worse for his cloacal passage, was exchanged for a can of American Autocrat coffee, which the man hoped to—and eventually did—peddle spoon by spoon for a big profit, thereby enabling him to buy a consignment of vacuum tubes whose original purchaser had died mysteriously.

These tubes were in turn sold for a larger profit, which the man plowed back into purchase of a brothel. (This brothel was left in his uncle's will to a man named Hills, thus becoming "all the flesh that Hills was heir to." Disdaining the trade, he was eager to sell cheap.) Now possessed of a steady income, the man was enabled to diversify his investments and to begin the establishment of a financial empire.

This man, of course, was Doctor Wu.

Thus, Impy stood in relation to Wu rather as did a certain Lucky Dime to one

Scrooge McDuck (the illustrated chronicles of whose career coincidentally began in the same year).

Unlike Dime Number One, tho, Impy was not kept cherished in a vault, but cast off like a spurned lover who had provided the requisite thrill, to make his own way in the world.

After a few dozen transactions, Impy ended up in Cambodia, in the till of a club called *Le Serpente*. One night he was given as change to a fellow named Phillipe deClosets.

Weh-hell.... When deClosets' met his untimely end, his lovin' daughter, Mekong Melusine, came into her inheritance. Not even knowing what money was, she polished Impy up and kept him as an ornament. When Nick Fury—*né* Harry Covair—reived her away naked from her only home, Impy was left behind. One day the peasants from the nearby village summoned up enough courage to investigate the disappearance of their beloved young *apsaras*. (The ruins had never lacked a priestess in living memory. The peasants felt the world was ending. And for them—with the establishment of the Khmer Rouge Year Zero not far off—it was.) Finding Impy, they took him away.

Many exchanges later, Impy came into the possession of one Lao Cohen.

Cohen was a *yakuza,* or Japanese gangster. His parents were Lilith Cohen, an aide to General MacArthur during his occupation of Tokyo, and a young Japanese mathematician named Hokyo Zammai. Zammai was a fanatical student of Taoism, the philosophy originated by Lao Tze, which explained his choice of a name for his half-breed son. He was especially intrigued by the researches of Chang Tao-lin, a Taoist alchemist who claimed to have discovered immortality in the second century.

Hokyo Zammai, to further his researches, abandoned his lover and son and emigrated to America.

Lilith Cohen, infatuated with Japan and nostalgic for the days of her courtship, remained behind to raise her boy.

Living in a society that placed a premium on racial purity, an illegitimate halfbreed endowed with a Chinese-Jewish name came in for a lot of prejudicial treatment. This early abuse led directly to young Cohen's choice of careers. Rejecting the society that had rejected him, he joined the *yakuza,* or "worthless ones," rulers of Japan's underworld. The *yakuza,* man—they were cool. They had the original Bad Attitude. They dressed all in white and took no shit from no one. (Hey, fella, you there tearin' up the street. If you wear that white tuxedo, how you gonna beat the heat?) They loved tattoos, these guys, up and down their bodies. The one required tattoo, the identifying mark of a *yakuza,* was a tiny dragon, located invisibly in a bizarre place: *under the eyebrow.*

Cohen acquired Impy in 1977 as part of a deal that involved several million yen and a mixed bill of lading of stolen silicon chips, sunglasses and M&M's. Recognizing the coin as a collector's item, Cohen sold it to a numismatist in the US, named Bongo Drummond.

Drummond lived in New York. One night his apartment was burgled. Impy ended up in the hands of a shady Boston dealer who went by the handle of L'Angelo Misterioso. Misterioso wanted some software written to catalogue his stock. He hired Ferdie Lantz, who was moonlighting from his job at Wu Labs. When asked to name his price, Lantz, his eye falling on Impy, felt a mysterious impulse to possess him, and singled out the coin. The dealer agreed. And when Lantz suffered his information-impelled decline, Impy was the one talisman he instinctively retained....

Cy stares at the coin. Holy-moly, wotta story. To think that this coin was actually touched—in quite an intimate fashion, too—at one time by the mysterious Wu. It somehow makes that invisible man, the web-centered spider, more real, gives him more substance and lends credibility to the improbable prospect that Cy and Polly will be able to get a handle on him and confront him. Cy hopes they can pry something out of Lantz—provided they can catch up with the renegade programmer—but if they can't, Cy's understandable impatience and anxiety is causing him to lean more and more toward his original impulse of simply storming into Wu Labs and demanding Ruby and Augie back....

Their train pulls into the station. Polly and Cy climb aboard. Seated, Cy tells Polly of his latest Universal Flash, distilled from his information overload (which disease, while still scary, is proving rather useful).

Polly seems excited. "This is a sign that we're on the right track, Cy. Stumbling on such a piece of Wu's past has given us more insight into the forces that have shaped him. We've got a better chance now of understanding what motivates him, and what he's after."

Cy feels good that he's helped their quest along so smartly. Still holding Impy, he flips the coin in an excess of spirits toward the ceiling of the car. Impy spins over and over, heads, tails, heads, tails, heads, tails....

On, off.

Dot, dash.

Yin, yang.

In, out.

Excited, inhibited.

Firing, not firing.

Thumbs-up, thumbs-down.

Charged, neutral.

One, zero.

Satori bursts on him then: *every coin is a binary switch, capable of registering two states.* Eight coins would comprise a byte, and could contain a byte's worth of information. And all the coins in the world, then, represent....*a huge computer!*

What programs are processed by this ancient money-machine, millennia older than its silicon brothers; what artificial intelligence does it strive to express? Where are the readouts, what forms do they take, and who interprets them? Who debugs M1 if the results are unsatisfactory? Is there a programmer of pennies, a compiler of cash? The velocity of money is defined as the rate at which it changes hands, but who has measured how many millions of instructions per second money performs, as coins flip and flop from one state to another? Is there a Heisenbergian Observer who witnesses the binary state of every coin, and thus causes it to signify? Is the money-engine *getting smarter*, with every coin added to the world's store? (And does it regard credit cards as a threat to its life?) Money, like information, seems exempt from the normal conservation laws that govern energy and matter. Both can be created from nothing, and proliferate effortlessly, as when banks float currency transfers and gain MONEY FOR NOTHING (except maybe they get a blister on their little finger). Is there an ultimate goal, an Omega Point, that the money-mind is striving for, a RUN STOP, END, or RETURN that will signal the Final Computation?

Heavy stuff, thinks Cy, as he catches Impy (who comes up heads—or is that tails?). But he can't solve such weighty metaphysical puzzlers now, for they're at their stop.

End of what transportation specialists call "dwell time," time spent in transit.

Aboveground, Cy and Polly orient themselves by familiar buildings—they're not far from Northeastern, their alma mater—and head toward the address given in the brochure for the flotation center. Usta be a saloon they patronized as students on Menlove Avenue, yeah, it's still here: THE TWANG BAR.

Polly wears a worried face, and Cy inquires why.

"It's been bothering me why Lantz, in his condition, would want to go to such a place. It just hit me on the train. You know how these tanks are sometimes called sensory-deprivation units, don't you? They're quite potent forces for altering one's mental state. John Lilly, their inventor, has actually called them 'a hole in the universe.' Well, you saw how Lantz was trying to muffle all his senses against any further input that would tax his clogged mind. Well, what better way than a flotation tank?"

"What's to worry about then? Shouldn't it have a calming effect on him, kinda restore him to reality, like?"

"In a relatively early case of AIDS—like yours, Cy—that would indeed happen. And in fact, if we don't get your life simplified soon, I might recommend such a treatment. But in Lantz's advanced case, where his brain has already started what's known as 'psychic fibrillation,' I'm afraid just the opposite might be true. Freed from external stimuli, Lantz might retreat totally inward."

"Catatonia?"

Polly nods. "Or worse."

Gah-rate.... Just when they thought they had his pressure points figured out, their one lead might be reduced to a mindless hunka jelly.

ZAQUICAZ AQUA RETREAT shows ahead. It looks sorta seedy.... Cyril and Polly pick up their pace and are soon thru the door of the Deprivation Den.

The receptionist is a young nebbish wearing a Walkman. He's tapping two pencils like drumsticks on his desk, in time to the music. Cy thinks nothing of it till he notices that the lid of the Walkman is open, no tape inside.

A nametag alligator-clipped to the guy's shirt reads: H. NUMINOSO.

"Gee," says Cy, "It's Mister Laocoon...."

"What?" puzzles Polly.

"Never mind. Let me talk to this guy."

When Numinoso shows no intention of acknowledging them, Cy steps up and removes his headphones.

"Hey, look what they've done to my song, Ma...." Numinoso gazes heavenward. "It don't matter, I can still hear it." He drops the pencils and begins strummin' an air guitar.

"Hyman, listen to me, there's no music playing."

"You're wrong, man, I hear it all the time now, it's all I can hear. It's only juke-box music, it's only rock 'n roll, but I like it. Rock 'n' roll is here to stay, rock 'n' roll music, any ol' way you choose it. Roll over Claude Shannon, and tell Norbert Weiner the news."

Cy sees there's no way he can really communicate with Numinoso, to ask him to resolve some of the questions raised by his fanzine. Best to just find Lantz and get out.

"Hyman, we need to ask you something."

Numinoso's eyes narrow down. "Did my sisters send you? They did, didn't they? Grace and Gloria, I hate those bitches. They did the rock 'n' roll hoochie koo with me, and I've never been the same since. You should see my little sis, she really knows how to twist you around."

"No, we don't even know them. We're just looking for a friend, Ferdie Lantz."

"You'd better be straight with me."

"We are."

"Let me check my sources." Numinoso picks up a stapler and holds it to his ear. "Yes....yes....no. The girl too? Okay." He sets the talkative stapler down. "All right, you're cool. Your friend checked in yesterday. Paid for a week."

"A week!" exclaims Cy. "You let your customers stay in for so long?"

Numinoso shrugs. "He said he could take care of himself. He planned to fast...."

"Quick, what tank is he in?"

"Number Ten."

"C'mon, Polly, let's get'm out."

Looking back, Cy sees Numinoso listening to messages from inside a coffee cup.

They're in Float Room Number Ten. An egg-shaped tank sits in its cradle, as in some kinda hatchery. The lighting is minimal.

Standing by the tank, they throw back the cover....

The artificial womb at first appears empty.

But wait, what's that...? Could it be...?

It is!

It's a tiny embryonic figure floating in the salty water, about as big as a minnow, a minature naked homunculus of Lantz, glowing and golden! Cy shuts his eyes in astonished disbelief. Incredibly, he can still see the shining image of Lantz! Howzat...?

An explanation suddenly occurs to Cy. He recalls how the early astronauts were puzzled by a certain high-orbital phenomenon. Even with eyes closed, they could still see "flashes of light." Turned out to be Cosmic Rays, unhindered by atmosphere, penetrating their eyelids and registering on their retinas! (None of the Kosmic Explorers ever turned into Ben Grimm, the Thing, tho. Too bad....) This must be how Cy is seeing Lantz!

The guy, whatever transmogrification he is undergoing, must be radiating! Hey, my balls could be frying! Talk about Blondie's "Fade Away and Radiate!"

It's a radiation vibe I'm grovvin' on. Don't it make you wanna get some son?

Cy opens his eyes. Same sight. An eensy-wheensy pitiful squeak comes from the Incredible Shrinking Programmer. Even as Cy and Polly watch in astonishment, the teensy figure continues to shrink, shrink, shrink, finally vanishing from their sight with an implosive POP!

Up or down Glashow's Snake of Sizes, it's all the same!

"What the fuck— Did I just see what I thought I saw?"

"It happens sometimes. His synaptic interconnections became incompatible with the physical structure of our universe, and the cosmos squeezed him out. He's moved to another level of existence."

"And that—"

"—could happen to you, Cy."

Holy Jacob's Ladder!

# EVERYBODY WANTS TO
# RULE THE WORLD

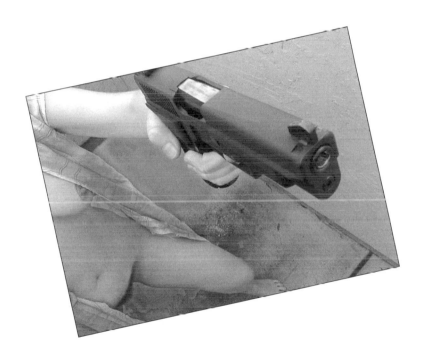

# K L U E S

## 00100100
"O sons of men, you add the future to the future, but your sum is spoiled by the grey cipher of death."
— *The Thousand and One Nights*

## 00100101
"Some people think [sequence banks for proteins and genes] are just repositories of information where people can go and pull out what they are looking for, like numbers from telephone books. But they are much more than that. They give new knowledge. They are 'connection machines' of a sort. Every time you add something into the pot, new knowledge can come out on the basis of the relationships that it finds in there. So they are information generators, not just repositories."
—Russell Doolittle

## 00100110
"To anticipate the future is the ultimate goal of the evolution of the human nervous system."
—Colin Blakemore

## 00100111
"By 1948 it began to take shape."
—Jack Kerouac

D amn my sophic soul, but life is good! So chortled a somewhat plump and positively placid fortyish Paddy O'Phidian to himself, this resplendently sunny Greek afternoon, with a bumper of sea-dark wine in his hand, a plate of snaky fried squid tendrils balanced on the arm of his canvas deck chair, a song longing to spring from his lips, a shine on his shoes and a melody in his heart, and a plethora of plans a-spin in his overactive brain, as he traveled gaily o'er the chop of the Ionian Sea, bound on yet another errand for his pair of sovereigns.

Neither of whom, he was fairly certain, knew just how much of a free agent he considered himself.

Ah, and wasn't this a grand and ancient land! Not as green and bountiful as the Old Sod, of course, from which he yet roamed in perpetual exile. (Homeward bound, I wish I was homeward bound...) But still, the sea-girt birthplace of Hecate and Medusa possessed a similar charm, Mediterranean fraternal twin to O'Phidian's Emerald Isle.

Seabirds raucous in the cloudless Homeric skies (white bird must fly, or she will die); dolphins cavorting off the starboard, diving down to the octopus's garden in the rain, where a certain city unsleeping lay; the stony sheep-speckled breast of the mainland off to port, haunts of ancient peace, holding the holy grail we seek; the pleasure of drinking wine spo-dee-odee....

Gonna take you on a Sea Cruise!

*Many's the time I've gazed on the open road, many's the time I've had a pocketful of gold*, thought O'Phidian, *but few times have been as glorious as this. Ialdabaoth, you wrought better than you knew! Grace and Glory still occasionally shine through the mud....*

So strongly did this marine scene harmonize with his mood that O'Phidian—much to the amusement of his fellow passengers, a motley collection of natives with a few foolhardy tourists thrown in—burst into song. Within seconds, someone was accompanying him on a bouzouki.

### O'PHIDIAN'S SEA CHANTEY

Oh, I'm just a Liddle Ion, um,
Sailing 'cross the Ionian Sea-hee.
Whether potassium or sodium,
That's strictly up to me-hee!

If it's the former that I'm bein',
Then the axon I am fleein',
But if the latter is my name,
Then floodin' channels is my game!

That's what's called Ack-shun Po-tent-shul:
A hot flame travelin' down a fuse,
A wave of chemicals tor-rent-shul,
That can enlighten or confuse!

Here I blithely glide, past the Node of Ranvier,
Just a few millimeters behind your very ear!
I'll make you see Heaven, or maybe Heh-hell—
Gee, ain't being an Ion suh-swell!

The Greeks, who had understood nothing of O'Phidian's Irish-accented English, applauded wildly at his bravura performance. The one or two English-speaking listeners twiddled index fingers significantly up at forehead level. O'Phidian raised his glass to toast these latter sardonically.

Nothing could spoil his day. Things were going too swimmingly just now.

The year was 1967, the month July.

Watson had been securely established at the Cold Spring Harbor facility. All the innovations and discoveries his team was producing were being siphoned off to Wu Labs, where they were instantly pursued and enlarged and tested on human subjects beyond anything permissible under the strict watchfulness of the NIH and other government agencies (excluding the lenient CIA, natch). And to think that the great Watson, on whom O'Phidian had eavesdropped a decade ago unknowingly in a London pub, should now be taking orders from him. (The Buddhist Wheel twirls and spins, spinning wheel got to go 'round, talk about your troubles, it's a crying shame, ride a painted pony, let the spinning wheel turn....)

Shannon had been rescued and rehabilitated, and now appeared to be firmly anchored in this world. Bejaysus, but that had been a close one! They had almost lost the old boy, due to his near-apolytrosis, and they certainly couldn't afford to let him slip away just yet....

The affair had begun in late 1960, early 1961. O'Phidian, well-established by then at Wu Labs, had taken the call at his home base in London. On the other end of the line was Robert Fano, one of Shannon's colleagues at MIT and a Wu mole.

"Mister O'Phidian, I just thought you should know. He's beginning to fade. I walk into his office sometimes, and I'm not sure whether he's there or not. What should I do?"

"Try to interest him in something new."

"Okay, but I can't guarantee anything."

A few months later, Fano had gotten back in touch. Not that O'Phidian needed the call to know what was going on. After all, Fano wasn't the only hook on his line. Fisher of men, fer shure!

"I think I've got him intrigued by something," Fano reported. "I happened to mention that no one knew how the stock market worked, and that was enough. Now he's off."

"Wonderful. Keep in touch."

The next week, Fano called again. Excitement was plain to hear in his voice.

"Listen to this: Shannon says that the stock market is merely an example of the partition of an independent time series, and that one can plot its fluctuations over a period of days! He won't tell me how much success he's having, but he just bought himself a GTO, a little deuce coupe and a hot rod Lincoln. This is sort of scary, Mister O'Phidian."

"I don't care if he buys all of General Motors, lad, so long as he stays out of Sophia's grasp."

But soon enough the market lost its allure for the Father of Info Theory. Too simplistic. For a brief time, John von Neumann succeeded in captivating Shannon with gambling, the essence of probability theory in the real world. They journeyed from Vegas to Ostend, where they met with Lord Keynes, himself a heavy-duty wagerer, to test out certain theories at the casinoes there, which featured roulette wheels lacking the double-zero slot.

But by late 1963, O'Phidian was facing the same crisis once more. Shannon's foothold in the world was slipping. Hey, Mister Tambourine Man, play a song for me. My senses have been stripped, my hands can't feel to grip, my toes too numb to step, I'm ready for to fade into my own parade....

To add to his worries, a telegram arrived utilizing Wu's personal cipher. Decoded, it read:

DON'T STOP STOP SHANNON'S TOP STOP YOU'RE MY BEST OP STOP YOU'RE A REGULAR MEPHISTO P STOP

Weh-hell.... Flattering as the message was, it still constituted a heavy responsibility.

It was then that O'Phidian considered the utility of Zona Pellucida.

He had recruited Pellucida in '54, when he had been in Alexandria during the Suez Crisis. (Alexandria, queen of cities, Gnostic hotbed! How could the burg be otherwise, named as it was after mangod Alexander himself, who had been born of the copulation between the deity Ammon in serpent form and Olympias, wife of King Phillip of Macedon? And what did Emperor Hadrian mean when he wrote from Alexandria, "There is not a single priest here who is not a mathematician"?) Pellucida had been thirteen then, a *uræus*-crowned orphan earning her living as a belly-dancer at the Sethra Cafe, run by sleazy Arab Sam al-Shammas. Watching her wiggle to the music of the house band, the Wholly Booleans, O'Phidian had intuited that she would be of use someday. By Basilides, she could really rock the casbah! And the audience—they loved to watch her strut!

Even O'Phidian, dat longtime member of the Wimmen Hater's club, had been turned on. I've avoided relations with girls from many nations, but just cuz I'm gay don't mean I'll turn you away!

He had officially adopted her, and taken her with him out of the country. Enrolled at the Isis Academy, a private Swiss girl's school jointly funded by Sandoz Laboratories and Siemens GmbH for the offspring of their employees, she had matured into a cosmopolitan young lady, adept at the arts of all the Nine Muses, not neglecting the Unacknowledged Tenth Muse, Eros. Now married to a Chinese diplomat of Tibetan extraction named Bardo Thodol, she lived at Number 111 Rue du Dragon, Paris, in a *pension* run by the elderly widow, Madame Groshorloge.

O'Phidian jumped right on the phone.

"Darlin' daughter—"

"Daddy O! How delightful! How may your little girl help you?"

O'Phidian explained.

"I'll be in Boston right away, before Mehen guides Ra through two more underworld passages."

"Wonderful. I knew I could count on you."

When Pellucida arrived in Beantown, she got right to work, posing as an ingenuous MIT coed, all lowered lashes and hiked skirts.

Don't stand, don't stand so close to me!

Before Shannon knew what had hit him, he had been screwed and tattooed, not to mention blewed. His *kundalini* serpent had been unkinked, his *qi* energy had been redistributed, his *prana* had been refreshed and his six senses had been throughly reattached to the mortal sphere. There was no way he'd be leaving for a while, now that the attractions of Sophia had been duplicated here on earth.

In a way, O'Phidian felt a little guilty, hindering another mortal's heavenly transition like this. But temporal affairs demanded it. The Final Day of this *kalpa* had not yet arrived—nor would it without help.

The whole incident had led directly to the formation of the Little Flowers, those tricky pro-teases, those daughters of the kaos who could make history. Pellucida had proven how invaluable a cunning cunny at the right moment and in the right place could be, and, with Wu's permission, O'Phidian had begun to recruit more women like his daughter, forming a corps of Mary-Magdalene-Mata-Haris. However, none of them yet, formidable as they were, had quite the range of talents he envisioned. Oh, well, he was sure his dream-girl existed somewhere, and he was bound to find her, given enough time. (Look East, young man! I wanted to say, until finally I myself dispatched Pagano to the Philippines....)

In fact, this quest for the High Priestess, the gal who, like Haggard's She Who Must Be Obeyed, would combine Machiavellian adroitness with sexual charisma, was part of the mission he was now embarked on.

"A little China doll down in old Hong Kong waits for my return, and a pretty Polynesian baby over the sea...." softly crooned O'Phidian.

O'Phidian paused in his reverie to refill his glass from the bottle resting on the floor beside his chair. Corfu had long ago dropped from sight below the horizon, while his destination yet remained out of view. He had plenty of time to ponder....

The diesel scent from the stacks blew briefly over him, engendering that petrol emotion of melancholy. Not everything under his supervision, natch, was a harem of cherries. For instance, Ché Guevara had bought the farm a few weeks ago—at 39, just a year younger than O'Phidian. Too bad, he had been such a useful cats paw, right from his first days in Guatemala. And then there was this pixeldrine thing.... It was proving to be a real dead-end. That idjit hippie, Flash, wasn't making enough converts, turning enough heads around. And although initially promising, the drug itself had proved to be insufficiently revolutionary to achieve the massive change in consciousness Wu desired. Production, therefore, had already been suspended.

(At this very moment, half the world away, Jumpin' Jack Flash was growing more and more anxious for O'Phidian's arrival, while doubts were beginning to trouble Emmett Demesne about the wisdom of his own choices as to which quarry to pursue.

("Man," said Flash, "this hot California sun is cookin' my brain! When it shimmies, I shimmy. I just ain't used to it. I'm a Michigan boy."

("I'm no native," replied Demesne, "but I love this place. It's like a dream, a California Dream. And the girls—I wish the whole world could be full of California Girls." *Except for you, Vivian....* "Why, I even love El Ay! Everything'd be perfect, if only your connection would show up...."

("Tell me about it. This place is cruel—nowhere could be much colder—and I'm just living for the city....")

But hey—was any of this anxiety O'Phidian's fault? The man had a lot of irons in the fire....

The engine fumes lifted off him, and with the shift in wind his spirits soared again. Such setbacks were minor, compared to the progress being made. And with the recent perfection of the IRS, PROJECT SNAKES AND LADDERS could now get off the ground. It would take dozens of years, and billions of dollars, but if it bore fruit—

Well, let's just say that there would exist more information about information than had ever existed before.

Sipping at his wine, O'Phidian picked up a book from the stack of three beside him. The trip from Corfu to Cephalonia was an overnight journey, and he intended to catch up on his reading.

The first book to come to hand was a familiar one. *The Great Revelation of a Voice and a Name*, by Simon Magus, had been his constant bedside reading since his days in the monastery, which had possessed the only extant copies. O'Phidian had thought it lost in the destruction of the Order. Imagine his surprise to receive this scorched copy anonymously in the mail one day. Father Gogarty, do you watch over me even now...?

O'Phidian put aside the well-thumbed text and picked up the next book.

LIVE IN THE PRESENT
Evil in the Serpent
by
Sally Salonika

The book had been written by one of the women he was traveling to see. He had best acquaint himself with her work....

The sun reached its height and began to sink as O'Phidian read. A steward brought him a fine lunch of stuffed grape leaves. Guinness being unavailable, the paunchy mick went to work on a second bottle of wine.

By mid-afternoon he flipped the final page and thoughtfully closed the book. Verrry interesting, as they said on that American television show. A book tracing snake-worship and mythology through the millennia and around the globe, drawing curious and frequently obscure parallels with the history of folk and popular music. Somewhat pedantic, yes, full of unnecessarily Kryptic Komments, but definitely heartfelt. No wonder Graves had fallen for this dame. But she wouldn't have anything to do with the randy poet, and, in a snit, he had given her name to his Wu Labs connection, hoping for some kind of bad karma to befall her.

To the contrary, Wu Labs wanted to do nice things for this lady. There should be little trouble recruiting one already so disposed.

O'Phidian got somewhat unsteadily to his feet. Two bottles of wine and the sun had no little effect. Maybe just take a little stroll around the deck to clear the head....

Movement in the sky attracted O'Phidian's eyes. A small speck gradually resolved itself into a large bird, some kind of raptor. It seemed to be having trouble flying. As O'Phidian watched, it folded its wings and dived straight for the steamer.

Holy Valentinus, it was going to land right at his feet!

Within a minute the bird crashed with a sickening WHUMP! onto the boards.

The impact made the dying bird vomit out a snake.

The dying snake vomited out a frog.

The dying frog spat out a metal capsule.

O'Phidian picked up the thrice-ingested slimy capsule and unscrewed its top. It was a message for him.

A. AGAPE LAIRS HI AND LO IN DELPHI.

O'Phidian pondered the note. This was good news. His other quarry, the little fox, had gone to ground. Yet—was he getting the entire import of the ostentatiously delivered note? There seemed more to it than was presented on the surface.

Insight suddenly struck him, and he was able to make out its *ubixic*, or secret meaning. It was cast in the form of an anagram of the plaintext.

I RAISE HELL, PAGAN O'PHIDIAN LAD.

Hmmm.... Wu hardly needed to remind him of that. Was the Doc promising unusual turmoil, an extra dose of disorder, industrial-strength chaos? Perhaps O'Phidian had unscrambled the message wrong....

A crowd of frightened Greeks had gathered around the corpses on the deck. O'Phidian picked up his wine glass and poured the dregs over the animals in a libation.

"Teleios, Keraunos, Lykaios, all praise be yours. I understand and obey."

He gathered up his books and made for his cabin. The Greeks fell back from him in awe.

Nothing was more fun than goofing on the natives. Kept 'em under control.

In his cabin, O'Phidian flopped down on his bunk. He thought for a time about the message he had received. He would act, he decided, on the plaintext, and reserve judgement on the anagram. Having made up his mind on this, he switched on the light to dispel the gathering dusk, and picked up his third book.

CAUGHT WITH A FINGER UP NATURE'S QUIM
Being Passages from the Life of a Philosopher
by
Charles Babbage M.A., F.R.S., F.R.S.E., F.R.A.S.,
F. STAT. S., HON. M.R.I.A, M.C.P.S., COMMANDER OF
THE ITALIAN ORDER OF ST. MELCHISIDEK AND ST. LAZARUS

### Preface

The world knows—or thinks it knows—its own history. But of course this is stuff and nonsense. For not only is the whole tapestry of history ungraspable by any single mind—and if one cannot apprehend a thing in its entirety, then in what sense can it be said to be truly known?—but also, past events are subject to manifold interpretations, any one of which, being resolved out of the morass, could totally crystallize the pattern of events around itself, like the irritant around which a pearl forms, or the mineral seed thrust into a crucible of molten silicon.

And as it is with the history of humanity, so it is with the history of any individual. Much as we might like to believe that we discern the true outlines of our own brief lives, we too often fall prey to mere delusions of understanding, mistaking information for knowledge, knowledge for wisdom.

And of course, all of the foregoing simply neglects the role of deliberate or accidental misinformation and lies, concealments and masquerades. Interpreting secular or personal history is like playing the parlor game known as Russian Scandal, in which an initial written message is sequentially transcribed. At every step of its transmission it undergoes some variation in the words in which it is related, producing noise and garbled meaning.

I preface my memoirs with such a long theoretical disclaimer only to protect myself against charges of misrepresentations. I am detailing my curious life in the most accurate way I know.

As the *Popul Vuh* says: "The sun that shows itself is not the real sun."

## Chapter 1

The first element of accurate knowledge is *number*, the foundation and measure of all man knows of the material world. Whenever a man can get hold of numbers, they are invaluable. Numbers are masters of the weak, but the slaves of the strong.

I was born in 1791, a banker's son.

One and seven is eight. Nine and one is ten. The difference between eight and ten is two.

No omen could be plainer. I was destined for great things.

From earliest youth, I manifested two main interests.

The spirit of nature.

The nature of spirit.

On the one hand, I avidly sought to fathom the workings of any physical process or man-made contrivance. In this sense, I was the most skeptical and hard-headed fellow imaginable.

On the other hand, I was a dreamy lad subject to mystical visions and odd fancies. I recall an attempt made at age ten to raise the Devil, and also the pact formed with my childhood friend, Dacres, that whoever of us died first should make an effort to reach the other from beyond the grave. Poor Dacres, upon making the transition, forgot the promise, it seems, perhaps lost in Sophic bliss. I also bring to mind the constant intimations from numerous sources that this life was not my first, that I had trod this mortal coil during other ages.

The former tendency was to culminate in my creation of the Difference and Analytical Engines, and in my invention of several splendid and ingenious ciphers. The latter, in my work such as *The Ninth Bridgewater Treatise on Miracles*, and in my vision in Salisbury Cathedral, when I perceived that there existed somewhere in decayed space an immense dragon whose breath produced all pestilence.

Let me speak a little now of my first sexual encounter. It took place when I was seventeen, and my amorous accomplice was an Irish lass, one Ruah Gogarty, she of the expansive freckled bosom and delicate wrists. In between her porcelain thighs I had my first confirmation of the numinous, yet substantial dualistic nature of reality. As my yang entered her yin....

This was not what O'Phidian was interested in. He knew all about it anyway, from Babbage's descendent, Father Gogarty himself. O'Phidian paged ahead a few chapters.

## Chapter 4

It was 1812. I knew the year would be propitious, for was it not composed of 1, 8, and 2, all powers of two? Yet I could not foresee the actual miracle that was to happen.

I was sitting in the reading room of the Analytical Society of Cambridge. Before me on the baize-topped table lay a chart of logarithms. Much pondering of this numerical chart had succeeded only in depressing me. I had long dreamt of devising a mechanical means of iterating such time-consuming matrices, useful as well for casting horoscopes and permuting primes, but the practicalities of the endeavor still eluded me.

It was at this point that Captain Fowke, a cavalier rogue, approached me with a proposal I leapt at.

"By the King's balls, Charles, you look unnaturally wan. What do "you say to accompanying me to Madame de Mallet's for a spot of exotic "crumpet?"

"A capital idea," I replied, and we were off.

At de Mallet's, I contemplated the menu offered to the *bon ton* clientele, finally settling on a flower-girl of Chinese extraction, who billed herself as "Yao Chi, the Turquoise Courtesan." With no little excitement, I allowed myself to be conducted up to her chamber.

I knocked, and entered.

The woman stood at a window with her back to me. She was dressed in a misty flowing grey robe; her dark hair was piled like a storm cloud atop her head and held in place with jade ornaments. Hearing my entrance, she turned. Her face was powdered white, her lips rouged and her eyelids done in moss-green. Her turning had wafted an astonishingly erotic perfume toward me, a melange of floral and spice scents.

"Ah, Laoyeh Babbage," she said, "welcome to my humble quarters."

Naturally, I was rather startled by her knowledge of my name. "Excuse "me, Tourquoise Courtesan, have we met before—?"

"No. But you see, I was expecting you."

Atop my recent megrims, this mystery was too much for my poor overtaxed brain. "Do you mind if I sit?"

"Excuse me, Laoyeh, I am remiss in my hospitality. Please, by all means, "sit. Allow me to serve you some of this splendid Dragon's Well tea. Most "refreshing in the summer heat."

Tourquoise Courtesan poured me a small cup of green tea, accompanied by a moist split peach on a laquered plate. Her mode of locomotion was so delicate as to make it appear as if she were floating. While I sipped the delicious brew, she took down a lute.

"Perhaps if I sing my tale to you, it will soothe your nerves...."

In dulcet tones, Tourquoise Courtesan began to sing.

She had been born in the Celestial Empire in the province of Szechwan, on the forested slopes of Wu Shan, within sight of the splendid Yangtze River. Her parents, woodcutters, had died when she was thirteen, killed when a tree they were felling crushed them. After that, Yao Chi lived alone. She had little contact with her neighbors, who shunned her for superstitious reasons.

Wu Shan, or Shamanka Mountain, it seemed, was reputed to be the abode of Divine Woman, the goddess of the Yangtze. The Shamanka could bring rain and bestow fertility. She could also lure men to their deaths with her wiles. As the only unattached female on the mountain, Yao Chi had come to represent the goddess in the minds of the peasants.

For many years, Yao Chi lived a peaceful life, subsisting on the offerings left by her worshippers. She spent the time cultivating her mind, reading the classics of Confucius and Lao Tze. Then one day a party of armed men rode up to her cottage.

They were representatives of the Emperor, who demanded her presence.

Soon Yao Chi found herself in the Forbidden City, kneeling before the Dragon Throne.

The Emperor seemed uneasy. He let slip a face-diminishing confession. "I have received instructions from above. We need the new Western "knowledge. You and others of your ilk will help us get it."

The next thing she knew, Yao Chi was being ceremoniously deflowered by the Son of Heaven. After that, she was enrolled in an intensive course of courtesanly theory and praxis. Only on the long trip to England did she have a moment to think:

Who was above the Emperor?

Tourquoise Courtesan finished her song:

"I sit long, the wind blows, the green damask is cold.
"Through the nine heavens the moon shines, a plate of crystal water.
"Do not think I will turn back, plunge, sink and be gone!
"For you, no regrets, just one night of joy!"

Her song had indeed calmed me to the point of lassitude. Or perhaps it was the tea. In any case, when Yao Chi began to unbutton my trousers, I made no objection. Soon, she had my stiffening manhood in one hand, the other fondling my ballocks.

"Ah, Laoyeh, this is no ordinary pantaloon-dwelling dragon. It is more "like the *chiao*, or kraken."

So saying, she commenced to fellate me.

Before I knew what was happening, Yao Chi was out of her robe and riding me where I sat in the chair.

"Laoyeh, we do not ask much. Just steady news of your progress in the "field of mechanical computation. The ancient abacus is much too limited "for modern needs."

"Uh, glad—um—ly. But I fear—uh—it's going rather slow...."

"Allow me to speed up the pace then."

With that, Tourquoise Courtesan began to accelerate her subtle rhythm, at the same time exerting a series of intractable pressures on my velvet-shrouded member.

"Now, Laoyeh, I roll you over, under, sideways, down. I could turn you "inside out, but that is what I choose not to do."

My ecstasy reached such a pitch that I lost all cognizance of my sur-roundings, of my body even.

I floated in a pearly void. Before me hung sixty-four golden arrange-ments of broken and unbroken bars which I recognized as the hexagrams of the *I Ching*. They were grouped in the Fu Hsi Sequence. As I studied these ancient symbols, I suddenly experienced a burst of insight.

If one regarded each broken line as 1 and each solid line as 0, then the sixty-four hexagrams represented the numbers zero through sixty-three in order, in base two!

As soon as this revelation broke on me, I spent with fury up Yao Chi and came to my senses.

Yao Chi was nowhere to be seen. I was drenched in water from head to toes; there was a piece of river vegetation in my lap. Duckweed, I believe.

Impossibly, I thought I saw a rainbow arc for a moment across the room.

After that inspiring night, I began construction of my Difference Engine.

Research soon revealed to me that I was not the first to discern the secret meaning of the hexagrams.

The great Leibniz had had the same knowledge vouchsafed to him by a priest, Father Joachim Bouvet, who had been a missionary to China. And like Leibniz, I too ran into trouble trying to design a machine that would employ binary addition. The materials I was forced to work with—so primi-tive compared to the ideal substances I could dimly envision!—were too recalcitrant. These gears and cams, chains and belts, pulleys and rods, how could they possibly be made Instinct with Reason? Surely it was not be-yond the Realm of Artifice to create a Machine that could Compute Sums, and, perhaps, even Parse Logic, using binary means....

Eventually, notwithstanding the aid of my Mechanical Notation, I was forced to retreat to the familiar base ten. Even this fallback, however, was not sufficient to bring me success.

Through the weary years of trial and error, I reported to the Chinese lega-tion, who in turn advanced me certain funds. Occasionally, I took advantage of my friend Count Strzelecki's travels to send blueprints to the Chinese.

But never again did I have the pleasure of Yao Chi's embrace.

For many years, I labored without a companion who could truly understand my work.

Until the arrival of the Countess of Lovelace.

There came a knock on O'Phidian's door. It was the steward with a tray bearing a glass of retsina and a plate of moussaka. As he ate, O'Phidian considered.

Who *was* above the Emperor?

O'Phidian was getting sleepy. It had been quite a day, and he needed to be on his toes for tomorrow. He would read just a bit more....

## Chapter 8

After the failure of my Difference Engine, I retreated for a time from the field. I assisted the Bank of England in designing new unforgeable bank notes. I worked on problems for the Postal Service. I designed a series of colored theatrical lights and composed a rainbow dance in honor of Yao Chi. I campaigned against street musicians, whose detestable tootlings grated on my ears, which the Tourquoise Courtesan's song had spoiled for any lesser music.

But I really longed to attempt the construction of another computational device, even grander than the first. It would be called the Analytical Engine, and be able to perform any feat of logic whatsoever.

Yet I simply could not motivate myself to undertake what I knew would be a long and arduous project.

Until I met my Ada.

The daughter of the notorious poet, Lord Byron, Lady Ada first visited my house in 1830, at age 15. (One plus eight equals nine. Thirty is divisible by fifteen twice. Nine plus two is eleven, or three in base two notation!) She was a little coquette even then, I swear!

I was showing her through my workshop, a converted stable. Her governess had chosen to remain in the parlor. We had already toured the forge and foundry in the old coach house. I had idly picked up an old riding crop which I used to point out various dusty pieces of my broken Difference Engine.

Ada asked such intelligent questions that I was moved to say, "Surely "with the blood flowing in your veins, your talents must tend more to poesy "than to ciphering."

"I divide my attentions equally, I would say, Charles. I may call you "'Charles,' may I not, please?"

I was much taken by her sweet voice which hinted at more than it stated. "By all means."

"Well, Charles," she said slyly, "I fancy I am equally adept at plotting "the Pearl of Sluts—oh, how silly of me; I mean of course the Pearl of "Sluze!—as I am in fashioning a good lay."

This reply somewhat discomposed me. I moved to hand her a portion of my Difference Engine. In my nervous state, I let it go before she had fully grasped it. It fell to the floor and shattered.

Before I could speak and rightfully take the blame, Ada said, "Oh, how "awfully naughty of me! I must be punished, Charles. It's only right."

The little vixen turned her back to me and lifted up her skirts. She wore no bloomers. I had a full vista of her pert little bare arse! She continued to hoist her skirts with one hand, while leaning forward and bracing herself on a workbench with the other.

"Switch me, Charles! I deserve it!"

Reluctantly, I gently laid the crop across her buttocks.

"Don't be timid! Lash it, whip it!"

I began to switch her bottom. Her breathing turned to panting. She emitted little yelps of mingled pain and joy.

"What force, what rhythm!" she exclaimed. "Hit me, hit me with your "rhythm stick!"

When her bottom was flushed crimson, I was bursting from my trews. I swiftly entered her.

At that moment, I received the second major epiphany of my life.

If the Switch isn't On, it's Off!

From that moment on, we were full partners and collaborators.

I owe so much to the Countess! For instance, the very notion of separate mechanisms for memory and computation came to me in a coital moment.

"And so, if we could only separate, unh—"

"Oh, Charles, harder, deeper!"

"—the Instructions—"

"More, more, more!"

"—from the Analytical Engine which, oh, God, carries them out—"

"Fuck, fuck, fuck me, Charles!"

"—we would have an All-Purpose Device—"

"Now, Charles, now!"

"—capable of anything! Ahhhh!"

And with a little similar sigh betokening a day well spent, Paddy O'Phidian let Babbage's memoirs slip from his hand as he himself slipped into the arms of Morpheus.

Call me up in dreamland!

The ferry docked in Argostoli around seven AM. Revivified by a good night's sleep and some strong coffee, O'Phidian disembarked.

Ah, birthplace of Carpocrates and Melusine! Stopover for Lord Byron on his way to Missolonghi! Home to Sally Salonika! Welcome now O'Phidian, the last real Gnostic!

O'Phidian trotted blithely with his light luggage to the Hotel Asclepius and checked in. Then he asked the clerk—one Niko Nike by name—a question.

"Who can I get to drive me to Aghios Georgios, lad?"

Nike crossed himself in reverse, following the Orthodox custom. "The ruins above the village of Kastro? Why, oh why, good sir, would you wish to go there? Nothing to see in those ruins! No, sir, indubitably much of a nothing."

"I understand a crazy Englishwoman lives there with her native lover."

"Oh, no, by no reach of the imagination! Could you imagine the scandal if such a thing were so? No, there is no possibility of such jiggery-pokery in our innocent villages."

"I'll ask someone else."

Nike clutched his head with both hands. "Aieee! You perverted foreigners will be the death of us poor Greeks! Go, ask around! No one will take you!"

Smiling, O'Phidian departed. Surely someone would drive him or loan him their car for enough money.

No one would.

This gal must be some tuff cookie! She had really earned the villagers' Are Eee Ess Pee Eee Cee Tee! Looked like he was in for a hike.

He walked through the dusty streets flanked by three-story buildings with walls the shade of old bone, windows shuttered against the heat. At an intersection, he saw a policeman directing traffic. The silver-helmeted officer stood in the center of the intersection in a large white concrete cylinder with flaring base, painted white with a dull-red wave-motif. He looked stuck in a large vase.

"The road to Kastro?" inquired O'Phidian.

"Turn left at Cuba," said the cop.

"Very funny. What's your name? I'm thinking of visiting the chief of police later."

"Spyro Gyro, sir, if you please. I am sorry you took my small joke amiss. It was merely a weak example of paronomasia. Now, you turn north at the Street of the Musicians...."

Gyro gave him directions. The ruins were nine kilometers away.

"And a good place to eat on the way?"

"Try the Memory, outside Fanariou."

The road was in bad shape, and so was O'Phidian. It took him two hours to cover the uphill four kilometers to Fanariou. There, he gratefully stopped for a snack at the Memory.

Seated outside, under the shade of a Cephalonian fir, O'Phidian contemplated what he would say to recruit Salonika. Her background was unique....

In 1941 the Nazis occupied the port of Thessaloniki. They would not be driven out until 1944. An English merchant named Vincent Craddock and his wife, Marion, were trapped in the invasion. Vincent was slain and his wife raped, the murderer/rapist being a young officer named Lambton Wurms. Nine months later, a malnourished and sickly Marion Craddock gave birth to a daughter, whom she christened

Sally with her dying breath. A priest named Kyril Bonfiglioli attended the birth and fostered the baby out of pity. When in 1949, at the very end of the Greek Civil War, Bonfiglioli was killed by right-wing terrorists known as The Snakes in the Pit, eight-year-old Sally ended up as one of many urchins on the streets, where she became known simply as Sally Salonika. A year later, when the country finally seemed stabilized, Mortimer Craddock, Vincent's father, arrived in the city, looking to reclaim any of his son's holdings. A lover of icons, Craddock was visiting Bonfiglioli's old church when what should he see but a dirty gamin who greatly resembled his dead daughter-in-law laying a frowsy flower on the altar. Making inquiries, Craddock soon learned the whole story and claimed his granddaughter. Brought to England, Sally Salonika stayed until she reached her majority, then returned to Greece, the land of her birth and of her heart. She had supported herself in a meager fashion as a writer since then.

Perhaps, thought O'Phidian, he could stress Wu Lab's pull with the publishing industry....

Finishing his collation, O'Phidian resumed his journey.

By midafternoon, the ruins of a medieval castle loomed above the small village of Kastro. Footsore, O'Phidian made the final ascent.

Among the crumbling battlements, a small hut had been erected, sheltered by a remnant of stone wall. O'Phidian stepped up to the closed door and knocked quietly.

There was no answer.

O'Phidian tentatively pushed open the door.

On a narrow cot, two naked women, illuminated by an oil-lamp, were performing sixty-nine. An empty bottle of ouzo lay on the floor.

The sight of all this oozy ouzo cooze temporarily unnerved O'Phidian, as he had a flashback to the love-feast he had experienced as a child. He fought to regain control of himself.

The woman on top—who was actually standing, straddling the narrow cot and the face of the woman below—lifted her head.

It was Salonika. Her platinum hair was cut short as a Marine's. Her half-German features bore an expression of irritated distaste.

"What do you want?"

"Perhaps later would be a more convenient time...?"

Salonika swung her leg off her lover, who sat up. Salonika sat down. "Too late to be sorry now, I'm afraid. Out with what you came to say. Unless you just want to gape."

"Not at all, Miss Salonika. I represent a very prestigious firm that is interested in hiring you, and I've come to speak with you at no small inconvenience."

She narrowed her eyes at him. O'Phidian could tell she was tapping into High Sources. "Did Graves send you? That old goat can't take no for an answer. He thinks I'm his goddamn White Goddess, and won't rest till he's fucked me." Salonika reached for cigarettes and matches. She lit two smokes and gave one to her girlfriend. "This is Palatina Persephone, by the way."

"Charmed, I'm sure."

Persephone licked her slick lips in a hungry fashion.

Salonika appeared jealous. "Save your compliments, she speaks no English."

O'Phidian hastened to reassure her of his good intentions. "In answer to your question, Mister Graves has only an indirect connection with my being here. As I said, my employer wishes to offer you a fine salary in exchange for certain services."

Salonika took a drag. "I can always use more money. My books haven't exactly been bestsellers. Hire me for what?"

"To write, of course. More or less anything you want in the direction you've already been going, with guaranteed publication. Of course, we would ask you to slant things a little, along lines dictated by our, um, Director."

"Sounds as if I could live with it. What else?"

"Ah, well—this part presents a problem, now that I've witnessed your, ah, proclivities."

"Not to mention my declivities."

"Yes. Well, to be frank, we need women of superior erotic and spiritual talents—and I believe you are certainly one such—who would be willing to put their bodies on the line to subvert the dominant power structure for the purposes of our organization."

"Both of which are overwhelmingly male."

"I am afraid so."

Salonika stubbed out her cigarette on a table that bore a dilapidated typewriter. "No thanks. I don't care to contaminate myself with all this macho nonsense, games without frontiers. Now, if you don't mind—"

He couldn't afford to lose this one; she was just the kind of Sweet Soul Sister Wu Labs needed. What could he offer—

The subject of his flashback recurred to him.

"Miss Salonika, have you ever heard of the Sisters of Melusine?"

Salonika's eyes lit up. "Do they really exist?"

"I assure you that they do. And I am perhaps the one person in the world who could provide you with an introduction to the head of the Order, Sister Michelle."

"Where do I sign, you devil?"

The harder they come, the harder they fall, one and all!

The next day, O'Phidian took the ferry from Sami to Patras, a short three-and-a-half-hour trip. He crossed the strait to Thessaly, rented a car, and was on his way to Delphi.

One down, one to go.

He parked the car at Castri, a mile from the excavations at the ancient shrine, and began to walk, weary already from the drive.

Bejaysus! He'd be glad when he was back in civilized London, where nothing he needed—including pints of dark brew—was more than a few air-conditioned yards away from his office.

As he trudged along the pebbled path, O'Phidian recalled the inspirational words of Alexander Graham Bell inscribed on the lobby wall at Bell Labs in Murray Hill, New Jersey.

"Leave the beaten track occasionally and dive into the woods. You will be certain to find something you have never seen before."

He hoped they applied today.

Trying to recapture the carefree mood he had felt on the ferry to Cephalonia, O'Phidian whistled a few bars of "Camptown Races." But he couldn't quite regain that frame of mind. So, knowing that if ya can't get over yer blues, ya gotta get behind them, he began to sing to the tune of an old Delta lament.

O'PHIDIAN'S BLUES

O, I'm just a Piece of Lint
In the Navel of the World,
Just a boozy mick in transit,
Always lookin' for That Girl.

From Dublin to California,
and to Cabezas, Dos—
That's in Arizona,
Quite a hike from Omphalos—

I've been on the *qui vive*,
Looking for that Heart of Gold,
A Heart that's always on my sleeve,
A Heart that's growing old.

A Heart of glass is what I own.
But I wish my Heart was made of stone.
A Heart full of soul from my Maker,
Saklad's just a rotten—doo, doo, doo, doo, doo—Heartbreaker!

(Since O'Phidian himself brought up his trip to Dos Cabezas, I'll mention that his visit to Arizona involved dealings with DIGITAL and the Hopi Indians, arranging the construction of a copper smelter. ((The Hopis, by the way, possessed a truly intriguing mythology. Worshipped their ancestors, the *moqui*, or Dead Ones, and also paid homage to Kokopelli, a humpbacked, flute-playing, priapic god who resembled more than a little the Dahomean Legba. Two interesting ceremonies of the

Hopis were the *tcuatikibi*, or Snake Dance, led by The Snake Girl, who was also, in another guise, Flute Girl (((not the last equation of serpents with music))); and also the *wuwuchim*, or New Year's festival, *wu* meaning to germinate, *chim* to manifest...)) We should also mention here the thesis of linguist Benjamin Lee Whorf, that the Hopi language mentally dictated a fine disdain for time. And of course the Hopis by this year of our Saklad 1967 had been trying to speak to the United Nations for decades, to pass on their prophecy of the world's imminent end, but only succeeded on their fourth request, in December of 1992.)

Reaching the southeast corner of the tumbledown wall that demarcated the Sanctuary of Apollo, a large rectangular area that sloped upward from south to north, O'Phidian stepped gingerly onto the Sacred Way. Still a lot of residual *mana* here, even after all these centuries. He began to climb the zigzag route, huffin' 'n' puffin' under the langorous Delphic sky, pausing to wipe sweat from his upper lip with the tail of his snake-tailed Queen's Messengers/Wu Labs tie. He wore a suit of Irish Tweed utterly incongruous with both the clime and the ambiance. Sure, he had been known to Go Native when necessary, but he prefered the styles of his Depression Era youth.

About 250 meters from the entrance, near the first bend in the road, O'Phidian paused in his uphill journey to rest a moment. He sat on the eroded face of a statue. *All I need is a cross....,* the self-pitying errand-boy thought.

Here, where the Sicyonian Treasury had once stood, O'Phidian pondered the politics responsible for his solitude.

The Colonel's Revolution of that April was an uneasily accepted fact of life, tho everyone could sense that King Constantine was planning some counter-stroke (which would, as things eventuated, occur in December, with embarrassing results for Constantine, causing him to flee), and the tourist-trade had almost dried up. (No more influx of them Imperialistic Dollars that you always reviled, folks, so tighten your belts as we prepare for A ROUGH LANDING!)

Thus O'Phidian found himself completely alone in the cliff-brooding, mountain-fast, sea-breeze-teased terraced ruins of Delphi on this fine summer day.

All around him he could feel the weight of history. The very stones seemed alive with memory.

The Parnassos Country was a place particularly rich in strange legends and allusive history, even for Greece. You had your sacred grove of the Nine Muses on Mount Helikon, not to mention the springs of Oblivion (Lethe) and Memory (Mnemosyne). Not far from Delphi lay Thebes, where Oedipus gave incest (that forbidden mingling of Genes Which May Not Meet) a bad name, and solved the cipher of the Sphinx. One of the most famous whores—whoops, 'scuse that, we meant *hetareæ*—of history, Phyrne, was born in the Parnassos region (which included the town of Lamia). Outside the village of Distomo sat Ossios Loukas, the shrine to Luke the Stiriote, a tenth-century Christian oracle. The hidden caves and crevasses of Mount Parnassos itself were the former sites of bacchanalian revels conducted by secret cults of women....

And of course, at the psychic center of the land lay Delphi, the Omphalos, or Navel of the World, former seat of empire (and how they do all pass and fade away, these overbearing sovereign states and earthly dominions that seem so imperishable, when the mighty information-river cuts a new channel through the land, leaving them high and dry, erstwhile ports from which the sea has retreated, as their harbors silt up with noise....)

Delphi, of course, was seat of that ancient Oracle, the pythoness. Place started out sacred to the antique earth-goddess, Gaea, whose emblem the Python was. Ol' luckless Mister Snake was soon despatched by Apollo the Sun, who took over the Royal Scam. We all know the trappings. Priestess sits on the tripod over the Sacred Crack and vapors waft up. (Anyway, *something* comes up. Remember, this cleft was the same one down which Apollo chased the Python, prior to killing him. *But what if he didn't?* Kill him, that is. After all, Apollo thereafter became known as Pythian Apollo, indicating he more or less subsumed his old enemy, co-opted him, so to speak. What if Mister Snake was *still down there* during the reign of the Oracle? Kinda inviting target he'd see, from below that perhaps open tripod, up the skirts of Fate Herself, the Sanctified Pussy....) Anyhoo—whatever came up outa that Cleft, it would quickly put the priestess in touch with the Numinous, and she'd fall into a stochastic trance, whereupon she would utter the prophecies. Said prophecies then would pass through the filter of her acolytes, where they would pick up whatever noise-quotient the priests intended.

('Course, the pythoness wasn't the only card up Apollo's sleeve. He also had, for instance, the severed head of Orpheus—which would issue forecasts—sitting in another temple. ((Orpheus hadn't fared too well after that trip down to the Underworld, looking for his stolen mate. He lost Eurydice from a snake-bite when he looked back at her, and shortly thereafter Orpheus himself had been dismembered by a buncha crazy women, the Mœnads....)) In any case, Apollo had plenty of strings to pull, for whatever purposes he had in mind.)

(The whole dust-up between Apollo and Python was representative of a world-wide battle between sun-gods and snakes everywhere. Tezcatlipoca and Quetzalcoatl. Marduk and Tiamat. Inaras and Illuyankas. Who knew what lay behind the age-old rivalry? Sure, snakes live in dark holes and go down thru cracks in the earth and in rocks, thus becoming an obvious emblem of darkness and subterranean realms, of night and the moon. But they could also be found soaking up Apollo's rays pretty regular. Oh, there were a few cases of solar-snake cooperation—such as the friendship between the serpent Mehen, who guided the Egyptian sun-god Ra through his nightly underworld passage—but for the most part, the sun and serpents were considered sworn enemies. Tho O'Phidian sometimes wondered if, as in the case of Apollo, it wasn't all a big snowjob, the kind of mock grudge found in pro wrestling and designed solely to stir the fervor of the audience.)

Yessir, taken all in all, a mighty resonant place, these olive-tree-covered hills....

O'Phidian, rested now, bestirred himself, lifting his arse from the rough stones.

Best to get this little recruiting chore over with as quickly as possible. The British embassy in Athens, headed by crusty old Ambassador Riboshome, would be wondering where he was if he didn't arrive soon. His ostensible errand, after all, was delivering a message regarding the current crisis. Still, no one would question him too closely about his side-trips to Cephalonia and Delphi. The Queen's Messengers had pretty much absolute discretion in their own actions. The important thing was that THE MESSAGE GET THROUGH ON TIME. This was the sole criterion by which a Messenger was judged. The service's centuries-old motto (which the U.S. Postal Service had shamelessly stolen and adapted) told it all: "Neither Noyse nor Constricted Channell nor Infelicitous Cipher shall stay these Messengers from the Swift Completion of their Appointed Transmittal."

Laboring up the slope, O'Phidian passed the sites of the Cnidian, Siphnian and Boetian Treasuries, masses of broken blocks and columns. Sure was a lotta money involved in religion.... A little further on, he reached the Athenian Treasury, restored by the French in 1906. O'Phidian could see the Sacred Fissure Itself higher up the hill. He dropped his gaze back to the Treasury. A Doric building with two columns supporting a frieze depicting the exploits of Hercules and Theseus, the structure made O'Phidian's sensitive antennae quiver.

There was someone hiding in the Treasury. A woman. He could psychically sense her Sweet Soul Music.

O'Phidian advanced on the small structure....

"Stop."

The single word was uttered in a woman's voice destitute of energy or emotion, yet carrying complete conviction and self-assurance. It issued from the shadowy depths of the Treasury. O'Phidian thought he saw the speaker within, a vague form that, despite all his esoteric knowledge, still had the power to tighten his balls. It had to be her....

O'Phidian stopped.

The woman emerged.

Young, dark-haired, wearing a soiled and ripped sky-blue summer dress, barefoot, her skin an enchanting sun-burnished Mediterranean hue, the woman carried a small pistol—a Beretta, or similar model—pointed directly at O'Phidian. Her strained features were smudged with dirt. Rebel, rebel, your face is a mess! Rebel, rebel, you've torn your new dress! Yet another hostile reception....

"If you're from the regime," she said with the same passionate tiredness, "you've come poorly equipped to take me back."

O'Phidian sought to lay on that old Gnostic Stare. Gotta get the upper hand right from the start with an Evil Woman like this'un. His eyes made contact with those of the woman, across the intervening meters. She flinched, staggered, recovered—then bounced his ol' snaky beam right back! O'Phidian was forced to drop *his* gaze! Whoa-ho, this gal's got the juice! No wonder Wu wants her.... Sorry, Father Gogarty, old mentor, wherever you might be, but she blinded me with science....

The girl *was* disconcerted, tho. "Who—who are you?" she asked. "It's obvious you're tired, darlin'" oozed O'Phidian. "Instead of standin' in the sun, couldn't we talk inside?"

The woman shrugged. "Why not? What do I have to lose? I'm tired of sitting here alone. Perhaps you might provide some entertainment while we wait for Papadopoulos's men. But I must warn you not to try anything. Although I haven't slept in days, I'm still quite capable of pulling this trigger."

"Talk is all I want."

"Very well, then. You first."

Stepping aside from the door, the woman motioned O'Phidian to pass in. He complied.

Inside the small single cool marble room was a heap of blankets and a half-empty bottle of wine. O'Phidian dropped to the floor opposite the blankets. Entering, the woman collapsed to the pallet without taking her attention from her guest. Her crossed legs projected from under her dress, revealing trim muscular calves taut with the tension of her lotus-position.

"My name's O'Phidian."

"Mine's Agnes—"

"Agape," interrupted O'Phidian. "I know."

And that wasn't all the wily Irishman knew. In fact, he knew more about Miss Agnes Agape's past than she probably knew herself. And that was—?

Glad you asked.

Let's bop back thru time to Italy, where George Gordon, Lord Byron, was involved in the secret society known as the Carbonari, who, among other things, were dedicated to freeing Italy from Austrian rule. Byron had left behind his wife, Anabella Milbanke, and his lascivious daughter, Ada, to pursue his scandalous lifestyle around the globe. That incestuous affair with his half-sister, Augusta Leigh, wasn't bad enough.... No, he had to go off getting involved in foreign wars and whoring after women and boys. Shameless!

In the year of 1823, while Babbage was displaying his Difference Engine to its backers, the London Greek Committee contacted Byron and convinced him to represent them in his beloved Greece, where he could aid the coming revolt. Byron agreed and went club-footing off (little noise in the translation of G.G.'s genetic blueprint here) to Metaxata on the isle of Cephalonia, where he was put up by the Persephone family. Weh-hell, needless to say, in between plottin', poetics, and posturin', Byron found plenty of time to dip his wick where it didn't belong. One of these occasions involved more than just your usual "Maid of Athens."

In the year 390 AD, Theodosius I silenced the Delphic Oracle for good. Or so he thought. All he succeeded in doing was driving the pythoness underground, where she felt right at home. The line of prophetesses continued unbroken, right down to Byron's time, each one remaining chaste and picking her successor before her death. However, Byron's cosmopolitan sexual wiles prove too attractive for the then-current pythoness, a gal named Kira Kychreus, to resist. (She was feeling a bit low at the time, having foreseen some of the drab materialistic philosophy associated with the Industrial Revolution, which would cast her trade into disrepute. Too bad she didn't get a look at Quantum Physics, which woulda cheered her right up....) For whatever reasons, private or professional, the reigning heiress of thousands of years of tradition copped out and copulated when Byron's copped a feel, thereby truly and finally ending the pure Apollonian tradition.

Byron split, leaving the pythoness holding her belly and wondering about certain stirrings, which would eventually manifest themselves as Agnes Agape's great-great-grandmother.

After Byron's contamination, inheritance of the Oracular mantle devolved by birth.

A year after his seduction of the priestess, Byron was dead, of a virus contracted thru exposure.

Like Byron's London daughter, who was already on her way to becoming the world's first programmer, his Aegean offspring, having been taught how to establish a Heavenly Channel by her renegade mother (as the daughter will in turn teach her daughter, and so on down the line to Agnes Agape), was heavily into some Binary Manipulation herself, only on the Kosmic Level.

Thus Byron's dyad of daughters had the plenum pretty much divided up between the two of them, one concentrating on the mechanical, the other on the spiritual.

After you, Miss Yin. By all means, after you, Miss Yang....

The current descendant on the spiritual side said to O'Phidian now, "So you know my name. So what? I imagine the name of Papadopoulos's ex-mistress, who has been revealed as a double agent for the King, is now fairly infamous. If you've come here seeking my trust for some reason, you'll have to prove you know more than my name."

"I know your parents' names also—Xenosis and Leucothea Agape."

Agape waved her pistol in dismissal. "Mere history. Surely you can do better than that."

"What of the looks we exchanged?"

Agape seemed a bit troubled by reference to that contest of wills, even though she had won. She spluttered for an answer to O'Phidian's question. "Only the heat, my fatigue— You're imagining something unreal—"

Now it was O'Phidian's turn to dismiss Agape's pretense. "Come, come, now, my colleen, you and I, we've been through that, and this is not our fate. Let us not talk falsely now, the hour is getting late. Surely you won't deny that we both obviously possess minds and abilities far above normal. My charged glance must have testified to that. I have the advantage of knowing your personal history. Perhaps if you knew mine...."

Signalling her willingness to listen, Agape relaxed somewhat on her heap of blankets, yet still maintained the bead of her sights on the Irishman.

O'Phidian proceeded to relate his life history. Condensed, of course, since in the thirteen years he had been working for Wu he had had more and wilder experiences than most people have in a lifetime (some of the meanings of which he was still sorting out for himself).

After O'Phidian finished, Agape remained silent for a moment, her dirt-smudged face unreadable. O'Phidian felt a rare uncertainty. Had he convinced her he was simpatico...?

Agape lowered her gun into the lap of her dress. "You worship the Snake also. I never thought I would meet— My life has been— I can't—"

Then the gal broke down in tears, tears for fears she had been holding in so long. O'Phidian was instantly by her side on the jumbled blankets, arm around her shoulder, consoling.

Well, hey now, just what is it about the order *Squamata*, ostensibly just a buncha nasty reptiles, that could cause such emotional devotion? In O'Phidian's case, of course, the Snake stood as the Fount of Knowledge, divine opponent to an insane and malignant Creator. (And don't forget that the Delphic temple was the one inscribed "Know Thyself.") This was the creed in which the Irishman had been indoctrinated since birth, and in which he still maintained belief in an adult fashion, on some pre-critical level. But could a liddle ol' worm really mean so much to Agape?

Yup. It could.

The Olympian mythos was saturated in snaky doings. Of course there was Python and his exploits. But in addition, one found the Scythian tale of Hercules' wife, a gal who possessed the lower body of a serpent. (This particular motif cropped up worldwide. For example, in the English ballad, *The Laidley Worm*, and in the *Arabian Nights* story, "The Tale of Yamlika, Queen of the Serpents.") There was the monster Typhon, with serpents for hands and legs, and the underworld serpent-goddess, Hecate (a favorite invocation of Shakespeare's). Hermes, the divine Messenger, bore his sacred staff, or Caduceus, around which were twined twin serpents in a kinda double helix, or Snaky Ladder. These twin serpents were believed to represent Ophion and his female consort (see below), and had an echo in the Chinese tale of Nu Kua, the Creatrix, and her male twin, Fu Hsi, who incestuously fucked the universe into reality.

The Caduceus, of course, was later appropriated as the symbol of medicine, and hence, we could say, biological experimentation in general. (Spenser seemed to have a different angle on the staff's powers: "He tooke Caduceus his snakie wand/ With which the damned ghosts are governed....") The serpent—because it could renew itself by shedding its skin, and because it was found in tombs, as if it were the soul of the departed—generally was held to exhibit healing powers, and came to be associated with Asclepius, son of Apollo, later meriting a constellation, which oddly enough was divided into two parts: *Serpens Caput* (the Head), and *Serpens Cauda* (the Tail). Poor ol' decapitated snake....

Some claimed the Elusinian Mysteries featured the mating of a Serpent and a Woman as the central ritual. Cybele, the great Moon Goddess, was frequently depicted offering libations to a snake.

The Primal Serpent, of course, was Ophion.

Created by Eurynome, the lonely Goddess Of All Things who danced alone in the empty universe, Ophion got the squamous hots for the Creatrix and coupled with her (she being nothing loath), whereupon Eurynome turned into a dove (talk about your polymorphous perversity!) and laid the Universal Egg, which Ophion hatched, bringing forth the material universe and all creatures in it. Ophion later got booted out of his Olympian love-nest for claiming to be the sole creator, and came to dwell on earth, hiding in secret places....

Steeped in all this sophic lore by her weird mother, Leucothea, Agnes Agape was more a child of the distant past than of the twentieth century. Isolated from her peers by her archaic beliefs and random stochastic trances (one of which had warned her of the impending betrayal of her status as a double-agent, and thus allowed her to escape to Delphi), she had developed a kind of invisible scaly integument which no one had pierced till now. Even those who thought they knew her as an ardent royalist would have been surprised to find that her only attachment to their cause stemmed from a vague desire to restore Greece to its prelapsarian Golden Age....

Agape's sobbing gradually tapered off into an occasional sniffle 'n' whimper. Her face was buried in O'Phidian's shirt, her upper body twisted toward him. Her dress, weighed down by the pistol, had ridden up her thighs. Her hair smelled like sunlight and sweat.

Weh-hell.... *Mirabile dictu*, O'Phidian was beginning to get a little.... *excited.* Unlike Salonika, this gal did not repulse him. His sexual tastes, fixed immutably from early administration of the Sodomic Sacrament, had never previously exhibited such overwhelming deviation before, not even watching Pellucida dance. Where's the Backdoor Man now? But there was something special about this young woman. Knowing that she represented in her slim body the culmination of several millennia of Serpentine Wisdom, O'Phidian experienced a kind of Holy Reverence or Higher Love that could express itself—because he was only human—only as lust.

He moved closer to her, knocking over the bottle of wine in the process. Neither one moved to right it.

Spill the wine and take that girl, you leaping, laughing gnome! We can share the women, we can share the wine....

To cover up this *faux-pas* and his embarrassing lack of recruiter-type professionalism, O'Phidian began to talk. In a low, seductive, almost crooning voice, he started to tell Agape of what he had to offer.

"Your trouble, my dear, is that you've had no control in your life. You've been unable to truly direct your own actions, or use the potent knowledge you've possessed to control others. That's why you're unsatisfied and empty, without direction or goals. You need to learn how to manipulate people, to feed them the information that will make them do whatever you want. Whether you influence them verbally or—physically."

It was no use. The words of his standard recruiter's speech couldn't distract O'Phidian from the agonizing hard-on in his pants. Almost volitionlessly, his free hand began to squeeze Agape's left breast, bound so loosely only by the thin cerulean cotton of her dress. She didn't object. Oh, no, she was a regular devil with a blue dress on!

"You've had inklings of this, I'm sure," continued O'Phidian smoothly, his hand busy with his lechery, while he spoke in confidence. "You thought getting involved in politics was a way of making people do what you want. That's a mistake many have made. Politics is a dead end, an illusion, merely the image of power. Politicians are simply boulders in the information-river. They can divert or dam the flow, but they cannot originate or alter the sequence. They have no access to the transmitter, they're merely amplifiers and filters spaced along the channel. And more importantly, they don't even know the code.

"My employer, Doctor Wu—ah, now there's one who has real power. He knows the strings to pull, the real sources of knowledge and—dare I say it?—wisdom. Why, he's as far above you and I as we two are above the blind masses of men, mired in *maya*."

To emphasize their kinship, O'Phidian began to roll Agape's nipple gently between thumb and forefinger. What the wily mick left unspoken was his dream of someday consolidating his secondary position to the point where he could supplant Wu as head of the old Chinese's empire, plunging the old tyrant into the Fourth Hell of Chinese myth, the one for misers, ruled by Wu-kuan Wang....

"The company I represent, and which I wish to invite you to join, has its corporate fingers in all the pies that matter. Styrofoam and icebox-magnets, pizza and television, all the seemingly innocuous instruments of social control.

"Consider the music industry, for one. Nothing could better illustrate my point. Music is more powerful than any number of statesmen. It's rich in information, both subliminal and overt. Bit for bit, byte for byte, music has a higher information content than words. Certainly a lower redundancy level. One can interpret most English sentences from which the vowels have been deleted, but can you imagine a song from which half the notes have been left out...? Wasn't it your ancestor's good friend, Shelley, who claimed not to care who made a nation's laws, so long as he could make its songs? Take Britain now, ostensibly a toothless old lion, yet at this very moment re-ordering the world through the music of those lads from Liverpool and others. We have a hand in all that, of course. Try to really listen to rock lyrics sometime...."

O'Phidian had opened Agape's dress, and now pulled it down over first her tanned left shoulder, then the right. As in a trance, she shifted away from his chest momentarily, allowing the garment to fall unencumbered around her waist. Now with free access to her naked breasts, O'Phidian continued to work her nipples erect.

"But music, although important in our schemes, is really the least impressive item in our armamentarium. We have taken advantage of, and integrated, the various scientific revolutions of our century as no other organization has ever done. Starting with quantum physics at the turn of the century, absorbing the work of Shannon, Weiner, Turing and von Neumann at mid-century, gaining impetus from the spread of digital machines and neurochemistry, we have picked up speed all the way. But the most important and potentially most far-reaching discovery of the century—which just crested last year—is the one we envision involving you in. I refer, naturally, to molecular biology and the deciphering of the genetic code."

O'Phidian dropped his posterior hand down to Agape's buttocks—she lifted one haunch obligingly—and began to fondle her ass, while still manipulating her tits.

"It's been fourteen years since Watson and Crick discovered the structure of DNA, but now the basic knowledge of cellular replication and protein synthesis, heredity and development, is complete. The symposium at Cold Springs Harbor last summer marked the end of the beginning—or is that the beginning of the end? What an incredible story it's been—with its oddities such as messenger RNA—this whole unraveling of the genetic code! Although actually, my dear, as Crick himself has admitted, we should call it 'the genetic cipher.' It all has to do with the way cryptographers define the two terms. 'A code has a separate arbitrary form assigned to every word, and so requires its own whole dictionary for encoding and decoding, whereas a cipher translates letter for letter and so requires only a small key.' And now we have the key! How simple and elegant it's turned out to be. Sixty-four nucleotide codons—two to the sixth power—make up the whole genetic alphabet. A magic number, much prefigured in history. Consider the sixty-four hexagrams of the *I Ching*, each, like the codons, made up of triplets. Or the sixty-four squares of a chess-board. What magic there is in the powers of two! Contemplate the beauty of cell division. Mitosis, meiosis.... One cell—two to the zero power—becomes two. Two become four, four become eight, eight become sixteen, sixteen thirty-two, thirty-two sixty-four! In just fourty-four generations, you'd have over seventeen trillion cells, all deriving from the first, the information in the original DNA replicated beyond its wildest dreams of dominion and subjugation, coiling and uncoiling its snaky yard-long double-helix self, providing the template for its own re-creation! (Do you know, by the way, that one cell in every person's body contains, of logical necessity, the original two strands of nucleic acid contributed by mother and father, from egg and sperm? Where is that Master Cell, with its ancient nucleus, and what special distinction does it bear?) And consider the spread of diseases too. One person infects another, then the two spread it to four, the four spread it to eight— Soon, if the disease remained potent long enough and there were no cure, the whole world would be infected! From the South China Seas to a beach hotel in Malibu.... All due to the powers of two...."

O'Phidian dropped his hand from Agape's breasts and began tracing patterns on her thighs, a sensual sign-language. Beneath her skirt, wandering north, detouring around the pistol in her lap, he found her Serpent Mound bare. He refrained from investigating further, but resumed his tracings.

"But I digress. These are merely side issues. At this stage we are concerned with one major project. The SNAKES AND LADDERS gambit. Wu Labs intends to map the entire human genome. We want to determine the location and function of every single gene. Naturally, this is merely a preliminary step to something larger, a prerequisite. After we possess this knowledge—well, isn't it obvious? When you know the alphabet, you write your own sentences. But first we need more information. We need raw material for our experiments. We need nearly naked DNA, preferably from a wide range of specimens. After all, there's really no such thing as a singular human genome, it varies from individual to individual, even if only by one percent. That's where you and others like you come in, darlin'. You see, Wu Labs needs information witches, black magic women, tantric tantalizers. More to the point, we need—your cunt!"

O'Phidian instantly plunged two fingers up the wet depths of the member in question. Agape gasped.

"We have a group called the 'Little Flowers,'" O'Phidian went on, still diddling the pythoness. "Become one of them, and you will be equipped with a small device similar to a contraceptive diaphragm, called an Eye Are Ess—Information Retrieval System. This miracle of miniaturization is actually an insulated cryonic sperm-trap, which will flash-freeze and store the little heads and tails wrigglers for our research. The reason we cannot simply ask for donations, under the guise of a sperm bank, is that those who volunteer would be self-selectively limiting. We need a wide range of contributions, many from remarkable and famous individuals, in order to fully determine humanity's parameters.

"And of course, we will take a few of your eggs, for more data. You Little Flowers are not hylics, but superior beings yourselves.

"Naturally, as a by-product of such liaisons, we will gain over some important individuals the standard measure of control that derives from sexual thralldom, as well as any conventional verbal information they might let slip."

Agape's breath was coming faster and faster now. O'Phidian removed his fingers from the Oracle's hot, moist fissure and laid her back on the blankets. She writhed bonelessly, only the whites of her eyes showing, fully into the Delphic trance.

Standing, O'Phidian quickly stripped. Confused and thrilled by Agape's religious ecstasy, he wasn't sure if she was a boy or a girl. All he knew was: Hot tramp, I love you so!

Holding his pagan prick, he got between her legs, which wrapped around him like Python's embrace.

After that, it was Ophion and Eurynome all over again.

Chapter 00001011

# The Demon Librarian

# K L U E S

**00101000**
"Say God is in a room and on his table he has some cookies and tea. And he's dreaming this whole universe up. Well, we can't reach out and get his cookies. They're not in our universe. See, our universe has bounds. There are some things in it and some things not."

—Ed Fredkin

**00101001**
"When a snake becomes a dragon, it doesn't change its scales. And when a mortal becomes a sage, he doesn't change his face."

—Bodhidharma

**00101010**
"When you spot anything true and clear you are at zero."

—Henry Miller

**00101011**
"Pop culture began in 1948."

—Griel Marcus

hen Cy had a job, he was always livin' for the weekend. Seemed there was never enough time to do the things he really wanted to do. I don't wanna work, I just wanna bang on the drum all day.... And wouldn't you know it, now that he's a bum and on a Permanent Vacation, a kind of seven day weekend, he's got too many worries to relax. Not the least of which is the whereabouts, whenabouts, howabouts, whoabouts and whyabouts of his missing girlfriend, lovely mullato who plucks his heartstrings *pizzicato*.

My baby left me, my one good thing. She took off her dress, floated up and moved into the universe, joining the world of missing persons....

Ruby, baby, when will you be mine again?!

Wait a minute. Missing girlfriend? Who's this a-snorin' like an asmathic grizzly next to him then? Guess ol' Pol qualifies as his current girlfriend, or lover, or sumpin. Wild thing, you make my heart sing, cuz we got a groovy kind of love! An exotic erotic narcotic hot chick in every port, looks like that's Cy's way.

But—

What the hell is Augie gonna say? Cy remembers when the Fractal Footballer kicked the ass of some guy putting the moves on Polly in The Twang Bar. What's he gonna do to Cy? My boyfriend's back, and you're gonna be in trouble....

Saturday morning confusion, fer shure!

Planting a little smack on Polly's forehead (Rose, darlin', Snake Mary's gone to bed), Cy gets up to drown his troubles in some coffee.

The apartment is clean. Our house is a very, very fine house. Two cats in the yard, life usta be so hard. . . . They tidied it up yesterday, for lack of anything better to do, after the disappointing events at the Zaquicaz Aqua Retreat. Then Polly went downstairs and disbursed from her purse the rent to Mrs Scozzafava in cash. (Who finds the money when you pay the rent? Did you think that money was heaven-sent?) Mrs Scozzafava was so pleased to get paid on time and with something other than a rubber check that she sent her son, Anthony, up with a huge casserole of eggplant *parmigiano* and half a loaf of crusty Sicilian bread. (He hung around so long, ogling Polly, that Mama S had to yell for him: "Tony! Toni! Tone!") Cy and Pol had noshed on that, then fallen sleepily into bed without making love.

Now he has no notion of what they're gonna do next. Will Max Parallax get off his fat duff—even metaphorically—and earn his retainer? Will they find out how to play the mysterious compact disc they are careful to keep close by them every minute? Will Wu Labs send thugs to kidnap or otherwise molest them?

Will you still feed me, will you still need me, when I'm sixty-four?

Cy shakes his head. Gee, he's really thinking in lyrics this morning. It's a bad habit, he knows. But his head is so stuffed with pop-songs—riffs and hooks, chops and licks, words and other scat-sung vocables, the residue of over twenty years of habitual ingestion of licorice pizzas—that he can't quit doing it. (I can sympathize, Cy.)

Well, there nothing like a little hair of the dog to cure what ails ya!
Cy flips on the counter-top radio.
Imagine his surprise when out comes—MUZAK!
Hey, who changed the setting?! Cy looks at the dial. It claims to be set right where
it oughta be, WBCN-FM. Cy spins the control. Static, MUZAK, static, MUZAK, static,
MUZAK.... No Top Forty, even? What's this, a woman's voice reciting numbers in
Spanish.... *"Cero, uno, dos, quatro, ocho. Cero, uno, dos, quatro, ocho ...."*
How about the AM band? MUZAK, MUZAK, news—"Cardinal Bernardin Gantin
of Benin appears to have a lock on bagging the post of head of the College of
Cardinals, according to our PopeScope...."—and more MUZAK. What the Christ
is going on!? He knew the radio was in the hands of such a bunch of fools, but things
couldn't be this bad, could they? She be listenin' to Channel Zero. Channel Z: all
static, all the time!

Suddenly Cy gets a telepathic message from the radio: *Now I will crush your
face!* He backs off in alarm. A frying pan echoes the threat. *I will crush your skull!*
Even the coffeepot blups out an unfriendly *I will scorch your tongue!* Cy drops into
a chair. Suddenly, he's gone all weak-limbed. It's the MUZAK, he realizes helplessly.
It's filling his cranium with mush, flocculent sonic cotton batting, depriving him of all the
usual nasty cynicism he relies on for motivation. (Discontentment is our engine.)

MUZAK. The deadliest foe to all real musical expression. MUZAK, the only arti-
fact of man's devising that is one-hundred percent noise. (And why is that? Because,
f-folks, "There is no information in a message that is *a priori* certain," and every
note and nuance of MUZAK is utterly predictable and foreknown.) MUZAK, the
abolisher of emotions and wit. MUZAK, the only sound meant to be absorbed directly into the subconscious. MUZAK, the last desperate unconscious hope of an
information-saturated culture in retreat. (But there is not, nor ever can be, any
retreat from the fix we're in. Just gotta push forward, hoping somehow to overcome
or transcend the limitations that got us into this mess in the first place....)

Cy is *so happy*. He's as empty as a record sleeve when the platter's on the turntable, or a jewel-box when the CD's docked. He doesn't have a care in the whole
wide world. Everything is syrupy strings. All the charts are by Chuck Mangione and
Kenny G. Why can't we all enjoy another silly love song? I just called to say I love
you. I write the songs that make the whole world sing, and I'd like to teach the
world to sing in perfect harmony. Tie a yellow ribbon round the old oak tree. Today
is the first day of the rest of your life—so have a *nice* one!

Fur-pajama-ed Polly trips sleepily in, rubbing her eyes, mumbles a good morning and takes a seat. Cy goofily gets up, manages to pour her some coffee and sits
down with her.

Perceptive Pol detects something amiss. "Cy, are you really listening to that crap?"

"Don't be rude, Polly. Besides, it's beautiful...."

Fuh-folks, can this be the same guy talkin' who once while working at Planet
Records told a teenybopper looking for a New Kids On The Block record to use a

cactus dildo on herself? Polly, for one, evidently can't believe her ears.

"What? Did I hear you right? Cy, what's the matter with you?" She gets up and shuts off the MUZAK. But it's too late for Cy. The destructive memes have sunk their barbs into his grey matter, and will not be easily dislodged.

"Gee, Pol, can't a guy express a little optimism and appreciation for the simple joys of life without getting jumped on?"

"Our mates are still missing, their trail is cold, and you're spouting Leo Buscaglia? It just doesn't seem possible...."

"Things are sorta peaceful now without Ruby and Augie."

"Peaceful! Cy, what *are* you talking about?"

"Did you ever notice how pretty the sunlight is...?"

"Sunlight? I don't see—" Polly poises a fingertip against a pearly tooth, pondering for a picosecond. "Cyril, tell me something. Who's your favorite group?"

"Group? People don't make music, machines do...."

"I thought so. Cyril, you sit right there."

"Here's as good as anyplace else...."

Polly leaves the kitchen and quickly returns with Cy's Walkman (with Dolby noise reduction B and C) and a tape. She clamps the 'phones on Cy's head. He makes no resistance, being too busy investigating the wonders of a toast-crumb.

Polly slots a tape home and turns the machine on.

Hoe-kay.... This ain't just any old pre-packaged cassette. Instead, it's THE TAPE, a hundred-minute compilation of some of Cyril's Favorite Toonz, guaranteed to loosen the roots of your hair, help you work it down to the ground, and make you shake your moneymaker.

### THE TAPE

SIDE A

1) "Less Than Zero," Elvis Costello
2) "Mayan Skies," The Stranglers
3) "Everybody's Everything," Santana
4) "Rikki, Don't Lose That Number," Steely Dan
5) "Medicine Show," Big Audio Dynamite
6) "The Future's So Bright, I Gotta Wear Shades," Timbuk 3
7) "Tattooed Love Boys," The Pretenders
8) "Sleeping Snakes," Translator
9) "Blue Money," Van Morrison
10) "I Handle Snakes," Tonio K
11) "Love Minus Zero," Bob Dylan
12) "You Ain't Seen Nothing Yet," Bachman-Turner Overdrive
13) "(We Ain't Got) Nothin' Yet," The Blues Magoos
14) "Day After Day," Badfinger

15) "Tuesday Afternoon," Moody Blues
16) "Hey Little Cobra," Rip Chords

BONUS TRACK
0) "The Mighty Zero," The Meat Puppets

SIDE B
1) "Accidents Never Happen," Blondie
2) "Tube Snake Boogie," ZZ Top
3) "Puzzlin' Evidence," The Talking Heads
4) "Papa Legba," The Talking Heads
5) "She's Not There," The Zombies
6) "Back to Zero," The Rolling Stones
7) "Forever Came Today," The Jackson Five
8) "Someday Never Comes," Creedence Clearwater Revival
9) "Saved by Zero," Fixx
10) "Funky Worm," The Ohio Players
11) "Love Epidemic," Trammps
12) "Play That Funky Music," Wild Cherry
13) "Our Day Will Come," Ruby and the Romantics
14) "Sunday Will Never Be The Same," Spanky & Our Gang
15) "Original Sin," INXS
16) "Time Loves A Hero," Little Feat

BONUS TRACK
0) "The Zero of the Signified," Robert Fripp

Now, if this tape don't get you shakin' your thang, you must be daid, bro'—or else you're Pat Boone. So Polly, in all confidence, expects it to cure her guy, Cy. And she's not disappointed.

As the tape spins, Cy's eyes glaze over, his lips go slack and spittle dribbles from the corner of his mouth. Man, it's just like *The Exorcist* or sumpin! The MUZAK virus lodged in Cy's synapses (which incidentally gained entrance because of his AIDS-weakened condition) is puttin' up a helluva fight for its miserable life, digging with its claws into Cy's neurons. If Cy's ears weren't covered, we could almost hear the virus's squeaky, Wicked-Witch-of-the-West supplications: "No, no, don't erase me, I just want to exist and reproduce like everyone else. I'm not a bad creature, just useless. How do you justify *your* existence? No, no, don't throw that rock 'n' roll cold water on me! Look what you've done, I'm melting, melting, aieeee...!"

Pretty soon the counter-programming has thoroughly erased the MUZAK-virus nucleotide-code bit by bit, recutting the old grooves in Cy's brain.

After one hundred minutes, when the second side of the tape has been played,

Polly removes the 'phones and waits to gauge the results of her last-ditch measures.

Cy opens his eyes. The old feisty light is there. "Thanks, Polly, I needed that. Thank you for letting me be myself again."

Hurray, hoorah, huzzah! His life's been saved by rock 'n' roll! Our hero's restored! He's cool 'n' clean as one of them Glass Masters used to press CD's. He's back to his prickly, touchy, self. He's Bad To The Bone, and he don't wanna be sedated no more.

What could he have been *thinking*? They've got a mystery to solve here, lost friends to track down, nefarious Fu-Manchu doings to drag into the light of day, perhaps, for all they know, a whole world to be saved....

Cy claps his hands together and rubs them manfully, as if preparing to grasp a sledgehammer and ring the bell at an amusement park.

"Okay, Pol, what's next? I'm rarin' to go."

"Well, how about hitting the beach? It's been really warm for May."

That's a curve he hadn't expected. "The beach? What's there?"

"Oh, sand, sun, waves—stuff like that."

"Jeez, I know that much. But how's it gonna help us find Rube and Aug?"

"Well, it won't help in any obvious way, but it will help us indirectly. Look how easily you succumbed to that cheesy MUZAK infection. You're a living wreck. You need a day off, to recoup your energies. And to tell the truth, I could use some downtime too. That incident with Lantz was too depressing. I just wanna shut my mind off for a while."

"How are we gonna get there? Should we ride the train to one of the North Shore beaches?"

"Too crowded. And I'm so sick of the trains! Let's really make a holiday of it. We'll borrow one of Daddy's cars, and go to the Cape."

Cy feels guilty at the notion of enjoying himself so brazenly while Ruby languishes under unknown circumstances. "If you really think it would help us—"

"I do. It's Doctor Peptide's prescription."

"Uh, Doctor, could you check my pulse too?"

"Oh, I see.... Well, we normally feel the wrist. But in your case, I'll make an exception...."

An hour or two later, they gather their sex-sated selves and a duffel full of beach-stuff together, and make the jaunt by mass-transit to the Peptide homestead.

Inside, Polly goes once more into her father's study to work her daughterly wiles on him, while Cy's left talking to Mrs Peptide.

"Do you know how great your daughter is?"

"She takes after her Mom," says Pressina Peptide with a sweet smile and a sexy wink.

Cy is overwhelmed with an image of the attractive Pressina naked and atop him, riding his cock. While her daughter sits on his face. Shame gets the better of his fantasy. Wotta pig! His very own something-similar-to-a-mother-in-law! He blushes, mumbles an excuse, and goes outside to hide his erection.

Next door, the flaccid Mister Wiggle lies on the grass. Was it only two days ago they fought the Sneaky Snaky to a standstill? It seems like a *kalpa* or a *katun*....

Polly comes out after a while to get him.

"It's all set, Cy. Daddy says we can borrow either car. And I fixed us a little lunch. Let's go!"

Out in the driveway, Cy surveys their choices.

One car—Mister Peptide's—is an Audi sedan, with its trademark of four interlinked zeroes gleaming on the hood.

The other car—Mom's—is an Alfa Romeo Julietta, flaunting its heraldic crest with fire-breathing dragon rampant.

"Pol, there is no question in my mind which car we are using. I will never in my life get another chance to drive an Alfa Romeo. That is, if you don't want to take the wheel—"

"Baby, you can drive my car."

Cy grabs the small cooler and duffel and puts them in the tiny boot. One sweet dream came true today: pick up the bags, and get in the limousine! This is the cure for the summertime blues!

What acceleration! My liddle 409! We'll have fun, fun, fun, till her Mommy takes the Alfa away!

Soon they are leaving the city behind. Oh, I love that dirty water—Boston you're my home—but I'm heading now for Rock-rock-rock-rock-rockaway Beach! No more summer in the city for a while, back of my neck all dirty-gritty.

This is what life was meant to be. In the summertime, it's all mangoes and cherries. Hot fun in the summertime, on the road with your baby. In short, an interval of

## MINDLESS PLEASURES

They drive past a Stop & Shop with the radio on (all stations seem to be Back To Normal). I'm in love with Massachusetts! I'm in love with modern rock 'n' roll!

Road runner once, road runner twice, it's the freeway of love, and it sure feels nice!

They're just a couple of love-cats, and everything is cool for cats today.

"Should we take four-ninety-five, or hug the coast?" asks glad-all-over Cy.

"I vote for the the coast,"

"You got it, girl."

So they pick up Route 3 and head south, passing Plymouth, where them Pilgrims learned the hermetic Indian lore from ol' Squanto, and, further on, the picturesque Bloody Pond.

Shade-wearing Cy switches from radio to tapes: he's had the foresight to bring along the five-volume Rhino history of funk, *In Yo Face,* as well as something by a gal named Angelique Kidjo, and they motor on in a cloud of song.

They sight an abandoned drive-in, its busted marquee still advertising its last show:

SCREEN 1
A– AB–ND
EL SA–ARI–

SCREEN 2
– FRE– RID–
SAL–MMB–

Before too long, they're on the Bourne Bridge over the Cape Cod Canal, and then they're on the Cape itself.

"Out to Pee-town?"

"No, it'll be full of tourists. And I want to get maximum beach time. Let's go to Sandy Neck. It's close and it's always quiet."

"Cool with me."

Within a few miles Cy sights the sign for the beach and hangs a left. Long narrow twisting unlaned blacktop bordered by scrubgrowth, with sand creeping over the road. Small dunes push up out of the earth, more and more until the landscape's all dunes dotted with tussocks of sharp grass. They round a curve and sight the magnificent heaving breast of the sea. Balboa, we are soulmates!

There's a booth at the entrance to a sizable parking lot, posted with Rules 'n' Regulations.

SANDY NECK BEACH
ZOSIMOS AND THEOSEBEIA JONES, PROPS.
NO PETS, FIREWORKS, ALCOHOLIC BEVERAGES,
CONTROLLED SUBSTANCES OR LOUD MUSIC
RESTRAIN YOUR ANIMAL INSTINCTS
PLAY CIRCUMSPECTLY
SWIM WITHIN BUOYS
OBEY LIFEGUARDS
DON'T CURSE
HAVE FUN

Anti-authoritarian Cy gets a little huffy. "Is this a beach or a concentration camp?"

"Now, Cy, don't worry, we can still enjoy ourselves."

"I hope so."

He brakes by the side of the booth, which is staffed by an elderly couple. The wrinkled old man—presumably Zosimos Jones—leans out.

"That'll be a dollar and a penny to park, son."

"How come the weird price?"

"There's a charity event going on and some radio station with call-numbers one-oh-one is sponsoring it."

"Here's the dollar. Pol, you got a penny?"

"No, I don't think so.... No, I don't."

"Listen, Mister, can't you just take the dollar and forget the penny?"

"I got to have that penny, son. Wouldn't be fair to the other folks that already paid, would it?"

"Jesus fuckin' Christ—"

Jones points mutely to the penultimate injunction on the signboard. Cy heaves an exasperated sigh and digs thru his pockets, at last, all unwitting, coming up with—

THE DIGITAL PENNY! Hopi counterfeit that once bit Cy's ass.

He hands it over to Jones.

Jones's eyes get real big.

"I'm so sorry, I didn't realize— Go right on in, please, sir and madam, do whatever you want, enjoy yourself to the limits. Look, here's a slip for free refreshments at our take-out counter. My compliments."

"Gee, thanks. Uh, sorry about the swearing...."

"No, no, that's quite all right. Listen, I'll swear too. By Ostanes, Agrippa and Thomas the Contender, my mother was a wicked serpent!"

"Uh, great. Excellent swearing, man. Well, catch ya later."

Cy parks the Alfa in one of the few remaining spaces, gets out and surveys the jam-packed lot. "Sandy Neck is always quiet, huh?"

"How could I know there'd be a charity event going on?"

"Well, maybe we can still find an empty stretch."

They flip-flop in their plastic sandals over to the changing booths and shower rooms, cement structures exuding coolness.

"You go ahead, Cy. I put my suit on under my clothes back home."

Cyril darts into the locker room, strips, and dons his trunks. He comes back out. Pol's still dressed.

"I'll get out of my clothes on the beach, so I won't have to carry them."

Cy lugging the cooler and Polly the duffel, they round the buildings and come upon the beach. People are everywhere, even under the boardwalk. There's a banner on two poles staked into the sand.

CELEBRITY SURFIN' SAFARI SPONSORED BY WTAC-101
TO BENEFIT THE JORMUNGANDR INSTITUTE

"Why, that's the special school Paulie Junior attends! Let's watch a little, Cy."

"Sure."

It's a regular Surf City at Sandy Neck today, with tons of local celebs in their wetsuits standing by their upright boards, looking either awkward or at ease depending on their previous experience at surfin' in the USA. Why, Cy can even make out the Governor, isolated by his natural reserve from the rest of the babes 'n' dudes. He's a lonely surfer, fer shure. And there's his wife, that plucky Surfer Girl!

People are betting money on how long each celeb will stay upright in THE PIPELINE before they (hee-hee-hee) WIPEOUT! The Jormungandr Institute gets the take from the losers.

All attention is focused on the current contestant, a real tall drink of water, blond gawky guy with a mustache. Can it be? Cy thinks. Yes, it is.

It's the great Larry Bird on a surfboard!

The crowd starts chanting to cheer Larry on.

"Bird, Bird, Bird's the word! Bird, Bird, Surfin' Bird!"

Larry gives a creditable performance before crashing, and the crowd applauds wildly and jumps up and down in a surfer stomp.

"Seen enough?"

"Yup. Let's find a place for our blanket."

By trekking down the hot sand for a quarter of a mile, they leave everyone behind. Cy spreads the blanket near the foot of a dune, where bejeweled dragonflies flitter among the grass. He weights it down with stones at the corners, and straightens up.

Polly has stripped.

Wotta knockout!

She's bustin' out of a Mucha' Linda creation: an itsy bitsy teenie weenie yellow polkadot bikini. Her juju bag hangs down between her tits. She pivots for Cy's inspection. The back of the bathing suit is a string running between her ass cheeks.

That Pol! She's a dedicated follower of fashion!

"Like it?" inquires the nearly naked semiotician.

Cy seems to have swallowed half the beach. After gulping several times, he can only say, "Hey Lawdy Mama...."

"I thought you would. The only trouble with this suit is that it leaves so much bare skin, you can go through a whole bottle of sunscreen."

"Well worth the cost."

Grinning, Polly unstoppers a bottle and squirts some white cream into her palm. "Want to help me?"

"I specialize in covering certain territory."

"I might have guessed."

After greasing herself up with Cy's enthusiastic help, Polly says, "Now you."

"Yuk! No way! I hate that stuff."

"You're gonna burn."

"I never burn."

"All right, it's up to you."

Cy asks, "Should we go in the water now?"

"After I just buttered myself up? Let's get some sun first. And I want to finish my book, too."

Polly digs in the duffel and comes up with *The Serpent Repents.*

"You're still reading that? Is it any good?"

"I can't say. It's weird, and I think I understand it. But like a lot of semiotics, it could just as well be doubletalk."

"How's she write?"

"Here's a sample. 'The name of God, the tetragrammaton, is hidden in the world, it shines forth as the *lumen naturæ.* Observe the flight of birds, the castings of earthworms for God's signature. Or if, like Alexandria Pope, you believe the proper study of womankind is woman, then examine your own words for hidden signification. Every sentence should be read backwards, every word deconstructed and reassembled to achieve the totality of messages. Let us all become lovers of cryptograms, or true philo-ciphers. "Madam, I'm Adam," was the first sentence ever spoken. The second was, "'S liar! Even Eve never ails!"' "

"Is there any part where she states her thesis?"

"That was it."

"Oh. Well, enjoy...."

Cy rolls over onto his stomach and closes his eyes. How peaceful. Polly had such a great idea. The salty breeze plays soothingly over his bare skin, the sun beats down, he gets drowsy, and falls asleep.

Inspired by his maritime surroundings, Cy begins to dream....

He is Christopher Columbus. It's October 10, 1492. He stands on the deck of the *Santa Maria,* surrounded by mutinous crewmen.

"We're all gonna die!" the crewmen shout, waving their belaying pins. "Let's head home!"

"Fear not," reassures Cyril Columbus. "Land is near."

Martin Pinzon, skipper of the *Nina,* steps forward as spokesman. "Land?! You're outa your gourd, Chris!"

"We must go on, for God and the Queen!"

"God ain't watchin'. And you're the only one who got to boff Isabella."

"A vile canard! There was naught but a French kiss to seal the pact. I have to succeed in reaching the Indies before I gain access to the royal muff."

"That still don't cut it, man. We're almost outa supplies! The quince juice is gone, and so's the violet conserve, the rum, the lard, the rose water, the lemon juice, the lily root, and even the tincture of honey, opium and dragontree resin."

"Have faith," urges Christopher Prothero.

"Faith no more! See how the mainsail swells. I'm tired, and I wanna go home. Let me go home!"

The crew advance at a signal from Pinzon. Cy cowers back against the rail.

The sea near the rail boils. An enormous whiskered horned and scaly head draped with seaweed surfaces, dripping water. It's Kraken! The crewmen drop their weapons and dive down the hatches. Cy is left alone facing the sea-serpent.

"What—what do you wish of me?"

Kraken grins with a mouthful of cutlery, then speaks. "You must continue. We have big plans for the New World. It must be discovered now."

"I'm trying! It's my crew that won't listen."

A web-toed forefoot big as an ox-cart breaks the surface. Poised between the tips of two mossy green claws is a gleaming pearl.

"Take this. They will not dare disobey you any longer."

Cy takes the pearl.

"Goodbye, Columbus. My advice is not to fill up with wrath."

"Wait! Am I heading in the right direction?"

"A tad more to the south. You gotta stop at Haiti to pick up syphillis."

"And can you tell me aught of my future? Will I live to enjoy my success?"

"You will make four expeditions in all, but die penniless and forgotten."

"Gah-rate.... Well, I suppose I'm committed now.... At least I'll get to fuck Isabella...."

"Bye, Beany," says Krakey.

"Bye, Cecil," says Cy.

The Kraken submerges and the crew emerges.

"What're your orders, Skipper?" says Pinzon. He's wearing a crush cap and looks just like Maynard G. Krebs (discoverer of the Krebs Cycle, natch).

"Alter our heading a tad more to the south. There's a virus waiting."

Wooden ships on the water, crew living on purple berries.... In two days they sight land. By December fifth, they've discovered Hispaniola.

"I will plant a colony here for the glory of Portugal. You, you and you—toss up a shopping mall pronto."

The crewmen so designated rebel. They gobble down some leaves from an information bush and suddenly become Little Black Sambos.

"Dis be de future lo-cay-shun ub Haiti, boss, and we is gonna hab us a liddle vodun sack-ree-fice now...."

His ex-crew members grab Cy and stuff him into a pot of boiling water.

"Help, help, Mister Peabody! Get me into the Wayback now!"

Someone is jostling Cy's shoulder.

"Cyril, time to turn over," says Polly. "You had fifteen minutes on your belly."

"Fifteen minutes? It was more like five hundred years...."

Cy lies for a while longer, then proposes a dip.

"Sure," agrees Polly.

They get up and step away from the blanket. Cy stops.

"The disc—"

Augie's CD, their one bargaining chip, resides in the duffel. They can't leave it unprotected!

"Cy, don't be paranoid. No one even knows we're here. And look around you. Yards of empty sand. No one can sneak up on us before we can reach the blanket. We'll be safe if one of us always watches the stuff from the water."

"Okay, if you say so."

They move toward the ocean. Cy looks back one more time. Nothing unusual. Just a harmless dragonfly sitting on the blanket.

At the highwater mark, Cy finds a corked bottle resting amid the wrack.

"Hey, message in a bottle!" He opens it and shakes out a tube of paper. Polly comes to look.

Unrolled, the message is an unintelligible smear of watery red ink, as if once written in blood.

"Oh, well...."

In the somewhat chilly water they frolic and play grab-ass, at first keeping an alert eye on their possessions. But as passions start to heat up, they drop their vigilance.

The next time Cy thinks to check it out, there's some kind of black iridescent shimmering haze obscuring their blanket.

"Hey, Polly, look—"

"Are those all *dragonflies?*"

Cy paddles to waist-deep water, then starts to run, Polly following. The sea strives to hold him back.

He's on the firm sand and picks up speed. But once beyond the waterline, it's slower going.

Cy can see the sand their blanket once covered. The horde of insects, clustered around the perimeter of the blanket, has lifted it off the ground. The airborne duffel makes the fabric sag, but the dragonflies are undaunted.

Some Raid, some Raid, my kingdom for some Raid!

Cy's huffin' 'n' puffin', drivin' and cryin'. Who knew he was so outa shape? Is he gonna make it? The blanket's three feet high and rising, heading north. By the time he reaches its former location, it's above his head.

"Yaaaahhh!" Our boy makes a superhuman leap and snags a corner, hand closing on a fistful of greasy dragonfly guts.

Hey there, little insect, don't scare me so! Don't land on me, don't bite me, no! Please come down, and we'll have fun and fool around!

For one brief millisecond he swears the superbugs are gonna fly off with him too. Then all resistance disappears and Cy falls back on his ass, the duffel landing painfully in his lap.

Polly's beside him.

"Oh, Cy, you did it! You're the greatest!" Polly hugs and kisses her man.

"I guess they musta been attracted to the lotion on the blanket, huh, Pol?"

Polly looks at him dubiously. "I guess."

"Well, in any case, that's the end of our swimming...."

"We can still hang out by the blanket, though. How about some lunch?"

"I could really use that."

They rearrange their blanket; Polly applies some fresh sunscreen, then cracks the cooler.

Inside is a six-pack of Dragon Stout from Jamaica, cold chicken, black Greek olives, peaches and some dates.

"You're a wizard, Pol. Let's eat!"

After their third beer apiece, Cyril and Polly, remembering what they had been doing prior to the attempted aerial theft, begin to feel kinda amorous.

"Let's go in the dunes," suggests Pol, putting an end to their stoned soul picnic.

They lurch drunkenly with all their stuff deeper into the dunes. When the blanket's spread on a gentle slope, they fall to kissing.

Cy fumbles with Polly's top, but can't unsnap it. She obligingly lifts her arms straight above her head so he can pull it off. He does, spilling forth her sunscreen-slick boobs, but the wet fabric twists and binds around her wrists.

"Leave it," gasps Pol, fit to be tied.

He tugs now at the bottom of her suit, which eventually ends up curling and tightening and pinioning her ankles together.

Cy skins off his own suit. He grabs Polly's bound ankles in one hand and lifts her legs up and toward her head.

Her cunt winks wetly from between the juncture of her thighs.

Eye in the pyramid, yeah!

Still holding her legs aloft, Cy kneels at her ass and drapes her legs over his right shoulder, holding them in place against his chest with an arm around her knees.

With his left hand he places the head of his cock at her pelagic pussy—and slides it up. Polly screams and starts bucking like a wild bronco-ette.

Cowgirl in the sand! It's the woman in you that makes you want to play this game! Will I see you in September, or lose you to a summer love?

Polly orgasms two or three times before Cy cums in a thankfully hallucination-free eternity of ecstacy.

Cy manages to twist around and lie down beside Polly without pulling out.

They fall asleep. Luckily, within an hour their face of the dune becomes shaded. When they awake, it is late afternoon.

"Jeez, we should think about getting home...."

"Cy, you are totally cooked. You look like an Indian."

"Shit...."

Dressed and in the car, they pull away from Sandy Neck Beach. A day to remember, fer shure, even without the enthusiastic hail-and-farewell from the Joneses.

Pleasantly weary, sand in their shoes, they ride back mostly in silence.

At the Peptide house, they immediately notice that the Audi's gone from the driveway. The front door's locked, and a note's taped to it.

GONE TO A SHOW.
PAULIE'S WITH AUNT AMELIA FOR THE NIGHT.
MAKE YOURSELF AT HOME.

Sounds good. But Polly's lost her keys somewhere on the beach.
She has to climb in thru the bathroom window.
Once inside, they contemplate fooling around some more. (Everyone's gone to
the movies, we're alone at last.) But they're simply too beat.
"Let's get some Noxema on you, Cy, and then have some supper."
"I'm gonna take some aspirin too. I feel a little feverish."
(Fever when you kissed her, maybe, Cy!)
No sooner said than done. After all of which they fall asleep, Polly in her bed and
Cy in her brother's, so as not to offend the sensibilities of Mom 'n' Dad when they
return.
Sunday and me: Cy wakes up out of confused dreams. When he moves, he finally
acknowledges how badly he got burned yesterday. His skin feels like the canvas
some merciless Artist has stretched prior to painting a bright scarlet. That'll teach
ya not to go messin' with Apollo, Cy, unless you know how to drive his chariot!
Borrowing some more of Paulie Junior's clothes, Cy gets dressed. The sensation
of even soft cotton fabric on his abused epidermis feels like being rubbed with
Brillo pads. He makes his way painfully downstairs.
The Peptide Family, *sans* Paulie, sits at table. Cy tries to be cheerful, despite his
discomfort.
"Thanks for the loan of the car, folks. We had a great day-ay-ay-ay!"
This last strange pronunciation being an exclamation of pain drawn from Cyril
as he tries to sit down.
Tender Pol is by his side instantly. "Oh, Cy, I warned you—"
Mister Peptide removes his pipe from his mouth. "Son, I think you could use a
little GreenGenes magic right about now. Luckily, I've got a tube of an experimental
compound that might just do the trick."
"Oh, Daddy, do you really think you could help Cy?"
"I'll certainly try."
Mister Peptide leaves and returns with an unlabeled silver tube.
"Apply this wherever you're burned. It's mostly Nerve Growth Factor, with additional
hormones and cytokines. We grow it in bioengineered Oh Ex One Seventy-Four."
"Come on, Cy, I'll do your back."
Polly accompanies Cyril into the downstairs bathroom and helps him slather on
the goop. He's too uncomfortable even to take advantage of her roving hands. When
the stuff is all absorbed, Cy notices an immediate alleviation of his condition. He
feels likes he's sheathed in a kind of protective integument. He redons his clothes
and joins the Peptides.
"This stuff is great, Mister Peptide," compliments Cy.

"Oh, Daddy, you'll make it big with this!"

"Now, Sugar, I told you not to hold your breath."

After a big hearty breakfast, Pol and Cy bid the Peptides goodbye, and set out for Boston, once more afoot.

At the Harvard Square T Stop, Cy says, "So, what's on the agenda for today?"

"I thought we could check out the altered Citgo sign in Kenmore Square again. Maybe there's been some new development."

"Sounds unlikely. But it's better than doing nothing, I suppose. Let's go straight there and get it over with."

On the Red Line leg of the trip (at one point during which, they pass mere yards away from the underground rooms of MIT's Media Lab, where Cybernetic Cabals cook up humanity's next info fix), Cy says, "You mentioned something earlier—God, I can't even remember when, so much has happened—it was about codes and channels. It's been bugging me ever since. I understand channels, I think, but codes—"

"In information theory," explains Polly, "a code is not a cryptogram, like you're probably imagining, but merely a way of insuring that messages are transmitted with minimum error due to noise. Any natural language, for instance, is a code. Theoretically, codes can be devised which reduce the probability of errors derived from noise to zero. Thus, without any increase in channel capacity, you'd attain an increase in information transmitted. I think I mentioned this when we were talking about becoming omniscient."

"Oh," says Cy, not really enlightened.

Once resurrected in relatively quiet Kenmore Square, they immediately eyeball the billboard. Much to Cy's surprise, the former formula has indeed been replaced, by a new version of the same equation:

$$C = \infty$$

"My God!" exclaims Polly.

"What, what?" frantically demands Cyril.

"Don't you see? Channel capacity is infinite. You were right. Wu is after omniscience, and probably immortality too. The question is, has he achieved it yet, or is he only boasting?"

Cy doesn't have any answer. Lowering his gaze, he looks idly toward his old store on Commonwealth Ave. What meets his eyes knocks him for a loop.

"Polly, they've destroyed the Planet!"

"What!"

"Planet Records. Look...."

Shure enuff, the building that once housed the record store is now a boarded-up ruin, roofless and charred. Welcome to the Workin' Wreck! A synthetic odor of melted records is wafted toward them by a vagrant breeze.

Cy feels a major mule-kick of sadness in his heart, remembering the happy times he had there, when the music blasting out of the speakers outweighed the misery of dealing with dumb customers.

Music. Real music. What it's meant in his life.... Most obviously, it saved him yesterday from a worthless existence as a mush-brain victim of the MUZAK virus. But aside from that, music has given his life meaning, boosted him up when he was down, shown him the way when all looked dark. (Imagine if Dante, wandering in his *selva oscura*, had only had a chance to hear, say, Van Morrison's "Listen to the Lion." All of history would have been different; kinda makes ya think....) It's provided the background and context to both his happiest and saddest moments, told him what was going down better than any other news-source around. Listening to music has been, for Cy, like taking part in a gigantic world-wide conversation some forty years old, (really millennia, Cy) whose terms constantly change, where witty remarks alternate with inanities, but whose underlying subject is constant: how to make it thru late-twentieth-century life.

There are certain areas, certain disciplines, certain fields, which are so deep that they can be studied and enjoyed and puzzled over for a lifetime. These subjects offer endless rewards to amateur and professional alike, becoming the basis for satisfying hobbies or vocations. Once perhaps merely shallow topics, they have broken through a certain barrier of complexity, emergent on a new level.

Obviously, the physical world is the ultimate model for such nearly infinite human-created topics. And while those who study nature are scientists, amateur or otherwise, there are other scientists, of a different sort, exploring similarly vast domains.

History.

Religion.

Literature.

Art.

Music.

You can lose yourself in any of these.

'Course, when Cy thinks of music, he's referring to Modern Music, Pure Pop For Now People.

Rock, funk, hardcore, punk, thrash, speedcore, reggae, world-beat, juju, new-wave, no-wave, fusion, skank, go-go, Motown, R&B, rockabilly, acid rock, cowpunk, ska, hip-hop, rap, bop, zouk, qawwali, black metal, speed metal, death metal, zydeco, rai, soukous, skiffle, rock steady, township jive, mbaqanga, merengue, house, hip-house, ghetto bass, tango, sampledelic, funk-punk, swampedelic, lambada, new jack swing, dancehall, skate-punk, griot, salsa, heavy metal, disco, calypso, industrial, bubblegum, straight-edge, ragamuffin, techno, mento, grunge, shoegazer, jit jive, afoxe, cumbia, palmwine, rara, al jeel, shaabi, Philly Soul, junkanoo, tejano, illbient, ambient, jungle, bhangra, salsa, quiet storm .... Endless Stax Of Trax. If it's got that post-Shannon sophic beat, Cyril will groove to it. Analog or digital, he can dig its overriding message: there is only Now, Eternal Present, no Past or Future, therefore LIVE!

Music. It's infinite. How could you ever hope to explore it all? It'd be insane to even try! You might as well attempt to encompass it all in a single book, a novel perhaps. You'd be bound to leave something out. Ah, well....

And to think of all that melted information in the ruins of Planet Records, gone to waste, incapable of influencing anyone any longer. It makes Cy, that clown, wanna shed a tear....

Weh-hell. Enuff melancholy. Cy tries to cheer himself up by speculating that Yarrow and Detmold might have been caught in the conflagration....

"It looks like an act of sheer desperation," opines Polly. "They probably broke in the same night they ransacked our apartment, and when they couldn't find the disc, torched the place."

As Cy ponders the implications of this violent act, it dawns on him that he is hearing the honking of several car horns, growing louder.

He looks up.

Kenmore Square is the confluence of five or six streets. The subway stop debouches onto a traffic island in the middle of the Square, from which Cy and Polly have not stirred.

There are four driverless cars and trucks coming down the major streets straight at them at about sixty MPH.

In a timeless moment, Cy manages to register:

A Sweet Life Foods truck with the slogan "Love is contagious."

A Montagnier Pizza delivery van.

A Melchisidek Liturgical Supplies hearse.

A black Lincoln Continental.

"Polly, down the stairs!"

They throw themselves into the subway entrance.

The street-level kiosk is sheared off and compressed by the impacting cars in a Titan's scream of tortured metal. Debris rains down into the subway station. Polly and Cy scuttle further away. There follows an enormous explosion.

At that moment a train pulls in. They clamber onboard. The train pulls out.

"I know it's only eleven-thirty," says Cy, "but I could use a drink."

"Me too."

They get off several stops away. Distant sirens can be heard. The shaky dismayed duo turn into the nearest bar, heedless of the sign above, which proclaims:

THE PEOPLE'S QUEEN'S VILLAGE
Fred McMercury, Prop.

The patrons are exclusively leather-clad guys with various parts pierced, arms around each other. They're all singing a song, to the tune of "Roll Out the Barrel."

## FILL UP THE CLOSET

Fill up the closet,
We'll have a closet of love!
Fill up the closet,
Let each push come to shove!
Fill up the closet,
We'll have a closet of love!
Fill up the closet,
Eeek! Oh my heavens above!

"Uh, you think we should try another place?"

"Yeah."

Next door is a more congenial bar called Danny's All-Star Joint (it's got a juke-box goes *doyt-doyt!*) Some guys are shooting craps in the back. Their voices drift to Cy and Pol, indistinguishable save for an occasional "Snake-eyes!"

Cy orders for himself. "One Scotch, one bourbon, one beer."

"Me too," says Pol.

The liquor does their nerves good. The bar is comforting in an innocently sleazy way, and they gradually regain enough confidence to think about venturing out again.

Cy scoops up the bills the bartender left as change, and they get ready to go.

Something makes Cy look at the cash before pocketing it.

The uppermost dollar has, as dollars sometimes will have, something written on it, black ink defacing the sacred green and white portrait of George. Cy squints.

*Come see me. —Max*

Cy accuses the bartender, whose embroidered bowling shirt names him as Gus Gusano. "Hey, did you write this?"

"Wotta ya, some kinda troublemaker? Geddoutta here, before I throw ya out!"

"All right, all right, chill out, Gus."

"What was that all about?" asks Polly, outside.

Cy shows her the bill with its message.

"Well, what did you expect? He can't use the phone."

"Oh...."

So here they are, shuttling off to Arlington Street and the Ritz-Carlton to meet with Max Parallax for the third time. Seems they're always running somewhere, carrying or seeking some new piece of this vast puzzle they're trying to solve. (And how exactly does one solve a puzzle of which one is an intimate part? We're talkin' problems of Heisenbergian nature here. Every push on the object hidden inside the black bag distorts it in a different dimension....)

Up in Room 1010, Polly and Cyril find Parallax in the same big chair. Something's changed, tho, something his Ray Charles sunglasses can't conceal. The fat man's normal Buddha-like serenity has been disturbed. His face is sweaty and marked with lines of tension. His suit is rumpled and he looks like he's been double-dipped in shit. Seems like somebody's gunning for the Buddha, fer shure!

Before Polly can even begin signing into his palm, Parallax speaks. "I've called you both here to warn you, and give you one last clue. The warning first: you two have stumbled onto something enormous. There is much more at stake here than the fate of your friends. I fear it may be too late to save them—to try might be as useless as painting legs on a snake, as the Chinese have it—and perhaps too late for the rest of us as well."

Forgetting Parallax's handicaps, worried as hell, Cyril yells, "Wotta ya mean, man, 'too late?' What have they done to Ruby? If they've hurt her, I'll kill someone, I swear it—"

"Don't be angry with him, Cy, it's not Max's fault. He's helped us all he can—"

Parallax interrupts. "I have to concentrate on defending myself now. I've touched the dragon in my search, and now he has my scent. He'll be arriving soon. I must be ready. You two are on your own now. Be careful. The clue is this: the number of the dragon will soon change. Go now—please."

Cy opens his mouth to protest, but Polly's grip on his arm halts him. She moves then to sign goodbye to Parallax, the old Hand Jive, and they leave the flustered Korean-trained savant sweating in his uneasy chair.

Feeling lower than a snake's belly, Polly and Cyril head for home. Their tits are really in the wringer now (to use a coarse idiom frequently employed by Detmold, who hopefully is now mere ashes on the floor of his store). They've lost their one ally, the guy they were subconsciously counting on to Save The Day, and now they're completely on their lonesome. If anyone's gonna save Ruby and Augie, it'll be them alone.

But how they're gonna do it is absolutely unclear.

Back in their apartment, they vege out.

Polly takes a long soak. The apartment becomes scented with bathsalts. Splish-splash, she was takin' a bath, long about a Sunday night. *Aprés bain*, she paints her nails, and then settles down to deconstruct a novel by Flaubert.

Cy, intrigued by the snatch of Salonika Polly read to him, spends a couple of hours trying to form anagrams with his full name, Cyril Otis Prothero. Among other combinations, he gets:

CRI ROI: SLOTHROP YET
"COP HER TIT" ROILS ROY
SIC HERO: TOIL, PRY, ROT

This last motto so dismays him that he desists from his wordplay and spends the rest of the day leafing thru the Sunday papers. If you wanna learn about anything, read it in the Sunday papers!

The melancholy pair take to bed early and celibate.

Monday, monday, can't trust that day....

Cy and Pol sit morosely at the breakfast table, their coffee growing cold, until Cy bursts out with "I can't stand this anymore! We've got to assume that Ruby and Augie are still okay, and that we can do something to help them!"

"Like what?"

Cy's stumped for a second. Then, winging it, he says, "Look, this is a mess bounded by information theory, right? What if I dig up some more information? On Wu Labs and the man himself, for instance? Research is the only thing I'm good at. Lord knows I spent ten years in libraries. Maybe I can find us a new lead."

Polly seems to take heart. "I've been thinking I might enlist Daddy's help. He's got lots of fancy technology at his company, and some pretty smart people working for him. Maybe they'd be able to find out what's on our disc."

Cyril smacks his fist into his palm. "Great! Now we're cooking! Let's go!"

Outside the Haymarket subway stop, Cy and Polly pause.

"I guess to maximize our time, we should, um, split up," says Cy hesitantly, almost hoping Polly will contradict him. But she don't.

"You're absolutely right, Cy. We'll meet back home tonight."

Polly squeezes his hand extra tight, gives him a kiss, and then disappears down the rabbit hole, carrying their precious disc in her butt-pack.

Cy experiences a moment of panic. This is the first time they've been separated in nearly a week. What if anything happens to her? He'll just die!

Then he recalls what that dream-Nazi said: "Her fetish protects you as long as you are together."

Holy Mother-Mary-fucker! What if something should happen to *him?!*

Cy manfully attempts to dismiss such nonsense from his mind. Astral fascists, indeed! He's got nothing to worry about. Why, he's safe as the master tapes of those great apocryphal albums, *Smile, Hot as Sun, The Everlasting First,* and *Black Gold,* all of which are locked in a Swiss safe-deposit box belonging to the Bilderberg Group, under the watchful gaze of Bank Manager Ludwig "Lewd" Scheiner, who won't even give you a glimpse.

Cy has a destination in mind, a place where he can begin his research. It's the Boston Athenæum, private library at 10½ Beacon Street. Cy first gained entry there thanks to the intercession of his old professor, Mal Sfortuna, and now has a permanent visitor's pass.

He sets out to walk crosstown, casting an apprehensive eye over his shoulder from time to time.

At the Common (Cy fails to spot *Peacock Feathers* adorning the Swan Boats), Cy notices a crowd. He goes over to check it out.

It's a Three-Card Monte Setup, a cardboard box presided over by a hustler.

Only novel thing is, the hustler has an accomplice.

His assistant is a gargantuan python, the mass of it coiled inside a wicker basket, head rearing up and swaying hypnotically above the three cards laid on the boxtop.

The python wears a cardboard crown from Burger King, secured by a string under its jaw.

"C'mon, laze 'n' jennelmen, who'll take a chance? Step right up, don't be shy, he don't bite, he just likes to squeeze. Lookee here, I'll show you how easy it is."

The hustler flips the cards to reveal the Ace of Spades as the middle of the three.

"All ya gotta do is keep track of the Ace, folks, while my partner moves 'em around. Go for it, King."

Faster than the human eye can follow, the python slides all the face-down cards around in a blur with its nose.

"Okay, who'll lay down ten bucks and give it a shot?"

A cocky B-boy wearing a rhinestone name-chain spelling out CROW steps up. "Here's your money, sucker. I say it's the one on the left."

The hustler reveals the card: a Joker. The B-boy looks inclined to demand his money back. Then the python hisses.

At that moment someone yells, "Hey, Millbrook—cops!"

The box is tipped, the hustler cuts out, the snake slithers down a storm drain, losing its crown in the process.

Adios to the Three-Card Monte Python!

Fer now....

Cy continues on his way.

He passes the bench where he discovered, a week ago, the graffiti of four decades.

It's been painted black.

At last the young scholar stands at the door of the Boston Athenæum.

The building is an unassuming four-story brownstone, long favored by the city's elite. Cy always feels sorta outa place inside, but enjoys its old-fashioned ambiance nonetheless, reveling in the presence of so much staid history, so much dignified Brahmin cerebral activity.

Curiously, there is something newly engraved in the stone lintel, beneath the library's name.

$$S = k \log W$$

Cy climbs the steps, presents his pass to a security guard (whose name tag reads RIDLEY SCROWLE) in the vestibule, then steps inside, anticipating a quiet day of roamin' the stacks.

Two Vegas showgirls are waiting for him. They wear three-foot-tall plumed head-dresses, G-strings, pasties, and high heels. Horsetails project from their rumps.

"Here, sir, please have a complimentary Zombie."

One of the gals presses a frosty drink capped with a liddle umbrella into his hand.

Cy instinctively takes the drink. He goggles at the showgirls, his mouth open like a fish's.

"Wha— What's going on?"

"Nothing out of the ordinary, sir. The Athenæum has been bought out and is under new management, and there have been a few minor changes."

"Do you still have books?"

The gals giggle. "Why, of course we have books. But we've also opened up the library to other media."

"Such as?"

"Oh, the Director could explain much better than we could. Do you want to meet him?"

"Uh, sure...."

The floozy librarians—highly informal information scientists—conduct Cy to an office door stenciled MISTER MAXWELL. They knock. A gruff voice calls out, "Whazup?"

"A patron wishes to see you, Mister Maxwell."

"Boot his ass in, whydoncha."

The girls open the door and push Cyril in.

The first thing Cy notices is that an invisible line had been drawn down his middle. The left half of his body feels chilly, the right half warm. (Like the old joke, that must make his average temp just right.) Must be something wrong with the air-conditioning....

The next thing he notices is Mister Maxwell.

The new Director of the Boston Athenaeum sits behind his desk with his feet resting on its elegantly inlaid top. Mister Maxwell is a squat, grossly corpulent fellow. His skin is brick red and spotted with suppurating whiteheads, zits big as dimes. His nose resembles a particularly ugly toadstool; his lips are big and liverish. Thick coarse black hair falls over his brow, concealing what appear to be two bumps on his temples. He wears a striped shirt, checker-board pants held up by suspenders, and a pair of combat boots. The crotch of his pants displays a bulge which, if unaugmented by padding, would indicate a male organ of non-human proportions.

In short, thinks Cy, Mister Maxwell resembles nothing so much as a certain drawing by S. Clay Wilson.

Mister Maxwell's hands are in continual motion. His right hand snatches unseen objects and passes them to his left hand, which tosses them away to that side.

"Take a load off your feet, kid."

Cy has his choice of two chairs, one on either side of the desk. He sits in one. It's freezing. He tries the other. Broiling.

"Uh, I'll stand...."

"Suit yerself. Hey, whatsamatta, drink not good enough for ya? C'mon, chug it!"

Not wishing to offend the burly and obviously capricious Mister Maxwell, Cy obediently sips his drink. Gee, it's quite tasty....

"Good, good, I like ta see people enjoyin' themselves. Now, how can I do ya?"

"It's nothing, really. I was just wondering about the, um, changes."

"A new broom sweeps clean, kid. I got big schemes fer this dump. Bring it inta the fuckin' twentieth century. I'm gonna make it a multi-media extravaganza, a honky-tonk on the info hiway! Lightshows, videos, some high-class tail— Just name it, ya got it. It'll be better than Em-Tee-Vee!"

"Don't you think you might alienate the older members? They sort of prefer a tamer atmosphere. You know: 'Keep it down now, voices carry.' Like that...?"

"Those old farts can stick their heads up their asses! I side with youth and chaos. Tho' I'm really an orderly kinda guy in my own personal life."

"Uh, what are your qualifications, Mister Maxwell? Not to offend, but I mean, have you ever run a library before?"

"Not eggzackly. But I'm a natural at sortin' things, and what the fuck is a library if not a collection of sorted things, I ask ya! And I got energy, boundless energy! Everyday I write the book on energy! That's my main strength, kid. Aside from connections in the right places, hunh-hunh, know-wutt-I-mean?"

Cy slurps up the last of his drink thru its straw. He rather likes Mister Maxwell, altho he suspects his program of changes will meet with more than token resistance from the establishment. Cy moves to set his empty glass down on Mister Maxwell's desk. For some reason he misjudges the distance by a foot and releases the glass in midair, whereupon it crashes to the floor. Cy senses that his head is almost touching the ceiling.

One, two, three, four, five senses working overtime!

Mister Maxwell stands. Cy wants to ask him something, but it's hard to make his tongue work. It feels coated with fungus. All he can say is, "Er, got— "

Mister Maxwell claps a hearty hand on Cy's shoulder, the other still in motion, chucking the invisible. "Don't worry about nuthin', kid. Just go upstairs and all your questions'll be answered. And if ya need me, just give a yell."

Conducting Cy to his door, Mister Maxwell shoves him out.

Cy stands in the main lobby of the library. He detects movement down at ankle-level. He looks.

The floor is crowded with small demon figures who bear a family resemblance to Mister Maxwell. They are zipping around carrying books, presumably filing and fetching for patrons.

Treading carefully, Cy walks to the elevator, pushes the call-button and waits only a second before the door opens.

A cloud of hot smoke and sassafrass issues from the elevator. When it clears, Cyril sees that the coffin on a cable is being run by a caped Mephistopheles.

<ciphe"Going down?" leers Nick.

"Uh, I'll use the stairs...."

"Win some, lose some...."

Cyril's on a spiral staircase. Demons bearing volumes rush up and down. Cy notices each step is labeled with a flaming letter: A-G-C-T-T-T-A-C-A-A-A-C-T-T-A-G-G-C....

He climbs and climbs; the way seems infinite. Thought this building was only four stories tall....

Finally he reaches the top.

There are stacks of books forming multiple aisles so long that they converge at a distant vanishing point. Cy has no notion of where to begin. Why didn't he check the Kard Katalogue...?

He notices an office door bearing the designation: INFORMATION.

Inside the office a Chinese man is seated in a lounge chair. Cy almost has a heart attack. Doctor Wu—

But he soon recognizes the man as the recently deceased An Wang, famous head of the ailing computer corporation that bears his name.

Wang speaks. "I have summoned my *hun* soul from the sky and my *pho* soul from the earth, at the bidding of certain important ones, that I may answer your questions. Begin without delay."

Cy doesn't think twice about the unexplainable presence of Wang, so eager is he to learn more about his nemesis.

"Doctor Wu—where did he come from? What does he want?"

"The Doctor emigrated from China soon after I did, but did not reach this country until 1950. He quickly built an empire with two main thrusts: physics and biology. The dead and the living, the hard and the soft, the dry and the wet, yang and yin. Originally, he dealt in vacuum tubes. He swiftly moved into transistors, then microchips. After the famous Nineteen-fifty-eight paper by Schawlow and Townes, he began to support laser research. He has extensive holdings in other firms, such as Siemens of Germany and Cipher Data Products of Los Angeles, as well as Oracle.

"At the same time he hotly pursued molecular matters. He supported the Worcester Foundation, which made crucial discoveries in birth-control and in Transfer and Messenger Are En Ay. He was instrumental in funding the discovery of endorphins, enkephalins and other neurotransmitters, and regulatory enzymes such as monoamine oxidase, or MAO.

"In addition, he is involved in many peripheral matters. He owns radio and television stations worldwide—not to mention his own private satellite, which he calls the Satellite of Love—as well as many brothels, legal and illegal. He is the secret backer behind several record labels, including Sub Pop. He manufactures a line of high-end synthesizers and samplers under the name Lusignan Nu-Signal. He is into registers on chips and registers for cash; musical scales, dragon scales, and produce scales; cellular promoters and concert promoters; coupling constants and constant couplings, bank notes and bent notes; G-clefs and G-notes.

"Aside from that, there is not much I can tell you. The Doctor enjoys candied ginger. He has chosen the dragon as his emblem—or it has chosen him. And he continually consults the *I Ching*."

Cy is reeling. "That's valuable, Mister Wang, and I'm grateful. But what's all this activity mean?"

"Mean? Who knows? Wu is too deep. I could never fathom his ultimate goals, and I've studied him for forty years. I often wondered if the Doctor had any."

"Yeah, the Doctor.... What's he a 'doctor' of?"

"No one knows. It's just a part of his name. Here, let me show you how many meanings there are to his single syllable."

Wang twitches aside a thick red velvet curtain, to reveal—

The Trapp Family Singers, led by Juh-juh-julie Andrews!

They begin to sing, to the tune of "Do, Re, Mi."

WU, WU, WU

Wu, a word that means a lot!
Wu—is there anything it's not?
Wu, a crow, a big black bird!
Wu, filthy, just like a turd!
Wu, the color we call black!
Wu, nothing, a plain old lack!
Wu, a house, an empty room!
Wu, move fast, or even zoom!
Wu, a witch who'll make you swoon!
Wu, the hour known as noon!
Wu, the number we call five!
Wu, to die, not be alive!
Wu, a mist, an awful fog!
Wu, a centipede 'neath a log!
Wu, a big mess or funky stew!
And that brings us back to Wu!

The Trapp Family takes a bow and disappears.

Cy smells flowers and spices. He turns.

A Chinese woman in a long robe reclines on a couch. She holds a lute.

"Mister Wang had to return to heaven. But I, Tourquoise Courtesan, will be glad to entertain you."

"I don't want to be entertained! I need information!"

"You should rather ask for knowledge or wisdom. But I will provide information, if that is what you truly seek."

"Okay. Tell me about the *I Ching*. Why's it so important?"

"The Book of Changes was first received by King Wen, in the year you know as Eleven-Forty-Three Bee Cee. There was much wisdom in it, even before it was further refined by his son and successor, King Wu."

"Holy— Not our Wu?"

Tourquoise Courtesan shrugged. "I do not say."

"Well, jeez, if he's already immortal, why does he need to master time like I thought?"

"Immortality does not necessarily imply mastery of time. Perhaps time masters Wu, and he wishes to turn the tables."

"And do what?"

"I do not say."

"Well, what's all this shit about dragons? There's no such animal—is there?"

"A dragon is a mutation of the spirit, no more, no less. It represents gnosis, satori. But it is also the unconscious mind. And a dragon is morphologically identical with snakes and worms. You will find a dragon in the Hesperides, at the foot of the World Tree. According to the vision of Saint Perpetua, a dragon guards the base of the stairway to heaven. Koshi the eight-headed dragon appears on Japanese currency. And a dragon possessed the Ring of the Rhinemaidens. You may visit dragon palaces beneath the waves or down a well. You may learn the Gödel Number of the Beast, but be careful not to wake him. Dragons enjoy their sleep, you see. If large, perhaps a thousand years or more. Here is a book you might like to read."

A slim volume materializes in Cy's hands: *The Book of Imaginary Beings*, by Borges. Suddenly, Cy can see right through the leather covers. An obstacle stops his vision at a certain page. Illuminated letters proclaim: "The Buddhists affirm that Dragons are no fewer in number than the fishes of their many concentric seas; somewhere in the universe a sacred cipher exists to express their exact number."

"The Buddhist monks were half right. There is a cipher, but it is equal to One. For the time being. And now, Young Scholar, I must be gone."

Tourquoise Courtesan starts to levitate off her couch, still in her recumbent position. Cy rushes toward her.

"Wait, wait, tell me more—!"

Space opens beneath his feet, and he falls, falls, falls—

Cyril's in a dark, dank, loathsome dungeon, a regular torture chamber. Skeletons hang in cages on the walls, instruments of excruciation await.

A red-haired man with a pinched, clean-shaven face stands above Cy. The man wears a sackcloth robe belted around the waist. His feet are bare and dirty.

Cy stands. "Who're you?"

"Ignatius of Loyola. You may call me Inigo. It is a familiarity I always permit my victims."

"Victim! What'd I do?"

"You are seeking after forbidden knowledge. Just like *Los Alumbrados*, the Enlightened Ones who flourished in Seville and Cadiz during my youth and were put down by the Holy Mother Church, you imagine that knowledge will permit you to transgress against God. But you will soon learn different."

"Jeez, I didn't expect the Spanish Inquisition...."

"No one expects the Spanish Inquisition! Did I expect it, after I underwent my week of trance and visions at Manrésa, during which I saw the Snake who lies coiled around the Tree, or after I wrote my *Spiritual Exercises*, which I hoped would help the mind focus on the Creator? No, I fully expected to be welcomed with open heart. Instead, I was clapped into chains and brought up by the Mother Church for examination, my devotion and holiness suspect! It was a painful experience, but I learned my lesson from it, learned it well. No one can rival me now in defense of orthodoxy! Death to all heretics and freethinkers!"

"Wait a minute, man...."

"Now, prepare yourself for the Anti-Sense Strings!"

Ignatius opens the lid on a box. The tips of dozens of pieces of twine and cord poke out under their own volition. They crawl over the side of the box and hump their way like inchworms across the floor to cluster at Cy's feet.

"What is your name?" shouts Ignatius.

Cy tries to resist but feels the words jerked out of him. "Cyril Otis Prothero."

As he speaks, one of the Anti-Sense Strings convolutes itself into an elaborate knot, like a South American quipu.

His name is gone from his mind. He cannot express it.

"Who do you love?"

"Ruby. Polly."

Another string twists on itself. The names of his lovers are gone.

"What was your original face before your parents were born?"

He opens his mouth to speak, but the knowledge is hard to vocalize. He tries to form the words, even as he realizes that if he speaks them aloud, he will lose the most important thing he possesses.

"Speak! Tell me!"

He starts to utter the answer to the koan.

Another man appears. He is clad in a white robe decorated with astrological and alchemical symbols, and is holding a beaker in his hand.

Ignatius jerks back. "Paracelsus!"

"Yes, it is I, foul traitor! You had your chance to join the pneumatics, but you cast your lot with the hylics instead. Now you must pay for your treachery!"

Paracelsus advances on Ignatius with his beaker raised up to pour.

"No, no, not the *aqua mercurialis!*"

Paracelsus starts to asperge the helpless Ignatius, while taunting him.

"Have you ever seen the divine rain, Inigo, or only the commercial rain? We will let it rain down on you. It will be raining in your heart, and you will be crying in the rain. Here comes the rain yet again! Dance to the music, the music of the mandolin rain! Who'll stop the rain for you, proud Jesuit?!"

Ignatius screams and begins to melt. When he's gone, Paracelsus deals in a similar manner with the Anti-Sense Strings.

Cyril feels his name and those of his lovers return. "Boy, I can't thank you enough, Mister Paracelsus."

"There is no debt between fellow seekers. Come now to my study."

Paracelsus's study is filled with alembics, retorts, crucibles and furnaces. He sits on a cushioned stool and bids Cyril do likewise.

"That stinking hypocrite and his kind really piss me off," Paracelsus confides to Cy. "They thought they exterminated us Gnostics when they killed the Bogomils and Cathars, but they'll never succeed in extinguishing the cold flame of our quest."

"You're a Gnostic? I didn't know alchemists were Gnostics...."

"Yes, child, we are all members of Eye Bee Em, the International Brotherhood of Magicians. Our terminology may be a little different, but our goals and motives are the same. Contact with Sophia, through her son, Mercury, and the acquisition of pure knowledge that leads to immortality."

"Say, didn't you guys talk a lot about the Worm Ouroboros, the snake that swallows his own tail?"

"Quite astute of you, child. Yes, Ouroboros is the symbol of the self-engendering, the self-destructive principle. He eats himself, then gives birth to himself. In that sense, he is identical to Ion, the Priest of the Inner Sanctuaries, who tortures himself—even decapitates himself—that he may be transformed, undergo metasomatosis or apolytrosis. And with tail in mouth, the Ouroboros also symbolizes the unification of opposites into the Tao."

"Gee, there sure is a lot more to snakes than I ever guessed."

"We have barely scratched the surface, child. A lifetime would not suffice to explicate the Holy Snake. For instance, what of the rod of Moses, which became a snake, and why was Egypt troubled by the horrible asp? Why did Christ later explicitly identify himself with this rod, in the Testament of John? You see, that is why I called Ignatius a hypocrite. He will not admit his own savior is a snake! And neither is his savior the final one, as he claims. We still await the *servator cosmi*, who will complete the work Christ began but did not finish and bring the *Dies Irae*."

"Could you look into the future, and tell me when this savior is due?"

"I will try. I'll be your mirror, but you might end up inside looking out. We shall use this special instrument, which I have borrowed from John Dee."

Paracelsus lifts a veil from a smoky mirror and begins his scrying.

"I see a country born in the New World whose first flag features a severed snake with the motto, 'Don't Tread On Me.' I see a Chinese Emperor named Mao proclaim that snakes have destroyed his 'Hundred Flowers' program. I see a mysterious terrorist named the Unabomber, one of whose messages reads, "Wu—it works! I told you it would!" I see a desperate prisoner named George Jackson in a shootout, yelling, 'The dragon has come! It's now or never!' I see a Presidential adviser call the President's wife 'a dragon.'"

"Gee, that's all old stuff...."

"It is still the future for me, child."

"Boy, I wish there was someone who could help me...."

"Shall I summon Mercury, child? He is the offspring of the Sun and the Moon. He unites all opposites, being both material and spiritual. He is God and the Devil, a saint and a trickster. He is the self and the unconscious, the *opus alchymicum*."

"If you think he can give me a hand...."

Paracelsus takes a bottle off a shelf, breaks the seal capping it, and sets it down on the floor.

Smoke billows from the bottle, taking form.

Mercury has descended.

The god is naked, a hermaphrodite, ball-less cock dangling above a woman's slit. He holds the Caduceus, whose snakes are crowned. An owl sits on Mercury's shoulder. A spear dangles from a wound in his side; silver blood drips continually from the wound.

Paracelsus addresses Mercury. "*Filius*, can you help this seeker?"

"Hmmm. It appears he could benefit from some of my Mother's milk. Let Sophia appear!"

A naked Junoesque woman, radiant as a quasar, manifests herself. From her jutting nipples drips sweet cream. Each drop sizzles when it hits the tiles.

She approaches Cyril, who sits in shock. Bending forward slightly from the waist, she cups a tit and brings it to his face.

"Suck it," she sweetly says, "and become one of the *filii Sapientiæ*."

Cyril obeys.

The milk has an ineffable taste. He feels his brain expanding. He can't stop swallowing.

One of the crowned snakes has slithered from the Caduceus and joined Cyril in suckling at the other tit.

Suddenly, Mister Maxwell materializes behind Sophia.

"Hey, kid, kin I get summa this action?"

Mister Maxwell unzips his pants and liberates his prick. His gigantic member is like a dog's, concealed in a furry sheath. His balls are spiky, like the coverings on two horse-chestnuts. He grabs his buzzcock and slicks back the covering to reveal a pointy crimson shaft from whose tip drools a long string of clear juice.

Grabbing Sophia's ass with both hands, Mister Maxwell rams his cock home.

It is all Cyril can do to keep Sophia's tit in his mouth, what with the violent coupling.

At the moment Sophia and Mister Maxwell cum, everything disappears.

Cy is lying in a field of poppies. All the poppies have faces and are playing plastic instruments, gyrating on their stems. The Rockin' Flowers begin to sing a song from dat ol' movie about Oz.


THE POPPIES' SONG


You're outa your tree,
You're outa your head,
You're outa your gourd!
So listen to me,
Fall into your bed
And prah-haise the Lord!

Mister Maxwell appears. Again. From out of nowhere he produces a giant silver hammer.

"Time for beddy-bye, kiddo."

He wacks Cyril on the head with the hammer. The hammer shatters.

"Hmmm. Guess I need the heavy artillery."

Mister Maxwell removes a tiny silver hammer big as a toothpick from his shirt-pocket. He taps Cy on the forehead with it.

Cyril goes out like a miser's lightbulb.

# Who's Zoomin' Who?

# K L U E S

00101100
"If you live long enough, you'll run into yourself."
—Carl Perkins

00101101
"Time is the purest and cheapest form of doom."
—Jack Kerouac

00101110
"Some mon just deal wit' information. An some mon, him deal wit' the concept of truth. An' den some mon deal wit' magic. Information flow aroun' ya, an' truth flow right at ya. But magic, it flow t'rough ya."
—Bush Doctor Nernelly

00101111
"Nature has a fundamental program: information, embedded in a source, directs assemblies through intermediaries, or messengers."
—Edward Rubenstein

'm in love with numbers.

Especially two and its powers.

Now, as one sweet lady once wailed, I'll sing my pæan to "the combination of the two."

When I was king (and emperor and empress), I would never have been as foolish as the ruler in the old parable, who agreed to pay his minister a chessboard's worth of wheat, one grain for the first square, two for the second, four for the third, and so on, till his whole kingdom couldn't provide the wheat due on the sixty-fourth square. (That greedy minister cheated a bit: he should really have taken zero grains for the first square, the true starting point of the whole sequence, the Taoist Void.) Depending on my mood, I would've either had the smug bugger chopped up into $2^{64}$ pieces, or given him $2^{64}$ nano-pico-milliseconds to get his ass out of my sight. (And I can see for miles and miles, cuz there's magic in my eyes. But nobody knows the pain behind blue eyes....)

The best justice, I've always believed, is capricious....

But enough political science. Back to math.

I must admit that I've always had a soft spot in my heart for four.

Four rivers flowed out of Eden. There are four strong winds that blow lonely across the seven seas. Four Kozmic Roads lead to Xibalba. Mandalas traditionally have a quarternary structure, akin to the Pythagorean *tetraktys*. The Mayan gods created the first humans as four all-seeing couples. And, for a fact, as Velvet Lou told me recently, two guitars, bass and drums are all you need to make some good music.

'Course, eight's no slouch either. Certainly much more exciting than the so-called "magnificent seven," of which just about all you can say is, "Seven and seven is." The mystic kingdom of Shambhala has eight districts arranged like the eight petals of a lotus. The Gnostic Ogdoad, the Eighth Level of the universe, is Sophia's home. Eight bits make a byte. In the Zen rebus, *The Ten Bulls*, the Eighth Bull represents satori, Nothingness, a white page. An octave comprises eight notes. And the Two-to-the-Third-Fold Path was good enough for my buddy Buddha.

But since we can factor eight into four and two, let's stick to four, shall we?

1

Parallax can feel it coming.

Seated in the cushioned chair whose every bump and depression has been molded by his unstirring butt, the man who inspired Stan Lee to create Daredevil (Lee hired Parallax to pull some astral industrial espionage on Lee's rival, DC Comix, which was why Marvel was able to whip their asses all through the 'Sixties) is outwardly phlegmatic, save for a line of sweat-beads on his barber-shaven upper lip. But Parallax is inwardly seething.

His Third Eye, opened forty years ago, sees day-glo wire-frame representations of seismic tremors, tsunamis in the Topographic Oceans. Complex wavefronts, aetheric disturbances in the universal Tao, Stochastic Ripples in the implicate order.... His Ears Which Are Not Of Parental Origin, the only organs that can hear the celestial music of satori, are filled now with static.

All the inputs transmit the deadly information to him with a minimum of uncertainty.

He's provoked the *hoary dragon that lies at the center,* and retribution will be swift.

Four decades ago, he was warned not to mess with that seething vortex of energies that he could sense at the nucleus of all he perceived. And all these years he has heeded the warning. But lately, he's been feelin' a mite stale and old, with no challenges left. Kicks just keep getting harder to find.... So, like a child taunting a leashed dog, he's been running in closer and closer to the Forbidden One, before turning at the last minute and darting back out of reach, safe from The Jaws That Bite And The Claws That Catch. (And if the dog turns out not to be chained after all, but merely waiting, biding his time...?)

When those two foolish children approached him, looking for their lost mates, it seemed the perfect excuse for him to bait the Dragon, aka Old Daddy Snake.

Laoyeh Snake, he sensed, was deeply involved in their troubles—if not the immediate cause, then surely the ultimate, as he was for so much. Certainly Old Daddy wouldn't resent his (Parallax's) probing and teasing if it was in a good cause, would he? (But in the all-seeing eyes of the Snake, is any cause that contends with His Own, possibly good?) What Parallax was relying on was the fact that his motives were pure. Wasn't he sincerely trying to help these two floundering kids? Wasn't he a selfless servant?

Well....maybe, and maybe not.

Parallax's motives are too mixed-up for even himself to dissect.

There is, he hopes, a smidgen of true altruism, a desire to correct injustice and tip the scales a little toward the disinherited and bereft. He can dig their plight, having been there himself. (His entire life hasn't been spent in the Ritz-Carlton and its cousins....) Parallax has always been a little uneasy with the elitism inherent in the Zen gnosticism of which he is an adept. He can't quite write off the mass of humanity as hylics, identifying himself with the one percent who have been enlightened. There's a part of him that still empathizes with the other ninety-nine.

So although not exactly Chandler's "untarnished man," Parallax does regard himself as somewhat dispassionate and above the fray, thanks to his unique condition. But behind this smattering of Samaritanism, there lurk less pleasant impulses.

A contradictory desire to assert his spiritual superiority over the unhandicapped *hoi polloi.* A flirtation with Ennui, Anomie and Angst, the Three Norns of Modern Life. And maybe a teensy-weensy death-wish as seasoning, just to keep things salty.

Ah, my....things used to be so much easier when he was blind. Blind to what he can "see" now, that is....

## The Chief

It was August 15, 1948.

On this day, the Republic of Korea—ROK—was officially inaugurated, marking the division into northern and southern portions of the ancient and much-abused kingdom of Choson (founded in 2333 BC by the Arch-Shaman Tangun, master of that brand of geomancy known as *p'ungsuchirisol*). (And hey, l-l-look at what a chance them gook politicians missed. If only they had called North Korea sumpin like Region Of Leninist Lackeys, we coulda had ROK 'n' ROLL six years early!)

The flag of the new nation was the yin-yang symbol surrounded by four of the eight *I Ching* trigrams:

*Ch'ien*, maleness, heaven, the father.

*K'un*, femaleness, earth, the mother.

*K'an*, danger, water, the second son.

*Li*, beauty, fire, the second daughter.

The twelve different hexagrams that can be formed from these codons are:

Army, Waiting, Conflict, Union, Peace, Stagnation, Companionship, Abundance, Progress, Intelligence Wounded, Completion, and Before Completion.

These hexagrams would soon pull a special man halfway around the world to this land.

Meanwhile, tho, let us turn our attention to General Douglas MacArthur, head of the Allied occupying forces, Commander in Chief of the Far East, seated on his proconsul's throne in the Dai Ichi building in Tokyo which he had commandeered for his HQ, separated by just a liddle old moat from the Imperial Palace.

Fresh from singlehandedly making the world safe for democracy (oh, all right— Captain America and the Submariner had helped a little too), MacArthur was now treating Japan like his private whore. Things were pretty well in hand in the Land of the Rising Sun. The whole country was under his thumb, and that's where she'd stay. *Like a squirming dog whose day has come, she's down to me, she's under my thumb. The way she talks when she spoken to, the clothes she wears, she's under my thumb!* You couldn't trust these crafty Asiatics further than you could throw an anchor. He'd been making a study of the Oriental mind since '22, and knew what they respected.

Brutality, force, cruelty.

Now in his office—where the portraits of his four heroes hung (Constantine, Tamerlane, Genghis Khan and Atilla the Hun)—MacArthur, be-sunglassed, chomping on his big corncob pipe, counseled the elderly Dr. Syngman Rhee, puppet leader of South Korea.

"We're counting on you to keep our beachhead on the continent strong, Rhee. Do you understand?"

"Yes, General. You are most worried about spread of Communism."

"You bet your yellow ass I'm worried, Rhee! This international Communist conspiracy is ten times worse than the Nazis ever were. It eats away at a man's moral fiber from the inside. Even America and her sons and daughters aren't immune. Thank Christ we've kept the Reds out of *our* hemisphere. Imagine if they were to take over, say, Cuba! We'd be forced to nuke 'em all! It might still come to that if Mao and his fuckin' guerillas win in China. But with your help, we'll see that the Red Tide is rolled back."

"I will stand firm, General."

"You damn well better, Rhee, or your ass'll be so much fuckin' fermented *kim chee* cabbage! Dismissed!"

Rhee scuttled out, stopping several times to bow and kiss the floor.

MacArthur toggled his intercom. "Cohen! Get your buns in here, chop-chop!"

In sashayed MacArthur's personal secretary, Lilith Cohen.

Cohen was a nice Jewish girl from Philadelphia. Raised since age ten by her aunt, Darryl Halle, Cohen had been sent away from Germany by her foresighted parents in 1935. Not so fortunate, her folks themselves—Hawa and Hewya Cohen—had perished at Dachau, under the rigors imposed by German doctors experimenting with psychoactive compounds.

Now twenty-five, Lilith Cohen was sloe-eyed and heavy-thighed, a zaftig dish. MacArthur had chosen her more for these qualities—and for her religion—than for her excellent stenographic skills.

MacArthur leered crudely at Cohen. She flinched inside, knowing what was coming.

"Controlling people always gives me a hard-on, babe. Lift your skirt, skin off them skivvies, and lay on the desk."

Cohen did as instructed.

MacArthur got between her legs.

"Say it," he ordered.

Cohen mumbled something.

"Louder!"

"Oh, Moses, stick your cock up me...."

"Who are you?!"

"It's me, Maria the Jewess, your sister."

"That's better." MacArthur, pipe still clenched between his teeth, penetrated her forcefully, then stopped, buried up to his heavy balls.

"Say the rest of it!"

"I'm a dirty slut, like all Jewish girls. Our religion demands it. It makes us just want to fuck all day, and we don't care who we do it with. Even animals, even our brothers...."

"That's better, sweetheart." MacArthur started pumping away. "Oh, honey, you've got a burning bush! Tell me what you wanna be!"

"I wanna be your dog," said Cohen.

But she thought to herself: *I wanna be adored....*

Ride, Captain, ride! You don't know what's just around the corner on your mystery trip!

Atop the desk, Cohen bore the intercourse stoically, her wedgies banging MacArthur's ass, her mind fixed on her new boyfriend....

## The Taoist

Hokyo Zammai lived with his parents, Amaterasu and Kwannon Zammai, in the pleasant precincts of Nagasaki. Young Zammai's main interest was mathematics, at which he had always excelled. He wore glasses, and had hands too big for his scrawny frame. As a teenager too young to fight during the recent war, he remained relatively untouched by the worldwide conflagration.

Until August 9, 1945, when, in a fine example of the utility of redundancy, the United States repeated the example of Hiroshima, vaporizing a third of his city and killing 75,000 people, his parents among them.

Burn, you're gonna burn, burn, burn! Fire! It'll take all you've got! Don't play with me, Uncle Sam says, cuz you're playing with fire!

Zammai, falling sick soon after with radiation disease, figured his own number was up too. Altho never what you'd call a religious lad, he recalled a visit once made to the Daruma Monastery not far away. It had been a peaceful place, and now struck him as the ideal spot to pass the last days of his life.

Barefoot, hairless, bleeding internally, his glasses lost, he made his slow way there.

He retained one souvenir of his past: the ring his mother had always worn: in the shape of a circular serpent with a small chain binding its jaws, it featured twin rubies for its eyes. Too small for Zammai's big fingers, it rested in the pocket of his shredded pants.

The monastery was empty. Zammai wandered listlessly through raked gardens and spartan quarters, finally dropping down exhausted.

He awoke to a feeling of vast peace. Opening his eyes, he was only slightly astonished to see—without myopic distortion—the glowing figure of the Buddha seated before him.

The World-Honored One was canopied by the hood of a giant Naga Lady coiled behind him. Music—possibly a naga raga—played softly.

The Buddha held up a single flower.

Scales fell from Zammai's eyes.

The youth felt compelled to speak, and signify his understanding. But what utterance, what concept, could possibly convey the depth of his vision? At last the words came to him.

"The square root of negative One.... Division by Zero...."

The Buddha smiled his approval, then faded from view.

And the healing had begun!

A week later, all traces of his radiation sickness had disappeared.

When the country settled down under the occupying Americans, Zammai, now miraculously in the full bloom of health, journeyed to Tokyo, intent on availing himself of the Imperial libraries and their vast store of religious texts, so as to further his understanding of his revelation and cure, the dovetailing of mathematics and mysticism.

Once in the city, he supported himself as a bicycle messenger-boy for Merku Ri Services, a small firm that would later expand into an electronics *zaibatsu*.

Delivering a message to the MacArthur HQ one day, he bumped into Lilith Cohen. Taken by her exotic looks, he summoned the courage to speak to her, voice quavering in his best Occupying Forces English.

"Hey, Hot Fujiyama Mama-san, how about you and me getting serious? Maybe some heavy petting under the old apple tree?"

Cohen looked at the boy. She saw a skinny, somewhat buck-toothed, eager-eyed young man, not distinguishable from a thousand others.

Save for a certain light, a certain knowledge, in his eyes.

Big Hands, I know you're the one!

"Sure," she said. "How about tonight?"


## The G.I.

Although he had no way of knowing it at the time—in fact, had barely heard of Korea before, could hardly point it out on a map, and had no idea that such a book as the *I Ching* existed—the twelve oracular signs contained within the South Korean flag corresponded, in a rough way, to the fate of Max Parallax, who, in 1948, was a seventeen-year-old boy in Murray Hill, New Jersey.

(Here Bell Labs had its buildings, in one of which, that same year, Claude Shannon had just finished scribblin' away on "A Mathematical Theory of Communications." Now, we don't mean to make Bell Labs (est. 1925) sound like Conspiracy HQ, but there sure was—and is—a lot o' brain power there, harnessed to who-knows-what. Even today Bell Labs has more Ph.D.s than any single university in the world. Seven of its employees are Nobel prize-winners. They hold 19,000 patents. They were instrumental in developing the transistor and laser. Nuff said....)

Young Parallax, a skinny, good-lookin' six-footer, graduated that year from high-school. It was an emotionally mixed-up time for the kid. On the one hand, he was kinda still smartin' from being too young to have taken part in the Big War just past. On the other, he was guiltily grateful that he *did* miss, say, getting his legs blown off at Iwo Jima.

Parallax's ambition, nurtured by his proximity to Bell Labs, was to become a communications engineer. (Parallax was the kinda teenager who'd rather be down in the basement solderin' connections than cruisin' in a jalopy.) Unfortunately, he had been unable to secure a scholarship, and his parents were too poor to pay for his schooling. (He wasn't no fortunate son.)

Mom 'n' Dad Parallax—Primavera and Pasquale (the family name had been anglicized a generation back)—were a pair of internationally famous (well, as famous as such folks ever got) cryptozoologists. They belonged to the International Society of Cryptozoology, and spent all their time hunting those mythical animals reputed to exist in the hidden corners of the globe. The yeti, Sasquatch, Nessie, the thylacine, the giant Brazilian sloth known as the *mapinguari*, who was fond of decapitating its prey, and the *ye ren*, or Chinese Wildman. They were frequently away from home, mounting expeditions to search out evidence of those creatures which the Unwashed Public generally denied the reality of. Such work didn't pay much, tho, and his parents struggled along from grant to grant.

During the periods of their field work, young Max remained home with his maternal grandparents, Gulabau and Dumuzi Ziggurat, Armenian refugees.

It was in this year that John Lee Hooker, he of "Crawlin' Kingsnake" fame, initially made the black charts, with a l'il number called "Boogie Chillen." Parallax first heard this witty ditty over the shield-shaped Seeburg speakers in a local Negro bar, where his high-school crush, a nubile Jamaican immigrant named Agatha Daymon, used to bring him.

Immediately falling in love with the tune, Parallax quickly became a convert to R&B, spending his meager allowance on numerous jumpin' sides. During that summer, whenever he got too down thinking about his future, he would plop a chunky 78 record on the RCA Victrola and let Amos Milburn or Lloyd Price wash his cares away.

(Speaking of black men, I must mention that during this year the Nationalists, with their funny word "apartheid," firmly established power in South Africa. Talk about retrogressive! These jokers just couldn't see that Genes Gotta Mix and Information Gotta Flow! Oh, well, people will always try pissin' into the wind....)

When Parallax's parents returned that September from deepest Africa, where they had been searching in vain for the hippo-swallowing snake of the Akikuyu known as the *ngakoula-ngou*, they found that their son had made up his mind about how to pursue his goals.

"Mom, Dad—I'm gonna join the Army."

Well, they would miss their boy, fer shure, but it seemed like the only way he'd ever get the education he wanted. And under the peaceful conditions that prevailed, he wasn't likely to come to any harm.

So Parallax made his sniffly goodbyes to Mom, Pop 'n' Agatha, and hi-de-hoed himself down to the local recruitment station. He got his communications training. He let himself be talked into re-enlisting. He was assigned to Japan.

Soldier Boy, you're my little Soldier Boy!

The world hit the century's halfway mark without blowing itself up with them there new-fangled nukes, and was chugging along nicely.

Then the first major shit storm of the Shannon Era broke.

On June 22, 1950, North Korean troops rolled across the 38th Parallel. The South Korean forces fell apart, their remnants pushed further and further south, right down to the last stronghold of Pusan.

Things looked mighty glum for the forces of goodness 'n' light....

## The Allies

Lieutenant Oliver Assipattle surveyed his troops. What a motley crüe! Not a Universal Soldier among them.... Just a bunch of lazy Buffalo Soldiers, so-called since they were always trying to "buffalo" their superiors. They had been assembled from all corners of the disintegrating British Empire at the behest of the United Nations. They would join the Turkish troops, the Greek troops, the French troops in this Korean Peacekeeping Action. Assipattle had his doubts about how many of them would ever return to their native lands. Not much he could do at this late date to whip them into shape. He was stuck with them the way they were. Oliver's army was here to stay....

Assipattle started out by haranguing his men in general terms. "You're a bloody crowd of apes! Apemen, that's what you are! You're all afraid to die in a nuclear war, you just want to live on your distant shores! You've got faces uglier than your butts! Could you be loved? I doubt it! No woman won't ever cry for you! Your only hope in this life is to do some good by fighting for the survival of the West!"

Assipattle turned his attention to an individual in the front ranks, trying to get some idea of his men's battle-readiness.

"You! Private! What's your name?"

"Goodness gracious me, sar, I am Rama Lamadingsingh, from the charming village of Tilpat, India, sar!"

"Have you ever seen combat before?"

"Oh, goodness no, sar! Before the King in his wisdom called me up, I was a humble snake-charmer, sar! Every man jack in our whole village is. If it please the sahib, I still retain my *been*." Lamadingsingh took a bell-mouthed clarinet-sized instrument from under his uniform shirt. "If the sahib wishes to hear a tune—?"

"None of your heathen tootling! As you were! You, what's your name?"

"Warnajarra Bangagong me, fella from Outback, yes, Abo boy at your command."

"Ever been in a battle, Private Bangagong?"

"In dreams yes, many time big fight. Also, clan of Rainbow Men gather at Devil's Marbles and wrestle kangaroos."

"Dreams! Kangaroos! Are you serious?"

"Dreamtime plenty important, yes, teach Abo boy 'n' girl path of Diamond Dove and location of waterholes. We light lamps full of midnight oil, and sleep on beds that are burning."

"Well, your dreams won't help you when you're facing the bloody Koreans! Back into the ranks! You, out with your name!"

"Me name Jumby Blackheart, mon. Trench Town rude bwai just like Rhyging."

"I've seen your kind before back in London. Not a Rastafarian, I hope."

"I and I follow de Lion of Judah, ya right 'bout dat, like all de members of de Thirteen Tribes."

"Thirteen? There's only twelve tribes, you ignorant heathen!"

"Nuh so. Jacob's daughter, Dinah, de rainbow, be de secret thirteenth. And anyhow, wha' fe ya gwine ta kass-kass me religion?"

"Your bloody religion is a bunch of trumped-up nonsense that inspires insolence. Worshipping Haile bloody Selassie! What a primitive lot of superstition!"

From thin air, Blackheart produced a wickedly sharp switchblade. "Me lickle ratchet seh de name of de King of Kings, *Negus Negesti*, not fuh de white mon's lips. Wha yuh seh ta dat, yuh bockra busha?"

"Uh, um— Company dismissed!"

## Chief

MacArthur sat in his office, awaiting the news from Inchon. The four military geniuses hanging on the wall gazed down on him with cruel smiles. It was September 15, 1950.

General Edward Almond entered.

"Good news, Commander. The Marines have secured the port. As we speculated, the city is so far behind the frontlines that's there's only a token force of Reds. We should be able to take Scoul within days. This is the beginning of the end for the North Koreans."

Slamming a fist down on his desk, MacArthur said, "Goddamn! Why should we stop with the North Koreans? We'll push them back to the Yalu River, and then we'll go after that goddamn Mao, on the pretext of securing a buffer zone. We'll drown him in the Amur before he knows what's happening. His ass will be draggin' when he's in the Black Dragon!"

Almond was taken aback. "Sir, isn't that over-stepping your command a bit? And would it be wise to antagonize the Chinks like that?"

MacArthur narrowed his eyes and stabbed Almond with his maniacal gaze. "If Truman and the electorate sees that I'm winning, I can do anything I want. And don't forget one thing, Ed. These are the Last Days."

"The last days...?"

"That's right. We're living in the time of Revelations, Ed. The Final Battle is coming, the forces of Jesus versus the Antichrist. World War Three will be the last war before the Rapture. Did you know that the Hopi Indians believed that when a black sun rose over the House of Mica, the world would end? And that the United Nations building corresponds to that very House of Mica, and that the pollution was so bad in Manhattan last year that the sun was indeed blackened?"

"House of Mica...?"

MacArthur resumed his normal arrogantly jubilant demeanor. "I can see you need some more time to digest all this, Ed. Why don't you come with me to Wake

Island next month for a little Are and Are? I'm scheduled to meet with that 'buck-stops-here' dipshit Truman. We can both tell him then about tackling the Beast. And maybe we'll rip a little tail off Cohen, the Whore of Babylon, while we're at it."

"Uh, sure....Chief."


Taoist

Hokyo Zammai shot a lovin' spoonful of jism up the bucking cunt of Lilith Cohen—ten cubic centimeters, to be precise.

When Cohen realized what her Japanese Romeo had done, she quickly squirmed out from under him.

"Hokie, you promised you'd pull out!"

"You see me extra sorry now, sweetcakes. But two things you should never believe: the bankdraft is in the post, and man will honorably remove penis prior to joy explosion. Sex just ain't fair for ladies in this man's man's man's world."

"Well, now I've got to douche. I've got no intention of getting pregnant just yet."

Cohen stood. She grabbed a warm bottle of Coke from the nightstand. Luckily, the PX was well stocked. She popped the cap with a church-key, covered the top with her thumb, shook it, then inserted the neck up her pussy, catching the outflow in a bedpan.

"Lucky soldier who redeem that deposit."

"Oh, Hokie, you're incorrigible! I suppose I should be mad at you, but I just can't be. You make me feel like a natural woman."

"That's ace, girl, because your little Hokie never mad at you."

Cohen climbed back into bed with Zammai and snuggled up. "Tell me how your research is going...."

Zammai suddenly looked serious. "I will never find the philosopher's stone, I think. The secret of how Buddha cured me is not to be found in the Imperial libraries. All the books I read! The *Wugenshu*, or *Rootless Tree*. The *Jindan Sibaizi*, or *Four Hundred Words On The Golden Pill*. The *Cantongqi*, or *The Triplex Unity*. The *Baizi Be*, or *The Hundred Character Inscription*. The *Qiaoyao Ge*, or *Tapping The Lines*. I'm imagining my brain is ready to burst, but not one of them a help! I think this country is not holding what I need. Old knowledge is fucked. I need to get hip to new paradigms, new theorems. Only America holds what I need."

Cohen frowned. "If you're thinking marriage again, you can just forget it. And besides, I don't know if I want to go back to the States just yet. I like your country."

"You can have it, babe. I'm up for hotdogs and John Wayne. I figure it would be nice to be on winning side for a change."

"Are you sure you can tell the loser from the winner?" asked Cohen, though she herself hardly knew what she meant.

Zammai lifted an eyebrow. "Very Taoist thing to say, babe. You surprise me. Like the old motto goes, 'Busy water seems dark.'"

Cohen giggled. "No. You mean, 'Fizzy soda cleans twat.'"

"Oh, yeah? Let me check this adage out."

## G.I.

Army and Waiting were over.

The hexagrams had changed.

Conflict came around.

Parallax found himself in The Land of the Morning Calm, an otherwise charming country which was about to become hell on earth for many American boys. Too bad they couldn't've all come as tourists. Lotsa keen things to see, such as the famous Korean Circle Dance, where women link hands to form a big ZERO, while in the background, no doubt, Seoul music is played. (Aw, shux, I know, I know, that was awful. But remember: Every pun packs a minimum of twice the standard information in the same number of bits!)

Assigned with one or two other Americans to the ROK First Division (whose chaplain was named Duk In Lee) as a U.S. communications expert, Parallax soon found himself far above the 38$^{th}$ Parallel, helping to push the Commies north.

On October 25, 1950, the First Division was encamped in the Chongchon River Valley, fifty miles south of the Chinese border, confident in their technological security blanket. Parallax was seated outdoors by his transmitter. He softly hummed to himself: "We're Gonna Rock, We're Gonna Roll," by Wild Bill Moore. Looked like this liddle dustup would soon be over....

Suddenly, the air was filled with blood-curdling screams, and the noise of bugles, whistles and drums. He looked up, to the surrounding hills.

From all sides poured down freakin' Chinks! The wavefront consisted of cavalry on short shaggy Mongolian horses. Behind them was a Golden Horde of footsoldiers. No tanks, no mortars, rifles old as MacArthur—

There were shouts of "Incoming! Incoming!" followed by mass confusion. The Chinese weren't combatants! They weren't supposed to be here! No troop movements had been reported over the border! It was impossible—

Then the Chinese soldiers were in the camp, firing and grappling in hand-to-hand combat, all the while shouting unnerving insults, Confucian proverbs and Maoist dogma.

"Your sister make ficky-fick with dragons!"

"No one use ox-cleaver to behead chicken!"

"A tyrannical government is more fearful than tigers!"

Despite the best efforts of General Paik Sunyup, the ROK forces were overwhelmed and scattered. Many prisoners were taken, among them two Americans.

Lieutenant Glen C. Jones.

Sergeant Max Parallax.

## Allies

General Almond paced with furious energy behind the curtain of the makeshift stage, berating his aides.

"What's the matter with these men? The guts have gone right out of them! Sure, the Chinese are a new element in the battle! Sure, there seem to be hundreds of thousands of them our intelligence boys missed spotting somehow! But what the fuck! We're white men, aren't we?! We're goddamn Westerners! We've got tanks, we've got jets, we've got modern rifles! The Chinese got shit! No guerillas will ever beat us!"

An aide entered, the stitched name on his chest reading T. ERDELYI. "General, here are those three average soldiers you wanted to see."

In came:

Lamadingsingh, turban on his head.

Bangagong, snakey tribal scars incised on his cheeks.

Blackheart, matted dreadlocks falling to his shoulders.

Almond goggled at them, speechless. Then he sputtered, "These—these are *our* troops?"

"You En, sir."

A look of immense pain passed over Almond's face. "Get them out of here! Get out, go on, enjoy the goddamn show!"

"Most immense gratitude, sar."

"Nijirana, him dingo god, him always by your side now."

"If me know de Soun' Systems be here, me be poppin' more style, yahso! Dis be heavy wunnerful!"

The soldiers left, and General Almond bade the curtain open. He marched out.

From the stage, he addressed an outdoor amphitheater full of troops gathered for the USO show.

"Men, I don't want to spoil your entertainment with a lot of palaver, so let me just remind you of one thing: You're fighting a bunch of goddamn Chinese laundry-men! And now, to phrase the message in musical terms, here's one of my favorite groups. They've come out of retirement just for this tour, so let's give 'em a big hand."

Four elderly geezers—dressed in straw boaters, bow ties, striped shirts, and suspenders upholding white pants—entered doing an arthritic buck 'n' wing, and took up their instruments. The leader spoke into the mike.

"We're the Al Gore Rhythm Quartet, boys, and here's our Nineteen-Twenty-Eight hit, 'Little Chinky Chinaman.'"

They started this Ragtime-Dixieland-Barbershop intro. But before one word of the vocals could be sung, rowdy catcalls, boos and jeers assaulted them, followed by a volley of cabbages, whole and in fragments, raw and fermented. The Quartet was driven from the stage.

"Quick," ordered Almond, "get another act out there!"

"Which one?" asked Erdelyi. "The nigger or the Numinoso sisters?"

"Sacrifice the nigger. I got my eyes on those sixteen-year-old honeys and don't want them bruised."

In a few seconds, a black man wearing a one-button suit with enormous lapels strutted out, carrying an electric guitar. The crowd calmed a bit, allowing him to speak.

"Here's a little tune Ah just worked up," said Lloyd Price. "Ah call it 'Lawdy Miss Clawdy.'"

Price plugged in and ripped off a chord; the troops went nuts.

Too bad Parallax wasn't there. He wasn't going to get a chance to hear much music ever again.

### Chief

The meeting with Truman had gone badly. It was the first time the General had ever met his Commander, and they had grated on each other's nerves from the start. Truman had been tougher than MacArthur had imagined. It didn't look as if he'd be able to pull the wool over his eyes as he had hoped.

And now these friggin' Chinks were up his ass! Well, okay, he had planned to tangle with them sooner or later, so he may as well get down to it. Nukes were still a possibility, if worse came to worst....

MacArthur spent a pleasant moment daydreaming about a one-on-one between him and Mao, perhaps televised.... But his mood soon turned glum. All this pressure was giving him a limp dick. He couldn't perform unless he was top dog. And now Truman was telling him to move it on over, little dog, there's a big dog movin' on in! Shit! He hadn't even been able to put it to Cohen in days....

There sounded a rap on his office door. "Come in."

A little Nip entered. "Message from the boys at Mitsubishi for you, Jack."

MacArthur was too despondent to ream out the Jap for his familiarity. He took the dispatch case. The native didn't move to leave.

"Reply?" asked MacArthur.

"No way, Jose. I'm just looking at you and thinking, 'This guy could use a Nipponese pick-me-up.'"

"Such as?"

"Oh, just some powdered rhino horn and black bear gall bladder, with a few secret ingredients."

"Not interested. Dismissed."

"Makes your willy hard as a year of Kay Pee duty."

"When can you have it here?"

### Taoist

Cohen slung down her purse and wearily doffed her coat. Even the relative luxury of her quarters at the old Imperial Hotel, located at 1-1-1 Uchisaiwaicho, failed to lift her spirits as it usually did.

It had been a rough day at the office. She should have known the peaceful interval couldn't last. Not only had the General fucked her six ways from Sunday—even going so far as to spank her with a riding crop that doubled as the Mosaic Rod

(I feel like I'm tied to the Whipping Post!)—but she had been overburdened with the typing of various communiqués relating to the numerous defeats recently suffered by the Western forces at the hands of the Chinese. The brass were running around like crazy, there were flights coming and going from the States, even Congressmen making the long jaunt out.

Who knew? Maybe MacArthur's lunatic talk about the goyish Last Days was on the mark. Moshiach on the way....

Zammai bustled in as she was undressing.

"Hey, flapjacks," he said, grabbing her ass, "how's about playing a quick round of dragon-in-the-cave?"

"Not now, Hokie, I'm beat. The General couldn't keep his hands off me."

Zammai looked guilty. "Ah, right. Hokie thinks he knows reason for that."

He explained what he had done.

Cohen sat down numbly on the bed, one seamed nylon around her ankle, the other still upheld by the garters of her girdle.

"Why would you do that, Hokyo? Why?"

Zammai joined her and put an arm around her shoulder. "I hated to, kid, believe me. But I got to get to America! The Tao tells me most ancient *hsien* is now there, the first and only Real Human, *chih jen*, or realized man, Old Daddy of the Mountain. He's the one guy what can end my quest—if I ever can see him, which is in doubt. And if you won't take me there, I figure General Gookhater is my best bet, even if he sucks bigtime in what he do to you. Sorry, Lil, but to quote Wayne-san: 'A man's gotta do what a man's gotta do.'"

Cohen started to speak, but a wave of nausea passed over her features. She clutched her stomach, bolted up and rushed to the bathroom, where she began to retch.

"Hey, kid, don't tell me—"

Cohen wiped her mouth with the back of her hand. "Yes, you testosterone-stuffed Taoist pig, I'm pregnant! Now why don't you just get out of here! I really don't want to see you...."

"Come on, girl, you can't be serious. Breaking up is hard to do."

"No, I mean it," asserted Cohen. But Zammai could tell she was weakening.

"I ain't lost that lovin' feelin' for you, babe."

Cohen smiled weakly. "Oh, all right, I suppose me getting knocked up is as much my fault as yours."

Zammai helped her to stand. They embraced.

"It's just like Lao-Tze says."

"Yeah?"

"'The best part of breakin' up is the makin' up.'"

G.I.

Union.

As the Communist troops carried Parallax and Lieutenant Jones high up into the mountains northwest of Bukjin, the two men formed an immediate bond, as they discovered a shared interest in R&B.

"You heard Ivory Joe Hunter's 'I Almost Lost My Mind' yet?"

"Sure did. Can't hold a candle to Mayfield's 'Please Send Me Someone to Love.'"

But even memories of wailin' R&B could not prevent their spirits from faltering.

"Looks like we trained in vain, Max."

"I 'spect my Mama's gonna be the first one on the block to get her boy back home in a box."

Eventually, a squad of Chinese peeled away from the main body of troops, taking only Jones and Parallax with them.

"Something tells me it's interrogation time for us, Max."

In the hills northwest of Bukjin they came to an old mining camp: assorted shacks, rusted cableway with buckets, timber-shored mouth of a played-out mine. Their escort conducted them to a cabin with blackened windows.

The inside was fitted out with a cot, a table, maps and a radio. At the table sat a middle-aged, dour, round-faced Chinaman dressed in the ubiquitous padded clothing. Standing beside him was a young Chinese teen who looked vaguely familiar.

The elder addressed the Americans in excellent English.

"My name is Marshall Peng. This is Mao Anyang, the Premier's son. Welcome to our headquarters."

Parallax looked around in disbelief. This was the nerve center of the whole Chinese war effort?

Peng got right to the point. "Let us not mince words, comrades. We want to know one thing and one thing only."

Parallax steeled himself for the question, trying to blank out any information on troop strength or logistics.

"Where," demanded Peng, "is Wu?"

Parallax was stumped. "Who?"

"Not 'who!' Wu! Do not play dumb with me, soldier-boy! You know we found the Laoyeh in the Caves of Yenan. But we did not realize at the time what he was. And so we allowed him to be trundled off to Shanghai, where we lost him. We thought for a time he had gone into Tibet, and we marshalled our forces there, but it was all a red herring. See, I am being honest with you. Now, be honest with me. We know Wu's in America now. Tell the truth: has the Doctor fomented this war? Does he want China back? Will he install himself as Emperor again? Be quick now!"

"Mister Peng, I don't have a blasted idea of what you're talking about."

"Me neither," said Jones.

"Bah! I have no time for frivolity. You will talk eventually. Meanwhile, you shall be securely held but not mistreated. We Chinese are not barbarians like these Koreans, who brainwash and torture. Take them away!"

Parallax and Jones were locked up in a shack.

Nearly a month passed. Each day they were brought out for exercise and questioning.

The topic was always the same: some guy named Doctor Wu. The two Americans continually maintained they knew nothing of him.

By the end of four weeks, it almost seemed Peng was coming around to believing them.

Then came the raid.

November 24th. Parallax and Jones were just leaving Peng's shack when an ominous drone made itself noticed. The soldiers in the camp began scurrying about, hustling important items into the mine shaft.

Peng emerged, carrying the radio.

"Your comrades attack. They do not even know we are here, they're simply bombing indiscriminately. It is our bad karma."

The B-29s were just visible now, black crows of death.

"Into the mine. Quickly."

Huddled in the mine, the Chinese and the two Americans awaited the bombs.

"Where is Mao Anyang?" Parallax ventured to ask the Marshall.

Peng calmly replied, "He went to Bukjin to speak with the Koreans. He will have to take his chances."

The bombs began to fall. The radio, tuned to the pilots' wavelength, suddenly crackled into life.

"Hoo-whee! Here's some hot napalm from Hiawatha Du Daanan! Have a liddle barbecue, gooks!"

The attack seemed to go on forever and a day.

Finally, it appeared safe to emerge.

All the cabins were flattened, smoldering piles of embers. Craters pocked the ground. Trees were splinters.

Parallax could feel the hatred emanating from the Chinese. All former civility was rapidly dissipating. He and Jones huddled together nervously.

Soldiers were dispatched to Bukjin.

They returned with the charred corpse of Mao Anyang.

Peng studied the boy's body gravely for a while, then turned to the Americans.

"This presents an interesting problem as to what I shall tell his young wife. Not to mention his honorable father." Peng paused, then broke down. "If I had a rocket launcher, some son of a bitch would die! I just wanna walk right out of this world, because everybody has a poison heart!"

With this, the soldiers began to beat Parallax and Jones with the butts of their rifles.

A blow to the back of his head put Parallax out.

The hexagram: Peace.


## Allies

Blackheart, Lamadingsingh and Bangagong sat together in a large foxhole. It was a wintry Korean night, the crescent moon showing, the wind howling. Each man was dressed like Ferdie Lantz: long wool underwear, two pairs of socks, wool shirt and trousers, cotton trousers atop the wool, boot pacs, pile jacket, hooded parka and gloves that allowed his trigger finger to be bared.

Blackheart shivered. "Dis here kind of night when duppies mek free an' roam ta vex." He drew an X in the dirt with his rifle muzzle. "Lucky t'ing duppy nuh count higher'n ten. Ex keep dem 'way. I and I duppy conqueror, yahso!"

Lamadingsingh concurred. "Yes, sar, *bhuta* stalk the air tonight. I will pray to Buthanatha, Lord of Ghosts, to aid us."

The Indian began to intone the sacred sound of AUM, where A stands for maleness, U for femaleness, and M for the marriage of the two.

Bangagong wringled his flat nose. "See white man's Milky Way. We call him *kadri-paruvilpi-ulu*, river-course-sky. That where *Wati-kutjara*, or first ancestors, still live. I make them call ghosts back."

The Aborigine began to keen.

After a time, the three sensed the departure of the spirits and ceased their precautions.

"Dis war of Babylon de Dragon be one manga bloodclot rax-up. Me nuh cyan seh why me even here...."

"Goodness gracious me, of course it is plain as *sukra*, the moon's semen which rains down on us from above. The white man has us all in bondage still. Even Mother India, so recently independent, cannot refuse to do the bidding of the British."

"Everything gone downhill since the dreamtime. White fella no have access to *jukurrpa*, dreamtime law. It natural for him to foul his own waterholes, kill everything, enslave poor Abo boys."

"Someday, praise Jah, dis whole fockin' mess gwine explode in de face of bockra busha. De craven bullbucker get his duma an' dudu soon enough. Den de black mon be free! Nuh more colonies! Exodus! Yahso!"

"Praise Shiva!"

"Yurlungur the Copper Python sees all!"

"It only tek one mon to turn dem all 'roun, mek black mon get up, stand up for him rights. De prophet yet to be made known. I t'ink maybe him be lickle bwai I know from Nine Miles. Nesta Marley him name, one blue-swee bwai. Him read palm, know obeah, cyan science a goat dead."

"The Maitreya Buddha will appear, yes, and then a new kalpa will begin."

"Big plane come from sky, bring ancestors back, land on Ayer's Rock, center of world."

For a short time, the soldiers comforted themselves with this prophecy.

Lamadingsingh absentmindedly stroked his serpent-horn.

Blackheart rotated his switchblade one handedly in a blur.

Bangagong rubbed his *churinga*, a sacred stone full of *arunquiltha*, aboriginal mana, inscribed with a serpent and approximately thirty thousand years old.

"Abo fella hungry for tucker."

"I and I lickle peckish."

"A spot of something would be most agreeable, yes, sar."

Bangagong removed from his pack a split stick holding several witchetty grubs and began to eat.

Lamadingsingh found a pot full of steaming curry.

Blackheart dug into some cassareep stew.

When they were finished, the Rastaman took a cigar-sized spliff from his kit, lit it, took a hit, and started it around.

"Ganja open up dem t'ird yeye, yahso!"

C

It turned out to be the Last Days indeed.

But only for old Mac himself!

The war had ground to a stalemate. His grandiose plans to push into China had gone up in smoke. The American public was sick of the lack of progress in this dirty little fracas in some far off land. Truman disagreed with everything he proposed to end it, even the obvious expedient of using nukes. MacArthur could tell his days were numbered.

And today, April 11, 1951, the axe had fallen.

While entertaining some diplomats with his wife, MacArthur had gotten the leaked news in advance of the official order. Now he was packing with as much dignity as he could muster.

He marveled at his calmness. The old MacArthur would never have taken this lying down. But something had changed. It was that drug the CIA had fed him. LSD, the spook had called it. What an experience.... Made a guy reconsider what was important.... Even peace didn't look so bad. Maybe they should give peace a chance. What was so funny about peace, love and understanding anyway?

The General snapped the locks on his luggage. Well, Korea was Ridgway's headache now. He himself would do the old soldier's shtick: speeches, rubber chicken banquets....

MacArthur picked up a phone. "Hello, get me Merku Ri Messengers. Hello, Merku Ri? This is General MacArthur. Send over your that kid Zammai who works for you. I need him. How far will he be going? Huh! About ten thousand miles...."

T

"So," said Cohen, "this is goodbye?"

"I guess so, babe. Unless you want to come back Stateside with me."

"No, I can't. Our child inside me has only made my feelings stronger. I feel myself turning Japanese...."

"Well, kid, most likely you go your way and I'll go mine. I know if I go there will be trouble, but if I stay it will be double."

"That's the way it seems"

Silence.

Cohen: "Do you—do you still love me?"

"The *Tao Te Ching* says, 'What is the difference between yes and no?'"

"That's an easy out."

Zammai moved to go, then turned.

"For you and the baby," he said, and handed over his mother's ring.

Then he went to join the retreating General on his plane.

And all poor Cohen was left with was a band of gold.

## G

Parallax awoke to silent blackness.

A blow to his head had damaged his temporal lobes, producing the blindness. Cupped palms repeatedly smashed on his ears had destroyed his hearing.

All he could think of was killing himself.

(This impulse, as we shall see, eventually dissipated, but the residue remained, tinting the rest of his days.)

His life was now a living daily black and noiseless hell. Cut off from a human's two main sources of information, he was trapped inside his own skull like an autistic child. He might as well have been decapitated. What was left for him? Was he supposed to invent a symbolism of smells, a talent for touch or taste? What, if anything, could ever replace what he had lost?

Weh-hell, as the Glimmer Twins say: "You can't always get what you want—but sometimes you get what you need."

After the savage beating at Bukjin, Parallax's special status was over. He ended up in what he soon fathomed was a regular POW camp. His universe had narrowed to a foul-smelling pallet in a cold hut.

From time to time, someone came to attend to his wounds, roughly dressing and bandaging them. But they couldn't do anything for his mind.

The next few months represented Stagnation.

Parallax became inured to the unvarying sameness. He would awake from dreams more real than reality, eat some dry bread, *kim chee* (a fermented cabbage and radish dish) for lunch, undergo a stumbling bout of exercise, drowse till supper (more bread), then go to sleep again.

One day, lying on his thin cotton pad, Parallax felt the steps of a guard reverberate thru the earthen floor. Was he to be brutalized again? He wished there were another prisoner here to stand up for him. (What happened to Jones, he never knew.) Having crawled around the entire hut this morning, he knew he was the only occupant. Most of the Americans came in with wounds more grievous than his, and they were dying off like frogs crossing an interstate. His last roommate had been taken away in the night.

The guard's footsteps ceased. Parallax could vaguely sense the nearness of the Korean. (Too bad he couldn't develop them viperine heat-sensors....)

There was a nearly subliminal impact of something light—fabric?—hitting the ground. Then hands fell on him—not harshly, but gently. He felt his pants being unbuttoned.

What the hell—?

Horrid images filled his mind: electric shocks to the genitals, bamboo splinters.... Even Parallax's lethargy and disinterest in his own fate extended only so far. Feeling his shorts being pulled down, he was about to jump up and lash out blindly.

Then a soft hot mouth encircled his prick.

Great Googly Moogly! What the Kee-rist *was* this? You and I know this was the war where the term "brain-washing" was invented, but does even Oriental Deviousness cover this?

As Parallax allowed the unknown lips to caress his cock, he had to ask himself: *Am I guilty of Cooperating With The Enemy by enjoying this? Am I Soft On Communism, or Is Communism Soft On Me? And oh yeah—which way am I swingin'? Odds are this is a guy, but could it possibly be—?*

Parallax reached down and felt two small naked breasts.

Good God, looked like the dude was a lady!

Parallax's cock swelled with this knowledge. "Don't look a gift whore in the mouth" became his instant credo.

The wonderful sensations continued for a minute or so.

Then the weird part began.

The woman left off sucking Parallax and commenced, with expert fingers, to poke and prod at various spots on his body.

Confusing fleeting visual images flooded his mind. Parallax took from them the general impression of friendliness. Well, okay, that just reinforced the initial impression of having one's cock sucked. My God, he had forgotten such things existed.

Suddenly the generous Mama decided to show Parallax she had a squeezebox that could work all night.

Two bare legs straddled Parallax's groin and his stiff cock was guided into a wonderful vise-like wet cunt. The woman began to rise up and down on Parallax, simultaneously fingering nodes up and down his body.

As you might imagine, he immediately felt better than he had in months. Strange, half-understood messages filled his comprehension, along with rumors of orgasm.

Just as he came in a fiery burst, an actual word registered.

*Kisaeng.*

Parallax had heard of them. The Korean geishas.

Companionship had done rolled around.

Over the next year or so, Parallax learned—via this unique mode of communicating, which improved in intelligibility with every act of Enemy Intercourse—what was what.

Due to extensive losses, the North Koreans had supplemented the ranks of their army with conscripted females from the lower classes. These women were assigned to non-combatant posts, thus freeing more front-line soldiers. Parallax's pleasant visitor was one such. Assigned the task of guarding Roundeye prisoners, bored and idle, this particular gal had set her sights on the pitiful yet still handsome American and resolved to engineer his rehabilitation.

Now, this gal—when they could mentally converse, she informed Parallax that her name was Ma Gee Mai—was one special honey. An ex-Zen nun, a follower of the Korean School of Buddhism known as *Popsong*, (founded by Wonhyo circa 650), and trained in accupressure, or *qigong*, she was able to manipulate the flow of Cosmic Chi, or Qi, within the Thirteen Meridians of Parallax's body by pressing various combinations of the 512 individual nodes on those Meridians in such a fashion as to convey very complex information. (If sixty-four codons contain enough information to build every kind of life, and twenty-six letters enough to build every kind of world, then imagine what can be conveyed with 512 characters....)

Pretty soon, just by running her hands over his body, Ma Gee Mai was able to communicate with Parallax as easily as by talking. (And no wonder. This gal had some special ancestors, most consequentially, for our story, Mai Won Song, wife of the Victorian-era Choson ambassador to Great Britain, she who taught Richard Burton how to marshall his orgasms to a female multiplicity....)

Parallax started to feel his old self again. Just being able to communicate with someone made all the difference. He exercised daily, building up his body so that Mai would enjoy their lovemaking. He was content to wait patiently between her visits.... He felt—Abundance.

Once Parallax had his self-esteem restored, Mai started to teach him more, stuff he never suspected was there to learn. Parallax reversed the slogan of the upcoming decade: he dropped out first, turned on second, then tuned in last. Mai expertly showed him how to extend psychic feelers to probe the Tao, gathering information both near and far. The first time he was able to make out the colorless whorls and subtle configurations in the Tao that represented Mai's body and soul, Parallax's useless eyes filled with tears.

He had his mojo working!

Pretty soon he was striding with eerie confidence through the prison camp by surveying a congruent landscape whose nature could be faintly—oh-so-faintly— hinted at by mentioning a topographic map, psychic isobars . The other guards and prisoners were creeped out by Parallax's blind certainty and deaf awareness.

It was a time of Progress.

One day Mai, lying in Parallax's arms, communicated this warning to her Yankee lover and student:

*I sense you are letting your mind range further and further. With the stimulus of your handicaps, you are becoming more adept than me. This is good, but I must warn you: never disturb the Dragon.*

"Dragon?" said Parallax. "What Dragon?"

*You'll see,* was all Mai would say.

Well, what would you have done? Right.... Parallax went lookin' for this Dragon like a wise-ass Saint George. Riding the gradients and contours of the plenum, he let his astral self be drawn down, down, down the entropy-funnel, from lesser order to higher, higher, highest—

The Dragon At The Center. Holy shit, whatever it was, it was impressively dense, maximum capacity, super-efficient code, minimum noise, Parallax extended a feeler—

*Yeeeooow!*

He was "miles" away before he even remembered "running." That hurt! And he intuited it was the merest warning, the gentlest love tap.

"I found the Dragon," said Parallax to Mai the next time they were together.

*And?*

"He took a piece out of my ass."

*So now you will stay away....*

"Nope. Now I want a piece out of his."

Mai shook her head ruefully. *You Westerners are all alike. Your hubris is incredible.*

"That's what makes us so fatally irresistible to you slant-eyes," said Parallax, grabbing a tit.

Adopting your typical Oriental bar-girl pidgin English (not the easiest thing to do via accupressure and Mental Modulation, but as we said, this was some special gal), Mai said, *Hey Joe, how you like-see if my cunny slant too?* Then she was atop Parallax for the second time that day.

All you did was break my bed....

Well, with his Intelligence Wounded by the Dragon's assault, Parallax formed your basic Captain Ahab obsession. Someday he would get that there Celestial Snake!

One morning Mai came to Parallax. He tried to pull her down. She resisted, and merely signaled, *Goodbye.*

Parallax knew then that this was Completion. He wept only a little.

That same day he was repatriated in a prisoner exchange.

Free Bird, take a free ride!

Soon he was back in the U.S., pensioned off.

More bad news awaited Parallax.

His folks had been killed while he was in his foreign prison.

It seemed they were boating on Lake Champlain, searching for Nessie's cousin, Champie, when they found her. Or rather, she found them. As witnesses described it, the huge coiled, scaled and finned length of the bottom-dwelling Lake Serpent surfaced right under the rowboat the Parallaxi occupied with their equipment, upsetting their craft and sucking them down.

Ah well, they went out as they would've wished, thought Parallax with a sniffle that was somewhat tempered by his own hard luck.... He chalked up another score against the Dragon.

Selling the family estate, departing the painful locale of his youth, Parallax relocated in Boston. Using his first V.A. check, Parallax bought into the stock market. Ya see, by now, not only could he see near and far in the present, but he was able to extrapolate future events with a high degree of accuracy. He could more or less cast the *I Ching* mentally, trace the *Afa-du* inside himself, pull a daykeeper divination *sans* corn kernels.

As soon as he piled up his first hundred thou, Parallax established himself in the Ritz, where his ultimately inconsequential physical needs could be attended to handsomely. (Eating was his one sensual weak point. Boy, could those Ritz chefs cook! Parallax began to put on weight, till he was big as the King of Dahomey.) One place was as good as another to someone who could travel anywhere without leaving his chair.

All Parallax was really interested in now was becoming wise—wise enough to eventually tackle the Dragon.

Living off his investments, he took a mundane case from time to time, just to keep his wits sharp.

For four decades, Parallax accumulated knowledge, building wisdom crumb by crumb.

Trouble was, he eventually realized, the Dragon had a 3,100-year headstart. Ain't no way he was ever gonna catch up....

This realization tended to sour everything for Parallax. He began to push his luck more and more.

Until he broke it.


A

Dawn was coloring the sky. Oliver Assipattle crawled into the foxhole containing Bangagong, Blackheart and Lamadingsingh. Marijuana smoke hung thick as the cloud from a smudgepot.

"All right, men, we're moving out. We're going to roll across the tundra— Gawd, looks like the enemy is laying down a smokescreen already.... Now pay attention. Our objective is Hill 101. Nothing special there, we just need it. It's held by hundreds of gooks with machine guns, and surrounded by miles of razorwire. We might lose a few brave men taking it, but, by Gawd, take it we will!"

The three men exchanged knowing looks. They raised their rifles.

"Good show, chaps! That's the spirit I—"

They cut Assipattle down in mid-sentence under a hail of bullets.

"Frag him raas! Bredren, I seh we gwine home."

"Most assuredly yes."

"Abo girls be painting breasts in welcome right about now."

"Let we nuh forget we talk. We meet after war, mek some changes somehow. Yahso!"

The moment is here.

For minutes now, Parallax has sensed the approach of his doom. Winging through the air, it's getting closer each second. At last he recognizes its form. Ah, so *this* is the chosen tool.... Well, he can take some pride in the magnitude of his executioner. Two of them, actually, one flying, one riding.

Parallax begins to concentrate all the *qi* energy in his huge bulk. He's preparing a last blow for his enemy. Oh, not the ones zooming toward him. After all, they're just pawns, and he can't win against two-to-one odds. No, if he's going to throw a final punch, it'll be against the Dragon himself.

High above the Boston Common a tiny speck begins to swell, diving straight down, heading toward the window of Room 1010 in the Ritz. People looking idly up spot it and begin to shout and scream. Look, up in the sky, it's, it's—

KUKULKAN, the glorious Plumed Serpent, insane god of the Mayans, who feasts on beating hearts ripped from sacrificial breasts! Like Time's Arrow, the beast and its rider, Eight Snake, plunge implacably toward their target.

As his antagonists burst through the wall of the hotel in an explosion of glass and bricks, Parallax releases his final bolt.

The sizzling *qi*-force travels faster'n light across the astral continuum, straight to the heart of the Dragon—

—and passes uselessly through!

There's nothing there any longer, realizes Parallax, as he smells K's hot meaty breath in the instant Before Completion. Sometime in the past forty years, the Dragon's vanished, leaving just a simulacrum! Where, why, how? And who's running the show—

—oooohhh!

## 2

There is the problem of money talking.

Always.

Call it, as does Emmett "Eminent" Demesne—victim of sanitarium-induced tardive dyskinesia, his ratso face incessantly a-twitch with horrifying spasms, his voice, whenever he can bring himself to speak, a cascade of stutters—Oracular Harangue.

"De mon," as they call him when he's down south in sunny Jamaica, sits in his cheap HoJo motel room in Newton, Mass (suburb of Boston, home to the Condor family), just off the Vandyke Parkway. He is on assignment from the DEA. One of their best, most implacable agents, Demesne has been sent to Boston to track down disturbing rumors of a new drug known as delta-sensorium.

Piled on the nighttable next to his slovenly bed are several antique Men's Magazines, which are Demesne's favorite reading material, representing as they do the only nostalgic reminder of life in his ancestral hamlet; for Grandpa Emmett used to collect them, and allowed his liddle namesake to peruse them.

There is a copy of *Valor For Men!* from September, 1957, whose cover shows a White Hunter shooting an angry crocodile, while the banner headline reads "Exotic

Snake Strip-Teaser!"

There is a copy of *Man's Life* from December, 1960, which contains the edifying article about "The Red Butterfly Horror—Revolt of the Tattooed Love Slaves."

And there is a copy of *Man's Magazine* from August, 1956, which tells of poor Dr. Robert H., who went "insane for science." "Why did I drink LSD-25, a drug that made me a maniac? Because I am a doctor...."

From the limited information Demesne has been able to gather, it appears that delta-sensorium is the first of an exceedingly dangerous new class of designer drugs. (In fact, the DEA has had to invent a new terminology for it. Traditionally, restricted drugs are labeled either Schedule Three, Two, or One with degree of danger and consequent penalties escalating in that order. So potentially devastating is delta-sensorium that the agency has had to create a new, fourth classification for it: Schedule Zero.)

Delta-sensorium has been engineered to deliberately alter natural synaptic reactions. It temporarily increases the speed and efficiency with which hundreds of neurotransmitters—acetylcholine, serotonin, dopamine, etc.—are released, channeled, received, degraded and recycled. The results of ingesting delta-sensorium are unpredictable. In some cases it has promoted what the users have taken as transcendental insights: chemical zen-gnosis. In others, Boschian nightmares, trips to the Avici Hell, have resulted.

Were this everything, the drug might not seem any different than, say, LSD. However, in certain dimly reported cases, different results have obtained. These run the gamut of the so-called psychic phenomena: precognition, clairvoyance, astral travel, telepathy, telekinesis, Chinese skin-reading, where printed characters can be apprehended by epidermal contact, and so on, and so on, like a particularly sensationalistic issue of the *Weekly World News*. There have even been reports of people who have, well, *disappeared forever* while on the drug. Not gone into hiding, but popped out of existence under the eyes of observers. Deadheads, being on the leading edge of mind-expanding drug use, have noted several of these mid-concert vanishments.

Weh-hell, guh-guh-gimme a break, thinks the rationalist, adult half of Demesne. Such shit can't be true. Then the child in him, huddling lonely and aloof in some deep cave of his shattered neurons, remembers the strange occurrences witnessed at the nightly ceremonies of the Therapeutic Church. Speaking in tongues, proleptic trances.... Who's to say this drug can't have the same effects as corn likker and handling enough snakes to contact the Gnostic Bitch, Sophia. (Jesus, Demesne still shivers whenever he pictures those unholy services, suh-suh-serpents crawlin' uh-uh-everywhere, up his muh-muh-mother's dress....)

He recalls the immense serpent that burst out of the earth at him, and his teeth begin to chatter.

Okay, okay, calm down, Junior G-Man! You're as burnt as that kid so long ago back in Frisco, the revolutionary, whatshisname. Holy Christ, my memory's shot, that was so long ago, another era. Whatever happened to that decade, who shut it down, who pulled the plug, wiped the disk? Or is that a misapprehension? Did it all just SUBMERGE?

Wheels within wheels, plots and counterplots, red herrings and *fata morganas*, it's all too byzantine. No sense in being a daydream believer, it ain't no day for a daydream. There a juh-juh-job to be done here—a big one, too.

And that's where the money troubles come in.

The DEA just can't get all the funding it needs for its world-conquering plans. Oh, sure, the Drug Czar tries to scare Congress into releasing the megabux, but what with national deficits and all and that ex-dope-smoker President in office, the money just don't flow in the gush they need. How are they gonna purchase all the trains and boats and planes they need to intercept the shipments, all the two-way wrist radios and semi-automatic, banana-clip, bayonet-tipped phallic symbols so beloved of Secret Service men and foreign fascists? And the public sheep-mass, dumb as a two-dollar whore, can't be counted on to remain forever on their side. Someday Joe and Jane Sixpack are gonna wise up to the fact that the government is playing both sides of the net, tightening and loosening their chokehold on Mister Illegal Substance so as to tweak M4.

The foregoing serves as explanation of Demesne's squalid lodgings; his difficulties in making buys, since the agency is reluctant to front any sum in excess of one hundred dollars; his shoes with holes in the soles, his off-the-rack suit and Cheap Sunglasses; his lack of expensive wheels; (Demesne is driving a local Rent-A-Wreck, a '78 Cadillac, in shocking pink, with the soft velvet seats); his general irritability at being unable to complete his assignment as swiftly and easily as possible.

What's happened is that Demesne has had to squeeze every penny so tightly, that they've begun, well, to *talk* to him.

Ever since Homer "Homo" Faber (Col., Incinerated) explained the intimate connection between money and drugs to him over two decades ago (M4 and all that), Demesne has become something of a bug about money. He has evolved a private symbology and theory of money (actually a quasi-mystical, Kabbalistic set of beliefs bordering on numismancy) which he invokes daily—nay, hourly—to help determine his course of action.

For instance:

Because the IRS—a branch, remember, of Demesne's old employer, the Treasury Department—has divided the country up into eight administrative regions, the number eight has assumed divine significance for Demesne. He brushes his teeth eight times a day. He shakes his mangled cock eight times after pissing. He watches for eights to materialize around him, and is not disappointed. Also, the keys and scales featured in the IRS's crest have acquired divine significance in Demesne's eyes. He carries and constantly rubs a talismanic key to his safe-deposit box, in which is stored the last existing print of a certain old stag film.

Demesne also practices a kind of divination involving money. Having heard that every piece of paper currency circulating in Miami is heavily impregnated with cocaine, because it has passed through the hands of so many dealers and users who snort with it rolled into a tube, Demesne has arranged through a contact in that city to have mailed to him a packet of random dollars from that city. These dollars he burns in an ashtray, inhaling the smoke, while simultaneously and most painfully jerking off, his only and infrequent sexual release. At orgasm, if he is lucky, he receives numinous visions which he will spend days interpreting.

(Demesne is unaware, or has suppressed the knowledge, that in this practice he is imitating the Mayan ritual of his nemesis, Eight Snake, only substituting Onanism for the piercing of prick by stingray needle....)

Demesne spends hours permuting the magic number 3172, which can be seen hidden in the shadows of the shrubbery engraved on the reverse side of a five-dollar bill. His most significant finding is that if one subtracts 1111—the year BC in which the Chou Dynasty was founded—one comes up with the year 2061 AD, which tallies with some of the theories of Jose Arguelles regarding the Harmonic Convergence.

Demesne also spends hours with reams of official statistics relating to the US economy. Using calculator, pencil and paper, he performs endless permutations on the printed numbers. Aided by a Wassily Leontieff input-output map of the American economy and several books by Fischer Black, Demesne searches for hidden patterns in the flow of dollars, goods and services.

His major finding to date relates to the Gross National Product, represented in equations as Q, or Quetzalcoatl. Demesne has discovered that the single figure cited each year as the GNP cannot possibly be derived from the individual sectors of the economy. For example—say you read one day, in the business section of your local newspaper, that the computer industry has, perhaps, fifty billion dollars of sales a year. The next day, you read that the music industry does twelve billion dollars of business annually. And so on, and so on.... If you start keeping track of these individual numbers, adding them up instead of ignoring them, pretty soon you've exceeded the GNP. And that's without even counting such minor but non-trivial sectors as the condom industry ("Consumer Merchandise, Non-Durable").

What, Demesne wonders, could be the reason for deliberately—and he's dead-certain it has to be intentional—understating the GNP? Isn't as large a GNP as possible the Holy Grail? Why diminish it? Is someone afraid of letting the public know *just how much wealth there is in this country* ? Is it the *money mind itself* that's rigging the figures? Does it have anything to do with the fact that only about fifty percent of the extant currency can be accounted for at any time, that the other half has simply vanished from official perceptions? Demesne doesn't know what to think. More research is indicated....

Connected with this whole issue is the matter of counterfeiting. If money is information, then counterfeit money is obviously disinformation, lies masquerading as truth. (Although it is interesting to note that information theory does not distinguish between lies and truth, any more than it does between nonsense and sense, worthless and valuable information. All transmitted bits are regarded as essentially equal. In this regard, information theory is a model of egalitarianism and democracy....) However, counterfeit money, regarded in another light, serves just as well as the real thing. As components of the money mind, as binary switches, fake bills and coins work just dandy. Therefore, counterfeiters, whether they know it or not, are *agents of the money mind,* laboring to increase that entity's brainpower.

For most counterfeiters, Demesne believes, this is obviously not the primary objective. For others, tho.... There is that Indian group known as DIGITAL— members from several tribes, but notably Hopis—who, with access to the copper mines of Arizona, are busy even now counterfeiting pennies. Trouble is, it costs them two cents to manufacture every false penny. (Their pennies are better than the government's, since they're one-hundred percent copper, unlike the zinc-sandwich-alloy true pennies.) Profit, natch, is not the issue here. Could they be hoping to destabilize their immemorial arch-enemy, the Federal Government...? Maybe. Maybe not.

(The connection between money and information transmittal is much deeper than has ever been realized. Altho the Chinese eunuch Cai Lun invented paper circa 100 AD as an information medium (("Hey, Doctor Wu, c'mere 'n' take a look at this. State of the art! Now we got something to burn for the ancestors!")), it was most useful for paper currency. And the debt goes in the other direction, too. In ancient Korea, the casting of coins was the direct precursor of cast type for primitive printing presses. ((The Koreans invented movable metal type in 1403, fifty years before Guttenberg.)) What goes around, comes around....)

Money, it's a drag....

But money—that's what I want!

All this feverish concentration on cash has caused Demesne, a loner since birth, to regard money almost as an individual, his only friend. He was hardly surprised when, caressing a filthy dollar one day, he heard it whisper, *Oh, honey, you got a nice slow hand....* Since that day, he has received innumerable intimate messages from coins and bills, so that now to plonk down a quarter for a pack of gum is tantamount to abandoning an old girlfriend. There must be fifty ways to leave your lucre....

But these sweet liddle nothings are not the most disturbing news from the money mind. No, that would have to be the omens and warnings, the auguries and presages, the adjurations and revilings. *The first one before shall now be the last, for the times they are a-changin'. Gotta serve somebody. You ain't goin' nowhere. How does it feel to be on your own, with no direction home? If dogs run free, why can't we?*

Demesne has no answer for these numismatic conundrums, and they disturb his sleep, trouble his concentration.

Now the retread fed hopes to relax a bit before hitting the streets. He picks up the receiver and dials the desk.

"Cuh-cuh-can I guh-guh-get a suh-suh-sundae sent over? Gah-gah-great. I'll tuh-tuh-take the Buh-buh-blueberry Hill with a Puh-puh-peppermint Twist."

Soon his treat arrives. The desk clerk himself has brought it. A black man with a crazed-look in his eyes, he says, "One of the waitresses's has her nose open for you, boy. Name o' Eleanor Rigby. All she does is sit in her room all day. You could make it big time with her."

"Tuh-tuh-tell her th-th-thanks, but I'll huh-huh-have to puh-puh-pass."

The clerk shrugs. "You give love a bad name."

Demesne ignores the insult and tips the guy a quarter, which, leaving his hand, says, *You don't know what you've got till it's gone.*

Jeez, everybody's a critic!

Just as he's diggin' into his ice-cream, the phone rings.

Demesne reaches over to a small black cube with a speaker-grille in its side and flicks a switch. Totally random artificial static issues from the white-noise generator. Gotta protect against eavesdropping, man. Then Demesne picks the receiver up, saying, "Yuh-yuh-yeah?"

The connection is awful. Gotta be intercontinental, if not intergalactic: pops, hisses, blurts and bleets. What with the white-noise generator going, Demesne can hardly hear the person on the other end. Sounds like some kinda gook....

"Tuh-tuh-talk louder," urges Demesne.

"A tip," says the voice. "Delta-sensorium...."

"Yuh-yuh-yeah?"

"GreenGenes. Paul Peptide. Goodbye."

There's a click, and the mysterious speaker's gone. Who could it have been? None of Demesne's regular informants. Can he afford to discount this? No way. It's his first solid lead.

Getting the dial tone back, Demesne, the original Excitable Boy, makes an instant decision. He dials the Boston office of the DEA, getting through to his contact at once by uttering the code phrase, "Your days are numbered." Then Demesne, knowing that if he's wrong on this one his ass is grass, shoots his wad:

"Suh-suh-send lawyers, guh-guh-guns and muh-muh-money, the sh-sh-shit has hit the fuh-fuh-fan."

Demesne cradles the receiver.

Half a world away, Lao Cohen—lying naked on his stomach on a plaited mat in Tokyo, in the hundredth building of Sony, on the hundredth floor, with a demi-nude Caucasian geisha kneading his back with demure facility—has just hung up on Emmett Demesne.

(Cohen has this thing for Western gals, a kind of Œdipal hangup. The Zammai half of his heritage is still trying to stick it up every *gaijin* chick available. His father's unthinking impregnation of Lilith Cohen is replayed whenever Cohen feels like a little slap and tickle....

This particular employee is Cohen's prize, the sweetest and the sauciest, the loveliest and the naughtiest, a former Miss Buenos Aires in a world of lacy lingerie. Named Veronica Eroica—tho she doesn't care what her owners call her—she was acquired in a recent flesh-for-debt swap with Argentina, the latest ploy in banking circles....)

Unable to fully appreciate the ministrations of the gal cuz of a troubled mind, Cohen raises a hand to finger the tiny dragon tattooed beneath one eybrow. On his pinky is the ring of Melchisidek, ruby eyes gleaming as if alive.

Cohen ponders what he has just done.

As best as he can figure things out, the legendary DEA man is making a minor nuisance of himself in the eyes of the Wu organization—with which Cohen's own crime-empire interlocks several Alternative Tentacles. The Wu group intends to rid itself of Demesne by setting him up and letting him take the fall in some sort of embarrassing *contretemps*, the exact nature of which is not clear to Cohen. In any case, Paddy O'Phidian has asked Cohen to place the call just terminated, and Cohen has obeyed, respecting and fearing the squamous Irishman more than he does Wu himself. (Wu, after all, is such a remote and nebulous figure, one Cohen has never met, whereas O'Phidian most manifestly exists and has the temperament and wherewithal to be very nasty if his wishes are thwarted.) Cohen has to assume that O'Phidian's wishes are congruent with Wu's, although they might very well not be.

Sometimes it gets so hard to know who's zoomin' who, who's yankin' whose chain in this ch-ch-chain of fools....

What was the couplet Alexander Pope had engraved on the King's pooch's collar?

I am His Highness's dog at Kew.
Pray tell me, sir, whose dog are you?

What Cohen is most worried about, tho, is the possible repercussions of his actions, the disturbances he has added to the Tao, the bad karma he might have engendered. Perhaps he should issue a Tokyo Storm Warning...? Maybe not. Doesn't pay to rush into things. He never likes to make a move without consulting certain oracles, but in this case his hand has been forced. Ah well, he can at least take a reading on the future in general.

Sitting up, Cohen claps his hands. The geisha scurries off and returns with Cohen's yarrow stalks. (No book, of course—Cohen has the *I Ching* memorized.)

The yarrow is a curious plant. Used throughout antiquity for its medicinal properties, it also gives an oil employed by certain American Indians for rubdowns. Swedes make a beer from the herb. The yarrow bears a connection with the goddess Venus, and is both an aphrodisiac and VD cure. Sorta an all purpose snake-oil....

Cohen grasps the forty-nine stalks firmly. He puts himself into the receptive state of mind, letting himself become a conduit for the Tao. (Due to his mixed Jewish-

Japanese heredity, he sometimes gets in touch with an angry old coot called YHWH—whoops, wrong number!)

Then he casts the stalks, thrice for each line of the hexagram.

Finally the sign is complete.

Ko.

Revolution.

Also called Change. (And out of the whole Book of Changes, to single one sign out as Change itself is pretty potent.)

Cohen knows the text by heart. But that don't lessen its impact.

JUDGMENT. What takes place as indicated by Ko is believed in only after it has been accomplished. There will be great progress and success....

COMMENTARY. ....Heaven and earth undergo their changes, and the four seasons complete their functions. T'ang changed the appointment of the line of Hsia to the throne, and Wu that of the line of Shang, in accordance with the will of Heaven, and in response to the wishes of men.

Great indeed is what takes place in a time of change. The new king and queen of soul will come around.

## 3

Mekong Mel was up a tree without her pants.

Literally.

She did have a shirt on, tho: a man's pullover, striped red, yellow and green and quite flattering to her gingery skin. Oh yeah—and a raspberry beret.

Seated in a tall ailanthus, the Chinese Tree of Heaven, Mel, that kaptivating Kampuchean kutie, her ass calculatedly overhanging her perch so as to present a splendid view from below of her moneymaker, peered down coyly at the Tuesday-born mullato standing by the base of the lofty tree.

The day was April 18, 1980.

The place was a luxuriously landscaped private estate in Salisbury, Rhodesia—this very day finally become independent Zimbabwe—not far from Rufaro Stadium.

The man watching was Robert Nesta Marley.

"C'mon down, pretty stuckie, I sick of yuh playin' me fe jegge. Me got nuh strength fe nuh more chase."

"You'll have to do better than that if you want me," Mel countered.

Marley folded his arms regally across his chest. Mel could see the old scar on the bicep where the assassin's bullet had entered.

"Yuh got de look, woman. I an' I would die fe yuh. Ain't dat enough?"

"Come up here and tell me all about it."

Marley glowered. "Yuh know me unhealt'y, girl. I gwine ta die soon, join Ras Tafari in Zion on de other side, yahso. I mek de prophecy t'ree year gone now, an' nothin' change since. I got nuh time fe ta waste. An' I got de show ta play tonight. Now get ya raas down here, so me cyan grease ya crease."

"Make me."

"So be it."

Marley fastened his eyes on hers like radar locking on a target. She felt her will melding into his. My sweet Tibetan Tara, he had an Ophite Whammy almost as potent as O'Phidian's! This was Radar Love, fer shure.

Her gamble had paid off. She had provoked Marley into proving that he still had the old mana, that the cancer that was killing him hadn't destroyed his spirit. Now she was certain that he was a sample worth collecting.

She only hoped she hadn't pushed the legendary Tuff Gong too far for *her* own good. She knew the history of how anyone who had ever tried to mess with Marley had ended up dead or insane. The hired guns who had tried to assassinate him in '76 had turned up wandering through the Dungle foaming at the mouth, claiming they were being pursued by duppies, that snakes were eating away behind their eyes....

Mel began to climb backward down the tree, her limbs not her own, fear the sleeper bubbling under her Top Forty thoughts.

Down on the grass, she faced Marley.

"I gwine ta cut yuh loose now, me la-la kriss-miss, so yuh cyan enjoy de jammin'."

As soon as Mel regained control of her arms and legs, she leaped on Marley and tumbled him to the ground.

He ended up atop her.

She helped him tug down his pants.

Mel was pumpin' pheromones like a cageful of tigers in heat. She willed every erg of her abundant $qi$ energy into Marley's cancer-riddled frame, loaning him the strength to really enjoy himself and provide a healthy shot of sperm for her IRS.

Her efforts succeeded. Marley was soon up her like the Lion of Judah, his dreadlocks a mighty mane.

My brown-eyed girl, making love in the grass behind the stadium! Stir it up, little darlin'!

Marley stuttered in his stroking for a moment, then exploded. Mel milked him dry.

Exhausted, played out, Marley fell asleep in her arms, pinning her to the fragrant African earth.

Sleep, Odysseus. The storm is surely past, it just might be that you're home at last....

Mel stroked his dreads. Poor lickle bwai.... A short life, but a noble one. Accomplished a lot, made people happy, wrote and sang some good songs. And now, tho fated to die within a year, he would make one last contribution. His flash-frozen jism would find its way to the Snakes and Ladders team at Wu Labs, where it would be multiplied by polymerase chain reaction (the Wu boys had tumbled to this trick several years prior to Kary Mullis's discovery of it) and teased apart. Then the one percent of the base pairs that made Marley unique would be identified, providing additional clues to the ability of some humans to transcend normal limitations of space and time.

As Marley's cock shrunk out of her, Mel luxuriated in the sensations of a job well done. She was proud of her work. She had never regretted signing on with Wu. How else was a girl gonna meet so many wonderful guys...? She only wished Wu had contacted her sooner. If she had gotten in on the ground floor, like O'Phidian's adopted daughter, Zona Pellucida, who knew what experiences she could have had?

As things stood, one of Mel's biggest frustrations was that she hadn't been able to get to Jimi Hendrix before he died. But it had been simply impossible. In 1970, she had been busy servicing Harry Covair as he dragged her out of Cambodia....

Not only would the Voodoo Chile's genes have been invaluable, but the guitar shaman was supposed to have had a really huge dick. This mattered not a little to Mel. She had never really found a guy who had the combination of spiritual and physical dimensions that would take her right over the edge, duplicate the sensations she had grown accustomed to from Daddy Snake back at Nokor Wat. Oh, sure, she always had a good time at her work. But it was never really transcendental. She wanted to be able to say of some guy, "I feel the earth move under my feet, I feel the sky come tumbling down, I feel my heart start to trembling, whenever you're around."

Sometimes she had a flash, an intuition that there was a guy out there, her other half, who would do it for her. But she just hadn't been lucky enough to meet him yet.

Not that she hadn't been busy looking.

Since she had been deflowered by Mister Snake at Nokor Wat thirteen years ago, Mel had fucked her way through a world of men. By her careful count, she had topped 5500 with Marley. This worked out to approximately 1.11 guy per day. Not that they had come (cum) with any such regularity. Even Mel took a day off now and then.

And what a history of VD she had! Syphillis, gonorrhea, herpes I and II, chlamydia, Pelvic Inflammatory Disease.... She had housed more microbes than Genentech. Wu Labs had cured her of all of them, sent her back out in the field fresh as a flower for the next conquest. Thank Vajrasattva they had just perfected a vaccine for this old-new AIDS-thing. Worrying about catching that nasty virus would have made her job absolutely impossible.

Her muscles cramping, Mel slowly rolled Marley off her. He continued to sleep.

Gently, she tugged a large black-stoned signet ring off his finger. She slipped it into her shirt pocket, and replaced it with a duplicate.

The ring had been Haile Selassie's. It contained fragments of Solomon's Seal. It would do neither Marley nor the world any good for it to be buried with him.

Looking down at the sleeping Rasta, Mel was confident that tonight, at the Independence Day concert, he would give a good performance, thanks to her ministrations.

She sighed. He hadn't been the one. Ah, well, maybe sometime in the next few years she'd get lucky. Perhaps the magic number 10,000 would do it. Let's see, at the rate of 1.11 fucks a day, factoring in a certain slowing down as she inevitably took on a few more administrative duties, she should roll over her odometer, um, about June, 1993.

Meanwhile, she would just keep her liddle motor idling, Our Lady Of The Last Chance Texaco.

4

In the monitor screen, Claude Lollolo watches Avalon sink away and dwindle behind and below him.

Adios, Shambhala, El Dorado, Hy Brasil, Cockaigne, Lyonesse and Poictesme.... No Pure Land for me permanently yet. Click your ruby slippers and say, "There's no place like home, there's no place like home...."

Now the party's over. He's so tired that he barely hears the samba music over the shipboard PA. How could relaxing wear you out so? Did R&R stand for Rest & Recreation, or Reckless Ruination? One thing about the employees of Wu Labs: they could sure party hearty. Why, he'd bet they would fight for their right to party.

Lollolo feels a little empty. Since he left Dahomey thirteen years ago, he's led a busy life. Almost too busy to permit any thought about what he was doing. Ah well, he's committed now. A little late for regrets....

He concentrates on the monitor.

Avalon is a towering transparent fairy castle built entirely of bond-strengthened superglass. It sits below a mile or more of ocean, atop a cluster of black-smoke vents which provide it with heat and power.

Boosting the magnification, Lollolo sees familiar forms inside the lighted galleries. Hmmm, looks like another orgy in the Garden of Eden.... Half against his will, Lollolo feels his 10½ inches of cock begin to stir.

As if drawn by the hidden writhings of his cock, two presences make themselves felt behind his back.

Claude shifts around in his seat.

It's Grace and Gloria Numinoso.

The identical raven-haired twins are dressed like female Hollywood pirates: pre-tattered white shirts with tails knotted under their half-exposed tits; leather hotpants that leave generous crescents of ass-cheek showing; thigh-high buccaneer boots. Each gal wears a gratuitous eye-patch. Thankfully, Gloria wears hers to port, Grace to starboard, so he can tell them apart.

The Pirate Twins are now fifty-six years old. Like Tina Turner (and for similar reasons), they look, tops, half their age, and a youthful half at that.

Devotion to that ol' snake is better for a gal's looks than your Oil of Olay!

As Taoist sage Liu I-Ming says: "If people are able to radically wake up and turn around, shedding attachments to things, to dwell in the realm of nothingness and formlessness, to uproot the senses and objects conditioned by history and sweep away the force of habit acquired in the present life, letting go everywhere to be open and clear, pure and clean, then even if the body is old, the nature is restored."

Sound easy? Give it a try!

The girls drop down beside Lollolo on the soft couch. In constant sub-etheric communication, they joyfully complete each other's sentences.

"C'mon, Claude—"

"—smile a little."

"We've got a new assignment—"

"—and it sounds like a lot of fun!"

Lollolo looks unbelievingly at the Numinoso sisters. "Don't you two ever have any doubts about all this? Don't you ever wonder what it's all about, whether or not we're doing the right thing, whether we're helping people or just using them?"

"No—"

"—not really."

"We leave that kind of useless thinking—"

"—to the big boys like you."

Lollolo shakes his head wearily, a cynical smile wreathing his lips. Back in Dahomey, he used to be disgusted. Now, he supposes, he should try to be amused.

The Jolly Rogerettes pretend now to be taken aback by the trouser-snake coiled in Lollolo's lap.

"Oh, how thick—"

"—and long!"

"This'll be good practice—"

"—for what we need to do later."

They lay their hands on his big cloth-covered prick.

"Tell me one thing—" begins Lollolo. The girls answer before he can finish.

"More than this   "

"—there is nothing."

Sometime during the fourth position of this quantum two-slit experiment, the fourth person aboard the submarine enters. (The sub is painted banana yellow: we all live in a yellow submarine!)

Ernie Europa is the Captain of the *Leviathan*. Once the commander of the US Trident sub *Harry S Truman*, he has been on the run ever since—under the influence of some acid called Neon Rainbow—he beached his vessel in the Solomon Islands, where he destroyed all its warheads and took his crew native, the whole lot of them becoming worshippers of Kahausibware, a local serpent goddess.

"Thank Weiner for cybernetics!" exclaims Europa, spying the tangle of limbs.

And as the good ship *Leviathan*—P.O'P.'s Sub—cruises toward its destination under the reliable guidance of its microchips, Europa, the Pirate Twins and Claude Lollolo try to rival its reactor for number of fusions.

Lollolo manages to enjoy himself. But something's missing. Sex just hasn't been perfect for him, ever since he fucked the Danhgbwe-no. He has dreamed continually of meeting her or her equal again....

Several nights later, the sub breaches. Its hatch opens. A rubber raft pops out and falls into the ocean, tethered by a rope. The Captain and his three passengers emerge.

"Where are we?" asks Lollolo.

Europa answers, "Just off Cape Cod. Little beach called Sandy Neck." He flashes a light toward land; a beam responds.

"Okay, folks, it's Inchon time!"

Lollolo and the Numinosos clamber down a ladder and board the raft.

"We'll paddle—"

"—so you can relax, Claude dear."

Gee, he never thought he'd get such royal treatment, being out of the Dahomean line of descent and all. Kinda feels natural and right somehow.... He's the King of America, where they pour Coca-Cola just like vintage wine....

"So long, y'all," says Europa. "Take care now. The seven seals have been broken, the Four Horsemen are abroad. If we can pull this off, it'll be the Year Aniadin, fer shure. Don't let them stop the Time of Perfection, when the Primordial Man shall rule. And watch yer asses. 'Specially you honey-tailed girls."

"Bye, Ernie sweets."

"See you in the funny pages."

The Pirate Twins cast off and begin to paddle.

Lollolo watches the shore draw near.

He can make out an elderly couple standing on the beach, lit by lantern light. A sagging banner reads:

-UR—' SA–RI

You are sorry.

He sure hopes not.

Chapter 00001101

# Funky Soup

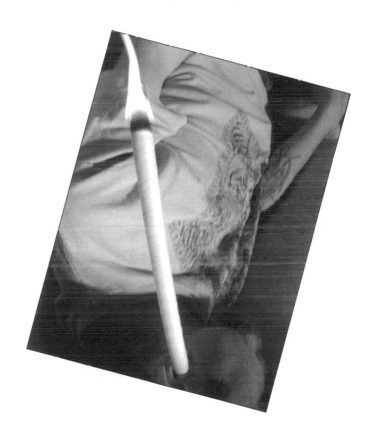

# K L U E S

## 00110000

"The parties of our day will be lyrical apotheoses of the proud cybernetics that is being humiliated and deceived, because cybernetics alone will be able to accomplish the holy continuity of the living tradition of festivities. In fact, at the algid period of the Renaissance, the party actualized the existential, quasi-instantaneous and paroxysmic pleasures of all the moral structures of information: snobberies, espionages, Machiavellian practices, liturgies, aesthetic deceptions, gastronomic Jesuitisms, feudal and Lilliputian disagreements, competitions between soft idiots.... Today only cybernetics, with the supreme potentiality of the information theory, could instantaneously deceive on new statistical subjects all the revellers...."

—Salvador Dalí

## 00110001

"Of all the forms of maya, that of woman is supreme."

—Buddhist proverb

## 00110010

"Indeed, the influence of music on the development of religion is a subject which would repay a sympathetic study."

—Sir James George Frazer

## 00110011

"Free your mind and your ass will follow."

—George Clinton

m y my, hey hey, rock 'n' roll is here to stay!
No, that's not what I meant to say.
Reboot....

My my, hey hey, it's better to burn out than to fade away.

Wrong, wrong, wrong!

Lift the needle and drop it again (but watch out for the needle and the damage done)....

Out of the blue and into the black, they give you this, but you pay for that.

Better, a little better. Shift the readhead to the next track (redhead to the next sack).

And once you're gone, you can never come back, when you're out of the blue and into the black.

Good, good, that brings us right around to our friend, Cy.

Mostly, once Mister Maxwell says to someone, "If you're just looking for one divine hammer, I wanna be your sledgehammer," and taps you with his liddle silver hammer and sends you out of the blue and into the black, you never *do* come back. But Cyril, our hero, has a Rubber Soul and a heart made out of railroad steel. It was not appointed that he should meet his end inside the Boston Athenæum. He has a part yet to play, his karma is fairly decent, the horny Norns don't want his bod—

Yet.

It's mid-morning. A van pulls up to a stop at the door of a North End tenement. The side of the vehicle is lettered:

MONTAGNIER PIZZA
CONTACT MAINTAINED BY CELLULAR PHONE
DRIVER CARRIES ONLY PENNIES
ALL 24-7 SPYZ
CALL 1-800-111-0101
TO REPORT DRIVER MISBEHAVIOR
(VEHICULAR JOKES DESERVE CENSURE)

Two men emerge. Both wear dark glasses. They scoot around to the van's side door, slide it back, and, together, struggle to lift out an insulated red pizza bag.

The pizza bag is six feet long. It contains a lumpy something.

The driver and his assistant set the bag down on the tenement's stoop.

"Dream baby, how long will you dream?" says one.

"Dream on, dream weaver," says the other, patting the top of the bag. "You slipped inside my sleeping bag."

The first guy reminds the other, "Let's go out to Egypt, cuz it's in the plan."

Then they ring the bell with the hand-written card PROTHERO/TUESDAY beside it, jump back into the van and race off.

In a few seconds, the door opens.

Polly's hair is greasy and lank. Saggy, puffy black crescents underscore her blood-shot eyes. There are coffee stains on the front of her white Gang of Four T-shirt. In short, she looks as bad as it's possible for a gal of her innate charm 'n' sex appeal to look.

Green-eyed lady, laughing lady, where have you gone?

Polly stares at the bag unbelievingly for a moment. She gasps, and raises the back of one hand to her gaping mouth. Then she falls to her knees and pulls on the long zipper, which untooths smoothly.

Cy is lying on his back, eyes closed, arms folded across his chest, hands on his biceps. He looks like King Tut. Several days worth of stubble is a first step toward the Pharaohnic chin-spinach. All he needs to complete the picture is a crozier and an ankh in his mitts.

Osiris in the pillar, fer shure!

When the light hits him, Cy opens his eyes.

He gazes with blank-souled innocence on the face of his beloved. The transition out of the everywhere and into the here seems to have affected him like being re-born. His mouth moves tentatively, as if unsure of how to form words.

At last he manages to croak out his first sentence, the words that will announce his return to the mortal world after the wiggly transreal events he has experienced.

"Juh-juh-just dropped in to suh-suh-see what condition my condition is in...."

"Oh, Cy!" exclaims Polly, bending down to embrace him.

After practically squeezin' the breath out of her boy, Polly straightens up and says, "Let's get you out of there."

The bag unzips only to the waist. Extricating the weak-limbed Cy is like pulling a mussel from its shell. But finally he's out, and standing on wobbly knees.

"Can you make the stairs, Cy?" asks his Maid Marion.

"I'll try...." replies Wordy Rappinghood.

It takes Cy half a minute per step, leaning heavily on Pol, getting both feet on a step before attempting the next one.

Up in the apartment, Cyril collapses into a chair. The apartment looks strange. He looks at Polly, and she looks strange. He looks down at his own hands in his lap, and *they* look strange! Ah, that's it.... Things and people look strange when *you're* a stranger!

Cy can tell from the slant of the sunlight that it's earlier on this unidentified morning than it was when he stepped into the Athenaeum on Monday. (No eternal reward will forgive us now for wasting this dawn....) It has to be Tuesday, a week since Ruby's disappearance.

"Sorry I was gone overnight, Pol. I know you must've been worried. But I couldn't help it—"

"Overnight! Cy, it's Friday! You've been missing since Monday! That day was manic! I've been going insane! First I went to the police. I saw someone named Inspector Dolan, and he promised to help. But they couldn't trace you at all. So I tried to reach Max, but his hotel door was locked, for the first time since I've known him. He must really be preoccupied with something.... Then I had Daddy hire more detectives to look for you. Some Japanese firm called Ningishzida Agency. But they couldn't turn up anything either. It was like you had vanished from the face of the Earth. Finally, I even called Wu Labs, but the receptionist—somebody named Vervain—stonewalled me. I haven't slept more than eight hours since Monday. I was just trying to motivate myself to go out and search some more. Cy, where have you been!?!"

Cy can hardly believe it. Four full days inside the Boston Athenæum.... How is it possible? Hold on—

One day to talk to An Wang.

One day to talk to the Tourquoise Courtesan.

One day to talk to (and be tortured by) Ignatius Loyola.

One day to talk to Paracelsus and lip the nip of sexy Sophia.

Tannhauser in Venusberg, fer shure!

What the *hell* had been *in* that zombie-drink?

Cyril relates to baffled Pol all that he underwent, omitting only the rather delicate issue of drinking milk from a Sophic teat.

When he's done, Polly says, "My god, Cy. How can you sit there so calmly? You took a four-day drug trip inside Boston's poshest, most respected library—which now seems to be run by forces allied with Wu—and you think nothing of it?"

"No, that's wrong, Pol. It's not that I don't dig the importance of it. I realize it was highly weird and sinister like, and that I could have gotten hurt, or even killed. But I didn't, for whatever reason. And now I can't bring myself to regret going there and getting drugged like I did. I learned too much. I seem to understand Wu on some wordless level now. I almost empathize with him! No, I think that what I went through is gonna help us get Augie and Ruby back. And it's not all nonverbal touchy-feely stuff either. We've got more concrete information about Wu now too. Assuming what the ghost of Wang told me is accurate. In fact—"

Cy pauses, running a mental inventory. It seems that there are a lot of uncollated facts lodged 'way back in his brain, a black mass of information that was never there before. He doesn't have immediate access to it, but senses that he might be able to tease some threads out of the tangle. Where the hell could this nest of sutras have come from...?

Cy suddenly remembers the feel of Sophia's big rigid pillow-backed nipple in his mouth, the taste of Her Milk, the Holy Lactation of Gnosis.

That had to be it.

"In fact," resumes Cy, a faint embarrassment lingering at the memory of suckling like an infant from the Sophic tit, "I might have learned even more than I can say right now. So don't be angry with me. How could I know Wu had taken over the Athenæum?"

A look of sorrowful repentence crosses Polly's haggard features. She drops into Cyril's emaciated lap. Our boy instinctively encircles her in a protective embrace.

Polly sure feels good! She might not be a goddess like Sophia, but then, who could live with a goddess every day?

"Oh, Cy, what am I saying? I'm not mad at you! I'm just so glad you're back safe and sound! You are okay, aren't you?"

"Sure—I guess."

"I hope so, because I don't know what I'd do without you! When I thought I had lost you, I nearly went crazy! Ruby and Augie being gone was awful enough. But at least you and I were facing it together. Then, all of a sudden, I was holding out so long, I was hanging on the phone, I was sleeping all alone— Lord, I missed you! I felt like ending it all...."

Polly lets loose then with a freshet of tears, all the sobs 'n' sniffles she's been saving up for the crying scene.

Cyril pats her head till she calms down. "It's okay, it's all right, Pol. If I had been in any condition to know how long I was without you, I would have felt the same way."

Polly kisses Cy's brow, then stands up. She's all competent and assertive now, her usual take-charge self. Being with her again—seeing her this way—makes Cy himself feel more normal. Like Pol says, they're so lucky to have each other. The times are tough, and getting tougher; the world is rough, and getting rougher. I'm looking for a lover who will come on in and cover me. And I would walk five hundred miles, and I would walk five hundred more, just to be the one who walked a thousand miles to lay down at her door....

"We're going to get you washed up and fed," Polly maternally mandates. "Then I'll fill you in on what I've been doing the last few days."

"Sounds good," tallies Cyril.

"Let me help you off with your shirt—"

Cy obligingly lifts his arms straight up above his head, and Polly grabs the hem of his shirt and pulls it up.

She stops abruptly with the garment still wrapped around Cy's head.

"Polly? What's going on?"

There is an audible gulp. "Cy. Something—something's happened to your skin."

Cyril jumps up and finishes shucking his shirt, a long-sleeved baseball jersey. He looks down at himself.

The sunburn he got nearly a week ago is gone. In its place, his epidermis has been transformed into an opaque white sheath. The effect ends at his neck and wrists.

Cy quickly pulls off his pants. His legs exhibit the same condition, from thighs to ankles.

Nervously, Cy looks under the band of his Jockey shorts.

He exhales a gust of relief. The condition stops at his waist. His second-favorite organ (after his brain) seems fine.

Polly is holding aloof, as if Cy's a leper or sumpin. "Did that Tourquoise Courtesan do this to you at the library?"

Something is tugging at Cy's memory. "No, I don't think so. It seems like— I've got it! That lotion your father gave me for my burn! I put it everywhere except on my face and the parts my suit had covered."

Reassured, Polly approaches. "Well, if it was Daddy's salve, it can't be anything harmful. Let me look."

Polly fingers the artificial terminator at Cy's waist. Before Cy realizes what she's doing, she's slipped the tip of a fingernail beneath the torso sheath!

She runs her nail halfway around him, to the middle of his back. Then with the opposite finger, she completes the circle.

There is now a little ruffle all around him, below his navel.

Polly pinches it with both thumbs and forefingers, and begins to peel it upward.

Underneath is revealed Cy's own new skin, pink and unmarked as a baby's.

Soon the thin plastic shirt has been entirely removed. (There are ragged holes where he failed to apply the GreenGenes liquid under his armpits.)

The inside of the garment is lined with Cy's old damaged dry and flaky epidermis.

Cyril peels off the leggings, then his Jockeys.

His hands, feet, groin and ass still retain his old night-owl complexion, his face showing the fading sunburn. But where the lotion was, he has been completely refinished in infant-perfect, hairless skin.

Cy regards his cast-off self, lying like a partial suit on the floor. He's never sloughed before.... Does this mean he gets two birthdays?

"All my old scars are gone," marvels Cy. "Can you imagine what rich old ladies will pay for this treatment? Your father is going to make a billion dollars with this stuff."

Polly starts to giggle, then actually laugh. "You look so silly! Like a patchwork doll!" Then she recovers her seriousness. "Cyril, listen. I'm sure Daddy's stuff is benign. But who knows what after-effects of that zombie-drink might be lingering? I think we should get you checked out by a doctor."

"Oh, no, man, I don't wanna—"

"Cyril, please! It's just a smart precaution. We'll zip over to Mass General and the emergency room. It'll only take a couple of hours."

Actually, Cy is not all that reluctant. He does feel slightly strange. The reassurance of a doctor would be nice. Who knows? After that meeting with Hermes, he could have Mercury Poisoning....

"Okay, let me have a shower first. I feel sort of grungy in the shorts area."

Cy quickly takes a rinse. His new skin is hypersensitive, not in any painful way, but as if the receptivity of all his nerve-endings has been notched up.

When Cyril emerges, fully dressed, he finds Polly waiting. Somehow during his shower she's managed to freshen herself up, so that now she looks almost like the old pretty Polly, untouched by sorrow and cares. A pang of affection mingled with sadness shoots thru Cy.

Polly seems to sense this. She smiles bravely, but does not allude to their troubles.

"I've called a cab. I just picked the first company in the phonebook. They said it'd be right around. We should probably go down and wait."

Outside, Cyril is confronted by the empty person-sized pizza-bag. He kicks it off the stoop and into the street. "These henchmen Wu employs are a bunch of goddamn nuts! Sticking a person in a pizza bag—! You know what bugs me the most about this whole affair, Pol?"

"What?"

"It's not even a proper conspiracy! There's no stealth, there's no ideology, there's no attempt at secrecy, there's no organization! There's not even any obvious damn goals! A million schemes just seem to diffuse outward from some nebulous center. And half of them seem to be at cross-purposes with the other half! It's not mechanistic, it's—it's organic! It's a big funky soup! You can't put your finger on what Wu wants or believes in or is doing. And instead of not being able to learn enough about Wu and the rest, there's too much to learn! It's not a conspiracy of silence, it's a conspiracy of noise!"

"And what else would a really modern conspiracy—one based on information theory, that is—be?"

Their ride pulls up then.

It's a stretch Lincoln, one long black limousine that can barely negotiate the cramped streets of the North End.

"Hey," says Polly weakly, "I only asked for a regular cab...."

The chauffeur powers down the window. He's a young guy with skin the color of Coca-Cola, and a little black mustache.

"Vishnu Ananta at your service, ma'am and sir. Most sorry to obtrude this vehicle under your unsuspecting noses, but all jitneys in our supremely efficient radio-dispatched fleet save this modest chariot were otherwise occupied. And our motto being 'You won't wait an aeon for an Aion cab,' we could not honorably do otherwise than offer you this humble coupe."

Cyril looks doubtfully at his mate. "Polly, not to sound like Roosevelt, but is this trip really necessary?"

"We have to get you checked out. And the car is already here...."

"Oh, all right."

They climb into the spacious passenger compartment, with its full audio-video entertainment center, wet bar and liddle refrigerator decorated with magnets.

Ananta's voice crackles over a speaker. "Where to, sahib?"

"Uh, Mass General."

"Please partake of a complimentary drink."

"No!"

"No thanks!"

The ride is uneventful, and soon they're at the emergency room entrance of Massachusetts General Hospital. The fare comes to eight bucks, but Polly makes it an even ten. Ananta gratefully tips his cap.

Inside, all is bustling antiseptic controlled chaos. The PA system is blaring messages: "Doctor Noah Drake, please report to the recording studio...."

Cyril and Polly explain themselves to the Triage Nurse, a mannish gal looks kinda like Patti Smith, name o' S. SALONIKA.

"Please take a seat. A doctor will see you in a minute."

They do so. Cy rummages among some ancient magazines. His eye is briefly caught by the cover of the January 11, 1988 issue of *Newsweek*, but he finally settles on a ten-year-old copy of *Arizona Highways*. He has barely opened it when another nurse pokes her head into the waiting room and says, "Mister Prothero?"

"Wow, that was fast! Okay, see you soon, Pol."

The red-haired nurse leads him backstage. Cy cannot help but notice the motion of her buttocks in her tight uniform. It's like watching a sackful of snakes. This girl is really walkin' in rhythm! She's got the action, she's got the motion—it's the Walk of Life! If this is a test of how good he's feeling, he's happy to report that he's functioning at normal libidinous parameters.

In the curtained-off cubicle, the nurse says, "Please strip down to your shorts, Mister Prothero. The doctor will be right with you." She leaves.

Cy undresses, fantasizing that the nurse will return and be so taken with his odd mottled appearance that she'll jump his bones right there.

The curtain parts.

Shux, it's a guy....

The Doc is an elderly yet sturdy Amerindian fellow with long black hair done up in twin braids. His stony visage is stark as a brass eagle's. A stethoscope dangles from around his neck, along with a big silver and lapis squash-blossom medallion.

Cyril immediately feels a trust inspired by the Doc's timeless countenance, generically familiar from a hundred elementary school textbooks.

The medico introduces himself: "Doctor Black Elk." His handshake makes Cyril feel as if his own hand is pinned in a mountain crevice. "They tell me you might be suffering from a possible drug overdose of unknown origin."

"That's right, Doctor. Plus who knows what else. I was practically kidnapped for four days...."

"I see." Doctor Black Elk listens to Cy's heartbeat. "A perfect sixty per minute. You are aware, I'm sure, that sixty beats a minute amounts to eighty-six thousand and four-hundred per day?"

"No, I—"

"And that one cosmic night and day of Brahma amounts to eight billion, six hundred and forty million human years?"

"Can't say I—"

"And that a single Brahma year equals three trillion, one hundred and ten billion, four hundred million human years? All deriving ultimately from the simple beat of the human heart?"

"Gee, that's interesting, Doc. But what about my health?"

"You are basically sound. But your inner forces have been disordered by your experiences. You have what we call 'snake infections.' If not treated, they could lead to swollen joints, itching skin, painful urination, dry throat, mental confusion, fear and loss of consciousness."

"Holy Jesus, Doc, I don't want that! What can I do?"

"Luckily, this was my shift. Most palefaces would not recognize your condition. I believe that with your complete cooperation, I can cure you right here and now."

"Sure, I want to get better. I want to be good, but good means being simple, and simple means forgetting—and I simply can't forget!"

"First we must apply the Hopi ear candle. Please roll onto your right side."

Cy does as ordered. The Doc sticks something waxy in his ear. There's the muffled sound of a match being lit, then a fragrant smell.

"This sacred candle is made of honey, Saint John's Wort, sage and camomile. It will exercise your lymphatic system and withdraw impurities. Your reflex zones and energy points will be stimulated."

Heat seeps down into his head from the candle. It's weird, but kinda soothing. Cy goes with the flow.

After a time, the Doc snuffs out the candle and removes it. "Your case is a relatively mild one. There have been instances when I've had to use sixteen candles.... Now, you must walk the Place of the Snake Pollen People. Stand up."

Cy gets to his feet. Doctor Black Elk pulls a rug off the floor. Revealed is a Navaho sand painting in the medium of hand-laid tiles. A circle, open at the top, is formed from the curving body of a stick-figure man. Four other human figures, colored white, blue, yellow and black, are arranged within the circle like points of a compass. From a small circle at the center of the outer one radiate four plants.

"You must tread the Beautyway of Rainbow Man now, to restore your balance. Begin—and move like a panther."

Setting one foot tentatively on the design, Cyril feels a surge of energy pulse up his leg. He puts the other foot down. The knowledge of how to move fills him on a somatic level.

As Cy shuffles hypnotized about the pattern, Doctor Black Elk begins to chant. "A-wop-bop-a-lulu-a-lop-bam-boom! Tutti frutti, all rootie—!"

After what seems like hours of tracing the Beautyway to the Doc's scatting, Cyril finally collapses. Black Elk helps him up.

"How do you feel?"

"Good. Tired, but good."

"Go home and rest for a few hours. If symptoms persist, take two tabs of acid and call out my name. I'll come running, wherever you are."

"Thanks, Doc."

Cy gets dressed and rejoins Polly.

"Did you get a clean bill of health, Cy?"

Out here, what the Doc did no longer seems so rational or unexceptional. Cy decides not to burden Polly with it. "The Doc felt there was nothing the matter with me that a little music and dancing couldn't cure."

"Oh, wonderful!"

They move to leave.

At that moment the Emergency Room doors burst open. Orderlies caroom in, pushing a special *ménage-a-trois* stretcher with two men and a woman on it, all unconscious and hooked up to IV's.

"Gunshot victims! The girl drilled both guys, then herself! Out of the way!"

Luckily, Polly, Cy trailing, is halfway out of the Emergency Room already, and so is spared the gory spectacle. *Poor Janey*, thinks Cy. Hey, Joe, where you goin' with that gun in your hand...?

The pair set off through the corridors of the hospital, heading for the main lobby, outside which they hope to catch a cab.

While still inside, they spot a knot of people clustered around a big window.

"Oh, look," exclaims Polly, "it's the new babies. Let's have a peek at them."

New babies remind Cy of grubs or worms. Basically, they give him the creeps. More souls reborn into *samsara*.... But he's so grateful to be leaving the hospital that he obliges Pol's whim.

Polly pushes her face up against the glass with the other visitors. Cy hangs back.

"Oh, Cyril, come and look! They're so cute!"

Cy steps closer to the window. He sees rows of plastic cribs full of shapeless pink 'n' blue bundles, their pathetically unformed and innocent faces devoid of all knowledge of the joys and troubles ahead of them. What a cryin' shame....

One baby is different, tho. Dressed in a brown shirt, this ex-embryo seems more alert, his eyes focusing on all the sights, his pitiful neck muscles causing his head to wobble about. As Cy watches, this days-old kid does something so impossible for its age that Cy just about wets his pants.

The infant rolls onto its stomach and pushes itself up, to glare with unmistakeable hatred straight at Polly and Cyril!

Then the tyke starts to wail. Cy can hear it even thru the window. Its face goes cyanotic blue, like baby Krishna's. Nurses converge on it. Nothing they can do seems to help or mollify it. Finally, the disturbed babe is jabbed with a needle.

By shading his eyes against the reflection in the window, Cy can make out the baby's nameplate on its crib.

LANGDON VERMICELLI

Cy hears subliminally: then you had to bring up reincarnation over a couple of beers the other night. Now I'm serving time for mistakes made by another in another lifetime. How long till my soul gets it right...?

The incident seems to have diminished Polly's enthusiasm for babies. "Let's go," she says.

Out front, they hail an innocuous cab and are soon back in their digs.

Polly goes into the kitchen to fix coffee and grilled-cheese sandwiches for brunch, with *Peaches En Regalia* for dessert. (It's not quite noon.) Famished from his four-day fast, Cy eats a hospital-purchased Nestle's Crunch bar while waiting. It's one of the special commemorative music ones, namely the "Funk" style.

After finishing the appetizer, while awaiting Polly's call to table, Cy sits in a chair and begins to probe mentally at the knowledge he earlier sensed lurking at the back of his mind. This black mass—the alchemical *nigredo*—of information starts to disgorge bits and pieces of itself.

But, to Cyril's disappointment, what he had thought would be answers turn out to be—questions. Wotta drag! Still, ya take what ya can get. He tries to reassure himself that sometimes the proper question is more useful than a facile answer.

Snatching up some scrap paper and a pencil, Cyril begins jotting down these questions as they surface in his mind.

When Polly enters with their lunch on a tray, Cy keeps right on a-scribblin', pausing only to absentmindedly consume his food. He's more fixated on his questions than Mae Brussell and her Brussel Sprouts on JFK. Polly, realizing the depth of his concentration, does not interrupt him.

At last, after approximately sixty-four minutes, Cyril has compiled:

### CY'S 64 THOUSAND-DOLLAR UNANSWERED QUESTIONS

1) Why is Elvis's middle name misspelled on his gravestone?
2) Why did Bhutan, independent in 1949, choose a dragon for its flag?
3) What was the real purpose of the RNA Tie Club, the association of biologists that limited itself to twenty members who took the names of the twenty basic amino acids?
4) What did Mark Ptashane of Harvard mean when he said that those investigating the workings of the cell must be prepared to take "psychic risks?"
5) Did sex begin in archaic cells as a viral infection?
6) Why was the concept of "zero" invented in India, and not in Europe?
7) Did the Mayans independently invent their zero, or receive it via diffusion from India?
8) Is the human body, topologically equivalent to a torus, not simply a big zero, or cipher?
9) Is it meaningful that "hadron" is a pitifully obvious anagram of "hard-on?"
10) Why did Niels Bohr use the yin-yang on his personal crest?
11) Why does the *Institut Pasteur* maintain branches in West Africa and Indochina?
12) Why is ARPA (formerly DARPA) funding Ed Fredkin's research into the highly theoretical notion that the universe is a cellular automaton?
13) Why does Haiti make all U.S. pro baseballs?

14) Who stole James Watson's luggage in France?

15) What was the connection among Monsignor Giovanni Montini, later Pope Paul VI, William Donovan of the OSS and the secret Masonic lodge, P2?

16) What was Nixon doing in Dallas the day JFK was shot?

17) Why did Liu I-ming's satori occur in 1776?

18) Why did John Cale wear a rhinestone choker in the form of a snake to open the Velvet Underground's first concert?

19) Who is the Dragon which Divine Right battles at the end of *Divine Right's Trip*?

20) Is Robbie Shakespeare related to Willy?

21) Was Carl Channell, player in the Iran-Contra scandal and Operation Black Eagle, gay?

22) Why does the Black Muslim group Five Percent Nation call all nonbelievers "snakes?"

23) Why is the time for Sly and the Family Stone's track, "There's a Riot Goin' On" listed on the album as 0:00?

24) Is it significant that one of Peter Tosh's killers worked for a firm named Hermes, Ltd?

25) Who are the Men In Black?

26) What did George Bush mean by his phrase "voodoo economics?"

27) Why was Bob Marley portrayed as Saint George on the cover of his *Kaya* album?

28) Did Papa Doc really command the spirits known as *baka* to kill JFK?

29) Does George Harrison still wear the ring bequeathed to him by his dying guru, Srila Prabhupada?

30) Was Howard Hughes's corpse secretly brought to Boston?

31) Why is a Boston gay-rights group called United Fruit Company?

32) What kind of bestiality was depicted on the 8mm films the DEA seized from Chuck Berry?

33) What did Chico Mendes's friend, Osmarino Rodrigues, mean when, in reference to Mendes's murder, he said, "The head of the snake was not hit"?

34) Why did Lou Reed subtitle *Metal Machine Music* "The amine β ring dextrorotory components synthesis of sympathomimetic musics?"

35) Why did Oliver Heaviside, the man whose equations allowed the large-scale implementation of long-distance telephony, end his life as a reclusive eccentric, assigning himself the imaginary degree "W.O.R.M."?

36) Why does the CIA refer to slipping people into the country without customs checks as "entering in black?"

37) Why did United Fruit Company—the corporation—fund a movie entitled *The Kremlin Hates Bananas*?

38) Why did Robert Gallo try to steal credit for the discovery of HIV?

39) What was the meaning of Carolee Schneemann's 1964 work of performance art, "Eyebody," in which she let snakes crawl over her naked body?

40) Is the dollar sign a cadeuceus missing one snake?

41) Why did the *Institut Pasteur* switch in 1989 to printing its journals in English?

42) For what purpose is Neil Sloane at Bell Labs collecting unusual numerical sequences?

43) Why was one of the first acts of the Allies at the end of World War II the confiscation of selected German radio frequencies under the Copenhagen Accord?

44) Why are certain Pacific Rim countries, such as Korea, called "Little Dragons?"

45) Why are ley lines called "dragon currents?"

46) Why is direction on the DNA molecule said to be either "upstream" or "downstream?"

47) Why are semi-autonomous computer agents called "dragons" and "dæmons"?

48) Why did the Japanese set up their A-bomb research station in Hungnam, Korea?

49) What does Benin do with the five million tons of toxic wastes it has contracted to dispose of each year?

50) Why have three-quarters of all national constitutions been rewritten since 1965?

51) Why was one of the early pioneers in the semiconductor revolution named Noyce (noise)?

52) Why did the ancient Chinese refer to death as "ascending the dragon?"

53) Why did Tertullian call the Gnostics "vipers?"

54) Why did a wave of decolonization begin in 1948?

55) Who replaced Paul McCartney after he died in a car accident?

56) What is the missing Tenth Commandment of Love?

57) If, as Ludwig Boltzmann believed, entropy is missing information, then where does information go when it disappears?

58) Why are there four basic mathematical operations, or cipherings?

59) Why was Sam Cooke shot?

60) Who puts flowers every year on Poe's grave?

61) Who replaced Bob Dylan after he died in a motorcycle accident?

62) Why did Elena Ceaucescu habitually call the Romanian people "worms?"

63) Is Thomas Pynchon one of the Residents?

64) Who, in New York, 1948, shot Chano Pozo, Cuban musician who was teaching Cuban/Yoruban riffs to U.S. hepcats?

Very good, Cy! But what happened to Questions 67 and 68?

Finished, Cy hands the list to Polly. She scans it carefully, then sits quietly for a minute, as if composing her response.

"Cy," she says finally, "have you ever heard of 'The Law of Disregard of Negative Information?'"

"No. What's it got to do with my list?"

"Everything. You see, as formulated by Alexander Luria, the Law states: 'Facts that fit into a preconceived hypothesis attract attention, are singled out and remembered. Facts that are contrary to it are disregarded, treated as exceptions and forgotten.'"

"You're saying you think my questions are all recursive and self-referential, just feeding off the same set of obsessions?"

"No, no.... It's just that some of them are, well—pretty far out."

Cy gets defensive. "Polly, I didn't invent all these questions. They're not a manifestation of my personal biases. They were put into my brain!"

"How?"

"Well, you see...."

"Yes?"

"It was, um, a second drink at the Athenæum, one I didn't mention."

"Who gave it to you?"

"Mercury."

"The god?"

"Yeah, the god! His mother, if you must know. Sophia. He summoned her, and made me drink milk from her tit!"

Polly blushes a little. "Cy, I never knew you were interested in that kind of thing—"

"C'mon now, gimme a break! Let's just concentrate on these questions. What's so unlikely about them?"

"Well, take Number Fifty. What do national constitutions have to do with information theory?"

"That's easy. Information theory showed people how repressive control is achieved through a one-way flow of information. Having seen this, countries everywhere knew they had to push for status as transmitters, not just receivers, and modified themselves. This ties in with Number Fifty-four. It's all totally cybernetic, and relates to discoveries about DNA too. The cell is a cybernetic organism, everyone knows that, thousands of feedback loops governing all its delicate cycles. And the way expression of the information in DNA is repressed by inhibitors until it's needed— It's the same with the colonized countries, the Third World, see— We need their information now, so Gaia—you know, the concept of how the world is really a homeostatic organism, governing our environment through feedback, so that no matter how much junk we pump into it, it remains basically livable— Where was I? Oh yeah, so Gaia, needing something from the Third World's 'genes' at this point in time, allows them to be expressed."

"Well, maybe. How about Number Six, though? What's so important about the concept of zero?"

"I had a vision last week, a vision off a barcode. Zeroes and ones. They're the foundation of everything, especially the zero, the Taoist Void. Zeroes, or circles, are everywhere! The sixty-four symbols of the *I Ching* are commonly arranged in a circle, as are genes on a gene map. Linear accelerators are circles where the tail of Glashow's snake is probed. And why does quantum physics use such goofy names? 'Quarks.' That's from James Joyce, ya know. And what about 'coupling constants!' Talk about one-track minds! And Glashow's snake, with its tail in its mouth, is a zero, of course."

"Okay, it seems to make a queer kind of sense. But the one I just can't fathom is Number Thirteen."

"Baseballs? That's easy. If you look at the stitching on a baseball from the right angle, it appears to be—the yin-yang!"

"Oh, Cyril, that's ridiculous!"

"It is not!"

Polly clams up, but Cy can tell she isn't converted. Guess this permanent disagreement will just have to be their Haitian Divorce.

"Okay, Cy. I admit that your list of questions does paint a subliminal portrait of some kind of worldwide secret history. But intriguing as they are, they're not going to help us find Augie and Ruby, whereas what I've learned will."

"You've learned something? What?"

"Well, while I was running around looking for you, I also had a programmer in Daddy's employ investigating our one solid lead: that compact disc. Yesterday he called and told me that he believes he's discovered what's on it."

Cy rockets to his feet. "My God! Let's go, where is this guy, can he see us now, what am I saying, of course he can, he works for your Dad. What kind of information is on that damn disc anyway? We know it's not video or sonic— Jesus, Polly, you're a genius!"

Cy makes a dash for the door, and is arrested by Polly's voice.

"Hold on, Cy! He can't see us until after business hours. And you're too worked up and on the edge now. That disc isn't going anywhere. You've got to relax first. We were supposed to take a nap, remember?"

"Well, I don't think I can sleep now, Pol...."

"Just try. How about if I give you a special massage that'll discharge some of your excess nervous energy?"

"If you think it'll do any good...."

"I do."

Whe-hell.... In a few seconds, two-toned Cy's lying on the bed belly-down, naked, with pantied and brassiered Polly straddling his legs.

"I'm going to use accupressure, or *qigong*," says Polly, "to balance your flow of *qi*. As Buddha said, 'The globe is full of rivers, as is the body.' Your rivers are clogged. We'll start with the *Tu-Mo* Meridian, the Governing Vessel, which begins down here at your coccyx."

Polly presses a spot on Cy's rump. Cosmic fireworks go off in his head. Whispers from the dead fill his ears. He feels like a silicon chip connected to its power source for the first time, suddenly aware that it's just part of a larger unit, a sandwich of circuits with a higher purpose. Burn me in, babe!

"Wow...."

"Quiet now. Just relax."

Cy complies.

Pretty soon, eyes shut, he's drifting off in a black universe, hardly aware of his body. No, that's all wrong, he's intensely aware of his body, in a completely different way. He can't feel it anymore, but he's seeing it somehow *from the inside*. Wow, what a busy place. L-l-look at all that's goin' on! This joint is hopping to a kind of blood music, the bio-beat. Speaking of blood, what mighty rivers the body contains! It's a whole world of red rivers: the Charles leads to the coccyx, the Bassac to the bowels, the Mekong to the medulla, the Niger to the nose, the Liffey to the liver, the Shannon to the spine, the Cam to the cortex, the Thames to the thyroid, the Knile to the knees, the Yangtze to my baby's ya-ya, Cripple Creek to the cerebellum, the Mississippi to the mammaries, the Yalu to the *yoni*, the Chongchon to the cock, the Amur to the anus, the Chao Phraya to the clit.... These rivers rise like a beast from hell, and we'll all be drowned in these rivers....

Halting his progress through the bloodstream, Cy pauses beside a random cell. Hmmm, seems to be a conversation of some sort goin' on inside, the voices of women. I just wanna hear girls' talk. I got a loaded imagination being fired by girls' talk.... I'm a girl watcher! Think I'll just GET small and slip thru the cell wall here. Hope my immune system don't catch me— Whoof! This ionic channel is tight!

Cy's inside the cell.

Boy, is this place cramped! It's packed fuller than a frat-house party. The interior is laced with microtubules. Proteins are wiggling by with their snake-like motion called "reptation." It's hard to see how anything gets accomplished in this tight confusion. (For instance, how does a literal yard of DNA get unwound for transcription in this zoo?) Big fat lipids go sliding by. Ribosomes churn out new proteins. Say-hey, there's the mysterious nucleus with the DNA inside. Hiya, Nuke! Good to see that at least my cells still have something at the center, even if the universe don't.... Golgi bodies, lysomes, zymogen bodies, centrosomes, the endoplasmic reticulum— Wotta trip!

Cy has forgotten for a moment about the female voices that initially attracted him. But now he suddenly notices that they've fallen silent. Looking around, he spots—

About a hundred identical, sensual, naked women! They're all dark-skinned Afro-Egyptian beauties. Seeing him, they begin to laugh and beckon. It seems Cy has stumbled on

## THE ANCIENT MATRIARCHY OF THE CELLS

These gals are the mitochondria. The mitochondria are the indispensable energy source for all cellular functions. Without them, nothing could go on. They break down the phosphate bonds (written, by the way, P-O-P) in adenosine triphosphate—ATP—releasing immense amounts of energy for all other cellular components to use. (Please don't confuse P-O-P with CY-P, which stands for cytidylic acid, a constituent of RNA, which in turn is not to be confused with psychedelic acid.)

The really fascinating thing about the mitochondria, however, is that *the information to produce them is not contained in the nuclear DNA*. Each mitochondria contains its own DNA, just enough to reproduce itself. They're like independent countries in the midst of an empire, tribal homelands in the heart of South Africa. Unlike every other cellular component, they are independent of Big Daddy Nuke.

Well, you may ask yourself: granted that the mitochondria can reproduce themselves, *where did the first one in every individual come from?* Good question. Turns out they're in the egg at conception. In other words, they're a maternal donation which reproduces as the embryo develops. Men have nothing to do with creating them, not even a half-stake. Every single mitochondria in every single human being—yes, I'm talking about you too, Mister Big Stuff (who do you think you are?)—has been passed on solely through females, in a straight line of descent from the first primitive hominid Eve. Your whole cellular lifecycle is based on maternal information. Can we say now that conception is still a fifty-fifty deal? 'Fraid not, folks. By whatever margin, females contribute more. How does that make you feel, babes 'n' dudes?

(As to how the aboriginal mitochondria hooked up with the aboriginal cell— that's buried deep at the bottom of the Mountain Of Time. *You* go digging for it....)

Suddenly Cy's surrounded by the energetically lascivious mitochondria, who have swum thru the cell's funky soup to greet him. They're rubbing up against him, hundreds of Gorgeous Glamour Gals, and he finds himself hard-pressed to keep down an erection.

Erection?

It's at this point that Cy realizes he's not a disembodied point-of-view, as he assumed, but a little naked image and representation of his big body inside itself.

"Uh, hi, girls...."

"Hi! Who're you? We don't get many visitors here!"

"Uh, Cy."

"Hi, Cy! I'm Mary. This is Marlene—"

"Hi!"

"—Magda—"

"Hi!"

"—Myrtle—"

"Hi!"

"—Maureen, Marie, Myrna, Moira, May, Mona, Margaret, Mabel, Millie, Margery, Michelle, Maria, Madeleine, Marion, Melinda, Marnee, Meryl, Miranda, Melody, Marsha, Misha, Molly, Mabel, Marguerite, Martina, Mara, Merilee, Martha, Morgana, Mima, Mya, Mliss, Mei, Mu Lan, Mu Tan, Mawusi, Morowa, Manidatta, Malini, Mairead, Mave, Mitsuko, Miyuki, Mwanatabu, Mi-Ok, Mitena, Mayuree, Mukhwana—"

"Okay, fine, I get the picture. Nice to meetcha all."

"So very nice to meet you! Wouldn't you come and say hello to our leader?"

"You mean Big Daddy Nuke?"

"Oh no! We do not owe allegiance to Laoyeh Nuke. We mean Queen Maya."

"Sure, I'll say howdy to your Queen."

The giggling bevy of wavy-haired beauties surround Cy and glide off with him through the cytoplasm.

They soon approach an out-jutting of the cell wall shaped like a throne. On it sits a mitochondria identical to all the others, save for a golden crown on her head. Her open thighs provide Cy with a enthralling shot of her plump mound. His cock swells uncontrollably.

"Queen Maya, we've brought you a visitor!"

The Queen surveys Cyril intently before saying, "We hope your visit is a peaceful one, young man. We do not care for outside agitators here. A cell divided against itself cannot stand. We want no snakes in our Eden."

"Oh, no, Your Majesty, I ain't no snake!"

Queen Maya gestures to Cy's stiff boner. "Yet you possess the primal serpent at your loins."

"Uh, well, I can't help that. Listen, maybe I'd better get going."

Cy tries to push his way out of the pack of fleshy amazons. Hard-nippled breasts and silky limbs yield, but do not give.

"Oh, don't go," pleads Mary—or is it Marlene? "The Queen's such a fuddy-duddy, just cuz she's the original. Don't listen to her. We could have such a good time together. Couldn't we, girls?"

"Yeah!" Marlene—or is it Mona?—reaches down and grabs Cy's aching prick. "We have so much energy, you see, we have to use it up somehow. And it gets so tiresome, just playing with each other. Can't you help us?"

"I don't know...." utters Cy unconvincingly as his prick swells even harder beneath Mona's—or is it Marion's?—randy squeezes. "I have to get back pretty soon...."

"Don't worry about *that*," says Marion—or is it Myrtle? "Time's different down here. We're operating on Molecular Time."

(What the wily mitochondria are refering to here is J.B.S. Haldane's division of time into five categories, based on the range of biological events. Molecular Time, where events culminate between 0.00001 and one second. Physiological Time, where events transpire between 0.01 second to one hour. Developmental Time, where the interval is .5 minutes to 70 years. Historical Time, which is N generations. And Evolutionary Time, which is 10,000+ years. Obviously, most of us are consciously concerned mostly with Developmental Time.)

"Oh, well," demurs Cy, "in that case...."

Gah-rate! This is all the horny mitochondria have been waiting for. Girls just wanna have fun, ya see! Myrtle pushes Cy onto his back onto a convenient organelle mattress, and he's instantly covered with female flesh.

He's fucking components of his own cells! It's a one-organism orgy! Girls, girls, girls—they go to his head like red wine!

There's one beautiful mitochondria sister riding his prick and one on his face.

His fingers are buried in two mitochondrial cunts, as are his index toes. These gals are collectively insatiable. As soon as one is satisfied by tongue or cock or digit, she dismounts and is replaced by another. Luckily, this little representation of Cy, this horny homunculous, seems infinitely potent also. Jesus, he must've come a hundred times by now! Are these girls lining up for seconds? How can he tell them apart? Even the Queen must've joined in by now! Cy starts to worry. How's he gonna escape? Has anyone ever faced this problem before, trapped within his own body by nymphomaniacal mitochondria? He can't even yell for help, with a succession of pussies shmooshed onto his face. Who would help anyway? Even Big Daddy Nuke don't have no control over these Man-Starved Bisexual Lesbians....

American Woman, let me be! Get these dirty pillows away from me! Take these hips to a man who cares!

Just as Cy is giving up the ghost, resigning himself to an endless existence as cellular stud, he feels himself slipping away from beneath the mitochondria, vanishing from within himself.

"No, come back!" the Cellular Sisters of Melusine clamor. "We're sorry we were so selfish. You have to visit our sisters in all of the other cells—there's billions. They want you too!"

"Arrgh!" screams Cy at the prospect. Then he's out, out of his own treacherous body, back in the bedroom with Polly—

—who, while he was gone, has stripped, flipped Cyril over, tied him to the bedposts with odds 'n' ends of Leather 'n' Lace, and is now riding his cock horse to some destination other than Banbury Cross.

He should have known it would come to this. By cooperating with Polly's unnatural desire for bondage, he's created a monster. How can he even sleep peacefully now at night, wondering whether he'll wake up tied to the mast like Odysseus, at the mercy of his personal Siren?

Cy tries not to cooperate, to express his displeasure at this uninvited Gulliverian treatment. However, Polly's exquisite manipulation of his cock with her canny cunny, the memory of his debauch with the sex-mad mitochondria, all these things conspire to undermine his resolve, and he's soon thrusting as fiercely as his bonds will allow.

Polly's slippery sliding accelerates, she screams, grinds her mons almost painfully against Cy's pubis, producing an upwelling of magma from deep inside him that jets out in torrents from his buried prick.

Then she falls forward onto his chest, unconscious.

"Polly? Polly, wake up! Cut me loose!"

Cyril wiggles under her. It does no good. Finally, he just gives in and lies there.

Five minutes later, Polly regains consciousness. "Cyril? Oh, Cyril, I'm so sorry! Here, let me get those...."

Breaking the sloppy bond between them, Polly moves to untie Cy, explaining herself.

"You were thrashing around so badly, I thought you were going to hurt yourself.

I had to tie you up. Then I tried to get you back from wherever you had gone, using *qigong*. But you didn't respond. Finally, sex seemed the only thing left. Especially since you had gotten so big...."

Cy is somewhat mollified. "Well, okay. But no more tying me up without my permission."

"Oh, of course," says Polly humbly. But with a smile, she adds, "Did you like it?"

"I think I would have liked it just as much without the gimmicks."

"Well, you never know until you try...."

Polly comes to cuddle with Cyril, and they briefly doze.

When Cy wakes, there is a new bit of knowledge in his brain, which seems to have been planted there by his experiences within his own cells. It is so important that he rouses snoring Polly to share it with her.

"Pol, listen. I know why we're so attracted to each other."

"I thought that was obvious."

"No, there's a predestined aspect to our relationship. It has to do with the four nucleotides that encode all living things."

"It does?"

"Yeah, it does. Look, it's so obvious I should have seen it ages ago. The four bases are adenine, thymine, cytosine and guanine. A-T-C-G. It's us, you and me, Ruby and Augie. Augie, Tuesday, Cyril—"

"How do I become 'Gee?'"

"Hmmm.... What's your middle name?"

Polly goes white. "Guinivere."

"Guinivere?"

"It was Mom's idea. She's such a romantic."

"Well, there it is. Adenine, Augie; Thymine, Tuesday; Cytosine, Cyril; Guanine, Guinivere. It explains our attraction for each other. Adenine always bonds with thymine, and cytosine with guanine. My God, I've been living with the wrong woman for ten years!"

"Cyril, I don't know about you, but I don't choose to regard myself as just a nucleotide—"

"You're not *just* a nucleotide, but on some level our nucleotides are meant for each other. Okay, I can deal with it if I have to. Ruby and Augie will just have to understand. Maybe they're even shackin' up together already somewhere. Lord, what am I saying, they're probably dead, killed by Wu for learnin' too much, just as we're gonna be—"

"Cyril, calm down. Our friends are not dead, I won't let them be. And we're on the way to finding them. Holy cow, look at the hour! We'd better get moving if were going to reach GreenGenes in time."

Cyril is half-dressed before he realizes something.

Polly didn't say, "Our mates."

She said, "Our friends."

Pretty Miss Purine and her base-pair beau, Mister Pyrimidine, finish dressing. Polly dons a shirt from Sam Ash's Bowlarama which she got for free (cuz of the misspelling of the name as SHAMASH'S BALARAMA) and a pair of your good old Black Denim Trousers, along with some retro Mucha' Linda Beatle Boots. Cy, his sartorial consciousness never raised (despite years of subtle and not-so-subtle hints from Ruby, such as burning certain of his clothes), simply slips into a black T-shirt advertising the Sidewinders and some grubby jeans. A pair o' shades completes his look.

Down on the street, Cy feels relief. Out in the street, I walk the way I wanna walk, I talk the way I wanna talk.... Anxious to learn the contents of the mysterious CD, he starts trotting downhill toward the fairly distant Haymarket subway stop, not even pausing to ask where they're going, or how. It's just an inbred reflex now, after years of shuttling back and forth in a subterranean fashion, for him to immediately dive underground. The boy's got what psychologists specializing in urban complaints call "The Orphic Reflex," or "metrotropism." Everything pulls you underground. The search for Eurydice just goes on and on forever. Leastwise, till the Mænads tear you to pieces....

A few paces away from his front door, Cy realizes that Polly's not following. He turns to urge haste, and sees her standing patiently with arms folded across her chest.

"What's up?" asks Cyril, rejoining her.

"When you went missing, I had to have some wheels to help me find you. So I had Daddy buy me some. And I was just so sick of travelling on that grotty subway. I thought we deserved to come up above ground, out in the open. Besides, the trains didn't go where I had to go."

Went missing.... That sure was accurate. I don't know why I went missing. It could have been the call of the night, it could have been a change of mind. But though lost, I found myself, right where I'd been all the time....

Cy shakes some musical notes out of his ears. "So why didn't we take these wheels to the hospital?"

"Well, I didn't exactly buy a little old lady's sedan. When I thought you might be sick, I felt you shouldn't be riding anything quite so, um, breezy."

"You got us a convertible?"

"I guess you could say that. C'mon."

Polly conducts Cy down the alley beside their tenement.

As they approach the small cloistered backyard hung with drying laundry—some wild shirts—furious barking resounds, followed by the rattling of a long chain. Two neighbors pass quickly by, one saying, "The Vice President's gone mad...."

The barking emanates from Mrs Scozzafava's Neopolitan Mastiff, Moses. Man, this beast is loud! He's making enuff noise for a dog with three heads....

When the pugnacious pooch recognizes Polly, he goes all wimpy, contorting his body into positions of doggie abasement. Polly fondles his massive head; Moses naturally thrusts his snout, conveniently at crotch level, right into Polly's recently be-cummed snatch.

Cy has never been able even to approach this monster, and is a little jealous, especially with Moses's nose occupying what he's come to regard as his turf.

"We've gotten very friendly since you've been gone," explains Polly. "When I was scared one night, Mrs Scozzafava even let Moses sleep with me."

"Yeah, yeah, great. Now, where's this— Holy Leader of the Pack!"

Cyril has spotted one slick road machine. Gee, it must be nice to have rich folks.... He lifts his Raybans to further appreciate the sleek steed. It's a 1000cc Yamaha Virago, this year's model. Born to be wild, yeah. Cy feels like Lou Reed in a commercial.

"Pol, this is just super! And you can drive this thing?"

"Was Pope Joan a woman?"

That Polly! Just when Cy thinks he's got her number, she pulls another surprise on him!

As his recent Intrabody Experience has left him disinclined and unwilling to argue about the relative superiority of male over female or proper gender roles, Cy indicates his approbation with a double thumbs-up. Polly swiftly straddles the bike, whereupon Cy slings a leg over the saddle-seat and snugs himself behind her.

"We're going to Lowell," says Polly. "That's where Daddy's company is."

"Oh, right, I forgot. Boy, that's quite a haul. Hey, isn't that where Wang Labs is located?"

Cy's referring, of course, to the Bay State ailing digital empire of the helpful ghost he met at the Athenæum, Doctor An Wang. The Wang syndicate, natch, fails to match that of Wu by several orders of magnitude.

"Yes, it is," affirms Pol.

"Maybe I should stop in and tell 'em the Doc looked okay when I saw him on Monday."

"I don't think that's wise, Cy."

"You know best, doll. So, what's it gonna take, about an hour to get there?"

"About. But don't worry, we can talk during the whole trip."

"Gee, Pol, it's sorta hard to shout for an hour...."

"Who said anything about shouting?" asks Polly, as she lifts two Darth-Vader helmets from where they hang by their chin-straps on the handlebars. Cy inspects his. Holy Marconi, it's one of them dee-luxe models, got the built-in microphones 'n' headphones. They're gonna be Two Transceivers On The Road Of Life, just a-sendin' and receivin' messages as they barrel along.

"I'm psyched," says Cy. "Let's go."

Dig it, f-f-folks! Before you can say, "Oh, Lord, would you buy me a Mercedes Benz?" the duo have left the city proper behind, heading north on Route 93, just chattin' easy like they was in their own home. Life's the same, except they're moving in stereo. Sweet dreams are made of this!

Cyril is still busy permuting the issues raised by his Sixty-four Questions, and takes this chance to share some of his thoughts with Polly.

"Did you know that both the Aztec and Chinese Han calendars incorporate the exact same theoretical flaw, which could never have arisen from actual astronomical observations?"

"No, I didn't. What is it?"

"They included too many lunar eclipses. As Professor Nathan Sivin says, 'They could never have noted so many, unless they had a branch observatory in Boston or thereabouts.'"

"Hmmm."

Polly drives very well, but very fast. Cy holds on tight and feels secure. If only they could just forget all their problems and race down this highway forever.... This road runs all the way to Paraguay.... Why *can't* this be love...?

Zipping through the slower-moving traffic, they pass a wildly painted schoolbus with the California license plate MAZ 804. Hippies are hanging out the bus windows, and the psychedelic relic is weaving erratically.

"The Dead must be in town," ventures Cyril.

"I can see why you'd say that."

Some little kernel embedded in Polly's response nags at Cyril for a few minutes, until he prises out its significance.

See why. He never thought about it, but the shortened form of his name's a rebus. C–Y = See Why. Has his christening predestined him to ferret out answers? Does this explain his fascination with the mysteries of history? It's too spooky to contemplate for long....

West for a short distance on Route 128, past the sign that boasts AMERICA'S TECHNOLOGY REGION, and the one that simply proclaims TOURIST INFORMATION, and a third which, in a child's scrawl, offers NIGHTCRAWLERS. Then north again on Route 3, bringing them soon enuff into Lowell.

Hit the road, Jack Kerouac, on your way to the Beatnik Beach! He was born on the road on the Fourth of July, and he'll live on the road till he sees fit to die! Did you possibly fuck Polly's Mom when she was young, and is Polly the way-gone fruit of your Beat loins...?

Polly maneuvers them into the parking-lot of the GreenGenes building, a modern, low-slung structure, all reflective glass and steel, set on a greensward licked by the tongues of sprinklers. (Cy recalls their recent, near-fatal encounter with Mister Water Wiggle, and shivers, despite the hot sun.) Dismounting and doffing their helmets, they head inside.

Polly gets the standard gushing Boss's-Daughter Treatment from the receptionist, a fetching Bengali gal named Shakti Shagbush, while Cy is tolerated as a harmless non-entity. Shagbush telephones the person they are to meet.

While waiting, Cy sizes up the public face of GreenGenes, as exhibited in the reception area. Very chic, yet suitably hi-tech. For instance, many of the framed prints on the wall look merely like abstract compositions in shades of grey, until you realize that some of them are blown-up photomicrographs of chromosomes. Others, resembling blurry barcodes, are magnified prints from the gel electrophoresis process. There is some actual fine-art stuff: mainly the numero-mystical paintings of one Alfred Jensen.

An inner door opens and a young Oriental guy with shiny black bowl-cut hair, round glasses and a big smile comes thru. He's wearing a hacker T-shirt that reads: DON'T GET EXCITED, IT'S ONLY ONES AND ZEROES.

"Cy, I'd like you to meet Tommy Tsunami. He's the one who got a readout on our disc."

Tsunami and Cy shake hands and avouch as how they're glad to meet. Then Tsunami says, "I never could have done it all on my own, though. I had to call in an old buddy for help. Hokyo Zammai. He works for—"

"The Lottery," says Polly somberly. "He's Augie's boss."

"Oh, you know him? Good, he's here right now."

Cy's so excited at the prospect of finally learning what's on the Kryptik Disc, that he hasn't much patience for all these pleasantries. "Can we get down to business now, please? This is very important."

"Sure. Follow me."

Tsunami conducts them down corridors and through mostly empty labs. They pass a rank of Hood gene-sequencers. These $100,000 machines can read 12,000 base pairs a day, sequencing one small gene in that time. Cy wonders what material the busy instruments are deciphering right now. Mystery achievement, so unreal....

Finally they arrive at Tsunami's own work area, a cubicle filled with books, papers and a power-user's Sun Workstation. Beside the computer sits a disc-drive of a sort Cy's never seen.

Resting in a chair next to the desk is a portly, balding Japanese. He gets to his feet and shakes hands all around. He's got large mitts.

"So invigorated by your acquaintance, Sweet Gams! Augenblick-san has spoken of you so radically. And you likewise, Cyril, dude. Now, up to brass tackheads! I'm understanding this disc comes from my buddy, Augie? It sure would interest me to know where he laid his hands on such a thing."

"I sold it to him," explains Cyril, "thinking it was just music. But since it was pressed by Wu Labs, and since they seem to want it back desperately, we're convinced it contains some secret information that we can use."

Zammai scowls at the mention of Wu Labs. "Once again, that big pain in the anus crops up in my worthless life. All I want since I came here forty years ago is to meet that *hsien*. I give up love of my life to become his disciple. But he eludes me forever. He can bite my Jade Stalk!"

Cyril recalls his talk with his nephew Arthur. "*Hsien*? You're claiming Wu is one of the heavenly immortals who walk the earth?"

"You can bet your bottom dollar-ninety-nine on that, kiddo."

"Oh, man, I just don't know. If Wu's already immortal, then that makes hash of our notion that he wants to control time."

"Not so fast, bunky! Maybe Wu is Time's Puppet, not the other way around."

Polly interjects, "This is all just speculation. Let's get to the contents of the disc."

Rubbing his hands together gleefully, Zammai says, "Ah, yes, contents are most interesting. But even more interesting than contents are the methods of encoding!"

"Why's that?"

Zammai ejects "Crawling Kingsnake" from the drive and holds it up for inspection. Rainbows shimmer. "As you hepcats have already dug, this disc cannot be played by either a conventional movieola or audio CD player. Number One Reason: you need Blue Light Laser to read it. Blue Light Special, ha-ha! Number Two Reason: wacky encoding. You see, this type of disc, which normally holds a mere six hundred and eighty megabytes of information, has been made to hold thousands of times that amount!"

"How?"

"First you must understand that there are two types of information on this groovy disc, each encoded differently. The first is a simple little sentence of three billion characters. The alphabet involved consists of only four letters: Ay, Cee, Tee, and Gee."

"The nucleotides!" blurts out Cy.

"You're locked onto the beam, Prothero-san! This disc holds the entire genome of an individual. But Gödelized! Each of the possible sixty-four codons has been assigned a different prime number, and those numbers multiplied to produce one enormous, yet easily encodable figure. Instead of three billion times eight bytes, the entire genome has been compressed into a few measly Kay!"

"And you've somehow been able to decompose this humongous number into its three billion factors?" asked Polly.

"Solid, Jackson! You better believe it! We now know the entire transcription of someone's DNA."

Zammai's somewhat unbalanced demeanor does not inspire total confidence. Polly and Cy look to Tsunami for confirmation.

T.T. shrugs. "Don't ask me how, but he did it. I would have sworn it was impossible, but I witnessed him work it out on a Hewlett Packard scientific calculator!"

Cyril says, "I thought that transcribing someone's entire Dee En Ay had never been done before. That's what Watson's Human Genome Project is undertaking, isn't it?"

"Don't believe everything you read in *The New York Street Journal*, kiddo!" advises Zammai.

Polly offers this salient slant on things. "Transcription is just information. But I'm willing to bet that whoever did this also has knowledge. I bet they know what genes are where, what the metastatements are which turn them on and off, the reading frames—all the higher order functionings."

"Now if we could only count on them having wisdom, everything would be copacetic, babe!"

Tsunami, echoing a K-tel record offer, says, "But wait—there's more! There's information elsewhere on the disc that seems to be—and this is just an educated guess, mind you—a record of all synaptic connections. A map of trillions and trillions of neural hookups, chemical gradients and action potential thresholds." Tsunami smiles proudly. "Deciphering that was my contribution. You see, I had just been reading about the work of Michael Barnsley and Alan Sloan, at Iterated Systems. They've developed a method for compressing graphics on disk at a ratio of five hundred or better to one. What they do is let recursive fractal equations represent the forms, instead of bit-mapping them. So I called them and got some tips that allowed me to reverse the translations that this data had been put through. The key seems to be those fractals known as 'dragon curves.'"

"So," Polly says slowly, "this disc contains the sum total of an individual's nature and nurture. The genes that originally shaped him, and a record of his brain—and hence all his experiences, a gestalt of his self—at some point in time."

Tsunami nods, and Zammai says, "Tell it like it is, My girl Lollipop!"

"But what the hell can you do with this information?" asks Cy.

"Good question," Tsunami says. "Of course, if you had some method of expressing all the genetic information—inserting it like a virus into an embryo, say—you could recreate the individual physically. Short of that, you might load the neural map into a computer and simulate just the personality. That is, if anyone could devise routines to mimic the functioning of the brain. It'd take an awfully big and fast machine, though...."

Cy slaps his forehead hard enough to hurt. "This is it, then. Wu's method of immortality. We know everything now!"

"Considering nature of your opponent," suggests Zammai, "I would not be so cocky-locky."

"Can we see some of this data on your system?" practical Polly inquires.

"Sure," says Tsunami, loading the disc into the CD-ROM drive. He begins to tap some keys. The clicks sound weird to Cy, as if he can interpret them as binary instructions. Is he a component of this system? Let's investigate. Give into it, Cyril, become one with the hardware, find out what your role is! Okay, our boy's getting into it now, it seems he's part of the optical disc drive.... Could it be...? Yowzuh, it is, he's suddenly become

## PROTHERO THE PHOTON

Cy has just emerged phrom the Blue Light laser inside the drive, travelling at the speed o' light. He realizes he looks like a gleaming white ping-pong ball. He's a photon, pure and massless, a Son O' Light. Particle Man, Particle Man, doin' all the things a particle can! Phunny, he doesn't pheel any dipherent.... Altho he has only a phew millimeters to traverse until he hits the disc, Cy's mental processes are commensurately phast, and he is able to look around himself as he zips along.

Millions o' other little white ping-pong balls—his phellow photons—are all neatly lined up and streaming along with him. It's like being in the army. Well, this *is* coherent light.

As the photons pass thru the phirst collimating lens, on their way to the polarization beam splitter, they begin to sing, sounding just like The Seven Dwarves.

### THE PHOTONS' SONG

Oh, we're just some phestive photons,
As weightless as a pheather,
Phlowing with our phellows
In Light's unbreakable tether!

We'll zip phrom Sun to Earth
In only eight phast minutes,
Bounce phrom a box into your eyes
And show you just what's in it!

Cy interrupts. "Hey, guys, what's up?"

"Oh," replies one photon, slightly different phrom its brothers, "nothin' much. We're just involved in a Read Operation. Say, you're new, aren't you? What's your name?"

"Cy."

"Cy? That won't do at all. You'll have to change it."

"How come? To what?"

"Oh, something like Phred, Phorest, Phrazier, Pharnsworth, Phelix, Phrodo, Phenton, Pherdie, Phrederick, Phaphnir, Phoghat, Phoster, Phloyd, Phabian, Phrancis...."

"Which name is yours?"

"Oh, I'm Phranc."

"Hey, wait a minute, you're a girl!"

"Shhh! Don't tell anyone!"

"Okay, I won't. Well, how 'bout if I call myself Philip?"

"Philip?" says Phranc. "I don't know. That doesn't seem quite right...."

They are dephlected by a mirror, and pass thru a phocusing lens. Looking up just then, Cy sees looming overhead a giant, shiny, whirling, rephlective rooph, philled with pits. The disc—

"Hold on to your head!" warns Phranc the phriendly photon.

Then they're hitting the disc.

Some o' Cy's compatriots, including Phranc, vanish into the pits. Others bounce phrom the non-pitted portion o' the disc. Cy is one such.

"Ouch! That hurt!"

Now Cy's heading back down, to a photodiode sensor. Wow, this is some trip. Wait one mo', bro', what's at the end o' the trip? Where do the captured photons go? No light leaks out o' the drive, therephore they all must be destroyed. This is death! He's going to serve his purpose, conveying inpho about the location o' the binary pits, and then croak!

Phuck that!

"Help, help! Get me outa here!"

Drizzle, drazzle, druzzle, drone, time phor this one to come home....

Cy's back in his regular bod.

Tsunami, Zammai and Polly are staring at him.

"Bad case of AIDS, kiddo. I suggest you go home and investigate your chick's Jade Terrace."

"Are you with us, Cy?" asks Pol concernedly.

"Uh, yeah, sure. Look, there's the nucleotides and some dendrites...."

Shure enuff, on the screen in one window is a portion of a seemingly endless string: ACCGGTCATTACGACCTACTCCATTTGTCCTTACGGCATGCATTG ACCTAGGAACTGCTGCCCGTAAACTGAACTGACTGACTGGGAACATTGTCAAACT CTACTGTGCTGACTGA.... (Hereafter refered to as GAG CAT.) In another window, a net of simulated synapses sprawls.

Cyril is suddenly impatient, wanting to apply this new knowledge. He can practically feel Ruby back in his arms....

"C'mon, Polly, let's take the disc and split. We've got something to bargain with now."

Cy reaches to eject the disc, but is stopped by Polly's puzzled expression. "Hey, Pol, what is it?"

"Just one last question for Tommy and Hokyo, Cy."

"Yeah?"

"Exactly *who* is *on* this disc?"

"Holy Lao-tzu, babe. You would have to think of that one, wouldn't you?"

"There's no identification I can find in the actual data," says Tsunami.

Cyril brushes the question aside. "I sure don't have any guesses, and I don't necessarily even want to know. Isn't it enough just to understand what the disc is, and know that Wu wants it?"

"I suppose...."

On the way home, Polly follows a different route which brings them into Cambridge from the west. Her voice reaches Cy over his helmet speakers.

"Dad's throwing a business party tonight, and he invited us."

"Sounds like fun. I feel pretty good, now that we know the full extent of Wu's schemes. Now it's just a matter of reaching the proper person in the organization and bargaining for the return of Augie and Ruby. Maybe that O'Phidian guy.... I think we deserve to celebrate, don't you?"

"Wild, wild horses couldn't drag me away from this party. Dad's affairs are usually pretty swinging. I think he's even hired the Mudmen to play. But I do suggest we grab some dinner first. There's usually not much besides finger food at the bash."

"Sounds cool. You have any place in mind?"

"I wanted to try this new restaurant in town. It's mixed Australian-Jamaican-Indian cuisine."

"I'm up for that."

As Polly manuevers them through town, Cy experiments with his headset. He learns that it can pick up AM radio. On the air now is the news.

"Our leading story: at Massachusetts General Hospital today, physicians were unable to save the life of a child born to the Vermicelli family of Brookline, who perished in a classic example of Sudden Infant Death Syndrome. Doctor Black Elk, spokesman for the hospital, commented: 'We do not expect a rash of SIDS deaths, as the soul of this infant was particularly malignant, and has doubtlessly already passed through Stage Two of the Chonyid Bardo, to reside in the Avici Hell of hungry ghosts.' Next up— One moment! We have just received reports of an explosion mere minutes ago at the world-famous Ritz-Carlton Hotel. Although eyewitness accounts differ, the explosion seems to be the result of an attack, possibly by terrorists, with a missile of some sort. All that is definitely known is that an aerial object impacted with the building at the tenth floor, resulting in the complete destruction of a single room. The only casualty appears to be one Maxwell Parallax, a private investigator. No body has yet been recovered from the rubble...."

Holy shit!

Cy's back on their private channel in a flash. So is Polly. Synchronicity—apparently she was listening to the same station.

Polly's voice is choked with sobs. "P-p-poor Max. It's all our fault!"

"C'mon, Pol, we don't know that for sure. Parallax's death might not even be related to the work he did for us. Anyway, he was an adult, he knew the risks."

"D-d-do we?"

Well, that Polly's sure one for posing Sphinxian riddles today. What can Cy say, except for, "Hey, watch the road!"

They're in a district sprinkled with eateries now: ALICE'S RESTAURANT—WE'VE GOT ANYTHING YOU WANT. PAAVO PAVONINE'S PEACOCK BURGERS. Also, a Taco Bell (MANAGER LOTTA ESTRUS), with a mock howitzer out front which is fired hourly: The Taco Bell Cannon!

Soon they're in the lot of the restaurant in question. They get off the bike, Polly sets its kickstand and they remove their helmets. Polly's eyes are bloodshot, her cheeks wet.

"Hey," offers Cyril, "maybe going to this party tonight isn't such a good idea. We could head home...."

"No, I'd just brood even more. And sitting around in a funk wouldn't help Max. Let's stick to our original plan. I'll try to cheer up, Cy. Honest, I will. After all, Max's misfortune doesn't change our good luck."

"If you feel up to it...."

They enter the restaurant, which is named THE LAMA'S BLACK GONG. A giant iron temple gong suspended by chains held in the mouths of two dragons occupies the lobby. In the darkened interior, Cy can discern that the interior furnishings are an eclectic mix befitting the multi-continental nature of the establishment.

A woman approaches. She appears to be an intriguing blend of African and Indian heritages. "Hello, my name's Rita Amrita, and I'll be your hostess for the evening. A table for two?"

"Please."

Amrita conducts them to a table in the exact middle of the crowded restaurant, hands them menus, and departs.

Now begins the part of their meal known as:

INTERPHASE

Polly studies the menu for a while, then says, "I can't decide. You order for me, Cy."

"Okay. If only—ah, here's our waiter."

A dreadlock-bedizened black man, exhibiting a smattering of Australian features, arrives at their table. "Bunny Bamapana here, yahso! State yuh preference fe drinks, Jah willin'."

"I'll have a Foster's Lager, and the lady'll have one of these Instant Karmas."

"I and I be right back."

"Gee, did you read this, Pol? This restaurant was founded by three Korean War Veterans. I wonder if they knew Parallax."

Polly starts to sniffle at the mention of the deceased P.I., and Cy regrets bringing the subject up. While Polly dabs at her eyes with her napkin, Cy eavesdrops on neighboring diners (which, natch, is half the fun of eating out).

Two secretary-type gals off to his left side, drinking what Cy recognizes as the latest in-drink—Vanilla Ice T's with colored Ice Cubes—are talking about work.

"Those wicked germs gave me the cramps I sure didn't have a Happy Monday this week."

"A jam like that drives me bananarama! I remember once I had this date with a real New York doll. He was a regular buzzcock, not a revolting cock. None of your sham sixty-nine. Well, wouldn't you know my boss, that deadhead Kennedy, kept me working till eight that night. When I got to my apartment, I felt like raising a black flag. That lush had gotten so drunk, he made a swerve, took the fall and was lying on the pavement, slanted and enchanted and knocked out loaded!"

"Men!" says the other with disgust. "Have you ever dated a crackhead? Well, I have, and let me tell you— He took me once to this chapterhouse, a regular house of pain. Inside, there's all these lemonheads and baseheads sitting around a water-pipe, smoking a superchunk of sebadoh. Well, against my better judgement, I joined them for some dee-lite, and soon felt like some kinda eugenius, a regular member of the Thinking Fellers Union Local 282. The Ace of Base was there, and he and my boyfriend got chummy. Before you knew it, it was Us3 alone, and we started counting crows, if you get my drift. They slipped their phish in and popped both my cranberries at once!"

Bamapana returns with their drinks. "Yuh ready ta order, mon?"

"Uh, sure. We'll both have the same thing. We'll start with this *ragout de cassareep*, followed by the *curry de kangourou avec witchetty larve.*"

"Good choice, mon."

Bamapana takes the menus and leaves.

Cy raises his glass of beer, and Polly lifts her frothy umbrella-topped drink. She seems to have recovered herself. They toast.

"To our success."

"Or something approximating same."

The drink goes right to Cy's head.


## PROPHASE

When they first sat down, Cy sensed a kind of social barrier around their table, isolating them from the other diners, who all seemed to be regulars. He wrote it off as imagination. But now he can sense this same barrier dissolving, opening them up to the rest of the crowd.

At the same time, Cy notices several busboys waiting patiently at stations on opposite sides of the room. They seem to be watching him and Polly....

When they're half done with their drinks their first course arrives.

Cyril's eye is caught by another waiter simultaneously arriving with the same dish at another table not too far off, where a man and a woman sit. Squinting, Cy thinks to detect something familiar about the other pair. The woman looks rather like Polly. She winks back at Cyril. You saw me in the restaurant, you knew I was no debutante.... Her companion, tho, is a real loser: a kind of snotty, confused, arrogant, badly dressed unathletic dude with pink skin wearing sunglasses.

"Hey, Pol, take a look behind you. That woman kinda resembles you."

Polly glances discreetly back, to find that the other couple is simultaneously looking at them. "And that guy looks just like you."

"What?! You're outa your tree!"

But then Cyril experiences a strange kind of split in his consciousness as soon as Polly identifies the guy as his doppelgänger. From that moment on, till meal's end, he feels like he's inhabiting two bodies at once, viewing the restaurant simultaneously from two distinct points of view.

Bamapana is waiting patiently with a giant combo spice-dispenser, and another waiter just like him is standing by the other couple.

"Want some Salt-n-Pepa, sir and sir and madam and madam?"

They squared decline.
"Let's try this stew," says Polly and Polly.
Cy and Cy raise two spoons to their mouths.

## METAPHASE

At that moment, the sound of an intense sudden summer shower rattles on the roof of the restaurant.
A leak begins to drip into the Cyrils' two bowls of stew.
Immediately the busboys rush over, several to each table. They are carrying cords and stanchions, which they set up in a complicated arrangement to mark off the area under the leaky roof.
"Excuse me, sir and madam, sir and madam. So sorry for this inconvenience. No, no, don't get up, we'll just pull your chairs and table back."

## ANAPHASE

The busboys begin dragging Cy and Cy and Polly and Polly toward opposite sides of the room, sloshing the stew out of their four bowls.
"Hey," says Cy and Cy, "watch it!"
"So sorry, sir and sir."
Cy's and Cy's doubled vision of the restaurant is growing more confusing as his two points of view separate further and further. He and he feel like their brains are going to burst. He and he can tell from the expression on Polly's and Polly's faces that she and she are feeling the same way. The vertigo is so bad now that he and he swears the walls of the restaurant are starting to move—

## TELOPHASE

The restaurant is pinching closed down its middle.
The walls are moving to meet, sealing one Polly and Cy off from their duplicates.
More bemused than scared, Cy waves goodbye to himself.
The walls are almost touching now....
They meet.

## END OF MITOSIS

Polly and Cyril are back in the middle of the room, which seems the same size it originally was, tho half of it must now be hidden away, along with their duplicates. The rain has stopped, and there is no leak. The social barrier separating them is back. Moreover, Cy cannot experience himself in two bodies anymore.
Setting down her spoon, Polly says, "Whoa, horsey.... That was some ride."

"We must be pretty beat if we let a single drink do that to us."

Bamapana arrives with their second course.

"How dat cassareep sit wit' yuh, bredren?"

"Okay, I suppose...."

"Good, good. Here de 'roo an' grubs."

Polly and Cy consume the rest of their meal in silence.

Presented with the bill, Cy asks, "What's a good tip?"

"I don't know. What does one customarily tip for an out-of-body experience?"

"I'll make it twenty percent."

When Bamapana returns with their change, he's also got two Chinese fortune cookies.

"Compliments of de house."

Cy opens his. It says: *A foreigner from Kansas—a judas priest, a motorhead night ranger, a loverboy—will rush on a journey past Cinderella's twisted sisters, past def leppards and gentle giant ratts from the sepultura, across the quiet riot of the poison Styx.* Not too enlightening....

Polly's reads simply: *Original Mind is the Way.* You don't say....

Outside, they hop on the wet seat of the Virago and bop around the block to the Peptide manse.

Once in the door, Polly heads upstairs to freshen up for the party.

Cy's left alone in the parlor with Mrs Peptide. He prays she will not make any lewd remarks to set off his overactive imagination. Luckily, Polly's Mom is busy stocking the bar, and merely comments, "So, Cyril, you work in a record store...?"

"Not since it was blown up by snakes."

"That's nice...."

Well, your mother should know....

Time passes. Night falls. Pretty soon, guests start to arrive.

Mister Peptide and Cyril greet them by the door.

"This is George Golgi, Cy. He works in the bio biz, as do most of the guests tonight."

"Goodtameetcha," says Cy.

"And this is Ralph Ribosome."

"Hi."

"Larry and Linda Lipid."

"Hello."

"Charlie and Cassandra Centrosome."

"Whazzup."

"Zoe Zymogen."

Wow, this gal is zaftig! "Very pleased to meet you."

"The same, I'm sure."

"Lionel Lysome."

"Howdy, Lionel."

"And the Mitochondria sisters, Millicent, Matilda and Mavis."

"Gaaahhh! I mean, ga-ga-glad to make your acquaintance."

"Say, you're cute!"

"Are you spoken for?"

"*We're* not."

"Uh, sorry I can't stay, girls, but I have to mingle. Suh-suh-see you later."

"We sure hope so, handsome."

"The night is young."

"And so are we."

Cy moves hurriedly away from the predatory Mitochondria sisters, looking for Polly. Jeez, wotta coincidence....

Sizin' up the ruckus. Mudmen are bangin' away at "Claude and Del Shannon Are Lovers." Anyone dancin' on the ceilin'? Are we havin' fun yet? Two-zero-zero-zero, party's over, oops, out of Time. Tonight we better party like it's 1999....

The main room where most of the people have congregated (many more have arrived after the M sisters), and where a buffet is laid out, is already very crowded. People are packed elbow to elbow. Everyone seems to be exchanging fragments of talk and touching with whomever they're with, then moving on to other groups. There's a constant interflow of people as little knots spontaneously disintegrate and reform. Only the group holding down the center of the room seems relatively stable.

Meanwhile, Cy can hardly move. He spots Polly across the room, signals, but is unable to get to her. Instead, peristaltic waves carry him to the food.

The caterers have laid out a chi-chi spread, mostly, as Pol predicted, nibble-type goodies. The waiter behind the table is dressed like a cowboy, altho he's a fat smiling old Asian whose nametag reads HELLO MY NAME IS SALOTH SAR. Must be Tex-Mex food. Hmmm, that Australian-Jamaican-Indian cuisine don't sit with you long. Kinda hungry. Think I'll grab some of this 'n' this 'n' this....

"Say," inquires Cy, mouth half-full, "what's this meat?"

"Rattlesnake."

Cy coughs up the masticated mess into a napkin. He's suddenly lost his appetite....

Mister Peptide arrives at that moment with his arm around a little Filipino gent. "Cyril, this is Epifanio Pagano. He represents a firm that must remain nameless for the moment. They're very interested in investing in GreenGenes."

Cyril abstractly shakes the guy's hand.

"Allow me to get you a drink, Mister Cyril," says Pagano. He dips a ladle of punch for Cy. Does his beringed hand hover suspiciously over the punchbowl for one brief moment? Does something plop and fizz? Does his inscrutable Asian face betray the teensiest leer?

Cy can't decide, then promptly forgets it. Sipping his punch, he tries a different tack to reach Polly.

Halfway across the room, the delta-sensorium with which Pagano has spiked the punch hits, seasoning Cy's funky skull soup.

'Scuse me while I kiss the sky at eight miles high! Let me take you higher, cuz everybody must get stoned! It's journey to the center of the mind time, no crystal blue persuasion necessary! I smell incense and peppermints, crimson and clover! Strange brew, see what's inside of you! What light! Shine on, you crazy diamond! It's all too beautiful! Hey, is that a girl named Sandoz, or just Lucy in the sky (with diamonds)? Maybe Judy in disguise with glasses! See Emily play in the Strawberry Fields forever! Are you experienced? Don't ask me, talk to the snake who's wearing the Crown of Creation. He lives in-a-gadda-da-vida, and you get there on the magical mystery tour....

Cyril stops, Polly forgotten, his brain totally rewired.

Something new has manifested itself. The room is apparently filled with a filmy network of tubules, a lacy three-dimensional organic web. Everybody seems to be attached to it, moving only as its structure dictates. Cyril tries to think what it reminds him of....

Of course, it's the ol' endoplasmic reticulum, the internal framework of the cell. Nothing to worry about, must've been there all the time, just like the Tao....

The party's getting rowdy now, as more and more people fall under the influence of the adulterated punch. They're gonna tear the roof off the sucker and give up the funk! The group in the center of the room have found a couple of leftover balls of crêpe paper from the decorations, and are playing some sorta game with it. They unwind its enormous snaky length—there's barely enough room in the crowd—lay a second length alongside it, then rewind the two strips in a supercoiled double helix....

Weh-hell, Cy's groovin' on this endlessly repeated ritual when all of a sudden, as trips will, his trip turns bad. If you see me getting high, knock me down, why doncha?

The endoplasmic reticulum becomes tuff dead strings tied to the limbs of the partiers, all of whom now look carved from wood: pictures of matchstick men. It's a dead man's party. All the strings merge and vanish through the ceiling, up to the Big Puppeteer In The Sky. When the strings jerk, the wooden people move in a horrible parody of life. Even Polly has been transformed into a hideous puppet.

Cy looks down at himself. He's the only one free and human. Nobody seems to notice anything's wrong except him. They don't even know they're being jerked around, they think it's free will.

It's your standard paranoid's nightmare come true. Mama told me not to come! I feel like I'm 2000 lightyears from home! How'd it go from mellow yellow to ball of confusion so fast?!

Cy screams.

The next instant, the room is gone.

Under the influence of the delta-s, Cy has somehow teleported himself upstairs, to the room of Paulie Peptide, Junior.

The autistic lad is under his usual restraints, helmet, gloves, etc.. But, thank Christ, he hasn't been transformed into a puppet.

Cy slumps down into the corner with Paulie, hugging him cuz he's real.

Eventually, after some indefinite time, during which no one comes looking for him, the delta-sensorium begins to wear off. At least, Cy thinks he feels more normal. He begins to consider rejoining the party, although his lingering vision of the puppet-people still creeps him out. What will he see if he returns? Can't put it off forever, he supposes....

Releasing Paulie, he stands. Say, what's the matter with the Kommunicationless Kid? His eyes are blinking a mile a minute. Never heard of that particular autistic display before....

Hey, is there a pattern to it? Both eyes are never open at once. It's either both closed or one open. Could it be—?

Zero or one! Paulie Peptide is blinking a binary message to him!

"Whoa, slow down," says Cy.

Paulie miraculously obeys, and Cy begins to translate.

At first, the message makes no sense. Then Cy realizes his mistake. It's EBCDIC configuration, not ASCII. Let's see, 1-1-1-0-0-0-1-1, that's T, 1-1-0-0-1-0-0-0, that's H, 1-1-0-0-0-1-0-1, that's E....

THE CENTER IS EMPTY.

Repeated over and over.

Gah-rate. A real heartening thought at a moment like this, on top of everything else he's just undergone.

"Thanks, kid, but I already suspected as much."

Cy heads back downstairs.

Halfway down the carpeted stairs, he encounters Polly coming up. Thank God, she looks like her old self. He must really be recovered.

"Oh, Cy, I'm so glad I found you, I was starting to get worried. The strangest things have been happening."

"Tell me about it...."

Linking hands, they begin to descend.

"Do you hear helicopters?" asks Polly.

At that instant, giant shafts of blinding light shoot in through every window of the house. Guests begin to scream. What the fuck is this, alien invasion? The next moment the front door is demolished by an enormous bulldozer poking its blade through and taking half the wall with it. (These are tactics approved by Presidential Directive 101 in the War on Drugs.)

It's a violation of Membrane Integrity! Every Organelle for himself!

Cy and Polly watch from their vantage-point as armed men pour through the gap and take up positions throughout the house. One sunglassed agent levels his Uzi at them in particular, and they raise their hands high.

Last to enter is a little rodent-like guy with a twitchy face, apparently in command.

He raises a bullhorn to his mouth.

"Oh-kuh-kuh-kay, duh-duh-dope fiends," bellows Emmett Demesne, Government Virus, "the juh-juh-jig is up!"

Chapter 00001110

# It's A Foxy World

# K L U E S

00110100
"The equation is more intelligent than its author."
—Paul Dirac

00110101
"As far down as you *can* go, you *will* go."
—Rickie Lee Jones

00110110
"Time will end
And Man must be
Mindful of Eternity."
—Hutterite Hymn

00110111
"One man's noise is another man's signal."
—Edward Ng

B e-bop-a-lula and shimmy, shimmy, ko-ko-bop! A-weema-weh, a-weema-weh and da-doo ron ron! Do-wah-diddy, diddy-dum, diddy-do and chicka-boom, chicka-boom! Boom-boom, acka-lacka-lacka-boom and de-do-do-do, de-da-da-da! Shoop-shoop and fa-fa-fa-fa-fa! Shoo-be-doo-be-doo-da-day and shu-doo-pa-poo-poop! Nee-nee-na-na-na-na-nu-nu and um, um, um, um, um, um! Shting, shtang and papa-oom-mow-mow. Karma, karma, down, dooby-do, down, down and mmm, mmm, mmm, mmm!

That's the inarticulate but persuasive sound money might make if it could talk! Money talks and nobody walks! (I hate to say it, but I know it's true.) The Golden Rule, natch, is: he who has the gold makes the rules. The money mind don't want much—just all you've got! Serve it for eternity! Carry around the coins that comprise your chains while you're alive, and smell the smoke of burning Hell Money after you're dead.... "Maybe, baby, I'll be your money honey. Would I lie to you? Would I tell you something that wasn't true?"

Anyone who says rock 'n' roll's only topics are cars, sex, drugs and love has forgotten money, the synonym for all four. Sometimes you can hear the clink of coins in every rattle of a tambourine, the whisper of bills in every slurred vocal. Bill on a hook, baby in a pool. It just makes you wonder why even the dumbest fun has to be touched by the Money Mind....

Weh-hell.... The money in question today, of course, is Mister Peptide's small fortune, and the not inconsequential prestige that goes along with it.

The lucre and status together are able to clear up very soon—well, at least by morning's bleary light—the whole embarrassing contretemps of last night's misdirected drug bust. In these Ruff Economic Times, the Commonwealth—scared of sinking lower than a "Baa1" bond-rating—has been bending over backwards anyway for the owners of any business that utilizes a technology more advanced than steam, and to have one of the state's leading hi-tech entrepreneurs and his family and friends jailed cuz of an obvious misunderstanding based on what in hindsight had to be a malicious tip is not to be borne for one minute longer than the slow wheels of justice need to release the injured parties on bail, with the assurance that all charges will soon be dropped.

Of course, it did not hurt that Mister Peptide used his one Konstitutional Fone Kall to summon his cadre of high-priced all-female lawyers in love, who peddle their legal expertise under the moniker of Jam, Lewis, King, Goffin, Spector, Holland, Dozier, Holland, Leiber, Stoller, Gamble, Huff, Oldham, Epstein, Parker, and Gordy.

With these sixteen high-powered paper-pushers, these affidavit Amazons, clogging up the station-house, tossin' off torts and droppin' their briefs, it was not long before the forces of Law 'n' Order threw up their hands and surrendered their captives. I fought the law, and the law didn't win!

After all, when you came right down to it, the cops didn't have a third leg to piss outa.

The trouble, you see, is that Agent Demesne arrived too late. The spiked punch was entirely gone when his forces broke in, and analysis of the sticky residue in the bottom of the bowl revealed only certain non-categorizable short-chain molecules that were the non-unique endpoint of the degradation of the delta-sensorium which Epifanio Pagano had dumped there. Blood tests on the arrestees were no more incriminatory. A simultaneous raid on the GreenGenes lab in Lowell failed to reveal the expected facilities for the production of the Schedule Zero drug, which was hardly surprising, since the real manufacturer was, as we all know, Wu Labs, one rogue organelle of which was still seeking to advance the numinous cause it had pioneered decades earlier with pixeldrine.

Thus did Demesne fall neatly into the trap engineered by Lao Cohen, *et al*. Busting a respected businessman and his guests on the strength of a phone call; causing thousands of dollars worth of property damage in two locations; opening the city, the state and the Federal Government to possible lawsuits for zillions of dollars; impacting the ecology of People's Republic of Cambridge without undertaking a prior six-months study (the chopper-noise had exceeded proscribed decibel levels)....

Weh-hell, you can imagine the level of shit Demesne found himself in. Not only was it up to his nose just a few hours after his ill-calculated raid, but it showed every evidence of rising.

Here we take our final leave of Emmett "Eminent" Demesne, treading the fecal soup of his own making.

(Oh, all right. For the incurably curious and those who like and insist on Happy Endings, this is what later happened. I shouldn't pander to you this way, but I've got a big heart to go along with my round-the-world Big Money.

(Demesne was recalled to Washington. At the Logan airport ticket-counter, facing a gorgeous Irish soubrette soubriquetted Brandy Finegal and embarrassed by his failure, he stammered an excuse that was to prove truer than he could ever imagine: "Guh-guh-gimme a tuh-tuh-ticket for an airpuh-puh-plane, my buh-buh-baby juh-juh-just wrote me a luh-luh-letter." He boarded shortly thereafter, full of trepidation. He knew he was about to be drummed out of the corps, and possibly jailed. He didn't think he could survive the humiliation and incarceration, and had already made plans to hurl himself into Moloch, the Treasury Furnace that had eaten his mentor.

(On board the air-shuttle, Demesne ate salted peanuts and drank eight beers. ((He overheard a stewardess say, "Sweet Regina's gone to China," but thought nothing of it.)) Over DC, the shipboard speakers crackled: "This is your pilot, Captain Hiawatha Du Danaan, folks. I regret to report we've just lost the contents of our toilet due to a little explosive decompression. Seems like we're dropping bombs on the White House. I thank you for your confidence, and fully expect to land this sucker without further snafus. And remember: Burning Airlines gives you so much more...."

(Miraculously safe on the ground, Demesne reported to his new boss, Jehovah Anguipede, Kennebunkport Yankee Jew.

(Anguipede pulled the same old control riff on Demesne that Faber had used over twenty years ago, making him stand on his gimpy leg while under silent inspection. Finally, just as Demesne's strength was giving out, Anguipede spoke.

("Demesne, you're a liability to the agency now. We can only do one of two things to you. We can stage a show trial and stick you in a Federal penitentiary. Or we can assign you a low-profile suicide mission. Well, what'll it be?"

(Programmed as he was by his Operation Fagin upbringing, Demesne naturally chose the latter, true to the valiant, albeit doomed cause he had long espoused, the worldwide elimination of illicit drugs.

(He immediately underwent cosmetic surgery to give his physiognamy an Oriental cast ((the surgery failed to alleviate his tardive dyskinesia, which had a neurochemical basis, so that his new face still possessed all the old twitches)), was braincrammed with a new language and identity, and parachuted into the jungles of the Golden Triangle, there to infiltrate the Doi Lang stronghold of the Burmese warlord, Khun Sa, and undermine his operations.

(Mission of Burma time, fer shure!

(Everything went hunkydory—up to a point.

(Demesne—or as he was now known, Bukdo No Rong—managed to insinuate himself into the warlord's confidence and become his second-in-command. One day, as a reward, he was presented with a harem of Burmese Giraffe-necked Women, also known as Dragon Girls. Having been celibate—save for the occasional numismatic wank—ever since his childhood infection, Bukdo faced his biggest challenge yet in satisfying these half-dozen Kama Sutra Succubi. He could hardly refuse them, for Khun Sa would take such an action as a personal affront. But to try to service his new harem and fail would lose him enormous face.

(Much disturbed, Bukdo took a lonely walk down a jungle trail, trying to figure out a solution to his plight.

(Far from the settlement, he was quite startled to see approaching him a mysterious figure he recognized as Khun Sa's own private red-haired mistress, who seldom strayed from the warlord's quarters.

(Bukdo stepped off the path to let her pass.

(She stopped, performed an ironic salaam-bow, and pulled aside the veil she always affected.

(It was Vivian Vervain!

("Hello, Em," she said sweetly. "Good to see you."

(His left eye and the corners of his mouth were twitching like a metronome. "Vuh-vuh-vivian. Guh-guh-good to suh-suh-see you tuh-tuh-too."

("I guess working different sides has kept us apart up till now."

(Bukdo grew serious. "Wuh-wuh-we're still on duh-duh-different suh-suh-sides."
("Oh, come on now, Em. Don't be such a stick-in-the-mud. We can still have a little fun." With this Vervain put her hand down Bukdo's native skirt.
("Duh-duh-don't be cuh-cuh-cruel to a ha-ha-heart that's tuh-tuh-true, Vi. I can't!"
("That's what you think, honey. I've learned a lot since I made that ol' poultice thirty years ago." Vervain whipped off Bukdo's skirt, dropped to her knees and, with fingers kneading various of his *qigong* points, began to suck him up to full alert.

(Braced for pain, Bukdo experienced only pleasure.

(Vervain had never worked or waited so long to bring about an orgasm, but it finally happened, and she thought:

(*Here cums your man!*

(When the blissful rapture had passed, Bukdo hung his head and had a good cry.

("There, there," comforted Vervain, "it's never too late to have a happy child-hood, Em."

(Bukdo looked up, his features calm. "Do you really think so, Vivian?" A look of astonishment passed over his face. "My god! I'm not stuttering. And my face— My tardive dyskinesia has disappeared!"

("That's Sexual Healing, honey. Now, let's have the booster shot!"

(The effect of this miracle cure on Bukdo's personality was nothing short of awesome. All his anal-retentive compulsiveness vanished. He became an easy-going hedonist who, when not busy screwing Vervain or his Dragon Girls, drinking or eating, was only too glad to help his liege extend his drug-dominion around the globe.

(A destiny that leads from the hills of North Carolina to the hills of Southeast Asia is strange enough; but one that leads from Treasury Agent to Oriental Opiate Poten-tate is touched by the dark miracle of chance which makes new magic in a dusty world....)

The sidewalks of Boston are privileged this early morning to a strange sight. Outside the main police headquarters on Berkeley Street, a bunch of White Punks On Dope are blinking in the dawn, which is howlin' while the mainframe shakes; these perps feel like they've been sleepin' in a cellarful of snakes. (Inspector Dolan and Offissa Bill "Bull" Pupp stand in the doorway, scratching their heads at the fucked-up outcome of this weird bust.)

Clad in party clothes, dressed up to get messed up, the partygoers obviously never counted on such an ending to their evening. One by one, released by litiga-tion-lysis from their jail-cells, they drift off, Golgi, the Lipids, Ribosome, and the rest, shattering the matitutinal quiet with goodbyes. (The Mitochondria Triplets, placed in the hookers' tank, made some new friends they were reluctant to leave. We woulda said the hookers were a bad influence on the M gals, but then again, angels and prostitutes may look the same.)

Finally, only Mom 'n' Pop Peptide and Polly and Cyril are left.

"Sure you won't ride home with us, kids?"

"Thanks, Dad, but I've got to stay with Cy. We've got some unfinished business to attend to."

"Oh my gracious!" cries Mrs Peptide abruptly. "We've forgotten all about Paulie Junior! They never booked him, so he must be home all alone—"

Mister Peptide's pipe drops from his mouth with a clatter onto the sidewalk. "Good gosh, you're right, Mother! Taxi, taxi! Quick, get in, dear. So long, kids—"

The convenient Aion Taxi roars off, under the capable hands of H. CHAPIN, otherwise known as Driver Eight.

Cy and Polly are left alone. Bone-tired, their Virago parked in Cambridge, they begin to walk toward the Arlington Street subway stop and home. So much for that old Jailhouse Rock! Have mercy, Judge, or we'll all spend Christmas in prison—but after thirty days in the hole, there's gonna be a jailbreak, fer shure!

"Okay," says Cy. "What's next?"

"I guess we just call up Wu Labs like you said, and try to get in contact with someone high up enough in the corporate structure to bargain with us."

Ah, Polly, such a straight-ahead gal! But the best laid plans of mice and men gang aft agley—which, translated, means, Expect The Unexpected and Don't Look Behind You—You Never Know What Might Be Gaining On You.

They're back in Cy's apartment only a second or two when the phone rings. It's Polly's Dad, sounding upset. Polly takes the receiver and immediately blanches and hangs up.

"Pol, what's wrong?"

"It's Paulie Junior—he's missing!"

"Oh, Christ, another one! Listen, we'll head over there right now."

"No, I mean, yes, I'll go alone. Mom's too upset to have anyone else around. They've already called the police, and that agency I mentioned, the Ningishzida people, so there's nothing either of us can really do. I just have to be there though. And I can pick up our cycle."

"Sure, Pol, I understand. Jesus, where could he have wandered off to? Has he ever done anything like this before?"

"No. He's incapable of it. That's what so strange...."

Cyril and Polly kiss goodbye. Then, still holding Polly, Cy voices a thought.

"You remember how I told you about that Nazi I saw during my orgasm, and how he claimed I was protected by your fetish?"

"Sure...."

"Well, I was thinking that it wouldn't hurt if we ever had to be separate again if I could, um, share some of it...."

Polly gets nervous. "You mean open my fetish and divide its contents?"

"Well—yeah."

"Cyril, I've never dared look inside that bag once since I got it at age three. It's like my own personal Jesus! What if I see something inside that destroys my faith? What if opening it ruins it?"

Cyril releases her, nobly protesting, "Never mind, then. It's all right. I'll just take my chances."

Polly bites her lower lip. "I'll do it, Cyril. Just for you, I'll do it. But I don't want to know anything about it. I'll close my eyes while you divide whatever's in there. And don't tell me what it is."

"Gee, Pol, I feel better already."

Cyril gets a ziploc from the kitchen. With Polly squeezing her eyelids so tight her lashes disappear, he draws her fetish from beneath her shirt.

The knotted leather cord securing the mouth of the bag is tight with the passage of so many years. Cy has to go for a fork, whose tine he slips thru the knot.

The knot's undone. Color me blue, and call me Alexander, son of a snake! He puts a finger in the top of the bag and waggles it open.

He removes his digit and looks in.

Space goes wonky, kinda like when they witnessed Ferdie Lantz disappearing inside the floatation tank. Looking into the bag is like looking out an open window.

Inside Polly's spacious fetish, Mister Maxwell, hardworking Demon Librarian, semi-reclines in a lawn chair beside a swimming pool, his hands busy moving molecules. Behind him is a green lawn with a flaccid Water Wiggle athwart it. Maxwell's gross and corpulent brick-red body is bare, and the resplendently naked Tourquoise Courtesan, her back toward Maxwell's face, her feet on the poolside concrete, her hands braced on the chair-arms, her head tossed back, black hair trickling down like a waterfall, is busy sliding up and down his jumbo cock, which, Cyril can now observe, is studded along its length with assorted fleshy wart-like protuberances.

Mister Maxwell spots Cy. "Hey, kid, good ta see ya! C'mon in, the water's fine!"

"Are you done yet, Cy?"

Cyril unfreezes. He hurriedly snugs the bag shut and ties a quick knot. Polly opens her eyes.

"Well, did you do it?"

"No, no, I changed my mind. You need it more than I do. I didn't take anything! You're all set. Have a safe trip, say hello to your folks, and don't be away long."

Polly stares at Cy. "Are you sure you're gonna be okay?"

"I'm sure. Listen, I'll try to get in touch with Wu while you're gone."

"Okay. Be careful now."

"I will."

After Polly's gone, Cy drops weakly into a chair. Mister Maxwell.... AIDS hallucination, or all too real? Polly's protection since youth? What does everything mean? Will he ever know?

Nope, you never will, Cy!

When his heart has slowed down, Cy hops on the phone. He keys in the number he called on the afternoon Ruby disappeared. (Was it only, lessee, twelve days ago?

It seems so much longer....) Call me on the telephone, ring it off the wall.... Two rings, and someone picks up.

Cy says, "Hello?" before he realizes it's a recording.

"The number you have dialed is no longer in service...."

What the hell—? Cy frantically punches up 411.

"Information. What city, puh-leeze?"

"Boston. Wu Labs."

"I'm sor-ry, that num-ber is now unlisted."

"Unlisted? Lady, we're talking about a multibillion-dollar company whose shares are traded on the New York Stock Exchange. They don't have no unlisted numbers."

"I'm sorry, sir, but that's the only information I have under that name."

"Goddamn!" Cy shouts, and slams the receiver into its cradle.

Weh-hell, this is a fine mess. All they can hope now is that the company hasn't pulled up stakes physically as well, and that they're still located out on Route 128, at the end of the commuter bus line Ruby used to ride each day. When Polly gets back, they'll just have to cycle out there and brazen their way in.

Meanwhile, tho, Cy doesn't know what to do with himself. Ain't it a shame how dependent he's become on Polly? What kind of guy is he, mooning around just cuz his girl's gone? I'm so tired, tired of waiting for you.... Run off to her family, will she? Leave him on his lonesome? He'll show her he's still independent! He'll go out and learn some more!

A destination has suddenly dawned upon Cyril. He's going to visit an old history professor of his, a man deeply versed in all of Clio's more intimate nooks, one who knows her very G-spot, who perhaps can verify or supplement some of Cyril's theories derived from his own researches.

Cy goes into the bedroom to change out of the clothes he's spent the night in. When he's dressed, he scoops some bills and coins—the pitiful remnant of the money his sister lent him—off the dresser top.

Hey, l-l-look who's here! It's Impy the Imperial Dollar, almost forgot about him. Fondling the dollar, hoping to get some more flashes from it, he puts it in his pocket. Donning dark glasses against the world's scrutiny, Cy departs.

Out on the street he reconsiders his recent passing vexation with Polly. What came over him? This whole mess is making him too irritable. He'll be glad when it's over, and his usual *sang-froid* returns. As it is now, what with the disappearance of Polly's brother, and the unavailability of Wu Labs (at least—and hopefully, only—by phone), he's feeling sorta low. He's got them rattlesnake, underworld, X-rated, zombie walkin', talkin' World War Three blues....

Maybe this visit to his old prof will help. Cyril experiences a sudden realization: he's not looking for additional information. He's already got more information from his own researches and celestial milk-suckling than he can handle. No, he's looking for—well, a different reading frame, one that will allow an innocent interpretation of everything he's learned.

Quite understandably, he just wants someone to reassure him that the last three thousand-plus years of history are not a record of the manipulations of a lone immortal Chinaman and his scattered serpent-worshipping followers.

Put that way, his request doesn't sound so unreasonable now, does it?

In a short time, Cy stands outside the home of his former mentor. The man lives in an elegant apartment building on the Avenue Louis Pasteur, not far from the campus of Northeastern U., within sight of the Fens. (Cy experiences a heightening of his unease at the name of Pasteur, recalling Questions 11 and 41 on his list.)

Trying to stifle these disquieting thoughts, Cy buzzes the proper apartment. From a rusty speaker grille above the buttons comes a burst of staticky syllables, sounds like a praying mantis trying to talk by rubbing its legs together.

"Zzzhurp. Krrrick. Vrrrrww. Pazzz. Gnnnert."

"Professor," yells Cy into the intercom speaker. "Is that you? It me, Cy. Cyril Prothero. Let me up, please, I have to see you."

"Hrrrix."

Simultaneous with this reassuring confirmation, the door-lock's solenoid is remotely activated with a click, and Cy pushes in.

The interior of this pre-WWI building is dim and old-fashioned. What must be the original faded floral wallpaper still hangs, patched with wood-framed prints behind glass so time-distressed as to render the illustrations invisible. The doors are massive oak slabs. Whenever Cy visits the Professor, he always feels as if he's just stepped into a Henry James novel.

Remaining on the ground floor (since there are no elevators here, the Professor is obliged by his handicap to live on the first floor), Cy walks to the back of the building. At the farthest door, he knocks, calls out, "It's Cyril, Professor," then enters the man's apartment.

Professor Mal Sfortuna sits, as always, in his electric wheelchair. His traditional black suit fails to conceal the full range of his deformities. His limbs are thin as crayons, and warped to boot. He's got one glass eye and a complete set of false teeth. One shoulder is lower than the other. His face is cadaverous; his pate shows through wisps of hair. Hawking *redux,* thinks Cy.

It's hard to believe that Professor Sfortuna was once a varsity track-star, but it's true. (The only lingering affectation the once proud-as-a-peacock fellow has is the wearing of fine cologne, namely Bijan's DNA scent.) Harvard Class of '54, Sfortuna was a true Renaissance man, athlete and scholar. Then one day in his senior year, studying in the Widner Library, he pulled the wrong book out of the stacks.

This book—although Cy doesn't know it—was a Victorian tome entitled *Serpent Worship*, by one James Ferguson, F.R.S. Its thesis was that the snake was mankind's oldest god, deity of a prehistoric, almost prehominid religion.

This volume, which Sfortuna so unthinkingly tugged on, was supporting the entire wall of shelves on which it rested. The book hadn't been touched since 1924, when Thomas Wolfe quickly flipped through it in his mad attempt to ingest the entire contents of the Widner. In the intervening three decades between the visits of Wolfe and Sfortuna, the shelves in this little-visited room had gradually buckled and deteriorated at various points in such a fashion that Fergusson's book came to function as the keystone of the whole edifice of knowledge, the entire primitive database. (Nice thing about electrons—they weigh less than paper and leather.) A stretch of shelves ten feet high by twelve long now pivoted precariously about the axis of this book.

When Sfortuna tugged the dusty tome from its niche—and for the rest of his life he would marvel at how easily it slid out, considering all the weight it bore—the entire structure with its tons of books collapsed on him. He was buried in history.

That Clio is one heavy main squeeze!

Sfortuna lay pinned beneath the wreckage, his hand still clutching Ferguson's book. It had come open during the avalanche, and one page of it was now pressed into his face.

Sfortuna knew he was close to death. The stress triggered an episode of psychic ability. He was able to epidermally read the passage pressed into his cheek. It said:

"Although fear might seem to account for the prevalence of the worship, on looking closely at it, we are struck with phenomena of a totally different character. When we first meet serpent worship, either in the wilderness of the Sinai or the groves of Epidaurus, or in the Sarmatian huts, the serpent is always the Agathodaemon, the bringer of health and good fortune. He is the teacher of wisdom, the oracle of future events. His worship may have originated in fear, but long before we became acquainted with it, it had passed to the opposite extreme among its votaries. Any evil that was ever spoken of the serpent came from those outside the pale...."

Sfortuna passed out then. His rescuers did not notice, beneath all the blood, the flaming words burnt reverso into his cheek, which later faded.

Sfortuna's resulting injuries left him paralyzed from the waist down and confined to a wheelchair. Deprived of most of the physical half of his life, he turned for solace to his undiminished mental abilities, eventually gaining Harvard's first triple doctorate (history, quantum physics, and ping-pong; due to his twisted joints, and by treating the ping-pong ball as if it were a massless quantum particle, Sfortuna was able to put unique spin on the ball, completely out-foxing his opponents, who had never before seen the celluloid spheroid behave in such a manner: zig-zagging, reversing, looping, stopping inertialessly.... He went on to play against the Chinese team during the era of Ping-Pong Diplomacy.).

For a time, Sfortuna taught at his alma mater, leaving in a huff only when Harvard awarded Henry Kissinger an honorary degree. (Sfortuna abominated Kissinger for his role in the destruction of Cambodia.) He then came to Northeastern, in time to have a formative effect on Cyril's intellectual career, most notably with his startling book, written in collaboration with the Oxford Biblical scholar Dr. Geza Vermes: *Lilith's Twin*.

Sfortuna's lap is filled with remote-control devices. These gadgets make his life easier, for he is able to activate many appliances in his apartment without stirring. Unfortunately, each appliance requires a separate unit, and Sfortuna is always getting them confused.

"Hello, Cyril," says the Professor now. He picks up a control unit, aims it at Cy and presses a button. Nothing happens.

"Was I supposed to respond?" asks Cy.

"No, no, of course not. I was just trying to close the inner door behind you, but this must be the wrong control. Oh my goodness, I wonder what I've done instead. I hate getting my signals crossed...."

"Professor—do you smell toast burning?"

"Yes, damn it, it's my breakfast! I must have changed the toaster setting. Quick, Cyril, could you get it? Oh, and you may as well shut that door, if you will...."

When Cyril returns from popping up the toast, he says, "Gee, Prof, you need a Master Remote...."

"Ah, if only life were that simple.... Now, what can I help you with? You sounded most urgent...."

As best as he can, without going into his own personal problems, Cy offers a precis of his findings. He tries to present them neutrally, not wanting to influence Professor Sfortuna's conclusions. At last Cy winds up his rap. He pauses, then remembers his list of 64 Questions, which he has purposely brought along. Taking it out and unfolding it before handing it to Sfortuna, he says, "Oh, yeah, there's this too."

Sfortuna studies the list for a few moments in silence. Then he raises his permanently canted head to confront Cy. His face shows disappointment. "Cyril, lad, just what are you getting at?"

Cy struggles to express his crazy, half-formed ideas, which have never seemed so nebulous as they do under the keen scrutiny of Professor Sfortuna.

"Don't you see? Take Number 54. All those countries achieving independence in such a short time span, after so many years of colonial domination— My God, the vast majority of the world's population has achieved self-government only in the last forty years. Why should the imperialist masters have given up after centuries of having things their way? What turned on the silent genes? And why does it all coincide with the formulation of information theory? It's too much to accept that it's just the result of blind historical forces. There's got to be some active motivator—a Prime Mover, if you will—behind it."

Sfortuna shakes his head ruefully. "I thought I taught you better than that, Cyril. You can't seriously subscribe to the Great Man theory of history. History is just what you denied: the result of huge blind forces, the myriad composite interactions of a faceless mass of men and women. It's useless to look for evidence of all-encompassing plots and conspiracies in the plethora—the superabundance—of historical data available to us in the twentieth century. Not because you won't find them, but for precisely the opposite reason. You can selectively assemble bits of evidence in infinite patterns that will prove anything. Have you ever heard of the work of the mathematician Frank Plumpton Ramsey?"

"No. What's the connection?"

"Ramsey proved that complete disorder is an impossibility. According to his work, every large set of numbers, points or objects necessarily contains one or more highly regular patterns."

"Okay, granted. But Professor, you don't know—"

Cy stops. What's he going to tell Sfortuna?

That he's suffering from a kind of AIDS which allows him to receive extra-sensory information?

That he was nearly killed twice, once in a pile-up of four driverless cars, and once by a rampaging Water Wiggle?

That people are disappearing left and right, one of them shrinking and vanishing in a floatation tank?

That a horde of dragonflies tried to make off with their beach blanket?

That Planet Records has been blown up because of a CD that possibly contains an encoded person?

That he's fucked his own organelles?

That he teleported under the influence of some kind of new drug?

That a Fortune 500 company has apparently cut off all communications with the world?

That his new girlfriend wears a fetish with Maxwell's Demon inside it?

No, it's ridiculous. No one who hasn't lived through it will believe it.

Cy retrieves his list and repockets it. "Thanks, Professor, I'm sorry to have bothered you. I guess it was a pretty crazy idea. I'll be going now."

Sfortuna tries to say goodbye, but Cyril has gotten him so upset that the academic has developed a wicked case of the hiccups. The crippled old savant is hic cuping so bad, in fact, that his speech is completely obscured.

"Hiccup! Hiccup-hiccup! Hiccup-hiccup-hiccup-hiccup! Hiccup-hiccup-hiccup-hiccup-hiccup-hiccup-hiccup-hiccup!"

Cy rushes into the kitchen to get the Prof a glass of water. Unfortunately, it has no effect. Various other remedies are just as useless. Finally the Professor signals by an impatient wave of his hand that Cy should leave, and he'll be all right. Fumbling for the door control, Sfortuna succeeds only in turning on the television, radio, cassette player, blender, coffee-pot, VCR, vacuum-cleaner, dishwasher, massage-bed, ceiling-fan, air-conditioner, stove, and several lamps. A little radio-controlled red toy Chevy skitters about underfoot, racing in a circle.

At last the door is opened, tho, and Cyril, shouting to be heard above the din, says, "SEE YOU AGAIN SOME DAY, PROF!"

Cy starts walking down the Fenway, feelin' kinda glum. Happy people are sitting out on the grass by the water. How dare they? Saturday in the park, thought it was the Fourth of July....

Having unconsciously raised his hopes that Professor Sfortuna might be able to clarify the farrago of information he has assembled, Cyril now suffers the consequent letdown of having been given no help at all—and in fact of being absolutely squelched. (Why didn't he just get down on his knees and say, *Build me up, Buttercup!?*) And there was so much more he had wanted to ask Sfortuna, information that was gradually seeping into his brain....

Why did the July, 1954, issue of *Vogue* feature James Watson ranked with other pop stars? (*Cf.* Kinski, 1981.)

Did Funk Software in Cambridge have any monetary connection to Wu Labs? What was the background of Otto Funke of Leipzig, who in 1851 devised the first method of deliberately preparing blood crystals, thus laying part of the groundwork for molecular biology as we know it today?

(Ain't it funky now? And if it's not, why then—make it funky! Animate your backside, you'll be my inspiration. Animate your backside, funk is our salvation....)

Was the passage of the domestic Freedom of Information Act karmically balanced by the strengthening of the United States Information Agency, which sought to control information in the Third World?

What was the significance of the expansion of the Group of Four (US, UK, France and Germany) to the Group of Seven? (The Group of Seven has as its primary chore the management of international rates of currency exchange. They drive the value of selected currencies up and down like yo-yos, according to their arcane policies.) Was there any connection with the demise of the Gang of Four (Madame Mao and associates, not the rock group of the same name)? And who are they waiting for to make it the Group of Eight?

Why was Cambodia the only nation ever to be ruled by a man whose name formed a perfect palindrome (Lon Nol)? And what of the recent internecine fighting between Siahanouk's sons, the Two Princes, one who adores the country but is poor, and the other who's rich? (If you wanna send me flowers, just go ahead now!)

Why was Haiti still the poorest country in the Western Hemisphere when it had such a headstart over the others, being the second country in that half of the globe to achieve its independence, right after the US (1804)? Was it because Voodoo required conditions of poverty (i.e., absence of the Money Mind) to flourish and thus perpetuated them? Also, as long as we're in the Caribbean, what explorer christened the straits around Trinidad "Dragon's Mouth" and "Serpent's Mouth"...?

Gaaahhhh! Walking down the street, Cy grabs his own head and shakes it, wishing he could pull it off. Stinkin' thinkin'! This action, natch, attracts a few horrified stares from passersby. He's *got* to stop thinking about these matters. (And does he even *want* to know the answers? What's an answer, and what's a question? I can't even see the lines I used to think I could read between....)

Cy finally admits there's nothing he can do until Polly comes back and they can visit Wu Labs. He's just tormenting himself with his helplessness, which at times is kinda fun (helplessness, after all, abrogates responsibility), but which right now is simply driving him around the bend. Like Elvis the Younger, he just wishes he knew "who put these fingerprints on my imagination?"

Without realizing it, Cyril has come to the Isabella Stuart Gardner Museum, site of a recent big art theft. (And why did the commissioned thieves pass up a Rembrandt, in favor of several lesser works?) It's ten AM, opening hour, and he decides to go in. What could be more relaxing than spending a few hours among humanity's cultural treasures, the results of lofty contemplation by pure-minded geniuses...?

In the lobby, Cy is greeted by a poster that proclaims: LAMIAS AND SUCCUBI: THE PAINTINGS OF FRANZ STUCK.

The image on the poster is a dark-haired naked woman, around whom is coiled a massive snake, its head coming over her shoulder and resting on her breast. Both snake and woman look directly out at the viewer. The painting is captioned "Sin."

Cy back-peddles out, nearly tripping on the doorsill.

So. Where's he gonna go now? Home seems so empty....

Mom. Mom and Dad.

Cyril has not visited his parents in over a year, relying on Sis to carry information back and forth. Things just got too tense toward the end. All they did was harangue him about Ruby. Couldn't he find another girl? If they were serious, then why weren't they getting married? Was he trying to send the ones who loved him to an early grave? Papa, don't preach! Cy often felt like shouting....

Out of everybody, Cy had thought his parents, given their own background, would have understood how it was between him and Ruby. But instead of making them sympathetic, their own history had made them bitter....

Rhiannon Powell was a nice Back Bay girl, born into a family a little down on their monetary luck, but still very intensely cognizant of their glorious heritage as Brahmin grandees. In 1962, Rhiannon was working as a clerk in Filene's. Also employed there at that time was a stockboy yclept Tyrone Prothero.

The two fell in love and announced their intention to marry, even on a farmboy's wages.

Tyrone's heritage was three-quarters English, as indicated by his surname, thus making him, he felt, in the eyes of Mr and Mrs Powell, a fitting mate for their blue-blooded daughter. Unfortunately, his grandmother on his maternal side, one Eva Sighbell, had, in 1914, an affair with a full-blooded blackamoor, a passing sailor named Sam Andriambahomanana, crewmember on the freighter *Shamanka*. This Karnal Konnection resulted in the birth of Tyrone's Mom, Iris.

And such a taint absolutely ruled out any linkage between Powells and Protheros. Against her parents' wishes, Rhiannon married Tyrone anyhow.

Her folks put them through some awful shit, even going so far as to invoke some Krazy Kolonial Law against miscegenation. (Don't folks like these realize that "miscegenation" is just nature's way of tossin' the dice, turnin' up new and valuable gene combinations? Don't worry, Rhiannon—one day you will win.) Eventually, the Powells had moved to Florida, rather than bear "the shame" in the company of all their old friends.

Thus, when Cy, snared by the lovely blue eyes of Ruby Tuesday, sought to repeat his parents' "mistake," they could only envision for him a life of misery, and sought to dissuade him.

All they succeeded in doing was alienating themselves from him, making Cyril feel like he had been born with a plastic spoon in his mouth. I look all white, but my Dad was black....

This all weighs heavily on Cy as he trucks crosstown to the Northampton Stop of the Orange Line, where he will board the train to his folks' home in Dorchester.

At the stop, he dives down the stairs before he can change his mind about this visit.

Heh-hey, what's this rubbish, millions of styrofoam packing cheetos. Cy crunches their little skeletons gleefully, remembering how they attacked him twelve days ago, intent on gobbling up his DNA. They seem helpless now, tho, and revenge is sweet....

At the turnstiles, Cy hesistates a moment before dropping his token. He senses a certain—well, lasciviousness, radiating from the ranked mechanisms. Kee-rist, what can he do but go on thru?

Shure enuff, soon as Cy's hand makes contact with the turnstile he's arbitrarily chosen, he hears: *Just put the coin in my slot, darlin', and come between my legs.*

Striving mightily to ignore this solicitation, Cy pushes thru.

Midway in its racheting, the turnstile stops. Cy's stuck in its chrome crotch!

"Help, help, help!"

A burly Greek-looking cop whose badge proclaims him OFFICER AMPHIARAOS responds to Cy's frantic cries. "Jesus, hold on, buddy, anyone'd think you was bein' murdered."

"Sorry, officer," lies Cy. "But I'm a claustrophobe."

"Yeah, well, I wouldn't boast about your sexual perversions if I was you."

Eventually freed, Cy makes it out to his folks' home without further troubles.

Standing on the steps, he rings the bell. No answer. Cy thinks he sees a curtain twitch at an upper window. He knows they're home; they never go anywhere on a Saturday. He peers intently at the window. Can you see your mother, baby, standing in the shadows?

Cy bangs furiously on the door. "C'mon, guys, it's me!"

Apparently, that's what his parents are afraid of. Cy gets pissed off.

"Okay, you two! This could be the last time, I don't know! All I really wanna do is be friends with you! Don't you even care I'm hurtin'? It's all right, Ma—I'm only bleedin'! And you'll just let it bleed, won't you?! I got some words of wisdom for you—let it be!"

No response. Cy deflates. He turns and trudges off, catching a train to the North End.

Once in his familiar apartment, he's at a loss for how to pass the time. He takes a shower and then a nap, making up for two deficiencies of last night's jail stay.

Waking at three in the afternoon, he eats a belated lunch of fried banana, peanut-butter and baloney sandwiches (the Presley Special) washed down with coffee. He listens to a few records, *Infected* by The The, Steely Dan's *Gaucho* (did "Time Out Of Mind" always contain that phrase, "Tonight when I chase the dragon....," which, Cyril recalls, is slang for smoking opium?).... Then he watches some tube, Leonard Nimoy lookin' for the Loch Ness monster—how hokey—and an old Bogie movie, followed by a commercial for a new Mexican restaurant.

1    LONG SHOT OF WHITE GUY WEARING FAKE MEXICAN SERAPE AND SOMBRERO, HOLDING MARACCAS.

WHITE GUY

*¡Hola, Señors and Señoritas!* Are you looking for an exotic dining experience? Then come on down to El Poco Lobo! We specialize in south-of-the-border cuisine, whether that border is the Mason-Dixon Line—sample our Hot Tuna Alabama or Black Oak Arkansas Bread, or any other of our 38 Specials—or the Rio Grande—nosh on our Flying Burritos, stuffed with meat from genuine Stray Cats, or try our Priest's Special, Sacrificial Heart with Leaves and Grassroots. Guaranteed to be served still beating, or your money back! And remember, all you Freshmen and Lettermen—Saturday is College Night. Free Tequila! So be true to your school and pay us a visit! If you don't drop by, how will *The Wolf* survive?

Finally, Cy settles on some new game show, *Oracle!*

The host is a smarmy charmer named Nikki Styx. "All right, audience, let's have a big hand for today's contestant, Mister Glen C. Jones. Thank you, thank you. Would you like to say hello to anyone in Televisionland, Mister Jones?"

"Just my old Army buddy, Max Parallax, if he's listening. Haven't seen him in forty years."

Cy goes rigid. Wotta coincidence! Sorry, Jones, but Parallax ain't in no condition to hear you....

"Good enough," continues Styx. "Mister Jones, did you bring anyone with you to cheer you on?"

"My wife."

"Ah, there she is. What a good-looking little woman. Me and Mrs Jones, we've got a thing going on! Don't look so bewildered, Mister Jones. Something is happening here, but you don't know what it is, do you, Mister Jones? Just kidding! Mister Jones, he's all right, drinking his beer from metal cans! But enough of this banter! Onto the game! If you can predict, Mister Jones, whether this rigged box, when opened, will contain a dead cat or a live one, you will win a set of gold coins commemorating the independence of all the world's nations, the *Encyclopædia Britannica*, and a deluxe Mr Coffee unit."

"Uh, gee, what are my odds?"

Weh-hell.... After a few hours of this boredom, Cy's eyes are glazing over. Polly still hasn't returned. Cy phones the Peptide home and speaks to a machine, leaving a message. Shit! It's getting late, beyond any possible Saturday business hours at Wu Labs. He can't blame Polly for being concerned about her brother, but they're not gonna be able to hit up Wu today either if she doesn't return soon. Another Saturday night, and I ain't got no one.

Cy works himself up into such a state of agitation that he can't sit still. He's so grouchy and miserable that if he were a girl, we could say he was on The Boston Rag. Pretty soon, Saturday night'll be all right for nothing but fighting.

As the last possible minute when Polly's appearance will still matter creeps by, Cy resolves to leave. Gotta get out, walk off these nerves.... I'm going down to Alphabet Street, gonna crown the first girl that I meet!

So-ho. Cy finds himself down on Washington Street around eight PM, having tromped the city pavements for three hours in a bout of R&R (Restless Rumination). Responding to twilight, streetlights have come on with idiotic precision, stupidly battling the inevitable night. (No Master Hand at the controls....) Neon glows, auto headlights flick Cy with their photonic lashes. (Is that you, Phranc?) The business suits of any Weekend Working Yuppies have been hung up in the closet (possibly with their occupants still inside), to be replaced by good-time nocturnal threads on slinky bods. People seem itchier, motivated more by their irrational, primal halves....

Looking up, Cyril notices he's in the Combat Zone.

The X-rated enclave is a faded remnant of its old self. Most of the strip joints are closed, along with the theaters and peepshows. Seems like the sex-for-money business has been driven underground these days, or perhaps merely democratically distributed across the land, every bedroom with a VCR a private Combat Zone.

It's funny, how close the seedy district is to touristy Chinatown. Cy's heard the hookers are bringing their johns there lately, under the ægis of the local Triad Society, the Ping On. There, on Harvard Street, under the mural that affirms "Love Conquers the Fire and the Dragon," the johns get their Saturday Night Specials.

Memories of Ferdie Lantz lying in his cheap rented room in the HOT–-L-AMI-A, bundled up against the information he could no longer tolerate, infiltrate Cy's brain. What a funky smell that place had. And h-h-how about the sound of couples banging away behind closed corridor doors, moans, slurps, wet squishings....

Ah, the unnatural AIDS-fomented horniness Cy has been subject to for the past two weeks is resurgent now. The whole world seems made of sexual components locked in binary ecstasy. Cy's utterly convinced that everyone and -thing is getting it on right now except him. He tries to fight the delusions down (little Warner Bros clip here of Bugs Bunny trying to lock the whirling Tasmanian Devil in a trunk), but it's too overwhelming. Pump it up, till you can't feel it. Pump it up, tho you don't need it....

Jeez, what's he gonna do? If only he were with Polly, he could bang her till he was blistered.... But he's not. Space and time separate them ineluctably.

A babe 'n' a dude walk by, hip to hip.

"Are you really gonna give it up or turn it loose tonight for me, Dandy?"

"Dandelion don't tell no lies," she says, and gooses his ass.

Holy Christ, Cy's gonna cream his jeans if he doesn't DO SOMETHING SOON!

The lively pitch of a sidewalk barker somewhere down the street leaps up out of the mix to Cy's ears. He moves almost compulsively toward it.

Thus begins a little episode which seems, to our hero's dazzled senses, to go on just about forever. Let's call it

### PROTHERO IN NIGHTTOWN,
### OR,
### ORPHEUS UNDERGROUND

Cy tracks the carny spiel down to the door of a strip-joint—indicated by two superimposed pink neon outlines of an impossibly busty female in slightly different positions, which strobe alternately on and off in a primitive form of animation. (Most of Boston's strip joints are owned by the notorious twins named C.B. and G.B. Omfug, and their cryptic silent partner, Squeamish Ossifrage.)

The barker is the crazy black wildman check-in clerk whom Cy has twice seen at the desk of the HOT—-L-AMI-A.

He recognizes Cy. "How's it hangin', brother? Still looking for a girl? We gotta get you a woman! Velouria? Victoria? Dirty Diana? Natalia? Nadine? Julia? Jennifer Juniper? Corrina, Corrina? Anna Ng? Tell Laura I love her! Say, why don't you come on in? We got plenty of girls here...."

Cy is having trouble swallowing. Altho he doesn't normally patronize such joints, he is unnaturally attracted to this one. Should he venture in? What could it hurt? Maybe witnessing some ecdysiasts shedding their skins will take the edge off his lust to the point where he can make it home. Oooo, I need a Dirty Woman....

The joint, he now observes, is called SHANNON'S DRAGON.

Cyril pays a ten-dollar cover and enters the lounge. Fulla Honky-Tonk Women carrying drinks on trays. The room is lit dimly with red and blue fluorescents; the predominant motifs are velvet and vinyl. Place smells of booze, sweat and musk. It's like being inside your own liver. Cy's reminded of the little journey he made into his orgiastic cells.

He looks around, expecting to spot the lifesize Mitochondria Triplets, but of course they're not here. More devious, Fate is keeping that ace up her sleeve. Cy takes a seat at a table near the empty runway, which is bordered by a rank of mirrors. Seems like a whole room full of mirrors....

Suddenly Cyril feels a stiff nipple in his ear. It's a blonde waitress clad only in a thong-bottom. "Uh, beer," rasps Cy. Guess I'm gonna have a cold one at the DRAGON....

The gal heads for the bar. Is that some kinda tattoo on her rump? Can't quite make it out.... She returns. "Four dollars," says she.

Reluctantly, Cy shells out the cash from his dwindling supply. Better make this one last....

Up on the runway an emcee has appeared, a little Oriental guy wearing Brylcreem, shades and a dirty pair of khaki pants. I'm a little pimp with my hair slicked back, pair of kahki pants and my shoes shined black.... Gee, this guy looks kinda familiar. If only the lights were brighter.... Where has Cy seen him before...?

"Now, gentleman, please give a big round of applause to Miss Zona Pellucida, formerly the toast of Cairo and Paris, now the boast of Boston."

Zona Pellucida? Wasn't that the name of the author of that bad fantasy novel Cyril read a while back? Jeez, guess writing don't pay that well, if the lady's gotta turn tricks here too....

Enters barefoot dark-skinned Z.P. to the accompaniment of anonymous music from a scratchy tape, dressed in her native belly-dancing costume, all spangles 'n' gold cloth. Little Egypt and her ying-yang, fer shure! (Gee, seems tattoos are popular among the employees here, Z.P.'s got one too. Cy glimpsed it briefly as she pirouetted to tantalize the audience.)

Now Pellucida starts to make with the Eternal Shimmy 'n' Shake, classic *houri* moves duplicated by her multiple images in the mirrors. Her dark eyes regard the assembled men 'n' their Ladies Of The Night with a heavy knowledge.

Shux, seems the old-fashioned action ain't enough for this rowdy crowd, tho, cuz they start to boo and whistle. One joker yells out, "We want Nastassia Kinski in a Brazilian shirt!"

Well, the catcalls serve as the signal for Pellucida to unlimber the heavy artillery.

Faster'n Cy can follow, Pellucida's naked—her costume tossed to one side—and writhing in a boneless way. The sight of her naked jiggling flesh is almost too much for Cy. Stop, stop, stop all the dancing, give me time to breathe! Even her reflections are urging him on: *Go to the mirror, boy*, they seem to say.

Suddenly, she freezes. With her bare feet firmly planted, she tosses her torso backwards, so that her palms touch the runway. Her body's now arched like a flesh-colored rainbow, her Mound of Venus thrust toward the clamoring audience.

Cy is so close he can see a liddle pearl of moisture on the tip of one tuft.

Pellucida walks her hands forward, further distorting her body, until her palms are even with her feet, and cranes her neck so that like a yogi she's looking out from between her calves at the audience, which goes wild. Whoa-ho, this girl has got a rubber spine! Rubber Band Girl, fer shure!

In a flash Pellucida uncoils. She's lying on her back on the filthy stage now, cunt still cocked at the audience. It seems the gal's intent on showing she's bi-flexible.

Grabbing her legs around the thighs, she curls up until her face is nearly in her own crotch.

Pausing a moment, she eyes the audience coolly.

Then she calmly extends an unnaturally long pink tongue (like the one that guy in Kiss had) and licks her own pussy.

Holy Kundalini! Cy thought two was the minimal number to make the Worm Ouroboros!

Pellucida jumps up and is gone. The crowd is bringing down the house. Cy is nearly fainting. Wrap it up, I'll take it!

This was not a Good Idea. His Condition is Worse Than Ever. Devil inside, the devil inside, every man and woman, the devil inside.... Maybe he'd better leave....

The emcee is back. Where *has* Cy seen him?

"Wonderful, isn't she? Our own Zona Pellucida. More non-stop entertainment now, gents, with Miss Gloria Numinoso and Friend."

And Friend? Maybe it wouldn't hurt to watch just one more act....

A black-haired Juno hits the causeway, wearing nothing but red high-heels and some prop—a thick length of rope?—draped around her neck.

The really weird thing is, one of her reflections seems to be duplicating her motions half a second out of sync.

Numinoso's weighty breasts bounce with each step. She seems to be alone, what's this jive about a "friend"? Numinoso capers sinuously about the stage. She's pretty and graceful enough, but compared with the antics of Pellucida, her act just don't cut it. The crowd is getting restless, as is Cy, when Numinoso, sensing the proper moment, removes the rope from her neck.

The "rope" is an eight-foot python.

But not just *any* eight-foot python. Cy recognizes it with dead certainty as Three-Card Monte Python!

It's Ophion and Eurynome, Daddy Snake and Mother Universe! (I think this girl's religious....)

Numinoso holds Monte just behind its fat spade-shaped head and at its mid-point. Her biceps are taut with its weight. The snake flicks out its tongue.

A collective shiver ripples thru the male spectators, like the Wave at a football game. They realize on some level that they are facing here their primal competitor, omnipotent power they can never match, let alone excel....

Numinoso begins to dance in earnest now. Her act before was just a tease, a buildup for the primitive carnal desire she now exhibits. The snake, her partner, is all over her, climbing her as if she were a tree in the jungle. It hugs her waist and licks her nipples with forked olfactory tongue. Hanging from her shoulders, Monte dives between her thighs and reappears like a tail above her ink-pricked rump. It slithers down one leg (a garter snake!) and pools on the floor.

Numinoso stands immobile before the coiled snake, eyes closed, sweaty legs braced wide apart on her stiletto heels, her thigh muscles quivering.

The snake lifts its head. Higher, higher, higher, aimed unerringly at her bush. Her crow-black pubic curls are plastered damply to her crotch. Mister Python's head touches her wet aubergine labia.

Numinoso gasps. The snake can be seen to push, push—

The head of the reptile, big as Hokyo Zammai's fist, vanishes up the woman's cunt.

Muh-muh-mother's little helper! Baby, you got what it takes to do the Snake! Is this samadhi, snake in a tube?

The girth of the reptile distends the outer lips of Numinoso's vulva, while forcing her inner coral lips inward. She begins to squeeze her breasts. More of the snake disappears, four inches, eight—sixteen? Holy Powers Of Two!

Medusaed, Cy watches unbelievingly, thinking only, *Its tongue*—

Dropping one hand to her clit, Numinoso grabs the python with the other.

She pulls it out a few mottled inches.

It slides slickly back inside her wet hole.

She pulls it out a few mottled—

It slides slickly back inside her wet—

She pulls it out a few—

It slides slickly back inside her—

She pulls it out a—

It slides slickly back inside—

She pulls it out—

It slides slickly back—

She pulls it—

It slides slickly—

She pulls—

It slides—

She—

It—

Numinoso reaches a visible climax, the Oracle's Orgasm. It's so strong that all at once she collapses to the stage, that slow reflection doing likewise.

The snake withdraws, glistening.

Cy can see its scales catch and release, in sequence, on the rim of her cunt.

Three-Card Monte Python slithers away on its own, and stagehands rush out to help the enervated Numinoso back to her dressing room.

There is no clapping this time. The audience is stricken mute.

Cyril remembers to breathe.

Of them all, he has been struck most heavily by this performance, uniting as it does many of the themes of his obsessive quest. He has to speak to this woman—

Taking advantage of everyone's stupefaction, Cy manages to sneak backstage.

The dusty unpeopled area is lit by twenty-watt bulbs. He walks past assorted debris—pipes, plywood scenery, paint buckets—until he comes to what he assumes is the dressing room.

Knocking, he enters.

The long narrow room—spotted mirror filling one wall above a cosmetic-cluttered counter, with stools before it—is indeed the dressing area. The hot air inside smells like stale perfume and funky sweat.

Numinoso is there, wrapped in a big towel, as are Pellucida and other performers. Three-Card Monte Python is absent.

Before Cy can speak, another person enters. It's a guy with a goatee carrying a cardboard box full of containers of steaming coffee. He sets it down, then tries to leave.

One of the dancers calls, "Hey, Tom—wait! Some small change—?"

"Oh, yeah," the guy rumbles, dropping some coins on the counter.

When Jamocha Joe leaves, the women eye Cyril coldly over the rims of their paper cups, making him stammer out his request.

"Muh-muh-miss Numinoso, can I just uh-uh-ask you a question?"

Well, the gals can see the kid ain't got no harm in him, so they lose some of their wariness and return to painting their nails, etc, save for Numinoso, who regards her visitor disinterestedly.

"Sure, honey—"

"—but which one of us—"

"—do you want?"

Cy spins about. Numinoso's behind him too!

"You're not—"

"—seeing double."

"I'm Grace."

"I'm Gloria."

Cy feels so weak, he has to sit. He bounces his gaze from one Numinoso to the other. "Two of you....? Then the slow mirror—"

"—was no mirror."

Cy waggles his head like a dashboard dog. "Why didn't you both just come out on stage with your snakes?"

"It'd be too much—"

"—for the customers."

"And besides—"

"—whenever you get two girls onstage—"

"—they expect a Lez act."

"Couldn't you just, uh, pull alternate nights?"

"We always—"

"—do everything—"

"—together."

Hoo-boy, Cy's imagination is hardly up to such a a visualization.

"Now, what was—"

"—that question?"

This bluntness leaves Cy at a loss. He can't just blurt out all his fears and suspicions

and demand that the Numinosos resolve them. Um, let's see, what's a good ice-
breaker? How about:

"Uh, your act. It's, ah, really something. May I ask where you learned it?"

The Numinoso sisters shrug, as if the question is completely trivial.

"We were in South Korea for a while—"

"—with the You Ess Oh—"

"—entertaining the GIs—"

"—those poor boys—"

"—and we saw a native gal—"

"—do the bit one night in Seoul."

"So when we came to work here—"

"—and had to develop a speciality—"

"—we thought it'd go over big."

"Not that it's something—"

"—you can do every night."

"Oh, no, of course not! Well, I can vouch for its effect."

Cy is suddenly struck by what has till now been merely a faint chord of memory.
"Do you girls have a brother named Hyman?"

The pythonesses smile, then grow sad.

"Yeah, we do—"

"—or did."

"Our kid brother—"

"—adopted—"

"and considerably younger."

"Not that we think—"

"—we show our age."

Cyril is too polite to inquire their birthdate. "And did he publish a magazine
called *Laocoon*, all about music?"

"He sure did."

"I remember—"

"—reading a copy."

"Crazy stuff about how you could—"

"—discover all sorta secrets by listening—"

"—to rock 'n' roll."

"I wish he had never got into that crap."

"It's what drove him around the bend."

"Worse than he was a week ago?" Cy inquires.

"Oh, much worse."

"He became violently unreasonable."

"Claimed dragons were following him."

"We had to commit him."

"Even electroshock didn't help."

"He's still in the bughouse."

This news sends Cyril's spirits plummetting. He felt a closet affinity with poor old Hyman, and sees his own fate in that of the publisher. Suddenly, he has no heart left to pursue matters with these women. At the same time, his implacable horniness delivers a kick to his gut, reminding him that he's surrounded by female flesh, and he becomes afraid of what he will do—or what will be done to him—if he remains. He has to leave.

"Thanks, Grace, Gloria. Sorry to bother you."

"Anytime—"

"—handsome."

Outdoors, Cy leans for a moment against the wall of SHANNON'S DRAGON. True night has fallen. The sidewalks are thronged with seekers after The Big O, or Ultimate Cipher. Taking deep draughts of the exhaust-thick air, Cyril pushes away from the wall and stumbles on....

He's standing in front of a seedy theater. He looks up at the marquee.

PILGRIM THEATER

UNDER NEW MANAGEMENT

XXXX HOURLY

The ticket-booth is occupied by a bored black girl reading a book: *Generation of Vipers*, by Philip Wylie. For one brief second, Cy fantasizes that the girl is Ruby, that he's found his lost mate. But that bubble of hope pops when she looks up.

Cyril is embarrassed by her apparent innocence, poor school girl trying to earn some book money, and chagrined at what she must think of him. To cover his shame, he flusteredly asks, "Uh, who's the new owner?"

"Some guy named Condor. You want a ticket or not?"

His own cinema-mogul brother-in-law.... How mortifying. What if Cy should meet him inside? What if word of his slumming got back to his sister, Anna Tina? No, he'd better not....

Cy turns to leave.

"It's a new feature tonight," advertises the girl. "Some new producers. The Woo-Woo Boys. Supposed to be really hot."

Before Cy's conscious mind can send a motor-impulse down his arm, he's pushing his last eight dollars thru the wicket for a ticket. Thanks for the loan, Sis. Can't say when I'll pay you back. Spent the last of it on a blue movie....

(Pornography, of course, literally means "writing about prostitutes." Since prostitutes typify the exchange of sex for money—one kind of information for another—pornography, when viewed with the right reading frame, becomes neither more nor less than underground information about information, a depiction of THINGS YOU WERE NEVER MEANT TO KNOW....)

There's a refreshment stand in the lobby. Cy's throat feels as if it's lined with wool. He'd like a drink, but there's always the problem of money, good old Auric Angst.

Cy scrabbles hopelessly in a sandy pocket and, miracle of miracle, brings out what feels like money.

Nope, it's only a slip of much crumpled paper.

To be precise it's the free refreshment pass from Sandy Neck Beach, courtesy of Zosimos Jones.

He presents it tentatively to the pimply kid behind the fly-tracked soda fountain. Miraculously, it's respected.

"One bottle of pop coming right up!"

Sipping his soda, Cyril stands for a moment in the deserted lobby. No sign of Alan. He figures he can still back out. The Woo-Woo Boys.... What could the movie be?

Cy drops his bottle in the trash and pushes thru the padded swinging doors.

Behind him, he hears a black voice call, "Whoa-ho! Let a man come in and bring the popcorn!"

Cy has just enough time to notice that closing credits from the previous showing are scrolling up the screen. Then a hand grabs his arm above the elbow.

"Hold on, son," says a mellifluous Southern voice. "Ah'm the usher here, and Ah got to do mah job."

Cy's arm is released, and a flashlight comes on, its light partly shaded by fingers. The light shines in Cy's face.

"Shucks, you remind me somehow of my twin brother, Jesse. 'Ceptin' he died at birth."

The usher shines the light on his own face.

It's the most famous dead singer's face in the world.

Cy backs slowly down the aisle.

He bumps into someone.

He turns.

It's John Lee Hooker.

"Shee-it, I ain't done this job since Beale Street, so don't mess me up! Let me show you to your seat, boy."

Cy lets him.

Well, this is all too much. Cyril really doesn't expect to learn anything from this show. But at least he can lose himself in X-rated fantasies and liberate his stifled desires by jerking off like a Times Square Popeye. Pictures of Lily made my life so wonderful....

Anyhow, that's what Cy *thinks* he's gonna do.

He's not counting on seeing something that is so riveting that he'll never even get his pants unzipped.

Lanced by a shaft from the projection booth, the screen comes alive.

NUMBERS
AN EDUCATIONAL FILM
DIRECTED BY
ERIC ENGST
PRODUCED BY
THE WOO-WOO BOYS
SCRIPT BY
ADA BLACK AND CLASS

STARRING
(IN ORDER OF DISCOVERY)
THE AMINO ACIDS

GLYCINE 1820
LEUCINE 1820
TYROSINE 1849
SERINE 1865
GLUTAMIC ACID 1866
ASPARTIC ACID 1868
ALANINE 1879
PHENYLALANINE 1881
LYSINE 1889
ARGININE 1895
HISTADINE 1896
CYSTINE 1899
PROLINE 1901
VALINE 1901
TRYPTOPHAN 1902
ISOLEUCINE 1904
METHIONINE 1922
THREONINE 1925
ASPARAGINE 1932
GLUTAMINE 1932

CASTING BY THE SOCIETE INTERNATIONALE DES ARTISTES
SOUNDTRACK AVAILABLE ON DYING DRAGON
INCLUDES
METALLICA'S "DON'T TREAD ON ME"
DIGITAL UNDERGROUND'S "DOO WOO YOU"
ROYAL TRUX'S "HERO ZERO"

Then the first scene.

It's a long-shot of twenty naked people, ten handsome men and ten beautiful women, revealed in various poses in a big, deep-carpeted living room. There's a picture by Rousseau on the wall ("The Snake Charmer") and a mobile in the form of slatted wooden helix hanging from the ceiling.

Seated on couches, lying on the rug, standing, the actors represent a dozen ethnic groups. It looks like a session of the UN, if that organization embraced nudism.

One by one, the people, staring directly at the camera like rank amateurs, introduce themselves, taking the names of the amino acids.

There's a closeup as each speaks.

Cystine is Cy's Tina.

His sister, Mrs Condor.

The camera seems to linger on her, but it's probably just Cyril's horror that makes it seem slo-mo.

Anna Tina Condor is quite fetching. High liddle tits, hourglass waist, generous hips, perky bush. Gee, she coulda been a fuck-film actress instead of an editor....

What is he thinking! Apparently, she *is* a fuck-film actress!

His blood runs cold, his angel is a centerfold!

Cy notices that his sister—as are all the others—is wearing a small earplug, as if to receive directions from someone off-screen. He can also see that Anna Tina, like all the others, is tattooed on her derrière with—he can finally distinguish it— a dragon, specifically, the Wu Labs logo.

The woman who named herself Lysine steps forward. She's a short demi-Asian babe with black hair down to her butt. Large tits, thin waist, knockout legs. Cy has a vague memory of having seen her somewhere long, long ago. (Poor Cy's seen and learned so much of late, tho, how can he be expected to recall that the mysterious Lysine once visited Planet Records, on the very day Ruby disappeared, asking for a record by the Slits?)

"I'm the most promiscuous," says Lysine, "forming the most bonds, so I'll speak for the group. We have a little lesson for you today. But just so it won't be boring, we promise to illustrate it just the way you like."

Lysine winks broadly before continuing.

"The first point we'd like to make is that information can be spread in a number of ways. Take both Gnostic sacraments, for instance. And while you're at it, why not take them together?"

This appears to be Anna Tina's cue. She steps forward. Two guys join her. They each nibble a nipple, Anna Tina holding their pricks. Then she releases them, and turns to embrace one guy. Bending forward, she slides her hands down his sides until she's hanging onto his waist. His prick slips easily into her mouth.

The second guy has moved behind her. He spits into his hand, wets his stiff dick, and positions it between Anna Tina's cheeks.

Still sucking, she backs up onto it.

There's a closeup of the cock disappearing into her rosy ouroboros, thick shaft stretching her asshole.

Anna's being banged from front and back. Her downhanging tits oscillate while she osculates.

My baby does the hanky panky!

These guys can really last. It seems she's been fucking for an eternity. But at last, the "money shot" arrives.

Hot cum sprays over Anna's blissful features, and up all the chakras of her spine. Double shot of my babies' love!

This display is the signal for the entire cast to get busy.

Cyril is beyond thoughts or feelings. His brain's been battered, he's in tatters, shattered! Bite the apple, Adam—don't mind the maggots!

The twenty people fall to fucking, sucking and fingering each other in the most astonishing display of positions and concatenations Cy has ever seen. Stiff pricks conjoin with wet cunts and tight assholes, and lips greet all three.

## COMBINATIONS

### 2
Man and woman, man and man, woman and woman.

### 3
Three men, three women.
Two men and a woman, two women and a man.

### 4
Four men, four women.
Three women and a man, three men and a woman.

### 5
Five men, five women.
Four men and one woman, four women and one man.
Three men and two women, three women and two men.

### 6
Six men, six women.
Five men and one woman, five women and one man.
Four men and two women, four women and two men.
Three men and three women.

7
Seven men, seven women.
Six men and one woman, six women and one man.
Five men and two women, five women and two men.
Four men and three women, four women and three men.

8
Eight men, eight women.
Seven men and one woman, seven women and one man.
Six men and two women, six women and two men.
Five men and three women, five women and three men.
Four men and four women.

9
Nine men, nine women.
Eight men and one woman, eight women and one man.
Seven men and two women, seven women and two men.
Six men and three women, six women and three men.
Five men and four women, five women and four men.

10
Ten men, ten women.
Nine men and one woman, nine women and one man.
Eight men and two women, eight women and two men.
Seven men and three women, seven women and three men.
Six men and four women, six women and four men.
Five men and five women.

To permute all the combinations up to ten has taken two hours, during which there has been only limited dialogue. The women consistently refer to their cunts as "ciphers." The men call their cocks "snakes." Screwing is referred to as "feedback" or "swapping info."

Cy has watched in brain-burnt astonishment. He hasn't really registered anything intellectually since he saw his sister milk two fat snakes of their white venom. The only thing he's really noticed is that each woman—as soon as a new man has shot up her—seeks out the other nine females one by one, whereupon they scissor their legs together and rub pussies.

This orgy of liquid limitless lust changes its nature at the point when there are two inexhaustibly screwing groups of ten forming two organic chains.

Suddenly the two side-by-side human chains coalesce, coiling around each other in a double helix.

Ambitious Amino Acids, Presumptious Proteins, daring to mimic their Daddy DNA!

They hold that shape briefly, until, merging, all twenty folks recombine heads to tails in a single huge daisy chain that travels up furniture and down, all around the room, twenty mouths connected to twenty assorted twats and dicks.

In a minute or so, a final collective orgasm travel like chaser lights around the circle, which promptly falls apart.

Out of the tangle emerges Lysine.

She stands, and the camera travels in for a closeup. (Cy can see, out of focus in the background, Anna Tina. She seems to be too tired to remove her face from the lap it's in.) Lysine's body is entirely soaked with sweat and other juices; her thighs sheen. Her thick black hair is clotted with cum, which also dribbles down her face.

She smiles. "Point two: if the switch isn't on—it's off."

Lys waves a hand at the limp cocks and swollen-lipped, bitten pussies of her fellow amino acids, who, after such a display, certainly deserve to be "off."

The screen goes black, and two final admonitions flare whitely:

EXPAND THE CHANNEL!
REVERSE THE FLOW!

Somehow Cy finds himself outside. It must be close to midnight. He hasn't a thought in his head. He's reached information overload. A whore and her customer walk by, the woman supporting the man. Cyril faintly assimilates the fact that the john appears to be the missing Paulie Peptide Junior. But our cinema-shocked boy doesn't even get excited about it. Nothing matters, and what if it did...?

A car pulls up sideways at the curb in front of Cy. It's a Little Red Corvette convertible with the top down, bearing a bumper-sticker that reads: ASS, GAS, OR GRASS—NOBODY RIDES FOR FREE. This car is really souped up. It's got seven headlights and ten horns.

Driving it is Lysine.

Cy has the absurd fantasy that she's just stepped off the screen, but of course, she's too neatly dressed and groomed for that. Jauntily perched atop her head is a leopard-skin pillbox hat from which depends a lacy 'n' racy black veil across the upper half of her face. She's wearing python hot-pants, complemented by a leather jacket open over a black bra.

It's the legendary combination of snakeskin suit backed with Detroit muscle!

"Hey, Joe, you go my way?" leers Lysine.

Cyril is shocked into response. "Haven't you and your amino acids done enough to me already, Lysine?"

"You jokey-joke with me, honey? We handled you with kid mittens. Now how 'bout you get in, chop-chop."

Resigned to his fate, Cyril opens the door and climbs in.

Sweet Hitch-a-hiker, take a ride in my mean machine! (But remember: hitch-hiking has its pros and cons!)

Lysine says, "You can call me by my real name, Melusine. Mel for short, since we're gonna be such good friends."

Melusine roars off, nearly flattening a wino in the gutter.

The night wind in Cy's face sharpens his wits somewhat, also wafting him the scent of Mel's White Eternity. Knowing that it would be useless to ask where they're going, he demands instead, "What's with the pidgin English, Lysine? Or Mel, if you prefer. You didn't talk like that in the movie. Not that you did much talking."

"How would you like me to speak, Mister Prothero? I must confess that my early career has left me most comfortable when making a pickup if I revert to the fractured lingua franca which was once my true speech, typical of a Saigon bar-girl. I could use French if you prefer. *Voulez vous couchez avec moi?*"

Cy stares at his sexy chauffeur. He does not deem it wise to trifle with her. "Uh, the pidgin's fine," says this pigeon.

"Oooo!" coos Melusine. "You make your little chinky girl so happy, Joe!"

Cy sighs. "Yeah, great."

They're heading out of town, leaving the bright lights behind. Melusine drives as expertly as Cyril has witnessed her fuck. Cy has a thousand questions—and none. Whatever happens, happens. He recalls what Polly once told him, how prophecy is merely a subset of information theory. If these clowns have the future scoped out, then it must already exist in some form, and there's nothing he can do to alter it.

They drive in silence for a time, passing thru suburbs and entering the forest-bordered section of the interstate south of Boston. Life in the fast lane....

Just when Cy expects only silence till the unforeseeable end of their trip, Melusine says, "How you like my Hollywood days, Joe?"

"You were inspirational. But I still don't understand anything."

"Not to worry. Wu will explain all mysteries to you and your pretty girlfriend tomorrow. Just drop by anytime. Oh yeah—be sure to bring that groovy disc too."

Cyril absorbs this invitation and promise for several miles. Melusine drives on. It's a Saturday night, I guess that makes it all right....

Pulling a sharp right, Melusine exits onto an arc of macadam intended as a rest stop. There's a phone booth and a busted streetlight on a tall pole. No other cars.

Melusine shuts the engine off. Crickets fill the gaps of silence between the noise of codons of traffic.

"Guess I'm out of gas, Joe, out here where the horses run free."

"Where's that leave us?"

"I'm lookin' for a man to love me like I never been loved before. I'm lookin' for a man who'll do it anywhere, even on a limousine floor."

"And that's me?"

"Well, not really. But I feel bad for you, kid. C'mon, don't you want to play my fantasy game? Don't you want to come with me into my nasty world?"

Melusine drops her hand in Cy's lap. "Oh, Joe, see! I knew you wouldn't disappoint your nasty girl! This leaves only one slight detail: I don't do nothing for free.

I'm a material girl. Like the Bad Brains say, 'You got to pay to cum.' What you got for your liddle Mel?"

Cy pats his jeans. He knows he spent his last dollar to get into the theater, and is about the say so, when he feels a heavy coin in his pocket. Reaching down, he digs out—Impy the Imperial Dollar.

Melusine grabs it. "That's Ay-Okay, ace, will do."

The circle is closed, the cipher of coincidence complete. The snake bites its tail.

Lifting her veil, Melusine pauses. "One warning, kid. In the morning, don't say you love me, cuz I'll only kick you out any door."

She leans toward Cy, lips parted.

Cyril grabs her boobs and squeezes, mashing his lips onto hers.

All his horniness is concentrated into an exquisite ache which is only magnified by the sudden notion that he is about to screw, in the person of this woman, the entire Wu empire which has so long tormented him.

Mel comes up for air. "Oh, boy, kid, I think you need the edge taken off you."

She unsnaps and unzips Cy's jeans. She tugs, and Cy lifts his ass off the seat. His pants end up around his ankles, as do, in the next second, his bikini briefs. The leather seat feels cool under Cy's rump.

Melusine drops her head down.

Her tongue snakes around the top of his prick, teases the cleft. Then her mouth encircles his cock, a burning ring of fire, flames going higher and higher.

Midnight Rambler, gonna stick that knife right down your throat!

It's paradise by the dashboard lights!

Cy cums in sixty-four seconds.

There's no money shot.

When Melusine straightens up, his sticky prick is not even soft, remaining hard as calculus.

Melusine shrugs out of her jacket. Cy unhooks her front-fastened bra and tongues her nipples, which she thrusts forward.

Pretty soon, she's unzipping her hot-pants too. Baby, I'm in shippin' if you're in receivin', cuz what I see I ain't believin'. The longest legs in the shortest pants. You got me doin' a matin' dance!

Cy's freed his ankles from his own entangling trousers and is ready to go. But Melusine abruptly halts their foreplay. From between them, she fetches a small wicker purse, a Mucha' Linda item known as The Sister Mystica handbag.

Mel reaches into the bag. She takes out a foil-wrapped Red Stripe condom, whose package shows a chalice entwined with snakes.

"You wanna use this, Joe? Prevents spread of disease. Or you like it bareback?"

In answer, Cy grabs the condom and flings it out the car.

"Ooo, my kinda man! Maybe you'd put this on for your liddle Mel, tho?"

She produces a jade ring a bit bigger than circled thumb and forefinger. It's carved into the shape of two dragons, head to head and tail to tail. A long thin ribbon hangs from it.

Before Cyril can do anything, Mel slides the ring over his cock, snug to the base. She reaches under his ass, finds the ribbon between his legs, and pulls it back, so that it divides his balls and runs between his asscheeks. She quickly wraps it around his waist and ties it to itself.

"Now you ready to show any girl a good time."

Cy's ringed cock is throbbing. He can't wait any longer.

Still seated, he clasps Melusine's waist with both hands, lifts the petite woman up bodily over to his side with supernormal strength, so that her back is to him as the Tourquoise Courtesan's was to Mister Maxwell.

Mel's poised above him, kneeling on the sides of his seat. "Oh, honey—stick your information in my communication!"

Cy skewers her on his cock.

Melusines gasps. Grabbing the rim of the windshield, she begins to work him, slow as a Brahma minute.

It's after midnight, and they're gonna let it all hang out!

She gives such a ride, she must be a limousine. Cyril can barely tame her little red love machine; he's gotta last like he never has before.

And, whether it's the ring or the pre-fuck blowjob, last he does.

As soon as Cyril shoots his second load up Mel's cunt, she pulls off him, jacks open the door, hits the ground and takes off running.

Cy leaps after her, snags her, and pushes her forward.

Melusine grabs the waist of a tree.

Cyril takes her like his sister was taken, up her ass.

When he cums for the third time, his knees go watery, and he falls to the ground, still clutching Melusine.

As he loses consciousness, Cy whispers, "I been searchin'.... Searchin' for the daughter.... Daughter of the devil herself...."

Mel replies to the snoozin' lad, "And you found her, kid."

Cy wakes up lying in the grass, on the cold hillside, his clothes beside him in a heap. The Kampuchean Kutie in her Liddle Red Korvette has dekamped.

Careless, careless, Cy! Don't mess with these folks unless you know the answer to koans like: How many tears in a bottle of gin?

Wearily, Cy dresses. An ache in his shoulder causes him to notice a bruise there, a set of fresh teethmarks. Do those teeth match the wound you got in Lovetown, boy?

He dashes across the southbound lanes (this traffic's trying to kill me!), the median strip, and the northbound lanes, positioning himself in the Breakdown Alley in order to trudge and thumb a ride back to the city.

He ain't horny no more. His body's satisfied fer shure. But that little daytripper took his brain only half the way there.

And now, li'l Cyril, who's gonna drive you home?

Outside of Boston, miles and minutes away from Cyril, the speeding cherry-red car decelerates when its driver spots a not unexpected figure by the side of the road. The lights of the car tighten around the figure like coils of a serpent. Tires crunch gravel beside the standing man, who blends darkly with the night.

"Hello," says Melusine with unwonted shyness. Underneath, she's more excited than she ever was as a girl during the annual Water Festival, Bun Umtouk, when the dragon-prowed ships flock past the Royal Palace.

"Hello," says Claude Lollolo, equally shy, fingering his fetish.

"They told me you'd be waiting here when I was done with our boy."

"And here I am."

"Would you like a ride?" asks practical Mel.

"I certainly would," replies Lollolo, and hops aboard.

Silence, save for the siren-song of tires on tar.

Then from Lollolo: "The Afa spoke to me of you. As soon as Europa dropped me off here, you appeared in its messages. Before then, I just never knew—"

"Nor me about you, Big Brother."

Lollolo seems embarrassed by the appellation, and turns the talk to business. "Things seem to be coming to a head now. Big changes just around the corner. They've kept me very busy casting the Afa-du at the Paris branch. A brief rest at Avalon—if you can call it that—and then, here I found myself." He tapers off as if embarrassed. "I hardly know how to speak to you."

"Me neither. Too bad Dad isn't here to advise us."

Lollolo laughs. "Poor Pop! You knew him better than I did, but I've heard some tales— He'd probably just tell us to cut the bullshit! So why don't we? We both know the real reason for our unease. You're my *soror mystica*, my shakti, and I am your animus. From the moment I learned of your existence, how you were born to a Cambodian Danghbwe-no, I haven't been able to get you off my mind. Something in you keeps calling to me across time and space. You are my other half, my binary complement, the parity digit that will complete my code. Together, we will produce heirs to the new future now gestating. I have to have you! Do you feel the same way?"

"As my pal Eight Snakes would say, 'Your words are in my stomach.' You make my soul tremble. I can see why Wu was keeping us hidden from each other till now."

Lolollo exhales with relief. "I'm so glad you share my feelings! Yet something still thwarts our destined *hieros gamos*. The specter of our shared genes. Poor foolish Phillipe! He hangs over our personal future like a worried grandmother."

"Phillipe is dead and gone. We're alive."

"How true. Now, more than ever, we must live in the present.... Listen, in the face of the immense transition coming up, it's wrong to stall any longer! Just because we both share half our genes with the same donor is no excuse not to—"

"To become lovers?" suggests Melusine.

Lollolo solemnly nods.

Neither speaks for a time.

Then Melusine ventures: "Is it true that your cock is over ten inches long?"

"Why, uh, yes, as a matter of fact, it is."

"Then, Brother, the time to hesitate is through! You can light my fire!"

Look at Little Sister smile! Big Sister won't, but Little Sister will! My sister is lovely and loose and—telepathic flash—she's not wearing any underwear! Lolollo feels instantly aroused, but protective too. He's not gonna let anyone mess with his little sister ever again....

An hour later, having climaxed ten and one-half inches up an utterly satisfied and sated, sobbing Melusine, while whispering over and over in her ear an involuntary "Sister, sister...," while she whimpers mysteriously, "Ten thousand, ten thousand...," Lolollo discovers that her post-fuck cunt tastes just like the Danghbwe-no's.

Except, of course, for the temporary flavors that are his and Cyril's.

# THE SUN SESSIONS

# K L U E S

### 00111000

EMPEROR WU: "What merits will my good works
bring me?"

BODHIDHARMA: "None whatever. A pure deed of merit
comes straight from the heart and is
not concerned with worldly achieve-
ments."

EMPEROR WU: "Then what is this holy religion all
about?"

BODHIDHARMA: "Vast emptiness, and there's nothing
holy about it."

### 00111001

"Now he's gone and joined that stupid club."
—Wendy O'Connor,
on the death of her son, Kurt Cobain

### 00111010

"The brain is a consumate piece of combinatorial
mathematics."
—Max Born

### 00111011

"God filled a mighty Cup with Mind and sent it down,
joining a Herald to it, to whom He gave command to make
this proclamation to the hearts of men: 'Baptize thyself with
this Cup's baptism, whatsoever heart can do so: thou that hast
faith thou canst ascend to Him that hath sent down the Cup;
thou that dost know for what thou didst come into being!'"
—Corpus Hermeticum

O'Phidian is beaten.
His ass is grass for old man Wu, that mad Nebuchadnezzar king, to chew on. (Unless, natch, P.O'P. will eat himself first.)

He admits his defeat now at last. He *tried* to give his Wounded Hand time to heal, but it was no use. He's only half the man he used to be. I'm a creep, I'm a weirdo, what the hell am I doing here? I'm a loser, why don't you kill me!

It's the end of Mr Under Assistant West Coast Promotion Man, your Ubiquitous Mr Love Groove, that radio-friendly unit shifter.

And boy-o-boy, does he feel like one of Saklad's Lowly Worms. (It's a rich and scary experience, to look in the mirror and see the eyes of a stranger....)

O'Phidian's like ten micrograms of LSD in a five-microgram neuron. He's got about as much energy as a dead skunk in the middle of the road, stinkin' to high heaven. (Oooo, that smell!) He's extended himself so far, threaded himself into the woof of so many lives, stuck a finger (and other appendages) into so many pies, that's he's got nothing left at the center of his being, nothing left in reserve to battle the infection that threatens to claim his physical self. He's dispersed himself Across The Universe!

The grand gamble he took—betting that he could stochastically predict Wu's ultimate plans for humanity and personally cash in on them before the Doc did—has failed. And the wager, his life, is now due.

That ancient devil Wu had proven himself just too smart! He knew too much, was too proleptically potent for O'Phidian to outfox. Even devoting only a fraction of his attention to O'Phidian's grandiose zoomin' 'n' boomin', even when absent, vanished, subsumed into Sophia (as rumors now had it) the Old Man had been simply too sharp....

Wu's schemes were too perversely elaborate to track. They exfoliated organically from their roots, sending up untraceable suckers half a world away from their subterranean heart. Millennia-old underground fungus, fer shure. From the Central Vertebrate Homeobox issued the subtle commands that guided all the embryonic development. Once set in motion, the Doctor's plots were self-perpetuating. And they synergized to become emergent on new levels, even growing parasitically on O'Phidian's own machinations, like eye-eye-eye-vee, Poison Ivy, or like viruses comandeering a cell. Redundancy too was a big part of Wu's success O'Phidian had failed to compensate for....

Wu's many programs had even survived the Ancient Chinaman's recent disappearance. Like the long-chain, elaborately folded proteins which, altho they ultimately and ineluctably derive from the master DNA template, possess an autonomous enzymatic life of their own, Wu's schemes worked their hormonal chaos far beyond the precincts of their origin.

In trying to divine Wu's intentions, to keep track of all his cats paws and cohorts, his feints and farces, his slights and slogans, his prizes and puzzles, O'Phidian had reached the limits of his information-processing capacity. Too much information, running in my brain! Too much information, driving me insane! He had matched his mind, that thousand-petaled lotus, against his employer's, and learned the hard truth. His was the inferior bloom.

Wu! Everything you do is irresistible! I run around in circles till I run out of breath. Why can't I be you, instead of the Mayor of Simpleton...? I'm sick of being your beast of burden, I've walked for miles, my feet are hurtin'!

It is early Sunday morning. O'Phidian is one of the few people present inside the rambling complex forming the headquarters of Wu Labs on Route 128, just outside Boston. The redundant apprentice devil sits behind his desk (on which is a plaque proclaiming THE BUG STOPS HERE), sweating profusely. He is dressed in a goat hair suit from the prestigious Los Angeles tailors, Slash and Rose. Beneath the suit, against his skin, he wears long underwear into which have been sewn sachets of blue verbena and yarrow. He is shod in boots he picked up on his last trip to Arizona. (That Arizona sky is so big, it always takes his breath away—and that doesn't happen every day! In a big country, dreams stay with you, like a lover's voice 'cross a mountainside.) The boots have small battery packs in them, which feed a magnetic field that Doctor Black Elk assures him is beneficial to his condition.

In short, our boy's got himself electric boots and a mohair suit!

Much good it's doing him, tho.

There's so little time left.... He runs a thick hand thru his sorrel hair, in which the first faintest threads of grey have recently begun to appear. (O'Phidian is fifty-three this year, over half a century, yet a mere Gnostic youth. How long that span sounds to mortal ears, yet how pitifully short compared with Wu's tenure on this sorry globe.... He'll never live even as long as Father Gogarty. Memories of a double-headed snake, the amphisbaena, trickle back....)

What occupies O'Phidian's mind now is a pointless exercise. He is busy trying to identify the exact moment in all his scheming when he fell irreversibly into Wu's trap. It won't help him escape, of course. Still, it would be nice to know just what the fatal miscalculation was. (Knowledge is power, after all, he's always maintained. What a laugh! *Wisdom* is power, he's realized too late.) He has a pretty good idea, but hasn't settled on it definitely yet.

In the last few minutes before he must act, must fatally commit himself, O'Phidian continues to noodle with the puzzle.

*Someone—possibly myself,* he thinks—*sold me down the river. Now I got less than twenty-four hours to live. The man's too big for me, and I got to ride across the river soon, cuz I been caught stealing, while I thought I was walking right thru the door. Wu knew it was probably a robbery, a bit of skulduggery— but when?*

Lessee, he came to work for Wu in '54, four years after the establishment of the Doc's Stateside operations. O'Phidian had missed out on the first wave of global action: the bulldozing of Sophiatown, South Africa, in 1948, f'rinstance. Also the infiltration of that revolutionary new medium, television. (In 1948, when the number of television sets in the US reached the Magic Sum of one million, the federal government instituted a freeze on the building of new transmitters, and carved up the US into various broadcast regions. When the freeze thawed, the fledgling Wu Labs had picked up at least one station in every market....) No, barring the recruitment of his *soi-disant* "daughter," Zona Pellucida, she of the Silly-Putty spine, his first major assignment had been in '56, with the establishment of the Federal High way Trust Fund.

For some reason, Wu had wanted the roads of his adopted country improved and expanded, and had lobbied Congress for the establishment of a fund for such a purpose. O'Phidian, with his experience as a Queen's Messenger, had been deemed the natural coordinator for such a project. How well he had succeeded could be seen from the amount of pavement currently binding the country like Gulliver's ropes. (At the present moment, there were 3.8 million miles of paved roads in the nation. Wu wanted an even 4 million, apparently regarding the figure as marking some sort of critical mass.)

Once, in one of their perennial telephone conversations, O'Phidian had asked him why—what was his ultimate goal for the Interstate System? There was dead silence on the line, save for a Snaky Kozmic Hiss. As he waited for Wu's answer, O'Phidian tried to picture the elderly wrinkled Chinese man, hidden away in some doorless, windowless sanctum flooded by merciless white light, his black-glasses reflecting nothing, his thin lips pasted shut.... So preoccupied was O'Phidian with this mental picture, that Wu's obscure single-sentence reply took him completely by surprise. "If we regard each road as a neural pathway, with destinations as receptors and the cars as molecules of acetylcholine...."

O'Phidian hadn't asked his boss to clarify that statement. The implications were too horrendous. An autobahn automaton...? Each cellular cloverleaf a switching mechanism, each roadside rest stop a register...? Each traffic 'copter an output device, reading the patterns...? Passengers and drivers merely nonsentient quantum particles...? The great American love of being On The Road merely a factitious passion contrived to further Wu's mad designs?

Holy Sophia, could it be? Wasn't the Money Mind diabolical enough?!

Still, for all its potential impact, the highway business hadn't been the fatal misstep. Neither had been manipulating Willy Dixon's transfer to Cobra Records in '57. Nor had been that tricky business of engineering a meeting between William Burroughs and Dean Ripa, a little-known surrealist painter and snake-dealer (speciality, black mambas). Sure, Burroughs had freaked when he saw Melusine emerge naked from the bedroom, the irascible old junkie claiming she was "an insatiable harlot from the swamps of my psyche!", thereupon pulling out a pistol and shooting holes in the walls and ceiling of Ripa's house. But they had gotten his jism in the end.

*Nor* had been the recruitment of Sally Salonika and Agnes Agape in '67, despite O'Phidian's having forgotten his self-control long enough to screw the pythoness and risk placing himself under her domination.

Could it have been—

A knock resounds on O'Phidian's office door, interrupting the Shaky Snaky's meditations. "Cuh-cuh-come in," trips unlightly off his tongue. God, he's really losing it, to be stuttering now.... Get ahold of yourself, lad!

The door swings open to reveal *M'sieur* Robert Norbert "Roi" Aubisson, Messenger Extraordinaire and part-time pizza-deliveryman, half-brother to Phillipe deClosets and Sally Salonika, uncle to Miss Mekong Mel. The Gallic-Teutonic halfbreed wears his ever-present dark glasses, and carries a pizza-bag—normal sized, this time—with his usual panache.

"I didn't order this," states O'Phidian chillingly.

Aubisson is slightly nonplussed. "I know, sir. It's something a few of us wanted to do, on our own initiative. We know you won't, uh, be around much longer—that is, in the flesh. So we all chipped in and had Mister Montagnier cook up a special farewell pizza. A kind of Last Supper, so to speak."

"I'm not hungry," says O'Phidian flatly. "And besides, there're only two of us."

"Come now, Mister Oh, don't be like that. Remember, 'whenever two are gathered in my name...,' and so forth. Look—you haven't even seen what kind of pizza it is...."

Aubisson unzips the bag, slides out the box and cracks the lid, holding the pizza under his boss's nose for inspection. O'Phidian peers at it suspiciously, then sniffs.

"Bananas? And are those peanut Em and Ems?"

"You bet," says Aubisson proudly. "And the crust was made from a dough with Guinness mixed in."

O'Phidian is slightly touched, his appetite piqued, but he don't wanna admit it. Aubisson has to prod him.

"Try a piece, sir. It'll do you good."

"You first," says the mega-hoovered megalomaniac.

"Why, thanks, Mister Oh. Don't mind if I do."

Aubisson sets the box down and takes a seat. He lifts up a mozzarella-dripping piece and has it halfway to his mouth when O'Phidian says, "That's the one I want."

"If you wish, sir."

The boss and his employee eat silently for a time, till sated. Then Aubisson speaks.

"What's on your mind, sir? Please tell me, I want to know...."

O'Phidian finishes patting his lips clean with the back of his tie, and sighs dramatically. "It's nothing special, Rowbear, nothing unique to me. I'm just feeling the pressure of time. Time is winding up, under the big blue sky. It's tick-tocking away, and the world hasn't found the wavelength of universal love yet. And even if it does, I won't be here to see it! The hourglass has no more grains of sand in it for me. No, I'm afraid my mortality has finally caught up with me."

Aubisson shoots to his feet. "Chief, you've got to enjoy whatever time you've got left! 'Live in the present,' right? When you don't have a body anymore, you'll regret the hours you wasted just sitting here and moping. Get up with me— Good, that's it— Now, just do what I do— First, put your hands on your hips— Now set your feet like this— Great! We're ready."

Aubisson begins to sing and dance, O'Phidian weakly mimicking his movements.

OOBY DOOBY

Oh, you shake it to the left,
And you shake it to the right!
You do the Ooby Dooby with uh-alla your might!

When you do the Ooby Dooby,
You got nothin' to fear.
When you do the Ooby Dooby,
I just gotta get near!

Suiting his actions to his words, Aubisson humps butts with O'Phidian, who merely smiles wanly. Shaking his head sadly at this lack of libido, Aubisson finishes up his song.

Oh, with the left leg you quiver,
And with the right one you shake!
Work it on down like a big rattlesnake!

O'Phidian drops wearily into a chair at the song's end, looking none the better for the exercise.

"Thank ye, lad. I appreciate the effort. But I fear my heart's just not in it."

"I know, Mister Oh. It's hard."

"Unfortunately, not any more, lad."

Gathering up the debris of their Last Supper, Aubisson prepares to leave. "Well, I'll download you sometime soon, Mister Oh, and we'll talk again."

"I'd appreciate it, Rowbear."

After Aubisson has gone, O'Phidian returns to his scab-picking.

Could it have been his mild-mannered acceptance of Wu's commands to shut down The 'Sixties? That action had always troubled him, felt somehow like too grand a betrayal. Arranging the death of all those musicians and politicians, artists and agitators, sideshow shamans and backyard *brujos*. Huxley, RFK, King, Malcolm X, George Jackson, Morrison, Joplin, McCartney, Dylan, Jones, Allman, Redding.... The list went on and on, right down to Vicious and Lennon. Shake it up is all that we know, using bodies up as we go....

It was not something the Gaelic Gnostic was particularly proud of, this covert wetwork. He had never really boasted about his part in the dismantling of this failed experiment. Nobody would've understood. Why, Mel alone would've killed him, if she had ever found out O'Phidian was the one who had helped snuff Hendrix before she could meet the part-Cherokee possessor of that prize prick.

But the Doctor had explained it all to him in such a convincing way, that he had consented, however reluctantly.

"I have unleashed forces," whispered Wu over the Heaviside-equation–smoothed telephone connection, round about '67, "which I cannot properly channel. I thought all the pieces were in place, but I miscalculated. The world is tearing itself apart. Humanity is not ready for mass enlightenment, egalitarian illumination. Dabbling in Zen without discipline produces only sickness. Remember: If you drink a bowl of water with a needle floating in it, the needle will stick in your throat, unless you know it is there. Let me redundantly restate myself: Humanity is as ready as they ever will be, but the vehicle of their satori is not perfected. All the drugs are lacking something; they are all temporary and artificial, even pixeldrine. I must rethink this matter for a couple of decades. Meanwhile, we need to restore the quotidian, put out some inhibitory signals. The Jewel-Mind Mirror must be veiled, the worms must continue to wallow in the mud a while longer. We must be cruel to be kind. If lust and violence tastes so sweet, is what they want, then we'll give it to them."

Well, Wu had Powers of Pretty Persuasion, he needed O'Phidian's cooperative confusion, and he got it. Into motion went all the overdoses and assassin's bullets and cancer injections, as well as the simple but effective public discreditings, such as the numbers he had run on Shockley—feeding him all those wacky theories about racial intelligence differences, so that no one would listen to his radical cybernetic proposals—and Lilly, whose work with isolation tanks and LSD went untrusted, simply because the scientist had been led to believe and state for the public that aliens were guiding him.

Still, despite the moral and ethical stains on O'Phidian's hands—which he judged by non-hylic standards—this task had not been the one that had undermined him.

No, right up till '77, there hadn't been a single assignment which he couldn't simultaneously carry out to Wu's satisfaction and also twist toward his own ends. (Those ends, inculcated by the Fathers of the Order of Saint Draco and never thereafter questioned until this personal crisis, were: first, eventual complete control of his environment—which, as things worked out, equated with Wu's organization— then, second, an assault on Sophia's maidenhead, an attempt to pop the perpetually self-renewing cherry, fresh for every aspirant, of the Wise Virgin, the Cunning Vixen, the Bold Virago, Ouroboros the Earth Mother....)

So-ho. That left only one major incident as the crucial juncture.

'77 had been the year of his undoing.

Was there any excuse for his not seeing it? True, he had been extremely preoccupied with managing the Little Flowers operation (those perfect air-brushed angels, who hurt your heart just by looking at you), which fed into the Snakes and Ladders project. Recruiting Information Sexperts, Ching Witches, from around the world. Making sure they were fitted properly with the IRS. (One defective unit had leaked its cryonic fluid, liquid helium, turning its unfortunate bearer into an instant corpsicle. Talk about Frijid Pink! O'Phidian had ragged the asses of the lab-boys good for that screw-up. How were his girls to have any confidence after such a snafu...?) Parcelling out the stolen DNA among the various Wu research operations around the world, all of which were striving to decipher the entire human genome thereby represented, so that it could be encoded on disc.... All this had distracted him.

When Mekong Melusine had come onboard in '75, his job had gotten a little easier. She had quickly advanced over those who had been doing the job longer, earning O'Phidian's confidence and proving she was capable of running the whole show. Mel's experience with maintaining her own financial empire, her organizational skills acquired thru managing everything from whorehouses to warehouses, brothels to hotels—these had proven invaluable, almost as crucial as her snake-hips and love-lips. She had taken over as cultivator of his Little Flowers.

Convinced that Wu was at last revealing his true aims, O'Phidian continued to pour heart and soul into the operation. This was where he first set the teensiest toetip on the Kozmic Banana Peel. Believing that he understood all of Wu's goals, he had fallen for his subtle disinformation campaign. He should have known that Wu wasn't telling him everything.

(God, sometimes you just don't come through! You need a woman to look after you....)

Still, he could have recovered himself at this point, could have pulled back his resources and tossed them at the real prize. But he hadn't spotted it, had been misled by the screen of noise.

Dahomey. He hadn't seen that Dahomey was it. That Saklad-be-damned Danhgbwe-no.... He never found out how Wu had tracked her and her cellular cargo down. Who the hell even suspected it existed?

*What* existed? you ask.

Now he can answer that question. But much to his undoing, he couldn't when it mattered.

O'Phidian had been taught as a youth, in those long drowsy days in the classroom and those frosty nights spent on the Archon Tracking Platform, that all mental powers exhibited by the initiated, as well as their longevity, came from extensive meditation, from psychic exercises which put one in touch with the Tao. So much was true, insofar as it went. But it didn't go far enuff. What he had never suspected was that there could be a biological substitute for such training, a cellular shortcut to gnosis.

It had been in the blood of the Dahomean Snake Mother.

A vatic virus.

Proleptic proteins.

Delphic DNA.

That sophic string of basepairs.

There were many ways, O'Phidian knew, of establishing temporary taps into the Tao, of deriving hidden information from the Koquettish Kozmos. Mechanical means such as the *I Ching* and the Afa-du and the tea-leaf-reading of O'Phidian's own Tinker clans. Chemical means such as drugs. Hypno-physiological means such as prayer and flagellation and ecstatic dancing. But all of these were exceedingly limited in duration. They were only temporary devices. After employing them, you always came back, imprisoned once more in "reality," limited to the small channel, fifty bits-per-second of bandwidth, the narrow spectrum of the senses.

And even the powerful mental reconditioning which Gnostic-Zen adepts achieved was limited in its application. If your attention wavered, if you fell into bad habits, succumbed to the tug of mundane affairs, you could regress to hylic blindness....

Wouldn't it be nice if there were a permanent, *biological* means of mind-expansion, allowing one to tap into the pleroma effortlessly and at will? A handy-dandy way to rewire your whole brain and nervous system?

You say you're looking for an Instant Cure, Boyo, a Quick Fix? Look no further, Son, we've got just what you want! Step right up to the snake-oil tent, and meet— the Danghbwe-no, the gal with the goods. Salvation hides below the event horizon of her wet Black Hole.

Africa. Birthplace of the human race. Your basic heart of darkness, ever-present in all our blood. Africa is so close to everywhere, despite what you think. Africa is the unconscious, the Third World is the netherworld. Why, it's nearly Africa right here and now in lily-white Boston....

The Romans knew: *Ex Africa semper aliquid novi*. Out of Africa, always something new. The new thing might not be anything you could even see. It might be an itsy-bitsy mutant virus, hardly bigger than a mitochondria, born just a few centuries ago when a sizzling quantum particle goosed a single basepair or three, rewriting the metaprogramming.

This virus was never contact-contagious nor exceedingly virulent—was rather fragile, in fact. It was passed on only thru intercourse. Nonetheless, it so unfitted the humans it lodged in for normal living, that the first tribe to harbor it was almost totally wiped out.

The bug survived in a lone individual, an anonymous woman.

She was adopted by a neighboring tribe, who found her wandering, ranting in the jungle. Some of her rants, it was later observed, came true. Hoo-whee, wotta we got here?! A leg up on our competition!

Her adopted tribe was careful to confine her to a hut, excluding her as a taboo object from your basic human connections, including, luckily, Karnal Kontacts.

They continued to milk her for Oracular Tips until, one day, she did not respond. A frightened young girl was sent in as an expendable sacrifice to check out what was happening.

She found the aging Snake Mother unconscious, suffering with a high fever. With local medicines, she nursed her back to a precarious health.

The first thing the randy old oracle did was have sex with the girl, making the old Lezzy She-Bop.

The original Snake Mother soon passed on to her reward. (Some died like all mortals; others, depending on their sensitivity, made the dramatic Ascent of the Dragon which Mel's mother had made.)

But the tribe found it had a new one, in the form of the infected youngster.

(This gal was named Latifah. Tho only thirteen, she had already borne a son. This lad, after the transformation of his mother, was raised by relatives, and was in fact the distant ancestor of Sam Andriambahomanana, Cyril's great-grandfather.) This accident—by which a new Snake Mother had been cloned off the old one—inspired, over generations, a rich set of superstitions.

During her lifetime, the reigning Snake Mother was the sole vessel of the sacred virus. Her daily erotomaniacal needs were met by the snakes that accreted naturally as her totem. At the proper time, the bug was passed down to the chosen new priestess in saliva and vaginal fluids, as the pair mated in a dark, serpent-filled hut, kissing first, sixty-nining, using a snake as a head-and-tail double dildo, then finally scissoring their legs together, squishing cunt to cunt, making the amphisbaena, The Serpent With Two Heads And No Tail.

(The virus never travelled to Haiti until recently, by the way, since the European slavers never dared, even in their most audacious moments, to kidnap the Danghbwe no.)

Weh-hell.... Somehow Wu, thru whatever arcane channels, contacted the Snake Mother and convinced her to violate generations of tradition by screwing Claude Lollolo. Thus, when Claude stumbled out of the hut, the virus was in him, swimming up his prick and down his throat, the first time in centuries it had been embodied in a male.

Back in the capital, Lollolo transfered it to O'Phidian via the Sodomic Sacrament. (Lollolo couldn't just deliver the virus to America himself at this point, since as a member of the royal family he was under strict supervision by the Kerekou regime, which didn't want exiles fomenting counter-revolution from abroad.)

And besides, O'Phidian sees now, as he toys with a blank WORM compact disc in its jewel-case at his desk, his orders to subject himself to the virus were part of Wu's scheme to put him, O'Phidian, in his proper place.

All this good stuff, as we've said, O'Phidian discovered too late. In fact just within the past few months. Piecing together various clues and bits of hearsay, digging deep into encrypted files, he learned the true nature of what he had allowed himself to be infected with....

A redundant knock-knock now re-startles O'Phidian out of his re-reverie.

"Who is it this time?" demands the Draconian.

Instead of a verbal reply, the door bangs open with explosive force, revealing—Mister Maxwell!

The Demon Librarian, his zit-studded face brick-red with the force of his emotions, rushes in and scoops up O'Phidian in a bear-hug.

"You old asshole!" yells Mister Maxwell.

O'Phidian, the breath crushed out of him, starts to say his Gnostic prayers.

"I love ya!" bellows Mister Maxwell. He plants a big slobbery kiss on the top of O'Phidian's head, then sets him down.

Drawing fresh air deep into his crumpled lungs, O'Phidian watches as Mister Maxwell turns toward the door and beckons for someone else to enter. Meekly, the Tourquoise Courtesan appears.

Now, this liddle China Girl is not, natch, the original T.C., immortal of Shamanka Mountain, or even the nineteenth century incarnation who was the consort of Babbage. She is merely—tho that adverb hardly applies—another of the Little Flowers. This avatar of the Tourquoise Courtesan, in fact, is the daughter of none other than our good friend Number 415, the leader of the Sick Poppies Triad Society, the corpse who donated Impy the Imperial Dollar to Doc Wu. Orphaned during the Communist takeover of Shanghai at age eight, T.C. eventually ended up working in one of Mel's houses, and was one of those gals whose options were picked up when Mel herself was recruited. A little younger than the Numinosos, she looks barely twenty.

Mister Maxwell draws the Tourquoise Courtesan tenderly to his side. "O'Phidian, pal, I can't thank ya enough. First off, ya rescued me from that circus sideshow where I was workin' under the moniker o' 'Bosco'—bustin' my ass for peanuts, liftin' weights and bitin' the heads offa snakes—and ya set me up with a classy desk job. Then, ya intra-duce me to this gorgeous broad here and tell me we gotta make a movie of us fuckin' by the side of a swimmin' pool. Well, I gave it my best shot, and, wouldn't ya know it, little Top Cat here was so stricken by my ee-mense charms—not to mention the heft of my ding-a-ling—that faster'n ya can say 'Vegas wedding,' we was hitched. Now we's here to announce our retirement from your company."

O'Phidian, grateful simply to be still breathing, can't be bothered at this late date to insist on Maxwell and the Courtesan fulfilling the terms of their contract (i.e., lifetime servitude). He himself will be gone soon, and the whole operation will have to struggle on without his guidance.

"What do you plan to do with yourselves?" O'Phidian asks, mildly interested.

"Good question, Chief. We sunk our joint savin's inta a roadhouse. Gonna call it 'Maxwell's Slipper and Hammock.' Gotta nice ring, don't it? Kinda relaxed, like. Anyhow, I'm gonna tend bar, and the Cat's gonna sing and dance. We should pack 'em in! Give the man a sample, Turk."

The Tourquoise Courtesan sweetly warbles:

P.O'P.'S LIFE

What's the matter with your life?
Is the money bringing u down?
Is the mailman jerking u 'round?
Did he put your million dollar check
In someone else's box?

What's the matter with your world?
Did u miss out on the boy and get the girl?
Don't you know straight hair ain't got no curl?
Life ain't real funky
Unless it's got that P.O'P.!

P.O'P.'s Life!
Everybody needs a thrill.
P.O'P.'s Life!
We all got a space 2 fill.
P.O'P.'s Life!
Everybody can't be on top!
But life it ain't 2 funky
Unless it's got that P.O'P.!

Mister Maxwell silences the Tourquoise Courtesan with a cutting motion. "Okay, kid, that's enough free sample. He'll have to pay the cover if he wants to hear more. Well, we're gonna be hittin' the road, Chief. Time's a-wastin'! But we just wanted to say thanks."

"Accepted, accepted," bemusedly blusters O'Phidian.

In an exuberance of spirits, Mister Maxwell yodels, hoists the Tourquoise Courtesan onto his shoulder and, one big hand firmly clutching both her ass cheeks, stomps out.

Now, let's see. Dahomey, 'Seventy-seven, virus and all that....

Oh, right.

O'Phidian wasn't totally obtuse. Far from it. He knew he was smuggling some sort of biological agent back from Dahomey. (Here's the scene at Customs: "You're coming into Los An-juh-lees, are you bringing in a couple of keys?" "Nope. Touch my bags if you please, Mister Custom Man.") But he didn't know what it *did*. For all he knew, it could have been the agent responsible for the Snake Mother's sexual proficiency and nymphomania. Wu was very interested in the ins and outs of sex, funding several clinics and foundations for study of same.

By the time he got back to Wu Labs, the virus was already proliferating in O'Phidian's system, subverting his own cells, using them to reproduce its DNA snakes, just the way O'Phidian used other people to further his desires, the same way all colonizers used the colonized—or in O'Phidian's case, the colon-ized.

The researchers took samples of his vital fluids and went to work making the first analyses of the bug.

They soon told him that it was ineradicable by current measures.

It had written itself by reverse transcription into the nucleus of nearly every cell of his body. Only the blood-brain barrier had temporarily managed to halt it. In short, there was a blot on his Western Blot.

They prescribed a daily dose of acyclovir, azidothymidine, ribavirin, and thirteen other drugs to keep the virus in check without killing it. If O'Phidian did not keep up this regimen—well, they didn't specify, but O'Phidian could guess. He didn't want to end up as a permanently tripping satyr in a dark thatched hut. He didn't think he could take a python up the butt, and fucking a snake's fanged gullet would not be pleasant.

No, O'Phidian had always planned that his long-awaited mating with Sophia would be more—not genteel, but controlled. He would not succumb to this bug! O'Phidian had patience. He could wait to taste omniscience until he had acquired temporal omnipotence.

So for the past sixteen years, O'Phidian had required a daily injection to keep the raw wild virus down. Science didn't know how to kill such a virus, but at least it could be temporarily stopped from completely colonizing his central nervous system and thence his brain.

(Lollolo, the only other person in the world to carry the original, unmodified bug, beat it by a different method. First, his African chromosomal inheritance— which included some of Halie Selassie's ((and hence, Solomon's and Sheba's)) genes—was superior to O'Phidian's for dealing with the intrusion. Second, his fetish and other Vodun rituals allowed him to integrate the effects of the virus into his already basically juju-warped body-mind system. But to tell the truth, even the noble Othello felt a little crazy from time to time.)

The drugs, natch, exacted a price. O'Phidian had always been a dynamic sorta guy, boundless energy to MOVE ANY MOUNTAIN, enough for myriad Machiavellian machinations, a kind of natural force. (After all, didn't his initials—P.O'.P.—match those of the phospate bond that underpinned all life: P-O-P?)

But in the last decade, and especially recently, he had gotten worn down more easily. The constant battle in his cells seemed to tire him out even if he was just sitting. Sometimes he felt like tossing in the towel, and letting the virus have its way with him. (If O'Phidian could have communicated with the invaders lodged in his cells, he would've told them: Hey, *hey*, you, *you*, get offa my cloud!)

But no matter how long he paused—bicep cinched with rubber hose, snaky veins swelling, needle in hand—he always shot up in the end, hoping that someday a more permanent relief would arrive from the bountiful beakers of Wu Labs. He was just Waiting For The Man to arrive with it.

So O'Phidian pursued his various goals in those years, never realizing that his feet had really shot out from under him on the Kozmic Banana, and that he was suspended, with the rest of the unwitting world, in mid-air, like Wile E. Coyote before he's aware he's overshot the cliff-edge, awaiting the results of Wu's conspiracies.

He had favored yang over yin, spark over soup. By forgetting to maintain a balance, he had toppled over like Humpty Dumpty.

Meanwhile, other employees of Wu Labs were tinkering with the captured virus—cultured from samples of O'Phidian's blood—engineering it for specific traits, using the new tools of molecular biology just then becoming available.

They produced variants of the bug, and proceeded to field-test them.

One cultivar was brought down to Haiti. Some genius figured that them island natives had a large preponderance of undiluted Dahomean genes from their slave ancestors, which might mesh synergistically with the virus to achieve the desired result.

Weh-hell, the engineering was bad, the virus didn't perform as expected, and to top the whole shebang off, it got loose in the general population, later arriving in the US in the body of Gaetan Dugas, Patient Zero.

This was '78.

The result was AIDS.

Not Ambient Information Distress Syndrome, Cyril's bane. That was strictly a numinous cultural virus which replicated via memes, and was transmitted thru the media. No, we're talking Acquired Immune Deficiency Syndrome, the plague of our times, a failed bioengineering attempt by Wu Labs that produced dementia instead of gnosis.

Hoe-kay, said those responsible, sorry about that! You can't make an omelette without breaking a few eggs! Back to the drawing boards!

(The anti-AIDS vaccine they quickly cobbled up, and with which all the Little Flowers were innoculated, only worked against the attenuated virus, not the totipotent ancestor O'Phidian harbored.)

O'Phidian knew all this only in a remote fashion. A lot was sheer guesswork. He hadn't been in on this small, seemingly minor project. There was just too much going down for him to keep track of it all. Information overload affected him too. Wu Labs had a hand in everything. (Who would staff the DNA Lounge and the Viper Room, for instance?) O'Phidian had to make decisions about what to keep tabs on. He just decided wrong. All the big money was going into deciphering the human genome and recording it on disc, along with a synaptic map. So that was where O'Phidian placed his bets. He was *sure* this was Wu's shot at immortality. (Altho why the 3100-year-old needed immortality was anybody's guess. Maybe he wasn't sure he would actually live *forever.* Or maybe he just wanted a Backup Copy.)

Anyhoo.... When the Snakes and Ladders Team finally announced success (Lantz's defection, they apologized, had slowed them down), it wasn't what O'Phidian had expected. Immortality carried a price. Still debating whether he wanted to pay that price or not, O'Phidian was hit first with Wu's disappearance, then with the revelation of the Ultimate Scheme he had set in motion before going.

And that was when ol' Wile E. knew in his aching, Sisyphean-punished bones that the cliff-edge was meters out of reach, and that gravity, claiming him as its own stone victim, was beckoning him down, down, down, to the canyon floor, where a cartoon-blue river meandered like a lazy snake.

One thing leads to another and another and another.... It's easy to believe that someone's been lying to me, but it was simply failure to see the Big Picture. The wrong antidote is a bone in my throat, and there never was a moment after I signed on back in '54 when I could have taken a different step....

O'Phidian pushes up from his desk and wearily stands. Feelings flying round, round up in the air, getting in my hair— There ain't no getting away from how I feel today. I've spoken with eternal angels and held the hand of the devil. But I still haven't found what I'm looking for. Nor will I ever on this earth. So I guess it's time to say goodbye—

With a song!

(All the music O'Phidian's heard already this morning has gotten him in a melodic mood.)

O'Phidian takes in hand a microphone connected to a karaoke machine given him as a gift by Lao Cohen. He activates the backing track, an old blues tune by Sonny Boy Williamson, and begins to sing, getting into that MHC Groove.

### FATTENING FROGS FOR SNAKES

It took me a long time
to find out my mistake.

It took me a long time,
long time to find out my mistake.

(It sure did, man.)

But I'll bet you my bottom dollar,
I'm not fattening no more frogs for snakes!

I was born in Dublin
back in Nineteen and Thirty-Seven.
(I started scheming right away.)

My downfall started from Nineteen and Fifty-Four.

(It sure did, man.)

I'm telling all my friends
(if I had any):
I'm not fattening no more frogs for snakes.

(All right, now.)

Here it is, Nineteen and Ninety-Three.
I got no more time to correct all my mistakes.
Whoa-ho, man, no time left to correct all my mistakes.
But I sure am thru with fattening frogs for snakes!

As O'Phidian finishes his song, the door to his office opens for the third time. It's Lolollo and Melusine.

The happy couple are holding hands like sappy teenagers. They obviously haven't slept all night. Melusine is radiant as a bride; Lollolo looks stuporously happy, dazzled but delighted.

"Hello, Patrick," says Lolollo reluctantly, as if this visit were not his idea. Melusine is more enthusiastic.

"Paddy, you hot number! Your fave babe is here to tell you what I learned last night: naughty girls need love too! I just had to find out who's got the ten and a half! I'm so extra happy, I got to share it with someone, and you jump into my mind like a bad penny!"

Lollolo coughs. "Ahem, Patrick, what Mel is trying to say is that we'd appreciate your blessing on our relationship. Could you, as the last Father of the Order of Saint Draco, sanctify our union?"

O'Phidian can't believe what he's hearing. Another wedding! What is this, a play by Shakespeare? No one has ever asked for his blessing before. He's been cursed and reviled plenty of times, but never supplicated as a friend and confidante. Somewhere down in his grinchy big gay heart, a tiny flame sparks, 'bout as proportionately significant as a single candle inside Saint Peter's in Rome.

O'Phidian turns aside for a moment to brush away a big ol' crocodile tear. When he turns back, Mel and her mate are waiting with hopeful and expectant looks.

"Step closer, my children," says O'Phidian. They do so. The priest makes two *mudras*: with his right hand, the *abhaya-mudra*, or fear-dispelling gesture, and with his left, the *varada-mudra*, or boon-bestowing.

"Simple words are best, so keep this short I shall. The *Popul Vuh* tells us, 'The first men were handsome, with looks of the male kind. Their women were truly beautiful. With their women, the men became wider awake. Right away they were happy at heart because of their wives. Perfectly they saw, perfectly they knew everything under the sky, wherever they looked. And as they looked, their knowledge became intense.' And let me remind you, in the words of Simon Magus, 'You twain are but One.' Take as your goal the injunction of Valentinus: 'Make death die.' Go now, multiply and be fruitful."

O'Phidian forms with his hands the *kataka-vardhana*, or "link of increase," and bows.

The newlyweds embrace and kiss. When they separate, Lolollo says, "Little Sister, who's your superman?"

"You're my sunshine superman, Claude. You build me up, inch by inch. Let's split now, honey. It's a nice day to start again. Thanks, boss."

"My thanks too, Patrick. And as your old Irish saying has it, 'May you be in heaven half an hour before the devil knows you're dead.'"

The visitors depart. O'Phidian sighs, and puts them out of his mind. Time to get going, or he won't make his appointment.... There's no time left for B-sides now....

But there is one piece of crucial business left to transact, one circle left to complete.

O'Phidian summons Epifanio Pagano.

Now, Pagano is the one person aside from Wu who can really creep O'Phidian out. This ability stems directly from Pagano's long-time association with Wu.

Some people—those who possess information only—regard Pagano merely as a particularly trusted messenger, one whose orders can be assumed with certainty to come directly from the spotlight-shy Wu himself.

Other folks—those who possess knowledge—realize that Pagano is Wu's cats paw, someone the hidden man can rely on to rake his nuts out of the fire with a high degree of discretion and ingenuity.

A third, much smaller set of people—those who possess at least a smattering of wisdom, such as O'Phidian—understand that Pagano is both messenger and cats paw and more.

He is Wu's catamite and plaything.

He is also Wu's Living Lucky Dime.

And it goes like this:

1949: Wu swallowed Impy the Imperial Dollar in Shanghai, then fled the Communist takeover of his native China, arriving in Formosa. There, he used the chance-found coin in a series of canny deals that laid the foundation for his multi-billion–dollar empire.

Now, you'd think, wouldn't you, that the guy would have a little sentimental attachment for the coin that had so fortuitously come into his hands and helped him rise up from penury. Maybe he would have used the the vast resources of his corporation to recover this important token of the Money Mind. Well, no way. Such feelings had been burned out in Wu 'long about his thousandth year, near as O'Phidian could figure out. Nope, Wu didn't care where Impy went after he passed from his hands. (When O'Phidian told Melusine that Cyril had Impy, she immediately recognized that it was the same dollar her father had carried, and resolved to get it back strictly for herself, as a keepsake of ol' Daddy deClosets, a romantic gesture by the daughter in keeping with that fog-headed Frog's whole ludicrous life....)

What really mattered to Wu was not material possessions, but people.

Wu recognized that the world was *maya*. (Not Eight Snake-type Maya, but Hindu *maya*, illusion.) Sure, inorganic objects were extrusions of the Tao, and thus capable of providing revelations, hence the yarrow stalks and Afa nuts, tea-leaves and coins. (And thus also Cyril's talking gadgets, mouthpieces for the Kozmic Konsciousness. In many ways, our universe *is* a cartoon one, where lips can sprout from teapots and doorknobs. Or as Willy S.—who *knew*, man—had it: "There are books in babbling brooks....")

But it was only people who incarnated whole universes larger even than the Tao within themselves, only people, vessels of spirit, who stood foolishly like boulders in the Flow, or wisely swayed with it like reeds, only people who had true randomness and independence, only people who could reverse Time's arrow, dismantle entropy.

The touchstone that Wu wanted always by him, then, was not the first money he had made, but rather the first person he had subverted in his new life.

That was Pagano.

In 1948, a thirteen-year-old Filipino named Epifanio Pagano, along with his twin sister, Dewey Pagano (named after Admiral Dewey, a hero for his role in the Battle of Manila, May 1, 1898), were sold by their destitute parents to a whoremaster. Dewey and Epifanio ended up in a Manila cathouse, where the owner hoped to use them for customers desiring bother-and-sister acts. Epifanio's recalcitrance and bad attitude, however, earned him a transfer to a notoriously strict Formosa brothel. (Dewey Pagano later went on to marry a US sailor named Billy "Bodacious" Budd and move to America, where—but that's another story.)

This brothel was the very one in which Wu had purchased half-interest.

One day the perfumed and talcumed boy was told to prepare himself to receive an extra-important customer: the new investor.

Almost before he could compose himself, Pagano and the strange old Chink were alone in one of the rooms, a lazy ceiling-fan spinning its rusty blades above the mosquito-netted bed in the twilight of early evening.

Wu was dressed in a Western suit and sunglasses. He smelled like candied ginger. He wore an old-fashioned queue and long mustaches.

He began to undress, until he was down to his sunglasses. These he never did remove.

Wu climbed into bed with the naked boy, who thought to detect—tho the shadows made it hard to be sure—a lack of balls on Wu's part. Was the old guy a eunuch...?

Pagano, on his back, lifted up his legs and spread, uncertain of what kind of pleasures a eunuch would take.

Wu backed up between them, until his feet were up under the boy's haunches.

*A weird position*, thought Pagano, *but not unheard of....*

What happened next, tho, was.

Pagano felt Wu manoeuvering a stiff prick into his asshole.

At the same time, Pagano's own prick was sliding into a wet cunt! Holy Mercury! Wu was a hermaphrodite, just like the Fon god Mawu-Lisa! Wu proceeded to simultaneously bugger and fuck the boy.

It's Venus as a boy!

It was the best sex Pagano had ever had.

For a 3100-year-old guy, Wu could sustain a remarkable hard-on and also produce buckets of pussy juice.

Pagano's reaction to this encounter was complex, to say the least.

Over the following weeks, initial shock and astonishment and revulsion segued into—well, not love, certainly (Wu was too remote a personality for that), but something equally deep and possibly more contorted. Respect mixed with admiration and awe for Wu's unique, primordial physiology, and for the commanding way Wu got what he wanted. Also, there was an intuitive sense of the immense wisdom this relic of antiquity (Pagano had a gut feeling, perhaps engendered by the intimate contact, of exactly how old Wu was) must contain.

From that moment on, Pagano became Wu's first and most ardent follower, his Living Lucky Dime.

Now the fifty-six-year-old man enters O'Phidian's office. The years have stamped the skinny Filipino with lines denoting a certain wisdom all his own. No genius— and unlike O'Phidian, possessing no formal education—Pagano nonetheless has managed to pick up a healthy measure of Wu's cunning and elaborate deviousness, just from carrying out their mutual leader's Byzantine schemes.

O'Phidian greets him still standing. Recalling that day in '54 when Pagano accosted him in London and escorted him to Wu, O'Phidian quivers inside. So innocuous a beginning....

O'Phidian and Pagano are only a couple of years apart in age. Odd to think that the Filipino looked so much older to the seventeen-year-old O'Phidian's eyes. (When I was young and full of grace, I was spirited by a rattlesnake....) He supposes that was because Pagano had by then already worked for Wu for five years, and acquired a patina of knowledge that aged him.

Well, O'Phidian has caught up with and perhaps even surpassed Pagano in deadly knowledge—he's a big noise with all the big boys—and no longer sees the Filipino—hasn't for thirty years—as someone more experienced. Yet his years of intimate bisexual contact with the Old Man Down The Road still endows him with something O'Phidian will never have....

Pagano regards O'Phidian with a calm indifference close to insulting, but is finally forced to avert his eyes when O'Phidian employs his still-deadly Gnostic Whammy.

Attempting to hide his own nervousness thru brusqueness, O'Phidian says, "Have you learned any more about Demesne?"

"Demesne's superiors at the DEA have already recalled him to Washington," Pagano replies. "He should be no more trouble to us."

"Very good."

O'Phidian feels a sudden spurt of affection for his henchman. If only conflicting ambitions and loyalties hadn't come between them.... Perhaps they could even have enjoyed the Sodomic Sacrament together.... The Irishman tries now to project some of that camaraderie, hoping to learn the answer to perhaps the most crucial question of all.

"Epifanio—have you seen Wu lately? Do you know where he is?"

Pagano shakes his head in the negative. "We both know he underwent a sun session, Mister Oh. After that—well, I haven't seen the corpse, have you? But I don't see how anyone could have survived—"

"That's enough," orders O'Phidian. The subject is too close to his own precious hide, now that he's decided. (He's decided? When did that happen? He could have sworn he was going to call up and cancel his appointment.... Has the decision been made for him on some cellular level, has the virus finally grown immune to the daily drugs and penetrated his blood-brain barrier, there to take over his neurons like some imperialistic colonizer? Ah well, for whatever reason, he *has* made up his mind. Life is what happens while you're making other plans, after all. And tomorrow is just an excuse away. But it's just as well. He's so tired, he hasn't slept a wink, so tired his mind is on the blink. And—he's afraid. Yes, big bad O'Phidian, afraid. He doesn't want to meet Sophia on the other side of life, he admits. He can't believe it's really time to stop the world and melt with Her. Isn't it ironic? The prospect of finally hooking up with the one woman this misogynist has longed for now scares the shit out of him. It's the Eternal Brick To The Head: to lust for a babe for so long, then to be impotent when there's a chance of getting it on....)

"All right, then, you don't have to tell me if you don't want to. I'm not personally interested. The only reason that I ask is that someone—or something—has just sent me a message thru the usual channels, signed with Wu's cipher."

Pagano looks interested. "Yes?"

"Wu—assuming it's really him—wants to thank you for so efficiently and elaborately shocking Prothero into a pre-illumination state. He assumes the lad will follow up on Melusine's invitation, and arrive here today, with Peptide and the disc."

Pagano nods humbly. "The Master has always appreciated elegance in the service of enlightenment. Thank you for delivering this compliment. And yes, I believe the boy is sufficiently intrigued to arrive on schedule. Now, if there is nothing else, I have much yet to do."

Pagano moves to leave. O'Phidian stops him with a cough. Pagano turns.

"I won't be seeing you after today, Epifanio. At least, not in the flesh."

"I know. You have perhaps chosen the safest retreat. The times are uncertain. You know, of course, that the *I Ching* has stopped working beyond a certain point in time...."

"Yes. Lollolo informed me that it's the same with the Afa-du. The future seems closed to us now, beyond the immediate stretch. I wish I knew exactly what it meant.

A true end—or a beginning?"

"We will find out soon enough," suggests Pagano, then leaves.

Weh-hell.... O'Phidian checks his watch. Almost time. There's nothing left to hold him here now.

Picking up the blank WORM disc from his desk, he steps out into the anteroom where his secretary—in rotation, any one of the Little Flowers on an R&R (Recovering from Rutting) break—usually sits. The desk is empty now.

All the girls are needed out in the field.

Only they ain't collectin' now.

They're givin'.

They've reversed the flow. No more withdrawals from the gene bank, it's all deposits now.

Can't have their asses draggin' at a time like this.

Out in the corridors, O'Phidian is startled by the silence and emptiness.

Normally full of hustling employees and purposeful noise, the various corridors, labs, offices, cafeterias, stockrooms, garages, and meeting-rooms of Wu Labs are empty now. Everyone has been sent home. There is no longer anything for them to do that truly matters. (Who're you gonna get to do your dirty work, when all the slaves are free?) Wu has played his ace and trumped all other players, who have folded their hands and abandoned the pot. (But—and here's the rub—is it the LAST TRUMP?) Already, cobwebs seem to be proliferating, dust accumulating. Time, not knowing that it's been defeated, attempts to establish its dominion over the abandoned empire of its enemy, stealthy and grasping to the last.... It's as though the vacuum at the center of Wu Labs has finally sucked everything else into it. Having lost interest in the universe she-he created, Mawu-Lisa, no longer content to let it function on its own, has begun to depopulate it....

Passing one room whose door is ajar, O'Phidian is attracted by a faint noise.

In the room, there is a mechanism running unattended.

A laser printer ejects endless copies of *The Diamond Sutra*, transcribing which was formerly thought by Buddhist monks to earn them good karma. The pages land on a conveyer which carries them beneath an Optical Character Recognition system, which apparently feeds back directly into the laser printer. After being scanned, the pages pass thru a shredder, whose bag is overflowing onto the floor.

O'Phidian shakes his head. Even at this late date, the useless schemes run on, self-perpetuating.

Leaving his particular building, O'Phidian crosses a greensward under the hot June sun on a path of cinders, and enters another structure. Here there is some remnant of activity, a few deferential personnel scurrying about as if engaged in something unwholesome, like counterfeiting or pornography. They bow and scrape to O'Phidian, who returns their obsequiousness with the proper magisterial nods.

He thinks of the wedding he's just performed. He really would have made such a fine priest, stepping lordly thru the streets of Dublin. How different his life would have been, if only the Order of Saint Draco hadn't been destroyed.... Ah, buck up, Boyo, no use now for what-ifs. He's taken everything about as far as it can go, and it's about to blow. There's nowhere to run, but there's hell to pay. But at least he can bleed when he wants to bleed. When you hear sweet syncopation, and the music softly moans, tain't no sin to take off your skin, and dance around in your bones....

O'Phidian enters a lab. A team of scientists and their assistants, gowned and seriously antiseptic, await him. This crack squad is known as The Wrecking Crew, masters of the Braintap Shuffle.

In the middle of the room is an enormous machine. Outwardly, it resembles a traditional CAT-scan device: a movable padded pallet extending into a huge toroid, where the scanners are located. (I made my bed, I'll lie in it, I made my bed, I'll die in it.) Inwardly, the machine's circuitry is much more complex. Not only does it incorporate CAT functions, but also NMR, PET, EEG, EMG, BAER, ECHO, digital-subtraction angiography, ultrasonic and infrared sensors, as well as some others which feature new technologies developed at W.L. and as yet unknown to the public.

It is this device that will map every synaptic connection in O'Phidian's brain and digitize the results, thus encoding his entire self. The resulting bit-stream will be fed down a fiber-optic cable to a Sun workstation, and afterwards, at a necessarily slower rate, to a CD-engraving device, which, with its little piece of captured sun, will laser-punch the ones and zeroes on the rainbow platter.

(Of course, such a system implies the ability to make many copies of an individual. However, pursuant to Wu's instructions, when his own disc was created, the Master was wiped.)

Already in storage is the readout of O'Phidian's entire genome, taken from a cell sample (specifically, a shot of his sperm, extracted, for sentimental reasons, with the help of Agnes Agape).

The technicians approach O'Phidian. The Irishman straightens his spine. He'll not appear uncertain before these underlings. *Control, control!* he hears the voice of Father Gogarty urging. Bejaysus, but he could use a Guinness right now!

"Sir?" tentatively says The Wrecking Crew leader, none other than Doctor Black Elk. O'Phidian inclines his head curtly, addressing the whole group. "Gentlemen—" They wait tensely for his commands. Go or no go, on or off?

"It's time to feed the tree! Let's kick out the jams, motherfuckers! We're gonna cut one helluva a record! Set the controls for the heart of the sun, cuz it's on to the heart of the sunrise!"

O'Phidian hands over the blank CD, a special gold-plated, felt-tip-pen-marked one.

The tension is dispersed! Their roles are clear! The Session Players have gotten the Beat! Now they know just what riff 'n' fills 'n' backup vocals to provide.

Time to meet that ol' Darkness on the Edge of Town, Down by the River. I'll be there on time and I'll pay the cost....

O'Phidian is undressed. Hands lift him up onto the pallet, where he is strapped down. (He's about to lose control of his limbs, and it would hinder things for him to thrash about....) Nurse Sally Salonika—O'Phidian notes the cadeuceus on her cap—approaches with a hypodermic filled with a mere ten cubic centimeters of liquid.

It's not O'Phidian's daily dose of anti-viral agents, but rather the mixture that will enable the machine to chart his brain.

A complex blend of radioactive tracers, neurotransmitter-enhancers, endorphins, enkephalins, opiates, barbituates, pixeldrine, delta-sensorium, and less likely compounds, the shot is intended to activate sequentially every single synapse in O'Phidian's brain, so that a complete recording can be made.

The mixture has what is called an $LD_{100}$—the standard shot is a Lethal Dose in one hundred percent of subjects. All neural cells undergo complete apoptosis.

The lab boys have dubbed it Love Potion Number Nine.

Salonika deftly slides the needle home.

O'Phidian wishes it were something else, in another portion of his anatomy.

The serum floods his riverine veins. The pallet is cranked into position within the cipher full of sensors.

Amazing that they could ever accomplish this, thinks O'Phidian as the Hot Juice races toward his brain. Just mapping the full genome alone was such an incredible task. Three billion base pairs, tedious repetitions of A, C, G, and T, a gag cat climbing up the supercoiled ladder. And the annoying thing was that, even counting the metaprogramming, almost half that information was shit, useless, redundant introns. God, is all life half useless? What of art? Jewels buried in equal amounts of shit. Three billion.... Funny, that's almost how much money W.L. had spent to map the genome: three billion dollars. Suddenly O'Phidian has an image of a strand of DNA where every rung is a greenback, ol' George the Liberator, Dead President, frowning three billion times, round and round the double helix. Lessee, each cell-nucleus worth three billion dollars, billions of cells in the body, that makes O'Phidian worth—it's an incalculable sum.

But he was already priceless to himself anyway.

What the fuck good is money? It's such a rip! That three billion was mostly obtained on the float anyway, or by other devious methods of credit. Easy Money. (But the easier it looks, the hotter it hooks!) Funny about credit, the way economists defined it: a standard of deferred payment, which permits the passage of value through time in the opposite direction from that of the store of value. Borrowing against the future, time-travel of money, vast piles of unearned future loot stretching their tentacles back thru time to ensnare us.... He's been a fool, they've all been fools, a cha-cha-chain, chain of fools, bowing down to the Money Mind. It's bigger than all of them, they can't win, can they...?

O'Phidian's been staring blankly at the ring of sensors while these jumbled thoughts swarm through his brain.

Suddenly they vanish.

Doctor, my eyes! Love Potion Number Nine has zapped his neurons. The man's got the funkiest skull soup possible now. In the next 1001 seconds, every synapse in his three pounds of grey matter will be excited, recorded, then inhibited. He will relive every single memory, even those he would swear he has forgotten, leaving him in the end a *wu naor*, or "no brain." And like a dreamer with failed muscle disengagement, his body will try at various points to obey a million different neural prompts, literally tearing itself apart in the process, a colony in revolt. But in the end, he will be imperishably preserved on disc, a Son Of Light.

I need a steamshovel, baby, to keep away the dead. I need a dump truck, baby, to unload my head!

We pause now to ask for a moment's Sympathy for the Devil....cuz here comes the Sun King!

One thousand seconds pass.

O'Phidian's body is wracked and destroyed, while his mind is exalted and recorded from a thousand angles.

By sheer chance, O'Phidian's last invoked memory is one of music.

As he lays on the pallet, unaware that his body is now a bag of fluids, torn muscles and osseous shards, rather a funky soup itself, he is simultaneously walking thru Hyde Park in London, along the Serpentine. It is lovely spring evening. The air smells of growing things. A full orchestra is giving an outdoor concert. O'Phidian, between assignments for both Wu and Liz, feels wonderfully, unnaturally relaxed. He's forgotten, for just a moment, all his schemes. Music wafts over him for several seconds before he recognizes it. "The Posthorn Serenade," by Mozart. How intricate, what a glorious assemblage of supernal, ethereal information. A fitting theme for a Messenger, one who's spent his life shuttling from point to point, urged on by a ghostly horn heard only by him....

Hyde Park disappears in a blaze of light.

It's the Sun, an Invisible Sun no one else in the lab can see. Invisible Sun, gives us hope when the day is done.... Black Hole Sun, won't you come and wash away the rain? I can see clearly now, the clouds are gone. Here's the rainbow I've been praying for.... I'm knock-knock-knockin' on Heaven's Door. Time the Avenger has arrived. But time loves a hero, loves him to death. There was a time before we were born.... Did you find me, Wu, or did I find you? Home, that's where I wanna be. Love me till my heart stops. Wu, I'm carrying the gold, you're watching me sinking! I saw the crescent, but you saw the whole of the moon.... But even the crescent is everything, everything you need, love and more. Look for me somewhere down that crazy river....

Keep away, Old Man! You won't ruin me with your history. I know there's no easy way to be free!

Wait—don't fear the Reaper....

Oona, my mother—is that you? The mother and child reunion is only a moment away....

Pythian Apollo! Time to eat the fruit and kiss the snake goodnight! Sophia, Grace and Glory! Holy Fucking Lucifer! White light, white heat! Light so white it's black! I'm cumming—

—coming home....

# ARE YOU WITH ME, DOCTOR WU?

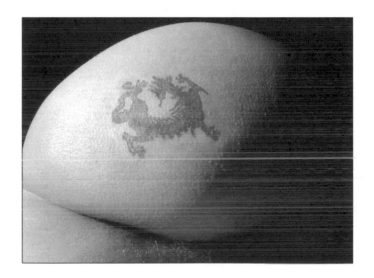

# K L U E S

00111100
"Very few ciphers are worth the trouble of unravelling."
—Charles Babbage

00111101
"The products [of eugenics], being superior to their creators, will inevitably discover that the latter should have produced something entirely different."
—Claude Levi-Strauss

00111110
"....like a journey that loses all meaning when it reaches its end."
—Jean Baudrillard

00111111
"This year turning sixty-four, elements
About to dissolve within me—the Path!
A miracle of miracles, yet where
The Buddhas and the Patriarchs? No need
To shave my head again, or wash.
Just set the firewood flaming—that's enough."
—Nangaku Gentai

Y ou say hello, and I say goodbye. Goodbye, goodbye! I don't know why you say hello, I say goodbye!

Please don't be offended, but just like a miotic cell, I gotta split! The Big Bopper's Wedding Day is here, and I'm gonna walk, before they make me run, cuz I'm just a Ramblin' Man. I gotta get outa this place, if it's the last thing I ever do. Hey, don't be mad and try to cut me down with those angry eyes! You touched my heart so deeply; you rescued me, now free me. There will be no more isolation in our secret separation. It's not that I don't love you—I do! (In fact, this whole story goes out to the ones I love, the ones I leave behind.) But I can't be your Forever Man. You're my everything, you're my soul and inspiration, but, baby, you're also on your own! It's time to get down and shake, shake, shake, shake your booty! I got news for you—I've made plans for two! Cuz I'm a stubborn kind of fella. But I'm also just a man whose intentions are good—please don't let me be misunderstood.

This little story of mine—so fragmentary, so incomplete, now almost over—is my legacy to you. Sorry I couldn't have made it plainer, but there was just so much to get in. And it was such a noisy channel. If you and I had been physically present together, I could have transmitted the Dharma wordlessly, just like a virus. But take my word for it: the pattern's there, if you just look hard enuff with your X-Ray Spex or your Third Eye, the one just below the Uræus.

F'rinstance:

I see the whole world from high, high above. It looks blank and perfect as an egg, the only living patterns being cloud-systems big as continents. Not much information here, but the totality is impressive and gives the illusion of being easy to understand, just like the Tao. Everything small and human has been subsumed in Nature.

Dropping down closer, more information becomes apparent: rivers, storms, dark ocean currents. The surface is more interesting, more complex, but harder to comprehend. We're losing the Tao, overwhelmed by its extrusions.

Closer yet: forests, cities, highways, fires, the Great Wall. The unity is shattered, the symmetries broken. But what we lose in wholeness, we gain in variety and novelty. Humanity begins to seem important.

Finally, we descend thru the roof of a certain house in the Western Hemisphere, on the landmass known as North America, in the country called the United States (One Nation Under A Groove), in the state of Massachusetts, the city of Cambridge, and are swamped with detail, a welter of data. All seems confusion and chaos.

But the Tao is still the Tao....

"This is awesome. I can't believe this. It's incredible. The whole world is going crazy."

Thus saith Cyril, our stupefied hero.

The disconcerted and nonplussed lad is striding agitatedly up and down the

Peptide parlor, cutting a track in the carpet just like a record-pressing machine. He's so upset he's taken off his shades, altho thick noontime Cambridge sunlight pours in.

Mr and Mrs Peptide sit side by side on the couch. Poppa P has found a replacement pipe for the one he lost outside Police HQ, and is clenching the cold stem tightly between his teeth. Momma P, having downed two Tolltex (a new trank from the pharmaceutical firm of Campbell and Campbell), is still upset enuff to be weeping softly. Mr Peptide now moves to console her in his manly fashion by draping an arm around her shoulder.

Polly, our Polly, sits on a comfy sofa, pretty chin in hand, musing. She's wearing one of Cy's Tees, advertising Anthrax's "Spread the Sickness" Tour. She endlessly curls and uncurls one, ahem, sideburn with her free forefinger.

Completing the family tableau is young Paulie.

Seated nonchalantly in a chair, the prodigal son has returned. And boy-o-boy, wotta return!

Paulie is freed of his usual restraints. Gone are the padded biking helmet, the boxing gloves, and, Cyril is willing to bet, altho it can't be immediately verified, the diaper he had to wear for incontinence. Paulie no longer looks like *Lear*'s Edgar pretending to be crazy. Nope, he looks simply great.

His face, without the overlay of insanity, bears a sibling resemblance to Polly's, all clean Nordic planes with a hint of Mom's Grecian complexion. (A few old self-administered contusions remain, but even these healing bruises serve merely as a foil to his good looks.) His arms are folded in a restful manner across his chest, his left ankle is propped insouciantly on his right knee.

Paulie seems to have taken a Personal Grooming Kourse during the thirty-six hours he's been missing. He's gotten a forty-dollar haircut someplace, as well as some new threads: pastel-green shirt, white linen pants, a pair of huaraches. He looks like the undercover protagonist of a trendy cop show.

Cy stops dead in his tracks and confronts Paulie Junior. Glaring at him, he says, "I've got it. You're a ringer. Admit it, you're a spy sent by Wu to keep track of us. That's it, isn't it? C'mon, what have you done with the real Paulie Junior?"

Even before Paulie laughs, Cy realizes how crazy his theory sounds. Why would Wu need to plant a tail on them this late in the game, after he's already gotten everything he wants, and has even invited them to meet him today? The wispy ghosts of Cy's desperate speculations offer no resistance to Paulie's resonant laughter.

"Cyril, how much longer do I have to say it? It's me, Paulie—but I'm cured."

Cy shakes his head. "I can't believe it. There ain't no cure for autism, no spontaneous remission either. It's just impossible. The closest anybody's ever come to alleviating the condition was in the early 'Sixties, during some legal El Ess Dee trials—"

BANG! Cy hits that ol' Brick Wall face on. LSD? What about that super-LSD that the Feds had been looking for during the raid on the Peptide party? Holy

Sandoz, could Wu Labs actually have such a beneficial drug? And what did they intend with it?

Paulie lifts his hands in a gesture of befuddlement. "What can I say, Cyril? I'm here. The evidence is before you."

Polly interrupts. "Cy, I believe him." She rises and moves to stand beside Paulie, reaching down to clasp his hand. "This is my brother. Somehow he's been cured. I can sense it."

With this pronouncement, Mrs Peptide increases her gulps 'n' wails 'n' snuffles to an alarming degree. Dad Peptide, at a loss, stuffs his pipe to overflowing, tamps and lights it, and begins to puff furiously away.

Lingeringly reluctant to believe in such a miracle being handed them on a silver platter, Cy tries one last tack. "Why can't he remember everything then? Answer me that."

Paulie looks genuinely hurt and confused. "I tried to explain that, Cyril, but you wouldn't listen. It was the chemical imbalance in my brain. It made everything so hard to grasp. The whole world rushed in at once. I had no discrimination, couldn't separate out the events in the sensory feed. Everything blended into one squall of noise. There was no filter on my channel, all the message packets got jumbled together. Oh, I retain memories of certain things: a touch, a presence, overheard names, sunlight, darkness. But for the most part, all that I can recall from those years is a big wash of overstimulation."

"How about language, then? How come you can talk so good?"

Pop Peptide speaks up. "Paulie's autism didn't become totally incapacitating until he was about four. He had the foundations of speech, and since we always talked naturally around him, he must have picked up the rest."

Cy contemplates the way Polly's gazing down fondly at her brother and squeezing his hand. The guy does look unnaturally innocent and guileless, as if he's indeed skipped from toddler to adult, passing right over the middle two of the Big Four Stages: Birth, School, Work, and Death. Cyril turns his attention to Mom P., who's ceased sobbing and is also beaming at her son. Paulie Senior puffs contentedly, and Cy can tell he's already calculating where his son will fit into the family business.

"Oh, Christ," Cy gives in. "Why am I arguing? Shake, Paulie, and welcome home."

"Glad to be back, Cyril."

"Paulie," says Polly, after the handshake is over, "tell us once more about what happened to you."

"Well, I have vague recent memories of explosions and bright lights—"

"The crazy raid," interjects Cy. "That guy Demesne, and his macho men in helicopters, swooping down as if they were on a rhino shoot...."

"I'll have to take your word for that.... Afterwards, there was movement, as I was carried or walked—to a car, I suppose. I was given something to drink. Then we drove someplace. The next thing I knew— This is quite embarrassing, Polly. Do you really need to hear it?"

"Yes."

"Well, there was an overwhelming impression of warmth and wetness at my groin, a feeling that a part of me was being surrounded, followed by repetitive motion. At the same time, I felt pressure points all over my body being fingered in odd patterns. Then came an immense flare of release, a sensation I had never experienced before.... I guess what happened—from what you tell me—was that I had sex with someone."

"My little boy!" cries Mom P.

"Oh, Ma!" says Polly. "Your 'little boy' is nearly twenty. He's just suffering from arrested development."

"I know, I know. Still...."

Cy remembers his hallucinatory glimpse of a Zone hooker supporting someone who looked like Paulie. (He's been so busy this morning, he hasn't had a chance to sort out his own busy Saturday night experiences, in fact has kinda sequestered the memories in his hindbrain.) Should he mention it now? He looks at the happy Peptide Parents seated on the couch. No way. He'll tell Polly later, when they're alone. Let Mom 'n' Pop think The Girl Next Door raped their son. That's the way it's spoze to happen anyway....

"After that," continues Junior, "my mental condition began to improve quickly. As if I were a television and someone were fiddling with my controls, the higgledy-piggledy picture of the universe I had always had began to cohere. Objects and sounds assumed definition. Instead of noise, everything was a song. Pretty soon I was functioning normally—at least I assumed it was normally—for the first time since I was four years old.

"Looking around, I saw that I was in a room with a bed, alone. The door opened, and a woman came in. I tried to ask questions, but she wouldn't answer. I couldn't talk so good at first, so maybe she just didn't understand me. She called someone on a telephone, and a man arrived with scissors. I had my hair cut. Then she ordered me these clothes. Did I mention I was naked? Except I wore a towel for the—is it 'barber?' Before the clothes came, this very nice woman and I, ah, um, had sex again. This time"—Paulie smiles fondly—"I learned how to lick the woman's private parts."

"Oooooh!"

"Ma! Quiet!"

"After we were finished and my clothes had arrived, we dressed and left. There was construction, repairs, going on in the hall. I saw by the room numbers we were on the tenth floor. Down in the lobby, I noticed the name of the hotel: the 'Rit-zee Car-el-ton.'"

"Yeah, that's another thing," quibbles Cy. "How come he can read?"

"Suh-*eye*-eye—!"

"All right, all right already."

"We got into a big, big car with a television in back—the driver was a dark-skinned man—and she—the woman whose parts I licked—said an address. Now I know it was ours. We rode in silence. The car arrived here. I looked at the woman.

She said, 'Tell them this is a little present from someone who's sorry for their other losses.' Then I got out and she drove off. You know the rest."

Mister Peptide removes his pipe and says, "Son, don't you remember any injection or operation, something that would account for your recovery?"

"Nope. Just a drink, followed by"—Paulie's face lights up again—"the sex."

Mom P gets her mouth open, but a withering look from her daughter stifles her. Polly then asks, "Was there anything unusual about the woman, Paulie?"

"Well, even considering that she was the first one I've ever really seen, I'd still have to say no. Oh, she did have a drawing on her, ah, bum. Some sort of crocodile. I guess that's not normal. I looked in the mirror for one on me, and didn't see any."

"Crocodile?" This from Cy.

"Paulie used to love for us to read to him about crocodiles when he was three," explains Polly. "I think we can safely assume it was the Wu dragon."

Cy nods, recalling the tattoo on the asses of Melusine, Pellucida, et al. After the changes he's been put thru, he ain't one to dispute the power of the libidinous, hard-boppin' Crocodile Rock. (And was not Sebek, the Egyptian crocodile god of the Abyss, cognate with Ananta, the Kozmic Serpent supporting the sleeping Vishnu?)

"Say," declaims Pop P, comprehension dawning on his face as he digests Polly's last comment, "you kids seem to know more about this whole affair than you're letting on. And wait one darn minute— Where's that jerk, Augenblick, who wants to be my son-in-law, been lately? And Cyril, didn't you used to hang out with a pretty black girl named Rosie?" Mister Peptide furrows his brow. "I hope you two haven't gotten into anything that'll take you over your heads. If you're talking about Wu of Wu Labs—well, they have a very cut-throat reputation—at least in the biotech field."

"Don't worry, Dad. We know what we're doing. Some day we'll tell you everything. But not now. Cy, let's go. We've got an appointment to keep."

Polly kisses her family goodbye while Cy stands itchily at the door. "Oh, Paulie," she says, "I hate to run out on you as soon as you're well for the first time, but we'll have plenty of time together later."

*If we're alive after today*, thinks Cy cynically.

Or is he just being realistic?

Soon they're on the Virago, a-zippin' down Mass Ave thru Allston via Pony Street and Rocking Horse Road, and onto Route 90, EXILES ON MAIN STREET, thence to Route 128, where the incommunicado conspirators await, a station no longer sending, a signal-source grown silent, a dead channel. It's time for our Basepair Buddies to travel up around the bend, out where the neon turns to wood.... (But remember: you who are on the road must have a code that you can know by; so teach your children well, because their parents' hell did slowly go by....)

Cy reflects on how impossible it is to tell your parents anything. Children, behave, that's what they say when we're together. And watch how you play. They don't understand! We're running just as fast as we can (in the Red Queen's Race). Look at the way we gotta hide what we're doin'. But I think we're alone now....

Cyril opens up a channel on his helmet transceiver. He explains to Polly about his chance encounter with Paulie and "the nice woman with the crocodile on her bum."

"You say this happened late last night in the Combat Zone?" queries Pol. "What were you doing there? You told me you spent the evening at Symphony Hall, listening to Yo Yo Ma and Itzhak Perlman perform the works of Don Van Vliet, backed up by the Antelope Valley College Choir and the Saint Louis Aquarium Choraleers."

Ah, yes.... Cyril vaguely recalls that this morning, his brain still functioning rather poorly from having been shattered, he improvised some farrago of lies to explain his late-night absence. He knew intuitively that he should not divulge the truth to Pol. She would surely be angry if she learned how he had foolishly endangered himself by plunging into Wu strongholds. (I've done all the dumb things. I've stood right in the middle of the tracks, with the Love Train roaring down....)

And speaking of plunging into things, there was the not inconsequential matter of his infidelity, his plunging into a genuine Wu Labs pussy. How could he explain that he had been tempted by the fruit of another in a moment of weakness...? He'd really be up the junction then. Nosirree, there was no way he could tell Polly half of what had occurred. Best to boil the funky soup of that night down to a rich stock of lies, purged of, ah, sensual details.

And that includes the celluloid image he can't bear to recall. The picture of his naked suh-suh-suh-sister— The sight of her buh-buh-buh-boobs getting— The cuh-cuh-cuh-cock down her throat and up her— Her fuh-fuh-fuh-face in a wuh-wuh-wuh-woman's lap—

No!

A twisted version of the horrible truth spills out of Cy then as an excuse, as they ride toward their destiny.

"I was meeting my sister there...."

"Anna? You met Anna last night in the Combat Zone?"

"Yeah. Hubby owns a theater there now. Al Condor passes for respectable, but he's really not."

"Oh. Well, if you were with your sister, there's nothing for me to worry about then—I guess. You know, that reminds me. Daddy gave me some more cash this morning. If you want, we can drop by Anna's house and pay back that money you borrowed. I mean, suppose we don't return from Wu Labs? All our debts will be discharged, our karma will be clean."

"No! I mean, that's nice of you and all, Pol, but no, thanks! It's just that I saw quite enough of Sis last night."

"Whatever you say, Cy."

Silence for some miles. They pass a ruined building set back from the hi-way whose partially smashed signage reads: —REE-L——-ENT—. Then, Polly speaks.

"You know, I'm serious about us maybe not coming back from this meeting, Cy. We know these people play rough. So I just want to say thanks for sticking by me these past two awful weeks. You were my only consolation and comfort. I couldn't have made it without you. I've been so happy together, even if we just were talking about the weather."

"Me too. And that goes double. Our love will be renowned in history, just like—like Romeo and Juliet! You can bank on my love!"

"How sweet! I'm glad you feel that way. And I just want you to know that if—I mean when—we get Augie and Ruby back, I intend to tell them everything about us, how we've become lovers. Then we'll work out some new arrangement like rational, civilized, mature adults."

"I'll choke the life outa that stupid quarterback if he tries to take you away from me."

"What if he wants Ruby?"

"I'll choke him if he tries to have her too."

"You want both of us women, leaving poor Augie with no one?"

Hmmm, did you ever have to make up your mind, to pick up on one and let the other one slide? "Oh, right. That is kinda greedy, isn't it? Well, lessee.... Good ol' Augie, he's my friend after all, I've known him lo these many years. He can join the three of us."

"How generous of you, Caliph. And what are we all supposed to do together?"

"You've got a good imagination, you work it out."

Polly pushes her ass against Cy's crotch. "If last night was any indication of your inclinations, I hope poor Augie doesn't fall asleep on his side."

Cy is mortified. He blushes beneath the obscurity of his black visor....

He got back into Boston proper around three AM, having hitched a ride from a trucker speedin' on uppers. The guy introduced himself as Horace Hourburrows, and then just wouldn't shut up. Kept yammerin' on about the Phantom of 309 and 30,000 pounds of United Fruit Company bananas.... But Cy didn't care, since he felt little like upholding his own end of any conversation.

Dropped off at an exit ramp, Cyril had to walk all the way cross-town, the subways being closed. It gave him plenty of time to think. His brain was clearing a little; the fog of disappointment, shock, lust and helplessness that had left him feeling like a puppet was dissipating ever so slightly. He felt able to think somewhat logically again. All the things he had been shown during his Nighttown Odyssey seemed to be subliminally arranging themselves into a picture that might one day show its meaning. Although he couldn't quite fathom it yet, he tried to summon up the faith that it would come clear, even if, like satori, it remained forever beyond words.

Wearily Cy trudged up the steps to his apartment and let himself in. He had seen the Virago parked out back—guarded by the unsleeping Moses, who let out a small growl at the smell of Cy—so he knew Polly was back.

There was a light on in the bedroom.

He went in.

Polly had fallen asleep, reading that Salonika book and waiting up for him. She was naked, lying on her side, legs drawn up. Her tufted quim beckoned pinkly.

Weh-hell.... At first, Cy felt too weak to even imagine taking advantage of this silent invitation. He had planned on no dancing when he got home that night. After all, three orgasms with Melusine, aka Lysine, had totally drained his batteries. Or so he would have sworn.

But then the strangest thing happened.

He realized with a start that he was still wearing the jade dragon-ring Melusine had fastened onto him.

And now it was radiating a hot sensation into his cock.

Cy quickly stripped. Polly snored on. He looked down at his private member.

It was wreathed in green luminescense emanating from the jade ring. (Who you gonna call? Ghostbusters!) As he watched, the corona stretched outward, drawing his prick with it to full extension and hardness.

Perhaps to fuller extension and hardness than ever before.

As Cy regarded this unwished-for aching boner, the emerald radiation suddenly took the shape of a couched dragon, its head at the head of his cock, its legs and folded wings laid back along the shaft, which was visible thru the glow.

A hologram condom!

Cy's mind suddenly held nothing but the desire to discharge his cock for the fourth time.

My ever-changing moods!

Start me up and I'll never stop, cuz you could make a dead man cum!

His love was like a button: he couldn't stop pushing it....

Get up—I feel like being a Sex Machine!

He doused the lamp. He could make out Polly's quim by the radiance of his cock. It beckoned: Read my lips, and what you don't know, find out!

Cy crept up behind Polly on the bed without waking her—as indicated by her uninterrupted snores.

He grabbed his demanding dragon and found it still wet with Melusine's juices of an hour or two ago, preserved by the unbreathing cotton-nylon fabric of the bikini-brief underwear he had worn instead of his traditional Jockeys.

Cy positioned the creature oh-so-gently at Polly's cipher.

Or so he thought.

As he nudged it past more-than-expected resistance, he realized that, in the immortal phraseology of Paul Krassner, he had mistakenly entered Orifice B, instead of the more traditional Orifice A.

"Zzshnrr— Wha—? Cy, is that you? Cy, *what* do you *think* you're *doing* back *there?!*"

"Let's swap info," murmured the demented boy, pausing halfway up.

"Jesus Christ! It's too big— Oh! You're pushin' too hard, you're pushin' too hard on me!"

Cy relented.

Polly urged, "No, don't you understand? I meant do it harder if you're gonna!" Cy felt Polly's hand drop down to her pussy, and he banged his dragon home.

Well, Cy lasted so long—he *had* come thrice within the past few hours—that Polly soon caught up with him, frigging herself to four orgasms.

At last Cy felt his own climax approaching. When it arrived it was pretty dry.

But just enuff of dem liddle heads-and-tails wrigglers with their new hitch-hikers escaped to do their job in Pol's system.

Tainted love! I've given you everything a boy could give....

When Polly could speak again, she said, "Cy, where have you been?"

Cy pulled out. He painfully snapped the ribbon around his waist and removed the dragon ring before it could make him hard again. "Inna mornin'," he replied sleepily, then began snoring himself.

There came to him a single dream in the night, which he told to Polly at the breakfast table, over coffee, along with the excuses for his absence.

"I was wandering thru a big control room full of switches and dials and meters. Suddenly I realized it was the headquarters of the Master Streetlight Man. I came upon a figure in a chair. It was Max Parallax.

"'Max,' I said, 'you're dead.'

"'No, I'm not. I'm just working for Wu now. Look at the great job he's given me. Why don't you join me?'

"Then Max began flipping switches and pulling on levers and I looked out the window that was suddenly there and the sun rose up at triple speed and raced across the sky and sank and rose and sank and rose again and again—"

Polly smiled. "Sorta like your cock."

"Jeez, Pol, get serious! What do you think it means?"

"Probably that you're feeling sorry for how you always insulted poor dead Max, and want to enshrine him now as one of your childhood icons."

"Oh. That makes sense, I suppose. You don't think it was a real message from him?"

"I doubt it. You told me how you got a phone call yesterday after I left, inviting us to visit Wu today, and it wasn't any voice you recognized. Well, if Max was still alive and working for Wu, wouldn't they have used him to convince us to come?"

"Oh, right," agreed Cyril, trapped in the logic of his own lies. "So, are you up for going there?"

"Of course." Polly leers. "And I know after your performance last night that I don't have to ask if you can get up for it."

"Sorry, Pol, I can explain—"

"Don't bother. The impulse was quite normal. It's just that your aim was off."

"Gee, thanks for bein' so understanding, Pol."

They were just stepping out the door when the phone rang with news of Paulie Junior's return. Hold on, troops, about-face!

And now here they are, travelling down the expressway to Wu's heart (or is that the expressway to Wu's skull?).

"Cy," queries Pol, "do you feel ready for this?"

Good question.... If we're being honest here, Cy must admit to feeling in less than peak condition. Too little sleep, nothin' but coffee and a nougaty Zero Bar for breakfast.... His stomach feels strange, and his brain stranger. It's almost the same set of sensations he experienced just before the spiked punch Turned Up The Gain on his neurotransmitters.... Hope he doesn't have a bug....

"Well, no, not really. My head feels spacey."

"Mine too."

"My vision is a little blurry."

"Mine too."

"And I'm hearing weird subliminal whispers."

"Me too."

"It's probably just a summer cold, huh?"

"Yeah, right."

Cy is not comforted by Polly's mordant tone. In fact, he is struggling to hold down a sense of vast, formless alarm, a kind of generic Cy-fear. Don't let this turn into a Motorpsycho Nightmare!

"I guess we don't have much choice except to tough it out, despite how lousy we feel. We can't let Ruby 'n' Augie down. We'll have to try to be heroes, if just for one day...."

They cruise on down the interstate, capable Pol firmly guiding the cycle, despite any visual impairment.

The events of the past twenty-four hours continue to tumble round and round in Cyril's brain like laundry in a dryer. Paulie's inexplicable return and cure, his sister on screen, his cock up Melusine's ass, Three-Card Monte Python emerging backwards like a newborn serpent-god from Numinoso's cunt, Horus out of Isis....

Would he ever get an answer to all his questions? More to the point: Wouldn't any possible answer raise more questions than it put to rest?

Cy tries to push it all out of his mind. He tightens his grip around Polly's waist. I got you, babe, to hold me tight. Nothing can change this love. Love will find a way. Polly rips thru a curve. Oh, yeah—and my love is in league with the freeway!

It's very warm today—or maybe it's just Cy. In any case, good ol' Route 90 feels like a rattlesnake speedway in the Utah desert.

They pass a traffic sign in the form of a Feynmann diagram: COLLIDING PARTICLES AHEAD.

Polly's voice crackles out of his earphones. "Have you noticed how weird the traffic is acting today?"

"Yeah, now that you mention it...."

"The road seems to have a mind of its own...."

(Polly, as usual, has brought up an interesting subject. Have you ever been driving along an Interstate when suddenly tail lights propagate down the line of cars ahead of you like nerve impulses materialized as red flashes, and you slam on your brakes? Traffic grinds to a halt. You can see the people around you, also stalled, begining to assume that mindless state suited to delays. *Oh-oh*, you think, *an accident*. For the next half hour or so, you crawl ahead a few feet at a time, anticipating that around the next turn, just beyond that lamp-post, that Jersey barrier, you'll see a scene of carnage, THE CRASH, where flesh and metal mingle obscenely. But before that ever happens, the pace of the traffic picks up slowly, the spaces between cars increasing from inches to feet to yards. Suddenly, conditions are inexplicably back to normal! You never see the reason for the delay, not even so much as plastic litter strewn across the lanes. What could it have been? A cop, who finally drove away? If so, why was he there interferring in the first place? Was it a self-organizing criticality? *Why the queue? Was The Controller busy polling another channel? Was your lane offline..?!)*

A few more miles pass.

Suddenly, a red car pulls up in the lane to their left and begins to keep pace with them.

It's Mel in her convertible Corvette.

There's a boogieing B-boy in the passenger seat. Even thru his helmet, Cy can hear that Mel's new boyfriend is groovin' to the sound of Public Enemy's *Fear of a Black Planet*.

Mel winks, and blows Cy a kiss.

Luckily, Polly does not notice.

Then the hip-hop jalopy races off.

Its license plate is 0X−174. And it bears two bumper stickers.

SUBVERT THE DOMINANT PARADIGM.

ONE DAY AT A TIME.

Cy breathes a sigh of relief. Thank God Mel didn't offer to accompany them. Introductions would have been awkward, to say the least....

The fading sound of Public Enemy prompts Cy to switch his own headset to an AM oldies station.

He hears four notes of Donovan's "Wear Your Love like Heaven," and is immediately catapulted into

## CYRIL'S LAST FUGUE

Cy finds himself wearing elephant-bell-bottoms and a paisley-patterned shirt. Around his neck is a leather thong holding a brass Peace Sign. Sandals adorn his feet. His hair hangs below shoulder level.

He is outdoors, in the middle of Nature Primeval.

There is a hippie chick next to him, clad in a flare-collared white blouse, orange micro-skirt, windowpane stockings, and square-heeled shoes with big buckles. Beside her stands a white guy with an Afro restrained by a headband. He is wearing a striped knitted jumpsuit.

"Hi," says the woman. "My name is Lady Sunshine. And this is Davey Burnout."
"Welcome to Utopia, man. Have some acid."

Burnout hands Cyril a tablet. Cy drops it to the ground as if it were on fire.

"Utopia? Acid? Where am I?"

"Hey, cool it, man," advises Burnout. "You're in good old America—Boston, in fact. This is Kenmore Square."

Cy looks around at the ancient trees. Liddle birdies are smiling down on them. A nearby river gurgles happily along.

"Boston? No, it can't be...."

"Oh, but it is," says Lady Sunshine. "You see, this is a different America from the one you know. This is the America where the 'Sixties never died, a place where there ain't nobody crying, no smilin' faces lyin' to the races."

"Right on, Lady! The Revolution triumphed on this timeline. We turned around the fascist military-industrial-consumer complex, and made a paradise on earth. Wherever there was a factory, now there are mountains and rivers. Wherever there was a shopping mall, it's covered with flowers. This used to be real estate, now it's only fields and trees. Instead of a parking lot, we've got a peaceful oasis. And we're all like Adam and Eve in the Garden of Eden."

Lady Sunshine squeezes Burnout's hand blissfully. "That's exactly how it is, Cyril. Everybody is happy here. Even my main squeeze. You know, Davey used to be an angry young man at one time. He got so catatonic that he'd pretend he was a billboard standing by the side of the road. In your world, he ended up in a sanitarium. But here he's mellow, like everyone else. Life is just one long groovy trip now."

Cyril is astonished almost beyond words. "All of the country is like this?"

"You've got it, you've got it."

"What the hell do you do all day?"

"Brew up some acid, turn on, make love, smell the flowers."

"What about music?"

"All acoustic, of course. Unplugged. Mostly reed pipes and log drums."

"No electric guitars? No synthesizers? No sampling?"

"Sampling? What's that?"

Cy shakes his head. "I can't believe this! What do you eat?"

"Well, we used to microwave," confesses Lady Sunshine, "but now we just eat nuts and berries."

"We just caught a rattlesnake," adds Burnout, "so now we've got something for dinner."

"Yuk! If this is paradise, I wish I had a lawn mower!"

"Don't be like that, Cy," pleads Lady Sunshine. "Isn't this what you've always dreamed of? A perpetual 'Sixties?"

"I didn't think it'd be like this. Where's the town? Look—this was a Pizza Hut, and now it's covered with daisies. I miss the honky-tonks, Dairy Queens and Seven-Elevens. I dream of cherry pies, candy bars and chocolate-chip cookies."

"Sorry, Cyril. Those are all gone now. And pretty soon, they'll all be gone in your world too."

"What? What do you mean? What are you crazy hippies gonna do to my timeline?"

"Oh, it's not us, Cy. It's you."

Burnout advances on Cyril and places a hand on his shoulder. "You're either on the bus or off the bus, Cy. C'mon, be a happy camper and take your acid."

Shrugging off the hand and knocking the second proffered tablet to the grass, Cy yells, "Keep away from me, you, you—Nazi!"

In the next instant, Cyril is facing Lambton Wurms in the room with the two analog computers and the desk. The soldier with the hole in brow looks weary. His head droops, his hand cannot even clutch his pistol.

*"Augenblick mal!"* he says. "Wait one minute while I assemble myself.... There." Wurms lifts his head to face Cyril. "So, we meet again. I must confess, you are beyond my reach now, *Herr* Prothero. I regret that my rebirth occured too late and ended too precipitously for me to reclaim my Regina. If I am incarnated again, it will be during the Year Aniadin, and you will all be beyond violence. Nobody's gonna touch you in those Golden Years. So be it. *Auf weidersehen*, my old enemy. Have fun with your new comrades."

Cy's back in Utopia. He's flat on his back, and a naked Lady Sunshine is sitting atop him, preparing to insert his cock up herself. Davey Burnout is kneeling on Cy's shoulders and is holding a sugarcube poised over Cy's open mouth.

"Time for some free love, honey," says Lady Sunshine.

Struggling, Cy yells, "It's not worth the price! I'm not buying into your hippie dream! Your wooden ships ain't no paradise! Polly, help! Don't leave me stranded here! I can't get used to this lifestyle!"

The motorcycle is decelerating. The altered kinesthesia shocks Cy out of his fugue, the body-mind balance temporarily swinging toward body.

Hastily switching back to their private channel, Cy is just in time to hear Polly say, "We're almost there."

They're on an off-ramp leading directly to a private industrial park.

The sign on the light-standard at the foot of the ramp reads FASCINATION STREET. Below that is a board listing the tenants of the park.

WU LABS
COSMO'S FACTORY
FANTASY FACTORY
PISS FACTORY

Wu Labs is easily the largest complex, a scattering of postmodern glass and steel edifices radiating a Welcome to the Boomtown air of wealth. This is the place where the truth is concealed for the children of concrete and steel.

Trying to summon up a bit of typical Cyrillic bravado, Cy says, "You'd better cover your ass now, Wu baby! We've got your number, and your number is up! We're gonna shout it to the top, and we won't get fooled again!"

Polly responds in kind. "We're gonna kick your yellow ass, Wu! It's time to face the face!"

They wheel into a vast asphalt lot, stop and set the kickstand. They dismount and doff their helmets.

"Gee, Cy—the lot's empty."

"Well, it *is* a Sunday."

"Oh, right. My sense of time is all screwed up. It seems like there's eight days to the week...."

"Hey, does anybody ever really know what time it is?"

Polly shivers. "Boy, even for a Sunday, it's so quiet. It's like there's a kind of hush all over the world...."

"Hey, no hype now," warns Cy. But he feels it too. It's Aboriginal dreamtime. The whole world shuts down. We're so tired, tired even of snowflakes on our eyelashes....

Cy tries to buck himself and Polly up. "Just forget it, Pol. Everything's okay as long as we're together. C'mon, we're not gonna learn anything just standing here. Let's go inside. Do you have the disc?"

Polly pats her butt-pac, slung to the front. "Right here."

Having verified this important point, Cy can think of nothing else to say.

They walk toward the front door of the main building. No security guard awaits them. The door is unlocked.

They step into an tall atrium reception area, filled with potted plants. No one's here, either. There are, however, four waiting pieces of original artwork hung on the walls to impress visitors with Wu's hipness and taste.

"Ouroboros," by Randolfo Rocha.

"My Dearest Cipher," by Doug Anderson.

"Indecipherable Narratives," by Julian Schnabel.

"Black Numbers," by Jasper Johns.

So. This is it, the culmination of days of frustrated questing, the arrival at the Forbidden City.

Why, then, is it so goddamn anticlimactic?

"Hey, is anybody home?!" shouts Cy.

Only echoes respond.

Where do we go from here? Still looking for my bluejean baby queen, prettiest girl I've ever seen (no offense, Polly).... Guess we just Rock On.... We've got your skinny girl, here at the Western World....

Polly rests a hand on his arm. "That's no good, Cy, it's obvious the hirelings are all gone. We have to hope Wu remains. Let's try to find his office."

They move further inside.

Weh-hell.... Our Heroes are really Backstage now. In the Kozmic Drama Of Life, they have jumped right out of their assigned roles. They left the Audience and entered among the Actors long ago, when Ruby and Augie first vanished. They were Onstage for what seemed the longest time, running around crazily at the wordless promptings of an unseen Director. Now they've Lifted The Scrim, hiked the skirts, so to speak, of Thalia (or is that Melpomene? Hard to tell the Muses apart from this angle—), and stepped beneath, into the musky dark. Wandering through the sterile corridors and unpeopled rooms of Wu Labs—as bare as the universe before Eurynome got the hots for Ophion—Cy feels the same eerie sensations as when he went backstage at the SHANNON'S DRAGON strip-joint, a kind of Jack-and-the-Beanstalk wariness, as if he's trespassing on the territory of a bone-crunching giant, about to confront the ineffable. It's a strange, strange world, Master Jack. You taught me all I knew, and I'll never look back....

Awright, enough of that! Indulging in such feelings will lead straight to the whim-whams, which Cy really don't need. Let "Eff the Ineffable!" be our motto, and full speed ahead....

Eventually, Cyril and Polly wander into what is clearly Executive Territory: the carpets are deeper, the furniture more expensive. Everything reeks of money.

It's the Land of Perks 'n' Jerks, Hacks 'n' Flacks, Bankers 'n' Wankers, Lawyers 'n' Destroyers, a place Cy has always instinctively hated. Will they really find the enigmatic, hoary Wu here, a mossy archaic dragon in this domain of newly coined MBAs who can barely grow one beard among them, and take-charge CEOs, elegant in their suits and greying temples?

"Cy," says Polly tentatively, "what do you make of this?"

"This" is a leather-padded, brass-studded, handle-less door with a single button set in the wall beside it.

"I don't know what it could be, but I know there's only one way to find out."

And with that, Cy presses the button.

In a few seconds a subtle *whooshing* noise is audible. This is quickly followed by a demure *ping.*

A hitherto invisible sign above the door lights up:

THIRTEENTH FLOOR ELEVATOR

The door swings open, revealing a luxurious elevator interior.

"Do we dare?" poses Cy.

"Do we dare not?" counterposes Pol.

They step in, an accordian-gate slides across, the door closes, and the elevator begins to move.

"Are we going up or down?"

"Does it matter?"

The elevator stops.

The door opens onto—

Majestic opulence? Corporate hedonism? Executive opium vice-den?

Nope.

Dimly lit, the room is quite Spartan, a replica of the interior of a Chinese house, circa Late Chou Period, time of Confucius and Lao-Tse. Mats, carved screens, paintings on silk, ceiling timbers, a potted bamboo. A closed door across the room mirrors the elevator entrance.

By the elevator door stands a wood sculpture laquered in the traditional red and black: two cranes back to back, with two snakes coiled at their feet: an ancient talisman warding against the intrusion of evil.

Water purls out of a fountain and into a pool filled with golden carp swimming around a submerged castle. Overflow from the pool trickles over a bed of time-smoothed stones, filling the air with moisture and sound.

Dominating the center of the room is a huge dragon sculpted from an improbably huge lump of jade, its mouth agape.

There's no human present.

But the room smells like candied ginger.

"This is it," says Cy, and they step in.

"What now?" asks Polly, when they've satisfied themselves that there's no one hiding under the rush mats or between the slim fronds of bamboo. (The second door is locked.)

"I don't know. Jesus, it seems that since we were called, there'd be someone waiting—"

"Hold on, Cy! Look at this!"

Polly's peering into the dragon's mouth. Suddenly she presses a tooth, and the dragon pokes out its tongue.

Which happens to be the receptacle tray for an optical disc, just like the mechanism in Cyril's player at home.

Polly reaches into her bag and removes the CD she carries, that much-handled disc which Augie thrust on Cy two weeks ago, the day he and Ruby vanished, and which has been so useless up till now.

She inserts the spuriously labeled John Lee Hooker "Crawlin' Kingsnake" platter into the tray and the dragon retracts his tongue.

Almost immediately there is an explosion of colored light from a hidden source, and Polly and Cy enter into that phase of their adventure known variously as:

CONVERSATION WITH A DEAD MAN,
OR,
THE GHOST IN THE MACHINE,
OR,
IS IT LIVE OR IS IT MEMOREX?

One corner of the room is filled with a three-dee projection, a hologram. The translucent figure is that of a thin Chinese man clad in a long robe, seated in a hologram chair.

His unique garment is colorfully figured with:

One Phoenix.

Two Dragons.

Four Suns.

Eight Snakes.

Sixteen Moons.

Thirty-two Buddhas.

Sixty-four Women.

This robe is the legendary Garment of the Maitreya Buddha, passed down thru the centuries from Zen Master to Zen Master until its rightful owner should be born to assume it.

The man's grey hair is in a long queue, and he's got them Fu-Manchu droopy mustaches. His face is lined, but not excessively so for a guy pushing thirty-two centuries. His eyes are concealed, natch, by shades. His knobby hands are folded in his lap.

A creature now of light, Doctor Wu has at last come out of the shadows. (I used to think that the day would never come, when my life would depend on the Morning Sun ((Mourning Son)).) No one except Pagano—and possibly O'Phidian, bless his Gnostic soul—has ever seen the Doc—or even his image—so clearly in modern times (i.e., post-1948).

"Please excuse me for a moment," says the Doctor, "while I catch up. You see, as Captain Beefheart once said, 'I'm not really here, I just stick around for my friends.'" Half a sec passes. "That's better," Wu affirms. "Old habits die hardest, and I find I must still have my daily dose of information. Please, take a seat."

Cy and Polly have yet to recover from this manifestation of Doctor Wu, invoked from the CD they carried with them unwittingly through all their travails. Cy is utterly frustrated. His fingers are half curled, aching to grasp. Where is the scrawny neck he often imagined strangling, until Ruby's whereabouts were divulged? Where is the physical Wu whom they could threaten and cajole? Gone, gone, into the realm of electrons and photons, bits and bytes, Number Heaven. Wu is now obviously only a Digital Doc, a Quantum Quack, a Hologram Hoaxer. I'm looking thru you, where did you go? I thought I knew you, what did I know...?

Polly—sane and sensible Polly—gets a grip on herself first, and, remembering their mission, demands, "Where are our friends you kidnapped, Doctor Wu? Ruby Tuesday and Augie Augenblick...."

Doctor Wu steeples his gnarly fingers, his eyes utterly unreadable behind his Raybans. "You begin with a misconception, dear."

Hey, thinks Cy, this guy's elocution and diction are flawless American. Is the buried distant supercomputer on which he's being recreated in realtime cleaning up his accent, via some Lantz-written routines, or is that the way the real Wu talked? Guess they'll never know....

"I was not responsible," continues Wu, "for the abduction of your friends—except insofar as I am ultimately responsible for everything my employees do. The buck does stop with me, after all. Although of late, distracted by my own problems and concerns, I must admit I haven't been as diligent an overseer as I might have been. Things have gotten a little out of hand.... No, it was not I who took your friends, they were kidnapped on the initiative of my second-in-command, a gentleman by the name of O'Phidian—"

"We know him!" interrupts Cy. "He was that Irish bastard in Ruby's movie. Callin' Ruby *darlin'*— Where is he? Let us at him—"

"As of this morning, Mister O'Phidian's existence is identical to mine. His mortal body is in bits and pieces. And I fear his disc is not slotted at the moment. If you wish—"

"No," says Pol, "just answer my original question. Where's Augie and Ruby?"

Wu has the grace to lower his face slightly toward his interdigitated pagoda of fingers. Cy tries to peer over the rim of Wu's shades—a feat which should be possible with a hologram—to get a glimpse of his eyes. (Can it be—? Are there— *images* of some sort flickering on the *inner surfaces* of Wu's lenses...?)

Cy's probing is ultimately unsuccessful, and he is shocked out of his inspection by a tearful wail.

"Oh, no, you can't mean it!" insists Polly half-broken-heartedly.

"Yes, I'm afraid it's true. I'm deeply sorry, Miss Peptide, I had no hand in it."

Cy's floundering. "What, what, what? Did I miss something? Where the Christ are they?"

Polly's clinging to Cyril now, weeping. Wu's voice cuts above the noise of her sobs.

"Miss Tuesday and Mister Augenblick now reside on Compact Disc, Mister Prothero. O'Phidian felt he needed, ah, volunteers to test the process. Even though I had endorsed it by going before him, he still suspected a trick. Your friends' deaths were totally redundant, and unfortunately quite final and irreversible. Allow me to be more precise: no one has been known to survive the process they underwent. Their remains were cremated and given a proper burial. If you'd like to have the discs—"

TNS time, folks: Temporary Neural Shutdown.

This is it, the end of the road, the karmic feedback that signals the end of love's expression, dearth of object—instead of overabundance—shutting down the soul's ribosomes, repressing the production of agape and eros....

Cy's fighting back his own tears now, but he loses.

As tears go by, as the rivers run dry and the tears flow high....

Goodbye, Ruby Tuesday, who could hang a name on you...? No more forever to feel your coffee-colored skin, to walk into a room where your scent lingers.... I remember the thirty-five sweet goodbyes.... Leaving like a gypsy-queen in a fairy-tale.... I never thought the girl could be so cruel.... Girl, I'm gonna miss you.... I was halfway crucified, and I'm still waiting for that taste you said you'd bring to me.... But Tuesday's gone on the wind, and the day you say goodbye will be the day that I die.... I don't know where the money goes, but wherever it goes that's probably where my baby went....

And Augie too—so long, old buddy! I hope you made it over the Heavenly Zero-Yard-Line for one last touchdown....

Polly's tears have ceased. Now she turns to face Wu's image and utters one fierce, harsh, implacable question four times, in four intonations:

"Why? Why?! Why!? Why!"

Wu hesitates before speaking. He shifts his wizened haunches in his ghostly chair, as if a hologram could grow uncomfortable. Wu, you ain't goin' nowhere, just sink down into that easy chair!

"Ah, my dear, you do penetrate directly to the heart of this old dragon. Why indeed? Some background is necessary first. I hope it will not bore you. Perhaps some music...." Asian strains sounds briefly, then stop. "No, Chinese music always sets me free, those angular banjos sound good to me. We need something more modern. Do you like Prince?" Notes of "The Ladder" sweep out. "Prince is something of a project of mine. I take a keen interest in his career. 'Little Red Corvette' was better than sex.... He's a mulatto, did you know that? But I see you aren't interested in such trivia. Where were we? Ah, yes— Why?

"My father was the Duke of Kau, later King Wen. He was a pale, slim fellow. They called him the Thin White Duke. Always had his nose in a book. Never enjoyed hunting or wenching.

"My mother—

"My mother was an apsaras, a celestial visitor from the Pure Land. She had—has—many names: Prajnaparamita, 'Wisdom of the Yonder Shore,' is one. Sophia's another. But she manifested herself to Dad as the original Turquoise Courtesan.

"She appeared to my father in his study one day, amid a display of many red birds holding documents written in red fire.

"'Fire is your ascendent sign, Duke Kau,' she proclaimed, 'under which you will rule, and your color is red. Your heir—the son and heir of nothing in particular—whom we must now engender, will rule under the sign of Water, and his color will be black. Now—fuck me!'

"Well, of course, my father could hardly refuse such a royal command performance.

"I was in my mother's womb for either eight days or a hundred years, depending on whether you believe Dad—who always claimed Mom was pregnant only for a week and a day—or the Courtesan herself, who maintained I refused to leave the womb at my proper time, and eventually had to be tricked out with promises of candied ginger.

"In any case, I was born, Mom disappearing for what seemed like good during the delivery.

"Upon examination, my father discovered I was equipped with two functioning sets of genitals. Doubly endowed, as a snake has two cocks, I united male and female, yang and yin, in myself. Dad knew then—had he ever doubted—that my destiny would be unique.

"I was never lonely, for I was my own fraternal twin.

"Like the Buddha, I had a conventional childhood, exhibiting no unusual talents, beyond, perhaps, the ability to piss out of either or both organs.

"My transformation occured when I was a young man.

"Dad had been jailed for his political scheming, a potential usurper to the Celestial Throne. Little did I know that while in prison he was busy formulating—under the tutelage of Mom—a mystic set of symbols that would become my undoing.

"Perhaps you know them as the *I Ching*....

"When my male parent was released, he took his scribbles out of jail with him.

"One day, while he was embarked on the renewed campaigns that would win our lineage the throne, I chanced to wander into his study.

"The naked *I Ching,* bare of later commentaries, lay unattended on his desk.

"I glanced down at the folio.

"Instantly I was entrapped.

"Contemplation of the symbols catapulted me into samadhi, a state where my body disappeared and I was only an intelligence, in partial yet nearly overwhelming contact with the immanent Tao. Trans-temporal, trans-spatial knowledge was opened to me. My former life fell away from me like a snake's husk. I was born again. I was elevated above the mass of men.

"What I gained at this time was not omniscience, nor complete wisdom. Let me emphasize the word 'partial' once more. My new knowledge was not total, and stopped just short of true wisdom. If I had attained this, the universe could not have supported me. I would have become a Buddha and disappeared, in the manner of many Enlightened Ones, humble and mighty, throughout history. I would have slipped down below Planck's Constant, or up through a quasar, mightiest of black holes. But due to some defect in my character or perception, I remained anchored to this earth, part of it, yet aloof, tethered by a string of flesh. My channel to the Tao was not perfect, there was noise that interfered with my complete understanding....

"It was my unique heritage, I eventually realized, half heavenly, half earthly, that put me in this in-between condition. Why all this should have happened to me alone, and so simply, out of the myriad scholars who have since wracked their brains studying the *I Ching*—some of whom had their own share of transcendental genes— I cannot say. I have ceased to speculate on this matter.

"All I know is that at the exact moment I made my permanent contact with the Tao, I became a singularity, the only man of my kind in the world, the one True Human, the most unconditioned *hsien,* able, to some extent, to interpret past, present and future from observation of the Flow.

"And oh yes, lest I forget—apparently immortal.

"Having tapped the energy of the Tao, I felt it suffuse my veins. I was deathless. Nothing could kill me.

"In the subsequent battles to overthrow the Shang Dynasty, alongside my father and, later, alone, I performed many brave feats until, being vouchsafed a sudden omen on the field of battle as to my lonely uniqueness, I retired from public life and began to search for my equal, having nominated a trusted minister to rule in my absence.

"You cannot imagine how tiresome this search quickly became.

"I will not waste your time recounting my entire history. The years spent in desperate travel around the globe, on foot, a-horse, aboard barquentine and caravel, alone and with traders and pilgrims, always looking for an out, either through soul-merger with my unknown mate, through death, or through Ascent of the Dragon. All options were equally unavailable.

"Once I thought I had met the man. Bodhidharma. But he spurned me. Claimed I owed something to the race of mortals. What nonsense, I thought then, and told him so. We parted on harsh terms.

"Speaking of the pilgrim that I was, you'll find a portrait of me at my most despairing in Chaucer, whose randy writings I humbly believe I had some influence on. My likeness is the ageless man who taps continually with his staff on the earth, begging incestuously, 'Mother, mother, let me in!'

"From time to time, for amusement, I retook the throne of the Celestial Empire. I was the Martial Emperor Wu, who ruled from 141 to 87 Bee Cee, and sent out the expeditions to search for P'eng-lai, the fabled Isle of Immortality. Thought any jokers there might have a clue to my condition. And I had some fun as the *Empress* Wu, from, oh, 684 Ai Dee, or thereabouts.

"Eventually, I despaired of travel and governing, and retired to the estates of my native land. Humanity bored and angered me with their petty mentality. I believe the last place and time I was physically abroad was Elizabethan England. In retrospect, a fascinating period, but dull as dust to me at the time. I was so weary of shouldering my years by then. Saint Paul—an interesting fellow, with his talk of 'secret doctrines'—once proclaimed that he who hated his life would be doomed to live forever. You gaze on the inspiration for his mysterious statement.

"Back home in China, I settled down in my ancestral estates, outside the Chou capitol of Laoyang. I began to sit in *zazen*, passing long periods in a trance, shutting down my painful, inescapable consciousness to a minimal level, doing a bit of astral travel. I abandoned hope of transfiguration, either through mortality or exaltation to another plane. I was resolved to await the heat death of the universe, the attainment of Absolute Zero. Surely I could not survive that....

"Naturally, I had no difficulties about money. Simple compound interest on a penny would soon have made me the wealthiest man in the world, but for amusement I had also dabbled in commerce and finance. With my stochastic abilities, it was like spearing fish in a barrel. My vast riches allowed me to hire faithful servants who would see that the minimal needs of my entranced body were tended to, and that my peace was not disturbed.

"I awoke briefly, in the early Eighteen-Hundreds, intrigued by the experiments of one Charles Babbage. His machines seemed to promise something new, an artificial enhancement of man's primitive brain. But when he failed to achieve anything, I soon lost interest and went back to my Golden Slumbers.

"My trance state became deeper and deeper. I took less and less interest in monitoring the affairs of mankind. My own infinite soul provided sufficient study.

"This was nearly my undoing.

"Neglecting to look far enough ahead into the future, I did not foresee the transition from Imperial China to the People's Republic. Like Pu-Yi, like Nicholas and his Rasputin-besotted Alexandra, like Halie Selassie, like King Constantine, like the Shah of Iran, I fell victim to history. But I should not rebuke myself. Fredkin's universe, a collection of cellular automata, is, to some extent, ultimately unpredictable anyway.

"I was dimly aware of Communist troops on their Long March entering my estate, slaughtering my servants—the multi-great grandchildren of my original ones—and appropriating my wealth. I tried to come alive.

"But I was stuck!

"When the Buddha meditated for nine years, he did not feel the bamboo shoots which sprouted beneath his legs and eventually grew right though his flesh. There have also been Zen Masters who have sat so perfectly that termites have constructed their mounds around them!

"This was my case.

"Humanity, those termites, had built a mountain around me with my cooperation, and I could not immediately escape.

"Taking my leave of Sophia, I began my mental descent from the Ogdoad. But it was painfully slow.

"Meanwhile, the Communists picked up my rigid form and, assuming I was some kind of mummy, carted me away, as a symbol of the old regime.

"I ended up with them in the Caves of Yenan, those mysterious caverns which connect with those below Rotten Cane in Guatemala. There I sat, occasionally pelted with rotten fruit and vegetables, unstirring for years.

"I was carried with the victorious troops into Shanghai, as a kind of totem.

"At last I regained control of my body, taking my first deep breath just in time to swallow a coin I believe you are quite familiar with.

"There I stood—penniless, though not dollar-less—with only the clothes on my back. I realized that, far from being omnipotent, I was subject to the whims of temporal rulers. This realization awakened me to the fact that I was not yet entirely above the mundane affairs of the human race. I still had to contend with man's stupidity and narrowness and short-sightedness. I decided I would never have peace until I did something about these qualities.

"I took then the Vow that Bodhidharma had urged on me. I would achieve the salvation of every sentient being. I would be no longer an arahant, concerned only with myself, but a Bodhisattva. Humanity and I had ignored each other, but the more they ignored me now, the closer I'd get! And don't you think I knew that walking on water wouldn't make me a Miracle Man? It would take something really big to make a difference. "This was when I resolved to alter the species.

"In modern terms, those of Haldane, I planned to force Evolutionary changes to occur in mere Physiological or even Molecular time.

"I knew it was the only way I'd ever get any rest before my longed-for death. 'Twas the only way I'd ever get the noisy world to shut its mouth!

"I believe you have some knowledge of my affairs from this point on. I set about recouping my wealth. I needed a new fortune to sustain the plethora of schemes I had in mind. I was hedging my bets by setting a number of plots into motion. One, however, always remained paramount.

"I had long been interested in selective breeding. Even millennia ago, I understood that within every human lurked infinite potential, held in check only by unscientific mating habits and the necessity of making millions and millions of crosses to achieve a certain trait. Nonetheless, I encouraged exogamy whenever I could in my travels. Before genes even had a name, I intuited that they could be engineered.

"After awakening from my long slumber, I caught up on the progress of science. I kicked myself when I read about Mendel's paper of 1865 going unheeded for so long. If only I had been awake then—! But what was a lost century more or less to me? Time was on my side."

The music has changed many times during Wu's monologue. Now Costello sings scathingly of "The World and His Wife," as Wu utters his peroration.

"Eventually, I settled on viruses as the means of effecting my changes. What marvelous little organisms, nearly naked DNA, and so pliable.... One natural variety—admittedly rare—already promoted a condition much like what I wanted. It also amused me that it was transmitted sexually, building up concentrations specifically in the seminal and vaginal fluids. It took several billion dollars, but I was finally able to make it do what I wanted, carry the proper traits...."

Wu pauses. His laser-generated face exhibits reflection. He resumes his speech in a more nostalgic, less boastful tone.

"In old China, the only land I ever loved, the peasants had a custom. When they needed an oracle, they would take up some of their precious paper money and bring it to a crossroads. There, each would ritually prick his finger and annoint the cash with a bit of blood. Then they would set it afire. The smoke would waft to the heavens, and, if they were lucky, a dragon would appear, bearing their oracle, speaking in a voice unlike anything you have ever heard.

"In a sense, this is what I have done.

"The human race—to which I no longer even truly belong—had arrived at a crossroads in its development. I have made a pyre of blood and money, and the oracle has been given. The oracle is: Change."

Cy and Polly, two rabbits, have been mesmerized by Wu's foxy spiel. His snaky voice has absolutely fascinated them. Cy feels as if he's been listening to the susurration of Egyptian sands over the buried Sphinx, or the lingering hydrogen whisper of the Big Bang filtered through a radiotelescope, something unutterably primal.... The cessation of the Doctor's speech is like an umbilical cord snapping, jarring both Cy and Polly back to themselves.

"What's the virus do, damn it?!" yells Cyril at the shining figure. Poor Cy's remembering rather guiltily his three bouts with Mekong Mel, how he rejected the condom she offered, and how he fucked poor Polly up the ass that same night....

The image of Wu opens its mouth to speak, but no sound emerges. Suddenly the hologram is shattered by audiovisual static. The image blinks on and off, warping and melting, like an insubstantial pageant fading. There's noise on the disc or the channel or the supercomputer, a failure somewhere along the line, all the fallible components....

"No, you can't!" shouts Cy. "Don't fade away! We've still got questions—!"

Are you with me, Doctor Wu? Are you really just a shadow of the man that I once knew? Are you crazy, are you high, or just an ordinary guy? Have you done all you can do? Are you *with me*, Doctor—?

Too late. The Doctor's gone, winked out.

"Oh, shit," exclaims Cy woefully. "Now we'll never know—"

"Know what, Mister Prothero?" speaks a redundant voice from the suddenly open, previously locked inner door.

"Gahhh!"

They whirl, clutching each other.

The living, breathing Doctor Wu stands in the doorway, immaculately unknowable behind his sunglasses.

"I told you I could not die, children. Nothing seems to kill me, no matter how hard I try. Nothing seems to break me, no matter how far I fall. I am the lone survivor of digitization. If anything as simple as veins flooded with isotopes could have ended my life, I would have been gratefully dead long ago."

"What's the big fuckin' idea?" demands Cyril. "Why'd'ya make us talk to that stupid hologram if you were still alive?"

"It is hard for me to concentrate now. I am finally changing, along with the world. It's time for me to shake away this disease, swim out past the breakers and watch the world die. I never expected it after so long, but I stand on the threshold of Ascending the Dragon. A kalpa has ended, a katun culminated. Is this tomorrow, or just the end of time? Isn't it ironic, that all my work was unnecessary? Or perhaps not. Perhaps the upcoming change in your species triggered my personal growth. Maybe the answer will be clear to you, my son and daughter, when the virus takes hold and increases your channel capacity. Soon the whole world will enter a permanent Now, freed from its limited reading frame, plunged into a state where everything makes sense, where all Times are Fused. Reversible Newtonian time replaced by one-way Bergsonian information-age time."

"We'll fight it! We'll kill the virus, we'll stop its spread!"

"Why would you want to? It means the abolition of Space and Time, mankind's oldest foes. Your perceptions will be vastly enlarged. Past, present and future become one, just as it was for the first Mayans, for Adam and Lilith and her twin. In any case, it's too late. This is no ordinary virus, it's of that class known as retroviruses. It encodes itself ineradicably into every single copy of an individual's genome. It's already a permanent part of the human genetic inheritance. There was a nice empty space that wasn't being used starting at base pair one billion, three-hundred million, six-hundred-and-twenty-nine thousand, and two.... As for its spread, it's ineluctable. Two, four, eight, sixteen.... Try to stop the world from fucking. You must face it—you've been colonized. The cipher of the dragon was always One. Myself. Now it will be equivalent to the earth's population. You are all my children, my heirs, a Blank Generation on which I have written my dreams."

Cy's burning mad. He knows in his very cells this ain't just another Pop Apocalypse. "Who are you to do this to us?!"

"You got another Bodhisattva, maybe?" sez Doctor Wu. Then the Doc cocks his head to one side. "Listen! Bells chime, and I feel I gotta get away. Bells chime, and I *know* I gotta get away. I know if I don't I'll go outa my mind. I'd better leave you behind, but don't worry—my kids are all right—"

Such insouciance is too much for Cy.

He hurls himself at the Doctor.

He's real, all right. It's like wrestling a bony snake. Cy tries to grab the Doc's balls and squeeze, but finds he's got none! The wrestlers fall to the carpet. Cy claws at the Doctor's face, gets a hand on his glasses—

—and Wu pops out of existence.

||||Mom! Amida Buddha! I'm home! Wotta ya mean, it's bedtime? Already? But I just got here! Please let me keep my ego for one more Brahma second. I just wanna see the end....]]]]

Cy has sprawled flat on his face. Polly helps him up.

He clutches in one hand the Maitreya's Robe. (Is it his size?)

In the other he still stupidly holds Wu's shades.

He studies them.

They're opaque. Each lens is a flat LCD display. A tiny chip and power source drive the screens. The hexagrams of the *I Ching* flash redly a dozen times a second in a dance of perpetual change, each permutation only subliminally perceptible, six solid bars that flicker in each frame, Innocence changing to Excess, the Perilous Pit to Breakthrough.

Virtual Transreality!

Polly looks at Cy.

Cy looks at Polly.

He wants to say something that will comfort, something suitably profound. Trouble is, as usual, only a lowly lyric runs ceaselessly in his brain.

From Miss Rickie Lee Jones.

"Is this the *real* real end?"

# THE FINAL KLUE

01000000

"If you don't know by now, the shock would probably kill you."
—Elvis Costello

# DOCTOR WU'S
# PORTABLE DECRYPTION OF
# CIPHERS

## Chapter 00000000

**live or am I Memorex**: A proprietary trademark concerned with fidelity of reproduction, elimination of noise. The answer, natch, is both!

**soup or spark**: In the early years of molecular biology, the method of propagation of the nerve impulse across the synapse was undetermined. Was it chemical or electric, soup or spark? Soup won.

**Nowhere Man**: The Beatles, "Nowhere Man."

**I'm a loser....kill me**: Beck, "Loser."

**Quit jammin' me**: Tom Petty, "Jammin' Me."

**Radio Kaos**: Roger Waters, *Radio Kaos*.

**radio head**: The Talking Heads, "Radio Head."

**Communication Breakdown**: Led Zepplin, "Communication Breakdown."

**Call it superbad**: James Brown, "(Call Me) Superbad."

**Hartley transform**: Mathematical operation similar to Fourier analysis, invented by Ralph V. L. Hartley, author of "Transmission of Information," 1928.

**pirate phages**: When Leo Szilard, the man who supposedly overthrew Maxwell's Demon, first saw phages in action at Cold Spring Harbor Laboratories, he had to go outside and pace up and down until he could recover his composure.

**all together now, all together now**: The Beatles, "All Together Now."

**Funky Chicken**: Rufus Thomas, "Do the Funky Chicken."

**Melchisidek**: King of Biblical Salem. "Without father, without mother, without descent, having neither beginning of day, nor end of life," sez Paul in *Hebrews 7*. A symbol of recursion.

**Sophia**: A hot babe.

**Thomas the Contender**: Jesus' twin brother, according to the Gnostic faith.

**Tathagata**: The Buddha.

**The sparkle of your china, the shine of your Japan**: Steely Dan, "Bodhisattva."

**one toke over....Jesus**: Brewer and Shipley, "One Toke Over the Line."

**make it all right....midnight**: Steely Dan, "Black Cow."

**keep it all in**: The Beautiful South, "You Keep It All In."

**Papa's got a brand new bag**: James Brown, "Papa's Got a Brand New Bag."

**Don't call me....fair to**: Pearl Jam, "Daughter."

**girl can't help herself**: Little Richard, "The Girl Can't Help It."

**Little Miss Can't Be Wrong**: The Spin Doctors, "Little Miss Can't Be Wrong."

**rockin' pneumonia....flu**: Huey "Piano" Smith and the Clowns, "Rockin' Pneumonia and the Boogie-Woogie Flu."

**dem ol' Kozmic blues**: Janis Joplin, *I Got Dem Ol' Kozmic Blues Again Mama!*

**I am a dj....play**: David Bowie, "I Am a DJ."

**THE RELIC'S RAP**: Based on a similar ditty by Ice-Floe.

**Joan of Arc....melt**. The Smiths, "Bigmouth Strikes Again."

**Where is my twin**: "Man and God are twins," sez the *Talmud*.

**Here we are....us**: Nirvana, "Smells Like Teen Spirit."

**implicate order**: The Tao of physicist David Bohm.

**One is the loneliest number**: Three Dog Night, "One."

**droplet....dragons**: The Lovin' Spoonful, "Younger Generation."

**Soul man**: Sam and Dave, "Soul Man."

**knocked off his cap**: a jimmy-cap.

**Ain't....fez on**: Steely Dan, "The Fez."

**Saklad**: Ialdabaoth.

**what a fool....away**: The Doobie Brothers, "What a Fool Believes."

**no satisfaction**: The Rolling Stones, "(I Can't Get No) Satisfaction."

**shook....brain**: Jerry Lee Lewis, "Great Balls of Fire."

**Hotei**: The Laughing Buddha.

**man's skin....hand**: *The Dhammapada*.

**can't buy me love**: The Beatles, "Can't Buy Me Love."

**whoever....tathagata**: *The Diamond Sutra*.

**This is hell....it**: Thomas Marlowe, *Doctor Faustus*.

**Missionary Man**: The Eurythmics, "Missionary Man."

**long strange trip**: The Grateful Dead, "Truckin'."

**the Georgia Peach**: Little Richard, a notorious bisexual.

**Oh, you hear....every day**: Sister Rosetta Tharpe, "Strange Things Happening Every Day."

**Where have all the flowers gone**: Peter, Paul and Mary, "Where Have All the Flowers Gone."

**enormous celestial dragon**: The Buddha could shrink dragons and confine them in his begging bowl.

**Book of Dreams**: Suzanne Vega, "Book of Dreams."

**circle-jerk**: A group (The Circle-Jerks).

**world drags me down**: The Cult, "She Sells Sanctuary."

**when the world....around**: The Police, "When the World is Running Down, You Make the Best of What's Still Around."

**Oh, my little....on a lay**: Stephen Foster, "Camptown Races." Only an Irishman would be dumb enuff to bet on a Nag Hammadi.

**king of pain**: The Police, "King of Pain."

**flatfoot floogie**: Cab Calloway, "Flatfoot Floogie with the Floy-floy." Floy-floy, natch, being money.

**Dirty deeds done dirt cheap**: AC/DC, "Dirty Deeds Done Dirt Cheap."

**little chinkie chinaman**: The Al Gore Rhythm Quartet, "Little Chinkie Chinaman," 1928, with R. Hartley on sax.

**Blood is a special substance**: The Talking Heads, "Swamp."

**blood on the tracks**: Bob Dylan, *Blood on the Tracks*.

**blood makes noise**: Suzanne Vega, "Blood Makes Noise."

**Give me just....change**: Chairmen of the Board, "Give Me just a Little More Time."

**If only this night could last all day**: Big Audio Dynamite, "Dragon Town," which also contains the sampled lines, "Mister Wu no longer has a laundry / I have to say the business was a flop."

## Chapter 00000001
## Day One, Tuesday, May 25, 1993
## Tribe of Reuben
## Day of the Reed

**world as we know it....feels fine**: REM, "It's the End of the World As We Know It."

**The sun....Tuesday morning**: The Cowboy Junkies, "The Sun Comes Up, It's Tuesday Morning."

**so wired up....cup**: Van Morrison, "Jackie Wilson Said."

**fourth cup**: Average coffee consumption in America is only 3½ cups per day.

**shooby-do-ANXIOUS**: General Public, "Anxious."

**time won't let him**: The Outsiders, "Time Won't Let Me."

**I told you....in the park**: Cream, "Badge."

**this year's model**: Elvis Costello, *This Year's Model*.

**time and space**: It should be noted that the brain is the only location where time is transformed into space. Events—a time sequence—are modelled in three-dimensional neurological connections, space.

**time keeps on slippin'**: Steve Miller, "Time Keeps on Slippin'."

**time is money**: An equation whose proof I am.

**Feed your head**: Jefferson Airplane, "White Rabbit."

**Yarrow**: Traditionally, the hexagrams of the *I Ching* were derived from casting yarrow stalks.

**buzzworm**: Western slang for rattlesnake.

**Mudmen**: Their lone East Coast hit being, "Claude and Del Shannon were Lovers."

**Kiwi record currently playing**: As I recall, it was "Heavenly Pop Hit," by the Chills.

**when we was Fab**: George Harrison, "When We was Fab." Fab, of course, is also the name of an immunoglobin fragment.

**ZZ Top beard**: The lone member of ZZ Top named Beard is the only shaven one. A modern zen koan.

**Eve of Destruction**: Barry McGuire, "Eve of Destruction."

**Jumping Jack Flash**: The Rolling Stones, "Jumping Jack Flash."

**get with the program**: Good advice.
**Tuesday's on the phone to me**: The
Beatles, "She Came in Through the
Bathroom Window."
**welcoming are....week**: Elvis Costello,
"Welcome to the Working Week."
**blue eyes**: "She was black, and her eyes were
blue," The Rolling Stones, "She Was Hot."
**Cinnamon Girl**: Neil Young, "Cinnamon Girl."
**hello....name**: The Doors, "Hello, I Love You."
**Who's this lady....home**: The Isley
Brothers, "Who's that Lady."
**Ruby Tuesday**: The Rolling Stones,
"Ruby Tuesday."
**that New York City....sack**: Steely Dan,
"Daddy Don't Live in that New York City
No More."
**Angel of Harlem**: U2, "Angel of Harlem."
**Harlem Shuffle**: The Rolling Stones,
"Harlem Shuffle."
**Smackwater Jack**: Carole King,
"Smackwater Jack."
**Bad Attitude**: not far from the town of Bad
Karma mentioned in *Gravity's Rainbow*.
**Golden Wedding**: Danny Wilson, "Ruby's
Golden Wedding."
**earn enough**: XTC, "Earn Enough for Us."
**blame it on Cain**: Elvis Costello, "Blame It
on Cain."
**UPC code**: The first bar-coded product
passed over a commercially installed
scanner in 1974.
**Sea of Love**: Phil Phillips, "Sea of Love."
**nature....conserved**: Cy is a little woozy in
his theorizing here. While it is true that
generally speaking in nature, matter and
energy are conserved, there are other
quantities that are not. Physicist Chien-
Shiung Wu was the first to disprove parity
conservation, for instance. And information is the grand exception, for it may be
created out of nothing and also destroyed.
Contrary to common sense, it is only the
destruction of information which seems
to require energy. This was the theoretical undoing of Maxwell's Demon.
**Get your kicks on Route 666**: Bobby
Troup, "Get Your Kicks on Route 66."
**children jumping rope**: And this is what
they chant: "Cinderella dressed in yellow/
Went upstairs to kiss a fellow./Made a
mistake and kissed a snake,/How many
doctors did it take?"

**White Eternity**: Sak Hunal, a Mayan deity.
**Femme Fatale....beat**: Velvet Underground,
"Femme Fatale."
**you're lost, little girl**: The Doors, "You're
Lost, Little Girl."

## Chapter 00000010

**as wild as 'Forty-Eight**: All right, since
you're so insistent, here's a partial
Katalogue of Konnections. The first of the
Nag Hammadi Gnostic texts, discovered
in 1945, is published in Cairo. Marvin
Camras perfects magnetic recording
tape. The Presley family moves from
Tupelo to Memphis. The classic Rockola
jukeboxes appear. Norbert Weiner,
ghostly double to Claude Shannon,
codifies his theory of cybernetics, based
partially on wartime work he did in
Room 2-244 at MIT and published in a
yellow cover. (It ended up being referred
to as "The Yellow Peril," for the formid-
ability of its prose.) Ralph Hartley invents
the Hartley Transform at Bell Labs. The
Frisbee is first sold. The Xerox company
unveils their revolutionary duplication
process. CBS announces 33-rpm records.
The General Agreement on Trades and
Tarrifs is signed. The U.S. National Security Act, establishing the CIA, is passed.
An Wang establishes his company in
Massachusetts. The International Tele-
communications Union is founded. Linus
Pauling discovers the alpha helix protein
configuration. A sculpture to honor
Raoul Wallenberg is erected in Budapest;
it shows a man dominating a snake. The
Boston Institute of Modern Art declares
its independence from MOMA. Les Paul
invents 8-track recording. Tito breaks
with Stalin. Henry Kloss and Edgar
Villchur start Acoustic Research in
Cambridge, Mass. The Alpher, Bethe and
Gamow paper on the Big Bang is
published in *Physical Review*, at the
same time the Steady State counter-theory
is proposed. The Universal Declaration of
Human Rights is signed by various nations.
A revolt begins in Burma's Golden
Triangle. Chuck Berry gets married.
Truman beats Dewey in a case of failed
stochastic prediction. The Epidemic
Intelligence Service is established by

Alexander Langmuir. Leo Fender starts marketing the first mass-produced electric guitar. The Bureau of Narcotics produces its anti-dope classic, *To the Ends of the Earth.* AT&T introduces area codes. The first statues of the Goddess are dug up in France, which is busy bolstering the African franc. Herman Blount changes his name to Sun Ra. And that ain't all she wrote!

**mix them races**: Rock 'n' Roll was originally called "mixed breeding music."

**Southern Man**: Neil Young, "Southern Man."

**Texas Instruments**: In this year also, British Telecom patents the modem.

**Kookie....comb**: Ed Byrnes & Connie Stevens, "Kookie, Kookie, Lend Me Your Comb."

**I couldn't resist....transistor**: Alma Cogan, "Just Couldn't Resist Her with Her Pocket Transistor."

**biological community**: In the same year, Rita Levi-Montalcini discovers Nerve Growth Factor in experiments involving snake venom, whose action mimics that of neurotransmitters.

**Lithium**: Did someone say Prozac?

**Unktehi**: Sioux water snake god.

**Peanut M&Ms**: Aside from candied ginger, my favorite sweet is my brown M.M.

**all go together....Eskimo**: Tom Lehrer, "We'll All Go Together When We Go."

**revolt of populace**: Prince Siahnouk, in a recent testament to the Cambodian love of fickyfick, refers to his countrymen as "*les chaud lapins*" and "*les chaudes lapines*," literally "hot rabbits."

**the heuristics and....line**: Brian Eno, "Backwater."

**HOLIDAY IN CAMBODIA**: The Dead Kennedys, "Holiday in Cambodia."

**Every generation....disease**: Fury In The Slaughterhouse, "Every Generation's Got Its Own Disease."

**well-respected man**: The Kinks, "Well-Respected Man."

*Laissez les bon temp roulez*: Shirley and Lee, "Let the Good Times Roll."

**How Much is that Doggie in the Window**: Patti Page, "How Much is that Doggie in the Window."

**Bill Haley**: On April 12, 1954, Bill Haley recorded "Rock Around the Clock" at New York City's Pythian Temple.

**Greasy Lake**: Bruce Springsteen, "Spirits in the Night."

**Good Rockin' Tonight**: Roy Brown, "Good Rockin' Tonight."

**BONJOUR TRISTESSE**: Françoise Sagan's controversial novel was inspired by this incident, which received much play in the French papers.

**Java Jive**: Milton Drake and Ben Oakland, "Java Jive."

**Hanoi**: Tenth century Hanoi was called Dhang Long, or the Soaring Dragon.

**hit the road, Jack**: Ray Charles, "Hit the Road, Jack."

**Run, run, run thru the jungle**: Credence Clearwater Revival, "Run through the Jungle."

**Bungle....grass**: Jethro Tull, "Bungle in the Jungle."

**walled pit**: Also found in Mayan ruins, where it is termed a cenote.

**got legs and knows how to use them**: ZZ Top, "Legs."

**Union Of The Snakes**: Duran Duran, "Union of the Snake."

**ride the snake....cold**: The Doors, "The End."

**quim and asshole**: Scientifically speaking, every male snake has two cocks, called *hemipenes*. Herpetologists assert that only one cock at a time is used during mating, but then again, they've never witnessed what deClosets saw. Interestingly, J. K. Huysmans affirms in *La Bas* that the Devil has two cocks which he employs simultaneously on the women he enjoys at the Black Mass.

**Johnny Mathis**: Apparently, a proleptic flash on the part of deClosets, since the song in question wasn't released until 1957.

**Sara Smile**: Hall & Oates, "Sara Smile."

**Because the sky....on**: The Beatles, "Because."

**cruel, crazy beautiful....goodbye**: Johnny Clegg and Savuka, "Cruel, Crazy, Beautiful World."

**ch-ch-ch-ch-ch-changes....time**: David Bowie, "Changes."

**Funkedelic Sperm**: Funkadelic, "The Funkedelic Sperm."

**tumblin' time**: The Chambers Brothers, "Time Has Come Today."

**squeezed the life out of him**: Q: What's a python's favorite musical group? A: Squeeze!

**time will crawl**: David Bowie, "Time Will Crawl."

**Four-way hips**: The Tom Tom Club, "The Man with the Four-Way Hips."

**hound dog**: Big Mama Thornton, "Hound Dog." This American hound dog has apparently succeeded in catching himself a rabbit (i.e., a Cambodian).

**Teen Angel**: Mark Dinning, "Teen Angel."

**Amerasian blues**: The Clash, "Straight to Hell."

**beyond all towns, all systems**: Rickie Lee Jones, "Flying Cowboys."

**majors and generals....war**: XTC, "Majors and Generals."

Chapter 00000011
Day One, Tuesday, May 25, 1993
Tribe of Reuben
Day of the Reed
and
Day Two, Wednesday, May 26, 1993
Tribe of Simeon
Day of the Jaguar

**Building 19**: Chain of Massachusetts salvage stores.

**Dyadic Intertribal Gathering of Indian Talismanic Archons and Loas**: Not necessarily the same organization as the computer manufacturer with Massachusetts headquarters.

**shooting its toxic wad**: The first of many Sodomic Sacraments.

**pressure....me out**: Queen and David Bowie, "Under Pressure."

**his own brain**: Cy fails to spot the anti-chance mechanism in his own brain which is all that is currently insuring that his thoughts and language do not degenerate into noise or entropy. But considering that there are only a thousand billion synapses in the brain, he can be forgiven for overlooking it.

**Shadows of Knight**: A group.

**Muzak**: Invented in 1933.

**Canon**: This company name was derived from that of Kannon, Goddess of Mercy. Alternatively, Kwan Yin and Kwan Seum Bosal, Tara and Avalokiteshvara.

**Secret Agent Man**: Johnny Rivers, "Secret Agent Man."

**Gonna walk like....man**: The Four Seasons, "Walk Like a Man."

**Woman Who Knows The All**: In Gnostic tradition, Mary Magdalene was the highest apostle, having given Christ a ride in her Pink Cadillac.

**recruit me**: Ruby Tuesday, bearing Jagger's genes, would indeed have been a valuable asset to Wu Labs. O'Phidian's ultimate actions were wasteful.

**slave to love**: Bryan Ferry, "Slave to Love."

**addicted to love**: Robert Palmer, "Addicted to Love."

**Operator, could you help me place this call**: Jim Croce, "Operator."

**Pennsylvania 6-5000**: Glenn Miller, "Pennsylvania 6-5000."

**Beechwood 4-5789**: The Marvelettes, "Beechwood 4-5789."

**853-5937**: Squeeze, "853-5937."

**867-5309**: Tommy Tutone, "867-5309/ Jenny."

**634-5789**: Wilson Pickett, "634-5789 (Soulsville, U.S.A.)"

**Here comes the night**: Them, "Here Comes the Night."

**no light can find him**: Tears for Fears, "Everybody Wants to Rule the World."

**hear me knockin'**: The Rolling Stones, "Hear Me Knockin'"

**way down....instead**: World Party, "Way Down Now."

**Boys don't cry**: The Cure, "Boys Don't Cry."

**driven to tears**: The Police, "Driven to Tears."

**lonely teardrops**: Jackie Wilson, "Lonely Teardrops."

**cryin' a river**: Julie London, "Cry Me A River."

**take me to that river**: Al Green, "Take Me to the River."

**let's spend the night together**: The Rolling Stones, "Let's Spend the Night Together."

**bed was too big**: The Police, "Bed's Too Big Without You."

**so far away....rain**: Dire Straits, "So Far Away." Those who play in the Sun frequently get Sunburned.

**tears into his pillow**: Little Anthony and the Imperials, "Tears on my Pillow."

**Chelsea morning**: Joni Mitchell, "Chelsea Morning."

**New Morning**: Bob Dylan, "New Morning."

**a beautiful morning....song**: The Rascals, "It's a Beautiful Morning."

**a-dreamin' about coffee**: Cyril seems to be recalling a cartoon he once glimpsed and forgot: Lee Marrs's 1973 work, "Caffeine Fiend."

**wild....seeds**: A group.

**bad....seeds**: A group.

**lightning seeds**: A group.

**caffeine in your bank account**: They Might Be Giants, "Don't Let's Start."

**Coaxihuital**: The morning glory vine, aka snakevine, which contains its famous LSD analogue.

**here-comes-Billy-in-a-skirt androgyny**: The Replacements, "Androgyny."

**Mandelbrot Set**: Mandelbrot worked with IBM on signal-to-noise problems. He also tangled with the Bourbaki, a secret society of top mathematicians.

**Brass in her pocket**: The Pretenders, "Brass in Pocket."

**the bond**: Obviously, a Peptide bond.

**Hokyo Zammai**: Zen work, *The Jewel-Mind Samadhi*. Samadhi, or the undistracted mind, has been likened to "a snake in a bamboo tube."

**NSA**: As an example of the deviousness of this cadre of spies and digit-diddlers, they have invented a method of encoding which, when applied to a message, leaves the message as before. In other words, it's an identity operation, rendering cipher-text which is *identical* to the plaintext.

**time to cry**: Paul Anka, "It's Time to Cry."

**tracks of her tears**: The Miracles, "The Tracks of My Tears."

**Industrial Disease**: Dire Straits, "Industrial Disease."

**Is the grey....grey**: Ned's Atomic Dustbin, "Grey Cell Green."

**Government Cheese**: The Rainmakers, "Government Cheese."

**Emotional Rescue**: The Rolling Stones, "Emotional Rescue."

**splish, splash....bath**: Bobby Darin, "Splish Splash."

**When you believe....superstition**: Stevie Wonder, "Superstition."

**If that disc....mine**: Inez Foxx, "Mockingbird."

**X-Ray Spex**: A group.

**von Neumann**: His father was a banker. "Emergence" is a term which refers to the appearance of qualitatively different phenomena when a system crosses a certain threshold of complexity. Von Neumann's colleagues, only half in jest, speculated that his brain was an emergent organ, having crossed a level of complexity not present in normal humans.

**down here the poets....at all**: Bruce Springsteen, "Jungleland."

**KALPA**: According to New Age millenialists, many different time schemes predict the end of our current era. The Mayan scheme of Jose Arguelles posits a date of 2012. Terence McKenna, using a computer program he calls *Timewave Zero*, also arrives at the year 2012. His program, moreover, is based on a scheme he claims to have extracted from the *I Ching* using multiples of 64.

**Shakyamuni Buddha**: When Elmore James wrote his "Shake Your Money Maker," he was really composing under divine inspiration. However, the astral connection was faulty, and instead of the name "Shakyamuni [the] Maker," he heard t he equally evocative phrase "Shake Your Money Maker."

**blind too**: If Max had been dumb as well, he would have resembled the famous "Triple Mute" of the koan, "How do you preach the dharma to a triple mute?"

**Blind Melon**: A group, led by the late *Shannon* Hoon.

**Def Jam**: A record label.

**so lonesome they could cry**: Hank Williams, "So Lonesome I Could Cry."

**Hey, Body....Again**: Steely Dan, "Turn That Heartbeat Over Again."

**Rage In The Cage**: The J. Geils Band, "Rage in the Cage."

**November spawned a monster**: Morrisey, "November Spawned a Monster."

**cum on....**: Slade, "Cum On Feel the Noize."

**The Big Guy**: Called by mathematician Paul Erdoes, "SF, the Supreme Fascist." Erdoes once defined a mathematician as "a machine for turning coffee into theorems."

**tell a soul**: The Replacements, *Don't Tell A Soul*.

**pleased to meet me**: The Replacements, "Pleased to Meet Me."

**roam, roam**: The B-52's, "Roam."
**Spooky**: Classics IV, "Spooky."
**oriented head to foot**: Rather like 69. Each single strand of DNA has a 5-prime end and a 3-prime end. In the double helix formation, 5-prime is aligned with 3-prime. Each doublet of DNA in every cell is doing 69.
**eat for two**: 10,000 Maniacs, "Eat for Two." If these folks had been binary, there be only 16 of 'em instead of 10,000!
**Hoodoo Guru**: A group (The Hoodoo Gurus).
**born on the bayou**: Credence Clearwater Revival, "Born on the Bayou."
**juju hand**: Sam the Sham and the Pharoahs, "Ju Ju Hand."
**zing, zing**: The Neville Brothers, "Zing, Zing."
**cha dooky do**: The Neville Bothers, "Cha Dooky Do."
**Dazed and confused**: Led Zepplin, "Dazed and Confused."
**Voodoo....Woman**: Bobby Goldsboro, "Voodoo Woman."
**Witchy Woman**: The Eagles, "Witchy Woman." Like Ruby, Polly too has a background that insured she would have been a valuable "employee...."

## Chapter 00000100
**all you young dudes**: Mott the Hoople, "All the Young Dudes."
**don't know much....geography**: Sam Cooke, "Wonderful World."
**Ding dang walla walla bing bang**: David Seville, "Witch Doctor."
**stop, hold on....destroyer**: The Kinks, "Destroyer."
**They'll roll you....dime**: Paul Simon, "Paranoia Blues."
**no future**: The Sex Pistols, "God Save the Queen."
**Nidhoggr**: Compare with Ndengei, the serpent creator of Fiji, and his cohort, Ratu-mai-mbula, serpent ruler of the land of the dead.
**Playing those my-eye-eye-ind games forever**: John Lennon, "Mind Games."
**It's all in the game**: Tommy Edwards, "It's All in the Game."
*Afa*: Otherwise known as Ifa. "Orunmila planted the sixteen parts of the secret in his head, and they burgeoned forth as Ifa, the force of divination."

**Only the lonely**: Roy Orbison, "Only the Lonely."
**Nana Buluku**: The redundant Creator one step above Mawu-Lisa.
**redundancy**: There are actually two types of redundancy: context-free and context-sensitive. Both lower the rate of errors during transmission, but the latter does so more economically. Only context-sensitive redundancy has allowed the human brain and genome to reach their current levels of complexity. Lollolo's sentence is understandable thanks to context-sensitive correction.
**black boys on mopeds**: Sinéad O'Connor, "Black Boys on Mopeds."
**too many people....trip**: Paul McCartney, "Too Many People."
**infested! The planet's infested**: Course Of Empire, "Infested."
***H.M.S. Rattlesnake***: Another famous Victorian battleship was the *H.M.S. Blacksnake*.
**Papa was a rolling....home**: The Temptations, "Papa was a Rollin' Stone." Note that the Tempts were originally billed as The Primes, before adopting their Eden-inspired name.
**You say....world**: The Beatles, "Revolution 1."
**language as virus**: William Burroughs, natch.
**kinky Afro....today**: The Happy Mondays, "Kinky Afro."
**purple toupee**: They Might Be Giants, "Purple Toupee."
**White man in Hammersmith Palais**: The Clash, "White Man in Hammersmith Palais." As an example of the strength of Lollolo's connections, this will do fine: the general public didn't get to hear this song until a year later!
**bit-per-second**: The figure commonly cited as the human bandwidth is 50 bits-per-second. Yet a CD uses 700,000 bits to encode one second of music (43,000 samples a second times eight bits per sample times two channels). Despite a certain incongruity in what's being measured in the two instances, human channel capacity is immensely greater than assumed.
**Mammy**: Al Jolson, "Mammy."
**Memphis Blues....end**: Bob Dylan, "Stuck Inside of Mobile with the Memphis Blues Again."

**back on the chain gang**: The Pretenders, "Back on the Chain Gang."

**fetish**: Compare the *tzi-daltai* of the Apaches, fetishes carved from lightning-split wood.

**Stone Cold**: Rainbow, "Stone Cold."

**Sail away**: Randy Newman, "Sail Away."

**Let my people go-go**: The Rainmakers, "Let My People Go-Go."

**Bad, bad....junkyard dog**: Jim Croce, "Bad, Bad Leroy Brown."

**Bodyguards....holes**: Bob Dylan, "Stuck Inside of Mobile with the Memphis Blues Again."

**Black Magic Woman**: Santana, "Black Magic Woman."

**Dance This Mess Around**: The B-52's, "Dance this Mess Around."

**Land of 1000 Dances**: Cannibal and the Headhunters, "Land of 1000 Dances."

**Cool Jerk**: The Capitols, "Cool Jerk."

**Watusi**: The Vibrations, "The Watusi."

**Twist**: Chubby Checker, "Twist."

**Freddie**: Freddie and the Dreamers, "Do the Freddie."

**Mashed Potato**: Dee Dee Sharp, "Mashed Potato Time."

**Gimme Shelter**: The Rolling Stones, "Gimme Shelter." Or I'll fade away.

**Black Snake Blues**: Victoria Spivey, "Black Snake Blues."

**Grazing In The Grass**: Hugh Masekela, "Grazing in the Grass."

**Good Lovin'**: The Rascals, "Good Lovin'."

**When love....up**: The Pretenders, "Message of Love."

**Jam up, jelly tight**: Tommy Roe, "Jam Up, Jelly Tight."

**brown sugar gal**: The Rolling Stones, "Brown Sugar."

**tantric energy**: According to tantric teachings, the Serpent Kucarini is coiled inside the abdomen of every man and woman.

**John Thomas**: A Wet Willie.

**Zoxathazo....zozazoth**: Chant recorded in the Gnostic text, *Discourse on the Eighth and the Ninth*.

**Ebony and ivory**: Paul McCartney and Stevie Wonder, "Ebony and Ivory."

**There is water underground**: The Talking Heads, "Once in a Lifetime."

**Black Rain**: The first atomic bomb had 32 points of detonation. Dropping radioactive slugs through a torus of uranium in an

attempt to measure rates of fission without starting a runaway chain reaction was called by Manhattan Project scientists "tickling the dragon's tail."

**Black Madonna of Poland**: The Black Madonna of Poland is Luiza Viorica Cziczczone, whose hit, "Like the Virgin Mary," went to Number One in Krakow.

*1000 Nites*: Arabic contributions to theology and mathematics cannot be overemphasized. In the former sphere, we should recall Cardinal Tisseront's theory that Jesus was really an Arab, born on April 16, 6 BC (Shakespeare's birthday) during a rare conjunction of Saturn and Jupiter. In the latter area, the Arab world transmitted to Europe the Indian concept of zero, and the word "cipher," derived from the Arabic, *sifr*, or void. Burton's translation of the *1001 Nites* was much admired by his descendent, Lollolo.

Chapter 00000101
Day Three, Thursday, May 27, 1993
Day of the Eagle
Tribe of Levi

**Pinball Wizard**: The Who, "Pinball Wizard." Note that The Who began their career as The High Numbers.

**Midnight Confessions**: The Grass Roots, "Midnight Confessions."

**live on Sugar Mountain**: Neil Young, "Sugar Mountain."

**girl like you**: The Rascals, "A Girl Like You."

**Tuesday Heartbreak**: Stevie Wonder, "Tuesday Heartbreak."

**Don't walk away, Renee**: The Left Banke, "Walk Away Renee."

**girl in trouble....**: Romeo Void, "Girl in Trouble (is a Temporary Thing)."

**My Mom....pain**: Everclear, "Heartspark Dollar Sign."

**Louie, Louie, Louie....mean**: The Stories, "Brother Louie."

**The Deadbeats' Club**: The B-52's, "The Deadbeats' Club."

**Janey's got a gun**: Aerosmith, "Janey's Got A Gun."

**she's getting serious**: John Astley, "Jane's Getting Serious."

**Sweet Jane's Revenge**: Times Two, "Sweet Jane's Revenge."

**Don't mess with these local girls**: Graham Parker, "Local Girls."

**Grafitti Bridge**: Prince, "Grafitti Bridge."

**ungena za ulimwengu**: The Temptations, "Ungena Za Ulimwengu (Unite the World)."

**MELCHISIDEK**: See Chapter 00000000. Turning again to Huysman's *La Bas*, we find that "the sacrifice to Melchisidek is, in some sort, the future mass, the glorious office which will be known during the earthly reign of the divine Paraclete." The ring of Melchisidek is "a serpent, whose head, in relief, set with a ruby, is connected by a fine chain with a tiny circlet which fastens the jaws of the reptile."

**Train keeps a-rollin'**: Dorsey Burnette, "Train Kept A-Rollin'."

**Pleasant Valley Sunday**: The Monkees, "Pleasant Valley Sunday."

**Money changes everything**: Cyndi Lauper, "Money Changes Everything."

**Blue Jay Way**: The Beatles, "Blue Jay Way."

**ain't too proud to beg**: The Temptations, "Ain't Too Proud to Beg."

**I want to hold your hand**: The Beatles, "I Want to Hold Your Hand."

**Mirror in the bathroom**: The English Beat, "Mirror in the Bathroom."

**T&A&C**: Thymine, adenine and cytosine.

**best friend's girl**: The Cars, "My Best Friend's Girl."

**No bozos on this bus**: Firesign Theater, *I Think We're All Bozos on This Bus.* It would not be inappropriate here to point to the figure of Doctor Memory.

**Mariah Carey**: A famous example of mixed breeding. Also known as Pariah Scarey.

**Word up**: Cameo, "Word Up."

**Rasputin**: Rasputin was a *starets*, or Holy Man. His traditional costume was black coat and trousers. He frequently indulged in Gnostic orgies. At one time he lived in St Petersburg at Number 64 Gorokhovaia. Many White Russians fled the Revolution to Peking.

**Maitreya**: In China, known as Mi-lo, and identified with Hotei, the Laughing Buddha. (See Chapter 00000000.) In Japan, Miroku-Bosatsu. A Redeemer figure whose coming heralds a New Age.

**the Genitorturers**: Included in their stage act is ritual prick-piercing, a Mayan hobby.

**Guns 'N Roses**: There is a small peptide of ten amino acids named after this band— GnRH.

**hsien**: What Cy's precocious nephew failed to mention is that there is a third sort of immortal, called *shih chieh hsien*. These immortals die, but do not go to heaven. They remain behind in limbo, bodiless. Earthdwelling Taoist immortals—among them the Famous Eight: Lu Tung Pin, Ti Kuai Li, Chang Kuo Lau, Ts'ao Kuo Chiu, Han Hsiang Tzu, Han Chung Li, Lan Ts'ai Ho and Ho Hsien Ku—practiced the five techniques: breath control, "wearing the sun rays," gymnastics, "the arts of the bedchamber," and diet. The Chinese character for immortal consists of two characters joined together: that of "man" and that of "mountain."

**Hope I die before I get old**: The Who, "My Generation."

**His sister Anna works....go-getter**: The Beatles, "Mean Mr Mustard."

**Peter Greenaway**: Once employed by England's Central Office of Information. The COI was the center of Britain's WWII propaganda. Another fine film by this director is *Drowning By Numbers*.

**thirteen steps lead down**: Elvis Costello, "Thirteen Steps Lead Down."

**It's my life....want**: The Animals, "It's My Life." Maybe Cy will even "ride the serpent."

**jammed with broken heroes....**: Bruce Springsteen, "Born to Run."

**WALK IT LIKE HE TALKS IT**: Steely Dan, "You Gotta Walk It Like You Talk It."

**cash ain't nothin' but trash**: The Clovers, "Your Cash Ain't Nothin' But Trash."

**I been runnin'....Saturday**: The Clash, "Police On My Back."

**I'm a bookkeeper's....night**: Steely Dan, "Don't Take Me Alive."

**tramps like us....**: Bruce Springsteen, "Born to Run."

**The words of....halls**: Simon and Garfunkel, "The Sounds of Silence."

**HI-HEEL SNEAKERS**: Tommy Tucker, "Hi-Heel Sneakers."

**Mucha' Linda**: This Beautiful Girl is plainly a *nagini*, a female *naga*, the serpent deities of India. Pictured as having the face of a human, with the expanded neck of a cobra and the tail of a serpent, they inhabit aquatic palaces, beneath rivers, lakes and seas, filled with continuous music. *Nagini* are known for their beauty, cleverness and charm. During a seven-day storm, the giant *nagini* Muchalinda protectively enveloped Buddha in her coils and raised her hood above him as an umbrella.

**watching the detective....lake**: Elvis Costello, "Watching the Detectives."

**satori....samadhi**: For a description of samadhi, see Chapter 00000011. Satori is gnosis or epiphany, attained through practice of *wu-hsin*, literally "no-mind," or contact with The Void. In Zen poetry, satori was frequently likened to celestial music "unheard by ears of parental origin."

**Hero takes a fall**: The Bangles, "The Hero Takes a Fall."

**end of Lonely Street**: Elvis Presley, "Heartbreak Hotel."

**Djean Djinni**: David Bowie, "Jean Genie."

**Sign in, stranger**: Steely Dan, "Sign In Stranger."

**Beat it**: Michael Jackson, "Beat It."

**Look thru any window**: The Hollies, "Look Through Any Window."

**Barbara Ann**: The Regents, "Barbara Ann."

**Peggy Sue**: Buddy Holly and the Crickets, "Peggy Sue."

**Linda Lou**: Lynyrd Skynyrd, "Linda Lou."

**Denise**: Randy and the Rainbows, "Denise."

**Black Betty**: Ram Jam, "Black Betty."

**Angie**: The Rolling Stones, "Angie."

**Peg**: Steely Dan, "Peg."

**Josie**: Steely Dan, "Josie."

**Rosalita**: Bruce Springsteen, "Rosalita."

**Layla**: Derek and the Dominoes, "Layla."

**Lola**: The Kinks, "Lola."

**Rita**: The Beatles, "Lovely Rita."

**Little Latin Lupe Lu**: Mitch Ryder and the Detroit Wheels, "Little Latin Lupe Lu."

**Roxanne**: The Police, "Roxanne."

**Suzie-Q**: Dale Hawkins, "Suzie-Q."

**Proud Mary**: Creedence Clearwater Revival, "Proud Mary."

**Sweet Loretta Martin**: The Beatles, "Get Back."

**Polythene Pam**: The Beatles, "Polythene Pam."

**Suzi Creamcheese**: The Mothers of Invention, "Suzi Creamcheese."

**Bertha**: The Grateful Dead, "Bertha."

**Sugar Magnolia**: The Grateful Dead, "Sugar Magnolia."

**Shanghai Lil**: Rod Stewart, "Every Picture Tells a Story."

**Cross-Eyed Mary**: Jethro Tull, "Cross-Eyed Mary."

**Candy**: Bruce Springsteen, "Candy's Room."

**Madame George**: Van Morrison, "Madame George."

**Lucille**: Little Richard, "Lucille."

**Avengin' Annie**: Andy Pratt, "Avenging Annie."

**One-eyed Fiona**: Lyle Lovett, "One-Eyed Fiona."

**love the one you're with**: Stephen Stills, "Love the One You're With."

**white room, with black curtains**: Cream, "White Room."

**twenty-five, or six two four**: Chicago, "25 or 6 to 4." Shades of deClosets' mixed-up escape: according to pop myth, these numbers supposedly refer to state highways!

**Number nine, number nine, number nine**: The Beatles, "Revolution 9."

**In the cheap hotel, time stands still**: Roxy Music, "Ain't That So."

**I dig U....dead**: Prince, "I Dig U Betta Dead."

**House of the Rising Sun**: The Animals, "The House of the Rising Sun." Apollo's favorite brothel. Or perhaps Sam Phillips's.

**Rocky Raccoon**: The Beatles, "Rocky Raccoon."

**paperback writer**: The Beatles, "Paperback Writer."

**can't get no satisfaction**: The Rolling Stones, "(I Can't Get No) Satisfaction."

**thanks for the information....zone**: Van Morrison, "Thanks for the Information."

**Stop, in the name of Platonic love**: The Supremes, "Stop! In the Name of Love."

**Jormungandr Behavioral Institute**: Run by Mister Wotan. Music therapy is attempted, employing mostly the soothing sounds of The Dell-Vikings.

**Heartbreak Beat**: The Psychedelic Furs, "Heartbreak Beat."

**Nineteenth Nervous Breakdown**: The Rolling Stones, "19th Nervous Breakdown."

**when I was a boy....**: The Beatles, "She Said She Said." A fine example of redundancy.

**I used to be....you**: Smashing Pumpkins, "Disarm."

**Cowabunga**: Originally a neologism from *The Howdy Doody Show*, this word became a battle-cry during the Vietnam War, and was in fact what Nick Fury, *né* Harry Covair, yelled when shooting Cambodians.

**greases Polly's hip like a big truck**: Dire Straits, "Roller Girl."

**Devil's Eighth Diurnal Ejaculation**: If the Devil ever succeeds in copulating and cumming eight times in a single day, he will become omnipotent. Much confusion has resulted from the fact of the Devil's two cocks, and experts are unsure whether a mere four double orgasms or sixteen whole shots are needed.

### Chapter 00000110

**hard to be a saint in *this* city**: Bruce Springsteen, "It's Hard to be a Saint in the City."

**Tuff Enuff**: The Fabulous Thunderbirds, "Tuff Enuff." 'Tis plain these lads follow the ways of the Dakota Indians, in their worship of Wakonda, the Thunderbird.

**the radio to heaven was wired to their purse**: Elvis Costello, "Blame It on Cain."

**Brother, can ya spare a dime?**: Yip Harburg, "Brother, Can You Spare a Dime?"

**That's all that money wants**: The Psychedelic Furs, "All that Money Wants."

**Soldiers keep on warrin'....won't be long**: Stevie Wonder, "Higher Ground."

**get fooled again**: The Who, "Won't Get Fooled Again."

**don't follow....medicine**: Bob Dylan, "Subterranean Homesick Blues."

**all we seem....in your heart**: The Style Council, "A Solid Bond in Your Heart."

**Don't sit under the apple tree with anyone else but me**: The Andrews Sisters, "Don't Sit Under the Apple Tree with Anyone Else But Me."

**I wanna be....sunglasses**: Human Sexual Response, "Jackie Onassis."

**I-wear-my-sunglasses-at-night**: Corey Hart, "Sunglasses at Night."

**Dalai Lama**: A rainbow over the home of a new tulku was one of the traditional signs.

**But if I....do that too**: The Coasters, "Searching."

**The Foggy Dew**: Traditional.

**he sat....tears on our cheeks....old hurley ball**: The Pogues, "The Broad Majestic Shannon."

**I've come....while**: Squeeze, "Take Me I'm Yours."

**midnight at the oasis**: Maria Mulduar, "Midnight at the Oasis."

**torn-down-à-la-Rimbaud**: Van Morrison, "Tore Down à la Rimbaud."

**higher....Oz**: XTC, "Merely a Man."

**Why did the Bodhidharma come from the West?**: To meet me.

***I believe....looking for***: U2, "I Still Haven't Found What I'm Looking For."

**gypsies, tramps and thieves....us**: Cher, "Gypsies, Tramps and Thieves."

**Cephalonia**: One of the Ionian islands, birthplace of Carpocrates. Melusine's Mom was the Fay, Pressina, whose other two daughters were Melior and Palatina. When exposed as a Gnostic, she fled with her girls to Cephalonia, according to Jean D'Arras in his *Chronique de Melusine*.

**Lady Jane**: A Pink Cadillac.

**The boys were back in town**: Thin Lizzy, "The Boys are Back in Town."

***That old black magic....your eyes meet mine***: Harold Arlen, "That Old Black Magic." This song came out in 1942, which would make these the memories of five-year-old Paddy.

**spirits in the material world**: The Police, "Spirits in the Material World."

**pulling a Johnny Ace**: An early rock star who allegedly killed himself on Christmas Eve, 1954, by playing Russian Roulette backstage. Another famous rock suicide, natch, was Del Shannon.

**Roll me in designer....enuff**: Blondie, "Call Me."

**The day's clear....five to one**: The Pogues, "Bottle of Smoke."

**Mindfulness....dead**: The *Dhammapada*.

**Lambton Wurms**: The fourteenth century Lord of Lambton, England, so the legend goes, kept an odd creature he had fished from a river in his well. The creature eventually grew to become a dragon—the Lambton Worm. A wise woman (!) told him how to slay it, and he did, by severing it with his sword and casting its

parts back into the river, where the current swept them away before they could rejoin.
**Michelle, *ma belle***: The Beatles, "Michelle."
**I want a pearl necklace**: ZZ Top, "Pearl Necklace."
**Celtic Ray**: Van Morrison, "Celtic Ray."
**Atum**: The Heliopolitan name for the Egyptian god, Re. His arch-enemy was the serpent, Apophis. Their whole legend is equivalent to the Babylonian rivalry between Sun-god Marduk and she-dragon Tiamat.
**Irish Heartbeat**: Van Morrison, "Irish Heartbeat."
**the ticket back from Suffragette City**: David Bowie, "Suffragette City."
**I won't worry....the light in your eyes**: Todd Rundgren, "I Saw the Light."
**In your eyes....complete**: Peter Gabriel, "In Your Eyes."
**You don't pull no punches, but you don't push the river**: Van Morrison, "You Don't Pull No Punches, but You Don't Push the River."
**Aryan Mist**: Van Morrison, "Aryan Mist."
**Orange Krush**: REM, "Orange Krush."
**Black Hats working for The Clampdown**: The Clash, "Clampdown."
**Helpless, helpless**: Neil Young, "Helpless."
**How can you run when you know?**: Crosby, Stills, Nash, and Young, "Ohio."
**Paranoia....creep**: Buffalo Springfield, "For What It's Worth."
**That's how....a-hey now**: The Searchers, "Needles and Pins."
**Sometimes I feel like a motherless child**: Richie Havens, "Motherless Child."
**Like a river....kept going**: Bruce Springsteen, "Hungry Heart."
**London Calling**: The Clash, "London Calling."
**Ferry 'cross the Mersey**: Gerry and the Pacemakers, "Ferry Across the Mersey."
**Waterloo Sunset**: The Kinks, "Waterloo Sunset."
**"I'm a Mocker!"**: John Lennon in *A Hard Day's Night*.
**mix those genes up**: It should be noted that all DNA is musical in nature, bearing both a "major" and "minor groove"! Also, DNA docking sites are palindromic.

**Brian "Blackie" Coffey**: Whose relative is King Coffey of the Butthole Surfers.
**Quicksilver Messenger Service**: 'Sixties San Franciscan followers of Mercury, or Hermes. Hermes invented the lyre, and functioned as a *psychopompos*, or guide to the dead. Hermes was a favorite of the Gnostics and alchemists, who called him The Awakened One.
**Eyes without a....grace**: Billy Idol, "Eyes Without a Face."
**Put the message....heard**: World Party, "Message in a Box."
**Road To Nowhere**: The Talking Heads, "Road to Nowhere."

Chapter 00000111
Day Three, Thursday, May 27, 1993
Day of the Eagle
Tribe of Levi
and
Day Four, Friday, May 28, 1993
Day of the Vulture
Tribe of Judah

**Just one Look...took**: Doris Troy, "Just One Look."
**Doing the Wild Thing**: Tone-Loc, "Wild Thing."
**Rocking the Cradle of Love**: Billy Idol, "Cradle of Love."
**Dancing in the dark**: Bruce Springstein, "Dancing in the Dark."
**Loco-Motion**: Little Eva, "Loco-Motion."
**Groovy Train**: The Farm, "Groovy Train."
**Banging a Gong**: T. Rex, "Bang a Gong (Get It On)."
**Big Time Sensuality**: Bjork, "Big Time Sensuality."
**Shaking, rattling and rolling**: Arthur Conley, "Shake, Rattle and Roll."
**Afternoon Delight**: Starland Vocal Band, "Afternoon Delight."
**Horizontal Bop**: Bob Seger, "Horizontal Bop."
*I get delirious, whenever you're near*: Prince, "Delirious."
**Doing It In The Road**: The Beatles, "Why Don't We Do It in the Road."
**Dancing in the Street**: Martha and the Vandellas, "Dancing in the Street."
**Mixed Coatings, Ltd**: Mixcoatl was the Aztec cloud serpent deity. His wife was Coatlicue, the earth serpent.

**I've got so much to give you**: Barry White, "I've Got So Much to Give."

**Tezcatlipoca**: Literally, "smoking mirror." The Aztec Apollo.

**I heard it thru the grapevine**: Gladys Knight and the Pips, "I Heard It through the Grapevine."

**Village People at the YMCA**: The Village People, "Y.M.C.A."

**It's like Beirut....cheveray**: Stevie Wonder, "Don't You Worry 'bout a Thing."

**I didn't mean to turn you on**: Robert Palmer, "I Didn't Mean to Turn You On."

**If it's just....train**: Willy DeVille, "A-Train Lady."

**Keep your hands to yourself**: The Georgia Satellites, "Keep Your Hands to Yourself."

**Love could make you happy**: Mercy, "Love (Can Make You Happy)."

**all you needed was love**: The Beatles, "All You Need Is Love."

**love was also a battlefield**: Pat Benatar, "Love is a Battlefield."

**love was a stranger**: The Eurythmics, "Love is a Stranger."

**love was a hurtin' thing**: Lou Rawls, "Love Is a Hurtin' Thing."

**love was strange**: Mickey & Sylvia, "Love is Strange."

**love was a many-splendored thing**: Four Aces, "Love is a Many-Splendored Thing." Half of a winning hand in binary poker.

**Only love could break your heart**: Neil Young, "Only Love Can Break Your Heart."

**put a little love in your heart**: Jackie DeShannon, "Put a Little Love in Your Heart." One of the many musical Shannons.

**love was like an itching**: The Supremes, "Love is like an Itching in my Heart."

**like oxygen to his lungs**: Sweet, "Love is like Oxygen."

**a whole lotta love**: Led Zepplin, "Whole Lotta Love."

**his love was bigger than a Cadillac**: Buddy Holly, "Not Fade Away."

**cheating heart**: Hank Williams, "Your Cheating Heart."

**torn between two lovers**: Mary MacGregor, "Torn Between Two Lovers."

**loved her madly**: The Doors, "Love Her Madly."

**could it be....too**: The Spinners, "Could It Be I'm Falling in Love?"

**Sneaky feelings**: Elvis Costello, "Sneaky Feelings."

**slippery people**: The Talking Heads, "Slippery People."

**he felt like makin' love**: Bad Company, "Feel Like Makin' Love." Cy definitely feels like this song, not the Roberta Flack song of the same name.

**love was here, and now she was gone**: The Supremes, "Love is Here and Now You're Gone."

**she'd be a woman....her man**: The Beatles, "She's a Woman."

**It's the season of loving**: The Zombies, "Season of Loving."

**Who do you love**: Bo Diddley, "Who Do You Love."

**the only flame in town**: Elvis Costello, "The Only Flame In Town."

**cyclone**: Not yet a practical goal.

**black satin doll**: Duke Ellington, "Black Satin Doll."

**I've got a girlfriend....in her eyes**: The Talking Heads, "Girlfriend is Better."

**Tell her no, no, no**: The Zombies, "Tell Her No."

**I've got a dirty mind whenever she's around**: Prince, "Dirty Mind."

**we're gonna do it all night**: Prince, "Do It All Night."

**You got me....lay you down**: Prince, "Dirty Mind."

**itty bitty pretty one**: Thurston Harris, "Itty Bitty Pretty One."

**I visited the....fountain**: The Indigo Girls, "Closer to Fine."

**Goodbye Girl**: Squeeze, "Goodbye Girl."

**Heaven is a place on earth**: Belinda Carlisle, "Heaven is a Place on Earth." This is very much a Zen statement.

**You were just....me instead**: Prince, "Head."

**Love me tender**: Elvis Presley, "Love Me Tender."

**Sex Packets**: Digital Underground, *Sex Packets.*

**It goes round....here**: Red Nicols and His Five Pennies, "The Music Goes 'Round and 'Round."

**I was a free man in Paris**: Joni Mitchell, "Free Man in Paris."

**When she was....friend**: Prince, "When You Were Mine."

she's gone Uptown: Prince, "Uptown."
West End Girl: The Pet Shop Boys,
"West End Girls."
she didn't even have....mine: Prince,
"When You Were Mine."
a broken heart again: Prince,
"Gotta Broken Heart Again."
spirits in the night: Bruce Springsteen,
"Spirits in the Night."
I will stand pat: And believe me, at times
it was hard to bear O'Phidian.
swallow every drop: Fellatio and sperma-
tophagy are sanctified Gnostic Acts.
Spin-the-bottle....you: Juliana Hatfield,
"Spin the Bottle."
Green Onions: Booker T and the MGs,
"Green Onions."
running scared: Roy Orbison,
"Running Scared."
Oh, pretty woman: Roy Orbison,
"Oh, Pretty Woman."
black coffee in bed: Squeeze,
"Black Coffee in Bed."
espresso love: Dire Straits,
"Espresso Love."
they'll be coming....ha-ha: Napolean XIV,
"They're Coming to Take Me Away, Ha-Haaa!"
She makes love....girl: Bob Dylan,
"Just Like a Woman."
stop your sobbing: The Pretenders,
"Stop Your Sobbing."
lay, lady, lay, across my big brass bed:
Bob Dylan, "Lay, Lady, Lay."
Alice in Chains: A group.
Mudhoney: A group.
Hole: A group.
Nirvana: The biggest.
love me two times, I'm going away:
The Doors, "Love Me Two Times."
slippin' and slidin': Little Richard,
"Slippin' and Slidin'."
Sugar Walls: Sheena Easton, "Sugar Walls."
Polly, he says....don't know why: Simon
and Garfunkel, "America."
run-run-runaway: Del Shannon, "Runaway."
There's more Shannons than Jacksons!
Since you're gone....tense: The Cars,
"Since You're Gone."
ain't love the sweetest thing: U2,
"Ain't Love the Sweetest Thing."
WHY DOES LOVE GOT TO BE SO SAD:
Derek and the Dominoes, "Why Does
Love Got to Be So Sad?"

As far as....coal-grey: 10,000 Maniacs,
"Like the Weather."
it rains like a slow divorce: Robyn
Hitchcock, "Balloon Man."
Until the Mighty Rivers....your man:
Graham Parker, "Mighty Rivers."
There is....wife: The Talking Heads,
"Once in a Lifetime."
Everything counts in large amounts:
Depeche Mode, "Everything Counts."
I'm the tool....: Frank Zappa,
"I'm the Slime."
fool in the rain: Led Zepplin,
"Fool in the Rain."
Messing with the Messer: Willie Dixon,
"Don't Mess with the Messer."
black is the color and none is the
number: Bob Dylan, "It's a Hard Rain
That's Gonna Fall."
who is that....Custerdome: Steely Dan,
"Gaucho."

## Chapter 00001000

Sinatra in the....duet: Frank Sinatra, Duets.
me and my shadow: Dave Dreyer,
"Me and my Shadow."
Mister Pusherman: Steppenwolf,
"The Pusher."
Going up the country....grows: Canned
Heat, "Going Up the Country."
Misty Mountain Hop: Led Zepplin,
"Misty Mountain Hop."
lazy houn' dogs....never caught a rabbit
yet: Big Mama Thornton, "Hound Dog."
Close To The Bone: Tom Tom Club,
"Close to the Bone."
just a funky....rusted: The B-52's,
"Love Shack."
answered by an owl: The owl was
associated both with Mercury and the
Lords of Xibalba.
Chinese New World colonists: The
prehistoric Japanese called the current
that carried them to the New World
Kuroshio, "The Black Current." And of
course, modern-day Chinese people-
smugglers are called "snakeheads."
Memphis, home to Elvis and the
ancient Greeks: Talking Heads, "Cities."
just "Em": M is a fine name. It was good
enough for David Hilbert to use, when he
wanted to name his complete theory of
mathematics.

**little pee-pee and little toes**: The Talking Heads, "Stay Up Late."

**he was a rock....no pain**: Simon and Garfunkel, "I Am a Rock."

**love him like a rock**: Paul Simon, "Loves Me Like a Rock."

**yellow-bellied blacksnake....to go....King of the Mountain....wall**: Midnight Oil, "King of the Mountain."

**poor young country....son**: The Beatles, "Mother Nature's Son."

**barefootin'**: Robert Parker, "Barefootin'."

**All the best cowgirls....eyes**: Pete Townsend, *All the Best Cowboys Have Chinese Eyes*.

**She's giving me....good vibrations**: The Beach Boys, "Good Vibrations."

**Up on Cripple Creek....mends me**: The Band, "Up on Cripple Creek."

**Down on the....hand**: Los Lobos, "Down on the Riverbed."

**Red, red, wine....need you**: Tony Tribe, "Red, Red, Wine."

**Shonen Knife**: A group

**takin' it to the streets**: The Doobie Brothers, "Takin' It to the Streets."

**Children, behave....hand**: Tommy James and the Shondells, "I Think We're Alone Now."

**freedom's just another....lose**: Janis Joplin, "Me and Bobby McGee."

**room to move**: John Mayall, "Room to Move."

**I feel free....reality**: The Who, "I'm Free."

**I'm not waitin'....friend**: The Rolling Stones, "Waiting on a Friend."

**What can make....girl**: The Temptations, "My Girl."

**crickets**: A group.

**beetles**: A group.

**katydids**: A group.

**buggles**: A group.

**falling down the mountain**: INXS, "Falling Down the Mountain."

**baby snakes**: Frank Zappa, "Baby Snakes."

**Spirit In The Sky**: Norman Greenbaum, "Spirit in the Sky."

**"The Viper's Drag"**: A toke.

**A tear fell**: Theresa Brewer, "A Tear Fell."

**Don't let the Sun catch you crying**: Gerry and the Pacemakers, "Don't Let The Sun Catch You Crying."

**TOMORROW NEVER KNOWS**: The Beatles, "Tomorrow Never Knows." Inspired by a reading of Leary's edition of the Tibetan *Book of the Dead*.

**Private Duncan Idaho**: The B-52's, "Private Idaho."

**Muswell Hillbillies**: The Kinks, *Muswell Hillbillies*.

**We put the past....totally**: Big Audio Dynamite, "Sony."

**Conquistador**: Procul Harum, "Conquistador."

**Night They Drove Old Dixie Down**: The Band, "The Night They Drove Old Dixie Down."

**Maggie's Farm**: Bob Dylan, "Maggie's Farm."

**Up, up and away**: The Fifth Dimension, "Up, Up and Away."

**How can I be sure**: The Rascals, "How Can I Be Sure?"

**Rock 'n' Roll High School**: The Ramones, "Rock 'n' Roll High School." It is interesting to note the changes that the passage of two decades has wrought in the academic proclivities of youth. In Sam Cooke's "Wonderful World," the singer laments that he "don't know much about history," while in *this* song, the singer brashly asserts that he "don't *care* about history." A most unfortunate attitude.

**without beneficial effects**: The major scare regarding acid, of course, was that it would "damage your chromosomes"—something much more likely to be caused by a virus.

**he never lost....head**: Lou Reed, "Walk on the Wild Side."

**1967**: In 1954, there were 50 computers in the world. By 1967, there were 35,000.

**Cortez the Killer**: Neil Young, "Cortez the Killer."

**printing and distribution of currency**: Dollar bills come 32 to a sheet. The paper for currency is all made by Crane and Company in, natch, Massachusetts.

**the Haight**: Chinese immigrants to San Francisco called that city "Old Gold Mountain."

**Mistra Know-It-All**: Stevie Wonder, "Mistra Know-It-All."

**spread of acid**: Was the CIA aiming for a critical mass of trippers? Would something new have become emergent, as in von Neumann's brain?

**Grab a flower....in your hair**: Scott McKenzie, "San Francisco (Be Sure to Wear a Flower in Your Hair)."

**bend you and shape you**: The American Breed, "Bend Me, Shape Me."

**light your fire**: The Doors, "Light My Fire."

**the Dead**: What does the band known as the Dead have to do with the dead band of satellite transmission? Probably as much as the Gap Band has to do with band gap.

**you never give me....situation**: The Beatles, "You Never Give Me Your Money."

**Mario**: Mario Savio stuttered.

**Brown shoes....it**: The Mothers of Invention, "Brown Shoes Don't Make It."

**Dirty Boulevard....suck**: Lou Reed, "Dirty Boulevard."

**I got fat....lifted**: Wu Tang Clan, "Method Man."

**Slow down....last**: Simon and Garfunkel, "The 59th Street Bridge Song."

**Wouldn't it be....together**: The Beach Boys, "Wouldn't It Be Nice."

**groovin' on a Sunday afternoon**: The Rascals, "Groovin'."

**Sweet Little Two to the Fourth**: Chuck Berry, "Sweet Little Sixteen."

**on the edge of seventeen**: Stevie Nicks, "On the Edge of Seventeen."

**twentieth-century fox**: The Doors, "Twentieth Century Fox."

**Foxy Lady**: Jimi Hendrix, "Foxy Lady."

**wang-dang-doodle**: Willie Dixon, "Wang Dang Doodle."

**Sunshine of his love**: Cream, "Sunshine of Your Love."

**bell-bottom blues**: Derek and the Dominoes, "Bell Bottom Blues."

**Jack Flash**: The Rolling Stones, "Jumping Jack Flash." These Rolling Stones are arrant rip-off artists, for just as they stole Ruby Tuesday's name for the song that debuted after her birth, so they've appropriated Mister Flash's name for their hit of 1968.

**suspicious of the food**: Demesne was, of course, suspicious of everything. Luckily, he had never heard of the 'Sixties band known as The Peanut Butter Conspiracy.

**time is on our side**: Irma Thomas, "Time Is On My Side."

**you oughta know....there, et seq**: The Talking Heads, "Life During Wartime."

**Street-fightin' man**: The Rolling Stones, "Street Fighting Man."

**Psycho Killer**: The Talking Heads, "Psycho Killer."

**Panic in Detroit**: David Bowie, "Panic in Detroit."

**I can't even write my own name**: All is not lost for Davey Burnout. As Master Bassui says, in his collected sermons known as *Mud and Water*, satori is attainable "even by those who don't know their own name."

**Reach out, I'll be there**: The Four Tops, "Reach Out, I'll Be There."

**keeps you hangin' on**: The Supremes, "You Keep Me Hangin' On."

**really got a hold on me**: The Miracles, "You've Really Got a Hold on Me."

**the hunter gets captured by the game**: The Marvelettes, "The Hunter Gets Captured by the Game."

**I second that emotion**: The Miracles, "I Second That Emotion."

**uptight, but everything's all right**: Stevie Wonder, "Uptight (Everything's Alright)."

**ain't no mountain high enough**: Marvin Gaye and Tammi Terrell, "Ain't No Mountain High Enough."

**the way you do the things you do**: The Temptations, "The Way You Do The Things You Do."

**bad moon rising**: Creedence Clearwater Revival, "Bad Moon Rising."

**if man is five....seven**: The Pixies, "Monkey Gone to Heaven."

**the fourth film**: The first three were: *Am Abend*, German, 1910, starring a young Lambton Wurms. *El Satario*, Argentinian, 1912, featuring three women fucking a devil. And *A Free Ride*, American, 1919. All three are to be found in the archives of the Kinsey Institute. However, no print of *Salammbo* is known to have survived the 'Sixties.

**Magic Bus**: The Who, "Magic Bus."

**Young Americans**: David Bowie, "Young Americans."

**Serpent Mound State Park**: Why do the convolutions of these mounds almost exactly mimic the snake depicted on the old flag of the Chinese Empire?

long and winding mental road:
The Beatles, "The Long and
Winding Road."
**Stunned and amazed....Ohio:**
The Pretenders, "My City was Gone."
**broken on thru to the other side:**
The Doors, "Break On Through."
**Manson:** One of Charlie's favorite pieces
of clothing was a cord vest embroidered
with snakes and dragons.
**Helter Skelter:** The Beatles, "Helter Skelter."
**Roland:** Warren Zevon, "Roland the
Headless Thompson Gunner."
**TVC-15:** David Bowie, "TVC-15."

## Chapter 00001001
## Day Four, Friday, May 28, 1993
## Day of the Vulture
## Tribe of Judah

**in and out of the midnight hour:**
Wilson Pickett, "In the Midnight Hour."
**I had too much to dream last night:**
The Electric Prunes, "I Had Too Much to
Dream (Last Night)."
**Vanilla Fudge:** A group.
**Chocolate Watchband:** A group.
**Burning Down The House:** The Talking
Heads, "Burning Down the House."
**Crowded House:** A group.
**You're my Venus....desire:** Shocking
Blue, "Venus."
**I'll stop the....you:** Modern English,
"I'll Melt with You."
**It's getting better....mine:** The Beatles,
"It's Getting Better."
**Indoor Fireworks:** Elvis Costello,
"Indoor Fireworks."
**when the levee breaks:** Led Zepplin,
"When the Levee Breaks."
**Yummy, yummy....tummy:** Ohio Express,
"Yummy Yummy Yummy."
**she's a rainbow:** The Rolling Stones,
"She's a Rainbow."
**What does sex....society:** Human Sexual
Response, "What Does Sex Mean to Me?"
**If I didn't love you I'd hate you:**
Squeeze, "If I Didn't Love You."
**Puff, the Magic Dragon:** Peter, Paul and
Mary, "Puff the Magic Dragon."
**This is Mission Control....right now:**
David Bowie, "Space Oddity."
**heavy weather traffic:** The Katydids,
"Heavy Weather Traffic."

**nothin' but a house party:**
The Show Stoppers, "Ain't Nothin' but a
House Party."
**Soul Asylum:** A group.
**Let them all talk:** Elvis Costello,
"Let Them Talk."
**Boy with a problem:** Elvis Costello,
"Boy with a Problem."
**Born under punches:** The Talking Heads,
"Born Under Punches."
**Keep it in....out:** Boom Crash Opera,
"Onionskin."
**Psychotic reaction:** Count Five,
"Psychotic Reaction."
**Shock that monkey:** Peter Gabriel,
"Shock the Monkey."
**cry like a baby:** The Box Tops,
"Cry Like a Baby."
**It's my party....wanna:** Lesley Gore,
"It's My Party."
**Are we not....Devo:** Devo,
*Q: Are We Not Men? A: We Are Devo.*
**I read a book....go:** The Mighty Mighty
Bosstones, "Where Did You Go?"
**Whatever gets you thru the night:** John
Lennon, "Whatever Gets You thru the Night."
**Who wrote this book of love:**
The Monotones, "Book of Love."
**Wake up, Little Suzie:** The Everly Brothers,
"Wake Up Little Susie."
**help me make it thru the night:** Sammi
Smith, "Help Me Make It through the Night."
**57 channels and nothing on:** Bruce
Springsteen, "57 Channels (and Nothin' On)."
**theme song:** David Bowie, "Cat People
(Putting Out the Fire with Gasoline)."
**Boy, you're gonna....time:** The Beatles,
"Carry That Weight."
**practicing human sacrifice:** Another
verified Mayan practice was drug
infusion via enemas.
**Blue Sky Mining:** Midnight Oil,
"Blue Sky Mining."
**owls:** In Mayan cosmology, the owl was
associated with the planet Mercury.
**Not in the long run:** Eight Snake was
remarkably prescient here. Almost
everyone connected with Operation
SUCCESS eventually came to a bad end.
Most notably: Ambassador Peurifoy,
transferred to Thailand, died in a car
crash on August 18, 1955. Allen Dulles
lost his job over the Bay of Pigs fiasco,

in which Rip Robertson was also caught up. Castilo Armas was assassinated. United Fruit became United Brands in the late 'Sixties. Its president at the time was one Eli Black. Over-extended, the company sustained tremendous losses. On February 3, 1975, Black smashed a window high up in the Pan Am Building and leaped to his death.

**I have been....tonight**: Bruce Springsteen, "Blinded by the Light."

**fur pajamas....wild life**:The Talking Heads, "Wild Wild Life."

**pretty in pink**: The Psychedelic Furs, "Pretty in Pink."

**I'll stick to....guy**: Mary Wells, "My Guy."

**Four in the morning....city**: Paul Simon, "Peace Like a River."

**here comes the sun**: The Beatles, "Here Comes the Sun."

**The sun is shining....ball**: Cyrkle, "Red Rubber Ball." Of course, a red rubber ball was what the Mayan *pok-a-tok* was traditionally played with, when they couldn't get fresh head.

**Wake up....head**: Livingston Taylor, "Wake Up."

**Sunshine go away....laughing**: Jonathan Edwards, "Sunshine."

**Ain't no sunshine**: Bill Withers, "Ain't No Sunshine."

**Riding along on....you**: The Hollies, "On a Carousel."

**We're captives on....came**: Joni Mitchell, "The Circle Game."

**looking for a cynical girl**: Marshall Crenshaw, "Cynical Girl."

**a Polly trousseau**: A rare item.

**We're goin' to....married**: The Dixie Cups, "Chapel of Love."

**I got you, I feel good**: James Brown, "I Got You (I Feel Good)."

**I just wanna....you**: Etta James, "I Just Want to Make Love to You."

**roll with me, Cy**: Etta James, "Roll With Me, Henry." Miss James is a well-known half-breed, the product of an Italian Dad and a Black Mom, which makes her Prince's mirror image (Black Dad and Italian Mom).

**Welcome to the Hotel California**: The Eagles, "Hotel California."

**Lips like sugar? Sugar kisses?**: Echo and the Bunnymen, "Lips Like Sugar."

**Bernadette**: The Four Tops, "Bernadette."

**Evangeline**: Matthew Sweet, "Evangeline."

**Sweet Caroline**: Neil Diamond, "Sweet Caroline (Good Times Never Seemed So Good)."

**Cracklin Rosie**: Neil Diamond, "Cracklin' Rosie."

**Windy**: The Association, "Windy."

**Allison**: Elvis Costello, "Allison."

**Carrie-Anne**: The Hollies, "Carrie-Anne."

**Charlotte Ann**: Julian Cope, "Charlotte Ann."

**Miss Molly**: Little Richard, "Miss Molly."

**Darling Nikki**: Prince, "Darling Nikki."

**Mustang Sally**: Wilson Pickett, "Mustang Sally."

**Sweet Jane**: Lou Reed, "Sweet Jane."

**Dear Prudence**: The Beatles, "Dear Prudence."

**My Sharona**: The Knack, "My Sharona."

**Sexy Sadie**: The Beatles, "Sexy Sadie."

**Jessica**: The Allman Brothers, "Jessica."

**Runaround Sue**: Dion, "Runaround Sue."

**Maybellene**: Chuck Berry, "Maybellene."

**Long Tall Sally**: Little Richard, "Long Tall Sally."

**Short Fat Fannie**: Larry Williams, "Short Fat Fannie."

**Jenny Jenny**: Little Richard, "Jenny Jenny."

**Mojo Hanna**: Esther Phillips, "Mojo Hanna."

**Miss Ann**: Little Richard, "Miss Ann." (Mister Penniman sure had his share of women—not bad for a switch-hitter!)

**Donna**: Richie Valens, "Donna."

**Sherry**: The 4 Seasons, "Sherry."

**Sussudio**: Phil Collins, "Sussudio."

**Sally Mae**: John Lee Hooker, "Sally Mae."

**Cecilia**: Simon and Garfunkel, "Cecilia."

**Bony Moronie**: Larry Williams, "Bony Moronie."

**Sweet Judy Blue Eyes**: Crosby, Stills and Nash, "Suite: Judy Blue Eyes."

**Gloria**: Them, "Gloria."

**Suzanne**: Lou Reed, "Suzanne."

**Melody Cool**: Prince, "Melody Cool."

**Kathy's Klown**: The Everly Brothers, "Cathy's Clown."

**Time is tight**: Booker T and the MGs, "Time is Tight."

**Go back, Jack....again**: Steely Dan, "Do It Again."

**"I'D GIVE YOU EVERYTHING I'VE GOT FOR SOME PEACE OF MIND":** The Beatles, "I'm So Tired."

**Nanking:** The perimeter of the modern-day capitol, Peking, resembles the head of a horned dragon with open mouth.

**Mao:** "The principle hallucinogens of the Amazon Basin are tryptamines of some sort or another, usually activated by being taken in combination with harmine, a monamine oxidase (MAO) inhibitor...." Terrence McKenna. It is also instructive to note that one of Mao's mistresses was named Lily Wu.

**China Groves:** The Doobie Brothers, "China Grove."

**ice-blink luck:** The Cocteau Twins, "Ice Blink Luck."

**Hey, fella....heat** Steely Dan, "Bad Sneakers."

**MONEY FOR NOTHING....finger:** Dire Straits, "Money for Nothing."

**Look what they've done to my song, Ma:** The New Seekers, "Look What They've Done to My Song Ma."

**It's only jukebox music:** The Kinks, "Juke Box Music."

**it's only rock....like it:** The Rolling Stones, "It's Only Rock 'n' Roll (But I Like It)."

**Rock 'n' roll is here to stay:** Danny and the Juniors, "Rock and Roll is Here to Stay."

**Rock 'n' roll music....choose it:** Chuck Berry, "Rock and Roll Music."

**Roll over, Claude....news:** Chuck Berry, "Roll Over, Beethoven."

**Rock 'n' roll hoochie koo:** Rick Derringer, "Rock and Roll, Hoochie Koo."

**You should see....twist:** Chubby Checker, "Twist."

**It's a....sun:** Fountains of Wayne, "Radiation Vibe."

## Chapter 00001010

**Homeward bound....bound:** Simon and Garfunkel, "Homeward Bound."

**white bird....will die:** It's A Beautiful Day, "White Bird."

**octopus's garden in the rain:** The Beatles, "Octopus's Garden."

**haunts of ancient....we seek:** Van Morrison, "Haunts of Ancient Peace."

**drinking wine spo-de-odee:** Stick McGhee, "Drinking Wine Spo-Dee-O-Dee."

**Gonna take you on a Sea Cruise:** Frankie Ford, "Sea Cruise."

**many's the time....gold:** Led Zepplin, "Over the Hills and Far Away."

**other government agencies:** The National Institute of Allergy and Infectious Diseases—NIAID—is no match for my naiads.

**bravura performance:** As we shall soon see, events will bear out George Clinton's doctrine that "The singer gets the pussy."

**spinning wheel....turn:** Blood, Sweat and Tears, "Spinning Wheel."

**GTO:** Ronny and the Daytonas, "G.T.O." Also, natch, Girls Together Outrageously.

**little deuce coupe:** The Beach Boys, "Little Deuce Coupe."

**hot rod Lincoln:** Johnny Bond, "Hot Rod Lincoln."

**Hey, Mister....parade:** Bob Dylan, "Mister Tambourine Man."

**single priest:** Hadrian didn't know the half of it, since, according to physicist James Jeans, "God is a mathematician."

**Wholly Booleans:** Sam the Sham and the Pharoahs, "Wooly Bully."

**rock the casbah:** The Clash, "Rock the Casbah."

**they loved to watch her strut:** Bob Seger, "They Love to Watch Her Strut."

**I've avoided relations....away:** Billy Bragg, "Sexuality."

**Isis Academy:** We can assume that the young ladies of the Isis Academy were trained to live up to the standards of the Academy's patron goddess, Isis, who fucked her brother, Osiris, and fashioned a serpent to bite the sun-god, Ra.

**Siemens:** This company with the off-color name bought up the Zuse computer firm after the Second World War. Founded by Konrad Zuse, ZC had manufactured the S1 and S2 computers used by Lambton Wurms.

**Don't stand....me:** The Police, "Don't Stand So Close to Me."

**pro-teases:** Hot juice.

**daughters of the kaos:** Luscious Jackson, "Daughters of the Kaos."

**A little China....sea**: Ricky Nelson, "Travelin' Man."

**that petrol emotion**: A group.

**California sun....shimmy**: The Rivieras, "California Sun."

**California Dream**: The Mamas and the Papas, "California Dreamin'."

**California Girls**: The Beach Boys, "California Girls."

**I even love El Ay**: Randy Newman, "I Love L.A."

**This place is....city**: Stevie Wonder, "Living for the City."

**reserve judgement on the anagram**: What O'Phidian never knew was that there was a second anagram, which he should have paid more attention to: I LIE, HE LAID: RA SIN ALPHA, NO GAP.

**Laoyeh**: Chinese honorific literally meaning "Old Daddy."

**over, under, sideways, down**: The Yardbirds, "Over, Under, Sideways, Down."

**I could turn....do**: REM, "Turn You Inside Out."

**whip it**: Devo, "Whip It."

**Hit me, hit me with your rhythm stick**: Ian Dury, "Hit Me with your Rhythm Stick."

**Call me up in dreamland**: Van Morrison, "Call Me Up in Dreamland."

**Are Eee Ess Pee Eee Cee Tee**: Aretha Franklin, "Respect."

**games without frontiers**: Peter Gabriel, "Games Without Frontiers."

**Sweet Soul Sister**: The Cult, "Sweet Soul Sister."

**The harder they....all**: Jimmy Cliff, "The Harder They Come."

**Heart of Gold**: Neil Young, "Heart of Gold."

**Heart of glass**: Blondie, "Heart of Glass."

**Heart was made of stone**: The Rolling Stones, "Heart of Stone."

**Heart full of soul**: The Yardbirds, "Heart Full of Soul."

**doo, doo, doo....Heartbreaker**: The Rolling Stones, "Doo Doo Doo Doo Doo (Heartbreaker)."

**Royal Scam**: Steely Dan, "The Royal Scam."

**Sanctified Pussy**: Marvin Gaye, "Sanctified Pussy."

**Sweet Soul Music**: Arthur Conley, "Sweet Soul Music."

**Rebel, rebel....dress**: David Bowie, "Rebel, Rebel."

**Evil Woman**: Electric Light Orchestra, "Evil Woman."

**blinded me with science**: Thomas Dolby, "She Blinded Me with Science."

**you and I....late**: Bob Dylan, "All Along the Watchtower."

**tears for fears**: A group.

**Backdoor Man**: Willie Dixon, "Back Door Man."

**Higher Love**: Steve Winwood, "Higher Love."

**Spill the wine....gnome**: Eric Burdon and War, "Spill the Wine."

**We can share....wine**: The Grateful Dead, "Jack Straw."

**devil with a blue dress on**: Mitch Ryder and the Detroit Wheels, "Devil with a Blue Dress On."

**lechery....in confidence**: On the island of Majorca, Robert Graves spotted a business sign designed to attract English patronage: THIS IS A LECHERIE OF CONFIDENCE. Meaning, THIS IS A DAIRY [*leche* + suffix] YOU CAN TRUST. Somehow, this explains why O'Phidian wanted to fill Agape with cream.

**From the South....Malibu**: The Specials, "International Jet Set."

**black magic women**: Santana, "Black Magic Woman."

**wasn't sure....love you so**: David Bowie, "Rebel, Rebel."

### Chapter 00001011
Day Five, Saturday, May 29, 1993
Day of the Movement
Tribe of Issachar
Day Six, Sunday, May 30, 1993
Day of the Flint Knife
Tribe of Zebulun
Day Seven, Monday, May 31, 1993
Day of the Rain
Tribe of Dan
Day Eight, Tuesday, June 1, 1993
Day of the Flower
Tribe of Gad
Day Nine, Wednesday, June 2, 1993
Day of the Crocodile
Tribe of Asher
and
Day Ten, Thursday, June 3, 1993
Day of the Wind
Tribe of Naphtali

**livin' for the weekend**: The O'Jays, "Livin' for the Weekend."

**I don't wanna....day**: Todd Rundgren, "Bang the Drum."
**Permanent Vacation**: Aerosmith, *Permanent Vacation*.
**seven day weekend**: Garry U.S. Bonds, "Seven Day Weekend."
**My baby left me**: Elvis Presley, "My Baby Left Me."
**good thing**: Fine Young Cannibals, "Good Thing."
**She took off....persons**: The Talking Heads, "And She Was."
**Ruby, baby....mine**: Dion, "Ruby Baby."
**Wild thing....sing**: The Troggs, "Wild Thing."
**groovy kind of love**: The Mindbenders, "Groovy Kind of Love."
**My boyfriend's....trouble**: The Angels, "My Boyfriend's Back."
**Saturday morning confusion**: Bobby Russell, "Saturday Morning Confusion."
**Rose, darlin'....bed**: Steely Dan, "Rose Darling."
**Our house....cats in the yard**: Crosby, Stills, Nash and Young, "Our House."
**Who finds the money....heaven-sent**: The Beatles, "Lady Madonna."
**Tony! Toni! Tone!**: A group.
**Will you still....sixty-four**: The Beatles, "When I'm Sixty-Four." A fine number to be, especially if it's 64 meg.
**the radio....fools**: Elvis Costello, "Radio Radio."
**She be listenin' to Channel Zero**: Public Enemy, "She Watch Channel Zero."
**Channel Z**: all static, all the time: The B-52's, "Channel Z."
**Discontentment is our engine**: Plan B, "Discontentment."
**silly love song**: Paul McCartney, "Silly Love Songs."
**I just called....you**: Stevie Wonder, "I Just Called to Say I Love You."
**I write....sing**: Barry Manilow, "I Write the Songs."
**I'd like to....harmony**: The New Seekers, "I'd Like to Teach the World to Sing (in Perfect Harmony)."
**Tie a yellow....tree**: Dawn, "Tie a Yellow Ribbon Round the Ole Oak Tree."
**shake your moneymaker**: As mentioned before, this Elmore James tune resulted from static on the line to the Muses.

However, this has not prevented it from being covered numerous times, most recently by the Black Crowes, whose name could be translated into Chinese as Wu Wu.
**Thank you....again**: Sly and the Family Stone, "Thank You Faletinme Be Mice Elf Again."
**His life's been....rock 'n' roll**: Lou Reed, "Rock and Roll."
**Bad To The Bone**: George Thorogood, "Bad to the Bone."
**wanna be sedated**: The Ramones, "I Wanna Be Sedated."
**Baby, you can drive my car**: The Beatles, "Drive My Car."
**One sweet dream....limousine**: The Beatles, "You Never Give Me Your Money."
**summertime blues**: Eddie Cochran, "Summertime Blues."
**My liddle 409**: The Beach Boys, "409."
**We'll have fun....away**: The Beach Boys, "Fun, Fun, Fun."
**I love....home**: The Standells, "Dirty Water."
**Rock-rock-rock-rock-rockaway Beach**: The Ramones, "Rockaway Beach."
**summer in the city**: The Lovin' Spoonful, "Summer in the City." The Lovin' Spoonful derived their name from the average measure of a shot of ejaculate.
**In the summertime....mangoes and cherries**: Mungo Jerry, "In the Summertime."
**Hot fun in the summertime**: Sly and the Family Stone, "Hot Fun in the Summertime."
**They drive past....twice**: Jonathan Richman and the Modern Lovers, "Roadrunner."
**freeway of love**: Aretha Franklin, "Freeway of Love."
**love-cats**: The Cure, "Love Cats."
**cool for cats**: Squeeze, "Cool for Cats."
**glad-all-over**: The Dave Clark Five, "Glad All Over."
**under the boardwalk**: The Drifters, "Under the Boardwalk."
**SURFIN' SAFARI**: The Beach Boys, "Surfin' Safari."
**Surf City**: Jan & Dean, "Surf City."
**surfin' in the U.S.A.**: The Beach Boys, "Surfin' U.S.A."
**lonely surfer**: Jack Nietzsche, "Lonely Surfer." Tho little known, this performer was the son of the famous German incestuous philosopher.
**Surfer Girl**: The Beach Boys, "Surfer Girl."
**THE PIPELINE**: The Chantays, "Pipeline."

**WIPEOUT**: The Surfaris, "Wipe Out."

**Bird, Bird....Surfin' Bird**: The Trashmen, "Surfin' Bird."

**surfer stomp**: The Mar-Kets, "Surfer's Stomp."

**itsy bitsy teenie weenie yellow polka-dot bikini**: Brian Hyland, "Itsy Bitsy Teenie Weenie Yellow Polkadot Bikini."

**dedicated follower of fashion**: The Kinks, "Dedicated Follower of Fashion."

**Hey Lawdy Mama**: Steppenwolf, "Hey Lawdy Mama."

**Faith no more**: a group.

**See how....home**: The Beach Boys, "Sloop John B."

**Wooden ships on....berries**: Crosby, Stills and Nash, "Wooden Ships."

**message in a bottle**: The Police, "Message in a Bottle."

**drivin' and cryin'**: A group.

**three feet high and rising**: De La Soul, *Three Feet High and Rising.*

**Hey there, little insect....around**: Jonathan Richman, "Hey There Little Insect."

**stoned soul picnic**: The Fifth Dimension, "Stoned Soul Picnic."

**Cowgirl....game**: Neil Young, "Cowgirl in the Sand." This fine song also contains the interesting line: "Hello, Ruby in the dust."

**Will I see....love**: The Tempos, "See You in September."

**sand in their shoes**: The Drifters, "Sand in my Shoes."

**She has to climb....window**: The Beatles, "She Came in through the Bathroom Window."

**Everyone's gone....at last**: Steely Dan, "Everyone's Gone to the Movies."

**Fever when you kissed her**: Little Willie John, "Fever."

**Sunday and me**: Jay and the Americans, "Sunday and Me."

**Oh, Daddy....hold your breath**: Adrian Belew, "Oh Daddy."

**Welcome to the Workin' Wreck**: Elvis Costello, "Welcome to the Working Week."

**Pure Pop For Now People**: Nick Lowe, *Pure Pop for Now People.* Allow me to present here a few curious musical fax. Jimmy Page had a favorite costume he called "The Poppy," which featured embroidered dragons. LaToya Jackson once sent her brother, Michael, a dozen black roses while he was in the hospital. Candy del Mar and Poison Ivy of The Cramps

have been known to sport snake earrings. Schooly D's partner is named DJ Code Money. One member of Urge Overkill is named Blackie Onassis. Vernon Reid of Living Colour has snakes on his guitar, and formerly played with the Decoding Society. The leader of the group Voivod is named Snake. Snakefinger was the one unmasked member of the Residents. Robert Cray's tour bus is named "Snakedaddy." Joni Mitchell's album, *The Hissing of Summer Lawns*, features a drawing of several natives carrying an enormous snake. John Lennon contributed a cloth snake for the cover of *Sgt Pepper.* He also included portions of *King Lear* at the end of "I Am the Walrus." Cher's home, especially her bedroom, is decorated with snake motifs. On *Another Green World*, Brian Eno is credited with playing "snake guitar." A spinoff of the Feelies is named Yung Wu. Jim Morrison wore snakeskin pants (when he wore pants at all). Edgar Winter has been seen wearing a Western hat with a gold snake as a band. There was a Renaissance musical instrument called "the serpent." Beethoven's gravestone features the Worm Ouroboros.

**Cy, that clown....a tear**: The Miracles, "The Tears of a Clown."

**black Lincoln Continental**: Graham Parker, "Black Lincoln Continental."

**Roll Out The Barrel**: Also known as "The Beer Barrel Polka" (composed by Lew Brown, Vladimir Timm, and Taromir Vejvoda).

**Danny's....doyt-doyt**: Rickie Lee Jones, "Danny's All-Star Joint."

**One Scotch....beer**: John Lee Hooker, "One Scotch, One Bourbon, One Beer."

**gunning for the Buddha**: Shriekback, "Gunning for the Buddha."

**Hand Jive**: Johnny Otis, "Willie and the Hand Jive."

**Splish-splash....night**: Bobby Darin, "Splish Splash."

**read it in the Sunday papers**: Joe Jackson, "Sunday Papers."

**Monday....that day**: The Mamas and the Papas, "Monday, Monday."

**Smile**: The Beach Boys.

**Hot as Sun**: The Beatles.

*The Everlasting First*: Jimi Hendrix and Arthur Lee of Love.
*Black Gold*: Jimi Hendrix.
**Keep it down....carry**: Til Tuesday, "Voices Carry."
**Everyday I write the book**: Elvis Costello, "Everyday I Write the Book."
**One, two, three....overtime**: XTC, "Senses Working Overtime."
**hot smoke and sassafras**: Bubble Puppy, "Hot Smoke and Sassafras."
**Satellite of Love**: Lou Reed, "Satellite of Love."
**Do, Re, Mi**: Richard Rodgers and Oscar Hammerstein, "Do Re Mi."
**stairway to heaven**: Led Zepplin, "Stairway to Heaven."
**Who do you love**: Bo Diddley, "Who Do You Love."
**Have you ever....rain**: Creedence Clearwater Revival, "Have You Ever Seen the Rain?"
**commercial rain**: The Inspiral Carpets, "Commercial Rain."
**let it rain**: Eric Clapton, "Let It Rain."
**raining in your heart**: Buddy Holly and the Crickets, "Raining in my Heart."
**crying in the rain**: The Everly Brothers, "Crying in the Rain."
**Here comes....again**: The Eurythmics, "Here Comes the Rain Again."
**Dance to the music**: Sly and the Family Stone, "Dance to the Music."
**mandolin rain**: Bruce Hornsby and the Range, "Mandolin Rain."
**Who'll stop the rain**: Creedence Clearwater Revival, "Who'll Stop the Rain?"
**rod of Moses....asp**: REM, "Everybody Hurts."
**I'll be your mirror**: The Velvet Underground, "I'll Be Your Mirror."
**inside looking out**: The Animals, "Inside Looking Out."
**buzzcocks**: a group, The Buzzcocks.
**a song from....Oz**: Harold Arlen, "You're Out of the Woods."
**silver hammer**: The Beatles, "Maxwell's Silver Hammer."

## Chapter 00001100
**the combination of the two**: Janis Joplin, "Combination of the Two."
**I can see....eyes**: The Who, "I Can See for Miles."

**behind blue eyes**: The Who, "Behind Blue Eyes."
**four strong winds that blow lonely**: Ian and Sylvia, "Four Strong Winds."
**magnificent seven**: The Clash, "The Magnificent Seven."
**Seven and seven is**: Love, "7 and 7 Is."
**Topographic Oceans**: Yes, *Tales from Topographic Oceans*.
**Kicks just keep....find**: Paul Revere and the Raiders, "Kicks."
**the other 99**: Big Audio Dynamite, "The Other 99." Ninety-Nine percent of the three billion base pairs in the human genome are identical from individual to individual. Only one percent of your DNA makes you unique.
*under his thumb....to*: The Rolling Stones, "Under My Thumb."
**I wanna be your dog**: Iggy Pop and the Stooges, "I Wanna Be Your Dog."
**I wanna be adored**: The Stone Roses, "I Want to be Adored."
**Ride, Captain, ride**: The Blues Image, "Ride Captain Ride."
**Burn, you're gonna burn**: The Crazy World of Arthur Brown, "Fire."
**Don't play....fire**: The Rolling Stones, "Play with Fire."
**And the healing had begun**: Van Morrison, "And the Healing has Begun."
**Fujiyama Mama-san**: Wanda Jackson, "Fujiyama Mama."
**Big Hands, I know you're the one**: The Violent Femmes, "Blister in the Sun."
**Bell Labs**: Now Lucent Technologies.
**no fortunate son**: Creedence Clearwater Revival, "Fortunate Son."
**Soldier Boy**: The Shirelles, "Soldier Boy."
**motley crue**: A group.
**Universal Soldier**: Donovan, "Universal Soldier."
**Buffalo Soldiers**: Bob Marley and the Wailers, "Buffalo Soldier."
**Oliver's army was here to stay**: Elvis Costello, "Oliver's Army."
**Apemen, that's what....shores**: The Kinks, "Apeman."
**Could you be loved**: Bob Marley and the Wailers, "Could You Be Loved."
**No woman won't ever cry**: Bob Marley and the Wailers, "No Woman No Cry."

**Rama Lamadingsingh**: In a proleptic
yogic trance, Lamadingsingh's mother
foreheard the Edsel's 1961 hit, "Rama
Lama Ding Dong."
**Bangagong**: Marc Bolan of T. Rex came to
know Mister Bangagong, and the song
"Bang a Gong (Get it On)" is a tribute to
him. I should note here that Bob Marley's
nickname, Tuff Gong, derived from the
Jamaican practice of banging on a gong
outside a Rasta temple to announce
oneself. Marley, natch, was a mulatto.
**midnight oil**: A group.
**beds that are burning**: Midnight Oil,
"Beds are Burning."
**Rastafarian**: The tiny island of Jamaica
(discovered by Columbus on May 4,
1494) possesses 134 rivers. Its
contribution to the world of religious
thought, Rastafarianism, derives from
almost that many sources. A startling
blend of occult features from Coptic,
Arawak, Amharic, Cromanty, Egyptian,
Hopi Kachina, and Mau-Mau belief systems, the creed relies on *The Holy Piby*,
known as "The Black Man's Bible," as its
main text, altho, natch, the *Bible* itself is
reinterpreted in Rasta's own peculiar
light, as well as such esoteric books as
*Sepher Yetsirah, Fama Fraternatis,
Book T, Book M, The Pimander,* and
*The Æsclepius*. The Rastas believe that
the Apocalypse has already begun, in 1977.
On a more mundane level, the practice of
*obeah*, a set of magical rites akin to *vodun*,
provides a means of achieving temporal
goals. United Fruit had extensive holdings
in Jamaica. And it should also be
remembered that no less an authority
than Bono has remarked that "Jamaica
and Ireland have a lot in common."
**lovin' spoonful**: The derivation of this
group's name has been previously
explained. The same explanation applies
to the next entry.
**ten cubic centimeters**: A group (10cc),
who upped the ante on the normal
ejaculate measure, 9cc.
**man's man's man's world**: James Brown,
"It's a Man's Man's Man's World."
**You make me....woman**:
Aretha Franklin, "A Natural Woman
(You Make Me Feel Like)."

**the secret**: Zammai is at a confused
stage in his quest at this point, since
the secret can be summed up in one
word: *wu-wei*, or non-action.
**move it on....in**: Hank Williams,
"Move It On Over."
**I feel like....Post**: The Allman Brothers,
"Whipping Post."
**Breaking up....do**: Neal Sedaka,
"Breaking Up is Hard to Do."
**that lovin' feelin'**: The Righteous Brothers,
"You've Lost That Lovin' Feelin'."
**The best....up**: The Ronettes,
"(Best Part of) Breakin' Up."
**trained in vain**: The Clash, "Train in Vain."
**the first one....box**: Country Joe and the
Fish, "Feel Like I'm Fixin' to Die Rag."
**If I had....die**: Bruce Cockburn,
"Rocket Launcher."
**I just wanna....heart**: The Ramones,
"Poison Heart."
**duppy conqueror**: Bob Marley and the
Wailers, "Duppy Conqueror."
**get up, stand up**: Bob Marley and the
Wailers, "Get Up, Stand Up."
**give peace a chance**: John Lennon,
"Give Peace a Chance."
**What was so....understanding**: Elvis
Costello, "(What's So Funny 'Bout)
Peace, Love and Understanding?"
**turning Japanese**: The Vapors,
"Turning Japanese."
**most likely....mine**: Bob Dylan, "Most
Likely You Go Your Way and I'll Go Mine."
**If I stay....double**: The Clash,
"Should I Stay or Should I Go?"
**band of gold**: Freda Payne, "Band of Gold."
**you can't always....need**:
The Rolling Stones, "You Can't Always
Get What You Want."
**looked like the dude was a lady**:
Aerosmith, "Dude (Looks Like a Lady)."
**a squeezebox that could work all
night**: The Who, "Squeezebox."
**he had his mojo working**: Muddy Waters,
"Got My Mojo Working."
**All you did was break my bed**: Rod
Stewart, "Maggie May."
**Free Bird**: Lynyrd Skynyrd, "Free Bird."
**free ride**: The Edgar Winter Group,
"Free Ride."
**roll across the tundra**: Royal Crescent
Mob, "Tundra."

**Time's Arrow**: According to classical physics, the Arrow of Time points inescapably towards entropy, decreased information. However, newer theorists, such as David Layzer of Harvard, believe that there are three arrows of time: the arrow of cosmic expansion, the arrow of history, and the arrow of thermodynamics. Only the last of these points toward entropy. The other two chart a course from lesser information to greater. The universe, for instance, started out as a monobloc totally devoid of information, but now contains many interesting structures, such as women and snakes. Social structures become richer and richer, too.

**Newton, Mass**: Not far from Canton.

**daydream believer**: The Monkees, "Daydream Believer."

**no day for a daydream**: The Lovin' Spoonful, "Daydream."

**trains and boats and planes**: Dionne Warwick, "Trains and Boats and Planes."

**Cheap Sunglasses**: ZZ Top, "Cheap Sunglasses."

**Cadillac....with the soft velvet seats**: Bruce Springsteen, "Pink Cadillac."

**keys and scales**: When the Third Seal is broken in *Revelations*, a black horse appears. Its rider carries "a balance." Try mentioning this the next time you're audited.

**Money, it's a drag**: Pink Floyd, "Money."

**money—that's what I want**: Barrett Strong, "Money (That's What I Want)."

**fifty ways to leave your lucre**: Paul Simon, "Fifty Ways to Leave Your Lover."

**The first one....changin'**: Bob Dylan, "The Times They Are A-Changin'."

**Gotta serve somebody**: Bob Dylan, "Gotta Serve Somebody."

**You ain't goin' nowhere**: Bob Dylan, "You Ain't Goin' Nowhere."

**How does it....home**: Bob Dylan, "Like a Rolling Stone."

**If dogs run....we**: Bob Dylan, "If Dogs Run Free."

**Buh-buh-blueberry Hill**: Louis Armstrong, "Blueberry Hill."

**Puh-puh-peppermint Twist**: Joey Dee and the Starliters, "Peppermint Twist."

**Eleanor Rigby**: The Beatles, "Eleanor Rigby."

**You give love a bad name**: Bon Jovi, "You Give Love a Bad Name."

**You don't know....gone**: The Neighborhood, "Big Yellow Taxi."

**Excitable Boy**: Warren Zevon, "Excitable Boy."

**Suh-suh-send....fuh-fuh-fan**: Warren Zevon, "Lawyers, Guns and Money."

**the hundredth building....floor**: Big Audio Dynamite, "Sony."

**slap and tickle**: Squeeze, "Slap and Tickle."

**the sweetest....lingerie**: Elvis Costello, "Tokyo Storm Warning."

**Veronica—tho she....her**: Elvis Costello (with Paul McCartney), "Veronica."

**Alternative Tentacles**: A record label.

**who's zoomin' who**: Aretha Franklin, "Who's Zoomin' Who."

**ch-ch-chain of fools**: Aretha Franklin, "Chain of Fools."

**The new king....around**: Santana, "Everybody's Everything."

**raspberry beret**: Prince, "Raspberry Beret."

**Yuh got de look**: Prince, "U Got the Look."

**I an' I would die fe yuh**: Prince, "I Would Die 4 U."

**I mek de prophecy**: Many a Zen Master saw fit to predict the date of his own death.

**Radar Love**: Golden Earring, "Radar Love."

**jammin'**: Bob Marley and the Wailers, "Jammin'."

**My brown eyed girl....stadium**: Van Morrison, "Brown-Eyed Girl."

**Stir it up, little darlin'**: Bob Marley and the Wailers, "Stir It Up."

**the storm is....last**: Steely Dan, "Home at Last."

**I feel....around**: Carole King, "I Feel the Earth Move."

**Halie Selassie's**: The King was crowned by Archbishop Kyril.

**Our Lady Of The Last Chance Texaco**: Rickie Lee Jones, "Last Chance Texaco."

**the party's....tired**: Roxy Music, "Avalon." The Mayor of Wu Labs' undersea city was, natch, one Uther Pendragonwagon.

**fight for their right to party**: The Beastie Boys, "(You Gotta) Fight for Your Right (to Party!)."

**he used to be....amused**: Elvis Costello, "The Angels Want to Wear My Red Shoes."

**More than....nothing**: Roxy Music, "More Than This."

we all live in a yellow submarine:
The Beatles, "Yellow Submarine."
Neon Rainbow: The Boxtops,
"Neon Rainbow."
P.O'P.'s Sub: A label—Sub Pop.
Europa, the Pirate Twins: Thomas Dolby,
"Europa and the Pirate Twins."
King of America....wine: Elvis Costello,
"King of America."

Chapter 00001101
Day Eleven, Friday, June 4, 1993
Day of the House
Tribe of Joseph

My my, hey hey....into the black: Neil
Young, "My My, Hey Hey (Out of the Blue)."
needle and the damage done: Neil
Young, "The Needle and the Damage Done."
just looking for one divine hammer:
Belly, "One Divine Hammer."
I wanna be your sledgehammer:
Peter Gabriel, "Sledgehammer."
Rubber Soul: The Beatles, *Rubber Soul.*
a heart made out of railroad steel:
The Georgia Satellites, "Railroad Steel."
24-7 SPYZ: A group.
Dream baby: Roy Orbison, "Dream Baby
(How Long Must I Dream)."
Dream on: Aerosmith, "Dream On."
dream weaver: Gary Wright, "Dream Weaver."
You slipped inside....in the plan:
ZZ Top, "Sleeping Bag."
Green-eyed lady, laughing lady:
Sugarloaf, "Green-Eyed Lady."
Juh-juh-just dropped in....in: First
Edition, "Just Dropped In (to See What
Condition My Condition Was In)."
pulling a mussel from its shell: Squeeze,
"Pulling Mussels from the Shell."
Wordy Rappinghood: The Tom Tom Club,
"Wordy Rappinghood."
people look strange....stranger:
The Doors, "People are Strange."
No eternal reward....dawn: The Doors,
"Texas Radio and the Big Beat."
since Monday! That day was manic:
The Bangles, "Manic Monday."
I was holding out....missed you:
The Rolling Stones, "Miss You."
the crying scene: Aztec Camera,
"The Crying Scene."
The times are....me: Bruce Springsteen,
"Cover Me."

And I would....door: The Proclaimers,
"I'm Gonna Be (500 Miles)."
Mercury Poisoning: Graham Parker,
"Mercury Poisoning."
long black limousine: Elvis Presley,
"Long Black Limousine."
walkin' in rhythm: The Blackbyrds,
"Walking in Rhythm."
She's got the....life: Dire Straits,
"Walk of Life."
I want to be good....forget:
The Judybats, "Being Simple."
sixteen candles: The Crests, "16 Candles."
A-wop-bop....rootie: Little Richard,
"Tutti Frutti."
Call out my name....are: Carole King,
"You've Got a Friend."
Hey, Joe, where....hand: The Leaves,
"Hey Joe."
Then you had....right: The Indigo Girls,
"Galileo."
*Peaches En Regalia*: Frank Zappa,
"Peaches En Regalia."
Howard Hughes: It is obvious, in
retrospect, that Hughes suffered from
Ambient Information Distress Syndrome,
and possibly just disappeared below the
Planck Level like Ferdie Lantz.
Tenth Commandment of Love: The
Moonglows, "Ten Commandments of
Love." Only nine are listed in the song.
Questions 67 and 68: Chicago,
"Questions 67 and 68." They are:
"Does the Cambodian political faction
FUNCINPEC stand for 'Funk in Pecker?'"
and "What were the secret Neandertal
findings from the Würm Glacial Period
made at Drachenloch, Switzerland?"
Haitian Divorce: Steely Dan,
"Haitian Divorce."
my baby's ya-ya: Lee Dorsey, "Ya Ya."
These rivers rise....rivers: The Call,
"In the River."
I just wanna hear....talk: Elvis Costello,
"Girls Talk."
I'm a girl watcher: The O'Kaysions,
"Girl Watcher."
immune system: "Lymphocytes can temp-
orarily take charge of communications
in an organ they colonize."
　　　　　　　　　—Claude Kordon
Also, "The immune system is an
alchemist's dream." —Hans Wigzell

**Cy's inside the cell**: Our Boy is down on the lowest level of J. G. Miller's chart of Living Systems, which goes:
1) the cell;
2) the organ;
3) the organism;
4) the group;
5) the organization;
6) society;
7) supranational.
We know what the Eighth Level is, but ain't telling!

**hard to see how anything gets accomplished**: "The problem is not so much to find out how cells address messages to each other as it is to understand how each cell manages to extract an identifiable message from the immense background noise...."
—Claude Kordon

**Mister Big Stuff**: Jean Knight, "Mr Big Stuff."

**Girls just wanna have fun**: Cyndi Lauper, "Girls Just Wanna Have Fun."

**Girls, girls, girls....wine**: Marshall Crenshaw, "Girls...."

**American woman, let me be**: The Guess Who, "American Woman."

**Get these dirty....cares**: P J Harvey, "Sheela Na Gig."

**Leather 'n' Lace**: Stevie Nicks and Don Henley, "Leather and Lace."

**Black Denim Trousers**: Cheers, "Black Denim Trousers."

**Out in the....talk**: Bruce Springsteen, "Out in the Street."

**I don't know why....time**: The Style Council, "Why I Went Missing."

**drying laundry....mad**: Bob Dylan, "Clothes Line Saga."

**Leader of the Pack**: The Shangri-Las, "Leader of the Pack."

**Born to be wild**: Steppenwolf, "Born to be Wild."

**Oh, Lord....Benz**: Janis Joplin, "Mercedes Benz."

**Life's the same....stereo**: The Cars, "Moving in Stereo."

**Sweet dreams are made of this**: The Eurythmics, "Sweet Dreams (are Made of This)."

**This road runs....Paraguay**: Steely Dan, "Turn That Heartbeat Over Again."

**Why can't this be love**: Van Halen, "Why Can't This Be Love?"

**Hit the road....beach**: Beatnik Beach, "Beatnik Beach."

**He was born....die**: Aztec Two Step, "The Persecution and Resurrection of Dean Moriarty (On the Road)."

**Mystery achievement, so unreal**: The Pretenders, "Mystery Achievement."

**My girl Lollipop**: Millie Small, "My Boy Lollipop."

**Particle Man....can**: They Might Be Giants, "Particle Man."

**Phoghat**: A group (Foghat).

**Wild, wild horses couldn't drag me away**: The Rolling Stones, "Wild Horses."

**ALICE'S RESTAURANT**: Arlo Guthrie, "Alice's Restaurant."

**Instant Karma**. John Lennon, "Instant Karma (We All Shine On)."

**germs**: A group.

**cramps**: A group.

**Happy Monday**: A group (Happy Mondays).

**jam**: A group.

**bananarama**: A group.

**New York doll**: A group (New York Dolls).

**buzzcock**: A group (Buzzcocks).

**revolting cock**: A group (The Revolting Cocks).

**sham sixty-nine**: A group (Sham 69).

**deadhead Kennedy**: A group (Dead Kennedys).

**black flag**: A group.

**lush**: A group.

**swerve**: A group.

**the fall**: A group.

**pavement, slanted and enchanted**: Pavement, *Slanted and Enchanted.*

**knocked out loaded**: Bob Dylan, *Knocked Out Loaded.*

**chapterhouse**: A group.

**house of pain**: A group.

**lemonheads**: A group.

**baseheads**: A group (Basehead).

**superchunk**: A group.

**sebadoh**: A group.

**dee-lite**: A group.

**eugenius**: A group.

**Thinking Fellers Union Local 282**: A group.

**Ace of Base**: A group.

**Us3**: A group.

**counting crows**: A group.

**phish**: A group.

**cranberries**: A group.

**You shame....debutante**: Blondie, "Dreaming."

salt-n-peppa: A group.
*foreigner*: A group.
*Kansas*: A group.
*judas priest*: A group.
*motorhead*: A group.
*night ranger*: A group.
*loverboy*: A group.
*rush*: A group.
*journey*: A group.
*Cinderella's*: A group (Cinderella).
*twisted sisters*: A group (Twisted Sister).
*def leppards*: A group (Def Leppard).
*gentle giant*: A group.
*ratts*: A group (Ratt).
*sepultura*: A group.
*quiet riot*: A group.
*poison*: A group.
*Styx*: A group.
your mother should know:
The Beatles,
"Your Mother Should Know."
dancin' on the ceiling: Lionel Ritchie,
"Dancing on the Ceiling."
Two-zero-zero-zero....1999:
Prince, "1999."
'Scuse me while I kiss the sky:
Jimi Hendrix, "Purple Haze."
eight miles high: The Byrds,
"Eight Miles High."
Let me take you higher: Sly and the
Family Stone, "Let Me Take You Higher."
everybody must get stoned: Bob Dylan,
"Rainy Day Women #12 & 35."
journey to the center of the mind:
The Amboy Dukes, "Journey to the
Center of your Mind."
crystal blue persuasion: Tommy James and
the Shondells, "Crystal Blue Persuasion."
incense and peppermints: Strawberry
Alarm Clock, "Incense and Peppermints."
crimson and clover: Tommy James and
the Shondells, "Crimson and Clover."
Strange brew: Cream, "Strange Brew."
Shine on, you crazy diamond: Pink
Floyd, "Shine On You Crazy Diamond."
It's all too beautiful: Small Faces,
"Itchykoo Park."
a girl named Sandoz: The Animals,
"A Girl Named Sandoz."
Lucy in the sky (with diamonds):
The Beatles, "Lucy in the Sky with
Diamonds." Or in this case, leucine in
the skin with dimers.

Judy in disguise with glasses:
John Fred and his Playboy Band,
"Judy in Disguise (with Glasses)."
See Emily play: Pink Floyd, "See Emily Play."
Strawberry Fields forever: The Beatles,
"Strawberry Fields."
Are you experienced: Jimi Hendrix,
"Are You Experienced."
Crown of Creation: Jefferson Airplane,
"Crown of Creation."
in-a-gadda-da-vida: Iron Butterfly,
"In-A-Gadda-Da-Vida." The phrase,
natch, means "in a Garden of Eden."
magical mystery tour: The Beatles,
"Magical Mystery Tour."
tear the roof....funk: Parliament,
"Tear the Roof Off the Sucker
(and Give Up the Funk)."
If you see....down: The Red Hot Chili
Peppers, "Knock Me Down."
pictures of matchstick men: Status Quo,
"Pictures of Matchstick Men."
dead man's party: Oingo Boingo,
"Dead Man's Party."
Mama told me not to come: Three Dog
Night, "Mama Told Me Not to Come."
2000 lightyears from home: The Rolling
Stones, "2000 Lightyears from Home."
mellow yellow: Donovan, "Mellow Yellow."
ball of confusion: The Temptations,
"Ball of Confusion (That's What the
World is Today)."

## Chapter 00001110
## Day Twelve, Saturday, June 5, 1993
## Day of the Lizard
## Tribe of Benjamin

Be-bop-a-lula: Gene Vincent,
"Be-Bop-A-Lula."
shimmy, shimmy, ko-ko-bop:
Little Anthony and the Imperials,
"Shimmy, Shimmy, Ko-Ko-Bop."
A-weema-weh, a-weema-weh:
The Tokens, "The Lion Sleeps."
da-doo-ron-ron: The Crystals,
"Da Doo Ron Ron."
Do-wah-diddy....diddy-do:
Manfred Mann, "Do Wah Diddy Diddy."
chicka-boom, chicka-boom:
Daddy Dewdrop, "Chick-A-Boom
(Don't Ya Jes' Love It)."
Boom-boom, acka-lacka-lacka-boom:
Was (Not Was), "Walk the Dinosaur."

**de-do-do-do, de-da-da-da**: The Police, "De Do Do Do, De Da Da Da."

**Shoop-shoop**: Betty Everett, "Shoop Shoop Song (It's In His Kiss)."

**fa-fa-fa-fa-fa**: Otis Redding, "Fa-Fa-Fa-Fa-Fa (Sad Song)."

**Shoo-be-do-be-do-da-day**: Stevie Wonder, "Shoo-Be-Do-Be-Do-Da-Day."

**shu-do-pa-poo-poop**: Travis Wammack, "(Shu-Do-Pa-Poo-Poop) Love Being Your Fool."

**Nee-nee-na-na-na-na-nu-nu**: Dicky Doo and the Don'ts, "Nee Nee Na Na Na Na Nu Nu."

**um, um, um, um, um, um**: Major Lance, "Um, Um, Um, Um, Um, Um."

**Shting, shtang**: Nick Lowe, "Shting Shtang."

**papa-oom-mow-mow**: The Rivingtons, "Papa Oom Mow Mow."

**Karma, karma....down**: Neal Sedaka, "Breaking Up is Hard to Do."

**mmm, mmm, mmm, mmm**: The Crash Test Dummies, "Mmm, Mmm, Mmm, Mmm."

**Money talks....true**: Roomful Of Blues, "Money Talks."

**Maybe, baby**: Buddy Holly and the Crickets, "Maybe Baby."

**money honey**: The Drifters, "Money Honey."

**Would I lie....true**: The Eurythmics, "Would I Lie to You?"

**Baal**: Our old friend, Baal.

**lawyers in love**: Jackson Browne, "Lawyers in Love."

**I fought the law....win**: The Bobby Fuller Four, "I Fought the Law."

**round-the-world Big Money**: Rush, "Big Money."

**Brandy Finegal**: Looking Glass, "Brandy (You're a Fine Girl)."

**Guh-guh-gimme a tuh-tuh-ticket....luh-luh-letter**: The Boxtops, "The Letter."

**dropping bombs on the White House**: The Style Council, "Dropping Bombs on the Whitehouse."

**Burning Airlines gives you so much more**: Brian Eno, "Burning Airlines Give You So Much More."

**Mission of Burma**: A group.

**Duh-duh-don't....tuh-tuh-true**: Elvis Presley, "Don't Be Cruel."

*Here cums your man*: The Pixies, "Here Comes Your Man."

*Sexual Healing*: Marvin Gaye, "Sexual Healing."

**White Punks On Dope**: The Tubes, "White Punks on Dope."

**dawn, which is....snakes**: The Waterboys, "Be My Enemy."

**dressed up to get messed up**: Roomful of Blues, "Dressed Up to Get Messed Up."

**angels and prostitutes may look the same**: The Talking Heads, "Ruby Dear."

**Driver Eight**: REM, "Driver Eight."

**Jailhouse Rock**: Elvis Presley, "Jailhouse Rock."

**Have mercy, Judge**: Chuck Berry, "Have Mercy Judge."

**Christmas in prison**: John Prine, "Christmas in Prison."

**thirty days in the hole**: Humble Pie, "Thirty Days in the Hole."

**there's gonna be a jailbreak**: Thin Lizzy, "There's gonna be a Jailbreak."

**personal Jesus**: Depeche Mode, "Personal Jesus."

**Call me on....wall**: Blondie, "Call Me."

**so tired, tired of waiting for you**: The Kinks, "Tired of Waiting for You."

*sang-froid*: Which snakes have in plenty.

**rattlesnake**: Charley Patton, "Rattlesnake Blues."

**underworld**: Beulah Wallace, "Underworld Blues."

**x-rated**: Little Elliot Lloyd and the Honeymoon Cats, "X-Rated Blues."

**zombie walkin'**: Tommy "Teacher Man" Grasso, "Zombie Walkin' Blues."

**talkin' World War Three**: Bob Dylan, "Talking World War III Blues."

**Saturday in the....July**: Chicago, "Saturday in the Park."

*Build me up, Buttercup*: The Foundations, "Build Me Up Buttercup."

**Ain't it funky now**: James Brown, "Ain't It Funky Now (Part 1)."

**make it funky**: James Brown, "Make It Funky (Part 1)."

**Animate your backsides....salvation**: The Tom Tom Club, "Close to the Bone."

**Two Princes....flowers**: The Spin Doctors, "Two Princes."

**Stinkin' thinkin'**: The Happy Mondays, "Stinking Thinking."

**I can't even see....between**: Brian Eno, "Golden Hours."

**who put these....imagination**: Elvis Costello, "Green Shirt."

**Papa, don't preach**: Madonna,
"Papa Don't Preach."
**farmboy's wages**: XTC,
"Love on a Farmboy's Wages."
**Rhiannon—one day you will win**:
Fleetwood Mac,
"Rhiannon (Will You Ever Win)"
**plastic spoon....black**: The Who,
"Substitute."
**Can you see....shadows**: The Rolling
Stones, "Can You See Your Mother, Baby,
Standing in the Shadow."
**This could be....know**: The Rolling
Stones, "The Last Time."
**All I really....you**: Bob Dylan,
"All I Really Want to Do."
**It's all right....bleedin'**: Bob Dylan,
"It's Alright Ma (I'm Only Bleeding)."
**let it bleed**: The Rolling Stones,
*Let It Bleed.*
**let it be**: The Beatles, "Let It Be."
**El Poco Lobo**: Two groups (Poco and Lobo).
**Hot Tuna**: A group.
**Alabama**: A group.
**Black Oak Arkansas**: A group.
**Bread**: A group.
**38 Specials**: A group (.38 Special).
**Flying Burritos**: A group (The Flying
Burrito Brothers).
**Stray Cats**: A group.
**Heart**: A group.
**Leaves**: A group.
**Grassroots**: A group.
**Freshmen**: A group (The Four Freshmen).
**Lettermen**: A group.
**Tequila**: The Champs, "Tequila."
**Be true to your school**: The Beach Boys,
"Be True to Your School."
"My girl will be shaking her pom-poms
now" might be a proleptic clue to what
Cy will soon experience.
**How will *The Wolf* survive**: Los Lobos,
"How Will the Wolf Survive."
**Me and Mrs Jones**: Billy Paul,
"Me and Mrs Jones."
**Something is happening....Jones**:
Bob Dylan, "Ballad of a Thin Man."
**Mister Jones....cans**: The Talking Heads,
"Mr Jones."
**Another Saturday night....one**:
Sam Cooke, "Another Saturday Night."
**the Boston Rag**: Steely Dan,
"The Boston Rag."

**Saturday night'll be....fighting**:
Elton John, "Saturday Night's Alright
for Fighting."
**I'm going down....meet**: Prince,
"Alphabet Street."
**Saturday Night Specials**: Lynyrd Skynyrd,
"Saturday Night Special."
**Pump it up....it**: Elvis Costello, "Pump It Up."
**give it up or turn it loose**: James Brown,
"Give It Up or Turnit A Loose."
**Dandelion don't tell no lies**:
The Rolling Stones, "Dandelion."
**We gotta get you a woman**: Todd
Rundgren, "We Gotta Get You a Woman."
**Velouria**: The Pixies, "Velouria."
**Victoria**: The Kinks, "Victoria."
**Dirty Diana**: Michael Jackson, "Dirty Diana."
**Natalia**: Van Morrison, "Natalia."
**Nadine**: Chuck Berry, "Nadine (Is It You?)"
**Julia**: The Beatles, "Julia."
**Jennifer Juniper**: Donovan,
"Jennifer Juniper."
**Corrina, Corrina**: Ray Peterson,
"Corrina, Corrina."
**Anna Ng**: They Might Be Giants, "Anna Ng."
Edward Ng's daughter.
**Tell Laura I love her**: Ray Peterson,
"Tell Laura I Love Her."
**Oooo, I need a Dirty Woman**:
Pink Floyd, "Dirty Woman."
**Honky-Tonk Women**: The Rolling Stones,
"Honky Tonk Women."
**room full of mirrors**: Jimi Hendrix,
"Room Full of Mirrors."
**a cold one at the Dragon**: Tom Waits,
"Shore Leave." Also: "....and a Filipino
floorshow."
**I'm a little....black**: Frank Zappa,
"Willie the Pimp."
**Little Egypt and her ying-yang**: The
Coasters, "Little Egypt (Ying-Yang)."
**We want Nastassia....shirt**:
The Beautiful South, "Straight in at 37."
**Stop, stop, stop....breathe**: The Hollies,
"Stop Stop Stop."
**Go to the mirror, boy**: The Who,
"Go to the Mirror Boy."
**Rubber Band Girl**: Kate Bush,
"Rubber Band Girl."
**Wrap it up, I'll take it**: Sam and Dave,
"Wrap It Up."
**The devil inside....inside**: INXS,
"The Devil Inside."

**Mother Universe....religious**: The Soup
Dragons, "Mother Universe."
**Muh-muh-mother's little helper**: The
Rolling Stones, "Mother's Little Helper."
**You got what....Snake**: The Isley Brothers,
"The Snake."
**small change**: Tom Waits, *Small Change*.
**Pictures of Lily....wonderful**: The Who,
"Pictures of Lily."
**Let a man....popcorn**: James Brown,
"Let a Man Come In and Do the Popcorn
(Part 1)."
**His blood runs....centerfold**:
The J. Geils Band, "Centerfold."
**My baby does the hanky panky**: Tommy
James and the Shondells, "Hanky Panky."
**double shot of my babies' love**: The
Swinging Medallions, "Double Shot
(of My Baby's Love)."
**His brain's been....maggots**:
The Rolling Stones, "Shattered."
**Nothing matters, and....did**:
John Cougar Mellencamp,
*Nothing Matters and What If It Did?*
**Little Red Corvette, *et seq***: Prince,
"Little Red Corvette."
**leopard-skin pillbox hat**: Bob Dylan,
"Leopard-Skin Pillbox Hat."
**snakeskin suit backed with Detroit
muscle**: Bruce Springsteen,
"The E Street Shuffle."
**Sweet Hitch-a-hiker**: Creedence
Clearwater Revival, "Sweet Hitch-Hiker."
**hitch-hiking has its pros and cons**:
Roger Waters, "The Pros and Cons of
Hitchhiking."
**Life in the fast lane**: The Eagles,
"Life in the Fast Lane."
**Voulez-vous couchez avec moi?**:
LaBelle, "Lady Marmalade."
**I'm looking for....floor**: Vanity 6,
"Nasty Girl."
**material girl**: Madonna, "Material Girl."
**you got to pay to cum**: Bad Brains,
"Pay to Cum."
**In the morning....door**: Rod Stewart,
"Stay with Me."
**mashing his lips onto hers**: From the
Gnostic text, *The Gospel According to
Thomas*: "Whoever drinks from my
mouth shall become as I am and I myself
will become he, and the hidden things
shall be revealed to him." (98:28–30)

**ring of fire....higher**: Johnny Cash,
"Ring of Fire."
**Midnight Rambler, gonna....throat**:
The Rolling Stones, "Midnight Rambler."
**Paradise by the dashboard lights**: Meat
Loaf, "Paradise by the Dashboard Light."
**I'm in shippin'....dance**: The B-52's,
"Hot Pants Explosion."
**stick your information in my communication**:
Spoonie Gee, "New Rap Language."
**It's after midnight....out**: Eric Clapton,
"After Midnight."
**I been searchin'....herself**: The Eagles,
"One of these Nights."
**How many tears in a bottle of gin**: Paul
Kelly and the Messengers, "Careless."
**Do those teeth....Lovetown**:
Peter Gabriel, "Lovetown."
**daytripper**: The Beatles, "Daytripper."
**who's gonna drive you home**:
The Cars, "Drive."
**the time to....fire**: The Doors,
"Light My Fire."
**Look at Little Sister**: Stevie Ray Vaughan,
"Look at Little Sister."
**Big Sister won't, but Little Sister will**:
Elvis Presley, "Little Sister." Of course,
not only did Isis screw her brother
Osiris, but Quetzalcoatl shagged his
sister, Quetzalpetlatl. And Erich Neumann
reminds us, "Wherever the incest motif
appears, it is always a prefiguration of
the *hieros gamos*, of the sacred marriage
consummation which attains its true
form only with the hero."
**My sister was....underwear**: Prince, "Sister."
**mess with his little sister**: Michelle
Shocked, "Don't Mess with Little Sister."

### Chapter 00001111

**P.O'P. will eat himself**: A group
(Pop Will Eat Itself).
**Wounded Hand....used to be**:
Stone Temple Pilots, "Creep."
**I'm a creep....here**: Radiohead, "Creep."
**I'm a loser....me**: Beck, "Loser."
**Under Assistant....Man**:
The Rolling Stones, "The Under Assistant
West Coast Promotion Man."
**Ubiquitous Mr Love Groove**: Dead Can
Dance, "The Ubiquitous Mr Love Groove."
**radio-friendly unit shifter**: Nirvana,
"Radio Friendly Unit Shifter."

**eyes of a stranger**: The Payolas, "Eyes of a Stranger."

**dead skunk....heaven**: Loudon Wainwright III, "Dead Skunk."

**Oooo, that smell**: Lynyrd Skynyrd, "That Smell."

**Across The Universe**: The Beatles, "Across the Universe."

**zoomin' 'n' boomin'**: The Tom Tom Club, "Booming and Zooming."

**eye-eye-eye-vee, Poison Ivy**: The Coasters, "Poison Ivy."

**Redundancy too was**: "Paradoxically, we note that the greater the redundancy, the greater is the ability of the system to fluctuate within limits compatible with the function."          —Claude Kordon

**Too much information....insane**: The Police, "Too Much Information."

**Everything you do....you**: The Cure, "Why Can't I Be You?"

**Mayor of Simpleton**: XTC, "Mayor of Simpleton."

**beast of burden....hurtin'**: The Rolling Stones, "Beast of Burden."

**That Arizona sky....day**: China Crisis, "Arizona Sky."

**In a big country....mountainside**: Big Country, "In a Big Country."

**electric boots and a mohair suit**: Elton John, "Benny and the Jets."

*Someone—possibly myself....live*: The Alarm, "Sold Me Down the River."

*the man's too....river*: Dire Straits, "Ride Across the River."

*I been caught....door*: Jane's Addiction, "Been Caught Stealing."

*probably a robbery, a bit of skulduggery*: Renegade Sound Wave, "Probably a Robbery."

**What's on you....know**: The Information Society, "What's on your Mind."

**Time is winding....sky**: The Screaming Blue Messiahs, "Big Big Sky." These folks are obviously worshippers of azure Krishna.

**It's tick-tocking away....yet**: The Vaughan Brothers, "Tick Tock."

**The hourglass has....me**: Squeeze, "Hourglass."

**OOBY DOOBY**: Roy Orbison, "Ooby Dooby."

**Shake it up....go**: Hall and Oates, "Out of Touch."

**cruel to be kind**: Nick Lowe, "Cruel to be Kind." This is the exact phrase used by Zen Masters to explain why they must administer blows of enlightenment.

**If lust and violence....them**: 10,000 Maniacs, "Candy Everybody Wants."

**Pretty Persuasion**: REM, "Pretty Persuasion."

**those perfect air-brushed....you**: Joni Mitchell, "Snakes and Ladders."

**Frijid Pink**: A group.

**God, sometime you....you**: Tori Amos, "God."

**it's nearly Africa**: XTC, "It's Nearly Africa." Why does the fiber-optic cable proposed by AT&T to encircle the coastline of the Dark Continent remind me of a Cell Membrane?

**She-Bop**: Cyndi Lauper, "She Bop."

**China Girl**: David Bowie, "China Girl."

**my ding-a-ling**: Chuck Berry, "My Ding-A-Ling."

**P.O'P.'S LIFE**: Prince, "Pop Life."

**Coming into Los An-juh-lees....Man**: Arlo Guthrie, "Coming into Los Angeles."

**MOVE ANY MOUNTAIN**: The Shamen, "Move Any Mountain."

**Hey, hey, you....cloud**: The Rolling Stones, "Get Off of My Cloud."

**Waiting For The Man**: The Velvet Underground, "I'm Waiting for the Man."

**One thing leads....throat**: Fixx, "One Thing Leads to Another."

**Feelings flying round....today**: Big Audio Dynamite, "Contact."

**I've spoken with....for**: U2, "I Still Haven't Found What I'm Looking For."

**naughty girls need love too**: Samantha Fox, "Naughty Girls (Need Love Too)."

**who's got the ten and a half**: Black Flag, *Who's Got the 10½?*

**big gay heart**: The Lemonheads, "Big Gay Heart."

**Little Sister, who's your superman**: Billy Idol, "White Wedding."

**sunshine superman**: Donovan, "Sunshine Superman."

**You build me up, inch by inch**: Elvis Costello, "Inch by Inch."

**It's a nice day to start again**: Billy Idol, "White Wedding."

**no time left for B-sides**: The Guess Who, "No Time."

**When I was....rattlesnake**: REM, "I Believe."
**Venus as a boy**: Bjork, "Venus as a Boy."
**big noise with all the big boys**:
Peter Gabriel, "Big."
**Old Man Down The Road**: John Fogerty,
"The Old Man Down the Road."
**Life is what....plans**: John Lennon,
"Darling Boy."
**tomorrow is just an excuse away**:
Smashing Pumpkins, "Thirty-Three."
**He's so tired....blink**: The Beatles,
"A Day in the Life."
**stop the world....melt**: Modern English,
"I'll Melt with You."
**Who're you gonna....free**:
Joni Mitchell, "Passion Play
(When All the Slaves are Free)."
**He's taken everything....pay**:
Bonnie Raitt, "Hell to Pay."
**bleed when he wants to bleed**:
Urge Overkill, "Positive Bleeding."
**When you hear....bones**: Tom Waits,
"Ain't No Sin."
**The Wrecking Crew**: Famed L.A. session
players.
**Braintap Shuffle**: Becker and Fagen,
"Braintap Shuffle."
**I made my be....it**: Hole, "Miss World."
**feed the tree**: Belly, "Feed the Tree."
**kick out the jams, motherfuckers**:
MC5, "Kick Out the Jams."
**Set the controls....sun**: Pink Floyd,
"Set the Controls for the Heart of
the Sun."
**on to the heart of the sunrise**: Yes,
"Heart of the Sunrise."
**Darkness On the....cost**: Bruce Springsteen,
"Darkness on the Edge of Town."
**apoptosis**: Or a-POP-tosis.
**Love Potion Number Nine**: The Clovers,
"Love Potion Number Nine."
**The easier it....hooks**: Rickie Lee Jones,
"Easy Money."
**cha-cha-chain of fools**: Aretha Franklin,
"Chain of Fools."
**Doctor, my eyes**: Jackson Browne,
"Doctor My Eyes"
**I need a....head**: Bob Dylan,
"From a Buick 6."
**Sympathy For The Devil**: The Rolling
Stones, "Sympathy for the Devil."
**here comes the Sun King**: The Beatles,
"Sun King."

**Invisible Sun gives....done**: The Police,
"Invisible Sun."
**Black Hole Sun....rain**: Soundgarden,
"Black Hole Sun."
**I can see....for**: Johnny Nash,
"I Can See Clearly Now."
**knock-knock-knockin' on Heaven's Door**:
Bob Dylan, "Knockin' on Heaven's Door."
**Time the Avenger**: The Pretenders,
"Time the Avenger."
**time loves a hero**: Little Feat,
"Time Loves a Hero."
**There was a....stops**: The Talking Heads,
"This Must Be the Place (Naïve Melody)."
**I'm carrying the....sinking**:
The Stone Roses, "Fool's Gold."
**I saw the....moon**: The Waterboys,
"Whole of the Moon."
**The crescent's everything, everything
you need**: China Crisis, "It's Everything."
**somewhere down that crazy river**:
Robbie Robertson,
"Somewhere Down that Crazy River."
**Keep away, Old....free**: The Who, "Slipkid."
**don't fear the Reaper**: Blue Oyster Cult,
"(Don't Fear) the Reaper."
**The mother and....away**: Paul Simon,
"Mother and Child Reunion."
**Time to eat....goodnight**: Soundgarden,
"Pretty Noise."
**white light, white heat**: The Velvet Under-
ground, "White Light, White Heat."

## Chapter 00010000
### Day Thirteen, Sunday, June 6, 1993
### Day of the Serpent
### Tribe of Dinah

**You say hello....goodbye**: The Beatles,
"Hello Goodbye."
**Big Bopper's Wedding Day**: The Big
Bopper, "Big Bopper's Wedding Day."
**I'm gonna walk....run**: The Rolling
Stones, "Before They Make Me Run."
**Ramblin Man**: The Allman Brothers,
"Ramblin Man."
**I gotta get....do**: The Animals,
"We Gotta Get Out of this Place."
**cut me down with those angry eyes**:
Loggins and Messina, "Angry Eyes."
**You touched me....separation**: Fixx,
"Secret Separation."
**this whole story....behind**: REM,
"The One I Love."

**Forever Man**: Eric Clapton, "Forever Man."
**You're my everything**: The Temptations, "You're My Everything."
**You're my soul and inspiration**: The Righteous Brothers, "(You're My) Soul and Inspiration."
**It's time to get down**: The O'Jays, "Time to Get Down."
**shake, shake, shake, shake your booty**: KC and the Sunshine Band, "(Shake, Shake, Shake) Shake Your Booty."
**I got news....fella**: Marvin Gaye, "Stubborn Kind of Fellow."
**a man whose....misunderstood**: The Animals, "Please Don't Let Me Be Misunderstood."
**X-Ray Spex**: A group.
**Uræus**: The circlet worn by Egyptian nobility which featured a snake arising from the middle of the brow.
**One Nation Under A Groove**: Funkadelic, *One Nation Under A Groove.*
**Birth, School, Work, and Death**: The Godfathers, "Birth, School, Work, Death."
**men in helicopters....shoot**: Adrian Belew, "Men in Helicopters."
**Crocodile Rock**: Elton John, "Crocodile Rock."
**Pony Street**: Elvis Costello, "Pony Street."
**Rocking Horse Road**: Elvis Costello, "Rocking Horse Road."
**EXILES ON MAIN STREET**: The Rolling Stones, *Exiles on Main Street.*
**up around the....wood**: Creedence Clearwater Revival, "Up Around the Bend."
**you who are....by**: Crosby, Stills, Nash and Young, "Teach Your Children."
**Children, behave, that's....now**: Tommy James and the Shondells, "I Think We're Alone Now."
**I've done all....tracks**: Paul Kelly and the Messengers, "Dumb Things."
**Love Train**: The O'Jays, "Love Train."
**tempted by the fruit of another**: Squeeze, "Tempted."
**up the junction**: Squeeze, "Up the Junction."
**Al Condor passes**: Simon and Garfunkel, "El Condor Pasa."
**so happy together....weather**: The Turtles, "Happy Together."
**Our love will....Juliet**: The Reflections, "(Just Like) Romeo and Juliet."

**bank on my love**: Hall and Oates, "Bank On Your Love."
**Did you ever....slide**: The Lovin' Spoonful, "Did You Ever Have to Make Up Your Mind?"
**Phantom of 309**: Tom Waits, "Phantom of 309."
**30,000 pounds of....bananas**: Harry Chapin, "30,000 Pounds of Bananas."
**no dancing when he got home**: Elvis Costello, "No Dancing."
**Who you gonna call? Ghostbusters**: Ray Parker, Jr., "Ghostbusters."
**My ever-changing moods**: The Style Council, "My Ever Changing Moods."
**Start me up....cum**: The Rolling Stones, "Start Me Up."
**His love was....it**: General Public, "Tenderness."
**Get up....Sex Machine**: James Brown, "Get Up (I feel like being a) Sex Machine (Part 1)."
**Read my lips....out**: The Katydids, "Lights Out, Read My Lips."
**You're pushin' too....me**: The Seeds, "Pushin' Too Hard."
**tainted love....give**: Soft Cell, "Tainted Love."
**expressway to Wu's heart**: Soul Survivors, "Expressway to Your Heart."
**expressway to Wu's skull**: Sonic Youth, "Expressway to Yr Skull."
**Motorpsycho Nightmare**: Bob Dylan, "Motorpsycho Nightmare."
**try to be....day**: David Bowie, "Heroes."
**I got you, babe**: Sonny and Cher, "I Got You Babe."
**Nothing can change this love**: Sam Cooke, "Nothing Can Change This Love."
**Love will find a way**: Jackie DeShannon, "Love Will Find a Way."
**my love is....freeway**: Robert Plant, "Big Log."
**rattlesnake speedway in the Utah desert**: Bruce Springsteen, "The Promised Land."
**place where there....races**: General Public, "I'll Take You There."
**Wherever there was a factory, *et seq***: The Talking Heads, "(Nothing but) Flowers."
**Nobody's gonna touch....Years**: David Bowie, "Golden Years."
**hippie dream....paradise**: Neil Young, "Hippie Dream."

**FASCINATION STREET**: The Cure,
"Fascination Street."
**COSMOS'S FACTORY**: Creedence
Clearwater Revival, *Cosmo's Factory*.
**FANTASY FACTORY**: Traffic,
*Shootout at the Fantasy Factory*.
**PISS FACTORY**: Patti Smith, "Piss Factory."
**Welcome to the Boomtown**: David and
David, "Welcome to the Boomtown."
**This is the....steel**: Living Colour,
"Type (Everything is Possible)."
**shout it to the top**: The Style Council,
"Shout to the Top."
**we won't get fooled again**: The Who,
"Won't Get Fooled Again."
**face the face**: Pete Townsend,
"Face the Face."
**eight days to the week**: The Beatles,
"Eight Days a Week."
**does anybody ever....is**: Chicago,
"Does Anybody Really Know
What Time It Is?"
**there's a kind....world**: Herman's
Hermits, "There's a Kind of Hush."
**The whole world....eyelashes**:
The Heart Throbs, "Dreamtime."
**Where do we....On**: David Essex, "Rock On."
**We've got your....world**: Steely Dan,
"Here at the Western World."
**It's a strange, strange....back**:
Four Jacks & A Jill, "Master Jack."
**THIRTEENTH FLOOR ELEVATOR**:
A group (The 13th Floor Elevator).
**I used to think....Sun**: New Order,
"True Faith."
**I'm looking thru....know**: The Beatles,
"I'm Looking Through You."
**bits and pieces**: The Dave Clark Five,
"Bits and Pieces."
**As tears go by**: Marianne Faithfull,
"As Tears Go By."
**rivers run dry....high**: The The,
"Love is Stronger than Death."

**Goodbye, Ruby Tuesday....you**:
The Rolling Stones, "Ruby Tuesday."
**I remember....cruel**: Steely Dan,
"My Old School."
**I was halfway....me**: Steely Dan,
"Doctor Wu."
**Tuesday's gone on the wind**:
Lynyrd Skynyrd, "Tuesday's Gone."
**the day you....die**: Buddy Holly and the
Crickets, "That'll Be the Day."
**I don't know....went**: Rickie Lee Jones,
"The Real End."
**you ain't goin'....easychair**: Bob Dylan,
"You Ain't Going Nowhere."
**Chinese music always....me**: Steely Dan,
"Aja."
**the son and heir of nothing in particular**:
The Smiths, "How Soon is Now?"
**Golden Slumbers**: The Beatles,
"Golden Slumbers."
**the more they....get**: Morrisey,
"The More You Ignore Me the Closer I Get."
**And don't you....Man**: Elvis Costello,
"Miracle Man."
**world to shut its mouth**: Julian Cope,
"World Shut Your Mouth."
**Time was on my side**: Irma Thomas,
"Time Is On My Side."
**Are you with....Doctor**: Steely Dan,
"Doctor Wu."
**Nothing seems....fall**: Soundgarden,
"Blow Up the Outside World."
**It's time....die**: Everclear, "Santa Monica."
**Is this tomorrow....time**: Jimi Hendrix,
"Voodoo Chile (Slight Return)."
**Blank Generation**: Television,
"Blank Generation."
**Bells chime....right**: The Who,
"The Kids are Alright."
**Is this the *real* real end**:
Rickie Lee Jones, "The Real End."

Paul Di Filippo was born in 1954, the year Elvis Presley first entered Sun Studios. One of his earliest memories is of lying on the floor and scribbling in a coloring book while "Hound Dog" played over a big console radio. In 1963, he missed the first appearance of the Beatles on Ed Sullivan, and felt so left out next day at school that he had his mother purchase him his first transistor radio: a Sears model big as a canned ham that came in its own leather case. While driving to college in the 'Seventies in his parents' Mercury Marauder, he would listen to Yes on 8-track tape. When he first heard Prince's "Little Red Corvette" he was completely convinced for the first time that an artistic representation of events could exceed the substantiality of the reality. Upon hearing of Jerry Garcia's death, he did *not* say, "What a long strange trip it's been," but rather, "All I want to know is, are you kind?" And, with the Smashing Pumpkins, he believes that "Supper's waiting on the table."